"Are you the man I am to kill with love?"

She is a captivating eighteenth century woman. And she is also that rarest of rare creatures—a white witch. BLACK BODY is Alba's story, told in the form of the testimony she gives when, imprisoned, she must reveal all the secrets of her race or be burned and become a "black body."

"H.C. Turk possesses the touch of a poet and the skill of a shaman. He has Barbara Tuchman's ability to bring the past leaping to life and H.G. Wells' to articulate the mysterious realms of possibility that exist enfolded in the familiar."

—Edward Stewart, author of *Ariana.*

". . . lip-licking lewdery. [Alba] looks like any mortal sinner (non-witch), albeit an extraordinarily beautiful one. She also exudes an odor or sensuality that draws men to her—and to their doom . . ."

—*Publishers Weekly*

H. C. TURK

BLACK BODY

PINNACLE BOOKS
WINDSOR PUBLISHING CORP.

TO DAD

PINNACLE BOOKS

are published by

Windsor Publishing Corp.
475 Park Avenue South
New York, NY 10016

First Pinnacle Books printing: May, 1991

Printed in the United States of America

CONTENTS

Being the True Testimony of a Genuine Witch
Condemned to Reveal Her Race

BOOK ONE:
MAN'S ISLE

One

When I slid in my baby slime between my supine mother's legs, I did not comprehend the expressions of her accompanying friends, did not understand that one was a crone, and two were hags.

I am now aware. As a matter of living I came to learn that Mother's ancient friends were surprised by the abnormal birth, for they saw not a child with the expected crooked limbs and jagged features, but a pale daughter unlike any known witch sister, one considered perfect even by the folk of societies and cities, those persons whom the witch calls sinners. Of any living category, the rarest member is the albino, the invert; and I am called white witch not because my magic is beneficial – for all born of Earth are evil – but because my skin is as soft as delicate petals, the hags and crones about me at my birth aware that I would not grow to resemble the average ugly witch, but pass as the loveliest of women.

None of Mother's friends had seen a white birth before, and only one could recall a witch born besides herself, Mother alone of these sisters in their centuries of living to have conceived, a rarity because witches are repelled by intercourse; for all men are sinners, whom witches shun. Impregnation occurs only through rape, the man to force himself on a witch the most extreme of sinners, the law of heritage alleging that the more despicable the man, the finer the daughter (in the sinning sense). My mother's friends presumed my father to be utterly incorrigible, so fine is my appearance. But although my character is adequate and I am beauteous to sinners, I am, in fact, the freak.

Although I could see at birth, I had scant capacity to understand, but those about me were able to predict more than my final appearance. They also saw too much sinner in this sister, a fact manifested as my love for the sinners' seductive ways, a love condemning me to prison and this treatise.

No more the fragrant wilds. After an early life of pure living in God's wilderness, I find about me man stench and metal bars, for my home is the sinners' greatest prison. Seduced too often by the city, I came to love its populace, came to love individuals and form with them a family. But my love failed and led to death, my family lost, and the white daughter in prison revealed as a witch and thus due to die. But I spare myself with words. Under Queen Anne's auspices I have vowed to expose every detail of my life and my sisters' ways, Her Majesty's good man and magistrate requiring my knowledge to end the mediocre evil of witches. With impunity I convey all my crimes, for my sentence of being quartered and burned as though meat for a sinner's mouth has been commuted, though my imprisonment continues until death. My love remains as long. I will save myself, for God saves only sinners, His folk with dying bodies and immortal souls. His witches have forms that if unburned may last as long as Earth, but no witch will see Heaven; for our souls are no more than personalities, our only eternity an endless death. But by exposing the truth of my sisters, do I promote the evil of treason or the virtue in salvation? And the moral revelation I offer here is not that witches are dangerous, but that we are as human as any persons with lives and loves.

Despite a witch's superior perceptions, my best recollections are of times after my birth, after the sisters' surprise and their celebration wherein they shared my mother's joy by sharing me, by licking me clean and consuming the materials of birth that arrived with the latest witch. Descriptions of that initial instance and many others in this dissertation are enhanced by details gleaned from sources other than myself, as well as the retroactive clarity of contemplation. As well, I understand sinners and the soulless not only from having lived both lives, but from having loved perhaps one too many.

I was born on Man's Isle in the Irish Sea, sinners' names used by witches, who are too naïve to invent languages or coffeehouses. We celebrate neither anniversaries nor holidays, and since our calendar is comprised of the seasons about us, I know not my date of birth, my numerical age. Suffice to say I was born near two decades before this testament, toward the end of King William III's sinning reign. I am told that the current date is the Lord's year of 1703, though at times the era seems Satan's.

I was reared near the hills, but within a hearty smell of the sea. The background for my early life was the verdant green of spring and winter's muddy slush, scampering does and rotting fish, the scent of fresh blossoms and all the wild feces; for whereas sinners love the beauty of nature, witches love nature, all of which is beautiful.

Our home was a trapper's cabin of timber whose floor was the soil below, the walls log beneath a thatched roof requiring seasonal maintenance. Within were furnishings to satisfy only the poorest sinner: a coarse wooden table used only to support our folded Sunday dresses, sheep sorrel snacks, and poultice of fly agaric for that rare crop of tainted lasot consumed by a careless witch—the white baby, of course—whose thick, uncomfortable tongue was soothed by Mother's medicine. Beside each dress were our shoes, items worn only in winter and when attending church in the nearest sinning village of Jonsway. Witches have scant use for furniture since they rarely sit except to appease sinners beside them in a pew. Our beds were uncovered straw kept tidy by daily raking with our fingers, occasionally scented with a naturally deceased newt placed deeply within to provide a fragrant character to the straw, which otherwise would smell like a sinner's barn, and barns are for livestock.

Seldom during daylight did we remain in our house. Our activities were gathering food, visiting friends, enjoying the forest, sitting on the cliffs and smelling the sea. After heavy rains we would re-mark our home with perimeter defecation so that bothersome, tasteless vermin would avoid us. (Although affected by the subtle smells of nature, sinners perceive poorly with their noses, missing current information of weather and animal behavior.) The personnel in these adventures could not have been finer, for Mother and I were always together. Here I shall bear no protests of prejudice on my part, for no superior crone was ever owned by the devil than my mother, Evlynne.

Winter somewhat curtailed our activities, for although no exposure to cold will kill a witch, we find pounding sleet unpleasant, and surely no witch would produce a fire for the warming. No witch would produce a fire except to court death. Most winters on Man's Isle, however, were made mild by the warming currents of the encompassing sea. We lived on the island's side facing England, whose coast could be seen on mornings of exceptional clarity. Jonsway was built near an inlet called Fairy's Bane by the sinners, their reason for this appellation surely sensible to them alone amongst thinking creatures. Our friends attending my birth lived nearby: hags Chloe and Esmeralda north, toward Maughold Head, and crone Miranda south near The Chasms. All these witches professed to be widows of seamen or generals (Mother was known as Mrs. Landham to the populace of Jonsway).

Mother and I attended church each Sabbath. Our friends were not so bold, preferring to avoid the sinners rather than mingle. Many years before my birth, Mother had found it necessary to move from her western home on the isle when sinners noticed that she had lived long enough to be dead. The settlement near which she moved grew to a fishing village, then a town with regular streets, combinations of buildings, and a population so large that only a sinner could be aware of every resident. Only recently had Mother allowed herself to be known, determining that her best response toward the ever-increasing sinners was to live amongst them to preclude their surprise at discovering her. Better they come to accept her as one of their own, though perhaps not one of their finest.

Living near sinners is both deadly to witches and necessary for our survival, for without the occasional rape, the race of human witch would disappear. That intercourse is unacceptable to the average witch is one of God's mysterious laws. All witches confirm perfect God as most righteous, as Creator of Earth and its inhabitants, including sinners, those folk with souls due eternal rest if only the truth of fine intention be fulfilled, God the Creator of good that sinners must promote in order to find Him in the Heaven they will share. Only those accepting evil need fear death, for Hell will be their eternal home. Soulless witches, along with animals on Earth for a temporary purpose, are not evil in themselves, but transfer evil through Satan's work of sexuality. Foolish, brilliant sinners, however, fail to comprehend that the difficulty witches

12

inspire is strictly sexual. We steal no livestock nor cause disease, but witches are so ugly that sex seems repulsive to sinners who pass them. (Surely our odor, so different from sinners', must aid in this repulsion.) As for the white daughter, at my birth friend Chloe asked whether this was the type that must be kept from men, and wise Miranda replied: Nay, this is the type who cannot be kept from men; a fact proven while yet in my youth.

We sisters are God's proof that sex can tempt sinners toward evil. To the sinner is left resistance, for those strong of spirit can reject evil's temptation in any form, sex or gold or political position. But even the finest sinner or witch is imperfect, and the former is sore pressed for sexual morality when a hag has been seen. The wife refusing her husband has that day viewed a witch. The seducer has brushed against a sister or heard her breathing. God tempers the sexual joys available to sinners by providing witches, repulsive women who are repulsive sex incarnate. But I, the invert daughter, was expected from birth to be the evil in sex that is excess enjoyment, my extraordinary sinners' beauty eliciting not love, but lust. This horror I carry with me, for even as Mother when walking through Jonsway would make wives frigid without intent, I, when mature, would pass a pious husband and draw his lust. Accepted by sinners is that intercourse shared between husband and wife to promote love and add to God's dominion is a joy they are due. Witches are from God for strengthening sinners, so that even while being poorly influenced, the pious will insist upon the purity of God's provided love. But since witches are Satan's tool as well as God's creation, an objective view of our truth will have us pitied. I do not testify, however, to elicit emotion, but to gain my own salvation, a selfishness that of all my sinning traits may be most human.

I was no surprise to Jonsway, for after being raped, Mother staggered through the alderman's doorway with a horrid tale of a harmless woman demeaned and damaged. Although amazed at her allegation—such a revolting wench raped?—the authorities' astonishment grew vastly upon later proof—a real child?—nearly exploding when the perfect daughter was seen. Mother had a tale for me as well, facts she felt I might later need. No rape, she mentioned, would have the barren invert bear offspring. Fine with me

13

considering the process of inception. First came a heinous man, Mother's beau so disappreciative and perceptive of his lover that he promised to leave for London if he could find nothing better in Jonsway to couple with than a dry witch. So enamored was he with the crime that his loins had been burned with a rod in punishment for a previous rape. His manhood had not been molested, however, Mother's final details being about men and their flesh sticks that they cram within women in order to squirt baby makings. Rather like shitting in reverse, is it not, Mother? I offered. After some deliberation, Mother could not disagree.

Mother was delighted to take me into Jonsway and prove her humanity with my presence, for one of the countless sinning misconceptions is that witches cannot conceive, that we are constructed by Satan from natural elements—perhaps pinecones and toad droppings. Such is the comprehension of sinners, their ignorance understandable in that they are more concerned with inventing new rules for city living than learning ancient truths of Earth, new rules about merchandising and taxation. The sinners' religions teach all of God's moral bases, but witches remain a mystery, known to be real yet unknown. In truth, great God has created all, Satan but a manipulator of the evil God supplies so that His people may choose themselves or His righteousness.

Seemingly I recall my first visit to Jonsway, but in truth my thoughts are a compilation of years of journeys; for although Mother necessarily carried me at first, clearly I recall the sensation of stepping upon a path made solid with flat stones. The failure of my memory and my experience to correspond is due not only to my youth during those early visits, but also to the very strangeness of a town never fully accepted. And though Mother offered forewarning of the site, I was too young to understand prior to experience.

Although we lived near enough Jonsway to ever smell the township, Mother and I distinguished individual odors as we approached in our Sunday attire. Soon I comprehended that this increasing intensity signified countless sinners and a vast source of their odd products. Evident at once were the artificial aspects of the upcoming land, for nothing done by the sinners seemed natural. The regular trail that turned to a packed dirt road was surprising enough, but a pasture where cattle were held in check by

14

wooden fences was stunning, my first sight and hearing of a horse-drawn cart a horror. Initially I could not believe that the lumbering construction was from our Earth, but then I was struck by this usage of animals as tools, as though sinners considered themselves the creators of these beasts, thus having a special privilege to control them. This notion departed after I discovered that sinners intended to control every part of the natural world for their own unnatural benefit. God created people, but only sinners could make a privy.

Mother at my side remained calm. Though apprehensive, I had little common fear, for the whole of my mind and senses was filled with a barrage of accosting surprises. At first I had no idea of my own position in this new land, whether the sinners or controlled animals cared about me or would respond to my presence. I only held my mother's hand most firmly, allowing the sinners and their products to engulf me.

As the buildings increased in number and size, the trail changed to a street made of stones laid with careful symmetry. Then came sinning women walking toward us. Burdened with sacks, they scarcely noticed the approaching pair, for evidently Mother and I were their peers. The notion that I was the same as these sinners struck me painfully, for the women's odor seemed spoiled—human, but rancid. And though Mother had said not to fear exposure in that we would not tarry in Jonsway, nevertheless, any perceptive person childish or mature can sense many terrible things in a brief duration. My next moment of terror came with an approaching wagon that brought the abnormality of men.

The first was baseborn, unusual because he wore breeches instead of skirts, though the man was virtually comforting because his smell and sight seemed more animal than sinner. He seemed a small bear, with even more hair on his face than Mother! Later I saw more social men able to afford ale who therefore stank additionally, men consuming tobacco who therefore stank incredibly, landowning males dressed with tall, useless hats and glossy shoes, and a surfeit of vests and buttons. Their wives were even more extreme, their bodies' normal shapes modified by hooped petticoats as though their hips should imitate a bush draped with laundry, the true odors of these "ladies" hidden by ghastly lotions and powders, some of these females so social as to cover their

15

heads with wigs like jumbled moss, hats or scarves applied above this. Then my experience worsened.

I smelled metal, a material witches find especially obnoxious, believing it should have remained in the ground, unaltered, where great God via Satan placed it. Metal in the form of silver bowls and cutlery and wheel hoops led us past a blacksmith's shop, then to fire. Here was one horror that disappointed. Even at this young age I had been taught that only burning or quartering would send a sister to her devil, that purveyor of unfulfilled death. From our distance, however, the heat felt no worse than a summer's day, hot stones beneath the feet, that new smell of coals nearly interesting. The flames themselves were revealed as having no solid form, as though the sun had produced a spray as do sea waves. The first significance of fire came after the smith's. I smelled metal and paint and glues and mortar and dyes and finally burning animals. I smelled burning animals, and since witches are a type of animal, I smelled my friends of Earth burning, smelled myself burning.

Beyond any anxiety I had brought into Jonsway, my perception of cooking meat was a horror beyond imagining. At once I understood the stench to signify one of Mother's primary warnings: Sinners burned animal flesh to eat it. Sinners burned living creatures for perverse consumption, and I smelled it, sensed it, experienced the evil, the terror, and could not move. I halted and prayed God to remove me from that revolting smell, which was surely direct from Hell. I ceased walking and thinking, unable to comprehend how a mere witch could experience such horror and continue living; and the world about me became oppressive and unclear as though dissolving from the malice of that smell. Nothing, nothing in my young life could have been more revolting, and for a long moment on the street as my sinner's skin turned more colorless than usual, Mother had to convince me and my chattering teeth that neither sinner nor witch was ever eaten by these folk, that no one would leap out and set me ablaze.

After I calmed incompletely and we proceeded, I found Mother to be a liar. Ahead were two sinners smashing their mouths together, and I knew they were eating one another and that I would be next. But, no, this was a type of kissing, Mother informed me, the sinning type in which teeth and tongues are involved, and most rude for even baseborn sinners to display on the streets. And, yes, certain other sinning folk shouted toward this young pair to find some decency within themselves or be stricken by Jesus. Stricken by the loud voice they were, the pair taking their tongues and departing.

My next fear as we continued was that sinners would find me a stranger and attempt to smell my bottom. Of course, this was normal practice for witches: Mother nosing my hindquarters to determine my health, I examining her droppings to ascertain her mood. Noting no such activity in Jonsway, however, I lost my fear, understanding that sinners had no truck with sensitive smelling else they would not stuff their noses with snuff.

The geometrics frightened me: square buildings and windows and angled carts and fences and signs. I presumed the marketplace to be the meal of a giant; but, no, sinners came in droves to *purchase* their foodstuffs instead of entering the forest to eat orache like any decent human. The buzzing of the sinners' speaking and their closing doors and creaking wagons and metal cracks were accumulated sounds to nearly madden me. Jonsway's unlimited nature was an engulfing intimidation: The buildings' endless heights and the quantity of sinners and the countless unfathomable smells all conspired to overwhelm my senses.

Not until many visits and several years would I come to distinguish and to understand. Social concepts were the most difficult of the sinners' inventions, such as their discovering a resource (fishing) that attracted more sinners who formed a village so that a government could be installed and taxes collected to allow the village to grow into a town requiring higher taxes to maintain, to pay for the constables and court system that controlled the sinners who built the town and no longer cared to pay all those taxes, so they turned to thievery and embezzlement. Mother and I avoided taxes by living outside the township, thank the good Lord, for our only social funds were coins Mother had gained so long ago that their source was forgotten, valuable to the sinners but revolting to me from being made of metal.

No more than politics were society's polite and aesthetic portions comprehensible to me. Drama in the form of plays held in the town square seemed organized deception. The accompanying music was a mocking of nature, exactly as per Mother's judgment. And what witch could understand smoking? To have a fire so near

17

one's mouth and to suck it? Scarcely more rational were undergarments, whose ownership I avoided, though Mother in later years padded my chest to reduce the protrusions of the youth's expanding nipples, parts not to be seen by sinners looking for God. Fine enough for a common fishwife were our Sunday dresses of linen, our daily burlap being inadequate for church, which is a social function and not a natural act as worship should be. At least services were not held in the forest where our bodies would have gone unprotected against rocks and brambles by the thin clothing, which was nonetheless adequate for sitting on smooth benches as a costumed sinner shouted, the audience itself rising on occasion to bellow en masse from a book.

Everpresent was the notion that sinners considered themselves so profound as to improve upon nature by modifying it, cutting the Earth into pieces that they moved about not for survival—simple shelter or food—but for grandiose pretensions: crops for those too lazy to feed themselves, churches for those who would learn of God by hearing the same prejudices each sermon, shops for dispensing social items needed not by people but by the township, and streets to connect all these pieces so that horses could be trained to pull carriages upon something, their destiny death and skinning if not moving properly, their hides tanned with a horrid acid to burn one's nose, one's sensibilities. The most shocking aspect of this entire process was that I wore shoes and appreciated them, thus was virtually a sinner myself.

The streets were a terror as soon as I could walk, because Jonsway was surely the true Hell of which the priest spoke falsely. What could be worse than people so alien as to hide their identities from sight and smell? How could they be considered human when all their acts were against nature? Leveling hills and digging furrows in flatland, making rounded stones square for buildings, demolishing trees to make lumber for houses and space for their placement, this latter a prime example of sinners' perversion that they considered an elegant solution to a problem they invented.

Mother and I were not appreciated in Jonsway, but neither were we annoyed. No children would dare approach me with the beloved crone protecting me with her presence, but on occasion the youths called out uncommon words I foolishly recalled. Mother explained the significance of crude epithets the day I repeated a phrase heard in Jonsway, mentioning to her that she was a bloody arse. Mother explained by calling me a sinner. My vocabulary was thereby improved by reduction.

They looked at us aghast. I learned the sinners' horror was due to contrast, for Mother and I seemed so different. But no sinner noticed the difference more than I, exemplified by my pale hand that Mother held as we walked, a hand like an animal washed onto shore, bleached by the salt water and sun. A blank hand held in Mother's fingers, her crooked joints and bulging knuckles signifying life, the thick skin and coarse hair marking her as lovable and alive. How can she bear to touch me? I thought, but did not fully understand the truth until the day we entered a clothing shop to replace my frayed church dress.

Within were manipulated materials of such an array that I could not comprehend the mass, the shop's interior of synthetic products seemingly an enclosed version of Jonsway itself. But hoods and high-crowned hats and pattens were not the greatest unpleasantry within. The endless, intimidating goods so numbed me that I scarcely noticed the sinning proprietress who came so near me I was engulfed by her smell, her average sweat obscured by powders, her breath reeking of spices instead of food. Changing my attire in the shop was of scant consequence in that I was allowed to do so behind a curtain. Once dressed in my insipid finery, I presumed the ordeal to be approaching an end, but then the woman showed me the greatest horror in the sinning world by placing me before a looking glass. I saw another of their dull children, an especially bland example from glossy, black hair to featureless face, one of no color, no character. This creature, however, had my mother's hand on her shoulder. Mother with her brown teeth and warty nose bent down to this blank sinner, smiling and holding this girl exactly as she held me, her daughter, her only daughter.

Never before in either world had I found something completely unbearable. I ran from the shop, from the town. I tore the dress away and waited, nude, on a rotting stump with grubs rubbing my backside, a condition preferable to the sinners' false luxuries and comforts that offered only torment. I waited for my mother, but even the clearest and firmest explanation from her did not change my understanding, because it did not change me. My face remained as weird as sinners' ways, and my life was yet a perversion.

19

Two

Several fine years of witches' living passed before I grew enough to look into my mother's eyes, though she was of no grand stature, crones being shorter than average sinning women, who are not so gaunt as the common hag. Because I grew at the same rate as sinners, my size described me as virtually a woman, for I had seen sinners of similar maturity married with children though virtually children themselves. A witch might have the age of a shade tree before bearing a child. I learned of sinning youths not by speaking with them, but by asking Mother, for I had no desire to associate with any person who wore pantaloons or peed in a bucket. My only communication with the Jonsway sinners was the occasional social greeting at church, for Mother's appearance did not encourage conversation, and I was never apart from Mother. As for my own appearance, imagine for yourself a conventional combination of comely sinning features and you will have an idea beyond my means to describe.

Mother consistently emphasized the advantages of being able to associate with sinners, to have them know that despite her appearance we both were of their people. Particularly this might prove valuable, she said, upon my gaining a maturity not of size, but gender, when men could perceive the sex witch in me, a condition beyond my imagination. Thus, I was instructed in the ways of sinners, practicing social discourse for use on Sundays, mouthing pleasantries of weather to my fellow parishioners. Beyond this, I saw no purpose in learning to speak politely and curtsy. Since Mother was known as a widowed commoner of the wilderness, she and I were not expected to have a full understanding of town politics, town gossip. Attending church was proof of our normalcy, especially since Mother sang hymns louder than any sinner, praising Jesus to the skies she was certain he had never passed through, unable to understand what a man strung to a stake like a witch had to do with the world's salvation.

One Sunday I was split from Mother by sinners who had planned against us. All were respected women, their husbands leaders of the alien community. The pack's doyenne, one Sarah Vidgeon, had observed me for years, occasionally speaking with me in her Sabbatical politeness, though she had always seemed terrified, doubtless due to my companion. Typical of sinners near Mother was a fear seen in their tightened eyes, smelled in their perspiration attempting to escape the restraints of camouflage perfume, this human stress not hidden to witches. Their fear, however, did not allay mine. Sinners, after all, were never burned by witches.

Amazed we were at being thwarted in our escape from church, for never before had the parishioners been eager to speak with us so personally; for as Mother was drawn in one direction, I was pressed in the opposite, Mrs. Hughbert being so bold as to touch Mother's shoulder! I was a more comfortable prospect, for the women were not afraid to touch a lovely girl, as opposed to her . . . unlovely . . . mother.

Lady Vidgeon and her cohorts stood with us witches outside the church building in the worn grass trampled by the sinning mass each week. From behind I heard the women babble on to Mother about all sorts of vital enterprises—from insurance practices to lotteries—of interest to no witch, though Mother feigned delight. Doubtless Mother was amused to see the sinners squirm beyond her grasp as she reached to touch their arms with their own ladylike gestures of crippled wrists and weak fingers.

I could smell Vidgeon's pity. I could sense how relieved she was that her part was to deal with me, so relieved that she took extra pains to grasp my shoulder and touch my hair as though a sinner baby's grandmum. But she was not aware of my response. The lady did not sense that she made me ill, for after I found that the most dangerous activity would be speaking, I became repulsed by the strange form of stiff crinoline and brocade before me. The tidy curls sagging beneath her commode as well as the powder dulling her skin chilled me and I could not look to her, staring fearfully over the sinner's shoulder when she sought my gaze. Though too old to flee on this occasion, I would have preferred to sit on a dead log with bugs crawling on my naked backside rather than have the sinner speak to me with her teeth so even, like brickwork. Like mine.

"Dear Alba, I would have your attention but a moment," she began, speaking rapidly. "I must say that in the years we have known you, though this has been to no great extent considering the area in which you live. Since we have known you, we have become quite fond of you, dear. You are such a lovely thing that we wish only the best for you, with your polite and quiet ways, and what is certainly a fine intelligence for a young woman, though you seldom speak. Potential for your becoming an excellent lady is evident in all about you. The difficulty as we see it now, dear child, is that living in the wilderness as though an animal, you will not be able to reach your potential. With your fine appearance and modest charm, any city would benefit from your presence—if you were properly reared and made to understand the ways of our modern world."

"Yes, ma'am; thank you, ma'am," I answered with a curtsy, averting my eyes. In those early moments, I lacked a definite reply, for I was uncertain of the sinner's meaning.

"The offer, dear Alba, that I make you now is for you to join a program we have begun for orphaned and other unfortunate girls wherein they reside with the finest families of Jonsway with whom they can live and learn the morals and manners of God and England. My associates speak with your mother now and apply toward her our wishes that a youth of such potential as yourself will be given to us to rear as one of our own beneath the eyes of God and King William."

I looked to my mother as the group surrounding her drew near. Though emoting smells slightly different sinner from witch, I was sufficiently familiar with the former's odor to judge that these women were expectant. Briefly I looked to their faces, then directly to their chests, their layers of clothing, their surface artifice. The generosity of these women described a true concern, but I could give them no thanks, for what they considered an offer to my benefit was in fact a horror.

By my side again, Mother was speaking, her common scent a relief.

"Have you heard, my daughter, these ladies' wondrous offer? Could any person imagine a more splendid future for a poor but penniless lass than to live with them and become their equal?"

I was too young for Mother's humor. Though recognizing her facetious air, I lacked the maturity to blithely accept so terrifying an idea. All I could manage was a failed attempt at the social decorum Mother had taught me as I conveyed to these churchwomen the truth.

"I must thank the fine ladies greatly, but I would rather burn in Hell than live without the only person in God's world I love."

Though I walked away from this sinning horror, what the value over running when I stopped so near that I heard their every word? The following conversation became ungracious. Certain ladies were disappointed, but Sarah Vidgeon was displeased, having found a type of anger available only to sinners, an artificial injustice as dangerous as the sinners' more direct, material means.

"Then we shall take her, Mrs. Landham. We shall arrange for the custodians to receive your daughter, for no English girl—despite impoverished manners—deserves to live in the wilds as though an animal. For the benefit of the child, I will show that even when spurned by the baseborn, I respond with generosity. Nothing more proper can I do than remove Alba from your inferior custody—and I will do so. There are laws to support me."

Though smelling of anger, Mother retained emotional control. Perhaps this was worse than mere anger. Next she spoke in a voice too rich for common sinners, looking toward Lady Vidgeon as though prepared to attack.

"Doubtless my daughter could be provided with a superior home for improving her station in society, but what could be worse than having her live with a witch like you?"

Since Mother's typical visage of impending doom was never manifested, Lady Vidgeon was fully startled as Mother lunged out to grasp her powdered and patched face with broken fingernails, rough stubs that drew blood.

The entire church body gathered about the conflicting pair as I stood to one side. Though cries issued from the congregation, no order to cease came to us witches as Mother and I departed. Stepping quickly through the town, traveling from street to trail to

23

wilderness, Mother held her bloody hand cupped before her like a vessel, but I would not ask her purpose.

"At least we've cause now for no longer attending their bleeding church," she told me, Mother's scent proving that her disposition had improved.

In the shade of an eroded hill that had always seemed a wall to separate us from the sinners' world, Mother and I stopped to perceive. With our feet we sensed them walking. We smelled the sinners near.

"They are coming, my dear," she said with a bit of a crafty smile, and touched my face with her bloody hand, applying thickening drops to my forehead and temples, beneath my eyes. "Some difficulty will come from the sinners' law, since I have damaged one of their finest of mediocre ladies, and I feel it best we not lead them to our home when they come for me. You shall return and wait, using utmost care not to disturb the lady's portions I have applied to your skin, which must remain to work with your smell and oil. With the efforts of your person, we may fully explain our position to Vidgeon and elicit a change within her thinking using the rare powers God has given us."

Mother's final words meant nothing; I had only heard that she would be taken by sinners.

"I cannot leave you for them, Mother," I told her with astonished fear. "Should we not move at once toward a new home?"

"Oh, but sinners excel at following," she replied with a smile. "But worry less than you feel you must, my daughter. Your nature is to kindle desire in men, a force their women recognize and would have near as though to gain this desirability. And though their laws can provide a force to take you from our home, much legal discussion would transpire first. Soon these women will have severe trouble with their husbands in bed, but none will recognize the cause as exposure to me. Immediately, however, the haughty sinner woman will have me make amends for striking her. That my goal was to take her blood now so that later we might take her intentions is a factor beyond her comprehension. Go now, Alba, and wait quietly at home with hands away from the makings of your face."

Since youthful or mature I knew that the essence of our lives was to be together, following Mother's wishes was impossible.

"Please don't send me away," I pleaded, my brain and body so weakened that despite the will to obey I could not move.

"On the contrary, young witch, I send you not away but to our home where I promise to briefly return. After producing a small show, the pompous sinners will be done with me."

"Mother, what will they do to you?" I cried out too loudly.

"Talk no more, Alba, for only sinners must speak to some undecided end before acting. I will neither deceive you nor encourage your fear, only ask that you fulfill my wishes."

The sinners were a stink a glade's length beyond. Within me was a youthful terror completely convincing of catastrophe, though disasters of later years would prove this trouble minor. Mother next became stern, and ceased her explaining.

"As though sinners, we speak endlessly when heretofore I have told what is best for us both. Move away now, child," she ordered, and turned from me as though I no longer were present.

I waited in a hollow near enough Mother to smell her thinking. Certainly she sensed my presence. She did not, however, look toward me nor order me farther removed as I watched her, watched the constables approach with their three-cornered hats and long staffs, firm men who did not expect my mother to speak first.

"Ah! and you come now for this old woman who only desires to save her family from the ruin of separation!"

Mother was wailing, a sound only sinners produce. She was bending as though collapse were imminent. Weakly she presented her arms and told the constables to remove her in chains if they must, for God in His creditable wisdom would protect those who love their kin more than wealthy strangers.

At first I could not understand why Mother applied humor in so grave a situation, but the constables were befuddled and unforceful, for they could only say they would bring this Mrs. Landham before the magistrate. They could not say, We will drag ye if need be; for Mother accompanied them without urging. And when she was beyond my feel, my senses, I understood another advantage of witches. I became so desolate that I could not move, but since witches cannot weep, there was no washing away the blood at work that would allow us correction, allow me revenge.

* * *

25

I did not return home, for the cabin was no home without Mother. I remained by that hill. Toward nightfall I sensed Mother return, my relief complete because her approach described her as unharmed: No animals shied from a known creature now damaged, no plant life was improperly stumbled upon by one familiar with woods' movement now too pained to walk correctly. And though our embracing was excellent, Mother could not provide me with the proper kisses about my face, for my skin was not to be disturbed.

She was wet, sodden in her hair and clothing. Mother explained.

" 'Tis no concern. With all my sinner's lament and mother's moaning, they found my crime minor, and insisted upon waiting till the morn before leading me to the ducking stool, for such punition is not given by gentlefolk on the Sabbath. With no remorse they will steal a child, but a moment's wetting must wait till Monday. But desiring to exit their fair town, I set upon them with such a great cry of my pitiful child's being left alone in the wilderness that they punished me at once, temporarily rescinding their Christian beliefs either for the child's best interests or to quiet the mother and be rid of her. Therefore, I am harnessed in a wooden chair hung from a long pole above the trough in the town square with a minor audience to view the immersion. A fine douse they provide me, so they believe, and I attempt to agree by appearing fully admonished. No doubt I neglect to inform them that no witch can swim, so she walks along a river's bottom when a fording is required. To the end I'm the humble Christian woman protecting her family, and there's a pity in the crowd although the women go home and sleep apart from their husbands, and the men drink to excess, then abuse themselves in the shed."

Mother shook her head in pity of sinners' ways as we stood before the segregating hill, within the forest's undergrowth. Then she asked what I could feel, and I told her, "Our friends."

"They will come," she said quietly, and touched the raw skin about my face where no blood was working. "Bodies and minds together are superior to those alone. All people, witch and sinner, form families on God's behalf. In their separate worlds, sinners form parliaments and armies, but witches make a gathering without request and without name wherein personalities become additive, where together the power of lives and experience conjoin.

26

Using our bodies and our living knowledge, together we shall apply natural abilities to correct what is most unnatural in our lives: the sinning woman's threats to steal our only daughter."

From a distance at the edge of my ability to sense, I felt unknown but welcome entities plan to draw near. I mentioned to Mother, "Are not friends approaching I have never met?"

"Correct, and all needed, for the effort must be great. Even as sinners rack themselves to cut forests or break stone, so must we extend ourselves to produce a vapor, a fume carried in the air so personal that only the single lady will smell it. The power of all our past lives and potential futures will be the force to modify God's elements and gain for us return, return to our state before the lady's generous thoughts. To do this, child, we will have to remove those thoughts."

We waited a day. Our most distant friends would not be present till the following afternoon, though the nearest were within smelling distance. We waited because the dreaded force of death would be needed, and our fires should burn before evening so that the sinners could not see.

Mother and I were in a strange state, for although not apprehensive, we were uncommonly somber as we ate the mushrooms that kill sinners, and drank dark water full of life. We did not, however, visit with the local sisters. All would wait until all were present.

We brought the clay barrel, emptied of rainwater, unused since the time sisters were hunted as though animals for the eating. Unable to recall where exactly on the isle she then had lived, Mother was only certain that she and her friends were saved by a forgetfulness carried in the air that caused the hunters to be lost and finally retire from their search. Only a few sisters burned, she told me, but a price was needed then from us, and one will be extracted now—but what price our soulless lives? Then she showed me her legs. White bones were visible beneath translucent skin, fleshless bones I had never before considered abnormal. I once was taller, she smiled with odd humor, but at least I remain alive.

No further smiling came. On a limb sled we dragged the waist-high crock all morning, Mother halting now and again to sniff and ponder before deciding the proper way. In folds of our clothing pinned with brambles we carried rare morsel of dulse and whelk stem properly aged for strong eating. Mother on occasion would

27

toss into the air splines of the cagewood plant, which traps seeds and ends forests. Then we read the patterns as the slivers settled.

"North," Mother said as she viewed the fluttering barbs.

"But all of those are tumbling, Mother," I mentioned.

"Toward water," she corrected herself.

"But so many never touched soil," I ventured.

"Stone and sea," Mother decided, looking firmly toward me for further interpretations. I agreed with her, however, saying nothing as I attempted to appear innocent, a difficult task for the sex witch even in her youth.

Eventually we determined to progress toward a rocky area near the western sea cliffs, stone ground enclosed on the inland side by the remnants of an ancient mountain collapsed to have formed an overgrown hill of rubble. Here we gathered as one with five sisters, a pair of triptychs to surround the white daughter, the invert child.

Five coarse dresses in a variety of greys and browns, one with a hood, two with full sleeves, a gathered bodice, one shift sewn carefully from seam to seam, perhaps repaired by a sinner. Crones and hags and a cripple: a taller unknown sister, smelling older than any other present that day, a bent hag who dragged her foot and poked the ground with an iron cane, an astonishing material for a witch.

We converged at once. Three of these sisters I knew. Crone Miranda as usual was blinking both eyes as though signaling. Considering speech to be a sinning disease, hag Esmeralda had vowed to refrain from any utterance while recalling some ancient, silent language forgotten by us witches due to sinners' exposure. Chloe might have joined her, for this hag's face was so flat that words could barely be squeezed from her mouth. The fourth I knew not, but her movements seemed stern, while the lame sister looked toward us all with a pleasant visage that would soon be shown not to describe her complete personality.

"Ah, and here's the spot we drop our crock," Mother sighed as she placed the barrel in a clearing the lame one had swept smooth with the tail of her dress after shamelessly dropping her iron cane to one side. "I bid you a moderate journey, Marybelle," Mother greeted her. The hag's reply was to step near and speak a few soft words unheard by me that made Mother smile. As they spoke, I was pulled aside by Miranda, who near tore my dress with the grasping, her former blinking yet to subside.

"And let us cook this white one, for I am shy a meal," she growled.

"Yes and yes," Chloe and her tight mouth agreed.

Although being dragged about so that I could scarcely retain my footing, I summoned enough effort to respond.

"I know not how you could consume me," I replied to Chloe, "for you've barely a mouth. And you, Miss Miranda, could not see where to place me within your face, what with the eye ailment you've contracted."

"Perhaps with no humor what I am saying should be true," Miranda submitted, "for one who causes such difficulty should be dissolved away," and she made a dainty gesture with her fingers as though emulating steam.

For a moment, I could not see them, only the truth I had disregarded, that I was the cause of Mother's trouble in Jonsway, the cause of my own fear, and now the cause of this great effort that might harm us all. I had to respond, but only sinners' words were available.

"God made me bizarre," I said quietly, having to blame the Almighty before telling them the truth I felt. "I am so sorry . . ."

The others were not so jovial now, Miranda gravely pronouncing, "No daughter so strange could be better loved." Then she held her arms out for me to run to her and be embraced by a friend who was truly family.

"Certain troublemakers," Chloe remarked sternly as she stepped near, "are worth their trouble." Then gently she reached to touch my weird hair, one pat—perhaps all the contact she could bear—confirming the truth of her words.

Aided by Mother and the firm stranger, Marybelle began placing dry sticks beneath the crock, the three silently at their task as though unaware of the activity surrounding me. Of course, they knew, but continued with their portion of the affair as we remaining sisters proceeded with ours. Silent Esmeralda approached me from behind to snatch me from Miranda's embrace, holding me like a bundle or a baby in her arms as she looked down to my face, her jagged brow knitted as she nodded to the crockery barrel, her visage and gesture as clear as her smell.

"Let's stew the wench regardless, afore she sucks us dry of pity," Miranda suggested with a horrid voice.

Gleefully Chloe agreed. Even the unnamed stranger glimpsed up to point her inverted thumb toward the barrel, but this witch had no smile. With a mutual roar I could only consider silly, the three began tossing me one to the other, the silent and the loud, the crooked and the bent. This brief bout of rough flying took my breath and left me with foolish giggles fit more for a sinning child than a troublemaking wench.

Chloe nearly dropped me before I was placed within the barrel by Miranda, who moved amongst the busy witches with sticks. Esmeralda with a great gnashing of her several teeth made as though to remove major portions of my face and neck, though of course she would have been revolted to touch me so intimately. Not being basically frivolous, the remaining adults ended their levity as a tapping sounded: Marybelle was striking dark rocks together, dropping sparks onto the tinder below.

Silence came. I looked about for someone to aid me from the barrel, for the sticks were now ablaze. My feet were becoming hot, and the surrounding witches were retreating from the fire they hated, the flames they required. I looked for Mother to assist me from the crock, but Marybelle, the eldest, turned to me and spoke a command.

"Pee," she said, but I did not understand, displaying an ignorant expression that at least was honest. Mother then clearly explained.

"Lift your dress and pee what you can, girl, before your feet melt."

I would as soon have complied, but my body would not cooperate. "My person is of no mind to pass water," I declared with some guilt.

"Pass what you can, child, and be quick," Mother said.

Unlike sinners who hide their wastes, witches accept the process as natural. Nevertheless, peeing before an audience was as unknown to me as being stewed, my anxiety so increasing along with the heat that I thought of leaping out. The smell of burning wood was not intriguing here, for my feet were hot—and hurting. Though the fire seen in Jonsway had seemed harmless, as soon as I felt heat as pain, I knew completely the witch's terror of flames, understanding fire as though sinners had tied me to a stake and set me ablaze. With a final grimace, I tightened my entire body and managed to squeeze a few drops of fluid from my bottom.

"Good a plenty!" Miranda cried as the smell of the sizzling reached my sisters.

The nearest witch then reduced the fire with kicked sand, approaching with Mother to lift me free. Though feeling somewhat foolish and a bit of a failure, I was thoroughly relieved to be away from the greatest fear in our world, a fear I had permanently learned.

Marybelle was next. Without comment she lifted her dress, one long leg into the barrel as she straddled its wall, her outside foot near the coals that smoldered. Revealed was a gash between her legs that seemed a scar, a coarse stigma I knew to be part of every woman's bottom, sinner or witch, though in my youth and whiteness mine was smaller and more . . . precise . . . and not coated with a fine crop of ragged hairs, but sparse fur as though from a black squirrel's chest.

Hidden by a clumsy boot, Marybelle's damaged foot supported her outside the barrel with a poor balance, her arm held by that second stranger so that Marybelle would not tumble into the crock—or into the fire. As Marybelle remained for a great period of wetting, her friends kicked sand near her foot to contain the flames, twigs added to the far side to keep the death fire burning.

She came out wet to her steaming ankle, aided by silent Esmeralda and Mother. Miranda proceeded with more difficulty, being briefer in the limbs than Marybelle. A moment and she was sweating piss, but remained within, turning stiff from the heat and strain. When she was removed, this sister smiled in relief, shaking her tough leg now wet to the knee. All but one remaining witch, including Mother, were spread and held above the crockery barrel, dresses crumpled in their hands as their loins strained and their abdomens pumped. From the stranger gushed a voluminous quantity that nearly filled the crock. The last sister, however, was dry.

"I had no pee within this year," Chloe informed us. Aware of the import of our task, however, she crammed her long hair into her mouth and attempted to swallow. After most of her coif was within her gullet, Chloe gagged once, then leapt forward with the second retch to throw herself over the urn and expel her hair with a loud belch and a sharp grasping of her entire body, her hair soiled with

31

unrecognized foodstuffs roiling forth in a continual, lumpy rush until the crock was full.

Turning away more bent than normal, Chloe pressed the dripping hair away from her face as the remaining sisters fed limbs to the fire with reluctance. Mother and friends examined the plant and animal portions each had brought, deciding none was required. All were tossed aside except the bug wings Chloe desired to begin filling her stomach anew.

Fires on occasion are entertainment for sinners about which they dance and sing, but flames are serious and unsettling affairs for witches. Dancing is so distinctly artificial that only sinners could have invented the process. To so chase about with no intention of catching anything witches deem foolish. And witches, not being troubadours, take no part in singing or chanting, most of them complaining about the current fashion of speaking to no end. Pronouncements and other speeches at earnest affairs are another sinning invention, witches when so grave as to *intentionally* initiate a burning being well aware of their purpose with no words needed. Nothing was said until the fetid mix was bubbling and spitting a nasty steam in our center. Then calm Marybelle turned to me.

"This one," she pronounced, "the cause. She seems not the mere sinner, but the sinner extreme."

Miranda then scoffed, "So perfect are her sinning traits that she could only be our sister."

Finally, Mother had to say, "She may not be the best witch possible, but neither are we. Nevertheless, she is the best I will ever have. And regardless of the person or appearance, I could not bear to love better."

"But the time is now for the proving," Marybelle declared, "for I believe no one has ever been within her."

No disagreement came. Initially the intended meaning was unclear to me, and to some extent I feared to learn. Then Marybelle stepped near, and I was not allowed an opinion. She lifted my dress and without requesting permission firmly held the bottom portion of my body with both her hands and—to my astonishment—began seeking the two major entrances that lead within any woman, every witch. This was no friendly smelling. Although aware even at this youthful age that the entrance for procreation existed, never had I imagined it subject to probing; whereas the anus, I knew, normally passed material. Now the passage was forceful and from without, Marybelle with twists and firm pressings inserting one crooked finger into each of my most private orifices.

The embarrassment I felt upon comprehending Marybelle's goal passed with her initial success, for these holes are sealed with muscle that Marybelle forced open, abrading the sensitive flesh of the area with her strong and stiff fingers. My embarrassment was replaced by pain, the greatest physical pain I had ever experienced as I attempted to pull away from her, feeling her bone rods enter as though ripping me; and I knew that my insides were being injured. The thought flashed past of Mother's described rape, and I could not believe something this horrible had occurred without damaging her for life. No child, even one perfectly normal, was worth such torment. Then all my thinking was removed, for in the next moment I learned how debilitating pain can be. At once I cared neither for a witch's honor nor for the foolish problems sinners cause us. The only salvation I desired was for myself—and immediately—the only love I felt for Mother the grateful relief to come only after she saved me. But she did not. With no concern for my own pride, I made no attempt to prevent the expression of horror coming over my face nor the rasping shriek I exhaled. I turned to my friends with these signals of damage and attempted to crawl away from the sister who dug at my innards, for I knew with certainty that I was being ripped asunder, and knew that nothing, *nothing* in the world was worth this agony.

So great was my pain that I thought Marybelle locked her fingers within me by ripping through the flesh separating the areas. But in the following moment, Marybelle removed her hands to hold them upward as I collapsed before her. The pain, though intense and continuing, was so mild compared to the previous misery that I was filled with relief and thanked the greatest God for reducing my torment. Thereafter, I was able to look upward and perceive Marybelle's actions, for her hands were now covered with my blood, this eldest sister extending her fingers for all to see as she spake with a witch's pride in her voice and stretched smile.

"This is no witch!" she cried, "this is a *white* witch, and as true as any—she has the internals for men!"

I did not understand the significance of her words, but was recovered sufficiently to accept her pride along with my sisters.

Marybelle then said to lift me, and they did. As I was raised to my feet, Marybelle began clawing my face. I thought she would smear my own blood against me as Mother had with Lady Vidgeon's, but feeling her nails dig about my eyes, I understood that she was scraping the sinner woman's blood where it had mingled with my sweat and skin oil. This abrading was unpleasant, but inconsequential compared to the previous distress. Then our sisters joined us, all standing near to claw at me, their rheumy eyes and ragged mouths a thrill. Mother was the center of their human force, and though I knew my skin as well as the sinning blood was being taken, I began to share their emotion, for I was part of them, we seven literally joined. So when they said, Raise your hands, white daughter! I did, I lifted my hands and together we formed a mass, individual scents filling my smelling, seven different touches against me, seven different manners of breathing, different tastes of spittle and textures of skin. Mother then rose in spirit to lead us, her hands upraised as she turned to the crock without the first sinners' word, kicking dust and dirt ahead to kill the killing flames, all her people following with flailing feet and lifted arms, all hands doused as one through the brew's steam and into the potion, body blood and piss and puke stirred by hands boiled to bone, skin that would blister, peel, and on some never heal, the agony increasing with the long exposure, pain far greater than Marybelle's fingers within me, for a witch can come no closer to burning than being boiled. The seven of us cooked ourselves with pride for salvation, yet none could believe that the joy in our family's success was greater than the agony of our melting flesh, for nothing more horrible nor valuable was imaginable.

Upon our conclusion, the gas began to function with no further aid from witches, and we were able to consider our damage, hands held out like animals eaten by a heat creature. An island's width removed, carried by the air, the season, fumes traveled to Jonsway, where sinners might have noted an odd scent, but only one woman began losing her hair. As we sisters slowly healed, so the lady lost her mind.

Three

Mother sought no guilt from me, though it seemed appropriate for our lengthy condition: hands wrapped in the soft leaves of the barrule bush, an intense, debilitating pain prevented only by constant applications of poultice made from the noxious brough fly's larvae. Time passed quickly, for we spent our nights seeking the brough fly by its particular buzzing, crushing the larvae with hands wrapped like a sinning baby's butt. We bore the price of our family's salvation, for this was one baby the sinners would not gain. Feigning hurt mortal feelings, we attended church no more; thus, had no need to enter Jonsway. Witch Miranda, however, made careful excursions, giving assurance that the sinners no longer desired to improve my social state. The witch they now sought was my mother.

Martin Vidgeon was lord of Jonsway's finest country manor, his estate known as far as Europe for horses of distinction. Humorless and mild, Martin had shown no great imagination in his life until his wife went bald and brainless. Since periwigs were so ubiquitous that a lady's true hair was seldom seen even by her spouse, the disease of baldness was of small concern to Lord Vidgeon, though his missus would have been most embarrassed had not such social factors become meaningless to her; for after receiving fumes of her own responsibility, Lady Vidgeon found her regained blood dangerous. Her memory became particularly acute, for she recalled each insignificant detail of her life, and described them to husband, servants, and every stranger on the streets of Jonsway. Lady Vidgeon, however, was soon no longer seen on these streets. After demonstrating an inability to perform average affairs such as dressing properly or covering her exposed scalp with a wig, Sarah was ordered by her husband to remain within the manor until her health returned.

The problem seemed mere illness to Lord Vidgeon until a neighbor mentioned a coincidence, that Sarah had begun suffering shortly after her plan for receiving the Landham child was rejected by the mother. As though delivered through the air like a thunderclap or sisters' fumes, the truth of Sarah's affliction clarified in Martin's thoughts to form a new enlightenment. Although punished with but a dunking, this Landham woman had bodily attacked his wife, drawing blood to engender a poisoning. And her ability to so damage with a touch was obvious: Since she was intensely ugly of face and frame and lived in a secluded hovel, was she not a witch?

But of course. Never before had the word of God inspired Lord Vidgeon to such passion, for as soon as the idea took hold within his mind, off he went to demand a private meeting with church rector and town mayor wherein he presented his evidence. Since witches were a dangerous breed known throughout Great Britain, the authorities found Martin's accusations reasonable, especially since they had seen his wife babble. Armed constables were thus dispatched to the northern forest to gain Mrs. Landham for an interview. Her child would also attend.

Mother had no forebodings regarding the sinners' retaliation for our boil. In her years, she had known witches blamed for bad crops, lame dogs, and broken wagons as the fashion developed, stemming from Welsh or European stories describing witches' current causal problems. Sinners would become so rabid over difficulties ascribed to witches despite how clearly the work of God or person that no predictions could be made concerning future allegations. Sarah Vidgeon, after all, was not the first Englishwoman to go bald or lose her mind, understandable asperities considering that the sinner's brain had never functioned properly.

Sensing men approach from the town, Mother and I at once made our home neat, squaring and flattening our straw piles to resemble the sinners' beds, discarding the insects lying about for meals. I suggested that we hide in the forest, for the sinners approaching would never find us in our own familiar wilds. Mother then explained that the men would return often, and if we were never found, they would correctly deduce that we understood their

36

approach. We would thereby brand ourselves as too special for sinners, imbued with metaphysics, dangerous as the devil.

I did not share my mother's calm. From similar experiences throughout her long life, Mother had achieved a resolve in dealing with sinners. My thinking was not so clear, for I suffered a fear so palpable it seemed an object lodged within me. Despite my terror, I managed to aid Mother in our preparation as she recalled to me how brief and harmless the last instance of sinners' visitation had been. But I could only see the opposing view, that my mother had been taken by creatures known to kill our kind who demeaned her before the eyes of God and made her suffer from their odd society. I expected no less on this occasion. Mother, however, intended to succeed and survive rather than worry.

We waited outside as though examining a damaged shutter. With no hesitation, three men approached from the forest's trail. Mother recognized at least one constable to have taken her before, but I did not understand how anyone could distinguish sinners one from the next—especially the men, who have more evil within any one of their persons than all of God's witches combined.

Two of the males did nothing but stare at the girl too lovely for her coarse attire. As the third man spoke, the staring pair began walking about our home, finding nothing of interest, passing our crock for rain water that reeked of Satan's power only to witches.

"We have come, woman, under order of Jonsway Township's alderman, Lord Bulkeley, to gain him your presence so that he and Reverend Corliss may inquire of you about certain activities."

"And what a delightful way to pass the afternoon it shall be," Mother cackled as pleasantly as possible. "Might I ask, then, of those activities concerning me as per your implied allegations?"

"You will be told by Lord Bulkeley, not by me. I am here only to take you, and will do so now."

This tallest constable would have grasped Mother's shoulder, but preferring not to touch this ugly female, he merely gestured for her to move. Before Mother could respond, one of the remaining males spoke.

"We've a bit more here, constable," he stated to his colleague, then earnestly confronted Mother. "We would enter the premises, woman, and seek evil within."

Mother at once gave a sweeping gesture of welcome toward our

37

door, announcing, "Please enter, constables. Simultaneously, you might recall the manners taught you by your parents and use my proper name, which is Mrs. Landham. Once within, sirs, thankful I would be for your removing all the evil you find, since we good women of God have no use for the stuff. If you uncover no evil, which is factually mandated by none existing therein, kindly leave none of your own production."

Although displeased at my mother's comments, the men were also amazed at a witch's speaking so fluently, a style Mother used to impress sinners, one so impressing me in those early years that I emulated her lingual abilities. The constables, however, remained mute while entering our abode, gaining even more displeasure to find nothing heinous. Placed on our general table were church dresses and shoes. The arbor vine that had entered years before, a welcome friend whose growth we enjoyed, likely seemed improper for even a decrepit home, for is not a house's function the exclusion of nature? Surely our non-evil beds were disappointing, for although the men pressed their sinning hands throughout the straw—a violation I could feel, the act more vulgar than Marybelle's fingers within me—nevertheless, they discovered no intimations of evil.

The sinning men's intrusion had so distressed me that their next vexing could scarcely increase my dismay, yet what words could have been more frightening than the tall constable's final orders?

"The girl," he submitted, "must be delivered as well."

Calm Mother offered no argument. Since this latest turn was unexpected, we witches had not planned a response. Our only preparation was Mother's experience. Throughout my life she had readied me for the sinners' suspecting my manner of living, and the time was nigh to discover how well I had learned.

Calm Mother was moved. Perhaps she noticed some sinners' reaction I was too young to sense. As we stepped from our home, Mother turned to one of the constables and declared with a voice calm as a witch's passion: "God forgive you for your thoughts, with your staring at my daughter too young for your wicked mind."

We then departed for the sinners' world where I would receive my strongest lesson in evil, where witches would be shown minor in dispensing Satan's malice, the sinners as dedicated in their inhuman destruction as the devil himself.

I was made to wait alone in a large room that was all edges and angles not existing in the forest. A guard stood outside while I waited in silence, hearing neither rustling leaves nor moving insects, only my own shallow breathing, my heart beating painfully with a rhythm ready to break. I heard no words, but would later learn of the "interview" then being held with my mother as subject.

Alderman Bulkeley and Reverend Corliss were accompanied by constable and clerk, as though the king's guard were required to contain my small mother. Fearful men, these decisive officials did not hesitate. At once they informed Mother she had been accused by Lord Vidgeon of witchcraft.

She swooned. Praying to God for salvation from lies to torment a poor woman, Mother wailed convincingly of her innocence and righteous fear. After further interrogation, the alderman determined that Lord Vidgeon's stature justified the township's bringing Mother to trial. Truly the authorities had sought a confession from her, thereby proceeding to her punition without a lengthy public display. Failing this, Mother was set aside with me in a jail cell, and Jonsway made plans to kill her.

Though having prosecuted alleged witches before, Jonsway began a persecution with my mother. Normal fare for an English town was publicly beating a woman adjudged to have been temporarily entered by Satan without her choosing, though she was held responsible for being a wicked vessel. Such crimes were considered minor because the corruption was not thorough, but Mother was formally accused of being a witch and therefore unholy, in league with Satan by choice, as though the devil existed on Earth as do peddlers and clergymen, individuals available to provide their services for a fee. Appropriate for such a heinous crime was the punishment of death. Here the sinners knew themselves extreme, for having never extracted this ultimate penalty for a crime so difficult to prove, they sought expertise from exterior sources. The priest requested the bishop of his diocese to attend the trial, the alderman hiring an expert in witchcraft from London. To our sisters' great misfortune, the fervent bishop knew his holy duty, and the expert knew her witches.

39

The sinning public soon displayed one of its more pitiable traits, for upon learning of the witch trial, they panicked and changed it to a witch hunt. A contagion began wherein gossip burgeoned until countless episodes of witchcraft were discovered in average lives. In brief days, Mother and I were joined by women placed in adjacent cells: five strange sinners, and two sisters we knew: Chloe and Marybelle.

I was not formally arrested, but the alderman found such difficulty in separating me from Mother that together we remained, his problem doubled because no Jonsway home would now accept the previously-fine child; and since the authorities would have me near and not in the woods, why not with the mother? Furthermore, since I was lovely though interred, Jonsway deemed it reasonable to arrest average-appearing women: a widow with a tiny farm who supposedly sold crops that rotted within the consumer's stomach, the truth being that one bad ear of corn terrified a foolish sinner into inventing an instantly-believed explanation as inspired by the original and only true tale of the bald and ebullient Lady Vidgeon. Another sinner was accused because of her numerous cats, too many black, the woman thus clearly responsible for all the wild felines roaming Jonsway, most of which had suddenly begun to steal the breath of human babes.

Additional stories of the kind developed, no truth being necessary for a panic to have set loose human fear. What explanation could exist for bad weather, bad crops, disease, and poverty? What more believable a cause for all these calamities than ugly women esteemed by none?

Our cell seemed pleasant with its roaches and rats, the smell of body waste more honest than any varnish. For days we waited, Mother so constant in her humor and strength that my youthful fear was contained—but no more than contained; for though I never screamed and raved and attempted to dig through the stone walls, this was my desire.

The alderman and minister also spoke with me. To Bulkeley and Corliss I praised God and Jesus, displaying honest fear as they described Sarah Vidgeon's condition. My response to their foolish questions of lizards' innards and spells was true incredulity. Mainly I spoke the truth, for the average witch displays no blatant evil; and magic is a subtle force, difficult and rare, unlike the sinners' easy

40

killing. The lies required I conveyed with ease, for although witches have an honest nature, we respect our lives too much not to lie for our own salvation. Our lives were given only by God, Who alone reserves the privilege of rescinding them. But since Satan supplies evil for all, sinner and witch alike must suffer.

Though largely unnoticeable due to Mother's variegated skin, the crock's contents had left pink blotches on her hands, a mark fully obvious on the white daughter. Separately Mother and I were asked of the injury. Equal were our descriptions, that a stew in its vessel had overturned upon us. The constables then noted that there had been no ashes in the fireplace nor at any site about our cabin. And there will be none, sirs, for we are chary of fire since it has recently damaged our persons.

The truth of witches' effects was never spoken; for although the men about us had more and more difficulty with their sexual lives, no mention was made of the embarrassing subject, not with so many wives revealing how they had always hated the act, and were it not to gain children . . .

Though unsatisfactory to the authorities, our accounts of eating wild herbs and sleeping on straw were no proof of witchcraft. Questions about lost livestock and moneys vanishing from the treasury caused neither Mother nor me grief, and we knew our nearby friends would fare equally. The greatest difficulty, Mother warned me, would certainly come with the trial. Then I asked her of our friends not enjailed, whether we might be saved by their hot activities. Our friends number too few for the effort, Mother explained, for more are captive than free.

Though neither of us was aware of any authority in witchcraft summoned from London, Marybelle—smelled compartments away—had gleaned from the alderman information on this expert. The name gained she recognized in reference to scandals on the Continent wherein women and witches had been burned like kindling. Marybelle knew that this expert was genuine, knew that each true witch would be discovered and killed. Though unable to communicate with her sisters, Marybelle devised a plan to save us, a strategy no youthful witch could conceive.

The next morning, Marybelle began moaning in her cell, producing such a commotion that the guards were prepared to beat her to silence. Upon drawing near, however, they heard Marybelle swear in her most pious voice that an angel of the Lord had visited her, and she was prepared to confess her true identity. Marybelle was thus removed to Alderman Bulkeley and one Bishop Dalimore, who had arrived that morning, replacing the local priest to the latter's holy relief. In private chambers, Marybelle swore with all the conviction she could simulate that Lord Jesus had entered her, promising a quick death and a quiet eternity if she confessed herself before God's man. Therefore, Marybelle on her knees before the bishop confessed to being a witch and Satan's aid, conceding that she and her kind were responsible for all the isle's problems. She then promised to reveal those other true witches imprisoned — if one request be granted.

"Oh, Holy Bishop," she pleaded, swooning to kiss the reverend's feet, "the greatest Lord Jesus has shown me the only peace for a witch — death, death and removal from the world where her evil does not belong! Reverend Bishop, hear the truth of my unholy sisters so that we all can be redeemed by death. But you must vow before the only true God as His Son has promised me, that our deaths will be without suffering. As we give you the gift of our dying, fine bishop and fine man, you must give us the certain death of drowning, not the horror of flames, of burning, burning. . . ." Then she could no longer speak, collapsing as the most reverend in his generosity bent to touch the evil one's shoulder, providing her with God's word.

"Be at peace, unfortunate witch, for God in His utter wisdom has shown you the only manner of rest, and so shall it be delivered to ye and your heinous friends who will end their wickedness in light of God's will. Name your fellows, and before Jesus I vow to fulfill His salvation for you by providing the death you have envisioned."

Breathing deeply, feigning such weakness that she could only roll onto her back, Marybelle looked up to the bishop, with a quiet voice speaking of God's visit that had come solely from her imagination.

"There came a vision," she whispered, "a vision where Jesus from the cross reached down to touch me, vowing that no witch who confesses in agony will be touched by her greatest fears, by metal or flames. Lord Jesus with His own right hand reached down to tie stout rope about my legs and to a stone my size from the cliffs of Man's Isle. His angels then descended with peace to lower me into the Irish Sea, to bury and slay me as the Lamb of God watched over me until I died and the evil within me was released, washed clean by God's sea and Jesus's blood."

Marybelle then blinked, and with a more worldly visage, looked upward to the bishop, touching his holy ankle as she concluded.

"This must be you, God's man. This must be you who binds my legs and my death in accord with God, who watches above me while I die and thereby gain the Lord's salvation. . . ."

The pledge was made and sealed with holy gestures, holy phrases. No hesitation had the bishop, for what more constant truths were known of witches than their fear of fire and that in no way could they swim? After the oath was given, Marybelle again grew agitated, asserting that her salvation could wait no longer, for she had suffered a century with her burden of evil. Now that God and His man had promised, the cleansing power of a kindly death could not come soon enough. Marybelle then spoke a desire to regain her strength quickly so that she might arise and point out each true witch. With his fine public voice, the bishop prayed aloud for God to grant this evil one a quick recovery. And, lo, as though her body were reborn by God the Maker, Marybelle rose renewed before Dalimore with an energy lost only to histrionics.

Rejoicing, Marybelle led the sinners to their victims. Accurately she dismissed the poor sinners for being only women, then revealed the true sisters. Though none of these witches was aware of the plan, Marybelle was able to describe her designs with only her presence as she stood before her sisters and condemned them.

Standing in our cell, she cried, "These are each a witch and Satan's own. Know now, unholy creatures, that your time of suffering is ended, for Lord Jesus sends His Father's man with salvation. Confess ye the evil of your lives and be cleansed with the healing death of an ocean drowning. Confess now before Jesus!" she shouted.

Mother said nothing. Carefully she smelled Marybelle before exploding. Tearing at her attire, she leapt into the air, thrusting her limbs about as she collapsed onto the floor, her torso jerking as she slobbered and screamed.

"God tears the truth from me past Satan! I am the witch and ever the witch—God's will be done if His men can do it!" And

43

she thrashed twice before calming, breathing roughly.

Panic in Mother was a lie. Kindly love for me and our friends was her life, not mortal passion. I could smell no such response from her. She reeked of effort and energy, but also of truth. Therefore, my response was not difficult. I was no ancient witch who had suffered from sinners for decades. I was a child, and came aware that I no longer needed to feign a strength I had yet to achieve, and suffer the stress of dishonesty. Looking from my mother and past Marybelle, I met the bishop's eyes, relaxing my efforts of salvation that were never more than hope.

"I am the witch God and Mother made me," I declared, then pointed to Marybelle with a languid imitation of her gesture. "I am the same witch as she." Then, with sheer honesty, I fainted.

Though smothering while bound in the sea seemed more cold destruction than salvation, this was not my greatest fear. From my first smell of the constables in the forest, I had been taken by countless visions of Mother's dying. So often had I felt my innards wrenched from this vision that the pain became normal, cramping me with a daughter's ultimate terror. But never did I cry out as the torment demanded, for this would have been cruel to my mother, unkind to the person I suffered from because I loved her most, Mother who retained the subtlest courage by never lying but never refusing to accept the truth. If we are to die, she said, consider beforehand the love we share, and praise God that our concern will be forever moved to His superior hands. Mother then smiled and held me. Then I loved her as ever, and again felt her die, then loved her more.

On a sinner's ship in a water world we imagined our salvation, imagined slow breathing, the water's air conjoining with the needed atmosphere retained within our lungs; even the witch child knew how to breathe within water. And she knew this plan was deadly, for a lengthy submersion in salt water was no assured salvation. Having passed beneath rivers before, I knew the breathing to be as uncomfortable as smothering with a wet cloth, knew that long immersion induces terror. The sea is worse because the salt stings the eyes and nose: After one attempt at the shoreline years before, I retreated with distress. At the shore again but unable to retreat, I saw child sinners frolicking in the sea waves, and knew that Satan had sent them to mock us. In their pleasure, however, they remained oblivious to our desperation; for not only would we have to remain submerged longer than any witch would choose, we would have to free ourselves of bonds hopefully mediocre from being secured by a bishop instead of a sailor, as per Marybelle's arrangement. And if we survived the long walk to shore, what if we were seen by sinners, evil people cavorting in a sea meant to kill us?

Upon comprehending Marybelle's plan as she identified us in jail, I had felt admiration for her courageous brilliance, felt genuine love for a sister I had previously found intimidating. But Marybelle was now on the ship's gunnel being tied to a rock that could crush her, while a sinner playing God's representative prayed above an evil creature who to her shit was his moral superior. Who had this man ever saved from death, and when had he jeopardized his eternal existence to aid his friends? The holy man proved his evil by waving a false Jesus stick, intending to cut God's creatures as dead as though he wielded the devil's sword. Certainly the words he murmured in some pretentious language were meaningful to either God the King or His Prince of Darkness, but which of the opposing forces?

The alderman attended. He at least was kind enough to have Marybelle and her stone pushed overboard as one instead of dropping the rock and allowing it to rip her asunder. I watched the deep splash and thought how awkward she appeared striking sideways, her visage lost in a tangle of hair as she disappeared, her personal wake lost in the sea waves.

Too numb to view Chloe being tied to her rock, I took scant notice of a sailor viewing through a metal tube he pointed toward shore. I took no notice, waiting for a salt rush about me to clog my breathing, to clean my disruptive life. But the next holy demise was interrupted by this same sailor buzzing to his captain, the captain conversing with the alderman and bishop, all these males looking toward a boat that neared.

The sinners waited. Stinking men from the two ships soon were speaking. Not so similar were all their faces that I could not discern a red flush about the bishop and smell his anger. He then sputtered with a twisted mouth as Chloe was cut loose. What manner of salvation could this be when my sister was released only to be beaten bloody by the holy man's metal cross? The alderman bid Dalimore cease, the bishop complying before Chloe was delivered a bloody sleep even a witch would slow recover from. But since Chloe was too dazed to be his audience, Dalimore moved to me and Mother, whereupon he screeched down with no Godly passion, his anger an evil no witch could match.

"What sin could you Godless wenches produce worse than lying to God and His man? The Lord's grace has sent truth in the form of Amanda Rathel on shore this moment. She has heard of your plotting and described how you would make fools of me and God by gaining the water that could be your witches' home. And though the devil has regained one of his creatures, the remainder of your unholy pack will meet God's judgment—in ashes. As quickly as this ship can be turned, we shall arrange the posts and chains to bind you as God's flames burn you lifeless. And you shall suffer the charred flesh and blackened blood due amoral liars and their immortal malice."

My last recollection of the return was the anchor's being raised. The chain seemed to be pulled through my person, for it was massive, metal, a loud and odorous symbol of sinners' murder. Beyond this, I recall nothing. The incarceration was as noticeable as common breathing. My sister and mother nearby were positions, not people. We had no praying to God nor mocking Jesus, no cursing the sinners, no torment so overbearing that dementia would result, witches babbling mindlessly like the balding sinner who guided us. No response had these sisters because the dead do not respond.

I recall utter sadness, the pitiful waste of the finest witches a girl could know, but have no recollection of the smell that ripped me breathless, the smell of Chloe beyond sight becoming rancid smoke.

She was beheaded first. As suggested by Lady Rathel, the witches would be separated from their heads; for although believing that under certain circumstances this cutting might not be permanent, Rathel knew that even witches with their heads at their feet would be immune to physical agony, for the lady was no torturer. Only a killer.

I did not notice them take my mother, though from the adjacent cell I should have smelled her depart. I should have smelled her cook, but this as well escaped me. Without intent, I had refused to die from the hell of perceiving my precious mother become burnt meat.

With no deliberation, I met the sinners, stepping toward the door as soon as it was opened. But they pressed me backward as an unknown woman stated clearly that I was no witch. For a moment I needed to recover, not from the surprising move but from the absolute lie. Quickly I stepped to the door again, for I was a witch, and since I could no longer have my mother, I demanded the pride in our love.

I moved again and they stopped me. The woman, whom I had guessed the Lady Rathel, astonished the alderman by insisting that she speak with me alone. I looked at no sinner who departed, nor at the murderess who remained.

She attacked me. Of course, this was her goal, to kill me personally. After looking behind to see that the males had departed, this sinner quickly reached out and cut my wrist with some implement concealed in a kerchief. But, no, she only produced a scratch barely felt. I looked to the wound, the fine line of blood, then up to this sinner, wondering what bizarre form her murder was taking.

"No human can have the oil of the nevier thorn in the blood without a pain to set her to screaming," Rathel began, looking carefully to my wrist. "But you have not even a redness—because you are no human. You are a witch. A more certain test is with the sexual tissue, but you are a youth and undeveloped. Perhaps not even your evil is mature." Then she looked to my face, and with a rapid tone explained herself.

"God help you, child, but I could not save your mother. By the time I learned of a perfect girl, the truth had been told of witches and water. Had I known before, I would have spared Evlynne, even though witches ruined me, and I would rid the world of their evil. But I have use for you, white daughter. As a witch you will kill a male whose father sought my ruin. For merely being natural, your life will be spared."

I became hot as any death flame with her words. Immediately I stood and shouted to the door, "I am a witch equal to any you have destroyed! Before God, I thank Him for making me a witch and not a murderous sinner!"

Moving loudly, Bulkeley entered with his constables. At once I

47

stepped to the doorway so that I could be beheaded and burned. But I was detained by reeking men as Rathel with calm confidence conveyed her latest lie.

"Your honor, this girl has been taken in the mind by witches who stole her as an infant, even as they later stole poor Lady Sarah's thinking. This child, however, can be healed. I will return with Alba to London, where with the grace of God, special practices will aid her recovery. But first I must prove not only to the world but to the deluded child herself that she is innocent and human. I have begun by scratching her with a thorn that will set a witch's skin palsied, but she has no reaction," and the lady nodded to the thin line on my arm. "Available, however, is a greater proof that even common folk may understand."

The alderman, familiar with a calm township wherein the devil rarely ventured, was weakened from the stress of killing, from evil and all its adjacent manifestations. Exasperated, he demanded that Rathel explain herself and be on with the proving or on with the execution.

"This girl is all the witch she appears," the lady told him, "for no witch can be sublime. As well, no witch can swim, but neither can many normal folk. But no human, we all know, can remain beneath the water's surface for any duration. The true witches were prepared to walk a league beneath the sea, allowing this girl to die in the process, a fact I shall demonstrate in verity."

The alderman agreed that I should be conveyed to the shore and submerged, but I would have no more of the sinners' evil.

"She lies for her own gain!" I screeched while attempting to pull away from men too strong for any girl. "I am a witch and will join my mother in Hell!"

"A pitiful delusion to be quashed," Rathel declared with sadness. "She will calm when the truth is shown and she becomes aware."

To avoid the crowd gathered to inhale witches' smoke as though perverse tobacco, the alderman had me led through the prison's rear door, into alleys and then to the sea. But once outside I found a greater cause to continue my screeching, for the odor in the air was stronger here, and if I were to concentrate, surely I would be able to determine its source. Impossible to determine was the source of that new, phenomenal sound; for with my smelling came a shrieking so near my ear, so near my heart, as to collapse me

48

with its power, throwing me to the ground where I lay—but why was my mouth open so wide as to pain my jaw? Why was my throat stretched and sore? What power had that sound to throw me, take me, yet allow me no feeling? With all the shrieking and ranting of my voice, my body, my brain, I felt nothing; for there is no higher life for a witch after death, and I had died from that smell.

The alderman's attempted prudence was thus ruined by the sensual blotting I required, that mutilation of my senses coming from me, coming from my mother. Surely this girl panicked as though stricken by Satan was a sight to rouse the populace. What thoughts had they of this screaming child with her neck stretched backward? What of the agony in her eyes and not a single tear?

Scores of sinners rushed from their buildings as insistent males pulled me to my feet. Young and old had to be pressed away from our entourage, unable to approach too near with their shoving, though removed they could remain and yet hear that groaning I had no control of, a sound as horrid as the previous shrieking, for both were sounds of death.

Once near enough the sea to smell salt and concentrate on this water rather than the smoke behind, I ended my noise, not only from exhaustion, but to give my mother her final due. With all my prideful resolve retained, I knew that verifying my identity would be a more important truth than revealing the dishonesty of this sinning woman, for it would be my final gift to Mother.

"I will take her myself in that I have handled witches from learning their revelations," Rathel proclaimed to Bulkeley.

Though balking at a lady's submitting herself to such danger, the alderman had no desire to be splashing in the sea or exposed to a witch's evil. Therefore, he agreed, the Lady Rathel a believable authority.

She led me into the water as constables restrained the sinning crowd. In my anxiety, I felt the lady moved us farther than required; so I slid beneath the water's surface to lie flat on my back in the shallows. Cooperative Rathel guided me down, then unobtrusively stepped upon me as she straightened, her weight on one heel and against my abdomen.

I could not breathe. Even in my depleted state, the water was no problem until Rathel crushed the air from my lungs and the sea rushed in. Then I suffered from both the force of her weight and

49

the terrifying suffocation. I choked and struggled to regain the surface – but the lady held me under longer, for she would not remove that foot from beneath my lungs. With the desperate effort of dying, I forced her leg from me and tore my way to the surface, gasping in God's dry air in accord with the lady's newest comments. As she straightened, drenched from having lost her balance as I fought her, Rathèl cried forth to the observing officials, delivering her latest false depiction.

"Do you see this human child and how desperately she fights me to breathe God's air again and not Satan's evil lies?!"

Constables were ordered to aid us ashore. With my lungs burning and my body bruised, I could not oppose Rathel, even more the authority now that she had jeopardized her own health to reveal the deluded child as innocent, to reveal the witch as human.

Due to a true debility, I poorly remember being conveyed along with Lady Rathel to a fine home in which she sojourned, poorly remember being dried and dressed in borrowed sinners' clothes, then made comfortable upon an elaborate bed. A clearer recollection is of my life's first nightmare, the first and worst sort for being true. Therein I found my sinning part, which seemed vengeance, and for the first instance experienced the true evil of witches.

Naturally I moved past the sinners in my sinning apparel as though the attire signified a part we shared. Through inactive streets I stepped with no sinners aware, smelling their presence or potential observation beforehand. The home I sought was not hidden to one sensitive to the reek of witch death, of piety as charred as black bodies.

Though guesting in an occupied home, the bishop lived alone, his sinner's station to be without a spouse as though witch himself. The cat sensing me once within cared no more for this witch than did any aware creature, a category not including the well souled and their corporeal evil. Surely the bishop considered the force to awaken him holy, for in me he viewed an angel of deliverance, not asking what or who was to be delivered, not wondering whether angels are properly nude.

With the sinner's gown at my feet, I was revealed by the dim lantern as a stranger known, the bishop unable to recognize Alba,

50

for he saw only a creature to become his most intimate friend—angels have neither age nor identity. As I removed his cover and pulled at his clothing, the bishop was replaced by a man, revealing a male's uniqueness, that central bone grown on occasion as though replacement for Adam's taken rib. This rib I smothered with an insertion foretold by Marybelle the swimmer. The former bishop swam against me, stroking through my body, receiving ecstasy from the special pressure of sex. Now the bishop was a man forcing his woman flat, holding her down with his bulk and his thrusting as he gained great pleasure denoted by his groaning, great pleasure from the muscle he stroked through. But soon he found the pressure of this angel uncommon, giving great pleasure that came immediately before equivalent pain. The force of her vagina holding him increased with his arousal until his ecstasy hurt. Until he had to cease his swimming. But the pressure did not end.

Careless was I, without intent, as the man failed to remove himself, the lust rushing out of him though his phallus was unchanged—too hard, too hard and hurting as noted by his silent grimace. But what equivalence had I gained to be equally pained? Was my sinning aspect the reception of the same misery in sex as any male invading me? Surely the bishop's misery could not have been worse, for my body was cramped as though crushing me, the agony so tortuous as to convince me death was next. This impression, however, was only feeling; the bishop's was fact, the former minister and temporary man grasping my thighs and attempting to remove himself as the agony increased, filling his life as completely as God's awareness. But awareness was soon lost to him as he fell away and the torture ended, replaced by a shocked numbness more terrifying than any pain; for when he fell away, he did not fall whole.

Too exhausted to move, too damaged to respond, the former man only temporarily alive looked to me, to the orgasmic contractions of my witch's muscle. Certainly no awareness was to be seen in my persona, only the same exhausted pain. And the man became religious again as he stared at the child's tearless eyes, became religious with guilt, perhaps, or had he ever felt remorse for fucking such a baby before she pinched his prick off? Whether awareness or shock, his attitude was ending, replaced by an empty sleep that

51

remained. Before morning, the bishop was holy again, for although without blood, permanently he was with his God.

Again I dreamed, for God had not allowed the interval between Mother's death and her daughter's new life to end. Hellish was this intervening era to provide dreams as tortuous as they were real, to be verified later only by further death. Within this reality that my memory made a dream, I remained upon a sinning bed. So sickly I felt the entire night that only vague impressions of lost Mother could penetrate, soon replaced with further pain, no comparison, no seeking a source for my illness in my family's death, only suffering as I perspired and shivered uncontrollably. Scarcely did I feel better when a vomiting came, an expulsion so forceful as to seem murderous. So weak that I could not lean toward the floor, upon myself and the sinners' bedding I vomited utter misery. Thereafter, my pain remained dense enough to make me oblivious to those sick materials. The Lady Rathel, however, was interested in my puke.

So ill was I that I could not distinguish that dream of illness from the evil health itself, could not be certain whether the lady entered in the morning of my day or the era of my imagining. But if not a dream, it became a dream, for what other source could generate such strange activity? Lady Rathel searched my vomit. With the sounds of sinning males outside the chamber of my nightmare, Rathel entered to view that literal illness coating the bedding and me, finding an item so desirable that she stole it. Into my vomit she reached to lift an object, and then she had six fingers on that one hand. But those nearing voices chased her hand away, men entering the room even as Rathel entered her own clothing, that increased hand swiftly into her bodice to come away with only five fingers, her stolen good safely stored against her bosom, both hands and their body bilge wiped upon her gown as though to lead the curious to that locale.

Then came street theater, the male sinners mentioning witches and asking of the girl's whereabouts as though some reasonable association existed, Lady Rathel insisting in the negative as per her recent proving. But with a new death and the witches all executed, it seems one was left, the men replied. Left in the world due to your inferior search, the lady retorted—or believe ye this child was out killing folk in all her illness? Rathel then moved aside to reveal a sickly lass with vomit everywhere and a personage too vanquished to be aware. Awake the night I've been with this child who has retched upon myself, the lady asserted, displaying her bodice. And if you need more convincing than this blatant proof, I suggest you find another occupation. Now, away with you to find the true witch, though doubtless the creature is escaped to the wild world, what with her cleverness to have eluded you while in your own town.

Away the males went to gather many witches, though Rathel pronounced them all human the following day. Thereafter, she refused her further expertise, for surely the killing demon had been lost, and work had she in greater England denouncing available evil. Away the males went, the lady allowing me to sleep, returning in my better memory to have the servants clean the bedding, though Rathel with a soft cloth wiped my face herself; for some stolen items should be handled only by similars, wealthy folk aware of an evil as expensive as death. On to London, then, for further malice, Rathel's greater task not denouncing evil but promulgating her own, the lady's best sin in the guise of a comely lass who ate men and discharged vengeance.

BOOK TWO: LONDON

Four

Sinners excel at calculation. From the firmament of nature issues the Earth in portions, all its living parts mathematical in growth: the geometry of a leaf's veining, the symmetry of a ferret's coat. Ponderously imitating God's superior ways, sinners effect nature's numerics by calculating exact lengths and widths of the stone rows they've heaped to form buildings. How profound these people are to emulate a tree by killing it, cutting it, and rearranging the pieces into shops. But how unnatural was this witch to approve of, even appreciate, their architecture?

No more unnatural than silence, a trait found only in the sinners' realm. In the deepest caves are scurrying creatures' feet or water dripping from cracks in the stressed but stabilized, irregular roof. No forest is without a variety of unsilent animals; every desert has a wind. And have certain oceans not been violated by the sounds of witches' feet dragging, dragging along their floors? In my dreams, every sea is defiled by this noise. But only in a sinners' construction have I heard utter silence. Only in a site free of life's activities did I begin to understand the lives of sinners.

The tremendous buildings of London I first saw in a daze, a dull delirium of living wherein my life of forest and family was exchanged for a land of city and enemy. The sea voyage from Man's Isle to England remains to me a poor memory of vague aching. That additional journey up the River Thames then deeper into London I recall no more clearly, my memory tainted by a death to last a lifetime and dreams to corrupt my recollection by becoming real.

Days after my arrival, I was scarcely more comfortable or actively alive, not speaking nor eating, feigning no interest in Rathel's world, which had been reduced to her massive town house that seemed a city in itself. Provided as my own was a chamber, a bed, and thereupon I remained, sleeping for constant hours, dark and light, until one morn when Lady Rathel stepped from my room and left me an exit. Having said something I ignored, Rathel vacated my chamber through a door, a door left open so that she or one of her countless servants could come with ease to speak with me fruitlessly. Since even witches know doors to be temporary holes in walls, after Rathel departed, I followed. Achieving my best awareness in this sinning world, I understood that more than one door existed in the house, and surely one to lead outside. Therefore, I searched until finding a door in a wall with a window that revealed the exterior. Since the door was locked, I waited behind drapery like an animal in the wilds, one hiding for prey or from a predator. Wait I did for the first person to quit the house through that exit I observed. Then brazenly I ran outside, past the departing Rathel.

Being no expert in counting, I knew not how many days I was gone. Being no specialist in surviving within a sinner's world, I was too weak to struggle with the constables who returned me to Rathel's house, her city. Then I consented to eat rather than starve, consuming uncooked food that would not sicken me, thereafter returning to that chamber designated as mine, returning for more sleep, further vagueness.

Sense enough had Lady Rathel to wait for my strength to increase before again speaking to me through that open doorway. Her next offer I reasonably heeded, for the woman offered to reveal London so fully that I might learn of quitting the realm. Of course, I agreed to travel with her through the city.

That day I experienced my first carriage journey. Immediately I felt an odd guilt for being dragged in a wooden box by horses that should have been free in the wilds; yet were they harnessed any less than I? At least I felt relief that I would never reek of sinners' contact as did these animals, because I was being shown an escape. But Lady Rathel lied. Her true goal in this journey was to display her world as so vast and complicated that one ignorant witch would never leave alone, and that to promote my own continued living I should remain with Rathel until . . . Until I somehow killed for her as she had mentioned on Man's Isle.

During that lengthy voyage, I came to understand that London had infinite directions all of which led to one another. The buildings were so massive and varied that the accumulation seemed an artificial seashore with abrupt, stone cliffs. Though different from the structures of Jonsway as the barrow vine is from the silkwood tree, nevertheless, the roofs and walls were recognizable as constituting a village, one whose mass and might changed its very species from town to city. No part of Jonsway was so dense that the wilds could not be sensed beyond, but London was terrifying in having no end. The very quantity of buildings and paved streets and the accompanying populace were so ponderous as to temper my reactions. I was not then capable of contemplating such a bulk of new experience, my perceptions lessened by the remnants of my former life, inundated with past disasters. But I understood that there was no leaving London, only being in London. Therefore, my reaction to this endless city was a sense of being both lost and trapped within its midst. Evoking this response was the lady's intent, but succeed she did beyond her plans; for whereas Rathel meant to intimidate me with London, she did not predict that I would also find an achievement of her people to inspire regard.

The sight to astonish me was St. Nicholas Cathedral. The largest building seen, St. Nicholas was the most excessive yet least possessive of constructions, being both extravagant

59

and selfless, this contradictory grandiloquence inspiring my awe.

Obviously a place of worship, the building seemed fit for Satan as its deity. The complexity of stone levels and probing spires, multiple peaks and curves thrusting upward, seemed endless rude jabs toward the sky, stone gesticulations denoting not calm worship but a type of passion; and is not passion a type of torment? Those acute roofs, complicated facades, and gaudy flashes of colored glass implied that the evil of excess was being worshiped.

A fog veiled the air between coach and cathedral, a structure that even when obscured seemed superior to such meager elements as moisture. But what influence made God's creation of airborne water seem subservient to piled stone? I then became dismayed that all the passing sinners found concern only in their own movement, as though their individual progress could compare to their massed religion's greatest manifestation. But no sinner displayed such enthusiasm, only London's single witch.

Beside me on a stuffed seat that seemed luxurious to no witch, Lady Rathel viewed her companion, noting my interest that drew her own. After tapping the coach partition for the driver to halt, Rathel spoke to me.

"Alba, your attention is unhidden. The honesty you display in not hiding your interest is typical of your people. But I find your concern with architecture surprising."

"My regard is not for this construction's being an edifice, but due to its being a church," I replied. "My concern is not for builders, but for God."

"And how is it you understand with no prior knowledge that this edifice is a church, and not a . . . a university?"

"No grander building have I seen," I returned. "Even sinners are sensible enough to save their greatest efforts to promote immortality."

Evidently the cathedral had caused my life's energy to return, for although I had previously muttered to Rathel, now it seemed we had shared a conversation, one whose lack of animosity implied that I might soon accept this sinner's presence as though enduring a hard winter. All my sensitive comprehension was disheartening, however, because I would reject the need to become accustomed to this lady—I longed for my natural life to be returned. But I allowed no clear thoughts of such desires, for they were impossible to manifest.

"This is St. Nicholas Cathedral," the woman told me, "a structure built two centuries past."

I could smell her attempt to enthuse me with longevity, but since the cathedral was scarcely older than my mother, the sinner failed to impress.

We would enter. The lady's mentioning that we might as per my choosing was a notion to secure my agreement. I found myself walking toward a mountain, a natural entity never seen by the white witch. But this mountain was a sinner's imitation. The structure seemed to grow as we approached, looming as though about to fall, about to crush me with its sensations. Nearing with Rathel, I could smell more than the odor of sinners: I could smell the stone fragrance of the building, smell that rare scent of glass seldom experienced by witches—and how was this material made?—smell dried resins applied to seal the timbers, smell the metal portions on the windows and doors, the forged and heated and beaten metal that had first frightened me in Jonsway and would ever be distressing. But these odors all became secondary as we gained the entry, an appropriately grand set of doors. Rathel opened one with some needed heft, its sound all mass and movement. Then we were inside.

The entrance chamber was as voluminous as the entirety of any home in Jonsway, but beyond I could sense the vast space of the cathedral proper. All about me were intricate surfaces the sinners had oversimplified. A deep frieze's rolling shapes of vines and flowers lacked the subtleties of an actual plant perceivable on endless levels. Unlike any natural mineral, the hard floor was flawlessly flat. Woefully had the sinners failed to improve upon nature: here a leaf's shape, there the colors of fruit, all superficial.

I waited to proceed from this chamber, waited for a superior experience, for I presumed that grandeur lay beyond. Lady Rathel for a moment spoke with men dressed in the manner of the Bishop Dalimore I had known. These folk I ignored more than that man of scant reverence, for beyond was the hollow heart of the cathedral hopefully filled with spiritual things. Rathel and I first filled the building with sound, our footfalls as we entered a corridor enveloping the air. The sound preceded us, becoming lost in an inner atmosphere more sizable than hearing. To either side were additional, smaller rooms, but at this corridor's end was the greatest cavern of this cliff, the main nave that expressed so profound a volume as to define space as another of God's elements. True, the floor was covered with pews as though a larger version of the common Jonsway church I had attended, but this hollow heart was filled with centuries of the sinners' finest attempts at holy grandeur, and I was moved by the sincerity of their worship.

The far wall was so distant that I sensed a faint haze, the cathedral encompassing such a space as to form its own weather. But this impression vanished when I saw that the same wall held a crassness turned sublime; for the heights of the vast surface were filled with elaborate panes of colored glass depicting scenes of Jesus and his cohorts. The characters, however, were of no import. The clarity of the hues extending toward me in the form of light, sheer light, was a true accomplishment of the sinners. This complexity of crystals seemed a sky itself instead of a mere usage of the atmosphere to transmit glassy hues, and the high sight led me higher. There went my vision and my breath, for the ceiling's reaching dome was another sky, a completed curve of sharp arches leading to the dome's center, a round row of glass shapes each larger than I, clear but colored connectors between God's sky and His witch below.

No Rathel existed in my world, for alone with God I stood in the center of His nave, enraptured by silence before the glass wall, the arched ceiling a clear cavern to house me. Then, without the unneeded intermediary of perception, I came to sense the concept of this edifice. Without sight or smell I achieved purest intellection, comprehending a most important aspect of sinners. Though I had known of their obsessions since Jonsway, the sinners' need to verify themselves to Lord God revealed their similarity to witches; for whereas no witch is obsessed, both mortal and well souled love God and love to worship Him. As I stood in the sinners' building that was their worship incarnate, I was filled with a contradictory grandeur appropriate for sinners; for even as they damaged their world, they worshiped the God Who made it. More understanding I became of Lord God's sinning people who by this edifice were shown to be imperfect in their sinning. As I stood motionless within this new universe, the experience affixed within me a change of living, change of life. And I could read the sinners' hearts in this machination, their edifice device not a vain display of craftsmanship, but a selfless conveyance of gratitude for expected salvation.

What inspiration was St. Nicholas Cathedral to Lady Rathel that following our visit there she changed her ways by changing mine? During my early days in London, I remained clothed in that dress lent by some Jonsway lady. After St. Nicholas, however, Rathel determined that I would be punished for my interest in London by dressing as did the city women. A servant would therefore educate me in the discipline of elaborate attire. Most of Rathel's slaves, however, seemed less than enthused with my presence, offering me neither smile nor kind word, but what was rudeness to a girl stolen from her mother's world? As for my response, what regard did the hirelings of a murderess deserve?

I gave them the regard of offense. A particular slave woman habitually entered my chamber to speak too often. With her I supped in a manner, achieving a social insect—a cockroach—which I retained until the servant came again for chatting. I then ate the creature, which resembled a beetle but tasted like sinners. The woman departed at once with the reddest face and tightest jaws.

All the servants thereafter ignored the new girl, this mutual disregard appropriate in that we presented no mutual danger. Especially safe the servants seemed in being female, none having the energetic smell of their mistress, though often they attempted to command one another to no fruition. The one sent by Rathel to instruct me in dressing was named Elsie, a solid but not large woman who smelled less than young but appeared less than old. Significant was that Elsie had been audience to my roach repast. Without mentioning bugs, Elsie approached me in that shadow aspect of my individual room, came to aid me, so she maintained.

"So I'm here to be helping you learn proper dressing, lass," she offered with uncertainty and insistence, a combination stemming from her desire to aid a youth who had proven herself distasteful, so to speak.

Elsie spoke with an odd inflection, a distinctive manner called an "accent" by sinners, who speak differently according to their locale of origin. In this manner were the sinning regions demarked, not by the natural delineation of glade and valley, but of suburb and estate, of wealthy homes and the dirt streets of workers.

"Not being one of your windows, I require no obsessive draping," I told the servant. "Attired enough I have been, and shall remain."

"Not attired enough, I'm saying, for a lady of any age," the woman retorted, "with no underthings below to hide your figure which one day might be womanly, though not if you don't start eating more properly than you're dressing."

Typical of Elsie was this characteristic of turning sentences into speeches, that initial speaking, remarkably enough, not an end in itself.

"And the purpose, now, is for you to become a lady," she continued, "for having a pleasant face is not enough in fine society. Neither is a handsome figure when its parts are being flaunted and seen within one's dress. A dress, I'm having to add, due more one of my station than an English lady, new or not. And your hair, then, is fit more some wild thing than even me; for at least I'm brushing mine each day and night, more than I'm saying for you, girl, in that your head is all a tangle."

"If Lord God had desired His people to brush their hair," I replied as though some clerical expert, "He would have made our fingers thinner and more numerous."

"If He'd had wished His lovely girls to seem ugly," Elsie retorted, "you'd be looking like me all along."

Yes, she was ugly, I noticed, her only charming characteristic. Though nearly as short as a crone, the servant had none of the subtle nuances of skeletal structure that delineate witches as a different race. Nevertheless, she lacked the pretentious odor of her employer, and required no titular addition to her common name as did ladies and bishops. And though she had the attribute of lacking sophistication, Elsie was a sinner nonetheless, not animal enough to provide me with pleasant company.

Within my (my?) chamber we stood, a site the servant would have me emulate by covering us both with fabric, on our seats and extremities and every vertical surface. Regardless, I had yet to determine why this servant's own attire was inferior to Lady Rathel's, since the fabrics seemed similarly rich. Of course, the gaudier the better was the rule of sinning clothiers. Elsie's frilly, white apron was servants' wear never seen on a lady, not even Rathel, who dressed mildly compared to some. And here was the basic difficulty of our conversation: not appearance but emulation.

"Learning to be a lady is not something I need accomplish and thereby become as calculating as the Rathel person," I declared to Elsie. "No witch would choose to live as bizarrely as she, not even one as odd as I."

Standing firmly before me, arms straight at her sides, Elsie reeked of patience as she looked directly to my face and replied.

"Ah, I'm hearing from our mistress of your delusions, lass, but you'd best not be calling yourself a witch, for it's unbelievable with your fine appearance and without you causing the first palsy."

"Only sinners bring plagues," I retorted. "Witches are a healthy folk who require no doctoring. Instead of commenting as to my 'delusions,' Rathel might have explained to you that the common sinning notions of witches are as fantastical and false as tales of elves and fairies."

"What Mistress Amanda is explaining to me," Elsie added patiently, "is of your former life tainted by evil. So I might be pitying your past, child, but since your present will be fine as soon as you allow it, I'll just be on with me job." Then she approached to aid in my ladylike dressing. But between us women, only I understood that the true delusion was the false life being forced upon me that I would continue to reject.

"So I'm showing you, girl," Elsie added, "the difference between petticoats and pantaloons." Then from a tall bureau she removed fabric items that she placed upon the bed, innumerable white parcels with crinkly edges that she would have me apply simultaneously. "The proper order I'm telling you, and an aid in donning them as well I'm being," she concluded, and stepped toward me, implying direct contact.

Though I made no aggressive move as the servant neared, I reached her first, taking the woman's wrist with no exceptional pressure, though I was discomforted by the contact.

Never before had I touched a sinner. But from the grip of sinners to steal me, kill me, I knew their flesh to be warm, and felt this heat upon grasping Elsie, unable to understand how they could bear such an inner fire. Was this not the aspect of their nature to make them so active? Always driven by their own, internal heat, the cause for flames being so desirable to them. Elsie's response was thus predictable. Unkindly, I intended to disturb her. Herein I succeeded, for with my firm touch, the servant looked down to my hand, thereafter pulling her entire body away.

The Lady Vidgeon had poked my hair and fabric. Elsie received all skin, cold skin.

"Blessed Jesus, lass," she hissed while looking toward me with a distraught visage, "you would have to be dead to feel so cold." And she continued to step away, quitting the room as though she had been asked to tend the dead. So absolute was her move that I assumed she also quit the Lady Rathel's household, as though such employ were abundant.

It is not. Rare is the witch with a servant. I retained mine, however, for Elsie remained. Though I desired only to have this sinner avoid me, I was surprised to find her soon returned. She wore gloves, the type used to protect sinners from winter. These would protect Elsie from a witch's coldness. Standing again with her arms comfortably straight at her sides, Miss Elsie stated her position.

"You and I, lass, shall become familiar."

Though making no move toward me, the servant controlled my dressing. Remaining in the doorway, Elsie pointed with her gloves that would surely insulate her from my cool demeanor. Firmly, literally, she pointed out how and where to apply each article of clothing.

I smelled her fear, but also her determination. And I complied, the witch not pleased but nearly amused with this stern servant. Because I was a witch, I felt shame for cooperating, but loneliness precluded my receiving torment from understanding that the next person to share with me familiarity would be a sinner.

A seamstress was hired to construct apparel in accord with my specific shape. Standing in thin undergarments as a humming woman hovered about me was less distressful than many previous manipulations of the sinners. And Elsie's observing every move of the seamstress was somehow supportive. Perhaps she had mentioned cold skin to this woman. Perhaps not. Days later, a raft of garments began entering my chamber and my personal furniture. Elsie was grandly

67

pleased at the finery, but I had no appreciation. Rathel was nearer in response to her servant than her ward.

"I am so pleased that your attire is now excellent, Alba. Despite your disregard for satisfying me, I thank you for pleasing Miss Elsie. Eventually you will find her a mild and cordial person. As a type of reward, I would like to show you a part of London that may refresh you in its wildness. Perhaps on our journey you may find a way of escaping the city. Perhaps not."

Perhaps I would agree to see Rathel's wild site with the briefest reply and no mention of escaping, a possibility I had not rejected, though flight is no topic to be discussed with one's captor.

Since the overall ambience of the city was oppressive, I continued to have difficulty in sensing London as I would a new forest whose parts would be comprehensible from familiarity with the genre. Being dragged about by captured horses was no aid. Along the street only moments before reaching our destination—but we did not stop. Through the window, I saw a green area of trees and grass, and though flanked by streets and containing a few walking sinners; nevertheless, this was wilderness compared to the brief frontage of Rathel's town house.

"This is not our goal?" I asked the sinning lady.

"This is but a park," she replied. "Our goal is grand."

We continued. During this journey, I noticed at the end of several streets smaller versions of that park, areas of natural land—with elms and brush—appropriately termed "greens." But since none was grand, none was visited by the heinous lady and her slave. We did not stop until after my first major horror in London.

The first experience to strike me with fear acute enough to be physical was another variety of sinning transportation. This was no coach nor carriage, however, but a bridge, in some intellectual manner the same as a boat in that both allow passage over water. But boats are sensible in floating like a log or animal; whereas this bridge seemed a road foolishly made to float in the air. Bridges I had seen before on Man's Isle, but they were low and short and encountered prior to a family member's drowning. Those of Man's Isle were sheds; the one we approached was akin to St. Nicholas Cathedral: so massive as to be of another species, like sinners and witches. Hershford Bridge was high to allow the passage of large boats below, and constructed not like a timber bridge of Man's Isle nor the lesser bridges of London. The latter had thick walls with cavelike passages for boats, but Hershford Bridge was set upon pilasters too thin to support its own mass. Perverse these sinners were to make lesser bridges more substantial than their greatest.

I was astonished to look from the coach and see myself above a broad river. Boats floated safely below, but I was suspended by poor idea, for roadways cannot float. They are heavy and must sink, sink to the bottom of this river and take the witch along, the witch utterly fearful of any water since Marybelle had been thrown into the sea. Looking out from the coach, I lost my breath, lost my ability to think; for I was held by the devil and about to be dropped, about to sink and drown and thereby manifest with my own death those nightmares I had been suffering of Marybelle's demise. For I knew not what had occurred to her beneath the Irish Sea, only knew that the ocean had killed my sister as the Thames would soon murder me.

My final fear was the smell of death, Marybelle gone without an odor, but I would smell my own body rotting on the bottom, the stench exactly as permanent as Mother's acrid deposit in the air. My upcoming death seemed punishment from Satan for my foolish inference that because I had never smelled Marybelle's dying, perhaps great God had again overcome the devil and allowed a witch to live. This imbecilic notion vanished as my dread peaked, the certainty that Hershford would hurl me into the water where I would smother with a death as sure as burning. But my terror extended as though a bridge itself, extended as the coach passed over the solid bridge no less supportive than the following roadway.

As we gained the bank and I frantically made an escape, Lady Rathel grasped me, insisting that I calm and explain myself. I then thought of her stepping upon me as I lay on the ocean floor, thought of her ruining my pride by ruining my proof, but what was the equivalence? My only reply was to reach for the door, but I could not decode the mechanism, fumbling at the metal latch as Rathel restrained me. Finally I spoke the single word, "bridge." Then the sinner understood, providing me with a comparison; for Rathel ruined me again by explaining that to return we would necessarily cross that bridge again. And though she insisted that our next passage would be as safe as the last, I could not heed her truth, defeated again by the sinners' heinous world wherein fear was not an evil to be avoided, but a byproduct of city living.

I was taken to a place of geometry; the trees and hedges of Pangham Gardens were cut into false shapes, cubes and spheres. Pangham's large pools held floating buckets of flowers, and metal fishes swam below. Yes, the fishes in these stone ponds were of the brightest gold—the astounding sinners had managed to coat God's creatures with their evilest material. And the fishes were real, for they emitted a smell no sinner could replicate. Forever I would walk on the colored gravel of Pangham Gardens where no carriage was allowed and stare at the fishes rather than cross that bridge again, stare at the fishes without wondering further of their organic gold, stare at the fishes until the sinning lady told me they were rare in England but grew wild in the Orient. Stare at the fishes and walk forever until Rathel understood that my prime sight was a bridge in my future, the one to haunt me in the real.

"We return with no delay," she said, "so that your fear will be alleviated. Within the coach, I shall close the curtains so that nothing frightening can be seen. Understand your safety in advance, Alba, for I am with you and have no desire to die."

Her tactic was successful until halfway across when I

ripped the opaque curtain aside to see, for I could smell the water and sense the height and needed to see the bridge collapsing so that I might react. So that I might grasp the air or watch myself fall and sink and drown. But Rathel was correct, for eventually we were over safely, the only damage to my memory, and not to be repaired.

Five

Water held me in the city. Within Rathel's house I remained, having no intents of escaping London since I knew that crossing a bridge would be required. After Hershford Bridge, I was entrapped not by the city, but by my fears, a rather insubstantial prison for so physical a witch.

After enjoying relief from surviving the Thames, I accepted an unusual feeling of security. Although in a city of sinners, I would not be found the witch unless revealed by Rathel, and she desired me for herself. No other dangers threatened me as long as I remained away from the Thames. And though this disposition continued into evening, the day's social end brought a change not to my thinking but to my life.

Donning that light gown for sleeping as per Elsie's education, I waited for a servant to enter my chamber and kill the hated candle, to reduce the evil oil lamp never known in my mother's home. So wicked are sinners that to provide themselves with light after God ends His true light of day they burn little parts of their households. The smells were unlike cooking animals, unlike any odors known to me, but they stank. Worse was the heat: not the quantity, but the immediacy. I could not bear to approach the candle and blow it out or use the snuffer, and the oil lamp was worse in being surrounded by hot glass. No sleeping would I have with those fire sources staring at me, as though prepared to attack, the witch so aware of her surrounds that she now could suffer from them.

Elsie's entrance was virtually joyous, for she was pleased to comply with my congenial request to quench the flames, though she wondered why the tasks were not within my capacity. This acceptable experience with Elsie recalled her assertion of familiarity to come. As I lay with improved feelings, I thanked Lord God that this bed had no major portion made of metal, not the posts nor canopy, only some fasteners ensconced in the joints they secured. But there my praying ended, and misery began.

I felt so secure that I remembered my past. At once I was overwhelmed by Mother's death. With all of my energy, I struggled not to consider her sight, her self, her companionship and love, all gone, completely gone. This anguish peaked with impossibility, for she could *not* be gone, could *not* be absent from every part of the forest, could *not* be separate from me forever. But she was gone, was dead, was in this impossible state, and would never return, gone with no fault of her own. But I felt no blame for myself, only sorrow, utter sorrow, a tormented state to negate the relief in survival I had found that day. Nothing remained but Mother's death, nothing but a void in my heart where my love for her resided. Then came pain, physical pain in my head and stomach and rigid lungs, a pain to weaken me so much that I could not think, only feel, feel the loss that was my mother, feel an agony that no person— witch or sinner—could be evil enough to deserve, mine nonetheless, my torment forever.

This suffering was the core of my beginning life in London, the awareness of Mother's death followed by bodily pain. But Elsie's kindness of that evening influenced me toward considering Mother's greatest love, which was her daughter, until I understood that Mother would have me survive and love her forever without torment. I thought of the sinners who killed her: the alderman and bishop, the ostensible Lady Rathel, the one to have stolen me—or was it merely borrowing? Had not this woman attempted to spare Mother? This contention of hers was reasonable in that Mother's continued existence would have been beneficial to me, and I was the witch Rathel desired, her

73

purpose to have me kill for her and thereby achieve some vengeance. Now Rathel had provided me with a safe chamber to encourage my cooperation, encourage further murder, but that act was of the future – that act was unbelievable. My current situation was more important: my new home and world and my need to survive therein. Then came recollection of grand St. Nicholas Cathedral, of heinous Hershford Bridge. Thereupon, I was struck not with memories nor details of these experiences, but their power, the inordinate energy they claimed within my existence. As though a chamber pot filled to the brim with urine, that excess energy spilled and slopped upon me, and it stank. My reaction was to demand that I survive the power and potential of my life in London. I determined to understand my current place and live as best as possible with Mother in my memory and God in my heart. I would begin with my chamber, my bed, but not that day, for I was exhausted from emoting. I slept, no dreaming, pleased the entire night to have no further heat within my personal quarters, no fire within my heart.

Eventually Elsie found me beneath the bed. What a fine place for hiding, the space below tight about me, the remaining world separated from the concealed witch. The liquid applied to the wooden floor was partially a natural stuff, for I recognized the scent of pine sap and walnut oil; but something had been heated here, the resin cooked to change it to a sinners' creation. I would make the product less noticeable by rubbing against the wooden surface as I crawled into this adequate hole, crawling out only when Elsie came with the broom to poke at me and complain.

"Aye, and you're trying me again, lass," she moaned as though damaged, "trying me by clambering on the floor in your lovely nightclothes. So you're coming out, now, to be dressing proper for the waking hours as I've taught you. Then you're hieing yourself for a meal, child, else I'm leaving your lamp burn the entire night, along with extra candles."

Fair enough, and out I moved, determining to be witch enough to have gratitude for this woman's kindly aid of the previous night. But not enough gratitude could I find to violate my stomach with the congealed animal grease considered food in this obscene universe. Instead of eating, I applied myself toward London.

Not all of the apparel Elsie provided could I connect alone. Included in my wardrobe were diabolical corsets and gowns whose laces and straps could not be secured by the wearer. How could even sinners be so foolish as to design apparel the wearer could not don unaided, and worse, not remove alone? What if a lady fell from a bridge into a river and had to unburden herself of a mass of fabric so sodden it prevented her climbing up the bank toward air?

Having sufficient familiarity with my bed and that satisfying space below, I continued with the remainder of my chamber, achieving a strange pride with that idea of possession: my chamber. The pride I received came from a sense of shelter and security. The accompanying strangeness was a taint of guilt from my taking any comfort from the sinners, strangeness being appropriate since my mentor's prime interest was death.

The ceiling was bordered with cornices as though a moderate version of St. Nicholas's entry with one more spider. Patterned carpet on the floor, patterned paper on two walls, wood on those remaining. The bed I knew, but how remarkably large it was, and extravagant with its layers of sheets and quilts, not unlike the clothing I was to wear, not unlike that bed in which I slept my last day on Man's Isle. Here was a blessed lack of concise recollection, for it seems I had become ill and vomited upon that clean surface. Of my current bed I imagined the deeper contents: some type of softest straw stuffed into a precise, rectangular form. But, no, that was imagination. The true substance had not been washed enough to remove its scent. From the first, I had found comfort in my bed and pillows because of their natural odor, but now I knew it dead.

75

The smell was of feathers and down, materials not to be removed from living fowl. Then I wondered of the hairbrush given me, wondered whether a pig's bristles could be removed from the animal while alive, and if so, would the plucking not be torture? Refraining from vomiting upon my new bed despite the good cause of my fowl awareness, I prayed that God might forgive sinners for their iniquities if only He could end them as well, prayed also in apology for my failing to recognize the dead smell earlier, finding selfish comfort instead.

That night I slept on the carpet. I thus discerned it wool, and that is a sheep's covering. At least this fur can be removed without destroying the bearer. How typical of sinners to develop so odd an activity as shaving, then apply it not only to themselves, but animals.

That day I completed examining my (my?) chamber. The soft blue and grey counterpane was not unpleasant, if only because it was not metal nor unfortunate tree flesh soaked in oil, merely woven from the bodies of innocent flax and cotton plants. As for the other fabrics, I remained uncertain of this "silk" on some of my clothing, though it smelled like a bug's excrement. How silly of my nose.

Trees were everywhere. The entire floor, the windows, their sills, and the myriad furniture were made of former trunks. Here was a tall construction with a surface folded flat to write upon. Many drawers and crannies in this thing, paper and ink and quills—and there were more deceased fowls to haunt me, praise God I could not write. Against the opposite wall stood a more massive piece: the armoire tall as a sinning male wherefrom Miss Elsie had attained some of my clothing, certain nether items brought from one of the paired bureaus rife with sliding boxes.

Shameful was this furniture for its artifice and waste. How unlike a flower, whose complex portions stem from a single seed, whose entirety grows from little; whereas furniture is false, made from butchered pieces of vanquished trees. Flowers come from life, whereas furniture delineates death, the death of plants like flowers themselves. The commode, for example, with its feet humorously carved to resemble the paws of some animal, with its lacquer coating and gilt appliqués and veneers. Exemplified here was sinners' craftsmanship, which means annihilating a natural thing to reattach its parts not with ease, but obsession.

Ah—but here was an item to examine. Upon a woody bureau with hateful metal handles was a timepiece. Of course, sinners had invented mechanisms that split the day into smaller pieces called hours, hours into tiny bits called minutes, minutes into virtually nonexistent packets called seconds, all of these sinners' moments unneeded by a witch. "Moment": how fine and broadly applicable an interval, but inadequate for sinners, since moments require no devices for measure. Furthermore, moments are silent; whereas all the sinners' time portions are as loud as their timepieces, for my clock clicked. A sinner's time is filled with noisome activity, having the same contents as a clock. Sound enough this beggar made that the witch deposited it beneath the winter clothing in her armoire. Therefore, when Miss Elsie came to set the pendulum into a motion to set me toward madness, she would find only silence.

Situated against the walls were chairs, standing cases containing books other than the Bible, adjacent shelves with those hated, hot lights. Also present were hygienic devices: a stand with lavatory and water jar made of clay with delicate paintings of flowers seeming no great art to me. Most imaginative of all was that final piece, the chamber pot I had been using since so instructed my first day in London: a sturdy pottery item unusual in utility, but attractive in its smell. Not that witches have an especial desire to be inhaling our droppings' fumes, but at least these matèrials are natural. And despite the servants' attempts to remove the thing's waste odor by removing the waste each day and occasionally splashing in some perfumed liquid, the pot had come to smell like me. Regarding utility, perhaps the invention was excellent; for if not in these pots, where would all of London's people be peeing? Pray God not in the parks. A further curiosity was of the site where these pots were emptied. Pray God not in the parks.

Situated against the walls were paintings that might have drawn my interest had they not been made of oil smears. A natural oil, I could smell, seemingly from the flax plant, but similar greases were used for cooking killed animals. So away to the walls' better view: windows. Windows in each of two perpendicular walls, for my bedchamber was situated in the building's corner, the second and uppermost story. Through one tall window I viewed the house's frontage, and across the broad street a largish stone town house not unlike ours (ours?). The chamber's rear, larger window had fewer, more expansive panes, none colored: Rathel's house, though elaborate, was no cathedral. I approached this window, pulling aside the curtains to find a revelation. Behind Rathel's home was her garden.

The dull witch had not previously noticed this area, but finally I was pleased in London, for here was my (my?) own park! Near my window grew a large and lovely elm tree. Beyond were sycamores and maples. Below were gravel paths winding through lush, well-kempt grass of a particularly bright green, hedges and bushes unfortunately cut flat or curved, but living organisms nonetheless. I saw flowering plants and spiky, unusual grasses in tall clumps, many plants unknown to Man's Isle, but loved by this witch regardless. Quickly then I attempted to decode the method and mechanism whereby I could part the glass panes and smell the garden, this living segment of the sinners' world enough to make me laugh with joy, then growl with perturbation since I could not open the blooming thing, unable to grasp that hateful, metal latch. And when finally I touched the handle from anger, all my manipulations were to no avail, if only because I would touch the metal, but barely. Then came an encouraging idea: I only had to move downstairs and exit the house to experience the entirety of the garden. So from my chamber I ran, left across the balcony, down the stairs with rapid feet and not a stumble, following the only route to the building's rear, through a swinging door into a

78

corridor terminating in a glassy door through which I saw shrubbery, a door I achieved but could open no more than the bloody window.

What a meager entrapment for the sinners' world of murder. How foolish of Londoners not to use the simple wooden latch of Mother's cabin. How disheartening not to gain that good life removed by a mere finger's thickness of glass due to mechanical ignorance. After sighs and slumping shoulders, I sadly contemplated my future. Either I would abandon my plans, endlessly attempt to open the door on my own, or seek the aid of a servant. Turning to discern my location, I discovered the kitchen at the corridor's opposite end. That locale emitted smells of burning animals and sounds of human voices. Help lay beyond. But no region could be more repulsive than that crypt of bloody baking. I would deny myself the garden rather than enter the kitchen.

Viewing the garden again, I espied a large woman hacking away at a bush with a metal implement. This was Theodosia, the one servant of the household never seen above the stairs. Soon this woman saw me, and gestured that I might join her. After some failed manipulation of the lockwork, I revealed to Theodosia an ignorant countenance. Herein I was successful, for the servant approached to call through the glass that I might come out if I so desired. More loudly I replied that I knew not how to open the door. No part of England exists so wild as to be without *doors*, she insisted. Briefly I hollered that such was my home. Theodosia then stepped to the door with no kind face to grasp the latch and succeed no more than I, for some witch had locked it from within. Thus, the servant became so exasperated as to howl in wordless consternation.

"What is your great distress?" I cried. "I am the one trapped with no escape!"

Soon we were pulling at the door from opposite sides, Theodosia leaning near the glass to point toward the door mechanisms and mutter unfamiliar terminology as though I comprehended her technical language. Pull on this and that I

79

did without success. What a scene we made to the next servant nearing, one noted in advance by a wave of sick cooking smell; for Miss Delilah approached from the kitchen to expertly release the bolt and activate the latch with a glare and not the first word, returning to the kitchen with a gait of annoyance.

Immediately Theodosia stomped back to her work, grumbling furiously. And though with the door's opening I smelled a raft of natural fragrances, my pleasure was polluted by the consternation I had caused. But with thanks to the good Lord I entered the garden, intent upon enjoying this realm whether I suffered from it or not. Enjoy the green sights and growing smells I did until coming to the well and finding a tiny river that in fact was a sinner-made ditch certainly meant to resemble the Thames, that small wooden bridge above bleeding well intended to represent Hershford. Around and to the house again, through the same door that in my genius I had left unlocked, to my chamber and beneath the bed forever.

"In that I am equal in this instance to my reputation of evil existence, you might believe me likely to chew away the feet beneath your ankles if you allow me not the small privilege of a familiar companion."

Distressing were these words to Delilah, the blood boiler and occasional chambermaid, whose current job was to clamber about attacking dust wherever it was encountered. No fond emotions had I for this servant, considering her curt response toward me when found innocent of doorways. Most upsetting to the servant was my final phrase, for worse than having her legs gnawed to gory nubs was this girl's having a fiend for a friend.

"But that's the greatest, nastiest spider I have ever laid me eyes upon, miss, and it's well lodged itself in a corner of your ceiling."

"Despite its size and impressive appearance, the beast is a kindly soul harming only those genuinely pesty insects whose place on God's ceiling, I am sad to say, is to provide my friend with nourishment."

"But the mistress will chew my feet off her own self if I do not smash the thing."

My next response was to cruelly bare my teeth, a display unbelievable to any witch. Delilah was duly cautious, unable to bear the thought of battling the spider, me, and thereafter Mistress Amanda for having failed with the former. Therefore, she accepted my own exhibited animalism in order to avoid the terrors of that well-legged beast, determining to worry later about the horrors of the wigged one. Taking her broom, she departed my chamber in defeat, grumbling unpleasantly.

"I'll send Miss Elsie up, then, who'll not accept such unkindness from a child."

Elsie did not come for the fiend, only calling for the young wench to lure her to the day's second meal. And though she eyed the spider upon entering my bedchamber, Elsie's comment was cooperative.

"Aye, and you're keeping the beast if you will, lass, but if you start rearing a mass of them, then you and I will be mouthing at each others' limbs to see who's coming away the shorter."

Blandly was I affected by her attempts to influence me with humor.

"Since I have dressed in the strange manner of sinners and have brushed my hair till it no longer is the protective coat God made it but more of a sinners' drapery meant paradoxically to obscure windows, I'll be trotting off for a bit of a bite now, unless you prefer I starve."

"So why is it, then, you're not eating this spider, if you've such a taste for bugs?" the servant brazenly wondered.

"Why is it you sinners eat pigs and not cats?" I returned.

"And what's your meaning, lass, in this word 'sinner'? 'Tis a common word, but not from your mouth, I fear."

"Bugs in the mouth are not common with sinners, one of which I am not. A sinner is any person not a witch. Therefore, you and I are one of each."

The woman pondered my explication long enough to understand that she was not being called a witch. Then her ideas returned to consumption.

"And what of you leading me to believe you've no use for luncheon, girl, if you're about to be doing all this normal eating?"

"I seek the nourishment of God's natural foods of vegetables and fruit," I told her. "It's your city dwellers' cannibalism in devouring dead animals who once were friends to all humans that sickens me. The kitchen itself seems hellish, and surely you are aware of the consequences of your forcing me to consume its bloody products."

"Aye, and the mistress is allowing you to eat raw greens after her fine meats have been removed. Rude you are, girl, to be eating with your benefactor only after she's finished. But that's better, I'm saying, than provoking your sensitive stomach. And a terrible organ it is, what with your huge puking on the table, right upon the cloth and the silver eating ware. And I am the miserable one having to clean it, when in fact it's due to your endless vegetables not being settled by some firm meat."

Strange was Elsie during these ravings, for although she sounded distressed, she had no smell of anger. Since she had begun to spew worse than my stomach days earlier, I interrupted her to explain my own anguish.

"The sensitivity I have is nasal. Never shall I become ashamed of being sickened by the stench of God's good creatures broiling in their own fat." Then, unavoidably, I retched, my hand at once going to my face, more to end those sickening thoughts rushing through me than any bodily fluid.

Thrusting her arm toward the floor, Elsie blurted, "This mess you'll be cleaning up yourself, girl!"

Controlling my choking, I replied, "Being a natural substance, vomit terrifies me not; whereas the eating of animal gore is . . ." Then I retched again, coming up with a bit of bile that I was certain to swallow rather than appear the total

82

wretch to Elsie by soiling her floor. But the gulp in itself was enough for the servant, who whirled about and quit my chamber, having had enough of my oral asperities.

Before eating, I continued with the universal assessment I had abandoned the previous day, having been defeated by that tiny, diabolical bridge. And though I would not abandon the garden proper, I required emotional acceptance before again entering that fine and growing place. But this day would see me situate myself in the sinners' world commencing with the house's interior, territory insufficiently familiar to the realm's new witch.

First I examined my bedchamber's door. This efficient latchwork required but a turn of the handle to activate. Looking closer I saw a hole for inserting a key. The thing could be locked, an achievement beyond me. I thus resolved to learn of these small, swinging walls lest they imprison me worse than the bulk of London itself.

Stepping to the balcony, I viewed the great main room below, an area with no apparent purpose but to separate north from south. Walking along the balustrade, I found additional doors like mine. Standing by the end door, the one farthest from the stairs, I leaned near the jamb, detecting a smell from within of Rathel. Away I went with no further interest, finding an odor of abandonment through the imperfect sealing of the other doors. Outside mine I was pleased to smell my own odor, but not sufficiently established was I therein; so I entered to pee a spot in each corner and make this place my own.

One door upstairs was odd. Past Rathel's chamber I stepped, smelling at this narrowest door. The area beyond somehow seemed both small and large. Being unlocked, the simple mechanism of this door readily opened, and there was a ladder. My, my, and up I went, finding at the ladder's top a flat hatchway in the ceiling. Here was a latch similar to the windows', but no despair came over me. Instead, I determined to attempt all the available motions of my hand until I unriddled the unpleasant metal. And succeed I did, mainly by force, not

83

intellection; for I grabbed the piece and pushed hard, producing an impressive click. Upward I leaned, the door swinging open, cool, exterior air and the light of the sky falling upon me. Then I stepped from the ladder onto the building's roof.

What magic I found there! Beneath my feet was a platform with a finished floor and a handrail. Though the purpose of this deck was to allow servants opportunity to repair leaks, my task was visionary. Beyond me in all directions was the sinners' world, an endless view of near and distant buildings to extend my thrill of opening the door onto nature's light and air. Although many buildings seen were taller than Rathel's, her town house was built upon high ground, and I peered over much of London. I felt the superiority of my angle, felt that endless space beyond, felt a thrilling location that seemed as much my own as that hole beneath my bed, this one an antithetical type of space: not one to conceal me but to reveal the world. And I cackled to have achieved this view, to look upon the sinners' endless architecture, seeing church spires and buildings nearly as great as St. Nicholas Cathedral, observing our lovely garden mostly hidden by treetops, but a fine sight regardless. At the end of the street was a patch of green, another type of garden though not enfenced behind a house: the park I had seen on my last journey into the city, a bit of wildness I determined to explore. But that greenery was too removed from Rathel's town house, too much a part of the sinners' world that was literally beyond me, and would have to wait for a more proximate familiarity. So down the ladder I climbed with a felicitous disposition, a feeling to satisfy even a witch removed from her true world.

Outside the door stood Rathel. Guiltless I remained, studying neither her smell nor her countenance. Instead, I explained myself, not having lost my pleased demeanor.

"Through this passage I have discovered the roof, and a satisfying view therefrom. I hope you are not offended by my pleasure." And past silent Rathel I ran, neither fleeing nor allowing the chief sinner to interrupt my function of determining my place in God's world apportioned to sinners.

Downstairs I found a large chamber full of books on shelves, another full of chairs and divans and other furniture, and that largest area filled with nothing, a mediocre space inferior to that beneath my bed. A significance shared by all of these lower chambers was a mortared hole with ashes. Beside each was a pile of felled trees. Not even I was ignorant enough to consider these holes sites for the burning of any witch coincidentally discovered downstairs. I knew them to be fireplaces, and hated upcoming cool weather in advance. How different from our cabin fireplace, which had less of a smoke residue than my nose. Praise God no such hell hole existed in my chamber.

Toward the rear of the house were rooms of no elaborate accommodations. These inner homes of Rathel's slaves I did not examine, though one of the denizens soon found me exploring and wondered of my travels. I mentioned having discovered the roof. To this, Elsie replied that brazen I must become to gain the house's opposite end; for this bottom was the basement, achieved only by passing through the kitchen.

"No other entry is available?" I asked her. "Certainly a kind woman such as yourself would not see me tormented by entering a bloody area proven to sicken me."

"And, no, girl, I'm not having you sick on my account, but neither am I being duped by your flattering talk. So I'm telling you now of the other entry, but it's outside, a door for receiving firewood. But locked it is to keep prowlers out, and can be opened only from within. If I've nothing better to do, lass, I might be opening the thing for you. But, then, perhaps I'm a better person to be teaching you bravery, for you'll not get far in London if unable to face cooking."

I then affected not courage, but timidity.

"Miss Elsie, I believe I do have potential for entering the kitchen in order to gain the basement. I kindly seek your assistance, however, for even if I summon the courage to approach that frightening area, ignorance will preclude my opening the basement door. I am pleased to thank you beforehand for describing how to conquer these devices."

The sinner went static as she examined my face, reasonably disbelieving that a girl of such fluency could not open a door.

"Very well, lass," she sighed. "And I'm telling you now that a key is needed, which you won't be gaining on your own, and won't be using without aid even if you did find the thing. So the key I'm getting for you and opening the door meself, because if I'm teaching you on that basement door, so long we'll be in that smell to pain you that a vomiting you'll commence to sicken me also. So our plan be this: I'm opening the door, then through the kitchen you run, then down the stairs carefully so you're not stumbling to die with a broken head against the firewood."

Elsie had me follow her into that rear corridor between garden and kitchen. As she opened the latter's door, a wave of hideous fumes came to me that inspired a rethinking. Surely the basement could not be worth my suffering that fog of destroyed animals. What need had I of the basement considering my conquests of the roof and garden? I thus decided to be off and under my bed before Elsie returned. But as I turned to flee, there she stood at the kitchen entrance, holding the door open to release a smell of burnt blood and death.

"Come, girl, and you're stepping quickly to get this passage done," she said, and waved me toward her. "The courage you're gaining here is worth a bit of upset innards." And she looked toward me with such a concerned expression that she nearly seemed a witch.

I ran. Glimpsing Elsie, I ran past, hearing her loud instructions: Move to the far wall, turn right, through that open doorway and down—and mind the stairs. So I ran, past Theodosia fiddling with death in a kettle steaming gore, past an open fire enough to burn me paces away, it seemed. In an endless moment, I ran while smelling steaming pots and a coating of dead fat throughout the room. Metal was everywhere: huge masses in the stoves and ovens and unknown devices for hot destruction. To the doorway and down, feet skipping quickly upon the stairs, into a darkened room that was cool and quiet and lacking any sense of death, with a smell of lichens and rodents. Then Elsie was behind me, moving down the stairs with an assured but heavy gait, viewing each tread as she spoke.

"Aye, and I'm hoping you find this no fond place, in that it seems a bit musty for any longish stay." She stopped nearby, looking only at the odd youth, not the familiar basement. "So when you're through with your exploring, lass, be up the stairs again and rap on the door. There I'll be, at some chores in the kitchen, but not many I have and not for long; so be making no encampment here as you do beneath your bed. A later day will have me showing you the ways of locks and latches, but for a spell I think it best we keep you inside if we're able."

The woman then departed, and I proceeded with my examination, which began with relief. Another sinning horror survived. Since Elsie had closed the kitchen door behind her, I received minimum smell from that death chamber, and virtually no sound of sinners' voices, clattering metal, of hissing steam escaping slaughtered creatures' pieces. In this basement I was alone, the only sounds my feet stepping on the soil floor and insects retreating from my intrusion. Here the only light came from small windows near ground level. And here I found a third type of space, unlike that of my bed's bottom or the rooftop, for those realms were of the sinners' world, and the basement seemed more of God's. The basement seemed a cave, and though no especial appreciation had I for these holes— preferring the dry expanse of the open world's air—this cavern was superior to corridors, even as my bed's bottom was a secure place in this land of dangerous sinning.

Superior, but not perfect, for my exploring revealed more of Rathel's furniture stored beneath thick fabric, but little metal beyond rake heads and hinges. Mostly present were soil and the mildew Elsie considered unpleasant. I also found wood: not planks, but limbs and trunk portions recognizable as parts of trees instead of flooring. The heap of rough coal pieces I discovered gave no satisfaction, in that their source was obvious: burnt wood whose ashes were compressed into lumps. Not likely would I again find the smell of hot charcoal fascinating as I had in Jonsway. Neither was I overjoyed to examine large, ceramic jugs whose fermented, fruity liquid I smelled as vapors leaking through one imperfect seal. Equally fruity was a sludge contained in smaller jars, the sweet smell of mulberries failing to entice me. A superior find were boxes filled with straw, a material with a bracing, subtle scent and a satisfying texture. But a better smell lay deeper. When I entered with my hands as though to have more of my person in the wilds again, I discovered the purpose of these boxes. They were not made to contain straw—the straw was inserted to preserve apples!

What a gift of God was this food. Not that I was starving, for I had consumed enough of the household's raw vegetables for sustenance; but this sweet find was so appropriate for this area that I rejoiced in God's love, which again He manifested in so simple yet profound a manner. Quickly I consumed a fruit, which offered an especially vivid taste because of my disposition. Then I placed the core behind a box, believing that possibly these fruits were a resource that Rathel had hidden for some sinning reason, and I would be burned for having consumed one. With a final inhalation of this cavern's air, I moved up the steps, fearing that if I tarried further, Elsie might quit the kitchen and I would have that hated chamber and two impossible doors to face alone; and how long could I live on a bushel of apples? But survive the kitchen I did, again with the aid of Elsie. Through that tunnel of dead steam I ran with her guidance, into a house that yet held me, though no longer was I lost therein.

Six

Wise was Lady Rathel to settle the witch in this new world by allowing me to apply my own sense of moderation and survival. No less intelligence she displayed by promoting our mutual accommodation through intermediary Elsie, who well accepted the new lass's challenge, though she remained displeased to learn that meat would never pass within me, only fruit and vegetables in their natural state. And, yes, those basement apples were provided me without request, but none of the cider, thank you, no preserves after the first sticky bite. I also found liquefied tea acceptable upon understanding it to be flavored, not filthy, water. Coffee, however, touched my lips only to be spat away, for this was the blood of burnt beans—but what a joy were onions! How appealing their shapes and hues: round and yellowish, long and green. What fine eating Elsie provided me with onions, somewhat to her dismay, since my breath became noxious to her after a meal of these tubers. And my eating was alone, at the huge, formal table where Rathel also ate with no companion, because I was her only peer in the household, and I would puke to be so near the molested flesh she consumed. And why the elaborate utensils? Clear, cut glasses, ceramic plates and cups, hateful metal tools for stabbing and cutting. These latter I would not touch, though I did relent to Elsie's demand that I accept my greens on a plate. Her assertion that only the lowliest of baseborn folk ate with their fingers caused me to dissent. No better way to eat apples, I declared.

The servants took their meals in the kitchen as was their proper place, and better than eating on the roadway, as Elsie professed. My place was more properly on the road than in this house, on the road and out of London, and this I would achieve, for my life's goal was to escape Rathel and regain the wilds. But I had no knowledge of any wilderness beyond. Regardless of the wind's direction, I smelled only local gardens and greens from the roof, the location of Man's Isle a mystery. I only knew that more familiarity with London was required for my escape. And never did I forget Rathel's design for my life. Though not spoken since Jonsway, her intents with me had not changed, I knew, for even her breath had the scent of vengeance. Neither was the nature of her plans forgotten: that I would kill for her as a witch, thus with either sex or magic.

I knew not how to explain to Rathel the foolish impossibility of her notions, for witches cause consternation with their sex, not death, knives and clubs more effective means of killing than any magic known to me. Deluded in her expertise, Rathel would not readily be convinced by one considered fit only for murderous servitude. But this convincing would further my life's goal, for if Rathel considered me useless for her purposes, what point in retaining me? But how would I confirm my inadequacy? If my only method of leaving London was to kill some man for Rathel, then long in this city would I remain.

"And I'm finding a smell of wetting in your room, lass?" Elsie demanded. "You're having trouble, then, in hitting your chamber pot?"

"Your pardon I most humbly beg, Miss Elsie, in that you well know I take satisfaction in cleaning my quarters and keeping the area perfect."

"Aye, that I know, lass, but perfect for you is sprinkling too much lavender petals and tea. Perfect for you is residing beneath your bed. But I'm saying we must have limits, child. If there's too much dust, another spider, or more pee on the floor

I'm smelling, then I'll be the one upkeeping your chamber, and I'm doing it with the strongest soap I can find, and that's a smell you'll not be fond of."

Sweeping was a task I enjoyed, for it brought me in touch with the natural element of dirt and allowed me to sprinkle too much tea on the carpet to provide the floor with a natural scent. Few other chores was I allowed, certainly not burying the household feces. Strange were the sinners to be human yet share little more than dung and tea with witches.

Theodosia and Delilah shared nothing with me, not only because I rejected their cooking, but because I made to usurp their employ, offering to launder attire and peel fruit—though not in the kitchen. But as Theodosia remarked, if I did all the servants' chores, would the mistress allow them to sleep in my bedchamber? Not blinking likely.

Rathel had no such duties. Being the inheritor of her husband's estate, the lady was a business person with fiscal responsibilities, the average day finding her out and about London to see of landholdings and taxes. Business sinners would also visit her town house, though only men, for rare was the lady in London who controlled her own wealth. And rare was I when the solicitors arrived, for Rathel suggested I remain unseen when men were present. Here the witch agreed.

Elsie was disappointed that these guests were never women from social clubs. Being a fine lady of English society, the mistress should be passing time aiding poor children or bedridden peers. Praise God at least, I told Miss Elsie, that Rathel is not out stealing other children from their homes as taught her by the Vidgeon fool.

Then I scowled and stomped away from poor memories attacking, Elsie with sense enough not to inquire of my distress. To her own misfortune, she later returned to that subject of social clubs; for most women of London—regardless of station—found satisfaction in craftwork, Elsie with modest pride displaying her crocheting. True appreciation had I for her peaceful efforts, but not enough to preclude Elsie's disappointment upon finding me with no desire to craft doilies of my own, though I well appreciated digging with her in the garden. Elsie's smell became one of disappointment because needlework was the nearest she came to being a lady, and a lady she would have me be, not a gardener.

"Oh! and Elsie—this is nearly the real world!" I exclaimed while looking above and beyond to see God's greenery and sense His sky.

"Ah, and you're not telling me again, are you, lass, of your terrible state for having to live in a beautiful home?"

"That house is but a brick cave, Elsie, an enclosure to separate sinners from genuine living. But this grass and soil and sky—this is the true world, miss."

"This is a garden, child, a fine garden and one I'm loving, but part of the world, not all of it."

"If you love it so, why the assaulting?" I asked Elsie, who was uprooting an epiphany only to bury it elsewhere. "The plant is secure here and living fulfilled. Is moving the flower traumatically a game you play wherein you imitate the mistress? Is this epiphany to your shovel a child witch stolen from her true home only to be taken to a false manse?"

With the term "witch," Elsie reacted with a discomfort to be smelled by one. Her words, however, were only of plants.

"Why is it, then, you're not condemning Miss Theodosia for plucking up weeds? Is this not a type of murder to one so wild?"

"Not to one who eats turnips without remorse," I answered. "Besides, Miss Theodosia is not so . . . compelling . . . in her speech as you are."

"And thank you, child, for saying how argumentative I am," she scowled, looking up from her dirty knees. "Be plucking a rose, then, and insert it above your ear if you're so displeased with my transplanting. At least your hair will then be smelling decent, in that you've not brushed the dust away from your last bout of rooting beneath the bed."

"Very well, miss, if I am so offensive in my preference for

God and nature, I shall move along and cause you no further misery. Perhaps I might examine the eastern gate to see where it leads."

Depart I did, along the hedges and across the gravel path. Toward the garden's eastern end were trees so tall and a stone fence so high that none of London could be seen, this area seemingly a wild place despite the sound of carriages beyond and the smell of the sinners' odorous city. But true nature is not bounded by sinning emanations. Wilderness is a place proven by its natural inhabitants. London, in comparison, seemed a moderated hell.

As though my comment were a threat, I continued to the gate, but this mass of lumber seemed a door not for a house but a fortress, an impediment as imposing as it was bulky. This huge door was not so temporary a hole as to be traversed by me. Besides, beyond was London, and that was a wall as thick as a city to separate me from the true world. If my window required a great effort to conquer, and the exterior doors remained unfathomable, how long before I would decipher London? But I was not lost in my journey from the city, for I had scarcely begun. Time I had to learn much and wait longer, for a witch lives not a life, but an era.

That current era became one of horror for me, for upon nearing the gate, I was attacked. Startled by a sound implying death, I whirled about to see Miss Elsie step near. With consternation, she began speaking, Elsie failing to understand my being terrified of so unspectacular a servant.

"And it's not an escape you're seeking again, is it, lass? On me own I'd be finding difficulty to leave this city, for it's too far to walk, and I have no coins for transport. And that if I knew where to go, for the wildest place about is Pangham Gardens, and that's but another green with fishes' pools. So be taking some food for your eating, child, so you won't be found half starved this occasion."

"In truth, miss, I had no intent of fleeing, since I fully share your position. This area, however, is the most sheltered in the garden."

"Aye, and you're saying, then, that it's not rife with people. And I would have let you be, Miss Alba, had I not thought there was a chance of your dangerous fleeing. So if you're weary of me now, you'll be letting me know, in that rarely have I found you bashful with your speaking."

"If I were so belittled by your presence, miss, the realm for me to seek would be that space beneath my bed rife with seclusion. Therefore, be less of a tender lass whose emotions are as easily disturbed as the water's surface. For who, in fact, is the stolen youth hereabouts: you or I?"

"Now I'm the one growing weary, child, not with your presence but your own soft emotions. So let's be forgetting your wicked life of kidnapping and be off with us to the tulip bed, in that wild persons are great eaters of bulbs, are they not?"

"I say, Elsie, your ability to comically rant is a virtue, especially compared to the dour attitudes of your peers and all our mistress. But if a plucking up from Earth be our next activity, let us not choose innocent flowers, but the fiendish bridge that pollutes the entire garden."

"And it's the tiny bridge, you're saying, that deserves to be ruined? What harm is it doing you, lass, in that it's only a bit of wood?"

"To me, miss, the material comprising the bridge is recollection; for a great friend of mine drowned in the sea, any bridge now bringing me wretched memory."

"And I'm feeling pity for your sorrows, Alba, but we can't be ruining the Earth to end them, for it's your own heart which gives the pain. My father himself it was who died beneath the wheels of a carriage when this daughter was younger than you, and each wagon is yet bringing those memories. But I'm bringing something of me own when I think of him dead: I think of the love I had as a child, which remains with the woman and the old woman I'll become. And I'm telling you more, lass, that I'm not making to preach on you as though I could end all the misery in your heart. But with God as my aid, Alba, never would I have your pains be worsened."

The woman then abandoned me to seclusion, her changed

94

countenance not the profound view of a minister with a sermon, but the preoccupied smile of a genuine friend.

In this manner my days proceeded. Boredom I avoided by sensing London from the roof: the confusing accumulations of masonry that were buildings, the sounds of misplaced horses, misplaced people. Sinning activities occupied my perceptions: the false weather of smoke haze from the sinners' producing oils and resins for paper and woodwork, perfumes and powders for their bodies, all of these acts requiring fire, all conspiring to make London impossible to accept.

My greatest emotion in this living came from death, my mother's demise oppressing me more than the bulk of London. Painfully predictable was this memory's sequence of reoccurrence: the black smell, black loneliness, the impossibility of our being apart forever. Whenever glutted with this distress, I attempted to change my thinking in light of Mother's last idea, that she would ever live within me as our mutual love. But what a sham my selfish intent became, for by attempting to save myself additional distress, I received an extension of my thought: that whereas sinners died and yet were loved by their surviving families, they also left Earth to spiritually exist with Lord God in Heaven. But my mother was not only gone in body, but had no soul to be transferred. Though undeserving of such a mediocre legacy, she would exist after death only as the love of her daughter, a child so shameful as to change her thinking whenever the distress of death returned, recalling only the acidic smell that was her mother's demise. Thereafter, the girl was so poor of heart as to feel remorse for her own inadequacies rather than dismiss them and return to loving her mother as that superior woman was due, the daughter instead causing enough misery to be a sinner herself.

This last idea seemed punition from God. By allowing my own torment, I was supporting the sinners who had destroyed Mother. Because survival was my due, I was correct to fit within London until able to leave the city. I thus became

95

profoundly aware of my position amongst the sinners. Their manipulating me meant nothing unless it meant retaining me. And though my detention would end if I cooperated with Rathel, her intents for me were murderous. My death was not being planned, however, but that of some male. Of course, I knew nothing about killing except those examples the sinners had shown me, but I might learn. And since the victim was a sinner with a soul to live infinitely with God, what ultimate loss had he? This soulless witch had no portion to bake in Hell for her part in the murder—so bring the victim on!

A decent enough witch I remained to reject this murderous thinking. I continued to believe that sinners had received their name by promoting evil beneath the perfect eyes of God; whereas witches had no such proclivities, lacking the lustful habits of sinners. The sexual distress witches inspired was not an activity, but an emanation, as though a smell. The sinners' evil, however, was a systematic intent called society. And to cause a person's demise would not make me a terrible witch but an average sinner. No greater failure at loving Mother could I achieve than to become one of her murderers.

"Would you choose to live again in undeveloped land, or is your preference to remain here as my servant?"

Rathel's astonishing words after one midday meal delivered me with uniqueness, for at once I desired to strike her as I never had any person. Such was the sinners' influence that I had begun responding to their social situations with the same immorality they displayed. But the feeling was gone with this awareness, and I replied without violence.

"My current situation here is one of peaceful survival, a state understandably incomprehensible to the typical, destructive sinner."

"And what of your future? Do you envision a house and home of your own in this city?"

"I envision living in a realm forever removed from the revulsion caused by your fantastic questions. To be your servant or to seek an abode in this heretical realm are ideas to sicken me. If God's will for me be done in accord with my natural state, my future life shall be in my past and genuine home of Man's Isle."

"No, you would not reasonably wish this," Rathel replied, "for more parts of that island each day are inhabited by humans. Any of the populace learning of your identity would be passionate to kill you."

"Am I to bless you, then, for rescuing me from that future, bless you for the estimable morality that beforehand drove you to murder my mother?"

Even with a moderate wig she was false. The more respectable persons in this house—witch and servants—wore only their own hair, but we had little fraud to conceal. I smelled the mistress to glean her secrets, the sinning odor so familiar to me now, so continually unpleasant. Well did Rathel hide her thinking behind controlled eyes and a moderate countenance, an ability doubtless learned from dealing with her sinning peers. I also believe she attempted to obscure her smell with an extra application of social scents, for being aware of a witch's superior perceptions, she would have the benefit of my not smelling her emotions. Since the woman could not disguise her breathing, however, beneath the creature grease in her mouth I might smell her heart.

"No, Alba. I believe you understand that had I not been too late in finding you, I would have saved your mother. Regardless, she and her racial sisters were guilty of damaging the Lady Vidgeon, a person who might now be dead from witches' vengeance. But no one died on Man's Isle by my choice. They were executed by human fear, a trait so dangerous as to kill human and witch unselectively, as you have seen."

"My people were not killed by fear, but by your allowance; for you were the expert to distinguish witch from sinner knowing full well that identification would lead to the witches' deaths, though in fact we killed no one, and therefore deserved no execution. Our only crime was to inadvertently harm a sinner who would have ruined

97

our family to satisfy her own lust."

"One saved is better than all lost," the sinner answered. "Your mistake is in believing that I could have convinced the Jonsway officials that your people were neither witches nor guilty. They were witches, and were guilty. Had I attempted a dishonest convincing, I would have lost my esteem with Bishop Dalimore and his colleagues. Without my position of expertise, never would you have been released into my care. Therefore, you also would be dead. Condemn me not for saving my personal world when it includes you."

"How sorrowful your existence is to be salvaged only with killing," I returned, "for is not the method of your salvation to have a peaceful innocent murder for you?"

"Be not so wise, young Alba, as to appear the total fool. No one your age knows all of her people, witch or human. Even in my elder state, I am not completely aware of my own race's potentials. But I know something of them as well as witches. I know that despite the witches' simple society, they are not so inhuman as to never feel murderous passion. My proof here is you. Family passion was your elders' justification for destroying Lady Sarah. Family passion was her intent in seeking you. Morally, however, you were all her inferiors; for Vidgeon's goal was to improve your life, not destroy your mind."

"Ultimately, morality is interpreted only by God; whereas death is evident to everyone. Therefore, God shall be my judge in ascertaining Vidgeon's evil in attempting to steal me and thereby ruin my mother's heart. But clear to any human with a mind is the vast gap of wickedness between Vidgeon's blathering and the stench of my mother's flesh."

"Condemn me or my race, Alba, but no good will you gain from it. Nor will you benefit from all your speaking, for you neither teach me nor learn for yourself a better understanding of our races."

"My understanding is sufficient to verify that you will never connive me into becoming a member of your race, into being your servant or peer."

"But this was my beginning query," Rathel stated. "My true

surmising was that you would depart London if given the selection. Thus, I would show you how such cooperation might lead you to wilderness."

"But previously you asserted that my original home would no longer safely house a witch. You thus suggest I live where—Pangham Gardens?"

"Pangham is a lovely place, one you will better appreciate when less fearful of the greater city. But Pangham is no more fit for living than that garden our own. Compared to the wilderness, these gardens are as trees to the forest. But England is a land of many forests. I can situate you in a place similar to Man's Isle for you to live as wildly as you desire. The site would be free of attacking humans; whereas Man's Isle is not. In your wisdom, you should see that I have brought you into a business to our mutual benefit."

"I recall your business, Rathel. And you shall never succeed if it entails my killing a man, by sex or magic or bludgeoning, for I have not the capacity, and your failure of wisdom is to disbelieve this fact."

"The capacity is not magical, but sexual, though you seem unaware. Understand that I only request you to be natural with this one human. My vow is to release you after your part of the business is attempted. I would have said 'concluded,' but no longer will I mandate success. Your cooperation is all I seek. Thereafter, whether I am correct or you, a wild place I will provide for your remaining years, and they are many compared to the lives of humans."

"I am human," I corrected the ignorant Rathel. "God made humans in many guises, but sinners within are all the same. So are murderers."

"So are witches," she replied. "Be natural for me is all I ask, and thereby fulfill my purposes. These were described in Jonsway. They existed before I met you, perhaps before you were born."

With her ending speech, I received from Rathel a sense of melancholy. I replied with appropriate sympathy.

"I pity your history for it to predicate future death. I pity your expertise as well, for it consists of imagination more than knowledge. If I am to kill some male, that person will live long, for no one dies from preposterous notions. Am I to strangle the gent with my body hair? Considering your understanding of mortal witches, perhaps he's yet a baby whose breath you expect me to steal in his sleep."

"Young he is, but no infant. Too young, however, for you to be given the opportunity to discover your true self as a witch with him."

"The person is too young for slaughter? When, therefore, will I have opportunity to prove your delusions and then be off to a natural land? Why does your expert misconception not consider me ready for slaughtering men with my pee hole?"

"Oh, and ready you are, Alba, though from delusion you do not comprehend. I am aware, however, and have therefore removed all men from the household. The problem is not your readiness, but the gent's. Not old enough to wed is he, and his parents would not allow him to be betrothed. Not to a charge of mine. My plan, therefore, is to await his attaining the proper age, in the meantime making you enough of a lady to be acceptable to London."

"Am I to be killing all of London, then?"

"London knows that I have brought you here to make your social graces fit your appearance. My peers would not understand if I failed to have you schooled in the ways of English society. Furthermore, although the boy will have you from desire, his parents will not accept you now. But if you become the boy's peer, his parents will fail to reject you when he asks for your hand. And ask he will, wed you he will, and you shall kill him on your wedding bed."

"So succinct, so certain? What if he does not care to wed the particular me? What if he has a previous beauty selected?"

"These potentials are no concern, for few men can resist the white witch, and none toward whom she applies herself. Apply yourself to my subject, be yourself with him, and with all my resources I shall deliver you to a wild land to satisfy you for your life."

"What, then, must I learn of becoming a lady fit for English, sinning society?" I returned. "If consuming animal flesh or tobacco is entailed, the remainder of both our lives shall proceed unfulfilled."

"Only the refusal to eat will seem odd in England," Rathel stated. "Nevertheless, we shall truthfully explain you as having a stomach too sensitive for animal products."

"What else need be done, then, in that my speech is adequate, and Elsie dresses me as she will?"

"You speak like a man: too aggressively and too often. With people not of our household your words must be moderate. Especially you must not embarrass the young man by displaying yourself as his verbal superior. You must also achieve the carriage of ladies, and learn enough of London to seem only new to our city, not an enemy thereof."

"Flailing a man to death with my baby dent might prove easier than this last you posit."

"Remember, Alba, ladies are not prone to overstatement. Remember also the satisfaction you have found in London. Would you not choose to visit St. Nicholas Cathedral again? Part of being a lady is attending church. A parish body uses these facilities for their services. This upcoming Sabbath will find us there if you desire. Since recently you have become aware of your surrounds only to find them less than ideal, I propose to improve them. Certain parts of London heretofore unseen by you may prove entertaining in their irredeemably sinning nature."

Humor was found in Rathel's mouth as often as insects. This last was not comical felicity, however, but mocking; for had not her final sentence been as portentous as many of mine? But comedy would not be the cause for my next experience in God's great house changing from inspirational to heretical; for the same as cathedrals, heresy is an invention of sinners.

Seven

What confidence could a young lady have in a tutor who smelled of snuff? Into her house the Rathel sinner brought a woman who seemed a tall version of herself, though not so reeking of vengeance. But no less diabolical was this Mrs. Cliffton, who upon espying me wished to insert a stick through my spine.

"We shall begin with sitting, which is easier to correct than standing, which requires one's weight to be balanced, not situated."

Apart from snuff, I sensed a bit of boasting in this woman, since the person she most desired to impress was her employer. Unfortunately, her pupil was the victim to be sacrificed on the altar of her expertise.

Sit I did, having been directed to a hard wooden chair made all of edges, Mrs. Cliffton immediately displeased because I was comfortable.

"Miss Alba," she declared, "you have dropped onto the chair as though an injured cat. A lady sits delicately, poised, not collapsed."

The woman then roughly grasped my arms to pull me upward, replacing my self with hers in demonstration. Upon only the chair's edge she sat, as though about to fall off, though Cliffton alleged with a prideful smell that her position was exactly correct, a statement I had to append.

"For a lady, then, a chair is not a furniture for comfort, but a perch as though for a bird by which she clings with her buttocks."

So flabbergasted was Cliffton that a moment of arrested breathing passed before she could state how shameful my speaking was to mention so low a body part amongst decent folk. Then Rathel with no pique explained my wilderness background, and et cetera, to which I replied:

"And sorry I am, mum, for mentioning the word 'perch.' In advance of the sinister deed, I herewith additionally apologize for the great slip I might make in using the term 'bleeding arse' instead of buttocks, and thus cause the lot of us peers some flipping embarrassment."

The next tutor was shorter and smoked a pipe, though not in the vicinity of employers. And though she seemed more of an intellectual Elsie than an extended Rathel, this one *did* manage to insert the yardstick down my clothing. In advance of Mrs. Natwich's arrival, Rathel and I had brief discourse wherein I was offered employ as chef and was told that I might remain as long as I wished, which would be a lifetime if I preferred untoward humor to a minimum of cooperation.

Natwich determined my curriculum. Of immediate import was the verbal realm.

"Your speaking is remarkable for one unschooled, Alba," Mrs. Natwich assessed. "Nevertheless, your enunciation is too harsh and quick, and your accent is only marginally couth."

"And cor, love," I replied, "me and the mum would praise yer bones to make me mouth fit a lady's face."

Rathel then calmly turned to Elsie, whose only purpose in dusting the library was to be part of the audience. The disgusted servant flicked her duster in my direction as though it were mine to take. Both these women I well understood. To sit prettily I learned with a speed to please both my tutor and my flipping mum.

"And I'm saying the mistress has a treat for you which you'd best be enjoying in a pleasant manner, else I'll be flogging you with bacon or other item you find wicked."

"Thank you ever, gracious miss, for your own most pleasant greeting, one of such incomprehensible content as to have flogged my sensibilities. Hereafter, however, you might feign the identity of a normal person and convey that simple message your plain mentality surely contains."

"And bless you, lass, for calling me the simpleton," Elsie replied with no rancor, such emotional distress scarcely available between us familiars. So comfortable was this woman in my presence that she no longer stood so starkly vertical as when before household guests. With me, Elsie constantly rubbed her fingertips on her white, white apron, a trait of informality, not tension.

"What I'm saying now, talking lass, is that the mistress has an offer, and I am sent to tell you. Into the city she's going to attend to some business, and you're to be traveling with her if you choose. I'm also saying that some cathedral is involved."

Startled was Elsie to see the bored youth lurch into attentiveness. But the servant was not so taken aback as to allow me to depart without the proper cloak and hat, correct attire for a lady on business in London.

Never before had I stepped through the front doorway. Cooperation was the source of this false feeling, for now I was part of the household and could be allowed to exit without Rathel's fearing my escape. As I moved to the covered stoop—in its columnar construction a tiny amphitheater for guests' collection—I scarcely noticed the lady waiting by a public coach. My first step in the sunlight brought the impression of my never having left the house before, when in fact I had never departed while fully cognizant. My fleeing in a rush past Rathel returned as recollection to strike me with my second step, strike me as though sudden fear or surprising joy. That escape I now found unreal, for though I had been gone days, scant memory had I of standing, sleeping, existing. The power in my current emotion was the triviality of that past experience, so significant yet so lacking influence over my further life. The falseness of that fleeing era dismayed me, for it was a separate life more real though less distressing than any dream of mine in which Mother died. I then wondered of unperceived existence, for how true is the life of a person unaware? How does God consider a human life unfelt by that human? How responsible can people be for acts obscured by ignorance, unforgotten days whose events are less real than the curiosity to follow?

As though I had tutored myself in that dull sort of living, I barely sensed the next moments as I praised God for having answers to questions I could only contemplate. What answer had He for the following time in which I recognized occurrences but felt nothing? Felt nothing as I walked across the green frontage between town house and street. Felt nothing as I approached the coachman and his waiting vehicle. Felt nothing as the male held out his arm toward me. Felt no ignorance, though I knew not his intent. Felt nothing as Lady Rathel grasped my hand and placed it upon the sinner's wrist. Felt no revulsion from touching a man. And what state had taken this witch to allow her to step inside the coach with no further prompting? The lady joined me, and I began a better life, for thereafter I was able to perceive. Beside me, Rathel beyond her smell of sinners' eating emitted an odor of satisfaction, for somehow she was pleased. And I found no shame in having satisfied a sinner, accepting God's likely interpretation that we were all the same, all His, even those diabolically manipulative somehow ignorant in living.

"The business I have is signing a paper with the manager of a landholding. Significant for you is the locale. Nearby is a cathedral. No, not St. Nicholas, but one called Christ's Cathedral, whose architect is the descendant of St. Nicholas's builder. I presumed you would be interested to see how such constructions are fabricated."

"How odd that such tremendous creations are formed by persons who are merely men," I responded with improved awareness.

" 'Architect' is the term for a person who designs buildings, even as Miss Elsie designs her needlework. The name of the 'mere man' responsible for Christ's Cathedral is Edward Denton. For yourself you may determine the coincidence of his being father to your future husband."

Again my living became incomprehensible. Not St. Nicholas Cathedral, but another; not an extant building, but one being constructed; not by any man, but one whose son I was to kill. And which of this man's traits would be more special: that he could envision such a construction, or that he was so involved with Rathel that his family deserved ruination?

"If this journey finds you satisfied and unfleeing, you will again be allowed from the household," Rathel stated. "Perhaps you might go with Miss Elsie to the park on our Feltson Street, or with her and Delilah to the farmers' markets. I am not speaking of being contained by a coach, but walking. This you might enjoy."

"I would enjoy the park," I told her. And with that rejoinder, I began my interest in such ventures, for I found myself immersed in the current experience.

I found myself immersed in fear, for I was locked in a box above rolling wheels that cut the air with their flight. How appropriate for the spokes to be enclosed by hoops of metal, that most Satanic material beloved by God's over-souled, over-brained race. These flailing spokes were the coach's greatest danger, for I knew they would either fly away and penetrate my body or reach out and pull me into their circle to club me dead.

This danger seemed definitive of city life. The carriage was a stampeding cabinet to crush pedestrians after one wrong step. Thinking of Elsie's parent, I knew my sense of danger to be recognition, not imagination. No help were these horses that smelled of acceptance in their task, so accustomed were they to having strips of their brethrens' hides slapping them, surrounding them, as though being lashed to wooden posts and a tiny house was natural for any earthly creature. The greatest horror here was that these poor beasts were controlled by metal rods HELD IN THEIR MOUTHS, which they bit against as though pleased to be eating Satan's meal. Drag the sinners in their furniture they did even as I dragged Mother and her rock through my dreams, and surely we would meet. I would be in London so long, I knew, that my sensibilities would equal these blasé horses', and we would become one.

Rathel's rods for stabbing meat were an equivalence here, and I knew that one bite of the holiest manna if supplied my mouth by the devil's metal fork would set me to being a sinner, not merely living in a sinning city. Then, from my horrorific mentality fit only for self-torment, I recognized that even then I was passing as a sinner. How long before I became not Rathel's servant, but her sister?

Scarcely could I imagine being upset at the sinning characteristics of Jonsway considering London, which seemed multiple, connected Jonsways, each taller and more intense than the one I knew, the accumulation greater than even a bright youth's imagination could envision. Rathel's was a moderate neighborhood of expensive dwellings, but in moments our box came to London's variety. The streets seemed unlimited, a new one extending to each side with every blink as I looked through the windows. Cobblestone, brick, clay, and packed soil. Satisfying areas I viewed down many streets, greens or squares with sundry natural growths. And the buildings themselves: high and low and painted and wooden and new and decrepit and stucco and stone. Red brick everywhere, occasionally yellow. Precise chalets there, gabled homes for Rathel's peers, shops and offices for their provisions, signs with names and numbers of all colors as though needlework of wood and glass made by a thousand Elsies.

I found the thousand Elsies, sinners dressed in working clothes, men and women passing on the walkways, merchants in their stores, folks guiding wagons transporting brick and cockles, printing presses and looms and tarpaulin-covered secrets. A street with grander structures held another sort of person, those whom Jonsway's best surely imitated, women and foppish men with white and silver wigs piled as high as a dunghill. Brocade and parasols were necessities in this realm of gaudy folks and coffeehouses, the men with patent shoes tight enough to hurt them and red stockings to hurt me from the sight, women with hooped petticoats to reshape their arses fashionably, their upper breast skin revealed, doubtless drawing more sexual distress than the common witch.

I felt so conservative. Elsie dressed me with no breasts leaping outward, no patch applied to my cheek. Perhaps I was merely too young for such finery. Perhaps next year, immediately preceding my suicide.

Turning often, we gained a dirt roadway with persons of less exalted apparel. This locale was unkempt, with no bright signs, only faded letters, no dandies with wigs, only people who worked with bent backs. On this poor street, women from upper floors dumped their slop onto crass merchants below whose cries had become tedious, peddlers licensed by city justices calling out the superiority of their merchandise, men with stacks of news pamphlets explaining this world and others for a ha'penny, men not so eager in their selling after receiving feces flying about them from the sky; therefore, on to the next corner.

This area was so inspirational that before the last poor folk were passed, I turned with suddenness to Rathel to ask whether we would be crossing Hershford Bridge. She answered that we would not. Thereafter, I lost the terror that had risen in me like water for drowning, but my emotions remained acute, akin to that initial intensity of my first step outside. Surely a secret language exists to describe the varieties of peculiarity I could only feel, not elucidate. Had the sinners themselves a language for odd emotion? No, for the products inspiring my sensations were familiar to the sinners by being their work, their world. No queer terms are required to explain the common.

Though my sensitivity to the cityscape about me persisted, not so definitively emotional was the balance of our journey. Passing a bridge caused me minor distress. Smelling a thick, secluded building reeking of men that Rathel termed Montclaire Prison aggrieved me little. But as we passed unoccupied stocks for punishment, I prayed great God that I would find no ducking pond. My attention was saved upon Rathel's mentioning that our goal was upcoming. Expecting to see a new, grand cathedral in some unfinished state, my attention was ruined by a pile of rocks.

Since ancient compacts had promised God limited land for His usage, the adjacent lots had been filled with sinners' buildings for commerce, not clergy. Therefore, we could not settle our box at a fond distance to view the creative act of pious people grow from the ground as though a mountain issuing from Earth. Instead, we were subjected to the stress of men's labors, for they were the prevalent element of this construction. Great wagons arrived full and departed empty of masonry parts and sacks of the unknown. Mounds of soil and channels in the land were formed. Huge stones were cut and adjusted. All these activities were produced by sinning men who were guided by other sinners. But not as the ants were they, gracefully working together for a communal accomplishment, for these massive insects were loud and conflicting. Well-dressed superiors shouted at incompetent, lazy workers, while individuals pushing barrows interfered with groups sighting the land's layout for whom an entire crew impatiently waited. God's implements here were males, their greatest effort anxiety, their grandest product noise. Near enough we were for a witch to smell them and feel their stress. The odor of their working seemed nearly a natural force, but their activities were unsatisfying. And in my imagination I was to infer St. Nicholas Cathedral from this beginning? At least I did not deny the possibility of beautiful worship for this building's future.

Rathel seemed prideful. Perhaps she was merely perspiring herself. Observing past the mistress, I noted that this site was adjacent to the River Thames. Brush and many trees were visible on the far bank, and though not a forest, was this countryside? Perhaps, for no twisting and stretching of my neck revealed more of the sinners' buildings. Here was a significant parcel of virtual wilderness.

Rathel was staring from the coach as though seeking a view of the wilderness herself. The mistress, however, was viewing a person. A man walking from the depths of the future cathedral had caught her interest. Rathel's mentioning that we might step out and stretch ourselves was an acceptable notion to the boxed witch. But upon exiting the coach, only I accomplished any stretching. Rathel merely stared at this expensively clad man until he noticed his audience. Then he could see nothing else. As though gaining a sight sought a lifetime, the male ignored his peers to stare at Rathel – and at me, stare as Rathel placed her arm about my shoulders, her scent one of gloating.

We entered the coach and departed. At some office, the mistress proceeded with her business, leaving me alone in the coach with her trust not to flee. Pleased she was to find me upon her return. During the journey home, some conversation transpired, but mostly the witch was tacit. The last thing said was a question from the mistress: As mentioned before, would I attend services with her at St. Nicholas Cathedral the upcoming Sabbath? Yes, I said, not fully certain of my decision. Yes, I said, agreeing with the sinner, with her world.

"Your words are exceptional, but your enunciation is archaic, as though you were reared in a swamp. An angry swamp, for you always seem prepared for distress. Ladies, however, are never perturbed."

I had asked to learn of writing; Mrs. Natwich insisted that my speaking improve as well. Any books on witches you got? I mildly inquired. But the tutor had learned to ignore my extremes, lest she become distressed, which she properly could not, being a lady. Being a sinner. Delighted she was, however, to ply me with lessons: grammar and enunciation, English history, household guidance, handwriting (despite the student's desire thereof), family economics, composition, and the lot.

"Cor, missus, and a right genius you are to be teaching me everything known to mankind."

Following this comment came another lesson in posture, and strange was my way to learn proper speaking by having a stick stuck against my spine.

"Could I inquire, kind and glorious Mrs. Natwich, what this 'composition' entity might be?"

"An arrangement of descriptions, Alba," the tutor described. "A set of events that transpire in the real or in the writer's imagination."

"What might the purpose of a composition be besides writing poetry, which is scarcely more useful than pimples?" I wondered.

"Having the ability to form a coherent composition aids one in conversation. Another value is in describing how the events of one's days have passed, as set down in a journal, for example. The Bible itself is not only a composition, but a collection of compositions. A more recent example is the opera libretto, whose story is a composition, as are the stories of nonmusical theater pieces."

"Street theater I saw in the town of Jonsway," I mentioned. "Truly I hope not to learn how to stand on a platform and shout."

"Ladies do not compose theater, Alba. Their tasks are of the home, not of so expressive a public art as theater. But fear not, for part of my task with you is to aid in your finding the best place in English society for the individual who is Alba."

"Out the flipping back door is best for me," I muttered.

"Alba!" Natwich returned sharply, "you must learn at once not to be mumbling so. Not only is the sound offensive and common, but if you have nothing to say, you should retain your silence."

"If people retained silence when not having something valuable to convey, most of England would be permanently mute."

"Alba!" she intoned, then taught me again with her stick.

The tutor did not come on the Sabbath. Though I had no desire to save my worship for a day selected by sinners, the grand cathedral remained a desired experience; whereas the sweaty, incomplete example was merely a curiosity. Come Sunday and I was set to voyage to St. Nicholas, despite the required carriage journey fit an explorer. Guiding my dressing with grumbling, Elsie threatened hideous crimes against my person because against that person I refused the choking corset, though Elsie insisted it was necessary to make so wild a torso svelte by eliminating rearmost waddling due to an uncouth lass's refusing to wear sufficient petticoats and et ruddy cetera.

I remain uncertain whether my next sight of St. Nicholas was equal in splendor to my expectation of that view. Though thrilled again, I was not startled as I had been before. Such awe, however, is not appropriate for my kind. The passion of profound mountain views is not a grandeur fit witches, who cherish all the small parts of God's domain, deriving worldly appreciation in constant, moderate portions, not in flashes like a sinners' fever. Souled folk save their awe for occasions in which they are not occupied by commerce, and thus can partake of items so meager as God's glory manifested in His physical realm. With its divinity of Godly salvation and worldly consumption, where was the rightful place of the great cathedral in my life? Where should a witch fit within this style of worship except to recognize that in their ignorance of the true world and their need to mock it, only sinners are profound and pretentious?

Certainly my renewed experience lacked some measure of the previous esteem, in that St. Nicholas on Sunday was surrounded by sinners. Though not boisterous, the accumulation seemed insufficiently holy in their common conversations to be worthy of the glorious creation they neared. Then dejection came with the awareness that this same species had formed the creation with their labors.

111

Perhaps not this exact type of sinner, I next thought, but some special members less in opposition to Earth, attuned more to God than tea societies. Then I recalled the brilliant creatures complaining as they hacked away at rocks that eventually would form Christ's Cathedral. Greatly did my regard for Rathel's basement increase with this thinking.

Green was their color. Out of the coach and into the cathedral's entry hall stepped the lady and I, finding that the prevalent hue this Sabbath was a pale green, not unpleasant except for its being of satin instead of ferns, the ladies here not so extravagant of bodice as they were in greater London when farther from God, with scarcely a bosom leaping forth. Somber in deep browns and greys, the men flaunted not the first red shoe. So conservative were these sinners in meeting Lord God that they sucked no smoldering pipes, those unable to resist Satan through his instrument of tobacco modest enough to keep their snuff stashes well concealed behind a gum, with nary a dribble from a lip, though even an untalented witch could smell the fetid crop with every respiration.

Too many characteristics inconsistent with God's house had they for me to catalogue, from vapors of recent liquor to talk of the neighbor's unseemly guests. Their one day for being godly, yet who was humble here? Then I became a member of the party as Rathel found acquaintances who of course would meet the new daughter.

They flocked around me as though otters at a salt lick. Hungered these ladies appeared as they stared at me and radiated delight toward Rathel, my mother. My *mother?* The comments came so quickly that I could not follow them all, though the mistress remained nonplussed. Not since spring I've seen you; meet the grandmama; and you're the lady who destroys evil? How courageous—how *British.* So, Amanda, this is the new girl, taken from a hole in the ground, I hear. No, from cannibals in the Borneo jungle. No, from witches in Wales, the place for them. All the ladies had to touch me, applying fingers to my cheeks while saying how sweet I was, grasping my forearm to insist that my comeliness was complete, squeezing my wrist while declaring me more fortunate than beautiful to be living with so fine a lady in so fine a city in so fine a nation, and et cetera, although I was so *cold*—you come

112

from Iceland, child? Being a young lady in education if not nature, I knew it proper to acknowledge these comments, if not all the fondling. Here the moderate talking taught me I was certain to apply, in that no advantage would befall me from extending a prolix insouciance. Therefore, I brought my response to them like a city horse its carriage box. "Pleased to meet you," and avert the eyes, curtsying at these ladies' names.

Next came men, a lot that had been lurking on the outskirts of the womanly mass. In comparison to their ladies, these males seemed starving, prepared to eat my presence; and I did not trust their nearing smell, for they emitted a faint, disturbing odor. As though smelling this herself, Rathel became adoring of her new lass, moving against me to wrap one arm about my shoulders, the other across my chest. In fact, this was not the loving mother, but the knowledgeable expert protecting me from that smell.

I was sated with these sinners regardless of gender, wishing only to pass them and enter the cathedral's nave, hopeful to find God somewhere in the building. His men were an unholy barrier that Rathel bypassed, pulling me away from the more aggressive males. Was she socially correct to press away this cuff and that wrist nearing her daughter? Her *daughter?* No embarrassment had she – and neither did the malefolk, though their ladies no longer smiled to look down to those reaching hands, then upward to the attached faces of their husbands. The women became protective of their own families, gently pulling their men away. And here was the height of society, for Rathel, these ladies, and even the gents all smiled as a lustful scenario was avoided, then to the minister's services, exchanging Satan in the foyer for God in the nave.

And so the services advanced, the process no more than a louder version of Sunday in Jonsway. Their organ had been portative; this was permanent, commensurate in volume to the edifice's entirety. The ministers were identical. I inferred that the presiding holy sinner knew in his experience the proper interval to keep his flock away from their smoking and liquor before they rioted. Lengthy enough were the services for me to lose my feeling of drudgery and look upward to the vaulted ceiling, so far away as to seem another land, countless paces above the nearest sinners, a breach they could not

113

close even with vision, for only the witch looked. Only the witch understood that the glory of the cathedral remained, that the sinners' taint was literally beneath the true grandeur available. Without this mass below, might not space be made for those special members who had manifested God's potential by constructing this edifice? Then, in a revelation that fit this holy place, I came aware that this building was older than my mother, and though the descendants of its builders built anew, why should a godful person believe them equal? Could the society of that previous era be as evil as the current? Though Rathel might believe Christ's equal to St. Nicholas, was she judging not these buildings but her own era, and therefore herself?

The end of a church service is ever the same, regardless of the grandeur of the edifice within whose bounds people meet to worship God and dip snuff. After the minister's, the choir's, and the congregation's benediction, these again-average people proceeded to mill about the pews, gossiping and politicking before returning home to attempt survival while plotting amongst their peers in the normal machinations of society. The difference here was that seldom are young ladies molested in church.

While I had been viewing the cathedral's vaults, the ambient men had been assessing me. Having noticed this examination, Rathel quickly hied me outside, maintaining to her friends that the girl new to society grew faint from the thick interior air, and—oh—breathless I attempted to appear. Despite our efforts to flee, we were met by folk whose curiosity had not abated: some appreciative of Rathel's presence, some offering new friendship toward me. One man, however, was offering his navel. The brother of a lady friend of Rathel, Mr. Georges Gosdale introduced himself with his smell; for as this mature sinner smiled and made to take my hand, I sensed a distinctive odor rising from the pit of his body. Since I refrained from accepting his hand due to my breathlessness, Mr. Gosdale offered words, stating that as well as a lovely face I had "quite a voluptuous fundament, yet without excessive girth."

What a silence he drew with that commentary. With shame staining his face, Gosdale made to explain himself by reaching around me to grasp that mentioned rump and say how prideful a lady should

114

be for having an appearance as vital as *this*. He did not, however, manage to gain *this*, for all the ladies assisted Rathel in intervening between Georges's grasping hands and my derriere. The remaining men poorly demonstrated their dismay, for with Gosdale's reaching, they began to smell the same as he. The sinners made a composition with their movements, only one aware that the central person was no beauty, but a witch; the cause not an evil she created, but wickedness released, held by men as lust, not sex, the latter Godly, the former Satanic, dark as the devil. In this scene, sinners disseminated both irresistibly, the witch so bland as to have no pity for their conflict, so selfish as to desire only retreat. God would instruct them if they could hear Him above Satan's call, the sound of their reaching for my body, black body.

Miss Elsie had known all along, and what guilt I had for not harnessing my rear with her laces. The next Sabbath found me yet without corset as I prayed in the basement, preferring God's mildew to His men.

Eight

On her knees she absorbed burnt blood on the planking, for what could ink be but the charred fluid of some plant? But I discerned no smell of cooking from this material, only a soil odor as though it had been drawn from the ground—but what Satanic niche of Earth could issue springs so black? But I had greater concerns in learning the ways of ink. Primarily I had to retain the stuff within its well and not go spilling it upon Miss Elsie's floor, for with dedication fit to build a cathedral she now scoured the smooth lumber. When I offered my assistance, Mrs. Natwich rejected my amends with a lecture on Miss Elsie's becoming a destitute heathen eating cheese rinds if I usurped her chores; and under no circumstance was an English lady to be found upon her knees.

Becoming more contained in my use of writing materials, I was pleased to gain the ability to settle my words upon a lasting sheet. Less satisfying were the words of my lessons, for I was made to write poetry and Bible verses and historical dates instead of words of my own imagining. But what loss here when I had nothing to describe but compositions about leching men and nightmares of dead family?

A certain influence I was allowed over my schooling. My curriculum would not include music after I heard Natwich blow into a hollow tree limb while fingering holes bored along the stick's length. Pleased was Elsie to hear this beaked flute; and, yes, it did sound like a duck having fingers crammed into its face.

116

Geography I found entrancing, the forthcoming lady an attentive pupil to learn of the world's great mountains and equivalent ditches called canyons. Eventually I made these lessons useful by pulling myself away from Africa and again to England. Of this area called London: Where are the nearest lands wild enough to discourage cities but not so dead as to reject animals? Thus, I was shown maps, seeing London as a drawing, and Man's Isle, the Irish Sea I had crossed, crossed in my sleep, the River Thames that I refused to cross, though this traversal was unavoidable certain nights. I was shown textures representing marshes, angled lines symbolizing hills, and was told of Wales. Perhaps Rathel might convey me there once I proved her notions foolish, once I let her victim grasp my fundament, his hands molesting me, eating me. . . .

Rathel's opinion of my murderous capacity seemed less foolish in light of that sub-navel smell of males. Regardless, I knew that disproving her theories would revolt me, for proximity to a sinning male would be required. All I could sense with these thoughts was Gosdale's leer, which seemed fundamental to him. And though Rathel was also concerned for my way with men, her response was even less comforting.

"Your cooperation so pleases me that I shall offer my own," she professed. "Since the parishioners last Sunday proved how men are drawn to you, we shall proceed to manifest that factor. I am arranging for your introduction to Edward Denton's son. When Eric nears you, he will not be able to look away. The more interest you return, the more he will desire my ward and nothing else."

"No fine liar am I, mistress," I returned. "How convincing can I be in displaying a false interest when sinning men disgust me? If your God be the same as mine, you understand His appall upon hearing the lies of His created folk."

"You were liar enough to feign illness upon departing St. Nicholas in accord with my suggesting that your health be poor. Surely God understands how your dishonesty aided in removing you from a difficulty. He will also understand that further pretense will send you to a compatible land. But with all your

117

learning in geography, Alba, please do not select another continent. As for convincing the male, I suggest that you speak only after Eric speaks. Conversation need be your only activity, for even sexual affairs begin socially. But do not batter the young man with your massive sentences. Philosophy is not romantic."

"Neither are witches," I mumbled, an assertion that I would soon have opportunity to prove.

The day of visiting the Dentons I sought a demeanor of acceptance. Eagerness I would have preferred, for disproving Rathel's notions and thereby quitting London was my great desire. But I could not feel eager to be with sinners, not with men, men from whom I drew expressions and smells of their gender. Therefore, I was no happy subject for Miss Elsie's dressing, the diligent servant delighted to wrap me with fabrics and secure the laces, for without question I demanded a corset to conceal my pervasive fundament, and a bit of chain mail for a vest, if you please.

Though gratified to find herself correct regarding my clothing, Elsie would have preferred a mannequin to a lass in order to dress it without complaints of her smashing the tender parts. Humming like the tutor's flute, she took extreme pleasure in piling my hair upon my skull as though building a cathedral, the purple hat attached as though a ceiling vault. And not the first necklace will be strangling me, miss, for the smell of silver so near my face makes my mouth dry, and wet it shall become when I vomit upon the brocade and show it to the beau with you to blame.

Pleased I was to quash Elsie's obnoxious purring. Her silence did not last, however, for there was the servant applying spittle to my shoes' dullness only to be babbling again about how deeply I would impress the Dentons; and what a thing to happen considering that the mistress was to have married into their family instead of Mrs. Denton. If only these elders could forget their past and allow the youths their future. . . .

"Miss Elsie, what are you raving about, with a marriage for Rathel and Mr. Denton?"

"And I'm telling you, lass, how improper it is to be talking

118

about other folk and things between them gone for years."

"And I am telling you, miss, of my accurate awareness that one of the great crafts of London is gossip. And since the person we deal with is family, I shall only benefit to learn more of our beloved mistress. Therefore, why did Rathel not wed this Denton, and what became of the man she had previously wed?"

"Ah, lass, Lord Franklin passed away to God from a long illness that finally took him to be with Jesus."

"Praise God for providing Christian folk with Heaven. Were you present at the time, miss, and was the disease contagious? Were you ill yourself? Is this the sickness to have made you what you are?"

"Ill I was not, lass, except for my poor feeling at Lord Franklin's own. A fine master he was, so I was pleased to be caring for him to aid his doctor. Aye, and God works His wonders in most circular ways, child, for the doctor was the same gent caring for him years before, when he was first taken by the fever, one known to return, though seldom murderously."

"But why should Amanda wish to marry Edward after Franklin's death? Was he immune to the realm of fever and thus a more permanent mate?"

"The men you're speaking of, lass, were in that same business of building things. Thick they were, so when the master took ill, Mr. Denton promised to be looking after this family should the worst occur. And occur it did, for it be Lord Franklin's death, Jesus comfort his soul."

"But if Mr. Denton's vow was to wed Amanda, why did the two refrain?"

"Ah, and I'm saying that marrying was not the vow he intended. His meaning was only to be caring for the lady's financial things."

"The misconception is surprising, in that Lady Rathel especially selects her words with care. How is it she misunderstood Edward?"

"Ah, and lass, but it were no misunderstanding, but a change toward our mistress's misfortune, so I'll not be saying more."

"But her current position seems fine," I remarked. "And Mr.

Denton is wed with children, so his life is likely as he desires. Therefore, wherein lies the continued discomfort?"

"And less it is, miss, with you here, for it deals with children."

"Am I correct in assuming that Lady Rathel has never borne children, or did she spew out dozens, all of whom sensibly ran away to the wilds?"

"No, she's having not a one, lass, and that is her misfortune, for more than anything was she wishing a child of her own."

"She had none because her womb is as barren as her heart?"

"Ah, child, and Master Franklin was ever insisting it be the wife's womb that's barren. Until the end he's asserting this."

"Miss Elsie, I smell imperfect accuracy in Franklin's assertion."

The servant ceased buffing my shoes to look toward me with concern.

"And how is it you're thinking you know this, lass?"

"I can sense it by your manner of speaking," I confessed. "And I offer to aid in your distress. If you've remorse for having gossiped about your employers, I shall pray with you to help alleviate your shame."

"And I've no shame within me, child," Elsie returned firmly. "I was not the one bringing the man a fever to make him barren since youth."

Elsie then sighed, reeking of foolishness for her lax speaking.

"Very well, miss, that revealing was not such a horror," I returned. "And though you should not feel remorse for your own part in the fever, how did you learn so completely of the disease?"

"It's the doctor who's telling me, child."

"You beseeched him for the shameful datum?"

"Ah, and lass, he's telling me because of his own part in it."

"He caused the fever?"

"Of course not, child," Elsie scoffed. "But he's following his patient's order and not revealing to the mistress that the lack of children was no fault of her own, as the husband had her believe, God forgive his own shameful soul."

"Did Amanda eventually learn?"

"Aye, she did, in that the doctor was feeling his own remorse for the deception, and would have the wife

120

know before her husband passed away."

"What was the mistress's response after the doctor informed her?"

Elsie then paused before speaking again and with her words came a smell sensed before, one I could interpret.

"Upon learning, she was—"

"Upon learning from you," I interrupted.

"Ah! I knew you're saying that, Alba," Elsie groaned, nearly ripping my shoe with her rag. "You're reading me heart now, child, and I'd appreciate you ceasing, if you're to condemn me for speaking."

"But, Miss Elsie, you are due no condemnation, having previously revealed that the doctor desired for Amanda to know this important truth. Did he ask you outright to convey the datum to her?"

"No, he was not asking me, child, but so strong was his desire that I could read *his* heart, and therefore was doing what he wished."

"And though the physician was relieved from this revelation, the mistress became distraught."

"That she was, girl, but the truth will sometimes cause this."

"Praise God for truthful people, Elsie, in that lies would ruin us all. And what of Lord Franklin regarding this major revelation?"

"Ah, I'm thinking he never knew, for he passed away before it could become important to him, though it did seem that he was finally recovering. But finally, Jesus bless him, he did not."

"After Lord Rathel went to his rest with Jesus, the lady was to marry Mr. Denton as per his vow, but did not in that something had changed. Am I to guess the modification, Miss Elsie? I think it easy. It must have something to do with Lord Rathel's impotence."

"Not so wise you are as you're believing, child, for it had naught to do with the lord's, but the lady's."

Then Elsie sighed and reeked of foolishness for her lax disclosure.

"But, miss, do I not denote contradiction? All along I thought

121

the lack of children in the family was due to the man, but now you say the woman was causal. Both persons were incapable, you tell me?"

"Both it was not, miss, until the lady took ill herself."

"Ah hah!—then she is the one to have also contracted the fever, becoming barren herself, and therefore is the person she is today."

"No, and wrong you're guessing again, lass, in your too-young wisdom. The lady's barrenness was from a different sickness, and a queer one it was, with her talking endlessly and losing her hair. . . . Uh, Miss Alba? And it's a strange look you're taking, girl, as though you were as cold inside your skin. Lass, are you feeling poorly now yourself?"

"Oh, and . . . and I was for a moment, Elsie. A . . . a quick chill come and gone. A . . . but a bit of dizziness. I'm fine now, miss. . . . Fine again."

But I was not fine. I was ill, too ill for further speaking, further gossip. What a paining loss was my reduced ignorance of the Rathel's expertise in witches. And the reverse.

As I departed, Elsie had a massive smile at the young miss's visiting the handsome Eric. Then I was with Lady Rathel in a rolling box, a container repulsive to any witch, especially one longing to begin the process of abandoning society's encasements.

The entry seemed on the wrong side of the building. Because the Dentons' town house was situated differently from Rathel's, it seemed improper, as though misplaced. But why this false impression? Why did I find strangeness where not truly extant, as though enough queerness did not express itself toward me without my active search?

Though the city's queerest person, I failed to comprehend how severe was Rathel's unbeckoned visit to a household whose master had ruined her life. The chamberlain explained. This smiling servant left us in the foyer to return with a strained inflection requiring no witch to interpret. The Dentons were in, but only the master would be able to greet us, since the mistress was ill, the witch yet unaware that this lady who had usurped Rathel's place would in no way on God's Earth or in Satan's London consent to see the woman to have cursed her, especially considering that she had brought her curse along.

We were led to the master's office, a colder locale than one's den. No casual remarks re the handsome decor had Lady Rathel, seemingly businesslike herself, but smelling excited or expecting excitement. The next oddity I found was the sub-populace of servants scurrying about the furniture like bugs about a tree stump. These servants included men, typical of London households except those with witches.

Male or not, the servants were concerned with Rathel's presence, not mine. The first person to stare at me was the sick mistress herself. Pale and smelling of illness as alleged, a well-attired woman stepped from a doorway escorted by a servant. After a glimpse at Rathel, Mrs. Denton looked toward me with a fear not for herself. And I could read her thoughts as though specially tutored. The sick mistress looked toward me and thought: She has found a weapon so powerful? Then to Rathel she spoke, her words more pained than her thinking.

"How admirable is your courage, Amanda, for you to enter my house when before you only sent misguided pain. But I can be no company due to a genuine illness that came through no coincidence. You will forgive me, then, to the extent you are capable of forgiveness. And truly I hope you've gained compassion enough to forgive when before you were unable; and how ready this should be when I have given you no offense. But agree or not, I know you shall understand, for a lack of intelligence has never been a weakness on your part. Adieu, Amanda, and may you gain peace from God instead of those sources you've been petitioning."

As Mrs. Denton turned away, Lady Rathel replied, "I pray, Hanna, that your health improves. As for your emotions, do not fear my presence beyond this introduction of my daughter to your household. Not again shall I intrude upon your health. Here, however, is a person you may be fortunate to see often."

Sinners have no measure for the brevity of Mrs. Denton's

123

glimpse to me; and how could such intense emotion be contained by an instantaneous moment? Then Hanna with a bent gait retired on the arm of her servant. My only thoughts were that I would not likely return to a household that became sickened with the first glimpse of visitors.

As the chamberlain led us onward, I recalled Elsie's words of refused marriage. What was marriage but another sinning business pact whose failure affected the heart—and was not failed marriage Rathel's intent for me? I then found that my exposure to this household had been too lengthy, for I was ill. Rathel was perfectly normal, stinking of success. I was also normal, dejected and confused, certain that every upcoming step would lead me not to the wilds of England, but to the evil of sinners wherever they might be.

Our personal bug deposited us at a doorway beyond which stood a man seen previously, at his site of construction. Within his home he seemed less the lord, having scant control over intruding guests. Though smelling of concern, even fear, Edward would remain polite; for English gentlemen respond graciously to ladies, as is supposedly their due. Apart from this position mandated by society, however, I could sense that Mr. Denton wished to hide, wished to oust the invaders from his kingdom. My mistress, however, was not to be thwarted by another person's fearful discomfort, for fear was one of her expert commodities.

"Lady Amanda Rathel and her new Miss Alba," was our introduction from the chamberlain. Though aware of the stress in this home, the man desired to witness the composition developing. Perhaps in their own social way these servants were an inferior race of crawlies.

I was uncertain how handsome Edward Denton should be considered. He was the same age as them all, and sturdy, but even a witch unfamiliar with sinners could sense that he was controlling his emotions because he had something emotional to control. Smiling was a chore as he bowed toward Lady Amanda and spoke her name. Rathel, however, seemed genuine as she called him "Dear Edward," producing a pleased visage rarely used with members of her own household. Simultaneously,

Rathel reached with both arms, Mr. Denton having to touch her fingers, a brief grasp, then gone.

"Dear Edward, how wonderful you appear," Rathel stated.

"You as well, Amanda," he replied. "I trust that you've been well."

"Especially well since gaining a new member of my household," she offered, and turned to me. "This youth is Alba, to be known as Rathel. I have taken her in to rear as a lady, one whose place in society might equal her appearance."

"A great pleasure, Alba," Edward professed, his smile no more comfortable or comforting than before. Then he kissed my hand.

He had to. Here was another move mandated by a society to torment a man even at home. Though aware of his intent in bending with a stretched arm, I had never been the one to suffer from such contact. Being an educated lady, however, I knew to lift my arm and allow my hand to be taken. Suave was Edward's shock to touch my frozen knuckles.

Grateful to God I was for Denton's having none of Gosdale's odor. Praise God again that he touched me with only his breath. But the act was so useless as to strike me, and I felt that he had bit me, bit my senses. After a hesitation that might have embarrassed some, I managed to curtsy, and Edward's mouth was gone.

I wished them to battle. Since their quarrel stemmed from mating, the butting of heads as though deer in rut would be proper. Then their problems would be resolved, and I could depart. But Rathel and Edward *were* emotional enemies, and as such would continue to dredge up unreal pleasantries to lay falsely at each other's positions.

Edward was not alone in this chamber. Another man had risen from his chair as the guests entered, Edward now turning to him. Perhaps this older man was affected by the liquor whose glass he set upon a sideboard, in that his visage and smell were cordial and unstrained.

Of course, Lady Amanda was well acquainted with Edward's father, Lord Andrew. Then her hand was kissed, which seemed normal in being between sinners. I was the witch, and strange I found the friendly father's approaching me to surround my shoul-

125

ders with both arms. He then stood away to look down at my face while squeezing my elbows, testing my fiber.

"And what a beautiful belle you have acquired, Amanda," Andrew declared, looking between Rathel and her charge. "More of London's superior meals in her and she will be quite the lady, for heretofore she has the poise. And so lovely she is that I must laugh with pleasure," he professed, and blurted a loud sound to startle me. Rathel then smiled enough to split her cheeks, I hoped.

Andrew was so active that my passivity was acceptable, but why was I not more offended by that smell of liquor so near? Why had this sinner's torso against mine not been a greater threat? The answer was found in his basic smell, for beneath the alcohol was a scent of innocence, a strange trait for a sinner, but as real as his son's distress. Unfortunately, that innocence seemed less than influential, and therefore could scarcely relieve me of the ambient anxiety.

As though startled into new thinking by his own chuckle, Andrew turned sharply to his son to announce a brilliant notion. Though I was not fearful of the elder Denton, I moved one step away as he spoke.

"Why, Edward, we must bring Eric down to meet London's newest lady. Here's a wonderful peer to strengthen the friendship between our families that somehow has grown slack, which I've scant been able to comprehend."

"Why, I . . . I don't believe that Eric is in the household, Father," Edward maintained while blanching.

"Oh, and of course he is. A moment past I saw him examining your hunting knives to the point—I say—of nearly losing a finger."

"No . . . I, I am certain he left the home thereafter," Edward attempted to assert. Failing again to comprehend, Andrew had stepped to the doorway, ordering a servant upstairs to retrieve Master Eric.

Further talking transpired, though none by Edward. Remain for tea, of course. I would love, but no, though the two youths' meeting would be grand. Yes, a new generation of friendship in our families, even as with Franklin—God rest his soul—and Edward.

A young male soon entered, unescorted, a person as common as his father, but not nearly so apprehensive. As Eric and I had our unspecial introduction—no kissing required by this youth, praise God—I managed some bland pleasantry that would have pleased my tutor. But my thoughts were with Edward, not his son. Rathel was the sinner most corrupted by drama, but Edward was the most distraught. On this household stage, the sinners improvised lines they had to live, not learn, their composition having entrapped me.

The youths were seated on the same divan, though between us was enough air for flying, Eric becoming nervous upon discovering that he was facing not a lady, but a girl. His first embarrassment was from Rathel, who commented on how manly Eric had grown. His next embarrassment was from the witch. As though tutored by Rathel or Satan, I asked him:

"Are you the male I am to kill with love?"

How appropriate this question seemed in being humorous yet insane, for was maddened love not the nature of these households?

The three Denton males reacted immediately to my words. Eric gained an uncertain countenance as he looked to me, then to his grandfather, who had burst into the loud, unfettered laughter heard before. Edward, the architect, was a building himself, static as a mortared wall.

Rathel, whose smile was as false as Andrew's was genuine, did not smell comical as she replied:

"Ah, London's youth, always with commentary to make themselves seem so important. We thus see that unimpeachable beauty must be more than artifice. Perhaps I know a greater factor weighing poorly against Alba's behavior. The girl was reared away from true society. This may be the cause of her *minor* humor for which we both apologize. With further exposure to London's superior etiquette, however, I am certain she will conversationally become the lady that she now appears."

"With God's grace and the influence of her new mistress,"

Andrew replied, "no doubt this fine lass can only improve, though she should never lose her humor."

I agreed. Understanding that we were now deeply into theater, I began speaking with compositional fluency. Though my inner disposition was similar to silent Edward's, our responses were disparate; for whereas Edward found himself in hiding, I found myself in battle.

"My truest apologies to all the Messrs. Denton. But with Mistress Rathel's expertise in demonology, I sometimes feel the witch myself."

Mad humor remains humor. I remained somewhat mad from my foolish response, while Andrew remained sane as he responded with the perfect humor of his familiar laugh. Edward then responded with words Rathel and I heard perfectly above the chuckling. Edward was staring at me now, having gained some controlled emotion I could not interpret, could not avoid, as he displayed the passion allowing him to envision cathedrals.

"Despite your fine humor, Alba, you might ask your mistress to guide you toward an area less dangerous to womenfolk. Inquire of her colleague, London's Magistrate Naylor, who has his own way with witches; for even as the lady's is being aware of them, the magistrate's is killing them."

And the theater ended. With that final phrase, the play became unacceptable to a witch most expert in the stench of blackened family. After a pause to accept Edward's words, I turned from him and looked toward the floor, seeing no true ground of God's, but deceptive planking precise yet sourced in destruction. I could smell his fear and sense danger within him, but the danger was not for me. This awareness saved me from fainting when thoughts of loved ones burned black filled me again, for I knew that Edward's fear of death included no desire for my own demise, only a plea to God for any death to come other than his son's.

Again the moderating mistress seemed to be aiding me in education.

"Certainly Mr. Denton is correct, Alba, in that neither dying nor witches are comical matters with godly folk."

Edward looked away from me after contemplating my wordless

128

response, examining my shame or sensitivity. Neither of us wished to view the deathly state between us, a theme to be reinforced if again we were to view one another. Being two persons whose preference was the living world, Edward and I looked away.

"Now, enough of dying and social chastisement," Andrew instructed all present. "Let us speak of the fond future, not the unpleasant past." And he chuckled mildly at his own humor. He and Rathel then discussed my schooling, church and social activities, and similar regarding Eric. Not a word in this conversation was emitted by Edward, who sat solidly behind his desk, chin lodged on his fist. Sane again, I said nothing. Eric, however, soon found his own cue for entering this evolving theater.

"You know of witches?" he asked, his tone one of profound graveness.

Though I had seen sinners scarcely older than this person wed with children, the boy was so commonly youthful as to be enthusiastic about a strange realm he considered dangerous. I then felt a lack of justice in my life for never having known a witch my age, for only having met sinning youths scarcely recognizable as human.

"I know sinners," I said quietly. My reply was unkind because I inspired Eric to seek resolution of that mysterious word.

"We all are sinners in the eyes of God," he stated, a comment that seemed a question, Eric wondering if he had grasped my meaning.

"And some well appreciated in the eyes of Satan," I told him.

"Such as witches," he returned thoughtfully, "for they cause plagues and steal the breath from babes."

"Cats in strange imagination cause the latter and liquor in actuality the former," I declared. "Your fantasies seemed misarranged."

Seeking to draw more of my sinister familiarity by impressing me with his own, Eric announced, "Oh, of course, witches curse folk with potions."

This pronouncement, however, was too aligned with true aspects of my life for me to respond facetiously.

"Clearly, sir, we have seen today that good Londoners in fact do curse one another. What potion could be worse than hatred?"

From the certainty of my idea as well as my loud voice, the seniors in the chamber noted my comment, though Andrew and Amanda continued with their speaking. Edward's reaction was to wander. As though literally moved by my speaking, he rose, stepping from one window to another. And though he settled behind the children and was thus unseen, the witch could smell his interest, could sense that Edward was now examining his son.

In reply to Eric's stated concern that witches in their increasing influence might draw us from God with the raw intensity of their evil, I noted that such active passion was a product of politicians, and therefore endemic to the realm of parliament, not potions. The young sinner in his maleness then began to stink, a mild version of that odor indigenous to his gender laid forth in the air between us along with equally undesirable words. Eric stated that I was not unpretty, and certainly on the subject of new smells and their inspirational pulchritude I was without response. Eric, however, received a most direct reply from his father, who ran to the boy as though attacking him, displaying the intensity required for a man to invent breathtaking cathedrals. He took his son's breath by taking his body, grimacing Edward snatching the lad of nearly adult size to his feet, hollering as he slapped the boy's midsection with a punishing hand.

"Your foul thinking in your mother's house!" Edward shouted, and slapped again at an odd projection of Eric's clothing, as though the boy had dropped a stick into his pants. This unfamiliar problem I would not peruse. Then the child-man was forcefully removed from the room by a father revealing the strength required to procure from within himself the design of hard constructions able to soften even death-ridden hearts.

With the departure of these persons, Lady Rathel determined that our own exit was next to be made, and here I had no argument. In farewell, Lord Andrew conveyed to Rathel his sorrow for that regretful final event, then turned to the young semi-lady to state his pleasure at our meeting.

More moving than his words was his nature, Andrew's consistent removal during histrionics from the play's poorer aspects. Of all those amongst us, Lord Andrew had never emphasized pain by recognition, avoiding the emotion not from ignorance, but amity.

". . . a superlative lass I am so proud to have met," he remarked in ending. "I wish your life to be as fine as your appearance."

His last remark was so clearly based on genuine goodwill that I could no longer be the firm witch set in her survival against sinners. I became the same human as he, providing Lord Andrew an emotional comment no less genuine in content than any of his own.

"God bless you, sir, and all your household that you may live happily as decent people deserve."

"Exactly as they deserve," Rathel concluded to Andrew with a smile, the lady as was her life's insistence unfortunately having the ending idea.

Nine

No especial concern had I for the male guest Lady Rathel was entertaining until he spoke of demons.

This sinner arrived the day after I met my future victim. Elsie answered the door as I crawled about my chamber, determining the damage from her latest covert bout of cleaning. While I was sighing on the roof, Elsie had obliterated my urine markings so small that no sinner should be sensitive enough to find them. At least she had not oiled beneath the bed, leaving me a surface recognizable as wood. But was this failure from her lacking time — in that the irascible lass might return any instant — or from friendly consideration? Perhaps the latter, for my sole natural friend, the spider, remained at peace in its corner. And it seemed that Miss Elsie was at peace in mine.

When the sinner in the foyer spake "demonic," I ran to the balustrade as Elsie guided a mature sinning man into the drawing room, though I viewed only his back. His suit seemed more severe than usual for men of Rathel's peerage, a dark, familiar jacket. Cursed with curiosity, I moved down the stairs and to Elsie, who was proceeding with her chores.

"Elsie, who is the male with Rathel?"

Having been violently scraping away encrustations inside a decorative flower crock, perspiring Elsie looked up to me with personal astonishment, proceeding to condemn me for shaming her person.

"Ah! you're having the gall to be traipsing downstairs in your nightclothes and without brushing your hair, you thankless waif?"

Theodosia nearby precluded my free speaking, for she and Delilah had rejected me outright for rejecting the state of ladydom.

Only a mad person, they believed, required convincing to become superior in English society, the servants willing to sacrifice any attribute shy of their presumably immortal souls for the opportunity being forced upon me. Therefore, no intimate revelations did we share. Only Elsie received my deceitful rantings.

"No more sorrow could I feel than to have offended you, kind Elsie, and to my chamber I shall rush to overcome my shameful state if only you would comment as to the identity of the gentleman herewith arrived."

Before Elsie could reply that Mistress Amanda's guests were not my concern, I quickly whispered, "I heard him say 'demonic.'"

She ceased her scraping to look firmly toward me, then continued with her activity. Her smell had changed, as had her face, Elsie with an odor of concern, an expression of apprehension.

"And the gent is London's magistrate, Lord Naylor, being the most important official of law in our city. 'Tis an honor we're having, child, for such a great man to visit our home," she advised. Only with a final sentence did Elsie regain her normal tone of comfortable scolding. "Now be up the stairs lest he's seeing you disheveled like no lady of his city."

Away I ran, Elsie seeing that my goal was not the upper story, but the great closet outside the drawing room. As I moved inside and to the far wall, Elsie wondered how I had learned this place the best for listening to the adjacent room.

I could hear voices a long walk beyond as polite persons travel, only paces away as the witch listens. Rathel had left the door to the drawing room open, in that a gentleman should not be privately met with a lady unless family, this another lesson learned by the witch though not considered sensical. And here was the subject to be discussed: not ladies, but witches. Within the closet, I listened improperly, though not inappropriately, for the subject was me.

"I must presume, Lord Magistrate, that you've some exceptional cause for placing such questions to me."

"Not so exceptional that you cannot call me Jacob, I assure you, Amanda. In fact, one of our fine citizens is the cause."

"Am I not one as well, Sir Jacob?"

"One of London's finest, and especially valued for the aid you've oft given England by helping rid her of demonic entities. Your

133

ability to distinguish witches from common women is a unique, inestimable faculty."

I could not smell this man, but his voice held no especial warmth nor a brazen lack of decency. How Lady Rathel was affected by him I remained uncertain, though it seemed that even her current firm position was being addressed to a peer, a sinner equal not only in society, but strength.

"I hope the time does not come when you doubt my motives regarding such malice because my aid to you is accompanied by a request for payment."

"A tribute of currency would be understandable, but since you request naught but a mention to the city's council or the king's chancellery, I find your fee temperate. Perhaps certain people care not for my wielding influence toward you, but as long as I publicly acknowledge my ideas as having come from yourself, I remain proper not only for the written laws of England, but also the established rules of political integrity."

"Then why on this occasion are you doubting my own integrity? Why is it you accept the word of the architect instead of mine?"

"The architect has responsibility for London's greatest new cathedral, and that is God's jurisdiction. Considering the man's position, he is due the benefit of my investigation."

"But accusing—"

"I present queries, Amanda, not accusations. Further, you might ease my task here by being forthright in replying."

"But what further queries could you have, Lord Magistrate? The first to leave your mouth virtually named my adopted daughter a demon."

"The query was not quite so crass, Amanda. And reasonable it was of Mr. Denton considering your familiarity with witches. Since by nature your profession deals with punishment, the possibility exists of your subjects' seeking retribution. To gain such vengeance, even demons influence people more than the elements. Considering that you now house a person previously under Satan's spell as per your own admission, Mr. Denton's queries must be understandable even to yourself."

"Understandable, but not agreeable, and presumably a type of vengeance of Denton's own, for even humans can be wicked."

"Please me, Amanda, by not being defensive when no offense have you caused. To obviate Denton's further distressing you via my office, answer me casually and quickly."

"Your answer, then, is simple, Jacob. Quickly and officially, my daughter Alba is possessed by great God alone, for truly she is as pious a child as any I have known."

"And as for the potential of the girl's somehow transferring the corrupt force that previously influenced her?"

"Never in my experience have I known of such demonic transference. Death can be conveyed via a witch's potion, but also by common poison. But do not misconstrue: Alba did live with witches. She did not, however, become one from this proximity. Either one is a witch or is not. No one dispenses Satan like a beverage."

"From my own experience, Amanda, I know demonic folk to transmit evil through every physical medium."

"But Satan is not corporeal on Earth, existing instead as malice. The black lord uses the witch as a means, not an equal."

"The means for my own worst experience of evil – my father's death, a sinister demise that well you've heard of."

"True, Jacob, the plague is the most wicked of illnesses."

"Most wicked exactly, and though some fools say it was brought by rats from the Continent, I know it was brought by witches from Hell. If rodents carried the disease, it was given them by witches. But here we disagree."

"I doubt that witches have the power to kill such a multiplicity."

"My own parent is the singular of my concern. As for your doubts, you may have them through your experience with witches; whereas I must accept your word, for little of that knowledge will you provide me."

"For a cause well depicted, Jacob. Those same witches would take my life through a charm long established if I tell their truths. But that past will change no more than the place of your father in Heaven. In our immediacy, however, is a current evil. You have come about Mr. Denton's accusations, which I would dispose of. Are we ended with his comments as to my daughter's transmitting plagues?"

"Denton's fact is that you brought your daughter to

135

his home in order to torment the boy Eric."

"I brought Alba to the Denton household to boast of my enviable state in having so felicitous a daughter."

"The architect has been specific in maintaining that the girl aroused his son as only persons married under God should become."

"Does he lie so daringly as to assert that my daughter lured his boy? That she made toward him either bodily revelation or a taunting with words?"

Rathel's last speaking was so intense that it caused a change in my own facial cast, as though she were speaking to me. The magistrate of London was doubtless undisturbed.

"He did not," Naylor stated with no soothing tone. "Mr. Denton alleged that the girl projected her gender via some evil emanation."

After scoffing, Rathel replied, "In fact, Jacob, evil *was* emanated. Evil was the wicked Eric boy who brandished the lust of his manhood. Alba revealed nothing but a lovely face. The ill-bred Denton scoundrel revealed the wickedness of his body. Does the architect deny this?"

"He suggests that some malicious flow from the girl caused the lad's maleness to be evident when it never had been before."

"If a beauteous face be wicked, then Alba is evil. But since Lord God created lovely girls to make all our lives pleasant, the wickedness is not from my household, but from the Denton boy's lust. As well, God was so gracious as to give the girl no understanding of beauty's power. Should I thus correct her deficiency by having lurid folk such as the Denton wretch teach her seduction? Should I scar her face to avoid the evil in wicked males? I say not, sir. I say leave her exquisite as God intended. I say speak with His ministers to correct the corruption in this situation, for it lay in the lewd Denton youth."

"Enough of this bother," the magistrate declared, and I heard him rise. "Enough of Denton's anxieties. And enough of my efforts' being wasted when I have true concerns of evil in this city. I will thus take my leave, Amanda, and thank you for your forthright replies."

"You will please remain for—"

"I shall not remain, lady, for I made appointments elsewhere, in

136

that two aspects of our conversing I predicted. The first: that you would be displeased by my questioning; and second: that you would nonetheless graciously offer the benefits of your excelling household. I thank you for both, and repay you by exiting, thereby allowing you to lose your displeasure with me. Adieu, Amanda, and my gratitude I give until again we have cause for cooperation."

The mistress allowed him to depart. I also withdrew, to my room to suffer a distress worse than Rathel's. She had referred to me as her daughter before, but now I was sickened. Ah, what a fool that Vidgeon woman to have desired me legally while possessing none of Rathel's resources—and what of Sarah's hair, her mentality? Had she cured as well—or as poorly—as Lady Rathel? Lord God, make Vidgeon average again, I prayed, not wishing known people to suffer further. And what a fool I had been, for if now an adopted Vidgeon, my station would be superior in not being subject to familial revenge. Sarah Vidgeon would yet be mindful and hirsute, and my mother would be alive. In that situation, could I not have secretly met with my true family to design a plan for being permanently together again? But with Lady Rathel, I was a sea removed from my home, and an eternity removed from Mother.

Typical of the sinners' outlandish affairs, my torment was not alone. Though resembling Jonsway's alderman in attire, this magistrate was more akin to the bishop in danger. And whereas Rathel sought a sinner's death, Sir Jacob threatened only witches. The true source of my melancholy was Naylor himself, an official who like the former in my acquaintance sought witches' demise for the sake of God and England. And I was certain that unlike the bishop, this magistrate I would meet again.

Less tidy in its artifice was that section of the grounds outside the kitchen. Here was soil made raw from traversal, not gardening, a path where servants walked to an unkempt mound for burying the household dung. The path's opposing course led servants through a thick gate to the depths of London for tasks of market-ing, the home's lesser members having an exit from the grounds separate from the lofty females' route. And which of my opposing portions would I emphasize if ever again I achieved escape: the

simple rear exit fit the witch in me, or the elaborate front metalwork appropriate for the lady I deigned to become not for social
status but survival? But how would I ever quit this sinning world
now that release via cooperation was shown to be false? False and
failed, I knew, ever since meeting the passion of the victim's father,
the incarnate architect, meeting the ambitions of another lawman
seeking witches as though a lode of precious metal. And though
Rathel demanded that I only attempt her plan, I knew that any
activity directly involving the source of man smell would be impossible considering the strain of simply visiting the family. I
thought of Gosdale, whose advances seemed fetid, thought of the
Eric boy growing a bit and changing from a person to a heinous
male due only to the fundamental lechery of men. No, no, I would
require a new means for achieving a true life. Therefore, I sought
the support of an army, which I would recruit in the guise of Miss
Elsie.

"And now it's plain water that's distressing you, I'm hearing? The
simple well which is bringing you water makes your poor self ill?"

"My meaning, stern and literal Miss Elsie, is that the bucket
induces a metal taste and smell in the water due to its iron surround."

"Aye, and it could be worsened, lass, by our having a lesser
bucket, one only of wood, and thus splitting as soon as you're
using it. But I'm telling you that the mistress is not having you at
servants' tasks, and if I'm to be chided, then the fault and the
shame both be yours."

Average servant and improper, learning lady sat on a coarse
bench fit a wild place and shelled peas. With a precise positioning
of this bench, we sat as though in the natural world, the adjacent
building's upper stories hidden behind leafy trees to shade us,
shelter us from neighboring witches seeking a view of space but
finding only humans concerned with future eating.

"Equally distressing toward Rathel's sense of etiquette would be
her young ward's preparing vegetables, would it not?" I asked
Elsie.

"Aye, it would," she confessed, "but it's one I'm enjoying, in that
your companionship improves as you learn to be less of the wild
creature."

"I also find your presence increasingly adequate, Elsie, a satisfaction stemming from your personality, not merely your physical presence, which nevertheless is compatible, since you've neither periwig nor paint to obscure your natural appearance."

"Ah, yes, lass, and what a terror for me to seem the lady," Elsie huffed, pods flying from her now-violent fingers.

Refraining to mention that no local witch was as sensitive as she, I continued to seduce this servant into my ranks.

"And with whom did you share such activities before I entered the household?" I wondered.

"Ah, but the chores I'm finding different are not the small ones of skinning, but the heavy ones of toting. That's where the persons are different, for once an older but everworking gent was here for the massive things. It's the mistress, then, who's having him leave lest the young girl coming be influenced toward menfolk too soon, though that's hard to figure with his age and ugliness. The more important man leaving, though, was Master Franklin, God keep him. But even with him, there was no true family, which the mistress was ever lacking." Elsie then paused, her face displaying an odd visage. "Before you, Alba."

"I must beg your pardon, miss," I replied with true offense, "in that your meaning hopefully eludes me."

"So I'm saying that since the mistress is never having a child from her body, at least she has one now for her heart. And no daughter from a person's own womb will be better kept than you, lass, I'm assuring you."

"I must say, Miss Elsie, that to become the child of a sinner is not merely an unpleasant thought, but one utterly revolting to any witch; for despite the rare individual's curse of seeming the sinner, we all are sisters in spirit. To inform you accurately, know that the purpose of Rathel's bringing me here is to achieve not family, but vengeance. Though knowledgeable in the ways of witches, she revels in the delusion that I, as a witch, am physically capable of destroying this Eric person in order to punish his father for that previous romantic dissent. As for family, having a sinner as a mentor is excruciating; having one as a mother would be perverse. I will ever have but one true mother, a soulless crone who although dead for God's eternity will live forever in my thoughts."

139

Elsie dropped her peas as though unable to support their mass, so weak she became, as though I had beaten her. In her ignorance of that second human race, poor Elsie was incapable of comprehension.

"Girl, I would be struck deaf from what I'm hearing!" she declared. "The mistress is telling of your delusions from that old life, but to be calling not only yourself but your poor dead mother a witch and a crone and soulless! Praise God, child, that even as He gave your resting mother a soul, may He soon be giving you a true understanding of yourself so that these fantastical things you're saying be ended, along with the pain you're now causing your true friend, this Elsie."

Having ejected her entire energy, Elsie was exhausted as she turned from me and regained her vegetables. I, however, remained calm and strong in my further speaking.

"Elsie, you are nearly acceptable as a person in that you have less the smell of the powdered lady and more of an animal's odor, but—"

"And thank you everso for calling me stinking!" she retorted.

"Therefore," I pronounced firmly, having to reestablish my speaking, "in order for our compatibility to continue, I shall display my true nature in evident proof and thus convince you of God's truth and mine."

"So, what is it you'll be doing, girl, since proving false things is not possible? You're beginning where with your delusions: showing how you'll be harming the boy or how your family is a pack of soulless fiends?"

"My gracious thanks, miss, for deeming me the fiend," I scolded. "With this basic tenet I shall begin: that although a witch, I am no more demonic than you, though somewhat less than Rathel. To provide you with this proof, however, I must first receive your promised word."

"And if I'm promising to believe your false things, child, then no proof at all will be coming."

"The vow you must give me in speech and God in prayer is to never reveal the scenes I shall display; for as you are well aware, witches in your sinners' semi-moral society are due grisly execution."

140

"And rightfully so," she declared, "considering the evil they're bringing to God's world."

Now I was the one affronted, though I mishandled not the first pod as I loudly retorted.

"No more outlandish delusion could exist than that my mother and her similars are heinous and worthy of a torturer's fire. I will cure your ignorance, Miss Elsie, by revealing myself a witch and yet worthy of your friendship. I shall also prove myself superior as a person to your opinion of me, for by demonstrating myself a witch, I prove myself honest and not the liar you believe."

Elsie's tightened breath revealed new tension. Though skeptical, the woman was also frightened by the unlikelihood of my truth. And, as was common with sinners, she was curious.

"Girl, if you're to be proving yourself a dark spirit, it would not be done with a palsy on me hands, eh?"

"Even as I verify myself a witch, I shall prove these additional assertions: that witches cause no illness, never harm crops and livestock, nor transmit plagues as though letters sent from Europe. If a reasonable person, Elsie, you will then comprehend those facts of my life that I've often mentioned. In fact, witches are repulsed by the eating of our fellow animals, and rightfully fear manipulation by sinners who would kill us. The former is my cause for stressing crops, not creatures, in my diet. The latter is the source of my opposing Lady Rathel."

"And how is it, young Alba, that you're proving yourself the witch in some way that an unbeliever might believe? It's no coldness of skin that's making a person the witch," Elsie added. "Perhaps you'll be showing some magic for me."

"I will display magic if you bear a child to demonstrate procreation," I retorted.

"Girl, and you're old enough to be knowing that making babes is not a thing done on one's own or within the span of a moment."

"Yes, miss, I do understand, and hope that henceforth you comprehend that magic is no less involved or difficult, an activity I care to undertake as much as you would bear a child for my entertainment."

"Aye, and it's for the best, girl, that you're not proving yourself wicked," Elsie sighed, "for I would have you as you are: often

141

deluded but occasionally sweet."

Moments before, Elsie and I had abandoned our shelling as though waiting for a brilliant method for confirming the lass either a genuine witch or a true fool. Then I was struck with an easy proof of witches that in my current era had mutated toward fear.

"Not from my rare felicity but a sought objectivity, I shall prove myself the witch, miss, by swimming for you."

"Ah, but it's known even commonly, lass, that no witch can be swimming," she submitted.

"True enough, but my reference is not to paddling like a coot, but remaining beneath the water's surface for a convincing occasion."

"But the nearest water, I'm saying, is the River Thames, unless you're to be ducking yourself in a rain barrel."

"I would not presume to impress you by immersing my head in a bucket as though promulgating a lark or washing my hair."

"And a fine offer that would be, considering how filthy you allow the stuff to become."

"No further deprecation do I require, miss. I have now decided that, yes, with this river you have arrived at an acceptable example."

I saw myself there. At the river's edge with Hershford Bridge viewed as though a painting on the sky, a harmless depiction akin to one on Rathel's wall. I saw myself not drowning in the depths as was implied by the bridge, but standing apart from the unsupportive structure, at the water's own level, not an intimate locale but one less dangerous than my dreams. I envisioned entering the water, not being hurled toward execution, but slipping at my will beneath the moderate surface. My best wish was my following imagination, that my dreams of drowning would disappear along with my sight of the bridge, vanish from my mind's night creations congruently with the sinners' span disappearing from my eyes.

Elsie and I departed at once, careful to exit the grounds without being espied by its populace. Traveling that worn path to the lesser exit, we entered an alley, then proceeded to verify Satan within me.

Our secretive retreat was tainted by Elsie's visions of doom. With every step, she moaned about losing her employ should the mistress learn of this journey. I was therefore made to vow convincingly and often that I would not attempt to flee, as though I had some reasonable goal, Elsie mentioning that this ignorance of locale had not stopped me before.

To achieve the river where I might gain an aide and rectify my sleeping, we traversed what seemed a huge expanse of London. Elsie at my side was a superior guide to Mother in Jonsway, for being a denizen here, the servant found no surprises in our travel. And she insisted upon remaining unobserved, Elsie feeling that any person recognizing her would inform Rathel of her servant's being out with the new lass for criminal purposes, a ludicrous fear, for in fact our purpose was evil.

Though no one interfered with us as Elsie shooed me along, a new torment found me as though to fill the vacancy of unimplemented anxiety. Through the London air came an unknown smell that was unpleasant yet not quite terrifying. Only the accompanying heat was frightening, Elsie and I passing a shop wherein a male was making bottles. The first sight caught me with a rushing sense not of danger but of alienness, and I had to whisper harshly for Elsie to explain how such an event as a sinner's blowing bubbles of molten sand could possibly be. Familiar with the girl's wilderness innocence, Elsie provided a clear explanation that in no way relieved my feeling that although I might come closer to being a simple person such as Elsie, the sinners' greater artificiality would always be unacceptable. And why was I uncomfortable with this thought when my unending innocence proved me the continuing witch?

At the River Thames, I found disappointment: No bridge was visible on this curving segment. Well removed toward that way, Elsie described. Without this prime element, I was certain that my prediction would not be fulfilled, and my dreams would remain like that bridge, imperceivable in the present, but as unavoidable as the past. No better was the water itself, which seemed incapable of cleansing mere dirt, much less imbedded dreams; for the river stank, soiled from the sinners' industries.

"And it's a foolish notion we're having, girl, and one yet changeable," Elsie declared, standing near me as she looked about for witnesses. "I'm saying we return now, before the mistress finds us."

"Let us find me the witch," I intoned, my voice so confident or so inhuman as to send Elsie a step away.

Expecting disaster to strike her like a storm, Elsie looked about for bystanders who might witness against us. Though previously she had attempted to appear innocent with her observing along the road, Elsie now looked stressfully everywhere for sheer danger. No worker nor passerby approached, Elsie and I shielded from most directions by an empty shed. But even Elsie's extended viewing revealed none of the true disaster, for one step away was the lass removing her attire.

"Alba! and you're mindless now to be denuding yourself on the Thames!" she hissed. As Elsie reached to pull my dress about me, I moved away with a step and a slip, and the garment was on the ground.

Miss Elsie then revealed her true intelligence, understanding that her path of curiosity led directly toward that inferred disaster. Therefore, she abandoned disbelief, proceeding directly to agreement.

"Aye, Alba, and truly I'm believing all you say about witches and plagues — and any thought in your mind, child, if only you'll be clothing yourself and return with me!"

But I would not clothe myself. Being of a race more physical than social, the witch readily pulled herself from the servant, dropping her bloomers to the wharf, then into the river with scarcely a splash.

As I looked to the water, the enterprise's most tactile aspect of wet suffocation became primary. Aware that the immersion to benefit my future would torment my present, I accepted a demeanor of dutiful accomplishment, intending to perform the task of convincing Elsie as though my continued survival were at stake. For no reason other than survival would I walk through water. Not to cross a river only paces long to gain food and end my starving. Perhaps to quench flames consuming my sinners' attire, but nothing less. But something burned me enough to force me toward that water, for the next moment I was not ensuring my survival, but losing it.

The last sound heard was a gasp from Elsie, my last thought to remain calm and procedural, to keep my eyes closed and pinch my

144

nostrils shut to avoid irritation in these sensitive membranes from the sinners' dank river. But once ensconced in the fluid, I found myself captured by it, and I was not retaining my breath, but bereft of it. After that first, smothering moment, I was prepared to push upward from the river's bottom to gain air again. But since any form of human can survive without breathing for a brief spell, I survived my airless moment and came to understand my problem. Of course, water supplies a witch air, a fact I had neglected in my concern for drowning. Less air comes from water than the atmosphere, but enough for survival. Then the water's filth became significant again, for I was eating it. I had opened my mouth to take in the Thames, allowing it to pass in and out via my pumping cheeks. I had to eat it like fruit, consume its saving juice that was wet air the fish know well, that a witch can smell and even sinners see as bubbles.

I calmed. I achieved understanding. Since I received little air, I knew to undertake equal activity. I calmed, allowing the water's air to seep into my lungs. Though continuing to feel some smothering, I breathed through it, a great fear ready to rush through me even as I was ready to rush through the water. But no further terror and no sudden movement came to me as I breathed enough for waiting, for survival.

Having no good idea as to the duration required to prove myself unsouled, I decided to walk about circularly as though on a journey of truth, as though a primping actor displaying himself to the public. Having gained respiration enough to provide me with energy, I began walking a distance I felt equal to a journey through Rathel's house, from the garden to the basement, returning through the kitchen and to the library, up the stairs and down again. The river's bottom here was strewn with sharp shards and hard-edged materials, surely the discharge of sinning luxuries. Since the water greatly reduced my weight, however, I suffered no stumblings as I slowly rose and fell with each step, the shoes I yet wore protecting me from abrasions. After twice traversing Rathel's imagined stairway, I returned to the river's edge, one hand outstretched to feel my way, my eyes closed to avoid a wash of effluent.

Dry Elsie was swaying, and she reeked of fear. Collapse seemed imminent, but with my rising from the water, the woman's disposition changed to surprise, Elsie becoming rigid as she stared.

"You might be so gracious as to assist me," I told her, "for certainly you see that the pilings here are steep and awkward to climb."

Instantly she bent to grasp my arms. As I moved out with Elsie's aid, she spoke in a voice implying anger, though her scent described relief.

"Ah, Alba, and I knew you to be drowned and myself insane for allowing it. But then I'm seeing you move, not your head with that dark hair, but your white skin like a ghost to chill me dead. No person who breathes could remain so long below without expiring, yet you're moving and I can see, lass. God praise, girl, that you're—"

"You might notice, miss, that I am having no difficulty with breath," I calmly advised as I reached for my clothing. "No distress on my part was involved, and I must apologize for yours. Also note that my original assertions as to my life and self are now verified."

Elsie's acceptance of these facts was interrupted by a new difficulty as obvious as the dimples on my hips, for it seemed that as soon as the servant ceased her vigil for witnesses, a parcel of them appeared.

Two men and three women ran toward us, gasping. Elsie's rigidity to have come upon noticing their approach thereafter changed to rapid movement as she guided my dressing, her intent to cover me with the gown and take the mass of underthings along. Her thinking turned most competent, Elsie explained the situation before the assemblage could demand the facts of this remarkable scene.

"Oh, and the courageous girl is throwing herself in the river to save her mother's imported dog from drowning! Oh, but what a thoughtful lass we're having to set her clothes aside and not be ruining them. God bless the poor child who'll be suffering now since the cat could not be saved."

"Dog," I mentioned.

"Since the dog could not be saved," Elsie added in correction.

During her speaking, Elsie attempted to hurl the dress about me so that we could flee without drawing the remainder of London's

146

populace. Because I certainly did not care to be centered in a pack of sinners whether denuded or hidden in a sack, I cooperated, though my movements were more restrained than Elsie's jerking stiff seams so violently over my limbs as to abrade them. But we of the Rathel household were not alone in handling me, Elsie finding it necessary to shove aside the hand of a male who was covering my breast with his fingers. Upon recognizing the move as no random slip, Elsie responded as she felt befit the man's behavior.

"Ah! you flipping rotter to have your hand on the child's bosom!"

"But I was helping the lass dry the water away," the man explained. "She'll catch the croup with such moisture."

Then I replied, "I've no special accumulation of moisture about my nipples, the ladies here especially will note."

Most astonished of all, the man's female companion proved herself the wife by spouting shouts and also spittle, so violent was her response.

"Satan take your bloody *soul* for fondling a lass!" she screamed, and shoved the man's chest so hard that he nearly toppled over. "Curse your black hands, untrue husband, for such corruption!" she mentioned, and threw her arm at the man's head in a tremendous arc, connecting soundly with his jaw, a blow to collapse him to the wharf and frighten all decent persons about regardless of their ability to travel in a submariner manner. Retaining his senses despite the combat, the male looked upward between his wife and me, attempting to ascertain why he had attacked the child, why one so young seemed irresistible.

"Not only a girl before my very eyes, but one not even a *wench!*" the woman continued, and kicked the downed man with her ending word, this latest attack inspiring him to evade so totally that his balance was sacrificed to dodging, the husband toppling into the Thames with a greater splash than mine, a blubbering noise from the intake of water silencing his previously blubbering lips and their inadequate explanations.

Now covered to the ankles, I was pulled along by Elsie, who held the unlaced fabric tightly about me to prevent further revelation of the man's fleshly goal or previously mentioned dimples. Though the greater scene had drawn additional sinners, the battle between spouses became their surpassing interest, a relationship

147

more interesting than a retreating child and her guardian. Away we went with a bundle of underclothes and a nonplussed witch, though the servant remained protective, an initiative clearly coming from her heart, and therefore worthy of my appreciation.

Once removed from the crowd and settled in a rapid pace to Rathel's town house, Elsie received a terrible revelation known as truth.

"Ah, this is why the mistress is removing the male servant," she wheezed, looking not at me, but somewhere far ahead, though she continued to hold my apparel tightly, even cruelly, about my torso. "The lady ever knew how you'd be drawing men, as you did in church—I've heard of it, lass—and just out of the river though you might be drowning."

"Of course, Rathel knew me a witch, my Elsie. As I explained, that very factor was her cause for bringing me to London. And what is more convincing to you: that normal men turn lurid when near me, or that I've proven myself impervious to God's waters?"

"I'm believing you, child, for whichever cause, and because never did I feel you dishonest. Deluded, surely, as the lady was saying, but not a pure liar. But of Mistress Amanda's dishonesty, it seems near justified considering your danger."

The servant then looked closely to me, emitting a strong emotion not easily described, though her own words were explanation enough.

"A lady such as ours going about her vengeance is understandable, Alba, when such damage was done her heart. We must be praying after her, child, for God to heal her spirit. But how can a lass such as this," she moaned, and squeezed me as though to crush me dead, to protect me with this eternity, "how can such a peaceful babe be dangerous? Yea, lass, I'm believing you much and might believe you more, but I'm having to ask God, not yourself, whether I should curse the witch or love her."

148

Ten

No more appropriate activity existed for my uncomfortable sleep than nightmares inspired by sinning men. And what more sensical setting than the sea bottom, for was not its stifling smother reminiscent of Rathel's world? My true world was now the sinners' stench, a realm of perception accompanying me when awake even as the sea held me during sleep as I walked, as I dragged a boulder secured to my neck with a chain taken from the anchor since mere ropes were not enough to bond a person so rapacious as to be both sinner and witch, and deservedly punished for crimes in both worlds. Dragged a boulder that was a sepulcher filled with family, stacks of charred bones and ashes, each with a name: Chloe, Esmeralda, Marybelle, Mother. Dragged a tomb through the sea as fishes swam apart from this lethargic scene, dragged that rock toward the shore in sight, a goal ever nearer until the boulder fell and I smothered, having lost my effort. Then the choking began, my only salvation to flee upward, but to do so I would have to swim. I would have to flap my limbs and frolic like the stinking folk who had sent me to the sea bottom, the only nearby sinner one in holy robes whom I dragged my rock upon until he turned the ocean red with his piety, not a human near except my mother in the stone attempting to gain the surface and thus be immune to the burning sting of the wet atmosphere engulfing her. I had only to swim like a sinner to gain Mother a single breath of air, but I could not, too much the witch to swim, not enough to avoid being cast into the ocean. And Mother waited with no odor of disapproval because her only daughter could not achieve the minor feat of salvation, having insufficient sin or insufficient love.

As though reversed inspiration, these nightmares revealed how my future might be fine, enlightenment striking me as though a view from God, which underreligious, overimaginative sinners on street corners oft assert to have received during a recent drunk. In truth, great God did deliver my future view, though through a stroke of sensibility, not passion. My latest plan was to learn enough of London to leave it. The city's intimidation was a problem to be overcome with familiarity. But could I achieve this self-schooling before time came for me to kill Eric, before Magistrate Naylor proved me the witch more terminally than I had proven myself to Elsie? And where would I go? Geographical tutoring had shown me Man's Isle on parchment, but that was slaughtered sheepskin—where was home within the real world?

When previously considering quitting London, my chosen method was cooperation. But foolish I would be to accept Rathel's honesty in vowing to deliver me to wilderness if I followed her scheme. Her alleging that Man's Isle was no longer fit for witches, however, seemed sensible. But were those wild lands she mentioned to be trusted more than she? No, the trust must come from myself. I thus established two requirements for my future: learning further of geography, and seeking a personal understanding of transportation. The former would come from the specialist, Natwich, but the latter must be sought from my friend, Miss Elsie.

"Miss, that is no natural product of God despite the wooden portion, for are not those endings *metal?*" This was my abrupt response to Elsie as I noted certain objects requiring condemnation. Until then, the woman and I had been peacefully accomplishing our workaday tasks in the drawing room.

Looking up to the wall where I pointed with an

intense gesture, the servant could not disagree.

"And I'm saying, lass, those are the crossed lances of the mistress's grandfather, a military person in the royal guard. Unnatural they may be, in that stabbing folk is no Godly thing to be doing."

"Neither is polishing silver," I declared as Elsie returned to that chore.

"Whatever you're saying, lass, for as natural as a weed or a worm you be."

"Bless you for the compliment, envious person," I remarked.

"And when is my thanks coming for not stoking the fire, eh, lass? You'll be noting that even on this chilly morn, I'm having no flames going, and only because you're setting up such a conniption about the fire, as though you're preferring to freeze."

"Thank you for your understanding, miss. But if your parent had been burned dead instead of run down, perhaps you'd prefer the cold yourself."

We shared no speaking for moments thereafter, and brilliant I was to prepare Elsie for deeper camaraderie by mentioning her squashed father.

"Oh, and Miss Elsie," I fearfully confronted her later in my dusting. "Are these objects as horrible as they appear? A box I've found containing more combinations of metal and wood, these with one curved wooden end and a dense metal tube smelling of evil."

"Aye, right again, clever lass, for those are dueling pistols by which affronted gents are confronting each other to settle their honor."

"Longer items of this nature I have seen attached to killing males called hunters. How utterly Satanic, Elsie. Made of metal and spewing metal balls along with fire in order to create death—how clever of Satan to settle all his worst ideas in so compact an object. Absolutely godless, and I pray the greatest Lord might take all the firearms in the world and smite the devil with them directly across his cleverness."

"Ah, but not all are the worst thing in the world, lass. Me own father was owning a musket, being a prideful gift from a

151

landed gent of his employ. A thing of wonder it was with its flaring end. So curse me dead father, if you will, for eating pigeons."

"Of course not, miss. I curse you for skulking about when Papa was unawares and playing with his firearm, certainly shooting all the children who did not acceptably do your bidding."

"And a shooter I was, lass, but only in the loading, for Father was allowing me this part in the hunting. Yes, lass, with all your terrible look to me, yes, hunting with him I did go. But his was not so modern as these," she continued, taking one of the pistols in hand. "His was needing tinder, which you place, here," she demonstrated, "and was ever falling out. But this is a flintlock, and holds its fire well. So all you're doing, then, is load a bit of powder here, then ramming in with the ball, have the flint secured, then pull back this hammer, and upon holding straight and steady, press the trigger to let loose the most huge sound and smoke and smell." Then she turned to me, reeking of accomplishment.

"But, miss, that was but a metallic click."

"Aye, lass, you're having to go through all the things I'm telling you in truth for it to be firing."

"Well, praise God that you went through insufficient things to be loosing a Satanic smell in the drawing room. And you say that *gentlemen* confront one another with these things for the purpose of *honor?*"

"Aye, and they do, lass, though it's no longer legal. They get riled upon one another for a quarrel and go to shooting to see who is correct."

"Ah! What a splendid idea that sinners should shoot each other. Why does the Rathel person not dispose of her problems with the Dentons by dueling them? Praise God at least that men go at witches with only axes and flames. At least these horrors cannot be promulgated at a distance."

We shared no speaking thereafter, and brilliant I was to prepare Elsie for deeper camaraderie by mentioning fried and filleted witches.

"Oh, thoughtful Elsie," I said apprehensively later in my

sweeping. "Have I mentioned that I must depart? A witch cannot live in London."

"And, no, I'm recalling no such foolish mentioning, child. My best thoughts lately are that whatever this word 'witch' is, it has no meaning to me. You're neither animal nor evil, but a lass unsure with herself from youth and from being in a great, new city. Apart from stubbornness, lass, your problem is that you're merely unaccustomed to fine society."

"The society familiar to me is God's realm of nature exemplified by the area in which I was reared, a land I recall and will ever love."

"Ah, but the problem you're having, child, is in thinking that because you once lived like an animal that you *are* an animal."

"We all are animals, Elsie, in that creatures and humans have similar bodies. The difference, perhaps, is only the human tendency to speak endlessly, attempting to accept things previously understood."

"What *I* am understanding, lass, is that a vacation in the country is fine, but that's not the same as a life of grubbing for bugs in the woods."

"I defy you to explain how a common grub is less nourishing than the butchered and burned flesh of God's complex creatures such as pigs."

"I'll not be arguing with you, lass, since lately I'm munching no bugs. What I'm saying is that because you lived wildly so long, you're thinking that way is best. Well, child, I was born in the most drab part of this city, and well I'm knowing that better a servant here than a queen there. And I'm saying that with more exposure to fine living, you'll come to appreciate the comforts. So give it a chance, girl—give *me* a chance, for you must know that my wishes are only the best for you. So be taking more time with this life and you'll come to enjoy your new family, and one day desire a husband and family of your own."

"As I previously mentioned, Elsie, the Rathel person has special plans for my having family. Her intent is destruction, her desire being that I, as a witch, will somehow kill the Eric boy. The Rathel has vowed to release me thereafter into a natural

153

land. Would it not therefore be better to exit now, in advance of attempted murder?"

"Aye, child, I'm hearing this part of your story, and have broached it to the mistress. Reasonably she's telling me that this is more of your delusion, brought about by a harsh life away from decent society."

"More of what delusion, you might explain. Since I have proven myself the witch ever professed, the remainder of my assertions should be considered equally true. Does my story not fit the Rathel's emotional background and her desire for retribution against Edward Denton, which you certainly believe and have implied to me?"

"I'm believing it nonsense, girl, since you—the great prover— have told how you're unable to be killing folk. You and the mistress, then, are convincing me that the killing's a delusion for everyone, wherever it began—with you or the mistress or Satan himself. So I'm saying that if you remain with us, lass, you and the lady might both lose your delirium and settle down into the fine life we have here. You're becoming accustomed to me, child, can you not then become accustomed to all of London?"

"I have not adjusted to all of your aspects, not to your lustfully eating butchered creatures of God, gleefully polishing metal utensils from Satan, and insisting that witches are intrinsically evil. Your sincerity I value, but not all of your concerns. Certainly not your regard for the Rathel, who allowed my mother to die, and would have the Denton child die also."

"Ah, I'm hearing it before, girl, but now I feel that you're planning more than talk. If you'll be astounding me by running off again, you'll be coming to no isle, but to your own personal grief when Mistress Amanda has the magistrate drag you home, for surely you'll be lost before gaining Gravesbury Reach across from Christ's Cathedral. No wild lands are in London, child. If you're off on an adventure, then, recall that all of Man's Isle was not enough to keep you, so you'll not likely be hiding in Pangham Gardens."

Elsie's speaking had proven her dangerous. By her own words, I knew she had discussed Eric's intended murder with

Rathel. Praise God she had not mentioned the Thames and me. Nonetheless, the servant might emphasize loyalty toward her mistress rather than the lass, if only for the child's own, deluded sake, and thereby ruin me from affection.

"Kindly refrain from the dismay of believing me so delirious as to throw myself into London's maw," I told her. "Instead of desperately leaving as I did before in a panic of sorrow, I shall remain in the safety of these surrounds. Perhaps in the future I'll fall into pleasant familiarity with your city. In the mean, I hope you find no opportunity to discuss with Rathel our present conversation, for certainly none will benefit from her learning that I expressed an idea of departure."

"And I'll not be telling this tale to our home's mistress, girl, for I'm only talking of you if it seems to be helpful. Seeing as how you've sense enough to remain where you're well looked after, I'm being quiet."

After our work was concluded, Elsie and I parted cordially, going about our different affairs as we proceeded to our separate places. The servant did not understand, however, that whereas her place was the household, mine was beyond any city.

"Alba, you shall accompany me to the opera this noon."

Rare was the directive given me by Rathel, who preferred to deal with her "daughter" via Elsie. Apart from involvement with my tutoring, the Rathel scarcely showed herself to me, having other affairs besides personal murder. Therefore, when the mistress approached me one morning with a statement beyond a mere suggestion, I was without preparation.

"I believe I have heard this opera described," I responded. "Is it not a type of theater wherein folk also dance?"

"No, Alba, that is ballet. Opera is the epitome of musical theater."

"I see. Opera is theater wherein sinners warble. But why would you elicit my presence at an affair certain to cause me discomfort? Am I in need of some torment as per a cryptic schedule of yours? Perhaps another male infant worthy of heinous killing at my hands is to be found screeching on stage."

"My, Alba, how pleased I am with your continued excellent speech," Rathel countered with no distress. "Your purpose in attending the opera is to be seen accompanying me and a most reputable friend during a cultural activity. Thereby your status in English society increases."

"Very well, then, I accept, for certainly some greater unpleasantry will follow if I reject your offer. But if so massive a likelihood seems imminent of perusing a pleasure by observing those who lie of their lives and screech simultaneously, might we also invite Miss Elsie, who is due a vacation, considering her good work with the difficult lass?"

The Rathel then smiled broadly, such a revelation of her teeth frightening me momentarily, the witch having thoughts of being eaten by a sinner gone mad with humor.

"How comical you are, Alba. But you've sufficient knowledge of society to understand that servants do not attend opera."

"Too advanced a race, eh wot?" I mumbled.

"Young ladies, however, do," she continued, ignoring my interruption. "Young ladies attend opera and have some familiarity with music. For your cooperation I therefore give my thanks."

"But reasonably, mistress, how much culture need I wield to kill a single lad? It's not as though I had to take on all of parliament."

"Elsie will see that you're prepared," Rathel concluded. "Noon." And she departed.

To my typical misfortune, Elsie was thrilled to truss me in her (*her*) layered finery. Only sinners have a propensity for wrapping: themselves, gifts, their food with chopped spices, the meal then placed on silver platters concealed beneath inverted bowls to be ceremoniously unveiled and ravished. So there I was, gleefully garnished by Elsie in my soft and crinkly cloth, to be consumed by London's elite.

A young lady I appeared except for my scowl and despicable posture, the latter a return to my days in the wilds where limbs need be dodged, the former a new product of English society. The Rathel relieved me of these poor responses to the opera via

156

her henchwoman, Elsie, who was a bruising social fiend as she wordlessly stretched my torso upward, cruelly pressing the curve from my spine until my carriage had the desired attitude. Not a word came from Elsie, only viciously pleased looks of power over her social superior, expressions I felt best applied to the true villain of the household, our mistress. And, yes, the strung oyster droppings I would accept about my neck, but away with the silver or it's back to the Thames, Elsie desiring to garnish me with little metal platters then cover me with pearls to be ravished by warbling actors.

Though informed by Rathel that we would not be attending the opera alone, I had no interest in the additional participant, busy preparing myself for the upcoming torment by garnishing my intellectual innards with dread. Therefore, I was stupefied to find Lord Andrew Denton in the foyer.

He attempted to bite me. No, of course not: Experienced I was in the ways of hand kissing, as demonstrated previously by this gentleman's son. Neither liquor nor tobacco I sensed from his person, and since from the first he had seemed potentially as decent as Elsie despite his wrong gender, I allowed him to grasp my hand and wave his lips near my knuckles. Praise God there was no slobbering and sucking as was the wont of romantic sinners seen before by the witch. Such lingual fondling seemed another type of meat eating, but with Andrew we had courtesy, not romance.

I recall Lord Andrew's saying how cold my hand was, that likely I lacked warmth from being undernourished. He made no mention, however, of a certain lower portion of my person perhaps approaching voluptuousness. Then we entered a carriage, Andrew and Amanda chatting along. And though the male had no odor of intended damage, he was in fact a weapon.

I understood the consequences. Rathel and this man's son were enemies, yet Andrew accompanied her in public. But he seemed without foul purpose. Was Lord Andrew more innocent of social ways than I, or was reconciliation his deeper motive? But the truest answer to my concerns was a broader comprehension, for with Andrew's presence, I came to understand the sinners. Despite forced and pretentious circumstances, were not the sinners' sought and lost loves similar to the love within my own family? But I did not think of Mother, did not grieve for her, only feared that one day I might grieve equally for these sinners who desired me for their familial purposes while believing my family the enemy.

The opera began as though church: amalgamated sinners sitting in rows within an ornate building. Here the surrounds were more luxurious than God's, like a giant drawing room, the audience overdressed with periwigs on their pates and brocade on their butts, and more sensibly with vizard masks so the people would either not be recognized attending so horrid an affair or would not be able to view it. Their pitiful patter of verbose verbalisms made my speaking seem compact, all their tiny talk adding up to a massive sound that nevertheless was thin, an acidic fog to surround me.

What a fool I was to be impressed by that sound considering the overture. The orchestra created a thick, tactile din with their glossy devices, a noise both hellish and ludicrous. The members sucking on their metal tubes and grinding at plank boxes with limbs were so earnest as to be comical, exactly the nature of the emanated sound.

Then the curtains opened, the stage further resembling church in being a huge dais, here disguised as an outdoor scene populated by several costumed preachers, their noisome activity completely dissimilar to the singing of birds. The Rathel had mentioned how special this performance was since the language was English instead of one of the sinners' foreign tongues. Yes, it seemed their "singing" was a method for enunciating common words uncommonly. With effort, I grasped their phrases, believing that strained attention might aid me in retaining my sanity, for passive acceptance of the "singing" was driving me mad. But distinguishing the words provided me scant relief, for their content was absurd, and I began to feel that I had lost my sensitivity for the sinners' relationships only recently gained, for were not the problems here like Rathel's but so exaggerated as to be unreal? The suicides, murders, accidental maimings, and dedi-

158

cated gender affairs came and went so rapidly I could determine neither cause nor purpose. The audience, however, was more appreciative, responding with bursts of applause here, moans and whistles there, as though they comprehended the loud histrionics. The only understanding I gained was that Rathel would burn me before I became so cultural as to attend the opera again.

The presentation ended only to begin again. This pausing I found convenient for declaring my condition to the Rathel.

"I am ill, Lady Rathel, and must leave or else pass out."

Finding no evidence of bodily illness in me, Rathel replied that I should avoid embarrassing a person in her position. An endless time later, the singers roaring again, I felt so clogged in my head that I had to turn to Rathel to call loudly that I was truly ill and must depart or be puking! But the crescendo ended with my penultimate word, the entire house hearing some unofficial singer cry out of her vomit. Satisfied was the Rathel to see me settle in my seat and in embarrassment.

The opera continued and I believed none of it. My sense was that the music, the words, and the audience's response were all falsified despite their consistencies. Not until the opera ended did I discover the truth. Not until the final, frightening applause had ceased did I find true emotion, a genuine scene more moving than all the sinners' screeching.

Audience members shuffled and chatted in the vast foyer, discussing the satisfying activity they had witnessed. Thoroughly theatrical, Lord Andrew was so experienced with this ending play that he discovered his son.

As we actors came together to form an opera, I was inadvertently included in the cast. Rathel played the Rathel, ever controlled, ever controlling. And though Mrs. Denton's smile was attached as though a misaligned patch on her cheek, Andrew was convincingly pleasant as he warmly greeted his son, the missus, and Eric.

The latter was least certain how to respond, looking to me, then to his father, but to no other persons. Eric's parents viewed me with a heat I could feel, but Hanna also projected a grief that even a partially-comprehending witch could understand.

159

Rathel received the worst view, but Lord Andrew was given disappointment. Then the Rathel party was told of Eric's unfortunate illness, though he seemed the epitome of youthful health, the boy needing to return home without further pause. Eric did not argue as he looked to me, then to his father, then to me. His father.

The Dentons made their exit from Rathel's stage with a final scene. As the two groups parted, Eric and I turned to look at one another, blank stares of understanding that told us mutually that between these two players a further story would be told.

Eleven

"And I'm thinking that protection from the weathers would be costing more, not less. I'm thinking that one with no roof is less costly to build, so the passengers should be charged fewer pence for journeying."

Elsie was comparing the tolls for open carriage versus enclosed coach. Carefully I listened, studying the ways of conveyance, for my chosen future would see me traveling again, traveling alone. I therefore heeded all aspects of our journey. Through the front gate we stepped with our market baskets, Elsie grandly raising her arm and calling for a carriage. I then learned that Lady Rathel had such a need of transport that the drivers of a certain company kept a tab for her to be paid at month's end. Elsie and I thus applied no hard funds to the coachman who recognized the servant and accepted our passage with a smile toward me perhaps exactly as lewd as I believed. Perhaps not. And to market we went.

"And I'm taking you to no common market, lass, but one that's selling Continental goods. There we're surely finding wonders to be pleasing a person with such strange tastes as yourself."

The first wonder I found was that the male vendors were not dangerous, if only because they were separated from me by odorous displays. The customers were almost exclusively women, commoners seeking expensive purchases for their lordly employers. Within the greater London of dangerous smells, this Continental market was intriguing with its exciting foodstuffs, most unrecognizable. Kumquats were my first thrill, litchis an equally divine discovery. The mango's stringy texture was pleasurable enough to have me cackle, though only once, since Elsie received such apprehension from the sound that surely she recalled the

River Thames and my failure to swim there, my success at being a witch. Then came the most red and expansive onions that so cleansed my breathing passages with the first bite that Elsie walked several paces removed from me, the sinner.

We purchased spices that seemed not sinning embellishments, but simply ground foodstuffs, despite their tin containers, which at least were thin and decorated with flower portraits, not Satan's visage nor epithets against vegetarians. And there were jars of pickled plants unpronounceable by British folk, and varieties of tea never smelled by the witch sold in paper wrappings bought by dear Elsie for her companion. But all our sampling and selecting to fill our baskets was not the best part of the journey, for our journey would continue.

"Aye, and I'm allowed by our mistress, child, to be spending time as though pence thrown at a beggar, if only you retain your vow of not running off toward some foreign jungle you believe a few streets removed."

"I pledge not to flee for the wilds without you, miss," I professed.

"And thank you, lass, but I'll be remaining in the city rather than nest with crawlies upon the dirt. What I'm saying, then, is that our chore of marketing need not be our only activity. I'm thinking you may care to stop at the Feltson Street park for a bit of walking."

I would care for this, yes, as noted by my bouncing on the seat so that the coachman turned to find the source of violence, seeing only exuberant youth; and, please God, not smelling the sex witch.

During our passage from the market to Feltson Street, the typical morning fog was dissipated by a rare wind that brought not clear air but smoke. A piece of this city not far removed had severely burned, though not recently. Expert Elsie I asked of this smell.

"Aye, girl, and it's Penstone Place you're smelling now. Years ago, a huge part of the city was horribly burned in the Great Fire. Not even London had the funds for rebuilding all the damage, and with your remarkable nose you're smelling an area left as the devil's fire rendered it."

"Never have I sensed so severe a fire, Elsie, and would be intrigued to observe the locale."

"At your choosing, lass, but it's only criminals you'll be finding, for so disheveled is the area that decent people aren't living there."

"I have no extreme fear of illegal folk, miss, in that Lady Rathel would make me a murderess."

"Of course, lass, and she's bringing you terrible girls in by the score to be slaughtering her enemies. But more importantly about this Penstone, lass, is that the menfolk there have a special fondness for young belles of the wilderness. So they're treating them well, girl, by roasting whole cattle on their burning buildings in the way of dining."

"And thank you, miss, for your tremendous humor. So it's off to the park, then, less you have more comic opera to purvey," I declared, and certainly Elsie's following laughter was a cackle.

"Oh, and look away, child, there's a tart."

"That is a foodstuff, miss?"

"That is a woman who goes about prostituting her person, and a fine lass should not be seeing."

"The woman there with the great periwig and patch on her cheek?"

"Of course not, and what are you saying, girl? That's a lady with most fashionable attire. The tart I'm seeing over there, with all the rouge upon her face and her hair so *loose.*"

"But, Elsie, she dresses as you would have me, does she not?"

Turning toward me to stare with a scarcely contained snarl, the servant severely replied.

"Aye, girl, it's a terrible time you're having in London if you're thinking that's a good appearance for a lass. And pain me it does, likely from your seeking it, that you think I'm not dressing you in a modest and proper manner. When am I revealing your chest and flinging your hair in the air and making your fine skin all reddish?"

"Never, miss, but you do have a wont toward attaching bright metal pieces to me, which seems a gaudier fashion tactic than the color red. And does this prostituting deal with Protestants?"

After turning from me to snarl and moan freely, Elsie replied:

"I'd be watching me talk of religions, girl, if I were a youth with a future. Here we're finding people most sensitive, they are. One mention of Lutherans and it's back in the Thames with you."

"Lutherans, then, are those musicians who play the lute?"

163

"Ah, and perhaps there is something to your being part the witch," Elsie groaned, rubbing anew her apparel with every free finger.

"Too late it is for compliments, considering your rude replies to my simple innocence."

The servant became so stern that I received no humorous response upon imitating the speaking of French persons we passed. Worse was her reaction to my seeking explanation of observed drunkards and gypsies, especially when mentioning that Elsie somewhat resembled the latter, and had not the mistress in her past been one of the former? What a fine compliment thereafter I received from Elsie as to my family heritage.

Elsie had the coachman halt at the very park I had seen from Rathel's rooftop. The driver was instructed to guard our purchases as we strolled. Elsie and I walked randomly, though the younger miss perhaps scampered about too physically for a supposed lady. And, yes, there were trees and wild plants in a pleasantly large space. We viewed hide-moths, smelled tansy and henbane, enjoying the natural world as we chatted. But too soon I found that we were not alone, for the park was populated by sinners and their children, small creatures with loud, meaningless voices who chased each other to no rational end. Upon complaining to Miss Elsie, I was told that they were "playing games," that the demonic lines they had drawn in the dirt denoted a "contest" — and was I so wild as to have never cavorted? Had I never been a *child?* I had never been a *sinner,* I returned. Elsie then described the nature of "contests": choosing sides to promote an arbitrary goal with artificial rules. The same as opera, I remarked, and Elsie punished me horribly with silence.

My godly judgment was that the children's greater contest was destroying the park. Girls chased butterflies only due to excess evil in their small, sinning bodies. Satanic boys attacked lizards with sticks and tossed rocks at birds. One captured moths only to squash them.

This last was the ultimate debasement to offend me. The murderous boy consumed not the first slaughtered hide-moth, for his purpose was not survival, but destruction. Then I came aware that this boy was Eric Denton's peer—and I was to allow such a demon near enough to kill him with body parts unique to women? But the mistress was correct, for such heinous entities should be destroyed. Therefore, I found a limb of my own that I applied toward the boy as though practicing for Eric.

I slapped the stick against his head, the boy throwing his arms upward for protection. As Elsie came running and the boy's mother hollered and flew to her offspring, I drew welts upon his exposed forearms, scratches whose blood matched the disreputable rascal's tears. Even when Elsie took the stick from me I continued, next applying snarling words in lesson.

"I inform you, wretch, in your own language of combat, that Lord God did not make harmless creatures for stinking, cavorting fiends to destroy in order to promote their own evil. And I vow that if you intend to damage the natural world, it shall strike you in return in the form of pious humans such as myself revolted by demons who hate life."

Elsie was occupied pulling me away from the boy so that I could not attack him with my empty hands. Though on the ground and weeping, the child looked up to me with hatred. This expression I would as soon slap from his eyes, but Elsie held me away from the fiend, his mother all offended as she bent over her son and asked of his horrible deed. As Elsie pulled me toward the carriage, I shouted that he was a perverted demon with a heart of urine that I would strike out from him, allowing God to inject some righteousness into its deadened place.

Upon determining that I had calmed enough not to be running toward the sinner to rip away his life with my bare teeth, the servant released me.

"Very well," I spoke as my breath returned, examining my attire for mussing. "Shall we be on with our journey and away from this uncouth locale? After such an exerted worship service, I could use a bit of nourishment, perhaps a berry to nibble upon while we calmly ride."

"Perhaps a child's heart to be eating while you breathe fire," Elsie returned with an astonished smell. "God help me, lass, but I'm never knowing such a person as you."

"If you remain upset, miss, we could go swimming instead," I replied.

How easy it is to enter a carriage when a thoughtful friend pulls one upward with force enough to rip both arms away. And to home we shoppers hied with our purchases and our education, the carousing one of us content to have won a moral contest with society.

Certain that one of Rathel's servants would be warily observing the rear door—where else would a combative witch escape?—the sinner within me decided to slip boldly through the front foyer. With deft clicks, I released the lockwork only recently learned. Then I was outside. With ease I lifted the gate's simple latch, though its feel was metallic. But, of course, this was the feel of London.

The sinners seemed such benefactors. As I stood at the street's edge, I came aware of the great difference between the two groups of sinning humans with whom I dealt. Those of Rathel's household had proven themselves harmless, even beneficial in providing me with my chosen foodstuffs. But those people were behind; the nearest sinners were members of a dangerous segment. As I stepped from Rathel's frontage, I sensed London stretching beyond, and again was the child terrified of Jonsway. But in Jonsway had been Mother. Then I thought of Elsie, a friendly obstruction to sinners who might interact with me. Without Elsie, the nearby sinners seemed immediate: That woman with the veil so loomed in my senses as to be treading upon me, that passing man so hurried as to notice nothing, though I felt that his cane was a weapon to be thrust through me at any moment. With no intervening Elsie, I felt the impossibility of avoiding these people who would soon be unable to ignore me.

The solitude I felt thereafter was so acute that I considered returning to be safe in Rathel's house, not comfortable apart from my true home, but at least not exposed to society. Then I forced myself away from that reverie of apprehension, looking toward the street to accept my position of safety. No one had set upon me to burn the blatant witch. Having dressed properly for being out on a young lady's errand, I drew no notice with my attire. And I prayed God that no male would notice not the witch but the sex witch, a special lust that men sensed with some hot and perhaps metallic portion of their bowels.

Not being the Rathel with servants to send ahead, I would have to hail my own carriage. Not one of the lumbering open wagons loaded with products, but a closed coach wherein I might hide. Had I seen that harmless man who conveyed Elsie and me that day of marketing and religion, I might have selected his carriage, though I had no desire to be exposed in the air without opaque Elsie to shield me.

Since I was becoming distraught from hesitation and excess imagining, I stepped forward to hail the nearest coach, in that instant having a new lot of exaggerated concern. Was my motion haughty enough to attract a professional sinner? And what if Rathel had no credit with his organization? Since I had no currency, would I be arrested for attempting to steal the coachman's services? Then I dropped my arm, deciding to retreat and rethink my foolishness. But too late, I had drawn the man instantly, and prayed God he had noticed me with his eyes, not his bowels.

My only concern with this horse-drawn shed was that it came directly toward me. But the animal remained on the roadway, not leaping the curb to overrun my person, and I was not flattened by those fiendish wheels. As the driver safely stopped his coach, I looked up to the male and his superior position, seeing an unrecognized sinner who knew me.

"Ah, and you're the new Miss Rathel, out on her own this day, and a good one to you," he said with a smile, tipping his cap. "Might the lady be aware that her lass is on the street with no benefit of chaperone?"

This unexpected confrontation I survived mainly because the man had elicited speech from me, words my most ready weapon.

"The extent to which Lady Amanda is aware of her household might well stun you, sir, in its thoroughness."

"Perhaps, miss, but I am certainly aware that the lady is a fine customer. And since my employ is to be carrying folks and not worrying of their households, I'll only open the door and ask your destination."

"In that I know you not, sir, I first ask you to pardon my ignorance, but I must ascertain whether the lady has credit with you that might be extended to her, uh, daughter."

"Yes to it all, Miss Rathel," he replied, and reached from his seat to open the door; and praise God he did not leap down to give a hand, to take one of mine, take more.

In a rush, I was grateful for not having to learn a new lock mechanism, grateful for not having feared this potential difficulty in advance. Then, in a weakness from relief, I lost my tutoring, clambering aboard in no ladylike manner to settle in the rocking box.

"And where is it you would venture, miss?" the coachman asked.

"Christ's Cathedral," I told him, for this seemed a fine beginning.

Behind the wooden panels, I felt protected, felt that the cab was not holding me in, but holding the sinners out, retaining me from their notice. And I journeyed in the city, moving with every moment away from Rathel, though not for an instant did I seem to be approaching my true home.

No removed vantage existed for perusal, the driver parking so near the ongoing construction that workers looked to us and wondered of our purpose, wondered of our proximity such that their missing teeth could be counted, their scars discerned. I remained obscured, however, peering along the curtain's edge, hiding that sight of a staring lady who viewed the pious stress of sinners extending the worship of their race.

The cathedral had grown. Now those stone portions seen before as though a broken form had been adjusted together into a foundation and budding walls. And though the overall site was yet a mass of rough elements, in my increased imagination I found less of the mess here and more of the creation. But the prevalent element remained effort, sinning men controlling heavy carts and sleds. And what of the one man imaginative enough to infer from this heap coherent worship?

I had not forgotten that wilderness across the Thames, but now I wondered how appropriate its name of Gravesbury Reach might be. I saw trees that implied a forest, and was pained with this thought, for memories of my forest home returned. And I considered the natural triptych of my part of London—this countryside, Rathel's garden, the city's parks—and wondered of their comparison; but were not all superior to paved streets, all laughable compared to God's removed wilds?

Feeling a shift in the coach as the driver turned to his passenger, I prayed the male was not moved toward insight by his fare's special smell.

"And you are the one, miss, who was here afore with her mistress. Is your interest, then, in architecture, or in men being worked?"

To make some polite reply without shouting, I would move across the seat to speak through the window opposite the loud men outside. But when I turned, one of those bodily males was at my door.

"So, here is the demon who will ruin my family. Has Amanda sent you to torment me, or is this visit your own wickedness?"

In that brief moment before my reply, I determined him. Immediately I was frightened, but the fear seemed to increase my awareness, for I noted attributes of this male previously unexamined. Unlike the perspiring laborers, this gentleman was dry and wore a wig, though his false hair was moderate. He seemed to speak with only the center of his mouth, the middle of his lips moving while the corners remained compressed. His nose was longer than usual for a sinner, his eyes moderately separated. All these features conspired to direct his speaking toward his subject as though thrust. But I was not aware enough to determine whether Edward Denton was frightened or displeased.

"The accord is my own, sir," I professed. "My goal is only to examine your construction, for truly I've been moved by St. Nicholas Cathedral and would view the new one nurtured by your talent. As for your utterance of evil, I must apologize for being its cause, apologize for my poor humor at our first meeting. In truth, I was damaged then by Lady Rathel's own delusions of evil."

Since I was deep in the cab, Edward pressed near the window opening to speak more directly toward me, his breath with a slight odor of snuff, but not liquor nor burning tobacco. And though he made no move for the door's latch, the man seemed immediately dangerous. I shied from his directed smell, drawing away from his ideas, not his eatings.

"I know of you," he declared. "You have not entered London without my agents' scrutinizing your past. Even before, I knew of Amanda and her witches. If I could prove you the witch, I would have you enjailed, for Lady Amanda is most expert here, and I

169

believe she has found a way to use her expertise to ruin me and my heir."

"How heinous of me to jeopardize that aspect which is your heir, as though the blood shared with your son is less important than transmitted wealth."

"Is this more of your ill humor, girl? No man could love his son as his own blood and life more than I."

Then he rushed away from the window, and I felt relieved that he had departed. But Edward had stepped around the cab to my door. Snatching the panel open, he commanded me to exit and the driver to wait. I allowed him to guide me out, his hand clasped on my elbow, for the only damage I sensed was not my upcoming destruction, but Edward's ongoing pain.

With his hand on my arm like a rein, Edward escorted me to his building. To one side stood men dressed as he, but Edward made no move toward his peers. In one hand he held me, in the other a cane that he poked at laborers in his path. Perhaps Edward was attempting to impress the lady by soiling her hem, but I was a witch and not fearful of mud. Perhaps he gained satisfaction in dragging me past his workers so they might leer at the young miss. And though these laborious sinners desiring to gnaw my appeal were as tangible as tobacco, they were less distressing than previous males anxious to eat my body with flames.

We halted apart from the workers, on high land with the growing building spread before us as though the array of a sinner's meal. Edward had led me to a vast mound of uprooted stumps, remnant trees to be taken away and burned as though witches who had cursed the construction Denton described.

"Is your interest, then, in the lintels to soon appear?" he intoned, finally releasing my elbow to direct my vision via his cane toward stone forms being developed. "Perhaps your interest in architecture is more structural. Would you examine the underpinnings of the pilasters to contemplate the vectored stresses they endure?"

"Would you impress me, sir, with your ability to pile rocks?" I returned as though admonishing. "The architect is an artist, is he not? Therefore, explain your true concern, and divulge for me the aesthetics of your son."

Edward turned away from his building and toward his true concern: the witch come to attack him. He stared for an instant in which he sought meaning, the young miss cryptic to him in all ways but her danger.

"I know not of witches as does your mistress, but I believe them real," Edward declared. "If you be any sort of demonic personage, I hereby warn you both of law and God. I warn that our king and all the Church of England shall support me in protecting my son."

"Sir, the sort of person I am is one steeped in morality, a lesson of life coming ultimately from God, Whose name you use as though He were one of your agents, a laborer with the task of protecting you from your own imagination. But I am of God no less than you, and being both fearful and loving of our greatest Lord, I wish harm to no person, not even the heinous Rathel, who has encaptured me. I wish only to live with my own people away from your family and Rathel's, which have no comfort for me."

"If you're a demon, girl, you're a glib one in asserting a love for God," Edward responded. "What, then, of your terrible speaking that day about killing my Eric?"

"Sir, it is not I, but the Lady Rathel who has an unfortunate delusion that somehow against my will and capacity I shall bring damage to your son."

"And thus is your reputation I have learned, that your past life was one with witches wherefrom you became imbued with their evil," Edward retorted. "How would you grievously harm my son if not demonically? But no need have you to understand a malice that Satan promotes through your person. Deluded you may be as to your harmlessness, but Lady Amanda is the expert here and she is your mentor. Her delusion is in believing that I wronged her intentionally by marrying my wife instead of herself. And Eric is *my* son, not hers, though she believes this improper to the point of ruining him and me. Amanda's delusion is in confusing contractual obligations with those of the heart."

"But, sir, was it not your vow to wed Amanda if her husband came to the worst, which was his death?"

"Glib again in knowledge you are, girl, but nevertheless ignorant of the truth's entirety. My vow was to financially support the wife of my partner, but Amanda confronted me with a misinterpretation after Franklin's death. Never was my promise to wed her, and all of honesty knows this, despite what your mistress might have told you. But I would have married her, girl—I would

171

have conceded—for time it was to begin my own family."

"An impossibility with Lady Rathel in that she was barren. Thus, we find the limits of your honor."

"Thus, we find the limits of Amanda's emotions; for upon my learning of her barrenness, she yet insisted upon wedding, though previously she professed no especial desire for me, only for a child Franklin could not provide."

"How wicked of her to seek a companion for life after her husband passed away, after she found herself incapable of a most desired offspring."

"Other companions were available, Amanda having some selection in being a significant lady. Better companions existed for her than I, for only misery would I bring in sharing her poor travail of being childless when a child was the companion I also desired most."

"Despite any incorrect honor, I pity you, sir. I also pity Rathel for her hatred, and truly believe you unworthy of vengeance because of your particular rejection."

"Amanda developed her hatred not from my rejection, but from my wife," Edward corrected. "Early in our marriage, Hanna bore me a son and heir. Only then did Amanda develop her poor emotion that she carries through the years. There is the pity. A fine life she could have with any of countless English gentlemen, but instead she has settled upon you."

"And thank you, continually gracious sir, for equating me with hatred."

"Pleased I would be to find you equal to the ostensible," Edward countered, "that child Amanda could never conceive. But I doubt this to be her satisfaction with you. I disbelieve that Amanda has been with her witches again to return with merely a comely girl. I believe the lady gained what she has sought these years: not a family for herself, but a weapon to harm me."

"Sir, I ascribe the true danger here to all of these delusions, which Rathel herself promotes as though real. Therefore, if you believe me that despicable medium the lady imagines, I suggest you best protect yourself by eliminating me. The most sensible method would be to aid in my returning home, thereby removing from London Rathel's greatest weapon—the delusion that I might be harmful."

172

"How am I to trust any presentation of yours when without question your adopted mother's motive is to pain my family via your person?"

"And correct she is, sir, but only in that you are pained by me. Your anguish, however, stems not from damage, but delusion, and can be corrected. The best correction would be avoidance of true or further distress. I suggest again, sir, that you remove this pain by removing me, for surely I cannot harm your son if we are separated by a sea."

"You would be at your former home again, this Man's Isle?"

"I would if God allowed me the selection."

"And you desire me to fund your living on this island as you now live? Am I to afford you luxuries that you in fact would take to your current home and thereafter gloat upon with your mother?"

"Sir, my mother is dead, my only mother, my true mother, and she was murdered by the despicable law you previously threatened against me. Perhaps your son would be satisfied to live in Rathel's home, but I am unnatural there, and would have my own home and nothing further of the Rathel, who compares to my mother as the blackguard compares to the businessman. And from you, sir, I have no desire but that your pitiful delusions leave my life. Being the only person about with no phantasms, I suggest that you provide me not with funds, but with direct transportation to my only and original home. This dangerous girl would then be beyond the bounds of your fear."

"I have no reason to believe this."

"Then believe your own desires, ignorant sinner," I admonished. "The position you now hold is conflictual. Can you deem me so wise in sophisticated city ways as to seduce you financially? Disbelieving my desires might be sensible, but to disavow your own is foolish. If you consider me so perilous, what could be better for you than to have me well removed with neither your luxuries nor the Rathel's knowledge?"

"Now I understand your plan," Edward announced, having gained deluded enlightenment. "I see that in fact you nearly are wise enough to have connived me, for with that last phrase you reveal yourself. Yes, you would have me plan your departure, yet all along Amanda would be informed by you. As soon as you left London at my behest and expense, I would be arrested for having kidnapped a child legally adopted by Amanda Rathel. Thereafter, I would be imprisoned for a term long enough for you and your mother to have your wicked way with my son, to overcome his own good sense and my weakened wife, gaining Eric's betrothal by seducing him with your worldly personage and beautiful, sinister visage."

"How talented you are, sir, to have constructed a composition more fanciful than any opera," I retorted. "How pitiful that Satan again has had his way with God's people by transforming another into a fool. My ending suggestion, then, is in the form of a wish: that your son receives the fine life any average person deserves, and that you are not burdened with the suffering your own ignorance should mandate."

Then I quit that site of deluded construction, no ushering from the operatic architect required, instructing the coachman to convey me to any kindly place where people do not reject their own salvation.

Of course, he took me home.

Twelve

On the roof, genuinely in my person, I believed that I sensed, unreally in my mind, a natural realm, wild land without constructions, animals without reins, plant life not in pots. I seemed to perceive the subtle intermingling of wilderness odors, their source not in sight but within my belief. But not even the keenest witch can retrieve sensation such a distance, though any person can sense home despite a separation; for this is not perception, but desire, and desire has no bounds.

True sensations were immediate, but only those of London's bulk. True thought existed, the fact that I would never leave this city by my own design, for I could not approach a park without finding evil to denounce, could not pass a major building without being accosted by impassioned fantasy. And sinning men were everywhere, some in the form of boys. True humans I saw below, the people to have improved God's perfection by building London. And what of this area before sinners? Had woods and witches been present, every tree and sister cut down because of their danger? Surely no witches remained, only Rathel's kind, Rathel's family. And that particular failure was present below, the child who should have been hers, for here came Eric.

The unaccompanied boy was not passing by, for he turned directly toward Rathel's town house. After stepping through the privet hedge, he left my vision, but then the knocker sounded. I knew Eric had come to prove the Rathel's assessment, that the white witch once presented toward a male would not be resisted. Could I resist him by remaining on the roof—but what of his next

175

visit? For how many years would I need to reject him? How long would Rathel retain me and my intended failure before having me burned? But I surrendered to the inevitable, moving from the roof into the house, returning to Rathel's family another failed member not hers by blood but through manipulation.

Stepping from the ladder to the balcony, I found earnest Elsie scurrying toward me.

"And it's the Eric lad who's coming to see you, Alba," she began, settling before me to speak importantly, fingertips rubbing her apron. "Since I'm last seeing him, lass, he's become a young man. And with you both being the age of betrothal, a wonderful bond might be made between the two families now separated by a past that should stay gone."

"Oh, Elsie, am I to be burdened with rescinding history? My tutor plies me with wars—am I to be mending the entire world retroactively?"

More concerned with appearance than content, the servant heard no word of mine, stepping near to pull upward on my collar and downward on my bodice, yanking my shoulders straight and patting my hair with effort and expertise as she nervously continued her own speaking.

"Ah, I'm praising God, child, that for once you're looking near decent, as though you've finally gained understanding of being a lady; for they must always be prepared for presenting themselves, and not to spiders, but to beaus. And after marriage, to their husband ever and to his business associates and fellow church members and—"

"Miss Elsie, the position you state shall never be mine. As I have made known before, the Rathel intends for this Eric child to wed me so that the witch in me will somehow kill him and make the final bond of hatred between the two families one of death."

"Ah, it's more nonsense you're tormenting me with, girl," the servant moaned. "Killing her husband's wilder traits is what a wife can be doing with love, but no more. Now, be pleasant with the lad or I'll be marrying him meself, since I've never gained a husband, and would as soon be taking one even if I had to kill him in payment."

"I wish you would take him, miss," I told her honestly, "for with your kindly spirit, you deserve him."

"Oh, Alba, so young a lad for meself . . . ?" she smiled. "Whatever are you thinking, now, in your often strange mind?"

"I am not thinking of his age nor yours, Elsie. I am thinking that such a person of appropriate age and similar position would be appreciated by you, with your good heart and elegant soul. Truly I have no desire for such a beau, but in you I detect a happiness wished for me that I would have for you, would offer as a gift if possible."

"Ah, and it's sweet you are, child, to be wishing for me something so grand as your own marriage. No lass from any land could be more generous."

"But here, my Elsie, is not all the generosity you imagine in me, but a desire for justice; for no person more fully deserves the love she would choose than you."

As the sinning woman was rendered static by my profession, I entered my chamber to drown myself and thus save Eric by discouraging him. Therefore, I denuded myself to douse my body—especially that baby-ejecting portion—with the strongest liquid scents Elsie insisted on procuring for my livery, though never had I applied them before.

Entering while my skin was yet exposed to the air, Elsie misjudged my last splash.

"Ah, and no more preparing, lass," she gently scolded, "for too great a heap of even the finest perfumes are making you seem tawdry."

Elsie with a drying cloth hurriedly wiped my abdomen—to no great success, since I had begun to reclothe myself, our arms becoming entangled, Elsie and I a skin spider in a fabric web.

"Oh, my, I do stink the terrible wench, do I not?" I submitted, my nose suffering from rising fumes. "But we can't be letting the lad wait while we tarry needlessly, would you say, miss?"

She would, though did not, flustered Elsie lacing me tightly, rearranging garment and coif one final time for my beau. Then I was guided downstairs not by my servant, but my friend.

Elsie released me to the auspices of our (our?) mistress, who waited outside the library. I refrained from smirking at her, though Rathel's smile was massive. Understandable, of course, for here was the prideful mother stuffed with pleasure from a significant beau come a-courting her daughter—or was she

177

thinking of this future victim of her old revenge?

"Master Eric Denton has come to visit us, Alba," she told me as I approached.

Her tone conveyed that the boy was near enough to hear. And, yes, with my final step toward Rathel, I saw him inside the library, seated neatly and looking toward us. Being a lady and necessarily haughty, I whirled about to show my back to the boy, speaking only for my, er, mother.

"Let us slaughter the victim at once, Amanda, while we have such a fine opportunity. I shall hold the creature down with my bulk while you let his blood with your teeth."

As I moved enough to expose Rathel's face to the boy, she continued smiling, though tightly. When she spoke, the lady leaned forward so that only I would hear.

"None of your speaking will change his desire, so be foolish at the peril of your own self-esteem. Neither will that excessive smell about you change the flesh beneath the odor. If in fact you have such pride in being a witch, then be on with your legacy and allow your influence to increase. You are the one to make great assertions of being natural. So be on with projecting your true nature, and sit with the boy."

Rude I was to step away while Rathel's last phrase lay in the air, for I had turned to confront the male. The lady had no difficulty in following me and my changed disposition.

"How pleasant to see you, Master Eric," I offered as I entered the library to approach my (my?) guest. "Especially felicitous, I must say, in that our previous meeting was naught but introduction. Now, however, in the comfortable and private security of Mistress Amanda's parlor, without murder or other extreme function of English society likely to confront us, might we become better acquainted and learn of potential diversions to share, such as shortened lives?"

Being not only the expert in witches but a proper hostess, Rathel seated the two youths on separate divans without so much as groaning at the demon's opening commentary. Cordially she offered the visitor tea, which he accepted, Elsie in the doorway told to bring the victuals; and I could sense this servant's interior. Containing her joyful satisfaction, Elsie smelled nearly of motherhood. Here, then, was my doom. How could Elsie

178

aid me in avoiding Eric when she felt it best we be together?

Since Eric had given no reply to my initial speech beyond a simple pleased-to-be-here, Rathel proceeded to converse with the boy in a manner fit a gracious host, but her speaking was common. Though the boy smiled pleasantly, I wondered how burdened he was being the gent as I was the lady, for he smelled less than enraptured with the Rathel's discourse. At least his odor of apprehension had no hint of that sub-belly man stink. Rathel smelled of unique pleasure, her glee approaching Elsie's, as though the occasion actually were of family bonding instead of breaking. Rathel then encouraged Eric and me to chat, mentioning that surely Alba would have some wonderful things to say. And, yes, I had thoughts of explicitly warning the boy that death was his designed future, but I said nothing. My silence was no version of ladylike coyness, however: My state was mainly melancholy. This average sinning youth meant nothing to me beyond a life with no cause to be taken, yet he was my responsibility. And though I hated the Rathel, I also pitied the foolishness that was her disease. But what could I do in that moment to change her? What could I do but chat?

The Rathel departed, ostensibly to modify her order for refreshments, but a noseless plant could tell she intended to leave the wild youths to their natural instincts; that is, sex and death. I remained silent, sitting pertly as is the lady's tribulation, only glimpsing the boy while waiting for tea, hoping that Elsie would bring me a guava if any remained, if greedy Theodosia had not stolen the last, for she . . .

"I wonder of your schooling, Miss Alba," someone said. "I am pleased to attend a private school, and would ask of your own education."

The boy began conversing even as important thoughts were coming to me, but I could form no immediate reply. His speaking directly to me was so odd that I had to allow a natural, sexless, deathless response to evolve.

"The, uh, year's term has ended for the summer with my own schooling," he mentioned. "Yours, perchance, might yet be under way?"

"Yes," I said, Eric certainly praising God for my long-awaited

179

reply. The desirability of my further response remained questionable. "No school with human pupils would have me because of my dangerous mouth that might jeopardize their sanity. I am thus made to undergo a form of torture called 'tutoring,' though for what purpose I have yet to ascertain."

"Well, the goal of schooling is to have the pupil fit within our society of England," Eric vigorously returned. "With you, being female, there is the additional purpose of teaching those special things known only to ladies."

"But already I've gained a gent," I professed. "What purpose has a lady in London but to secure a gentleman, formulate a family, and thereafter be on with conniving its members?"

"Well . . ." Eric replied with all the brilliant wit he could muster. "It's certainly a tremendous speaking you're capable of, Miss Alba. I hope that one day I might learn to speak so well. My poetry mentor tells how wonderful words are for displaying our ideas. Might I guess that you've been tutored as to increasing your talents with words?"

"I speak well because my mother did. Of course, she is dead now, and scarcely opens her mouth."

The Rathel returned with tea and cake and Elsie. The latter was such a humming, smiling thing that I gave her a terrible grimace as she bent to me with the tray. She responded by smiling even more brilliantly. And when I made to trip her as she moved away, I missed. Having interrupted the conversation even as I was becoming charming, Rathel began chatting again in her own unexalted style.

"Since you were speaking of schooling and society," the mistress remarked to Eric, proving that she had been eavesdropping, proving she entered in order to quash my charm, "I would ask of your own place there in becoming a gentleman."

"Well," Eric remarked boringly. "A man must learn society in order to advance society. He must learn of England and her place in the world in order to better that place. Men are those in society meant to achieve wonderful things such as architecture, which is my father's work."

"Oh, yes, your father makes churches," I mused. "Does he also make prisons?"

"Well . . . no, miss," slow Eric replied. "My father's structures

180

are not the type to house unworthy folk—those who hate their surroundings—but persons who love God and England and all their laws."

"But how could criminals sensibly hate their citified surroundings when the city is their source?" I pondered aloud. "Criminals are made by society. Thus, might you in the future as a man make England's place in the world better by achieving the wonderful thing of creating more criminals in England to thereby aid in the work that is society's advance?"

Weak Eric then looked to Rathel for guidance. The false lady was smiling as though her false daughter had created incredible comedy. Guidance enough for Eric, for he was soon able to continue.

"I must leave," he said. Brief salutations later, the boy was gone.

After the door closed, I lingered in the foyer to discuss my success with Rathel. Sensibly I would have returned at once to my place in the house if only to dream of being in a better site. But I was so spiritually weak as a witch that I could not resist my own misplaced joy.

"Praise God I've driven the brat away with my eloquence," I told the pseudo-lady. "Despite your grand smile drooling pleasure like dog spittle, the boy would not remain."

Smelling of both success and relief, the mistress stated, "The boy will return, and one day you shall go with him." Rathel then left me, returning to other parts of her home, if only to dream of being in Hell; for what site could be superior to so successful a fiend?

"By your pardon, Lady Amanda," Mrs. Natwich replied to her employer, "I have been secured to educate but the single child."

"You shall be recompensed for any additional effort needed to accommodate the boy," Rathel stated.

How crude these social folk were to speak of my personal education in my personal presence. At least Rathel had left the new pupil in the great room while discussing him with the tutor in the library. There I sat, map on my lap, geography lesson interrupted by a certain sinner first come two days before now returned as

181

though another of Rathel's hirelings with no purpose in life but to fulfill her desires, which unfortunately for this agent was his death.

"Allow me to explain, Lady Rathel —"

"Allow me to interrupt, felicitous missus," I interjected, "to mention that your dedicated disregard for the lady's vast finances is appreciated by me, since my background is of poverty. But my additional background of experience with the mistress suggests that in order to defeat the lady in her own home, you must arm yourself with weapons beyond mere principle. Might I suggest something sharp with a long handle?"

"You might make no additional suggestions in your rudeness, young miss, lest I have you recite Latin with pebbles in your mouth," my tutor scolded.

"I'll rip your heart out with my bare hands first, demon," I mouthed, but not a sound left my lips. And no further arguments came from Natwich, for the Rathel had defeated her. Then I recognized how foolish I had been to inadvertently aid Rathel. From that day on, through my own failure, the Denton boy was a persistent guest in my (my!) home.

"How is it you are here?"

We were alone. Toward the end of a difficult day's learning in which Eric proved himself well educated and I thoughtless and lazy — according to the tutor — Natwich quit the library. Though her alleged goal was to speak with Lady Rathel, I smelled that the tutor's true need was to be draining her urine, a natural process not to be mentioned in unnatural society; and whose pot would she use? The Rathel's, I hoped, the mistress not likely to notice an unfamiliar scent; whereas the semi-social witch would be offended to smell strange pee in her crockery. But only such desperate needs could separate the tutor from us, in that children were not to be left to themselves. This exact situation, however, was the Rathel's fond desire, in that I might kill the boy with my bosom or other gender portion as he innocently nibbled crumpets. I, however, had a more certain torture for him, attacking the lad with my verbosity.

"How is it, I say, that you are able to journey here?"

"Well, miss, in that I fail to glean your meaning, I must beg your pardon."

"Of course you must, but enough of this begging. My inquiry is to your presence here considering that your parents hate my skin and bones, and certainly have allowed you no permission to attend my library."

"Well . . . in fact they did not refuse me permission to visit here."

"In that you did not ask, I assume."

"Well . . ."

"Sir, if you reply again by invoking vertical water sources, I shall swoon and need to be hoisted from the carpet."

Having to reset his entire existence in order to avoid uttering that term, Eric paused a moment before responding.

"As for my parents, miss, my father during day is at his employ, in his office or about his construction locales. My mother, though busy with household or church affairs, allows me a generous liberty with my time."

"Which means you lie to her and say that you are out with the boys."

"We—," he began, interrupting himself to note if any swooning had transpired. Discerning my continuing consciousness, he proceeded. "I make no mention of coming here, only that I am out at a friend's house."

"Is there not a thing called 'apprenticing' that a young man enters with his father to pursue the latter's profession? Will that activity soon keep you away from our street?"

"Being a professional and not a craftsman, miss, my father will accept me under his employ only when I am sufficiently educated to suit the guild of architects. This will require my tenure at a university."

"Is this university so proximate that you might connive the educators into believing that each day you attend local colleges when in fact you ramble toward me?"

"No, miss, I'll not be so conniving, in that the university chosen by my father is not within this country."

"Is the locale a wild land of valleys and forests without coffeehouses and hard streets?"

"Not exactly, miss, being Italy."

Before I could delve further into ridding myself of this male, our (our?) tutor returned with the smell of powder about her groin as though a young witch attempting to secrete her true identity from lusty lads. Thereafter ensued a lesson of proper public interchange between ladies and gentlemen; that is, between sinners of different sexes.

"A premise to promote society wherein womenfolk have less influence than men is that ladies are most honest persons," Natwich told her students. As usual, studious Eric was the pupil to reply.

"Since the Bible tells us that all persons sin and come short of God's glory, one might respond that ladies, though more honest than even gentlemen, are nevertheless imperfectly so."

"Sir, I surmise offense in your impugning a lady's honesty," I returned. "I would have thought that a true gentleman would support ladies by ignoring their imperfections instead of implying that they lie."

Eric looked toward me with a startled visage as he considered the consequences of his speaking. The consequences were deep embarrassment, for Eric was at the age when lady peers were most important to him; yet according to his favorite lady, Eric had attacked our entire feminine race. The young man stood rapidly, looking between the two women present, his complexion darkened with rushing blood. I could smell the heat of his embarrassment, and was thankful that unlike our first meeting, never in those days of mutual schooling had I smelled the heat of his crotch.

"I do so apologize, Mrs. Natwich, Miss Alba," he implored, Eric facing each lady in turn, his speaking affected. Then he bowed, his spine stiff, and quit the room, the household.

Though I expected a scolding from the tutor, Mrs. Natwich seemed more disappointed than angered.

"Perhaps, Alba, you can be made to learn that shaming a gentleman is no measure of a lady's sophistication. I have noticed how well you accept the pridefulness that a lady of your station should display, but too intense an application of pride makes one haughty and unpleasant in the eyes of English society. Never forget, Alba, that although no lady, Jesus was not burdened with pride."

That last unique interpretation I would not likely recall, but the previous ideas I agreed with, though not due to having failed Natwich's social order. From the morality of persons, not cities, I felt shame for having harmed the emotions of a person who meant no harm, no shame. This lesson was taught me long before by my own family. But the young witch, in her bigotry, had not learned the lesson enough to apply it to sinners, to those other humans.

"And it's the Sabbath, girl, so of course you've no tutoring today."

"Oh, of course not. The days have so leapt past."

"Aren't you noticing, child, that the other folks in this household were attending church this morn as is God's desire while you were lounging beneath the bed?"

"How presumptuous of you to deem the sinners' selected day of worship God's," I retorted. "I have no remorse for worshiping the God we share in a manner pleasing to Him, not you. And because you are personally aware that public men will have at me if able, I am surprised you admonish me for remaining in the house. Would you have me bring my attraction to your parishioners so they might reveal their lust to Jesus?"

"Aye, you can be ending your assault now, lass. Ah, I'm thinking one day you'll be having me apologize for hoping to better your young life."

"No, one day you will be required to vanquish that excessive sensitivity of yours as though you were a child attempting to grow properly; whereas I in fact am the blinking lass made to become a lady in a strange, opaque world wherein she does not comfortably fit—and so on—yet yours are the tender emotions continually injured."

"Yes, miss," the snide servant replied, "and I'm thanking you for the lesson in existence, miss."

"Please, Elsie, you sound like Eric. All day I have to hear his mewling."

"Ah, and now we're finding your true concern: that your beau is not appearing this morning."

"Elsie, I vow to render my chamber into a most wildly natural area if you ever again refer to that sinner as my 'beau.' "

"Now, Alba, there's no shame in having a friend who's also a young man. Are you having only me as a friend the rest of your days in London?"

"You've taken your final breath as a friend of mine if you torment me further with the Denton creature," I snarled, and hastened to my bed cave.

I had so shamed the boy he would not return. This was the concern to lead me to Elsie that morning. I had found myself loitering in the great room, expecting the tutor's approach, for she had always come before Eric that first week of his visiting. But no one came, and though I inquired of Elsie, the true answer I found in myself. I sought Eric not only to allay my guilt at having disgraced him, but because he was not the typical male. Eric was not the same species as those creatures in the park, was not at all like Georges Gosdale and that man on the Thames's bank. He was neither boy nor man, but Eric, and not an unacceptable companion. And though he had no fragrance of the witch about him, he had a morsel of their ways, for Eric lacked the pretension of most sinners. Unlike Elsie, who made to be motherly but was in no way my mother, Eric was my social peer. And, yes, I was a member of this society as long as I lived in their city and shared tea with their populace. Eric was also peer to me in certain personal respects: His age was similar to mine, his thinking acute, whereas Elsie's was kindly. Perhaps Eric was similar enough to substitute for the witch friend of my own age I had never known. . . .

Certainly. This sinner who upon first smelling me had unleashed his baby stick to stuff inside my bottom was the same as a witch sister. Because my absurd thinking dishonored me more than I had Eric the previous day, I entered a deserved bout of sulking to last the entire Sabbath. Not a second did I spend on the rooftop. Not a moment did I pass in the garden. The following morning, I opined my situation to Rathel, who waited in the foyer to greet the tutor and the extraneous student.

"What is the continuing purpose in retaining the tutor's services when the victim Eric is heretofore taken with my presence?" I demanded. "End this teacher's dreary work and let us be on with proving you ignorant so that I might exit London."

186

"The purpose is for the boy, not yourself," Rathel replied with a calm I could be tutored toward disliking. "In Mrs. Natwich he has a chaperone of professional stature. Furthermore, tutoring allows the boy justification for coming here that he might provide his superiors. He would not, of course, convey his true rationale, which might yet be unknown to him. So we shall continue with the tutor's services, unless you have some superior idea. But this I doubt, for you have yet to learn how to think, only speak."

"Oh, the pain you deliver scars my heart," I intoned. "My best idea, then, is to be on with your foolishness to thereby more rapidly prove you the fool."

I then left Rathel to greet her guests. The tutoring with Eric passed normally, the boy having no evident effects from the previous day's disgrace. Much of the morning passed, however, before I overcame my displeasure. Thereafter, I was merely bored, too concerned with myself to allow the young man to be a diversion.

In the following days and into autumn, Eric was a constant visitor, occasionally arriving before the tutor, an initiative that drew unspoken joy from Rathel, but firm lessons of being unchaperoned from Mrs. Natwich. Thereafter, Elsie or Rathel would rush Master Eric out of doors through the garden only to return him via the front entry once the tutor was settled within. My part was to become so bold that I waited in the foyer to greet him one morning. Drawing scandalous looks from Elsie for usurping her servitude, I rushed gleefully to the now familiar latchwork with the first rap, expecting Eric but finding Georges.

Arduous surprise came over the sinner upon viewing me, the man's shift of visage exacerbated by my unhesitant greeting.

"And a proper welcome to you, Mr. Gosdale, the sinning gent with his hellish hands and Satanic soul."

"Miss Alba!" Georges cried, "I must propose serious marriage to you!"

Immediately Elsie rushed beside me with a loud inhalation. Of the three humans present, this servant was most passionate.

"And you're a bit old, are you not, sir, for so young a lass? And a bit mad, too, for any type of person. So you'll be away from the door before the whole household is set upon you and your criminal thinking!"

"Do not threaten me, hag, with your household of women," Gosdale retorted. "No gentleman will accept abuse from an utter commoner."

Elsie then produced the most severe anger ever in my time with her.

"I am the hag, you blackguard! A flipping scoundrel you are without even a scum of decency!"

These two were then interrupted by an ostensibly calm Rathel.

"Miss Elsie, you will no further confront this person. Go instead to the drawing room and attain my grandfather's lance upon the wall so that I might skew the criminal directly in his bowels."

So passionless was the sound of Rathel's words that a fool might disbelieve. But no fool with a witch's nose. As Elsie withdrew, Gosdale proceeded with his goal as previously described to the servant.

"Lady Amanda, I must ask—nay, I must insist upon your daughter's hand," he began, then thrust forward for that mentioned extremity. Now in a literal mode, Gosdale gained my wrist with his fingers and my bosom with his forearm as he jerked my hand to his lips, leaning so near me that I could smell his scalp. As Georges pressed ahead and grabbed, Rathel inhaled an affronted breath, achieving a startled demeanor from face to rigid posture. More direct was I in snatching my hand from the thief and smacking him with a hearty push of both my palms against his head.

I felt no hatred, but under no circumstance would accept such an assault by a sinner. My action was enough to send the gent beyond our threshold where he paused with smarting eyes, but Rathel was set to even greater redness in all her skin as though a natural tart, transmitting a terrible glare to Gosdale as she ordered him away before Magistrate Naylor in person was brought here to arrest this trespasser, this molester.

That final word inspired Georges to again seek his honorable goal of my hand, as long as my fleshy torso portions would also be forthcoming. Though he reached for my limb, there was no contact, the lass leaping backward as the lady thrust herself between the lass and the lech.

"Never again will you touch my Alba, vile despot!" Rathel cried.

"And I say, Mrs. Rathel, that such contact is acceptable for a fiancé, one to support and love your daughter for her life," Gosdale professed with attempted reason.

"You shall steal the crown jewels before you again corrupt my girl with your immoral touch, Mr. Gosdale. Now, away with you before your only available spouse is a guard of Montclaire Prison."

By then, a minor audience had gathered on the street, another forming within the house: the two remaining servants peering fearfully from the great room. Our theater soon turned most dramatic, for Gosdale in his Satanic passion became increasingly insistent upon grasping my hand, upon touching me, having me in marriage, having me in the flesh.

"If this be your prejudiced thought, Lady Amanda, I should change it. I shall correct your misgivings by taking your daughter now, and proving my worth by loving her properly."

With a bulk beyond us, Georges pressed forth to take me as though a side of beef for his table, grasping me so intimately that surely some law would have us necessarily wed. Then the molester paused to look beyond the foyer, seeing Elsie dashing near, outraged from the man's latest honorable advance. Elsie was met by her mistress, the two sinners stepping together to exchange the lance.

"Sir," Rathel demanded, "you are off at once or I demonstrate English law by preventing your further assaults at the price of your health."

"I suggest you not threaten a swordsman of my experience," Georges declared as though familiar with such military activities.

"A swordsman unarmed, I see," Rathel observed. "Then take this, sir, to be your weapon," and she stabbed him.

Sufficiently experienced was the man to avoid receiving the head in his bowels, which was the lady's aim. Not so proficient in combat was he to avoid all damage, however, for the lance sliced into his side, through clothing and into flesh as proven by his grimace, by that grasping throughout his body; and there was no acting here, no opera. No expression could have been more real than his face distorted in astonishment.

The exterior audience responded with a communal gasp at this theatrical turn. Strong from her righteousness yet weak from unsought violence, Rathel ordered Delilah to the constables. Scarcely near enough to smell blood ran the woman past the downed sinner, outside the grounds and away.

As the servant passed him like a storm, Gosdale looked up to his assailant, the man showing no remorse as he spoke.

"A wench you are to have attacked a gentleman come only to beg for your daughter."

"You might find time to seek Jesus's absolution for your sin of lust before Satan takes your soul," Rathel told him. "That immortal passage will transpire in but a moment, sir, with your unchecked bleeding."

Looking down to his side and the wet welling to color him like an unnatural tart, the non-famous swordsman could only agree.

"Yes! I am killed. Have the girl fetch a minister instead—you worry of the law when I am murdered? God alone take my soul!"

"I shall fetch a mortician for you, sir, in that none other alive will have use for your corpse."

Again I was overwhelmed by English society. And though I had no conceptual argument with the Rathel's defensive actions, nevertheless, I could only feel maddened at the world she had forced me to enter.

"You need me for your killing with the power of death you wield?" I demanded of her in a harsh whisper.

"His wound is not of the consequence he believes, else he'd be crying less and bleeding more," Rathel stated, quashing my operatic response.

The mistress then looked toward the crowd, to the persons stretching above the privet hedge, those collecting to see through the gate. She focused there as though unable to notice them until the danger had been reduced.

"Any physician or woman of nursing might aid him," Rathel called out loudly, then ended her speaking with a quieter voice as she turned to her home. "I, at least, will let him bleed until the authorities arrive."

"Cauterize it!" Elsie proposed with a loud whisper, but made no move to apply her own medicinal expertise.

Rathel then stepped inside, closing the door behind.

"I doubt the graveness of his wound," she told her household, "but I'll allow none of my home to be taken by madmen."

Though feeling more revulsion than terror, I considered the madness Rathel had ascribed to Gosdale most appropriate here, and I for one felt no less extreme. Extreme enough to step past the lady and open the door, moving outside to Gosdale.

Alba was the word, a barely heard gasp from Elsie, a name that was both question and order from her mistress. My only reply was to continue.

Though the gent moaned loudly, his smell was of illness, not death. As I stepped to him, I seemed somehow removed. Gosdale's legs were separated, knees bent and unsteady. A bit of red on the spear's metal point I could see, a portion of the shaft hidden toward the wet end, ensconced in the sinner's clothing. So I grasped the clean section of the smoothed wooden limb, lifting and twisting until it came free of Gosdale's wool, taking no flesh along, causing some cowering in the male but no additional damage. Then I left him with the same concern as Rathel.

I returned inside with the weapon, having seen more of the audience than Rathel, but the same as she, only after the intruder had been stabbed, only after the impediment to my perceiving something as common as a crowd had been removed. But this crowd was not so common, for there stood Eric at its edge, no more or less involved than the other members. The same as they, after the constables had removed Gosdale for care or adjudication, Eric went on his way, passing no nearer the Rathel's stage than any of the observing audience.

Tutored enough to know of firearms, I was aware that this wooden stick despite its forged metal was a primitive weapon, one appropriately used by grunting folk in grass huts, not social persons in London. But, oh, what a modern weapon it was compared to witches, who are best to reflect evil, not invent it.

I dropped the Rathel's heirloom at her side, as though being workmanlike in retrieving a lost object. I then explained.

"Perhaps we shall again need to protect our home against evil," I stated, and resumed my place in the household.

Thirteen

Though Eric was not seen further that day, the tutor arrived as per schedule, Natwich becoming so distraught upon hearing of my suitor that she was taken by sickening emotions, and returned home without giving lessons. Having more interest in current affairs than Natwich, London's constables remained longer. Their main chore was to convey Gosdale away, his wound or situation impressing certain constables enough for them to kindly wish his recovery, though none predicted an impending demise. The constables' interrogation of the household was left to their superior.

Lord Jacob arrived in the following hour. Though familiar with Naylor's voice from that day of eavesdropping, no imaginings had I of his appearance as I was summoned downstairs to be interviewed. And I cannot say that Naylor's visage matched his voice, for whereas the sinners' faces are nearly all alike, the significance of human communication provided visually is in the changing nuances of a person's face and carriage, not the thickness of one's beard nor the supposed beauty of one's snuff-filled lips. Likely Naylor's being a wigless person though his scalp was balding held some import for the sinners, but the witch was not amazed at his lacking both hair and vanity. The consequence of this sinner's words, however, was clear without my needing to search for subtlety.

"Kindly forgive me beforehand, Lady Amanda and Miss Alba," Naylor began, "but I must query you about this violence. The gentleman Gosdale has not been known to drink excessively, and we have no beliefs of his being one to carouse with the womenfolk. Yet he tells us from his ill bed that Miss Alba has offered him provocation toward matrimony."

Despite the magistrate's beginning wish, Rathel at once became angered.

"I defy the lying blackguard to describe the slightest prompting on my daughter's part that encouraged his extreme, unhealthy desire."

"Your anger is justified, Lady Amanda, and again I apologize. But surely you are one to understand my position in needing to determine the cause of Gosdale's injury. I will add, however, that in fact the gentleman was unable to convey those specific activities on Miss Alba's part that so provoked him. Nonetheless, he was firm in insisting that it was she who drew from him desire."

"Of course, a lass so beauteous as my Alba is the center of men's desire," Rathel answered. "But a man's ungodly passion makes her a victim, not an instigator. The evil here is all in Gosdale and his lust, not my daughter and her innocence."

"Being a normal man, I well appreciate beauteous femininity," Naylor conveyed as he bowed to me. "Certainly the lovely Alba can inspire esteem in men with no intent on her part. Nonetheless, I am not here uniquely on this topic. I recall a certain architect with allegations similar to Gosdale's, therein regarding his son."

"Allegations proven meaningless in accord with my explaining the boy as too young," Rathel declared. "Proven by the fact that Eric Denton and my Alba are now friends; yet the boy has caused no further difficulties since growing into a young man and acquiring gentlemanship."

"I ask specifically of this latest passion," Naylor continued, "ask whether on any occasion the girl behaved in a manner that allowed Mr. Georges Gosdale to believe that one day he might gain her hand."

This ultimate constable remained directed in his attention toward me with that question, the witch requiring no subtle deception to reply.

"The notion, sir, that I would encourage such a sinner to procure intimate contact with me is so revolting an idea as to have me ill."

What a normal man Naylor was to be so confused and inspired by the term "sinner" as to provide me with a sermon.

"In that the Bible tells us that we all fail to achieve God's perfection, even you—an excellent youth—are not free of sin, and therefore in imperfection might not be distinguished from Mr. Gosdale."

"Lord Naylor, I suggest that Mr. Gosdale and I are distinguishable not by our separate sinning, but by our relative morality; for so well do I glory in God's perfection that I am never inspired toward assault. No man nor child have I molested. And never would I allow a male person to wrongly believe that he receives from me potential marital regard."

The magistrate then viewed me completely, staring briefly with static eyes that seemed to perceive every nuance of my life; and I was frightened by his depth. Then he rose with a firmness that told of no pleasure, though as well I sensed no anger from him.

"The difficulty is hereby determined," he announced, looking down to the seated Rathel. "King William's bureau having jurisdiction here might correctly be ecclesiastical, not criminal, in that I judge the Gosdale person to have been taken for a limited time and degree by Satan, who delivered him with a lust far beyond decent appreciation for one nubile. Therewith, this bother concludes."

After businesslike salutations amongst us three, Naylor departed. Perhaps the man was not pleased, but as an official he was adequately satisfied. His position as a sinner remained unknown to me.

"So I'm telling you, lass, that this is a city with people, and most of them talking more than me. The tale of Mr. Gosdale and his lancing is being heard throughout London in this very moment. Being no foolish person, your young visitor will not soon be coming around so that the city will see him here and think him like Mr. Gosdale."

Experienced Elsie was proven correct in her estimation, for the Denton boy was not seen in days. Then the subject of his presence was broached again, though by Elsie, not me, for was not my young man to be missed?

"I should long for this sinner because he is more bland than his elder peers?" I retorted. "Lust is the cause for his presence here, a motive no different from Gosdale's. The difference is that the

194

younger man lacks the initiative to insist upon his goals."

"But I'm seeing that you take no offense in his company, girl."

"Neither do I take great pleasure, but his presence is a distraction in that I gain no vast satisfaction from the other activities offered me."

"Aye, 'tis true, lass, except for sweeping and peeling onions. But who's to be curing you, girl, of having more interest in a servant's tasks than those of a lady? Your mother has—"

"Elsie, if ever again you refer to your employer as my mother, not once thereafter in your entire remaining life shall I provide you with a word or look or notice of existence," I growled to the unmitigated sinner.

"Oh, and everso, lass, with your extreme sensitivity, I *am* apologizing. But what I'm saying is that I've no idea how to interest you in things of a lady. My employer, the Lady Rathel, is offering you a most wondrous harpsichord, which you rejected, and I'd be showing you work with the needle, but you refused, and you've no interest in fashion and are saying you've none in marriage, so what kind of lady will you ever be?"

"Oh, Elsie, you sinners are so, so *appreciative* of your own ways, as though God made no other humans, and the world is your marketplace. Yet a person such as yourself, with no wealth, is like an animal in that you're but a device to implement the Rathel's whims—an upstairs packhorse. Does some subtle, social reason exist for your being less worthy of Rathel's place than she?"

"But you're thinking too much of social things, lass. God loves us simple folk as well as the wealthy, and has made us sensible enough to appreciate what He has given us. My life is not the finest as far as luxury, but it's happy I am, and understanding I am of how much worse I could be. I had been worse afore coming to this household—and much worse I'd be in the woods living like an animal with no shelter or law. And because my place is not the best, I'm wishing my friends better than me. I am always hoping the best for you, young Alba."

"Your generosity and kindliness I cherish, Elsie, but you mistakenly believe that our types of satisfaction should be equal. Though I am satisfied with my own class of person the same as you, I would also allow you and Rathel your particular living. I wish you all the best, Elsie, for you are not only friend but virtually family. Nevertheless, I understand that no forest life would please you. I allow Londoners the life you would have, why can you not accept my given nature?"

Not replying with her usual verbosity as to my deluded, wilderness thinking, Elsie responded instead with tears.

"You've never called me family before," she blubbered, then shuffled away her burden of sentiment as though an emotional packhorse.

My mouth fell open like a sinners' mechanical trap for flies, and I could not reply until Elsie was away from my hearing.

"Ah, you flipping sinners are a sensitive lot," I muttered, and sought an onion to attack in catharsis.

"But, Miss Alba, your humor is extreme. What life could be better than that of a lady in London? Would you be a commoner on a farm?"

Eric's cautious vacation from me had ended. As though disgusted with Rathel's treachery, I did not concern myself with her ability to schedule Eric and me so that we were often alone, now on a day when Natwich was not due, the male and I walking in the garden without the burden or benefit of chaperone. How coincidental of this household that none of its members was out of doors but the lass and her visitor. Rathel, however, was surely observant, peering through some glass wall to gauge her success. I had no intention of seeking her gaze, fearful of seeing bliss ooze from her pores like a hot sinner's sweat, a failed suitor's blood.

"Yes, and I say again, sir, that I do not care to be a lady in London. For that position's replacement, I might choose to be an average member of God's humans in a wild land away from chamber pots and metal utensils for stabbing dead meat and mad gentlemen."

We touched sycamore bark, viewed a vining grey-bush, stepped upon the path's imprecise stones, one of us avoiding that tiny, nasty bridge. This late in the season, most of the trees' leaves had fallen and been raked away by Theodosia and a certain witch. Though I smelled a late and mild winter coming, I made no mention of this sensing, thereby avoiding a wild form of explication the sinning male would not readily accept.

My woolen dress with sleeves to the wrists was all I required for this weather. Eric, not to be climatically bested by a girl, had left his overcoat within the house, though his skin had a bluish tinge. Such are the travails of the virile sinner.

"I as well can understand, Miss Alba, that being in wild land might be adventurous for a time, but for a life? Are not the advanced ways of our city superior to a coarse life without implements? Devices are made to better our lives, not burden them. Chairs and beds give us comfort where reclining upon stones cannot."

"Lizards recline on stones, sir. Humans in the wilds have sense enough to find soft segments of the world to provide them adequate comfort. Excessive comfort is the slothful way of Londoners."

"And sturdy homes to protect us from paining weather, and carriages to provide us with transport."

"And to carry all our needless implements about."

"And Continental gardens to supply the edible rarities that some of us require."

That rejoinder stopped me like a lance's stabbing. Intensely I stared at Eric for some explanation of his commentary, as though he were the witch, not I. And I could smell a smirk in him, though he looked to the trees as though having some especial fascination with poison oak.

"How dare you, sir, insult me by developing a sense of humor akin to my own."

"My, my, miss, have you noticed the fine crop of poison sumac growing this season? Surely some person in our world exists who considers this plant a delicacy."

"The Greeks have gods who curse young men of comical discourse beyond their station. I suggest you restrict your imagination to the construction of jails for boys away from home without their parents' consent. My understanding is that these criminals abound in our London, and must be quashed before they multiply like cockroaches in the basement."

"And I say, miss, that prisons are another of our useful implements. What life could we have if such wanton criminals as you mention were allowed to roam freely

197

through every library and garden in their path?"

"I've done this to you, have I not?" I returned with unbelievable solemnity while staring at Eric, who continued to view limbs. "Prior to my wretched influence, you were an average, arrogant sinner. A few years in the wilds would improve your haughty disposition, sir."

"Oh, and we are in the wilds again," he remarked, glimpsing me peripherally, and we began walking anew.

"Yes, in the wilds where we might live better by concerning ourselves with God's products of Earth and animal rather than our own conceits."

Having been quietly contemplative, nodding in agreement, Eric turned acute as he quickly looked to me, his thoughts made pellucid by his reply.

"I have been to the seashore."

I understood. I understood that he had visited the seashore and been moved by the wild ocean, the natural smell, the overwhelming mass.

"What a tremendous force the sea is, Eric—would you agree? All the endless water of such a space as to render England meager. And the complexity! Beneath the ocean's surface is a second geography populated by animals and plants both enormous and unique."

"Yes, yes," he whispered, and we halted to lean near as though sharing a secret we needed to retain. "No land creature is as great as a whale—not even English cathedrals. And what living thing could be more wondrous than a sea horse—have you seen one, miss?"

"Etchings, I have seen a lovely etching of a sea horse."

"In actuality I have examined one," he asserted eagerly, so decent as to share this great event. "One in a jar, not alive but perfectly preserved, yet indescribable. Indescribable."

"Coquinas," I added, looking to Eric's face to denote his interest as I matched his revelation and thereby increased our mutual wonder. "Occasionally upon the beach of Man's Isle near Maughold Head I would find coquinas. Do you know of them?"

"I do not, but I would—please!"

"Tiny paired shells," I described softly, importantly, holding my finger and thumb a nail's width apart. "As though a miniature

198

clam, containing a miniscule, unseen creature that propels the joined shells into the sand and away from the seeker, away from one's digging feet."

"Do they bite or snap at one?"

"Not at all! Harmless and therefore not to be harmed. But lovely to see and fascinating to seek and touch, then leave undamaged and alone."

"Mountains," Eric mentioned. "You are correct regarding the sea's second geography. On the ocean's floor, at the water's greatest depth, are mountains taller than any of land."

"This I readily believe considering all the other wonders of God's oceans. And though the great mountains mentioned would be an extraordinary sight, I'd be partial to those wet and wonderful animals."

"I have noticed in your speaking, miss, that you've a special fondness for animals wet or dry."

"I do, Eric, because my people have always believed that humans are a type of animal, in that the mutual aspects of body are similar."

"The reference to 'your people' is not new, Miss Alba, and I wonder of your meaning. Are you of some different nationality? This is not readily accepted considering your excellent speaking, though you do have a bit of the dissimilar accent."

"Yes, 'tis true that I'm a foreigner in coming from Man's Isle, a land so alien as to be seen from greater England on a clean day. As for my people, I refer to my mother and our friends who lived on this island a life simpler in goods than yours. Some folk would consider us animals ourselves in that we chose to exist without a raft of forged implements."

"But as the Bible tells us, miss, the difference between person and beast is that animals lack the immortal soul that only humans possess."

"Apart from the Bible's lessons, I have always lived according to those laws of God as presented by His Earth, not His scholars; in that within the wilds, one finds immortal laws and God their Maker everywhere, always. Being in that manner subject to God's glories and His rules simultaneously, I live my life as taught by my superiors with the view that animals are special in their simple honesty, though of course inferior because they kill one another, this surely God's manifestation of their being without soul. Therefore, do not humans behave as though without immortal spirit by emulating animalistic murder?"

"What became of the whales, miss?" Eric returned. "The wonders of the sea seem to have been replaced by philosophy. And within your thinking, did I not understand you to say that we humans are animals yet emulate animal behavior? Have I found a paradox not intended?"

"Sir, I remain unaware of whether you deliberately discovered a paradox I did not intend. My meaning is that humans have a similar nature to animals. We are animals in the way we shit, not the way we think."

Eric had no comment, for he had been struck by Satan in the form of a devastating word. Of course, even a pseudo-social witch understood that term to be indecent. God forgive me for my error, and Eric, too, if able; for although with a riotous visage, he remained completely silent. Quite red as well, as though a natural tart, his cool blueness made hot by my speaking, Eric doubtless attempting to convince himself that, no, he had not heard such a word from Miss Alba. And if he had, how was he to respond? Recalling that first instance of my shaming him, I quickly moved to end Eric's discomfort.

"Needless to add is the fact that animals do not trample human environs in order to build their houses thereupon, nor systematically destroy people for their hides and flesh. Perhaps one might say they lack the ability, and do not because they cannot. But as well I might posit that animals lack the . . . spirit . . . for such destruction."

"I see, miss," Eric muttered, looking anywhere but toward me.

"Therefore, you might understand that I have moral argument against not only killing animals, but enslaving them for selfish human purposes."

"And, um, what of pets, miss?" Eric replied with an improved tone.

"I would beg pardon of your query, sir."

"Pets, miss. I wonder of your beliefs toward pets considering your thoughts of other animals."

"Sir, whereas I certainly have heard this term before, I lack full understanding of its defining. What, pray tell, is a 'pet'?"

200

Appearing alive and with me again, Eric explained: "Why, a pet, Miss Alba, is a creature who is kept in one's home for the benefit of himself and the people there. These animals are often the finest of companions."

"Oh, I now comprehend. Prior to my arrival here, the Rathel had cats in the household likely for the very purposes you state."

"My mother has a most exquisite cat from Asia, fully regal and of the purest white—even moreso than your lovely skin, Miss Alba," Eric mentioned. Then, aware of his blunder—his lust—the boy blushed and stammered through a breath before attempting to continue.

"Oh, and I am sorry, miss, in that . . . I, I . . ."

"Sir, I promise not to say shit again if you vow not to term me lovely."

Although his mouth then formed a proper shape for speaking, scarcely could respiration commence.

"Now that our mutual embarrassment is ended and forgotten, perhaps we might return to our conversation regarding pets," I said while viewing the bare limbs above us. "I mentioned cats. You described one in particular. Currently I say nothing while awaiting your words to return."

"Well, and, yes, miss. I, uh, I—and my father has a parrot."

"Which is?" I asked, fulfilling our agreement by saying nothing of pulchritude or feces.

"A parrot is a bird from the South American continent, the size of a falcon with a curved beak and the most beautiful red and yellow feathers."

"More beautiful than my plumage, sir?" I asked coyly, looking to Eric, who could not view me, unable to see through that plumage of redness on his face (as though a feathery tart), the witch feeling true but minor guilt not for the embarrassment, but for failing to resist the verbal temptation, for depleting her pact.

"The bird sounds lovely, Eric," I said, attempting to rectify my crass speaking. "I did not, however, notice any such extravagant flying thing that day within your home."

My, the witch brings another plague; may as well have said shit again. That day within his home was a time of Eric's passion, not his pets, and well to be forgotten by him. Therefore, I attempted another comment that might remove the edifice of shame I had

201

erected between us, currently a cathedral in size and approaching the bulk of a mountain, underwater or otherwise.

"And you, sir, with your parents so luxuriously endowed with pets, have you some welcome animal of the type?"

"I do, miss," he stated with a vague, attempted friendliness, a disposition increasing with Eric's continuing words. "I have a dog that is perhaps superior to a brother, for Randolph is most loyal and honest. And I can see your meaning. Yes—his nature is such that he seems to have a soul, a spirit of generosity and concern as full as any person's. Perhaps his is another type of soul, one God has seen fit to describe not in His Bible, but in the world as you mentioned. Perhaps animals have souls lacking intellection, though not permanence, which quit their bodies along with their lives. What do you think of my speaking, Miss Alba? It seems so fine a notion, and fitting. Perhaps the soul of an animal goes not to be with God to exist after death with people of His image, but remains within the animal portion of the universe, which is the Earth whereupon God placed them, the Earth God made for humans only for their lives, but provides His animals forever. Does this seem sensible to you, Miss Alba? Miss Alba?"

He had to repeat my name, for there was no ability within me to respond. There was no apparent life in my countenance, for I was static and breathless. Then in a swoon that frightened Eric, I bent at the knees and waist to cover my face with my skirt, hiding from a revelation to affect me as though the sight of God Himself, hiding my senses so I could neither hear nor see further, for I was filled with enlightenment and could bear no added perception. Completely filling me was Eric's idea that we soulless creatures had a permanent part in the universe, as though our aspect of glorifying God and loving Earth was so valued by Him that He would allow His world to retain our essence. Therefore, I would not be burned one day to exist forever as ashes, but upon my demise would become as though an idea, the disembodied kindliness and intended generosity inherent to decent folk. Thereafter, I would be on and of the Earth like an essence: I would be with my mother, who since her death had existed equally. I would be with Mother again, her form the great value of her living that had never left Earth, left existence. As I leapt upward to run away, fearful of my state, I loved the Lord God as never I had before, in

202

my selfishness thanking Him with my life not for my life, but for its greatest love, my mother. Before running to be alone with God and my mother who was my mother's love, so choked that I could scarcely breathe, I found myself able to thank another entity, one so excellent as to be unworthy of further shame.

"A most wonderful idea, Eric. No idea could be so superb," I whispered, and entered the house to stumble upstairs with Elsie's aid, the servant finding me distressed and wordless in the corridor. But I could explain to her no more than I could weep, yet no more deeply could I feel. From that moment hence — from Eric's idea proceeding — I gained another sinning friend perhaps no more immortal than I.

Fourteen

Rathel expressed interest in my swooning if only because I had frightened her victim from the property, the lady not likely fearful for my health. I told her that the unclean meat in her system so emitted grease from her pores that I was made to faint.

Having well met the lad the next morning, Rathel departed on her business. How unfortunate having to be the honest citizen instead of the vengeful murderess. I imagined her crawling outside the library during tutoring to find a weak spot in the wall for extended listening, her vigil one of monitoring the increasing relationship. No talk of murder would she hear, however, for I was certain to allow no further, foolish revelations of Rathel's intending to vanquish the lad with me as her medium. Therein lay only more investigation by a magistrate whom I surmised from the first to be cunning and competent, and willing to execute his authority by executing me. Spies on the border of my education would only hear of geography and whales.

"I do apologize for not being more of an aid to you the previous day, Miss Alba, but I could not determine the nature of your affliction."

"Have no unease, Mr. Denton, since my attack was only the passion of God's understanding as delivered by your own enlightened reasoning."

"Miss Alba, although I praise God if I have influenced you to be nearer Him, I nonetheless have no feeling for profundity in my speaking. Yet, is it not simple to be profound regarding the Creator? Merely think of any wonderful thing beyond our poor normalcy, and more of God's glory will be found. But even if my idea of yesterday were valued, the responsibility in main be yours, for truly any thinking I had was from your inspiration."

"You may not feel profound, Master Eric, but perhaps the lack issues from your modest nature. Despite your current ideas, which again are of great value, your generosity is such that you posit me as the source of inspiration, when truly the cause must be your own, inherent spirituality."

I was no longer displeased to find Eric engaging, for his holy notion yet stunned me with visions of a future I had never believed available. Unlike a meal after a period of hunger, the concept was sustenance to last: not until the next weakness, but for a life. And though too grand to casually bear, Eric's idea was discomforting because its source was a sinner, one due to die by my body.

"I would suggest, sir, that we be about our routine and thereby end a greeting that causes us each to near embarrassment, and that is a state we've promoted enough for an era."

Embarrassed at the mention of embarrassment, pink Eric agreed. With no tutoring scheduled that day, the guest and I entered the drawing room to chat apart from the library's endless books, endless lessons, preferring the more luxurious settees of this less intellectual chamber; and who was offended by the asymmetry of a weapon display with a missing stick?

Even in this mild weather, the fireplace was functioning, Eric remaining near a terror I could survive only at a distance with my back to the gassy heat. Socially I survived by mentioning my fear of flames. I wondered whether Eric's positioning was habitual, or had this weakling sinner gained a chill from walking in mellow autumn? After losing his assumed or genuine coldness, the male moved nearer me. Alone we were, but not encased, having left the door open, chaperone enough.

Settled but less than talkative, we felt between us a new closeness that filled Eric like the blood yet coloring his neck. Here was his desire, to be near the girl as social folk, not students. Continually pleased by Eric's revelation, I was not dismayed by the male's desires, not so bodily here as to be smelled. Nonetheless, my feeling was also moderated dread, for how could even my peripheral satisfaction from this relationship not encourage Rathel's desire for Eric's death?

"In that I am being smothered with silence, Master Eric, I might continue yesterday's subject of household animals. Within me you have found a natural interest, and I would care to hear more of your pets."

My words reduced his red romanticism. Enthusiastic Eric described his dog and its feeding, his dog and their mutual play, his dog and its endless tongue. With difficulty, I attempted to not consider pets more animals stolen by sinners for the latter's benefit. But were servants not in a similar situation? Both groups were fed and sheltered and had problems with their tongues.

"Truly, Eric, I would enjoy meeting your pets. Especially your particular dog, in that Randolph seems an agreeable sort."

"I would also have you see him, Miss Alba, for I am certain that you would become friends. However . . ."

"However, your parents are pleasantly disposed toward neither me nor Lady Rathel, so my visiting your home would be problematic. And I assume that conveying the dog here is no reasonable suggestion."

"Having him walk with me would be unwise, and bringing him via carriage would be foolish. Randolph, however, is oft left outside to avoid his begriming the house with, um . . . Therefore, if ever you are near my home, we could arrange for you and his walking to coincide. Being outside the household, you would not draw notice from my parents, and I would draw no great shouting from the same source."

"Sir, I shall not be satisfied in London without achieving Randolph's acquaintance."

"I don't suppose, Miss Alba," Eric pronounced slowly, "that there's some method by which you might travel nearby my home . . ."

"Yes, there is—let's leave at once," I whispered, then bowed my head, covering that foolish brow with both hands, certain that Rathel a wall away was inhaling our every syllable like a witch stealing the breath of babes.

"I say, Miss Alba, what a wonderful idea. Unfortunately you seem displeased by your own speaking."

I made no rejoinder, turning to the door while gesturing for Eric to be silent. Then I waited for Rathel to roll through the doorway like a runaway cart and toss me into the fireplace.

No attack transpired. Viewing into the great room, I shook my head for Eric to do nothing. Perhaps Rathel was yet out on business. Perhaps she simply had not heard, for my blundering words had been whispered. Then I thought that perhaps Rathel *had* heard our speaking, and found no argument with our intent. After all, I had mentioned journeying to the boy's house, not Man's Isle. Perhaps Rathel at the moment was hiding her own sounds, her palms rubbing together enough to blaze, her skinny throat cackling worse than any witch; for would she not well desire the two students out on their own where terrible things might transpire? With this new awareness, sensically I would remain lodged in my chair.

"We leave at once," I repeated.

Eric's leaping upward like a toad was hardly gentlemanly, even to a witch. Motioning for him to remain, I nonchalantly approached the door. Seeing no person, I ran across the great room to the foyer, gesticulating for Eric to follow. He complied with commendable silence of his feet. As I retrieved the boy's outer coat, he whispered of the exterior chill, suggesting that a lady might need gloves and the like. Unconcerned with cold, I nonetheless decided to hide behind the conventions of apparel, walking oh so casually to the stairs and up, past Delilah with whom I shared a friendly greeting, to my clothes cave for a hat and cloak. Then downstairs to the male.

Moving furtively, we achieved the front entrance. There we halted, adopting guiltless visages, which Eric accomplished less consummately than his previous success in retaining silent feet. After searching in all directions for Rathel to be peering at us like a cockroach viewing sinners abandoning their dinner table, we stepped into the London air.

About me I found a compelling space that seemed completely new, though certainly this impression was due to my company. In this atmosphere, our positions were reversed; for whereas within my (my?) home, I was the instigator of activity, once on the street, Eric confidently led the way. As we walked, London's size and smell accosted me without the insulation of Rathel's household, for the city was about me now, not beyond. Then, noticing that Eric was swiftly walking ahead, I felt a brief panic that he would abandon me. Eric then looked behind.

"In that we should hurry, miss, I suggest pressing onward."

I agreed with a mumble, following the boy who now seemed a man, certain and sizable in familiar surrounds. I seemed to be in tow, like a public coach, but where was the occupant of this box? for I felt vacant. Since Eric was an expert guide in walking precisely between oncoming persons and crossing streets without being run down by metal-mouth horses, I followed his sinning influence without hesitation.

After a moment's rapid walking, Eric halted to present a changed idea.

"We'll take a carriage to my home," he informed me.

In my bold experience, I espied a coach used by the Rathel household, suggesting its usage to Eric as I prepared to signal the driver.

"Oh, no, Miss Alba," Eric declared. "Those are too slow and too expensive. We should seek the company whose vehicles are brown." After a tall stretch for searching, Eric found one.

In his genuine knowledge—unlike my semi-familiarity—Eric called the coachman with a word and gesture. And we ran, not needing in our youth to be slow and sophisticated. But we were educated enough in England's social order for Eric to automatically assist my entry into the carriage. The boy's demeanor changed as he opened the door, for he became less of the rushing youth and more of the gentleman as he looked to me closely and offered his hand.

He wished to touch me. The boy sought to play, the young gent knew to aid a lady, but this maturing man was desirous of my touch. Ignoring two of the three, I scurried into the cab with more the rapid grace of an animal than the vapid oozing of a lady. Within, I smiled toward Eric, who was happy to leap beside me without bothering to accept hurt feelings, for was not my felicitous visage a type of intimacy? Ultimately, however, the smile we shared was not of affection, but mischief.

"Kindly enlighten me as to the divergences I encounter, Master Eric; for when in the past I've made use of public conveyance, the coachman informed me that his hiring would be charged to Lady Rathel's account."

This was my response to Eric's passing to the driver some coinage from his pocket never smelled by me in that fabric locale.

"Well and good, miss, unless you would have your transport unknown, for carriage drivers on account must notate all their charges. That person of the household responsible for billings will therefore be aware of everyone's travels. Thus, I pay with my own coin, which cannot be followed to its source—me."

"And by what method, sir, have you appropriated such wealth?"

"My father's favorite gift for birthdays is coinage, and I have no argument with his choice. However, I have been known when desperate for finances to hock some of my less passionate possessions."

"Kindly, Mr. Denton, define for me that unpleasant word."

"Hock?"

"Hock."

"It means to take some item like a fob to the pawnbroker, who will pay less money than the item is worth. Hocking is a type of selling in which one has opportunity for a time to retrieve the goods before they are resold. But I suggest, miss, that you avoid this business, since usually the item of your own possession that you sell is immediately found missing by your guardians. Remarkably, the item then gains for them great emotional value, as though in retrospect it were an heirloom instead of the common object received each holiday from relatives."

This economic method I would certainly recall, though how I might apply Eric's expertise thereof was a mystery fit a sinners' fantasy of witches. But any deliberation on the subject would come another time, for currently we had arrived, Eric having the coachman halt shy of his house as we exited with no handling of one another. The building yet seemed located on the wrong side of the world.

As I stood away from the Dentons' windows, Eric entered for

his pet. More than desiring to see the dog, I was passionate not to see the parents. I remained in the shade of a shop's portico until a bearlike creature with a pleasant gait came running, dragging a young man attached via strap as though horse and wagon. As the two approached, I stepped from the shadows, the dog appearing and smelling quite friendly until he gained my scent. Then he ate me.

The dog began growling from the bottom of his throat, baring his teeth, hair sticking upright on his neck like ruffled feathers or the pants of an excitable lad. Unfrightened but confused, Eric bent to hold the dog while looking between his two friends.

"I . . . I don't understand, Alba. Never before has he been unfriendly toward strangers."

"I am no stranger," I told Eric, "I am unknown. Never have I seen one of God's creatures respond to me so viciously, except for sinning humans, and the influence of the latter has certainly caused the former." Then I stepped toward the dog with no fear to display.

"Perhaps he'll revert to a savage state if we force him," concerned Eric proffered. "If he bites you, my father will have him shot."

"If he bites me, your father will have him canonized," I corrected. "We will not force the creature, but allow him to understand."

I then reached with one hand for the dog to smell. Randolph stepped nearer, the large, tan animal stretching to present no more than his nostrils to my fingers. After he had smelled enough to place me in God's kingdom, he leapt against my chest to knock me flat and grasp my throat with his reverted animal fangs.

Immediately Eric grasped Randolph with all his body, attempting to pull a creature nearly as weighty as himself off my prostrate personage as people began noticing me: one woman shrieking, a man calling for a sword to slay the beast before it kills! I, however, promoted restraint with my words, able to speak because the dog was holding me, not consuming me.

"Please remain calm, Eric, in that Randolph and I are," I stated with some difficulty. The dog's smell and tactile proximity produced a rich sensation to please me were it not for our relative positions. I then spoke quietly, my words only for this creature.

"You need not taste a witch to understand her."

Randolph then released me, pulling his face away to pant and drip saliva on my lips as though oozing the emotions of a lustful sinner.

"Oh, and thank you for the refreshing drink of your spittle, ingracious beast," I remarked while wiping my mouth. As I rose, Randolph cooperated by moving aside. The dog then sat between me and his master, reaching to lick my hand, as I tended to my sinning apparel.

"Apologies beyond that token display are in order, sir," I told Randolph. "Perhaps you might explain your disreputable behavior to the crowd you've collected."

Though the dog had scant concern, Eric noticed that too many people had stopped nearby to buzz excitedly and stare, though after my mentioning that drink of spit they held less concern for my jeopardized life.

"Let us be stepping away," I suggested to Eric, looking between the two social males, the garbed one comprehending at once as he pulled his pet's strap, the shorter creature with the superior coat moving as per his master's bidding, both beasts looking to make certain I followed.

"And you'll be excusing us, folks, in that we've other young ladies to be trampling," I called out to the audience, my convincing imitation of Elsie either an astonishment or further embarrassment to Eric, who continued to walk his dog and the witch.

Moving past the accumulated sinners, I found myself cackling. Though more disruptive than the common laugh of sinners, the cackle of this white thing was not the shattering richness of a decent witch. Since I attempted to contain the sound with a hand before my mouth, the cackle became more of a chortle, Eric sensing this foolishness and snickering in kind, though he was sickened from the taste of dog spittle against lips, despite the mouth's being mine.

As we continued in fine spirits, I came to appreciate Randolph, and again was delivered with enlightenment. I learned that humans and animals could live together not merely as accepted familiars—as I had coexisted with animals on Man's Isle—but as desired companions, Eric and his dog an even more compatible pair than Elsie and her witch.

He responded to Eric's every given sound and gesture with a look to his master, a wag of the tail. I could sense Randolph's satisfaction in this excellent travel. Eric here was not taking his dog walking, but walking with him. In his familiarity with the locale and the society, Eric led the dog even as he led me, but neither Randolph nor I was subservient to this man, neither of us inferior nor forced to proceed.

"I usually take a different route," Eric described, "but since the people there are neighbors, I would be hallooing the lot, and thereafter they would be asking my parents of the girl with their son. What impossible explaining I would then need attempt."

Eric's character increased with his speaking, for he revealed himself as active and humorous, the latter appreciated by me in any type of person, the former considered dangerous by witches, in that sinners' unchecked activity oft reduced our populace. And I hoped this boy would not reveal himself as too active, too much the conventional sinner—like Rathel—but would remain discreet in his destruction, like Elsie.

"Forgive my rudeness, Mr. Denton, but I notice that lately you become less congested in speech. Perhaps the exterior air has loosened your breathing."

Displaying unreal indignity, Eric replied, "Forgive me, miss, if my gentlemanship has been lessened through inattentiveness. In fact, my breathing comes easier as I find myself less intimidated by my company."

"Whyever should the dog your virtual brother intimidate you, sir?" I asked, then feigned enlightenment. "Oh, your reference is to she who has brazenly slid from her combative lessons of ladydom to cause all those about her approximate shame. Aye, and I'm sorry now, lad, for the pain that I'm causing you," this last spoken with my Elsie imitation.

Responding in accord with his emerging personality, smiling Eric asked, "Think you, miss, that you might fancy a pet of your own? Truly I consider dogs the best. Of course, besides

212

the enjoyment, one must accept responsibility. Alone in a great city, a dog would have difficulty finding decent food. Also, on his own he might be run down by carriage wheels or stolen by another person desirous of a pet."

"The ownership itself I yet find discomforting, Eric. How odd it seems to accept such broad responsibility for a creature who by nature should be free to control its own life."

"Not while living in a city, Alba, which is not a natural life for beasts. Therefore, we pet owners repay the joys of our animals' companionship by caring for them properly. In a way, is it not like man and woman rearing children?"

"I most lavishly hope not, Eric, but let us consider. God's intent in the latter is for the race of humans to continue. The former is more akin to a man and woman marrying for lust. No, that is too bizarre a comparison. I've overextended the definitions of passion and friendship, and certainly pets are of the latter."

"I am hopeful that Lady Amanda would allow you to acquire a pet, Miss Alba," Eric submitted, to my great relief not begging for a wedding in that I had broached the subject. "Certainly a person with such concern and understanding of animals as yourself would be a superior mistress."

Quickly then I turned to Eric, having been struck with revelation.

"Eric! I have a pet!" I exclaimed, grasping Randolph in emphasis.

"You do, miss? I am surprised that only now you mention the fact. Is the creature so boring that you lost recollection?"

"No, my sir, the lack is not in remembrance, but comprehension. Only upon considering your explanation of the concept of pets have I come aware of my own example."

"You do not refer to good Miss Elsie," Eric wondered slyly.

"In fact, humorless lad, I am more that servant's pet than the reverse, and better stationed in this uncomfortable land because of her concern. No, Master Eric, in fact my pet is one I've had as long as I've been in London, a beast who's been a friend throughout."

"What type of animal is your newly-comprehended pet, miss?"

"A spider."

After a pause mandated by disbelief, Eric responded: "I might have been correct in mentioning boredom, this being your possible cause for misinterpreting the beast."

"A simple spirit, but a calm companion. Unquestionably the spider is a pet by your own definition, since I am friendly with the beast, though uncertain of its feelings toward me. Nevertheless, my protecting the spider from wanton servants allows the animal to survive in the artificial environment of my chamber."

"I am not fond of spiders," Eric commented, "and would prefer a different bug."

"Remarkable are our pets, Master Eric: a common insect that never leaves its corner, and a fiend dog that nearly killed a lady. But regardless of preference, what be our choice? The horses about are all occupied in slavery to the folk of London. If we could gain a regard for rats, however, an endless supply of pets would be available."

Not through mimicry but excited interest, Eric duplicated my earlier act of grasping Randolph's coat as he called out, "Oh, and Miss Alba, I have this tremendous thinking!"

"I would be most happy for you, sir, if your intellection did not cause such anguish."

"Anguish may be the eventual result, if recent history proves consistent, for the subject again is animals."

"Oh, praise God, you've a plan for entertaining us enormously by gathering London's rats and constructing tiny leads for them to drag us about the streets in wheeled crates!"

"You approach my true thinking, miss, as the spider approaches the dog in size. The wild animals I suggest that we study are heretofore harnessed, for they are in . . . the animal faire!" this last phrase acutely spoken as though worthy of excited acknowledgment.

"How thrilled I am, sir, with your wondrous presentation, if only I had the foggiest notion of your thinking. What, pray tell, is an animal fair? A court of justice for God's furry creatures?"

"No, miss, faire with a terminating 'e.' A place of public entertainment, a place of amazement and uproarious laughing."

"Oh, you mean the opera. That's 'era' with an anterior 'op.' "

"Miss, you mock me, and how apologetic I am to have irked

214

you. But of course, I now recall your wild background, which is surely the cause for your lacking interest in a mere animal faire, considering the beast populace of your former home. Is it therefore true that elephants and zebras and giraffes were your neighbors?"

"Forgive me, sir, but my Latin studies are not current, so I know little of your foreign terminology."

After Eric described the named creatures, I assured him I had no familiarity with such beasts, had even less belief in his own veracity.

"Sir, I say that whereas the former of your imaginative constructs revealed some ingenuity, the last is too simplistic to impress. Why stripes of such dull colors? And why that common animal? Why not a house-sized coquina with metal feathers each a different rainbow hue? A horse with black and white stripes is scarcely worthy of a lad whose father invents cathedrals."

"To beg your pardon, unkind miss. Gentlemen seldom lie, though moreso than ladies, all of whom are perfect as you've shamed me into believing."

"Since previously we've established that social graces are wasted on us, let us skip society and proceed anon to nature. These . . . things . . . you mention: Are they in fact amongst God's living entities, or part of Satan's strangest dreams?"

"Real they are, miss, and God's own creations. Furthermore, I am pleased to find you unfamiliar with them, pleased to say how utterly astonishing they are, as per my own knowledge; for I have seen them myself, and smelled their unique presences."

"Tremendous smells, you're saying now," I Elsied him. "Here my interest resides, sir—in my nose—for we wild folk are sensitive to revelatory fragrances. I therefore challenge you to convince me of your descriptions, not in words, but in the real world we have come to know." And I grasped the dog with both hands. Aware Eric understood.

"Any friend of Randolph is an acquaintance of mine, miss, and I would not lie to an acquaintance, being occasionally the gentleman when not overly influenced by folks from the wilds."

"Influenced to the point of creating sentences that grow unwillingly in no comprehensible manner until

215

achieving the category of composition," I remarked.

"Yes, miss," he replied.

"And where in the world of our acquaintance do these astonishing real animals reside? I speak not of flat geography, sir."

"Is Millney adequately real for you? Having journeyed from the African continent, the animal faire presently draws audiences in Millney's locale."

Turning harshly to Eric, I demanded, "Sir, we travel there at once."

"Yet I am the one accused of loose activity?" he uttered. "Millney is such a distance that we would not likely return before nightfall even if departing now. I doubt that even your imagination, Miss Alba, is so loose as to save us after we are discovered alone, together all day."

"Cannot we simply lie?" I countered. "Is this not the way of sinning Londoners?"

"No, not intentionally, as any lady knows. Though we might decide to lie in order to retain peace in our lives, not likely would we convince our superiors."

"The Rathel will be of no concern."

"Perhaps, miss, but my parents will be outraged. In all honesty and in genuine shame to me, my father is convinced that you and I should not be acquainted, though he has failed to provide me with an acceptable motive for this belief. Therefore, were he to learn of such a journey as Millney—nay, even one as simple as this, one conflicting with his orders—I would fear for the continuity of my existence."

"You are correct," I stated while looking down to Randolph. "My suffering would be scant. You are the person whose eternal being is in jeopardy."

" 'Tis true, I fear," he returned with a sigh. Eric then inhaled a huge, loose breath to call out loudly, "We're off!"

The socialite then established our plans.

"I return home with Randolph, gain funds for our carriage hire and entrance into the faire—and we depart at once for tremendous glee!"

"Or," I returned, "for astonishing danger."

* * *

216

I smelled the creatures a distance removed, and became frightened. Such odors perceived on Man's Isle would have sent every witch and animal fleeing to seek protection, yet here I was approaching. Eric then explained that the beasts were not only peaceful in essence, but also constrained and thus unable to attack persons if any wild reversion overcame them. But I was no person—I was a witch, and imagined fantastical creatures leaping upon me as had Randolph, imagined having to make friends with a hooved tree trunk with spots as it chewed my neck.

We approached a dress, a huge hooped skirt with a roof, this latter appropriate in that the garment was the size of a building. Eric stated that the impermanent structure was known as a "tent," the animal faire being housed within. Exiting the carriage, we stepped past a sign denoting THE DRS. IMBRIATI TRAVELING EXOTIQUE OF ANIMALES. After Eric provided a sinner with the required coin, we moved inside with other Londoners.

The next smells to accost me were of soil and straw tainted by the wastes of Unknown Animal. After a few anxious steps, I saw the first. Though Eric's descriptions were excellent and my view was lengthy, I am yet without words to fit a giraffe. And I was not disappointed to find upon nearing that the beast had no especial concern for the witch who stared up to those ears, down to those bony legs, side to side at those spots, all along that neck. Scarcely could I imagine living in any portion of God's world wherein such a creature was indigenous.

Eric and I promulgated suitable awe. Then my sinning guide led me to monkeys. These beasts seemed virtually normal compared to the giraffe. Considering their boastful screeches and frenetic scurrying bar to bar, was not their imprisonment appropriate? Given a few tools, they could have been sinners.

Then we arrived at the elephant.

"Master Eric, your accuracy in having measured this beast in my mind is astonishing," I wheezed.

"Yes, miss, and let us so observe as to revive these sights forever, sharing them long after we have departed this faire."

The elephant's texture was its most impressive initial characteristic. Sensible it seemed for such a wieldy beast to have sturdy grey hide instead of fur. The hooves resembled those of a pig, but the bulk of those toes! The elephant's nose was remarkable for being out of place, for it seemed either a boneless leg or a fat, hollow tail. And if my responses seem mad, truthfully I was moved toward distracted sensibility by the creature, and was amazed fully anew at God's ability to effortlessly imagine animals that common people could only wonder of insanely.

Familiar from his previous visit, Eric provided a name for that nose-snake. But the witch was too moved by the grand sensation to heed his composition, viewing the creature's unerring flexibility, its infinite neck, the impossible ears flapping like a sinners' bedsheet. But why should such a portion be called "trunk"?

"Come, you massive lout, show the good citizens your entire bulk."

Within the temporary rope room that was the elephant's home, the creature puffed up dust clouds the same color as itself in response to a sinner's influence. About the beast walked a man with a Continental accent tapping the elephant with a stick, lightly striking diagonal feet to incite the silent animal into rotating.

"The trainer there, one of the Drs. Imbriati," Eric whispered.

First I thought the trainer remarkable to have tutored such a brute into accepting guidance from taps so meager they would not crack an acorn. But further examination of this thin timber brought me distaste. I perceived with sight the pointed object secured in its end, for one nail is not enough metal for a witch to smell.

With no thoughts of ladylike propriety, I called out firmly to adjacent Eric, "The sinner is stabbing the poor creature with a lance!"

Uncertain whether to temper my speaking or to agree with my protest, confused Eric remained silent. The trainer, however, replied in affront.

"I bring this great animal across oceans for you to see and am called a sinner for it? I am subject to Satan's eternal fires because I tap the creature with a tack?" And he held the stick's poking end up for the crowd to see. "Notice, friends, the size of the tack compared to the size of the beast. See the big difference here. See that the creature shows no pain at all. How could something tiny hurt that skin, which is thick as a thatch roof?"

While speaking his theater piece, Imbriati approached me, finally having words specifically for the offender. Preferably I would have retreated, but more people had drawn about this grey exhibit, and I would have to jostle them to change positions.

"You'd best thank me, girl, for the control I have over the beast, else she'd go wild as is her nature and be stomping you to be eaten."

The crowd began jostling its own members with that assertion, but though loud and fearful, these sinners refrained from panicked flight. I remained firm in my position, for the trainer's assessment was insulting to a witch's sensibilities.

"Sir, I defy you to convince these reasonable folk that such an obviously peaceful animal eats anything more bloody than straw."

He was looking too closely at me. Too many strong, uncommon odors were about for sensitive smelling, but his countenance implied checked desire; and I knew how foolish I had been to attract this man with words and thus lure him near enough to be attracted by my person.

"I tell that the young miss is both correct and incorrect," the trainer announced to the crowd, making me part of his theatrical speech. "True, the creature is harmless now, but only because of my expert control of its heathen instincts. To prove to all ye fine Englanders my success in having tamed the animal, I invite one of you now to feed the thing these nut meats," and he pulled from his pocket some shelled peanuts, "which the elephant shall eat in her manner." Then, without looking to the animal, the trainer held forth his hand, the beast uniquely grasping the foodstuffs with her boneless tail, curling it up to her comical lips.

"Have we a volunteer to prove the elephant's peace?" Imbriati queried, looking out to the crowd only to snatch his gaze again to me. "Here we have a fine one, in that she has proven herself both knowing and courageous in the ways of great beasts, as though they line her path in life."

Holding out his hand to signify me, the trainer then asked the

219

crowd, "Will the miss not do?"

The witch-hating sinners surrounding me of course agreed most heartily—even Eric, the traitorous lech—loudly deciding that I, from amongst them all, would be the elephant's victim.

"Oh, please, miss," some revolting wench reminiscent of Elsie pleaded, "might not one of us have the courage to confront the beast?"

"Oh, and, yes, miss, for do you not know better than us the monster's harmlessness?" some sinning fool reminiscent of the Rathel declared.

As I stepped to the rope as aided by the crowd's rowdy encouragement, my words were only for the young sinner who had led me to this doom.

"My death via trampling shall live with you ever," I cursed Eric.

He returned a look of utter innocence. Imbriati had a more tactile response, reaching with thick fingers like an elephant's toes to give the girl a hand, a contact the witch was certain to avoid.

"Thank you, sir, but although I have been connived into entering this realm, I prefer to do so without the aid of your digits."

Remaining away from Imbriati, I moved beneath the rope. Once beyond that segregating string, the huge beast was immediate, seeming more landmark than living thing. But I found ingratiating the grace of its swaying head, the kindliness of its eyes and delicate lips.

"Here now is a nut for the young miss to feed the beast and prove it only formerly a killer," Imbriati stated, and held out a peanut for me.

With confidence and no contact against the trainer, I accepted the foodstuff. Supporting the nut on my palm so the beast would not bite away my fingers with its "trunk," I extended my arm to the elephant, which reached for me with its thick, misplaced tail, removing the food with scant pressure. The sounds of its muscles contracting were massive though quiet, as though a muffled moving of the Earth. Louder were the trainer's clear but foreign words to the elephant. Only after transmitting the meal to her true mouth, however, did the creature respond to Imbriati's commands, leaning forward to uncoil that frontal tail and push me to the ground.

"Hold, Sheba, you're no longer the killer, you'll recall," the trainer cried as the crowd responded with sharp breaths whose scent was fear. And the elephant refrained from killing me, taking no note of my presence as I looked up to its mass, which had seemingly increased. As he bent to aid my rising, Imbriati spoke again in that strange language—but the elephant was also moving, stepping toward the crowd, which retreated from the murderous beast. Once near the rope, the elephant halted, lowering her slow bulk until reclining between the audience and actors, the male half of the latter aiding the lady by grasping her bosom and thigh.

"The girl is not injured, but is slow to regain her feet from the startling occurrence," the trainer called out over his obscuring animal while reaching into my apparel to knead my crotch. The only member of the audience with a good view of this molestation was the young man who had passed the rope to stand above the groping sinner and the struggling girl.

He could not speak. He could not move further nor act, Eric only looking downward—more pained than I—unable even to say, "Sir, you will move away if you are a decent fellow," unable to cry out to the crowd, to shout for constables.

I was astounded at how thoroughly the trainer was able to hold me down, astonished to find he had circumvented all of Elsie's clothing to gain an entrance to my body, managing to insert a finger within my baby slot, a contact I found more offensive than painful, though I was angered enough to revert to a wild state no witch could imagine without sinners.

I emitted a thin grunting from the exertion of pulling at Imbriati's arms and kicking at his torso as the trainer continued to press within me as though a mole making a new tunnel, digging first through the grass of my lace, then into the soil of my sex. But not until my struggles and the trainer's efforts caused my thigh to be revealed was Eric able to act. His mouth drooping, his face red as though burnt, as though a perverted tart, Eric moved stiffly to the trainer's stick. His face displaying both fury and dismay, Eric grasped the tool to give this exotic animal a lesson, one not to be assaulting the audience of his opera, not to be reverting to his natural instincts of lust. Not a studious pupil, the trainer paid no heed to the threatening youth until Eric smote him against his head, the educational nail striking the sinner's skull and remaining.

Breathing as heavily as the elephant, Imbriati fell to his side, reaching with shaking hands to his head, to that wood and metal limb, one completely unlike a trunk, more akin to Satan's horns.

The witch did not remain. Retaining a fury that Eric had lost, I leapt to my feet to tutor this static youth who stared at the trainer's fantastical extremity.

"You wish your stick returned?" I hissed, then grasped his arm, turning Eric from the animals. "We're off. We leave him as he is and flee," I concluded, and pulled the sinner away.

Eric responded, moving more quickly now, around the elephant and beneath the rope without a word. I was the only person speaking.

"We go for the elephant doctor," I announced to the crowd, "for the beast is fevered."

The audience then viewed the departing girl expert in great animals, turning to the fallen beast and wondering of its illness.

"I'll bloody well not have the magistrate lured to us for saving myself," I whispered harshly to Eric as we ran.

We gained a waiting coach and returned without being questioned, without being caught. Night remained too distant to endanger the cab's inhabitants, a pair of distressed humans slow to calm, one a maturing male, the other an angered witch. But she was not the person weeping.

222

Fifteen

My journey with the lad was to the street of his home for the purpose of dog walking. No thoughts had I of attempting to escape London as per your accusations of yesterday. In fact, I was ever mindful of returning before Eric was discovered on the street by his punitive parents.

"Ah, and it's thoughtful you are, lass, to be sparing your friend difficulties. But as oft you're learning as an English lady, it's no prideful thing to be journeying with no permission and no chaperone."

Displeased Elsie then turned to withdraw, but I was not through with her, requiring the servant to perform her fond task of gossiping.

"Before you depart in anger, miss, I must say how believable I find your warning, for Eric and I late yesterday heard an odd tale describing a faire for animals and difficulty there with children. As I understand, these youths also were out of doors improperly."

"Aye, it's a tale I'm hearing this morning, child, from a passing friend. She's saying, then, that an elephant animal and its keeper were having a fracas with a youth who wounded him with a club."

"Your story, therefore, is not of two girls whom the faire owner attempted to hire as hedonistic dancers, becoming so adamant that the young ladies beat this person to death with a limb?"

"No, and I'm hearing of no girls and no killing, only a boy

223

and a wound. Your tale may be the better, lass, but such stories are changing as they move from one person through the next. So it's young Eric, then, who's telling you these . . . compositions, as you say?"

"Similar to you, Miss Elsie, Eric has friends with whom he shares described tales both true and modified."

"Likely he does, lass, in that we're all having our friends of a similar station. You'd be having your own if you were of a mind to be friendly toward other young ladies, for a few there are about our neighborhood, and from fine families."

"Oh, what a wonderful idea, Elsie! Kindly introduce me to any capable of walking beneath the sea long enough to terrify their servants."

"And I'm thanking you again, lass, for the torment," Elsie grumbled. "As for friends of the Eric lad, perhaps we're seeing one now, since a boy his age has been looking toward our door the morning with no purpose. Friend or foe, though, I'm about to be learning who this stranger is on our street parked like a waiting carriage." Elsie then stepped outside with the official air of one about to instruct armies.

Separated by a window thicker than sound, I watched her approach a young male, but could not hear her brief speaking. In response, the lad delivered the servant with a slip of paper. With no reply evidently required, the youth turned to run, the witch denoting his relief without need of smelling.

Elsie looked down to the paper, then up to the window, to me. Having the same ability to read thoughts as any witch or servant, I was left with reading her countenance, Elsie returning inside with a folded note.

"And the urchin is only saying that this paper be for Alba," Elsie told me. "I'm confessing I might be reading the thing meself if I'd not known you to be looking. But I'm hoping you're taking in no news you can't be telling me, for even witches should be ladies."

"But never the reverse, I assume," I mumbled while unfolding the note. There I read: "I survived. I thought I had the other end."

"No shame have I in describing this communiqué, Miss Elsie. Although no name is signed, the paper is from Master Eric. He tells me—to some relief, I confess—that he survived. That is a quote from him, its meaning that yesterday he received no severe punition from being out on the street with me and the dog, but no chaperone."

Elsie looked down to the note, then up to my face. The paper was folded again, not offered for the servant's perusal.

"Yes, miss," I added with a mischievous tone, "the remainder of the writing is secretive in nature as fit an English boy and girl. Its content I shall retain, but I vow that nothing therein would cause you shame in your Alba."

"Ah, and you should be selling riddles on a corner, girl, with all of your comedy," she retorted, and walked away with less of her previous anger. The messenger, it seemed, had improved both our spirits.

The entire morning I remained satisfied with my relief. And though the problem alleviated was my concern for a sinner, I felt no regret for misplacing my emotions. I appreciated Eric from God's inspiration, not society's corruption, for Eric was the source of that profound and permanent idea affording me a type of immortality. Even sinners, I knew, were human enough to love God.

Another male of profundity soon returned, for that afternoon I found Georges Gosdale. With no tutor due, I was being so generous as to apply tea outside my chamber, sprinkling the fragrant grounds in the drawing room when I discovered selfishness. I understood that again I was providing for myself, since no person occupied this room more than I and my guest. With a guilty glimpse to see if anyone had noticed my failing, I saw instead a change on the wall: the Rathel's military heirlooms. That second lance had been cleaned and returned. The stick that had stabbed Mr. Gosdale. The stick tipped with sharp metal. Sharp metal that had stabbed the elephant trainer, another sinner lying wounded due to his lust. Due to me. As I stared at the dark grit on the carpet, there as though before me on the grass lay Georges Gosdale. There on the soil lay Imbriati, each man

225

shaking with pain, their expressions of surprise never forgotten. And there before me dying was Eric. As surely as the previous men had lain wounded, so would Eric. The nearer he came to being part of my life, the nearer he would approach his death, exactly as intended by foolish Lady Rathel. And finally I understood that the fool was I. The potential for death from my sex promised by Rathel even then had twice been proven true. She had spoken of a "sexual capacity" for killing, and I was so foolish as to believe she expected me to smother men with my breasts, strangle them with my vagina, when in fact death from this white witch was well specified in demonstration. Gosdale and the trainer through their lust for me had accepted steel into their persons, and Eric — I knew — would somehow gain the same gift.

When would my sense come to equal the sinners' lust? When would I no longer endorse the sinners' evil with passivity? For their torment had found me even when I was least cooperative with their ways. When would I learn the lesson of leaving? But I knew. I knew to become active in seeking survival by removing myself from the sinners' path. And now I had a new excuse to spur me. Without my presence, the Rathel's threat against Eric would be removed. I thus became determined to preserve not only myself, but also my religious mentor.

I expected Eric to have taken from the animal faire caution enough to keep him apart from me for days. But the days were few. Passing through the great room one morn, I heard a familiar sound. The same as a person's gait, one's knock is distinctive and identifying. That sound at the door was surely Eric's, and I found myself moved by anticipation. Delilah then answered the door to find Eric, as expected, but not only Eric, for behind the young man came his father.

How strange to see these family members' divergent states. Smiling at Delilah and even moreso upon sighting me, the son stood unaware that stalking behind him was his angry father set to snatch the boy away, to scold his kin while ignoring all of the Rathel household.

And so the theater transpired. Eric learned of the upcoming opera by the strange looks thrown past his shoulder by Delilah and me. The younger Denton turned only to receive his father's forceful grasp on his shoulder, the more massive adult heaving the youth around without a glimpse to the servant or me paces beyond.

"You thus disobey me and English decency?" Edward harshly confronted his son. "Are you so lecherous as to dishonor both your parents?" And with his hand on Eric's shoulder, he pulled his boy toward home.

I watched them depart, Eric embarrassed and unresisting, shamed worse than ever by this witch, no crowd collecting for this compact encounter, one that moved me as deeply as the victim. Of course, Eric was ever meant to be the victim. And despite the scene's clean lack of bloodshed, the violence here was imposing; for these people were of import to each another, not enemies, the Rathel through her selfish auspices harming the truth of their family love via the encompassing evil of revenge.

"Miss Elsie, you might please aid in my understanding London, for Lady Rathel and her tutor have failed to grant me adequate knowledge of English finance."

"And I'm to be telling you business things that the mistress and Mrs. Natwich haven't? You're burdening me, child, with knowing about the wealthy as though I be one. But I'm helping you if I can, lass, though don't be expecting from me learning that a simple person is not having."

"I would ask you, miss, from whence people obtain money."

"Why, of course, child, but your question is easy. One asks their mistress for coin to be buying a batch of fish or a peck of kumquats."

Elsie then smiled so pridefully as to be purely the sinner.

"Thank you, miss, for your fulfilling humor. As well, accept my forgiveness for your taunting me when I seek only to better myself. Or is the truth I now discover that you have no desire for me to become a lady?"

227

"Aye, a few things you're learning about being the lady, girl, for even now you're excellent at being unkind to servants. As for moneys, I'm saying that Mistress Amanda has gained a fine estate from Master Franklin, from both his ownings and his business with Mr. Denton. And I'm hearing the mistress is most wise in handling her husband's wealth."

"Therefore, the Rathel in her business dealings obtains money from other town houses and brings the coinage home."

Laughing, Elsie added, "Girl, I'll feign no awareness, then, of your taunting me out of vengeance. And I'm pretending I believe you don't truly know that in cities like London, most funds are in the form of paper, promissories and drafts being held by banks. And afore you're asking what is a bank, I'm saying it's a business which holds your money so it won't be lost. When you're needing some currency, you go there and they're returning some of which you gave them previous."

"When you require funds for fish and other slimies, Elsie, do you hie to a bank and acquire some of the Rathel's money?"

"Ah, and no, lass, because they're only giving moneys to those that were placing it there to begin with. They're giving Mistress Amanda's money only to Mistress Amanda."

Learning nothing in this conversation, I decided to invoke boldness with my further deceptions.

"How exactly would you manage to gain funds for purchasing a slimy thing as a gift for the mistress, therefore being unable to ask the recipient for money?"

"Girl, you're a terror to society with your tremendous lack of learning. So I'm telling you now that servants buy no gifts for their masters, and the blooming opposite as well is surely true. But if a person would be purchasing a gift for any cause, there are other sources. Some are gaining a bit of honest money from craftwork or home gardens. Things such as knittings and veggies can be sold, you know. Another way is in turning criminal. Then you can be visiting honest folks' banks and take all the money you can—until you're caught and hanged, that is."

"What other things of a household can be built and sold?" I asked. "Are all these tapestries and porcelain as valuable as are goods from a garden? In that you would teach me needlework, can you teach me to produce these objects as well?"

"My stitching a welcome mat is not the same as a tapestry it's taking a crew of Frenchmen a year to make. And you'd best be understanding, lass, that selling such artworks if not your own is called 'thievery,' and for such acts the magistrate will be making your new home his old prison."

"I now comprehend why I have not been made aware of finance's complexities, for this is an area no person of God should enter, since the process ever ends with one's being hanged. My tutor I thank for this ignorance, and hope to retain it along with my unstretched neck."

"Aye, and it's the attitude of a lady you're now taking, girl, for finance is best left to the menfolk. If you're needing money, be marrying a rich man, is what me mum ever said. Since I'm a commoner and having no need of funds, I'm sending away the countless barons always after me apron strings."

Again Elsie had produced a humor to sicken me by being so similar to my own. As the servant moved away to proceed with her baseborn affairs, I concluded my interpretation of English finance, conjoining her ideas of money with Eric's of hocking. Because no more than Elsie would I be marrying a wealthy sinning man, and unlike her I was subject to the magistrate's ultimate punition via the Rathel's whim, to attain the funds required for my purposes, why not become a thief?

Since I sought release from London, not incarceration, I would heed Elsie's speaking and not attempt to gather bits of Rathel's fortune directly from her bank. And though not so abjectly foolish as to remove portraits of British kings from the lady's walls, since I possessed no fobs or similar gifts, I would necessarily pawn the Rathel's belongings. As explained by expert Eric, items for the merchants of hocking must be carefully selected. At once I was terrified by the thought of taking a ring long unused by Rathel though purchased by Franklin and vowed upon by his wife to retain for her lifetime, the item never worn but touched each night by the lady who renewed her vow before praying to God, immediately after promising Satan to eke for him Eric's existence. With less fear and more sensible thinking, I selected an item to be my economic victim.

"Good morning, Miss Rathel, and is it that you would take the clock for a ride?"

Had I a source of coinage, I would have hired a different coachman, for one unfamiliar with me would not have asked semi-humorous questions as to my temporal companion.

"Sir, you would be so good as to convey me and the timepiece to a shop of pawning where I might sell the item."

"I would aid you, miss, if I could, and will apologize because I cannot. Instructed I was directly by the Lady Rathel not to transport you to any place alone, in that she feared for you without chaperone. This I can agree with, in that you are from a mild place which lacks the criminals of London."

Again I felt enslaved by Rathel, that mistress of human manipulation. But I also felt social enough to be embarrassed before this coachman. And blushing or not, I was more apprehensive to reenter the house with my booty than to proceed. Therefore, I continued with the same sinner rather than beginning anew with a more dangerous male.

"In that my task is decided, sir, I must proceed without your services. Nonetheless, I ask you with kindness to inform me of the whereabouts of the sort of enterprise I seek."

"Miss, I fear that telling you this would lead you to go there and gain for yourself difficulty. I would not bring a problem upon you. And certainly you would not be walking, I'd wish."

"Sir, I begin walking immediately. If you are such a minister of my household as to inform Lady Rathel of my plans, may you rest peacefully with your thoughts. But you would aid me without jeopardizing your employ by providing the directive I seek. Furthermore, I would have you understand that I came to London from the wilderness, which was my home. In the wilds are no thieves, but giraffes and other creatures certainly no more difficult to avoid than London's average criminals."

"If you are one to deal with a thing as great as a giraffe, then human murderers should cause you scant pause," the coachman responded. "Thus, I shall direct you to the place you seek."

And so he did, the witch listening carefully to instructions for gaining a shop supposedly not far removed. Thanking the coachman, I retained the haughty mode fit an English lady and a witch so ignorant as to accept insufficient directions. Foolish these sinners were to be deceived by a witch, one to convince them she was a young lady instead of a child. Even sinners know how easily children can misplace themselves, this one so wild as to be lost paces beyond her doorstep. Though reasonably the complex streets should have been marked, only a few signs were posted, those names the coachman had given me so unfamiliar that I forgot them regardless. But the man had also mentioned the tall office of a basket manufacturer whose braided sign would be missed with difficulty.

Not at all. The walking was difficult, however, because I stubbornly continued to search long after losing my landmarks, fooled by the false belief that I would eventually find the proper shop if only because every shop in London I would eventually pass. My grand mistake was continuing toward a semi-hated smell, for ahead were the remnants of a great burning. Proceeding, I soon came to poverty, and what direction then? No fine carriages awaited on these narrow streets, for no elaborately dressed gentry lived here to hire them. No intricate houses with elegant vines gracefully coating the buildings' fronts beneath high, peaked roofs and multiple panes of glass. Only unpainted clapboard and broken windows, dirt streets, the only brick covered with soot marks from a hot history.

From behind a partially boarded window came the sound of a sinner woman cackling like no witch; whereas in the Rathel's locale, no person of any gender or station would display such a loud lack of etiquette. Neither did any men in my neighborhood slouch as did these, as though to be nearer the dirt that covered them. Though many males in wealthy locales found interest in me, none had ever stared at my torso only to imitate a wild pig hungered to the point of madness, salivating and swallowing their spittle from lust, a putrid desire extended to verbal obscenity upon my passage.

"Ooh, cor, bloke, and there's a thing to be mouthing on."

Here were children never influenced by a tutor, numerous examples of the wretch I had deservedly beaten in the park,

231

quasi-human creatures who sneered at me worse than any in Jonsway, calling out as though viewing a giraffe grazing their streets that I was "Carrying a bleeding clock!"

At the next intersection, I turned onto a street even less desirable due to its increase of destroyed buildings. The advantage here was that no populace was seen beyond, and I wished no more exposure to sinners far worse than Rathel's kind, their response to a harmless stranger describing their society as one ruined—as though paradoxically—by a lack of wealth. If wealth were a prime evil to have spoiled the whole of London, how could its removal be responsible for this inferior part? Why did these people, in their lack of materials, not become like witches? Though I could not determine whether poverty or wealth were more akin to wild living, I was convinced that despite its pretension and waste, luxury was preferable to human filth; for squalor is not only unnatural, but unpleasant. Unladylike.

Having walked too far without discovering anything to lead me home, I found instead a despicable reversal, found certain aspects of the wilderness present but perverted. This region also held a populace whose members remained in shadows. And strangers were not intruders, but victims.

Three persons met me individually, separate illnesses but the same disease. Though I formed no incisive descriptions of them—as though one were tall with long limbs and neck, another agile and hirsute, the third bulky with a greyish cast—they were akin to the giraffe, the monkey, and the elephant in being alien. But whereas the exotic beasts of the animal faire were honest and unviolent, the three new creatures were human in those respects, having the humanity of sinners, not witches.

"Aye, good lady, I'm taking the gift you brought me now," a sinning male professed as he blocked my path, startling me as he stepped from the shadow because he seemed a shadow, manifesting his form from the darkness.

I halted to avoid walking against him, whereupon another building's niche exuded a second man to confront us two.

"You'll not be bothering the miss, blackguard. She's mine in that long I've followed her wanderings."

232

As these males faced, a hole decanted another cretin to confront those three persons (in broad terms) heretofore assembled.

"Ignorant bleeding slime you are to be discussing what I own," the latest scowled, snatching the clock from me with such certainty that I had no opportunity to resist. His forcefulness so intimidated me that I could form neither sound nor deed.

"Take the bleeding clock, cur," Giraffe snarled at Elephant, "but be watching I don't take it from you as you sleep, along with your eyeballs."

These two then positioned themselves as though flesh-tearing beasts prepared to battle. Before my fear could increase enough to choke me breathless, the remaining creature had his own and least pleasant say.

"The pair of you fools fight over the useless clock, while I do what is sensible and fuck this wench until my pecker drops away."

Though having good notion of his meaning, I lacked knowledge of all these criminal terms. The latest speaker, however—this Monkey—began actions I was overtly familiar with, for at once he had his hands on me. Immediately this cretinous entity much larger than I displayed his expertise, for he seemed proficient in molesting girls, so assured were his moves as he grabbed my body, squeezing my breasts as though pests to be squashed lifeless.

With extreme speed in his words and moves, Giraffe was inspired by Monkey to proceed with a shared immorality.

"I'm fucking her rear hole standing," he squealed as though surprised by his satisfying imagination, stepping behind me to lift my skirts and have at my flesh with both hands, his touch and breath of a more desperate mode than the elephant trainer's, this man more excited, more criminal.

At once I was leaping and flailing, but uselessly. The sinners grasped me with such forceful economy that I could not believe their ease in controlling a person. And though this ravaging was not my first, every new initiated rape taught me that each succeeding molestation would be worse, more painful, more obliterating to my senses and my spirit.

"What a cold bitch—I'm reaming her fuckable arse," Giraffe

sighed grotesquely from behind, moaning as he slobbered roughly into my ear, both hands pulling on my naked buttocks as though to pull them apart, my apparel pressed between us in a bundle offering the animal no impediment, not enough fabric in England to prevent his sex smell from rising to violate my senses.

"Stuff her cunt full with my prick I'm doing," Monkey earnestly groaned as he dug against my baby portions.

"Off of it, half man, I'm lapping her cunt and arse hole dry only to fill them with my prick snot," Elephant moaned, and attempted to force the other animals aside. Before he could substitute for his Satanic friends, this last beast found himself so conservative as to run from a noise. A clomping from the perpendicular street: horses' hooves, a man loudly urging the animals onward, a whip snicked through the air, first above the horses' heads, then against the hides of monsters.

He could say nothing. All of us looked to the coachman who had refused me, his face so clenched that no words could exit. But his activity came easily, the man whipping at Monkey, who immediately grasped and turned me so that I shielded him, he and Giraffe having no place to run, for the coach had forced us against the nearest building. Since the driver would not be whipping the girl, he jerked his reins so the horses stepped to the side, stepped near us entangled three all of whom fell, the horses stumbling but remaining upright. A hoof like a sharpened stone thrust down by a brown, beautiful leg beside my ribs nearly struck me, but only soiled my skirt loose about my torso and those men. Well trained and peaceable in nature, the neighing horses avoided us, necks thrown down, then back, loudly straining to move away with erratic steps likely to break and bloody us. But with fortuity or God's guidance, no contact came.

The nervous horses were calming as the coach wheels rolled inches farther, then stopped. So near me was the vehicle as I lay against a wall on my backside that the driver could not exit downward. After looking toward me, the man moved to the cab's opposite side, knowing not how to aid the fallen girl while retaining control of those horses yet too near her. Then I arose, surprised at not being ravaged by the men, crushed by the horses, nor rolled upon by the coach. Since the vehicle was static, I retrieved my clock where it had fallen to the dirt. Continuing to the cab's rear and around, I pulled together the ripped ends of my apparel, brushing the soil from my skirt and my timepiece. Covered and cleaned acceptably in my social modesty, I moved to the coach's door, the driver nearly reclining on his seat to stretch and reach down for the handle; for if nothing else, he had to open the door for the lady. Without a word, I entered, not needing to ask the sinner to take me home.

Sixteen

"Sir! You will cease this fleeing!"

A young lady in the street's center shouting at a coachman was most unseemly, especially since she held a clock. Because the driver had looked toward her, stared—reeking of disbelief—then ordered his horses away, what could the girl do but rush out and stop him? Was she not so selfish as to hold this sinner partially responsible for her previous day's distress?

"Miss Rathel, you cannot mean to proceed with your intent of yesterday," he declared. "How is it you are even let out this morning?"

"Because none of the household has seen me depart. And since the only damage received the prior day was to clothing I scarcely value, an explanation of a carriage accident to the servant was enough to allow me freedom to contemplate another journey."

"But I am most unbelieving that you would choose my hire again."

"Your selection, sir, is due to the understanding we have formed between us, since I would have never suffered distress had you not forced me to walk. Yet again today I find you abandoning me to my feet."

"Yesterday, miss, it was I to be aware of your harmful situation, and I to thereupon come seeking you."

"For which I now gratefully thank you, sir, and applaud you equally for not describing the situation to Lady Rathel."

"I retained my silence for my own purposes, miss, in that I

feared to be seen as not preventing enough of your woes."

"Thereby you demonstrate agreement with the notion of culpability I first presented. And since we have arrived circuitously where I initially began, let us fulfill this compatible concept and continue to the pawnshop as we should have upon my first requesting, feigning now that we never suffered the discomfort that was yesterday."

With no further word, I entered the coach, receiving no aid with the hinging, the only assistance from the driver his tacit acceptance.

The journey was brief. So simple was the travel that yesterday's expedition seemed impossible, a painful experience attacking again as a dream. Perhaps maddened by the nightmare, I found the coachman at fault again, now for my memory, for no warmth had I for the sinner as I exited the coach. If only due to my temporal burden, the driver stepped down to open my door and offer his hand, which I left him, nearly forcing myself to say, "I will thank you to wait," in my coldness and needless imputing certainly more of the English lady than ever before. Such were the lessons of London.

Within the shop, I waited for prior business to be resolved. This interval allowed me to study finance, as I listened to a nervous customer attempt to sell a ludicrous firearm with a terrible metal smell and a flared end as though a funnel for decanting flour. I thus received a lesson in hocking from this man seeking a fair sum for his "blunderbuss."

The sinner would have ten guineas for this weapon used by King James himself to fend off burglars when yet a prince. The proprietor offered him tuppence for a weapon whose only usage was as a rusty truncheon. This valued addition to any lord's arsenal the man would virtually provide gratis for only five quid. The pawnbroker offered two pounds for the heap he would melt down for fishing weights.

"Three quid," the customer either pleaded or moaned.

"Done," the proprietor agreed; and this was finance?

He was asking my business. With the previous bargain completed, my time had come, the proprietor's speaking snatching me from an innocent numbness again into the fiscal world.

"I would sell this, sir, if in your generosity you'd be willing."

His opening and closing one hand meant to approach. I thus stepped forward and set the clock upon his counter. After the pawnbroker examined the mechanism, I received his perusal, for both items were significant in such business.

"I would ask you, miss, if you are the owner here, for you seem too young to be possessing such an article."

Though unsurprising, his implication affronted me, and I was not a lady receptive to insults.

"Am I the only person in London so disrespectfully queried?" I returned from true offense. "The former customer you in no way embarrassed by implying him a thief."

"No discourtesy meant, miss, but that man lives in a home he owns. Being licensed by city justices, I am liable for the receiving of unowned goods. What you have here is from a mantel, likely belonging to the house's owner—your parents, perhaps, if you'll forgive my need to ask."

"I forgive you for being unaware that my parents are dead. And I tell you, sir, that whereas I have never received a firearm, even ladies in their youth have requirements of time, and families so generous as to provide them with fine, unneeded items on their birthdays."

"I thought young ladies were required to know of time, yet to you this clock is not needed."

Having stumbled over my mouth again, I had to quickly reestablish my thinking. Soon I found a most sensible reply for the acute proprietor.

"I'll take three quid."

"Now you've a deal," the sinner replied, and reached into his money drawer for coins, which he placed on the countertop before me, and the clock was his. With scant satisfaction I reached for my funds—but they were stolen by the woman behind.

"You will keep your miserable price, thieving merchant," the Rathel snarled past my shoulder, "and I will take my timepiece." And she flung the coins at the man's face, then seized the clock from him. "And I defy you, dishonest sir, to make the first query as to my ownership of this item or this girl." Then she

238

snatched the latter as though another timepiece, pulling me toward the door. There she halted, calling out loudly past me.

"Never deal with my daughter again, or Magistrate Naylor I'll have look into your questionable business."

The remaining customers with their guilty or well-owned merchandise stared at us three and wondered. But Rathel, in having no embarrassment at being involved in public theater, seemed even less the lady than I.

Onto the walk with her objects, Rathel next confronted my driver, a person of public business now punished as though family.

"You, sir, shall find yourself this day with no employ," she vowed, proving herself a lady equal to me, blaming the coachman for his cooperation as though it were cause.

The mistress had another coach for our conveyance. As we entered the cab, Rathel released my arm and calmed. A moment of travel passed before her next speaking, and there was no anger in her odor or sound.

"I will ask of your seeking money. If you've some desire, you have only to request it. You would likely be surprised at the wealth I would expend to satisfy you, Alba. Not lately have I been so pleased as upon seeing you and Eric become friends."

"Being an average person with some attempted kindness, I can befriend those people not plotting to harm me. As for your wealth, a small portion would be required to send me home to Man's Isle."

"For this reason, then, you sell the timepiece?"

"In truth, I have no purpose for the price I would have gained. I only know that cash is required in London for acquiring things that other folk would disallow, but I have no notion as to the price of my liberty."

"Your freedom is being purchased now," the Rathel informed me. "Continue as you are with Eric and you shall be free for a long life in any remote area you choose. Since I will pay for your transit then, Alba, you have no need to collect advance funds you know not how to spend. To discourage you further, allow me to explain your criminality. Even if my legal daughter, you have no right in English law to steal my property and sell it. The punishment is a flogging and perhaps incarceration."

"How mild you are, Amanda, not to threaten revelation of my true witch's self and thereby subject your daughter to burning. How kindly you become to offer me only prison and a legal beating."

"I'll not threaten you with prison, Alba, for your confinement there would aid no person. My vow is that your accomplice will long live in jail if ever you attempt such thievery again. And I assure you, Alba, that Elsie will suffer terribly in Montclaire Prison."

With dullness my days proceeded, and never did I apologize to Elsie for a personal mien any human could construe as moping. Too long in bed I remained each morning, rising only at the hour of expected visitors, one of whom never came. The tutor I would see only to practice my scripting, having learned too much of local geography. Husking tubers held scant interest for me, and no initiative had I for fiesty conversation with Elsie. No other source of wit was available, Natwich hardly a peer, hardly humorous, and Eric was no longer a visitor to my household.

Despite our different races, this male was most like me of all the sinners. Whereas Elsie was a friend, Eric in certain ways— God forgive me—was an equal. As well as being more actively intelligent than Elsie, the male had revealed to me parts of God never known before. But why had I never considered the possibility that our most evident difference might be emphasizing our compatibility? In that sinners formed their greatest bonds of friendship between sexually opposite spouses, might not the same be true for a pair of humans half sinner, half witch?

Potentials of this idea I sensed most acutely that morning I waited for visitors, and smelled one. Upon my roof spot I stood, my intended observation a view of space, not the locale of London polluted by sinners, but the air above this land, the uninterrupted atmosphere. I then sensed part of London without intent, for a person approached whose scent was familiar. But I took no pride in my increased nasal sensitivity, for I felt that I

240

could sense sinners like witches because I was becoming more and more the sinner. Then came fear, of death and vengeance; for of all the sinners I knew, the only one I recognized by scent was Eric.

I moved downstairs as Rathel answered the door. I did not look to him. I had no need, remaining in the great room, though not in sight of the household's guest. I could hear the boy, however, and smell his body changing. No sub-navel stink was this, but a terror without to be faced from within. I could hear him, smell him, and though removed, yes, I could feel him.

"Good morning, Lady Amanda, and I would see you briefly if you've the time. No more than a moment have I, but no more is required to offer you what I must."

"Of course, Master Eric," the mistress replied. "What time I have is yours. Will you please enter and be seated before a warming fire for our speaking?"

"Thank you, no, in that I must be gone virtually as soon as I've arrived. Forgive my curtness, Lady Amanda, but if I might speak with you in your doorway a moment, my business will become evident."

"Speak, then, Eric, and be assured that you alone have my attention."

Odd was his voice, odd as his odor, Eric boy and man simultaneously now, wishing to be adult in his decisiveness, but cursed with youthful anxiety.

"Lady Amanda, I have come—in that I am of an acceptable age—I have come, that is . . . I come to offer myself in betrothal to your daughter, and so vow as proven by this paper that bears my signature. I must first ask if my offer is acceptable, but no more time have I, because even as you learn of my wishes for your daughter, you know my father's opposition and that of his wife. But my life one day will be my own, and my only desire is to fulfill it with your Alba, who is surely God's greatest lady. I am not uncultured, Lady Amanda, and you must understand that although my parents currently keep me as though a prisoner, when established in my career, I will have a position to support your daughter as is her due. And though we speak of years, not months, no time known will separate me from my emotion for Miss Alba."

The Rathel responded as though finally able to rid her household of a most revolting and aged offspring.

"With joy and God's graces I accept your betrothal, Eric, and welcome your vow toward my daughter above all others imaginable!"

"Praise God for your acceptance, Lady Amanda, which I required for life's relief. Further apprehension I have from my parents, but please understand that whereas their obstruction is one to overcome with time, my emotions for Alba shall overwhelm me as long as I remain the same person."

He then departed. I heard his running footsteps. But was this a man pursued by a fiend, or a boy chased by his father? Was he running from a bogey in the night, or fleeing the witch in his heart?

Though I cared not to smell the Rathel's pleasure, she passed me nonetheless, for I was unhidden paces behind her. The lady displayed no flaunting, though she had no activity like Eric's running to relieve her of excess energy. She had but a paper, a folded page sealed with wax as though to purchase a servant or other object.

She would not have spoken to me, since all of Eric's words I had obviously heard, but I halted her passage with my own speaking.

"Am I to treasure this achievement? Being God's greatest lady, perhaps I should retain my modesty and merely curtsy at your document, the wishes of a young lady in the area of her own marriage having less influence than passive pen and paper."

"You are not satisfied to be on with yourself, on with God's way with you? To be on with my plans that will end with your deliverance to a homeland as desirable to you as you are to Eric?"

"Should ladies be so inquisitive as to batter their loved ones with queries?" I responded. "Regardless, allow my own wonderment; specifically, might I be curious as to the flaw of your intellect that presumes this paper able to engender the connubial death you crave?"

"You are wise to understand the value of this paper, Alba, for it only describes, not decides, Eric's passion. He believes it important as proof of his emotion, as though to be wielded against his father in verification of his lust. But no proof is required here. Documents are for matters of finance, not for bonds of passion. Take you then this paper, Alba, as proof of my own. Take the thing and treasure it as you will, or burn it from your own desire. And be wise enough to understand that to end Eric's vow, you must destroy not this paper but his heart."

"Oh, Miss Alba, and tremendous excited you must be in receiving a life's offer of betrothal from one such as Eric!"

"But of course, Miss Elsie, do I not reek of enthusiasm?"

Away went the servant's rapture with that response, a more subdued woman replying.

"Your heart is one I'll never be reading, girl, so perhaps it's best I'm not asking what's in there."

"But what of the contents of your own interior, miss? Since doubtless you were present at the enthusiastic occasion within some hidden niche, did you not wonder of the boy's not mentioning me except absurdly? That is to say, for years he might store his lust like pickled herrings, but no mention made he of intervening visits, of my own opinion of the proposed betrothal, no question as to whether I yet resided in the house or were functionally alive."

"Now, Miss Alba, I'm reading a bit of your heart here, and am telling you not to be concerned with the truth of his love. These are only the ways things are being done in better society."

"Now, Miss Elsie, if truly you've an ability to read my heart, you find the same dull thumping as before. As for love, you might recall I've made no mention of Eric's love, only his whereabouts. Neither was this lusty term used by the impassioned one himself."

"Aye, but you're worrying yourself too greatly, lass, about mere companionship. His parents are needing some convincing, I'm told, but the boy's love yet is true. And this will be proven by your 'whereabouts' with the lad for all your lives, as proven

243

by the paper of avowal."

"With all your interest in compositions, miss, next you'll be attending the ruddy opera," I grumbled.

"Ah, lass, and you should not be speaking so of the young man's heartfelt promise," a disappointed Elsie intoned.

"Allow me, then, to revise the composition of my previous speaking. As symbolic of my own heartful appreciation for your supporting this betrothal, I would present you with the very document in measure of my gratitude. There, lying upon the commode: Take the paper, miss, and treasure it as would I."

The sinner nearly swooned, needing to place a hand before her face to keep her heart in, I assumed. As though crippled, Elsie walked to the aforementioned furniture, reaching for the document as though it were holy. But she was unable to touch it, certainly due to all the glory steaming from the ink.

"It's not a scab from the Stigmata, miss, but a mere earthly paper," I told her. "Continue, then, and take the thing."

So she did, lifting the flat pledge as though it were Jesus's toenail clipped for her alone.

"But . . . but, Miss Alba, it's not been opened—the seal remains intact. You're not reading it, child."

"But, of course not, miss. To have ravaged the wholeness of the penned pledge would in some way taint the vow itself, believe ye not?"

A thought to become her own conviction, Elsie holding the paper as though the world's only untouched blossom. And though I would have told her that I hoped she loved the pledge on the paper as much as I loved the pledge in Eric's heart, this was too much mocking, for it was mocking her and Eric and me. Having regained some morality in this sinners' wicked world, I sent her away with the same love she had brought.

"Take the paper, miss, and with it my wish that you might cherish it as much as Eric must cherish me, or at least with the same affection that I hold for you."

In this manner my days proceeded, more comfortably barren of Eric in that Rathel had changed him from companion to future spouse. But was not this ruination of friendship sought by English parents? Friends must become family for society to continue. But I sought no family and had lost my friend. I had also lost my activity, for I no longer attempted to quit the Rathel's world now jointly owned with Eric. Seemingly I was waiting, a term perhaps too active for a phase of hibernation. And grateful I was for blandness, because stagnated heads produce no racing thoughts. Thus, I had no endless attacks of perusal on my attempting to leave London, but not attempting enough. Nevertheless, my waiting precluded Elsie's meeting the magistrate, and Eric's meeting Satan or God, depending upon his soul.

A bit of sweeping I yet enjoyed, though lavender petals were not available in English winter, tea slipping from my hand to anoint the carpet a refreshing pursuit. As though convinced by Elsie to have pity on those emotionally impoverished due to their tormented pasts of ungained spouses, I held no hatred for Rathel and her increasing success. Lord God one day would have Rathel forever in His immediate presence, and since I should live much longer than any English lady, could I not wait for God's greater plans with Rathel to overcome her mundane ideas for me?

In this manner the Rathel had my life proceed. A fortnight was the era here, my senses so insipid that I failed to appreciate winter's cleansing, cathartic snow that hid so much of sinning London. Occasionally my sluggard thinking settled on absent Eric. Thereafter came despondency, for had not our walking Randolph been my finest time in London? Yet not again would we attempt such activity, for Eric had changed. And if he returned, what would the witch do with a boy grown into a man as though that single near-killing had aged him?

In this manner my nights proceeded. Long they were, beginning early, for witches are accomplished at sleeping, having few cathedrals to build, few vengeful lives to plot for years. And they ended late, the witch no longer so concerned with visitors; for if the Eric man showed himself, would not he be dealing with Rathel? If I needed to kill him on the stoop in my version of Gosdale's stabbing to thereby leave London, could not the

245

servants arouse me for the task?

No servant was the sinner to awaken me deep into a night cold enough to have me close my window. And I would not have opened it for that sound against glass, for I knew a man had come to kill me. At once I understood the significance of my having vacated the streets, for beyond my walls were males set to affront, then maim and murder me. But what salvation had I gained in being sealed inside, for had not a man worse than Imbriati come to break the glass of my container and kill the poorly preserved girl?

Not likely, since the man at my seal was Eric.

On its axis I pivoted the pane of glass that would knock him to his death below, the fool having climbed my wall like a cliff. Not so old had he become, for his smile held the mischief of youth. Dim moonlight did not deceive me here, for I also heard a ration of youthful pleasure.

"Excuse me, miss, I've been working nights sweeping chimneys and wonder if you've seen one about that might hire me."

"Impoverished humor for a boy about to fall to his death," I advised.

"Beg pardon, chimneyless lady, but my grip remains secure."

"Less secure, unsooted sir, if I find a chimney with which to smash you in repayment for your attacking my sill."

Eric laughed—and thereafter terrified me, for with that sound he slipped, as though having lost his hold due to meager comedy. He slipped and I instantly reached to grasp his shoulders with both hands, leaning heavily on the windowsill as a brace. But I saw the fallacy with my initial touch, for Eric smiled, not grasping the building for his life, revealing himself as well set and having more poor humor. He also revealed some surprise in my action, startled that I would fling myself through the window to save him.

As though ever calm, I retreated to tell him, "Sir, I will gain no fevered chills from your bizarre activities. Enter, then, or leave so that I might close the breeze."

"I leave then," he stated quietly, then laughed with the same light tone. "Only a person of your fine thinking could imagine the long journey on foot I've shortened by traipsing through

246

snow-filled alleys past people of a type to frighten the devil. And the climb up this wall had to be accomplished properly the first attempt. But off I am this instant, since I fear my father has spies outside my door to peer within during the night and count those persons in my bed. The sum zero found would be a poor number for me. But I come, Miss Alba, because of elephants."

"Elephants, you say? What became of chimneys?"

"The trainer, miss," he said with a type of fear. "With the trainer, what I . . ." And without further sound, devoid of humor, he looked down, and departed.

I leaned through the window, for I would watch him exit. No dream was he, but a night visitor desired; and I viewed him lengthily to study that emotion, to comprehend exactly what I wished of Eric. I did not wish him to leave. Whether boy or man, Eric would not be changed by maturity: Age would not rescind his personality that once developed should be admired. With age came more substantial emotion, and feeling only refined his character, but this I had learned without watching him depart. Along the ledge, then to a brickwork corner providing holds for his extremities, down to a window's cornice, then the ground, a path as supportive as the street, the witch observing each move not to discern his safety, but to share the best moments achieved in an era.

I remained enough of a witch to escape discomfort though winter's wind blew through my window left open so that Eric, upon his return, might enter without waking the household with his glass tapping. An alternate form of announcement was cause to leave the window loose, for proven beforehand was Eric's scent being familiar enough to inform me of his approach, perhaps even during a light sleep. But this was not the smell to jerk me from a sleep deep enough for convincing dreams, though none as real as family.

Mother walked the ocean floor, safe because the sinners above floated in coach boats with emptied harnesses, the pulling sea horses having fled to their true home, finally able to leave after an era of drawing sinners to faires only to have trainers grind their gender organs into sausage, proper treatment for creatures so bizarre as to have abandoned family and promoted evil without Satan's sexual intervention.

Mother walked the ocean floor. I attempted to reach her, failing in that being half sinner, I half floated and was ever above. And though I drew near with great effort, I could never touch her, for the seawater was too thick for me to smell Mother but a single reach away. Then the current changed like smoke above London, carrying my mother's scent to the ocean's surface, and I could only perceive her by floating—by swimming. I finally located her by writing wax documents sealed with ink, following the boy delivering my pledge of salvation. To gain Mother below, I had only to sink, but I had drowned too often and was too much the sinner to remain below long enough to retrieve Mother even from water that had proven me the witch. As I threw myself to the ocean floor only to float to the surface, I smelled her again, then dove below only to awaken.

So vivid was the sensation of having smelled Mother that even when awake in bed with blinking eyes as though stung by salt water I smelled her. Then I sat and understood.

I ran to the window, for outside was a witch. A fresh odor this, and nearby. Not my mother, no, not my dead mother, but a witch as true as I, and here, below, in London.

I pulled a dress over my nightclothes, no shoes—no time for fine dressing, for I was not attending church, but visiting family. I ran to the window, recalling Eric's vertical journey. Sinners had no special ability for climbing their own buildings, so a spry witch should manage.

After turning and stepping out, I learned to look at my feet or the building, but no farther down, for with this view came an unsteady head. Retaining caution and silence, I imagined this structure a tree with square limbs or a clean cliff, down to the grass, run to the gate and through to the street.

Cautiously I moved through the thin, fresh snow with no shoes needed, my eyes sensitive to the minor light of a partial moon. As I moved to the witch, I passed an elder male who ran into the shadows upon sensing my approach, a sinner more frightened than I. The next fearful person I sensed was a sister. A narrow space between buildings' outcroppings held her smell. Nearing the site, I slowed, aware that by then she had sensed my approach. Though I recognized her as my kind, I also discerned that she was no person I knew. To the niche in the brickwork, my heart loud yet seemingly weak, as I turned to my sister with light breathing and apprehensive eyes. The hag was dressed with much clothing, not only to protect from winter's cold, but to cover a visage unpleasant to aesthetic sinners. I could sense that her state was the same as mine, both of us aware that neither belonged in a sinners' city. And though witches hold no danger for each other, the nearer I stepped, the more frightened this sister became; for whereas I discerned her as rich in a witch's features, she saw me as a stone-smooth sinner. Not the coming together of like humans, but the fear of our dissimilarity forced her to speak.

"Great God, now help me—what manner of creature are ye?"

I reached beneath my apparel to my backside. Rubbing my finger against the anus, I spoke to this sister.

"Your senses are God's gifts, and do not lie," I told her firmly. "Take my hand and find that I am the same creature as thee," and I pressed my hand to the stranger's face. "My appearance may be as odd as the sinners', but my smell is your smell. I may look like none you know, but, witch, I am your sister."

She knew upon inhaling, her squinting eyes staring at my featureless face. And though believing the witch, she could not bear to view the sinner; so the woman moved where I could not be seen, reaching to grasp me fully with both arms, her face beside mine as we held one another.

We separated, and I led her deeper into the shadows, farther from the street and the hearing of sinners. Then I quickly spoke, my subject more important than our meeting, for the subject was our future lives.

"Person, why are you here? London is a place to be killing our kind."

"I know this, girl, in that me friends are killed from our wild home north by sinners, and only I the one left. And I am here

249

not for you, but for a Lady Rathel. But upon my coming, I smell you and do not know what to do, such is my confusing."

"I am held by the Rathel for her purposes," I explained, "and currently am unable to escape. How is it you know this sinner?"

"I know of her, but we're not met. Lady Rathel lived with my people for a time, because women elder than me thought to be friends with the sinners, but I kept away except when a magic was needed. Lady Rathel was joyed with this living and learned much of our ways. Then she was gone, and later returned not friendly toward herself, but with a sort of terror inside, the sinners' sort where they must hate. She then had us do a thing for her else be telling our site to men to burn us and thus kill."

"This occurred long before the present?"

"Before your birth, or near it."

"Presently she is forcing a similar pact with me wherein my life is threatened—and so remains. What thing were you to do for her?"

"And we did it, child," she answered as though surprised, "and to this time the only one alive—this Lucinda—is begging of God to forgive us. But the sinner lady would have them kill us all, was her vow, and it was proven by her doing it later."

"What exactly was your act?" I repeated.

"She had us do the magic things of which she had heard. This we knew little of, but witches getting together to do this learn of it. We were to do the thing of having her husband die, and she brought clothes and hair and a footnail of a man, which shows her lack in knowing, for no one knew of using the stuff—it were done of a person's life, not his pieces. We were the ones to lose our pieces. But at first we would not do the thing, especially me, for I would remain apart from the sinner, but could not remain from needy sisters. No killers we be, so we got together with our lives to make her forget her desire to kill, and that ever she knew us. But we did not do what we wished, though we thought so, for the sinner lady was not soon returned. But later she gained us again and with a fury, for we made her forget nothing, but changed her so sickly that she could not have children, ever. So to keep her from bringing the men to our homes and kill us, we had to do the magic thing again—but now to do the first for true, and to kill the man her husband. And we did, Satan take her soul or God forgive us, girl, we did."

The last confession was spoken with a sorrow I could smell, but the witch remained controlled. But as remarkable as her revelations were, they existed in the past. This sister's present was of more import to me.

"Why do you now come to Lady Rathel?"

"I am here because I am driven from my home. All of my friends are dead by sinners from towns that grew too near our wilds. I alone am remaining, and have been moving toward here, with nowhere other to go. So I come for the Lady Rathel and her aid, in that I and my sisters did her bad deed. So might she owe me, else I tell what I and my friends have done to the Lady Rathel's own people. If I die by that, so be it, for the sinners must find who I am one time or the next."

"But you are not fully aware of the sinners' ways, especially Rathel's," I declared. "Her greatest act in payment for your deed was in allowing you to live. Woman, I tell you that Rathel will do no more than have a servant point the direction by which you may exit London. Worse, if she fears you might convey your story to others, Rathel would have her friend the magistrate capture and kill you."

"But what am I to do, girl?" Lucinda asked in presumed failure. "How much longer can I walk in this city without being known? How far beyond it must I go to find a place of peace?"

"For this I have no answer," I confessed. "Where have you lived and slept recently?"

"The city has much holes to hide in, and they're easily found in that the unpeopled areas are my travels."

"And you eat?"

"Enough for a witch."

"The cold for you?"

"Not cold enough for a witch."

"Then remain where you are safe, Lucinda, and return here the following night in this hour. I then shall have either arrangements for your leaving the city, or firm plans for the near future."

251

"And I do this, girl, for on you I smell a city you know more than me. But if you live here without harm in that you look it, do not take trouble from me, in that I will not bring you a pain I have and you do not need."

"You bring no difficulty, but a friend I must love at once, and happily," I told her. "Please return as I ask, Lucinda, and both of us will soon be free of troubles."

We then parted with a grand embrace. Less apprehensive than before, I found with my improved perception that this woman stank. Lucinda was too filthy and had consumed too much trash for food for me to find her odor pleasant. I knew that witches were not the cleanest animals, though I remained uncertain whether my recent sinners' cleanliness was preferable because I was accustomed to it, or because objectively I might prefer the odor. Regardless of preference, I knew that the smell of this witch signifying her type of person amongst God's variety was always and ever beloved. But another truth that pained me was that the better sinners also had an acceptable smell. This acceptance I might not lose, might not have wished to lose, but most of all I wished to regain the fragrance of witches that was their life.

Seventeen

Helpful was Lady Rathel to leave in her chamber coins that I stole with scant regret. Not enough were present to buy Lucinda's freedom, but my first requirement was carriage passage. The sister's freedom would come from later, greater thefts.

Aiding Lucinda to depart would be no practice for my own rejection of London, but more akin to substitution; for if I could not send myself, at least I would have my family conveyed to a new home of safety. If not for my upcoming success, her next home would be Satan's. Yet if Rathel again found me beyond her town house, Elsie's home would be prison. It seemed my very being had come to jeopardize my friends, but above all my friends, I knew to aid the one nearest in blood, the one nearest death.

I chose a new exit. I would feign a visit to the basement, then steal through the rear gate. Beneath my apparel I concealed a cloak and hat, exiting the house to walk past the servants in the kitchen, entering the basement to make enough sound for the sinners to notice my presence. Only Elsie would disturb me in my hiding spot, and Elsie I perhaps could manipulate. Perhaps not. Then I quietly departed, to the gate and gone.

Down the street I walked until finding a brown, open carriage. The driver I hired with stolen, immoral coin. And pleased was the man to hear me requesting his knowledge.

"Oh, and no, miss, but we only provide travel about the city. What you seek is a different sort of service. Those folk have not the fine, sleek carriages we offer, only the large and crude ones needed for long journeys you refer to. But, yes, I can take you to one of which I know, although there might be others."

His would suffice. Then I thought of the assistance received from a previous coachman, previous friend, and was saddened to think that no longer was he either. So I wished him fine employ with another company, one not having to deal with such an opera as the Rathel and her family.

No further acute feelings had I as the carriage proceeded. London before me was scarcely noticed, previously unseen streets with new commons and decent greens, a university building larger though less grand than St. Nicholas Cathedral, ladies and gents and then an old, unpleasant sight: constables at work, males with long staffs and distinctive hats pressing coarse persons away, surely leading them to a prison that even with new inhabitants would house a young witch.

As though my current business were common, I blithely had the coachman wait before the travel agency's unimpressive office. Behind were expansive stalls with horses and those great carriages mentioned by my driver. This rear compound seemed a barn, a farm for nurturing sinners' transport; and how could I apply this travel beneficially when before I had failed? My business, however, was not for me, but a sister. And these folk, curse Satan, were rarer than angels.

I demanded decisiveness to accompany my fear. Succinctly I would learn of this travel and the needed price, then return to buy passage after pawning half of Rathel's household. Therefore, I affected the identity of a young lady in a rush, stepping quickly past those people on the walk and through the flimsy door of the Mortwaite Agency of Travel to find sinning men cursing their peers.

"Aye, and indeed I did have the gent at our carriage in the agreed time, but damned if the bloke did not call me watch a liar. With one hundred bleeding miles to go and he thinks he's late to begin."

This speech came from a male standing before another settled at a desk. Upon noticing me, the latter displayed a severe visage toward his obvious inferior. As the males turned to me, I initiated my part in the theater, facing only the superior sinner as he stood.

"Sir, if I might interrupt your foul communications unworthy of great England and her king, I would discuss my business rather than your previous client's temporal inadequacies."

The inferior looked toward me as though smothered by my words. As the superior spoke to his new patron, the lesser changed his gaze, viewing me now as though meat for the eating rather than a lexicon whose content was unreadable.

"My truest apologies, miss, for the coarseness of this driver. But surely a young lady of your evident quality understands how difficult it oft is to obtain employees of culture."

"Understand I might, but understanding is neither acceptance nor agreement," I countered haughtily, and turned to the inferior as though he were meat for the puking.

With an ungentlemanly grimace, the superior informed this "Percival" that he would be out of the room at once. After bowing to me, the latter complied, appearing chastised though his hunger had not abated. Then I attacked the remaining male.

"Sir, my time is severely brief. You might aid me, then."

"My greatest pleasure, miss. Please be seated," he replied, and ran around to offer a chair—which I accepted—thereafter reseating himself posthaste, looking toward me with a desire to assist.

"Now, what may I do for you this day?"

Enough geography had I learned to know the location of wild places. My selected wilderness I mentioned to this sinner.

"You know of Wales?"

"Yes, miss, I do."

"You provide transport to this area?"

"We do, miss, but few are the towns in this region."

"Aid me, sir, in my lack of knowledge. My position is that I've an aunt in London for a funeral so distraught that she cannot recall her village's name. My intent is to have her returned as quickly as possible to that most comforting site of home. Can this be arranged on your part?"

"Certainly, miss, in that such passage is our occupation here, as well as my great pleasure to so accommodate you. Readily it will be done if your aunt has retained the paper that tells of her departure."

"Unfortunately, sir, she came in the wagon of a friend, who, er, drowned when his carriage tumbled from Hershford Bridge."

"My true condolences for the misfortunes of your family," the man replied, looking toward me with uncertain pity. "Nevertheless, if you can somehow determine the specific village that is your aunt's home, we might yet provide conveyance."

"I had hoped to receive from you a listing of names to spur my recognition. In that my aunt lives on the edge of a wild region, and few are the towns in this Wales, the listing should not be excessive. Thereof what know ye, sir?"After a pause for contemplation, the sinner leapt to his feet, moving to a portal in a wall that he opened, an old man in an adjacent room thereby revealed.

"Jack, have me a map of Wales at once."

"And you will have it, Mr. Wroth," a high, gentle voice replied. Moments later, a map was passed sinner to sinner through the square hole, which was rapidly shut thereafter by the superior.

Placing the paper flat on his desk, Mr. Wroth studied briefly, then applied his finger to a spot and looked up to reply.

"Well, miss, everything in the mountain region is coarse and undesirable for the building of towns. North and south before these Cambrian Mountains are towns reachable by us."

"Therefore, our determination proceeds with your map, sir, in that your stating those townships' names might elicit recollection."

"I shall so state, then, miss," he agreed, and looked down to his map. "Available on our route are the towns of Laerffgniogwrtyd, Wystghllaen-niomb, and Cwynhdaeth Rhaneddfsmawrt."

What a horror to suffer nightmares while awake.

"To what, sir, did you say?" I asked, for those names spoken were incompatible with my hearing, much less my mouth.

"The towns of Wystghllaenniomb, Cwynhdaeth Rhaneddfsmawrt, and Laerffgniogwrtyd, miss."

"Oh. So I thought. These towns, then, are near unpopulated locales?"

"They are, miss, in that not far beyond all is virtual wilderness."

"Well, sir, in that they all sound so similar, what might the difference be? Which is most remote?"

"I would have to judge, miss, that they are equally remote," Mr. Wroth determined while studying his map.

"Then, sir, which town is the nearest and most easily achieved?"

"That, miss, would be Cwynhdaeth Rhaneddfsmawrt, which is nearly due west, and a fine, small town to which we may provide conveyance."

"Sir, you now have struck me with a certainty of recognition. Yes, this, er, this town you mentioned is unquestionably the site I seek. To be absolute in my identification, however, kindly write the name upon a paper that I might verify it with my aunt."

Pleased he was to comply.

"Additionally, sir," I continued while reaching to receive the unreadable paper, "because my aunt requires her home to cure her increasing despair, some urgency we have as to her leaving without delay. Therefore, what day is most reasonable for her departure, Mr. Wroth?"

Before I had concluded my query, the sinner was delving into a book of bound listings, looking closely with his eyes and a finger.

"A coach goes so far as Lucansbludge this Tuesday next. Space yet exists for one or as many as two persons and their baggage. An additional yet nominal fee will allow us to take your aunt thereafter to Wales, the further sum required since she alone will occupy the coach to Cwynhdaeth Rhaneddfsmawrt. Therefore, miss, an advance payment will allow me to add your family member to our schedule."

"The total sum might therefore be?" I asked, and Mr. Wroth stated a quantity that revealed the limits of my tutoring, for I knew not whether the amount was parsimonious or extreme, knew not how to translate his pounds into quids.

"Very well, sir, I leave," I stated, and rapidly stood.

"But, miss, I assure you the fee is especially reasonable," Wroth asserted as though fearful of losing his only income. Finding his reasonableness believable, I continued with our dealing.

"Sir, I have no argument with your fee. But you say no coach departs sooner."

"No, and I am sorry, miss, but no coach of ours can leave before Tuesday for this section of the island."

"What island, sir, is that of your reference?"

"Why, the main island of Great Britain, miss."

"Oh yes, of course. I was thinking of another island. Know ye of Man's?"

"Certainly, miss, Man's Isle is well known."

"And which is the nearer journey, Man's Isle or . . . this?" I asked, waving my paper.

"Cwynhdaeth Rhaneddfsmawrt is quite the nearer, miss."

"Very well. Then I return tomorrow with your fee, its receipt to expectedly induce you toward formally arranging my aunt's being scheduled to . . ." and I waved my paper.

"At my personal doings, miss, the arrangements shall be made.

257

A draft from your bank will be most welcome."

"I ruddy well wager it would, sinner," I mumbled incomprehensibly.

"To beg your pardon, miss, I failed to hear."

"I said a good day I wish you," I concluded, and turned to depart, stepping away as though in a race, since Wroth desired to leap from his desk and open the door for me. But I won, onto the street and into my waiting carriage.

Before I could begin to wonder what item of Rathel's to steal and where to sell it, a man came running alongside the carriage, begging for the young miss to please halt as he waved his hands. I had the coachman fulfill the sinner's request, for this was the Percival male of crude linguistics from Wroth's office.

"Sir, your business with me I must demand," I demanded.

"Ah, miss, and I can get your auntie to Wales before Tuesday," he replied with some respirational difficulty.

"And how might this be, sir, in that Mr. Wroth cannot?"

"In that I've a carriage of my own that I drive as well as driving the company's. For a minor fee I can have your aunt departing for Wales tomorrow. If you come with me to my office at the agency, I shall begin the papers."

He then opened the carriage door, and held forth his hand.

"Have your man leave, in that we've a company of coaches," Percival stated, "and I shall return you to any locale within the city you please."

Being desperate or deluded, I agreed. With Rathel's coins, I paid the coachman his due without displaying my distaste for the nasty metal, receiving a tip of his hat but no thanks in that I was too ignorant to provide him with a gratuity. As I stepped from the carriage without accepting Percival's hand, the rejected coachman departed. Somehow I believed that the driver whose employ I had ruined would not have left me so easily.

"This way, miss, and I'll be careful with my leading to avoid scuffing your shoes," Percival promised.

And so he was, looking down to the street's surface and walkway with but the rare glimpse behind to see that I followed. Followed to the stables for horses, the garage for coaches and their repair.

"Thank Jesus for mild winters," the male said, seeing that no snowy slush existed to soil me. "This way, miss," he instructed, looking about in a manner I considered furtive, as proven by his next speaking.

"Ooh, and we should wait here a moment, miss," he said after peering around a corner. "An unpleasant person is there we're best to allow pass."

We soon continued, Percival leading me past a massive coach with missing wheels and into the realm of horses. Other men were perceivable in the near distance, but my guide's path precluded our being seen. The rich smells of animal bodies and their droppings were reduced by the wooden crates called stalls containing the horses. Through the rear of the stables to a small room with a bed, boots, and the smell of this Percival, my night sister's fragrance exalted in compare.

He had me enter first, then closed the door behind.

"My, what a poor office you have," I observed.

"My business is simple and needs no fancy desk."

"Business with a fool can be simple, can it not," I replied, and turned in a rush to the door, grasping the latch to run out, fumbling with the mechanism as usual. Finally I had determined that although a certain illegality was ever expected to be part of this business, my being alone with this man meant the enterprise might be painful as well.

Then he attacked me. Before I could open the door, the sinner grasped my shoulder. Surprisingly, however, Percival after that first contact released me, standing away to speak rapidly.

"Please, miss, you've come this far, please hear me out—for your own benefit."

I paused. Percival stood across the small room, making no move against me. Because I said nothing, the male continued.

"I think I know you, miss. I think I know your social place is unusual to follow a stranger into the stables. Therefore was the cause for your accepting Mr. Wroth's huge fee. And I think that when you made to get it from a bank, you would have difficulty. But my fee is more reasonable."

"Your fee for what?"

"Why, for taking your auntie to Wales in a coach with my own horses."

"And what sum would you ask?"

"Why, I would have you lie with me, miss."

259

Not wholly predictable was his price since he began by asking for his desire instead of grasping it as had his brethren.

"I know little of such things, mister sinner, but know I can expect no conveyance for my aunt if you receive payment in advance."

"But, miss, I have papers for booking," he asserted, and stepped to a table by his bed, attacking a paper with a pen and inkwell, signing and blotting his writing before handing me the form.

"If I do not hereafter complete my agreement exactly as per my promise, miss, you are encouraged to impart my failure to Magistrate Naylor himself."

I accepted the paper. I could not be certain of its legal aspects, but the sinner's encouragement to set the magistrate upon him seemed significant. But I continued with our business because of a more remarkable fact, for this male had written the name of the selected Welsh town exactly as had Wroth.

"And to lie with you," I asked warily, "is this not what the criminals call 'fucking'?"

"Oh, and it is, miss, damned straight—I mean, I mean, so wise you are," Percival replied weakly as though I had beaten him; and did I not sense the first odors of the male's perturbed bottom?

"During which, as I understand, you are to insert your baby stick into my child port and rub it about awhile."

"Oh, and yes, miss, how wise you are, and how grateful I would be for a bit of this rubbing."

I thought of Mother's description of procreation, that it was harmless to witches, though the mad sinning men were ludicrously enthralled with the activity, their women disappreciative beyond the production of children, which seemed sensible to me. Then I thought of Marybelle's examining my innards, and recalled the considerable pain.

"Show me this thing you would insert within me," I ordered.

At once the man began tearing at his pants, tearing at a lump forming beneath the fabric, this growth in a male's clothing one I had seen before. So prejudiced was I as to consider Eric's sex smell cleaner, virtually decent. And though I was unfamiliar with Eric's sex flesh, I next learned of Percival's; for he pulled forth a part of his body resembling a large finger made red and tender from the nail's being ripped away, this little limb attached to a patch of body hair beneath the man's belly. Compared to Marybelle's

260

hand, this extremity seemed of no consequence.

"At least the thing is of no ponderous size," I mentioned.

"Yes, miss. Thank you, miss," Percival returned.

I thought of stealing valued items from the Rathel and attempting to pawn them. I thought of walking to that burnt part of London, thought of being discovered by Rathel with her clock, thought of failing at these miserable activities again and again. Therefore, I asked this sinner:

"What further process do we now commence?"

"Why, why, why you lie on the bed with no clothes and I lie on top of you."

"That is preposterous," I exclaimed. "I will not have your odorous bulk upon me and squashing."

"Well, well, well . . ." the male continued, thinking at the greatest rate possible as he stared between his baby stick and the floor. "You might lie on the bed's edge and I will kneel before you upright."

"I see," I returned. "But since you have use for only one restricted part of my person, I shall expose no more than that area," I conveyed, and proceeded to fulfill my notion. All of these garment layers I pulled up, my pantaloons going down. Then I waddled to the bed's edge whereupon I sat, partially reclining with most of my weight supported by my elbows.

"Oh, yes, miss," the sinner cried as though moved by a great minister's sermon. Then, as described, he knelt before me. Because of the impediment of my underthings collected about my ankles, I found it best to lift my feet above the sinner's head to allow him access to my arse, so to speak. As the man moved near, I viewed his sex stick through my vertical thighs, saw a drop of sticky liquid at the tiny hole or slit in its end, and I thought of the baby fluid Mother had mentioned; and from stuff like snot Lord God makes babes?

With some groping of a shaking hand, the driver grasped his pinkish limb and poked that body hair of mine corresponding to his. After tiny, curled hairs loose from my person inadvertently adhered to his stick due to its viscid liquid and the master's inaccurate aim, the sinner managed to gain the proper receptacle; whereupon he entered me with some force — and some discomfort on my part, until I understood that the muscles there should not be constricted. Thereafter, I had no pain, though Percival seemed about to die; for he proceeded with his rubbing, moving his limb-stick to and fro as though unable to determine whether it should best remain within or be removed. His face was a passion I had never seen on a grown sinner, more like a child at play having harmed himself. Then the sinning male leaned heavily against my legs, reaching to grasp my bosom.

Harshly I shoved his shoulders and gave him my greatest scowl.

"Sinner, leave go with your hands! Lean against the bed if you fear collapse. Your lust shall not be my peril, so fall on the floor, not me!"

As though drunk, the unsteady driver complied, his hands going to the bed's edge for support.

I would not look to him further, not caring to see signs of his unusual pleasure, but the man was sickening me. After moments of his pumping, I grew weak, collapsing upon my back, head lolling to one side, my feet and their surrounding apparel falling before Percival as though a curtain shielding an operatic actor from his suffering audience. And though my torso was limp, my bottom felt hard, all my blood seemingly collected there to surround the attacker, for the flesh was hot. My baby region felt like stone, and there my pain gathered and intensified, for the muscles about my pee hole and buttocks grew tight, then cramped, so cramped I felt agony, frightful agony. This pain was not from the male's limb moving within me, but due to my own response, for my muscles would not relax despite my effort to go calm about my crotch. The tightening and the pain increased until I could not even attempt to shove the sinner away. I became delirious, my eyes unable to focus, for all my energy was stolen by this sex. And here was a dream, a nightmare from Jonsway instantly, acutely returned, one of a male with more authority but equal agony. But here I suffered reality, and I prayed for the crushing spasms to subside; for if the torment did not soon end, I felt I would die.

Finally the acute, concentrated agony subsided, only firm contractions of my baby muscles continuing, leaving me with a dull pain that was filling, though not murderous as the former sensation had been. After a moment of deep breathing, I sat, then noticed that the male had pulled away from me, now lying on the floor, apparently asleep on his face. If his pain had been as great as mine, his fainting was understandable. Impossible to comprehend was how sinners could seek such activity, could enjoy this procreating. If the activity were not agonizing for the male, but desirable as alleged, why had this man collapsed? But no intellection was within me, merely fleeting thoughts passing through my delirium as I stood unsteadily, determining to quit the sinner before he called out for aid or understanding. From my own distress, I had no concern for the sinner's: He could heal himself as had I. Thinking only enough to take the signed paper, I folded the form and left. Through the door, the stable, I reversed Percival's path to gain the street.

Stepping along the walkway, I soon regained clear deliberation, and halted. Though my movements had been so slow that I was either demonstrably ill or very much the lady, I had drawn scant attention, since my clothing was barely ruffled and my face stern, not astounded. But how much walking would I have to undertake? No carriage awaited me, and I saw none for hire. The sex sinner had promised to convey me home, but I would rather die than return and ask him, even if he were conscious again. And I could not ask Mr. Wroth, for how to explain my unhidden illness? I am sick, Mr. Wroth, from being unaccustomed to fucking your drivers. So I remained, leaning against a storefront without idea or energy until a man approached, reaching out to kindly touch me as he inquired of my health.

"I am well. Be away, sinner," I growled, and leave my sight he did.

I remained leaning against the cut clapboard of a building until a pair of finely dressed elder women approached with the same concern as the previous man, but without that faint odor about them that I would never again accept. So when they asked of my health, I feigned no strength, but replied weakly, truthfully.

"Ill I am, madams, and in further difficulty beyond health."

"What is your problem, dear child, for of course we would aid?" one lady returned.

"I am out of the household without my mother's permission. My carriage is departed, and I find none to hire, and in fact feel that I've scarcely the strength to hail one regardless. I would walk home if not so distant, but it seems I can scarcely stand."

There would be no walking as long as they had a coach. They

had a coach from their own stables as though a company for conveyance themselves; and as though angels they insisted upon conducting me home and summoning a physician if need be. With all honesty, I told them I praised God for their gracious concern, but no physician would be required, only my own bed. The ladies assisted me into their vehicle, understanding when I closed my eyes that I was unable to respond to their inquiring of my difficulty. Therefore, these sinners kind as any witch asked nothing further of me. Once before the Rathel's, they insisted upon guiding me to the doorstep, but I had strength enough to convince them of impossible difficulties to befall me if discovered by Mother. Only assist me from the coach, and God's graces and my greatest thanks go with you forever.

My walking was adequate as I stepped to the town house, turning to wave at the departing women and forcing myself to smile where I had no such strength, but a kindly expression was the least they were due. As the sinners moved along the street, I moved through the rear gate, then to the basement and within. Beneath covered furniture I concealed my papers and hat, then lay on the cold ground that soothed my hot illness, falling asleep with no concern for punition.

"Ah, girl, and you're in the basement again all day like a mole, and I know you're not eating. Lying on the ground in this cold will be taking all your warmth and make you ill, lass. Are you never learning even that?"

Above me was an oil lamp attached to Elsie, who was shaking me awake. Again, it was effortless to tell a tale when truthful and beneficial to me.

"Miss, I have grown ill, so much that I am unable to climb the steps."

As though angered, Elsie placed the lamp upon a box and turned my face to peer carefully at my features, thereby determining my state.

"Aye, and you're sagging in the face and nearly panting, lass. It's your eating, it is. Either you've had nothing for too long or else you've been eating too many of those scallions. Or — pray God, no — you've eaten some crawly to upset a person. Whatever, child, you'll be throwing this nasty stuff up worse than you throw up the meat you hate, and then you'll be feeling better. Come, then, you're making it up the steps with me aid, are you not, child?"

"With your aid, miss, I am," I responded, and together we moved to my chamber.

We passed the Rathel. She inquired as to the difficulty, and Elsie conveyed her presumptions regarding bad food. The mistress asked whether a physician should be summoned, but the healer Elsie was offended, replying in the negative. Neither had she need of further servants, for Elsie had always managed well with me.

"We have no spare girls in this household," Rathel countered. "I have no extra daughter and you have no extra lass. I believe you would agree with this assessment, and therefore I hope your justifiable pride in your own fine abilities would not disallow your having me send for a physician if one is truly needed."

With her supporting arm around me, Elsie looked to the Rathel more intently than I had ever seen, and between these women long together I viewed an understanding they well accepted yet seldom displayed.

"I have no extra lass, mistress, and you've no extra daughter. And there's not enough pride in God's world to keep me from begging for any help needed to cure her. So she'll be coming along fine for me, or I'm running for the doctor myself."

Into my chamber with the irreplaceable lass who was disrobed by a sinner finding blood on me where I should have been private. This wise woman was aware of the situation.

"Aye, and you've become a woman, Miss Alba. This is no aid to your feeling ill, likely much of the cause." Then she departed, returning with a warm, wet cloth with which she cleansed me.

"We'll be talking more of this later, child, and I'll be showing you how to dress so as not to be staining your clothing when this next occurs."

She then had me drink some nasty syrup to draw a grimace from me, which of course pleased nurse Elsie.

"The worse it tastes, the better it's working," she crooned. "You'll be feeling better if this clears your stomach."

The servant physician was then satisfied to leave, but I stopped her at the door. I thought of the ladies on the street. They had received true expressions of my gratitude. Elsie now received further truth, in this instance perhaps too much.

"I hope you do not mind, miss, but I find I have to love you."

Here was my syrup for Elsie, for it drew from her a grimace as well as tears. And she left like the sinning man against me, so pleased yet seeming in misery.

Into the night, I reposed without sleep until the healer's material began to function, for I felt a rising within me, an uncomfortable swell as though from food's sickness. So I rose to move to my chamber pot, voiding myself of such material that part of my innards seemed rejected. But Elsie had been correct, for her syrup and my vomiting delivered a true improvement in my feeling, for thereafter I was well enough to sleep. Sleep too comfortably, too deeply.

My only dream was horrible, for it was virtually real. Therein I had a friend to gain, my greatest friend. Unseen she was yet well smelled by me as I walked in the dark, traversing bridges to lose me even when well, but I was not. In my illness, every step increased my pain so greatly that without ever approaching this friend, I became so agonized as to faint and fall asleep as though dead. Despite my great desire to rise, I was unable to awaken, remaining alive in my mind but dead in the body. When finally I awoke, however, it was not within this dream but from my true sleeping, and outside was morning light. Then I knew the dream to be genuine, for that lost night held the sister whom I had vowed to meet and to save. And though I leapt from bed and ran to the window, further moves would be useless, for all my sense and every perception told me that the witch outside was gone.

Eighteen

"So, are you feeling better now, girl, in that you're walking to the window, or so bad you're about to be hurling yourself out?"

"I am feeling less ill, miss, for which I must thank you. And I have no intent of moving through this window."

"Then you'll be returning to your bed, lass, in that you've nothing better to do this day than rest."

"Perhaps I do not, Miss Elsie. Perhaps not."

She had brought me water, a servant's daily task used by this miss as a mechanism for entry, as though her true purpose were not to examine the patient. After satisfied Elsie filled my urn and departed, I considered my response to her, contemplating my needed activities of the day. Seeking Lucinda would be useless, for the witch would not have remained into day's light. Reasonably, however, she would return this evening although I had not been present as promised. After all, I had informed her of my own subjugation by a sinner. Assuming her return, I could proceed to acquire funds for Percival. Was not his paper valid? These documents from promising men collecting about me like flies on the chamber pot — should I value this latest as I did the first? And if its worth be nil, should I then expose that mutual act of bodies to Mr. Wroth or to Naylor? But if only married folk in England were to be partaking of such rubbing, was I not a tart and subject to punition? If sufficiently illegal, I would be imprisoned by the magistrate regardless of the driver's felony. Here, perhaps, was the factor to allow Percival such ease in threatening himself with Naylor. Therefore, I should first determine the validity of Percival's document. If it be valueless, then return to the Rathel's, steal much wealth, attempt to sell it without being discovered by the mistress or rejected by the broker, then again to Mortwaite to pay Wroth's price. Typical business in my sinning London life.

As I stood at the window in my reverie of uncertain contemplation, Delilah came to fulfill her daily chore of emptying the household chamber pots. With mine came a warning.

"I was most unpleasantly ill in there last night for which I do apologize," I told her.

"Can't be worse than what is normal in them things," she muttered. "I've learned by now to look little and breathe less when I deal with the pots, with folks sick or well."

She then took the ceramic pot to a bucket in the corridor covered with one cloth and situated upon another to catch the slopping. Dumping my pot into the bucket, Delilah seemed well able to prevent her sensing the materials, in that no retching ensued, the servant then returning my container empty, on to the next.

My reverie ended with the decision that, yes, I had more important things to do that day than rest in bed. Again I must pursue severe activities, and I wondered if every aspect of achieving a new home for my sister would begin as easily as Wroth and end as impossibly as Percival.

Elsie returned after I dressed, mentioning that she was off to the market for foodstuffs; and I would not be attending even if I so desired, not with my weakness and the cold outside, but was anything special to be brought me? No, nothing special desired with the yet-improper stomach.

I looked through the window as Elsie stepped across the street with her basket. Yes, I desired to accompany her, to partake of an enjoyable, unimportant journey without danger. No journeys for me that day would be less than profound if recent history be a measure. But Miss Elsie's excursion became no less provocative than my last. Scant minutes later, I heard her moaning outside, and saw the servant with her basket being dragged home by constables as she called out for her Mistress Amanda.

Downstairs I ran as Theodosia and Rathel opened the door.

Out of sight I remained, having an adequate view and excellent hearing. On the stoop stood a pair of average constables and an exceptionally frightened woman appearing small and useless between the men as though a creature destined for slaughter and well aware of her fate. At once the speaking ensued, the visiting authorities first.

"A good day is wished to you, ma'am, and is it that you are the Lady Amanda Rathel?"

She was, and why had they her servant in their hands?

"Instructed out we were at sunrise to gather all women likely demonic, in that witches may be in our city, in that yesterday came a crime as only one with the devil could do."

With true affront, the mistress declared, "This woman is a servant of mine and entrusted with the entire household. Moreover, not a moment the previous day did she leave this building, and for her I vouch absolute godliness. If you lack acceptance here, then speak with Sir Jacob Naylor himself, for he and I are colleagues."

"Lady Rathel, your name is known to us as well, and well regarded. We ask not of you, but of this woman, that she is of your house as she asserts. Learning now that this be true, we return her, and suggest you retain the servant inside until more comes of the problem mentioned."

"And what is this crime of which you speak?" Rathel inquired.

"A man was killed in a demonic manner not to be described to a lady," was the official response.

Rathel then pulled her servant away as though a toy misused by a greedy friend, patting Elsie's back and telling the poor miss to return to her room and rest. Theodosia accompanied Elsie from the foyer. Unkindly I concealed myself from Elsie's sight, for although I would not refuse her my sympathy, this demonic situation must first be heard by the demon.

Again Rathel confronted the constables, speaking with less passion, now more professionally.

"Through Magistrate Naylor you might know that my life is one of confronting witches. Therefore, you shall convey to me details appropriate for my expertise."

After sharing a look, the constables acquiesced.

"A man Percival Bitford was killed most sexually, in that his male member was torn off his body and too much of his blood lost for him to live further."

"Perhaps this man had enemies," Lady Rathel returned. "Humans are also channels for Satan's evil."

"Sir Jacob is thinking witches."

Rathel looked to the constables, but had no denial. When she spoke again, her words were final.

"The magistrate knows my home. I know witches and servants. I wish you a good day," she concluded, and closed the door, turning to walk away.

She sought Miss Elsie to soothe her, telling the servant not to broach this story to Alba, for the girl's weak condition would not bear the distress. Elsie, of course, would tell no one, ever, of being arrested for wickedness, tell no other servant and never Miss Alba, dear Miss Alba.

Rathel did not come to me. Was she so expert as to know I would have no comprehension of my own witch's act? Of course, she would not mention the event to me, lest I be influenced to avoid performing the same activity with Eric, exactly as Rathel had intended and asserted in verity from the first. But men were all sinners, no more, and killing them would send their souls to God. Besides, if the specified person were ended, would I not thereafter be conveyed to a land where no sinners existed to kill? What care had I for these folk with more of Satan's evil than any witch?

I had never seen Elsie so frightened. Had she been present with her evil lass, her absolutely evil charge, perhaps she would have noted our new similarity; for my own fear was unparalleled, even greater than when Mother was taken to her burning, or when I awaited death in Jonsway. Those horrors had come from without, but this latest was so inherent to me that I felt responsible for all those previous deaths, not merely Percival's. So foul was my core that surely it permeated my past, an evil implemented in the forgotten real, and obscurely revealed in dreams.

Elsie would have discerned no great difference with her sight, though surely that hot blood burning my head made the white witch somewhat pink, rare meat she was, unique in her corruption. Standing by the window, I thought of Elsie's words, of my being so ill I might leap. And I had the thought, but knew that Satan or Rathel would catch me. Then I thought of Percival and was relieved that no more dealings could I have with him or his company. I thought of my pain and of his, and knew I had felt both during the event, the dying, and now felt them again: not in my crotch, but in my heart and my head and my spirit, and this was Satan's glory. I felt pain and impossibility, for I could *not* have killed that man. I could not have killed any person, not with my body—the idea was absurd. But the intensity of that pain now seemed fit for death, and how dead the driver seemed in retrospect. How deadly the Rathel was to know this all along and use my trait as a weapon, use me as a weapon: a person more vile than even Satan could imagine. A person so wicked as to have killed a man by plucking away his most prideful part and letting him bleed for it. And I felt it. I felt myself locked onto that male and felt our pain and felt his piece pulled loose and that piece was my brain. I felt Percival's blood oozing away and it was my blood, for I felt my heart being pulled from my body. I felt the pain of my killing, and as well as God Himself I knew I deserved it, deserved the agony again and felt it so fully that thereafter nothing in my life existed but that horror returned. But I did not suffer enough, for I continued living; whereas that poor, average sinner had not. I felt abject moral misery so completely that I was nothing but that concept, an idea of evil so pure that only a devil could bear it. But I was only a girl, one hating herself enough to die, but Satan only let me faint.

That day I remained ill, but from no distressed stomach. Each moment awake or partially aware I prayed God for understanding, believing deeply that within His wisdom some reason existed for the incredible evil in me, a divine plan that let me love both Him and humans, yet kill the latter. But I received peace only upon accepting Lord God instead of seeking from Him the aid of explanation. Only then did I approach divinity, understanding that a design only God could devise He alone could comprehend; and this was satisfaction enough. Then, exhausted with my religion, I managed to sleep through the uncomfortable afternoon. When I awoke, I found myself no less evil, but no less a part of God's enduring plans.

Evening had come. I arose to stand by that desperate window, aware that outside lay my future that soon I would need to follow again. Beginning my preparation, I applied effort to tidy my apparel as though the killer were a lady; for in this world of God above and Satan everywhere, a lady she best be. I even brushed my hair, then quit my chamber to show God I yet accepted myself as part of His world, not Satan's. Unfortunately, Satan seemed to be part of me, for my bottom was evil, the musculature there so sore as to affect my walking, for I limped as though elderly. Was this, then, the cause of old sinners walking poorly: a life of sex coupling? Sex killing?

Though the evening was not late, Rathel and her servants had retired, all but Elsie, who met me downstairs in her dressing robe as though waiting. Unimpassioned but pleasant was our meeting, wherein we mutually determined that each of our conditions had improved; and, yes, perhaps we were hungry. Entering the kitchen, Elsie was thoughtful enough to eat only an apple instead of rendering me ill with meat. For Elsie's benefit, pomegranate instead of onion was my meal.

As Elsie and I departed the kitchen, the servant proceeded to her room. As though an insect in the evening, I was drawn to the light of her doorway. Following the miss, I stood outside as she entered. Never had I been within nor viewed this chamber. Elsie moved to her bed and sat. I had never seen her settled upon a surface all her own, and she was mildly prideful in having a place, any place, though this room was the size of my armoire, with a tiny bed and tiny chair, and two shelves and all of Elsie's things: her crafts and comb and Bible, a clean and neat apron the next day she would be rubbing with her fingertips. One oil lamp whose light filled the small space, and I saw myself there. Upon a round table lay a crocheted doily with a pamphlet of Jesus, a dried flower from our garden, and a ball of black hair tied with a ribbon. Elsie's hair was brown.

I looked toward my friend. Instantly I would have exchanged chambers with her, for clearly we were misplaced. Elsie would have loved the grand expanse of my room, and I would have

272

been more comfortable in a modest space. I looked only at Elsie, and cursed her properly.

"Sleep perfectly, miss, and rest as you deserve," I said.

She was embarrassed. I departed, the servant and I wishing one another a good evening. Only Elsie's, however, would soon end. Midnight for the witch was a literal center.

By the window that connected me to the sinners' world, I awaited a sister's smell, but none came. Perhaps the witch was present a wind away, her odor masked by a breeze. Believing that Eric would not be so foolish as to come on a day whose bright hours had seen officers collecting sinister women outside my door, I had concern only for my sister whom I prayed to appear one additional night, bringing me new opportunity. I then departed through that plane incapable of separating me from the wickedness without, for did not the devil have a daughter within?

Down the wall with no slippage. Across the street through a minor snow and to the site where my sister again would be found, please. The same aged sinner of my previous journey was so gracious as to have returned, a consistency I prayed for in Lucinda. Again he scurried away, frightened that I might be danger. How wise was this man. The person of my true concern, however, was not present. For hours I walked the street hoping to gain Lucinda's odor, but no person was sensed, sinner or sister. Near dawn, after I had stopped myself from falling as though waking from a flying dream, I returned to the Rathel's. Though exhausted, I traversed the wall unharmed, all the while wondering how to find Lucinda again, crawling into my chamber to find a sinner asleep on my floor.

As I stepped past him to the door, Eric was startled from his sleep as though on the street half-conscious looking for his kin. He sat upright to watch me lock the door to exclude Elsie if she were to awaken before the sun to look in on me. What a joy the Rathel would receive from finding Eric here. But what a disaster for Elsie's heart.

"Surprised I am, miss, at your being out this hour," Eric quietly stated, standing as I turned from the door.

"I explain before you ask, sir," I told him. "Outside I was to meet a poor friend of my true family to describe the path

273

whereby she might exit London. These things are done at night for the same cause as yours, for my friend would suffer greatly if discovered by superiors."

I then sat on a chair, bending to remove my shoes, having a true need to sleep and beginning my preparation despite the present guest. Before the first dead cowskin was loosened, however, I came aware of the tart move I was making, even God's greatest lady no more than a common wench to tempt a man by revealing her lower extremes. At once I ceased, but surely Eric had seen an ankle. As I sedately dropped my hem to the floor, did I not smell from my visitor an odor usually present when men were about to die by me?

Eric turned from the semi-lady, distracted or attempting to appear so.

"Did you succeed in aiding your friend exit our city?" he asked.

"My friend was not present," I replied. "In that she is disheveled and unhandsome, I fear the constables have taken her for a witch, arresting her as they did our Miss Elsie."

Surprised, Eric quickly turned to me despite the potentials of stockings revealed.

"Surely the latter is not yet detained."

"Surely not, in that Rathel was a fury to take her servant from the men, officials or not."

"But if your friend is detained, can you not as Lady Amanda's daughter vouch for her bonafides?"

"Without the complexities of deep exegesis, let me inform you, sir, that entities in this world exist more convincing to constables than I."

After staring toward me a moment, Eric stepped to the window, looking out as I had earlier and seeing the same, viewing nothing but his thoughts.

"Might I provide some aid to help with your friend's departure?"

"Accept my gratitude, sir, but I find no use in your involvement."

Looking through that window, the young man seemed full distracted.

"I leave, then, miss," he sighed. "In fact, I have come for the

274

purpose of describing my departure, for not only your sill but London sees me exit."

"Interpret your riddle, sir, in that quitting London has become a horror for me."

"The purpose, ostensibly, is to convey me to education, when in fact the object is to remove me from you."

"Who so takes thee, master?"

"My father and the wife, who've made payment for exclusive education in Italy. This was expected and gratefully appreciated before, but no longer. Not when it comes a year early. The true goal is not to increase my intellection, however, but to decrease my exposure to you. The parents, though unaware of these meetings, yet read my heart as though Jesus my soul."

I believed his speaking, though it seemed unreal, a dream. Eric was being forced to leave London while I remained a prisoner? Shaking my head as though to clear the clogging injustice, I asked of his travel.

"You depart for the Continent? How far removed, sir, and for what duration?"

"A brief journey over water, then days on land, the stay to last for years. Truly my parents hope for me to find and wed a peer newly met in Europe, but I am heretofore betrothed. You might know of this."

"I do," was all I needed to say, for Eric had not ended his speaking.

"What your feelings thereof might be, I know not, shan't ask, and in a way I find irrelevant. For in fact, I am dispassionately convinced that after years when I return to London, I will come to you."

He then moved through the window and down, not having looked toward me again.

"I'll be wedding no other," I sighed, and nearly laughed. Then that faint smile to have come over me was lost, my ironical feeling exchanged for melancholy. And I was confused because I knew not whether this dejection came from my failure to remain emotionally apart from sinners, or merely because I would be without Eric.

* * *

275

About me bubbled fumes effervescent in the air, animal fat and blood turned to acidic vapor that etched my sensibilities. I continued with my chore, sitting on a simple stool on the coarse kitchen floor, the falling, green husks of the corn unnatural to this fumy atmosphere. With my back to the stove across the room, I wondered if Delilah used excessive heat in her cooking as punition for my being in her kitchen, the girl who puked at excellent pork when these servants were pleased to get bones for soup. Though interested only in planning Lucinda's exit of London, the husking an exercise to relax me, I found myself again in a conflict with English society. Instead of contemplating my true family of witches, unavoidably I was attempting to measure these sinners.

Then came the shouting.

"Ah! you're burning the beef, ignorant woman!"

I turned to see Theodosia and Delilah congregate before the unattended stove. One woman with a thick cloth removed the large skillet from the heat, setting it aside as the other peered closely at its contents with eyes stinging worse than mine.

"It is most black on the bottom and that which is not is surely overcooked," Theodosia reported. "And you know how much the mistress detests unrare meat."

"Perhaps we can dice it into some concoction and thus save the stuff," Delilah submitted, her cohort responding with derision.

"Best worry, woman, about saving your own hide and not this blackened beast's which you have ruint."

Delilah's reply was a glimpse more of guilt than glaring. Then up from the wet ashes she looked and to the kitchen door, for there was the final servant, one recently polishing metal and therefore without my accompaniment.

"Aye, and you'll not be worrying about the upcoming meal, in that the mistress is not attending. Off she is with constables to be aiding the magistrate."

"Gone the night she is?" Delilah asked. "Out of London? We've not seen that in a time."

"And you're not seeing it again this day," Elsie replied. "Likely she's returning before evening, was her goal, time enough to be preparing a proper meal for our weary mistress."

"Ah, the relief God grants well-meaning folk," Delilah sighed, and moved to dump the burnt mess outside where cyclical dogs eating house to house might find it.

Elsie departed, and I followed her involving news. Noticing my rapid standing, the remaining sinners wondered of my rush.

"And you are complete, Miss Alba, with your chore?" Delilah asked as I gathered the stripped corn.

"Done, miss, and on to another."

"You need not be doing these things, Miss Alba," Theodosia added as I scooped the bright green remains into the mulching box. "The mistress might not relish her young lady peeling vegetables."

My disturbing the organic mass brought forth fresh odors of old food, old plant remains, a smell enough for me to notice above the reduced fat steaming the room.

"I trust I am not improper in aiding the preparation of food that I also eat," I stated with a smile, wiping my hands as I stood paces from these servants, a proper space for women other than Elsie.

"You're a helpful lass, though, and thank you, miss," Delilah added.

Another smile and no further speaking as I left. Solely concerning me was that Rathel might again be the determiner of a witch's life. As though I might learn something from Rathel's last position, I ran to the entrance foyer, but sensed nothing. I therefore waited, an enterprise not always satisfying even to people as long lived as mine.

I lingered near that temporary hole. Not within sight of Elsie was I when she heard the coach halt before the household to divest itself of our mistress. After Rathel entered and spoke briefly with Elsie about weariness, the sinners separated, the witch stepping out from behind a curtain to grasp the lady's hand and smell it.

Startled Rathel attempted to snatch her fingers away, but long enough and near enough I held her to gain the smell I sought.

"Clove is not strong enough a scent to conceal a fragrance so personally known, lady sinner," I declared.

"Alba, if you have lost your mind, I shall confine you to a home for the mad," Rathel retorted while retrieving her hand.

"Not with an ignorant sinner of your huge village do you speak, Rathel. Wise enough I am to have surmised your task with the magistrate to be identifying witches. And on you proof is found, for the odor is lodged deep in the crevice beneath your nails, neither to be soon washed away nor hidden with additional scents. Not hidden from me."

"Partake of brevity in your wisdom, Alba, and describe the ultimate goal of your speaking."

"You have been with witch Lucinda—I know this."

"How is it you know a witch never near your home island?" Rathel replied after an unsubtle pause.

"I know her from *your* home, former missus. Inadvertently she found me here while seeking you and your typically sick business."

"The home of a woman not known to her, else my examining her would not have been required. Does your wisdom not tell you this?"

"But you are known by her friends: those instruments used to kill your own spouse, and thereby gain—fail to gain—Edward Denton."

"You confront me with these stories as though to achieve some advantage in your life," Rathel retorted. "I suggest, however, that you not display your wisdom to Edward Denton. Even now he considers you demonically tainted, and to the pyre of Magistrate Naylor you would go."

"Yes, mistress, with you as companion. How believable shall I be in alleging that you have me here to kill as in the past you so wickedly used witches? Might you tell Naylor that my identity be unknown to you? That display of insanity would gain you no home for the mad, but a prison for criminal fools. How readily shall you convince rational officials in light of my evil that Franklin died without your aid and effort? But I've no desire to inform tax man nor king of my identity merely to have you burned beside me. My silence I would retain if only you continue to humor your daughter."

"And what would this comedy cost me, Alba?"

"Dismissal, mistress. Have the witch Lucinda dismissed

from incarceration and from London."

"Is this a studied goal on your part, or one frivolous?" Rathel queried.

"A most studious goal I have been attempting to implement. Before Lucinda was encaptured, I had initiated her departure."

"Therefore, you killed the Bitford man for her passage."

"Satan ended this sinner through my unwilling, unknowing body. Perhaps the devil used you in a similar manner to kill your husband. At least I sought gain for a person other than myself. To purchase Lucinda's conveyance, I intended more thievery of your excess goods."

"Your generosity is moving, Alba, but will not likely convince a magistrate who shall only see the witch in you, not the sister. As for your business, I understand now the aunt of yours I was yesterday."

After a pause mandated by Rathel's nonsense, I replied, "You ascribe madness to me then speak insanely?"

"Upon learning of this Bitford's death, I also learned of his employ, and believed you on the verge of a foolish attempt to withdraw from London. At the agency of his hire, I inquired of a young lady with your face and fine speaking. Being told that you sought conveyance for a senile aunt, I took great offense, insisting to be that person and you a hateful niece attempting to rid me from your home. Thus, I canceled your papers with a generous gratuity to Mr. Wroth. More importantly, I concluded a business that if left unconsummated at the time of an employee's death might lead a thoughtful superior to have you sought. None shall seek me, since I used no true name, and my face was unseen. I suggest that when next you endeavor to kill a man with your sex, Alba, wear a veil to hide your distinctive face. But feel no need to thank me for saving your life again."

"I die the witch with a cunt virginal or murderous, so I need not thank you for your self-salvation. You would have me executed at once were it not for my continued success with Eric."

"Your further success, however, is required for your return to the wilds."

"How wise you are to not promise my continued living, only a conveyance to the wilderness."

"Both of these I will have for you if you wed the Denton lad."

"Easy is your business when the boy's true betrothal is written on his heart. I so consume his thinking that at night he climbs the wall for me—do you doubt it?"

"I do not, Alba, but take not this boy between your legs without a wedding, lest you ruin our chances for surviving his end."

"How could that be, mistress? I understand how you might secrete me out of London after Eric's death, but you remain, do you not? If available to justice, how shall you survive a murder that clearly you intended?"

"Because the death is one that clearly *you* intended, Alba. Besides myself, only witches are aware of the white one. I shall have even the king believe that you were the one seeking vengeance, vengeance against me for allowing your sisters on Man's Isle to die. You thus concealed yourself in the guise of a human girl until able to destroy me by killing your marriage, thereby ruining any mother's most beloved hour."

"Convinced I am, mistress, and in my guise as king's counsel, I adjudge you well connived by the witch though innocent of murder. But you shall require no such adjudication from the genuine law unless a new death transpires. And none shall unless Lucinda's be avoided. For me to continue with Eric as I am, you must have Lucinda released and removed from London."

"But here exists difficulty," Rathel returned. "Without your concern, I have no interest in this witch. My objectivity was revealed to the magistrate in my identifying Lucinda, then leaving her for the law. How am I to now tell Naylor that I care for the witch when earlier I did not? Should I mention Mr. Bitford's death?"

"Along with Franklin's, of course. Ply me not with your foolishness, sinner. If you have arranged for Eric to die by me and your husband through other witches, no doubt you've the ability to have one woman released, the reason by your own invention and convincing of the magistrate. But I suggest you not tarry, for I will tolerate no pretext that too late you were or too inconsistent toward Lucinda. So let the deaths fall where you will them, not where they must, for you are the center around whom your people perish. And remember as you journey, mistress, that I've developed my own resources for influencing London. Know ye, wench, that a sinner needs no prick to die by the will of witches."

There our speaking ended, the Rathel looking toward me firmly as though to read my will. And she walked away before I, walked away to have Elsie fetch her cloak and gloves, for again she need leave on business.

With the lady gone, Elsie found me near the foyer to ask of the Rathel's departure.

"Forgive me, child, but I'm hearing this harsh whispering between you and the mistress, and praise Jesus I'm hearing not enough to know what was said. But as I'm worrying of your arguing and the mistress being out again, can you be telling me how much I should fret?"

"The discussion, miss, was more negotiation than exchange of distress. As for Rathel's business, the mistress is to the magistrate's again with no difficulties expected, and none, I pray, forthcoming."

Expressing her relief, a fond demeanor with these servants, Elsie withdrew to the kitchen, one of their favorite sites. I soon smelled cooking, my first thought being that Elsie had opened the door to release a whiff of Delilah's burning meat. But no beef was that odor, and not from our kitchen. On Satan's pyre a witch was now frying.

I ran to the foyer, opening the door to be certain of my smelling, at first convinced I was as mad as the Rathel had mentioned, so distraught that my worst dreams now came awake. But I found no mistake and no nightmare, only a full breath of London's air now containing the black fibers of a burnt sister.

As though eating the dark flesh instead of smelling it, I retched and bent as though broken, my stomach's contents so exploding from me that I was thrown to the floor by the force of my contractions, not those of my stomach, but my heart, for my spirit was vomiting. I felt another loved one dying by torture, felt my morality destroyed from having allowed another sister to die by not being witch enough to save her.

281

Bloodless and filled with blood, I rose to move into the drawing room for an item of household protection, removing a metal heirloom to apply to that person most ruinous to the home, sitting within smell of the door, waiting for the Rathel to kill her.

Why she was so long in returning I did not know, but soon I came aware that Rathel had no initiative with Lucinda. Though she had identified the witch, this activity was old with her and familiar to me. She had no opportunity to save Lucinda as per my demand, for the sister was set to Hell's fire before Rathel could arrive. I had been correct when retching, understanding then that I was to blame: for being too active, too passive, too improper as a savior, a sister. I asked myself if Lucinda were less worthy of death than Percival; and, yes, the answer in God's name was yes. Regardless, I had killed them both. Having murdered enough for that era of my life, I replaced the lance and retired to my chamber, closing the window passage to night London because the incoming odor could be nightmarish.

I imagined Eric climbing the wall. At the window, I would kick his face, the boy falling to his death, an accident to English law, the Rathel satisfied and I on my way to Man's Isle. Eric's death would be accepted in this land as normalcy, for was he not innocent and unworthy? I imagined Eric coming and dying, for was he not next in queue for my killing? First Percival from unknown, unavoidable evil, then Lucinda from incompetence and a lack of courage. Therefore, why not Eric next from clear intent? Was this progression not reasonable?

I imagined Eric but had no dreams of him, lying on my bed without sleep, my only thoughts of dinner gone bad, of a negligent cook having caused a harmless burning of a meal, nothing lost, nothing worse than this mistake. I attempted to justify the soot in my brain until a drunken wench came stumbling into my chamber.

Rathel had been imbibing liquor, a taste of hers I thought she had recently tempered. Sinners drank as a social enterprise and to hide their cares with the dull foolhardiness that alcohol provides. But what was this sinner's state that she had to share it with me?

"You smelled the witch gone before I arrived," Rathel snarled, "and somehow—I know—you sent me to become a fool before Sir Jacob."

"Satan made you the fool, wench. I sent you to save my sister. I prayed to a God you have never loved to save my sister through you."

As though not having heard me, Rathel continued speaking, directing her composition—an opera—toward her audience.

"I told Naylor I should speak with this witch to learn more of the demonic activity in London. I then heard of her dying, but Naylor mentioned more on the subject of recent evil. The Bitford man dead. Then an older tale about a pale girl under water much too long, and how an average gent was drawn to touch her. After a story for his minister, this man was sent to the magistrate. Sir Jacob asserted that so much demonic now lay in London that people fear for their children. Sharing a drink with him to get the taste of the Thames out of me, I learned more. Learned that one family sharing a school with Lord and Lady Naylor had sent their boy to Europe this very day. And since the youth's name was Eric and you've been speaking with him at night as per your boasting, did you not encourage him to leave? Was this not your best initiative, moreso than pawning my possessions to abandon me for the wilds? Perhaps in your criminal journeys you've noticed that other pale girl about, she in Penstone Place nearly ravished before being driven off. Her appearance not unlike my goddamnable new daughter, I am told. Sir Jacob would have mentioned this earlier had I not been so insistent on being with my new family that I had no time to work with him. But this was understandable to the generous Naylor, that I preferred my lovely lass to those possessed with demons, as though anyone could be taken by a demon worse than you."

"Your mouth is perverse from liquor, unnatural creature," I retorted, but again the Rathel seemed not to hear.

"But many pale girls live in this city. When they're all discovered to be the same and all mine, she'll be enjailed before finishing with Denton—exactly as planned, is it not, witch?"

"Yes, you idiot blackguard," I laughed. "It all is true. As though God Himself, I've been manipulating this city to irritate you. So foolish are ye, drunken wench, that you'd believe I would burn myself to thwart your plans."

"You've made a mistake in deceiving me, witch, in stabbing me from behind with your deception."

"Bleeding right, you ferocious whore, I've made a mistake in stabbing your back!" I shrieked, and leapt from the bed to run past Rathel and downstairs, having achieved a most objective intent, as though a formula to correct my living, and it would be the Rathel's death. Into the drawing room to gain the lance and slaughter heinous Rathel, Satan take her soul if he could find room for her infinite evil in his Hell. But energized with drunken anger, Rathel was with me like Lucinda's final smell. As I stepped onto a chair and reached for the lance, Rathel attacked me from behind, having taken another object in her life I purportedly had wielded against her.

"Here is the clock you would sell, when you meant to sell my hide, bloody witch!" she screamed, and struck my shoulder, the bones becoming so numb with pain that I could no longer reach.

"You've driven Eric off, but I will have you wait for him!" she cried, and struck my spine, the clock's corner biting into me so solidly that I shivered with an agony both unique and unbelievable.

"Your demon kind has ruined me before, but I'll have you make amends or have you quartered!" she screeched. "You'll be outside killing me piece by piece no more, but ill and inside until your betrothed returns!"

Stunning pain collapsed me. Then against my face fell the ceiling, which was only the timepiece; but this blow removed my ability to sense pain and to see, though I was startled by the force, wondering how any head could accept such a blow and yet live. I could not move, only hear, more babbling from the Rathel now obscured by screaming Elsie, who ran to her mistress as a final strike took my hearing and my mind.

Nineteen

A sinner was wetting me with her face. Was my mind so deteriorating that each dream became more bizarre than the last? No, it seemed my life was now so bizarre that all my nightmares came true, came in a vague succession like days, eras of witches burned with salt water, a tiny boy lamed by the Rathel standing over him like an elephant, myself retching to death for having loved a sinner, for having touched him with my head as he crawled up my body toward my entrance. Now this damp dreaming came true, for the real Elsie was weeping above me, separated by a cache of bandages.

"Oh, praise God, child, you're returning to us at last!"

Her weeping shook me, a not unpleasant vibration, this sinner's proximity not discomforting since I could not smell, though I felt I should be smelling something most profound, more moving than this unimpressive weeping. But at the time, I had no comprehension of emotion, and tears were for another race.

"Are you hearing me, child, are you hearing, dear Alba?"

I looked to her, but attempting to see this fuzzy face was painful, so I ceased focusing.

"Alba, are you with us, now? Are you with us again, lass?"

"I'm out on an errand," I attempted to say, amused by the odd voice coming from beneath the bed, it seemed.

Then the sinner threw herself against that bed and partially against me, praising God and His offspring, Jesus, for whatever return she presumed, my clearest thought being that Elsie had enough concern for us both, and might she enjoy it. After stroking the fabric cache covering my head and weeping additionally, Elsie moved away, returning in a dream moment or a sinners' minute with a wet rag to dab about my face as though I had use for further moisture, babbling all the while.

I was beginning to comprehend. As I became more aware, I became more uncomfortable, for throughout my person I felt an unspecifiable pain. Finally I had a clear reply to Elsie by stating simply, "It hurts. . . ."

Because my words were understood, more weeping came— God help me. "Sleep . . ." was all I said, though I wished to ask the woman to step away and allow space for my breathing, since the atmosphere seemed as dense as water; but, no, this was due to a swollen nose. Sleep, sleep, I told her, but closing my eyes was painful; so I left them in a slit as Elsie blubbered, kissed the fabric about me, and withdrew.

I next awakened to hear Elsie's prognosis. She said the physician had done his best, but was uncertain of my recovery, what with all the damage from my having fallen down the stairs, as the mistress told him. But you're not to be worrying, Alba, in that I know you're healing, know your lovely heart and God's great generosity will . . . And I slept again.

I was bright and dim as though an oil lamp, but never fully illuminated. A constant with my coming and going was pain, pain to take my thinking, such pain that each awakening brought a desire for more sleep, but after days or years or lifetimes, I oft felt too much thick agony for rest. Another constant with each awakening was Elsie, the woman as everpresent as furniture. But one day the sinner before me as I awoke was not the servant, but her mistress and mine.

No tears from this beast, as though she were a witch, but nearer to Satan than any type of human. She moved to my bed with an uninvolved look, and I knew my additional pain would be in hearing her speak.

"No witch can be harmed by a minor beating," she informed me. "Both of us well know this, Alba. Yet you have been so

286

foolish as to walk about London causing yourself grief and potential death with every step. Be thankful I have rendered you safe here."

For long I had recalled the cause of my position on this bed as though a stain, but the story seemed operatic: seen, comprehended, but unmoving despite its noise. But with the Rathel's words, I felt only the truth, only her evil.

My voice was too strange a sound for any actor, but clear enough for revenge.

"When I walk," I whispered, "I kill you."

Though I clearly heard her ending words, I remained uncertain whose final speaking was more important.

"You are the murderess, Alba, as both we know. Best keep the fact to yourself."

In this manner my living proceeded. A sinning male occasionally entered to pull white apparel from my head and prod about my face. Then some poultice he would apply, the fabric replaced, some speaking by him or Rathel. When this male physician was near me, Elsie and her mistress were immediate, the latter to preclude the white witch's being handled by the doctor's possible lust. Elsie's purpose, it seemed, was to look between me and Rathel with facial expressions not easily described.

My body wastes were collected in bed by Elsie holding a type of skillet, the metal about my sensitive areas causing me to shudder. Meals consisted of vegetables selected by Elsie, a bit of chicken slipped in with the parsnips, always dropped from my lips with no toothmark, thereafter more odd expressions from Elsie, but these seen often before, perfectly describable.

Eventually I was walking enough to use my chamber pot. Being separated from that skillet was the best desire I could form, except for ending the pain. With my consciousness returned, the pain increased by having my senses to invade. Misery from my damage became so great as to awaken me as though someone were gouging my eyes. Nothing else, nothing else in the world could I perceive but that agony when it peaked. As though suffering tortuous theater, I stood away and watched my pain in disbelief that any force could be so relentless, so large, as though an elephant above me with frightening details and bulk enough to kill me if it fell with its entirety, this oppressive agony one of God's creatures so exotic as to steal my mind.

Something old was missing. Looking up from my bed one morning, I found myself blinded, for a part of the chamber I could not see. High in the corner was a clean locale where there should have been a pet. No dust lay against my ceiling— and no spider, for it had been vanquished web and all, its home removed from my home. Only two friends in this household, and one had been expelled, or murdered. And I knew my other friend was not the sinner responsible for this exile, this death.

No future was mentioned by friend or enemy, no plans for my being lame until Eric returned, no comment from Elsie as to how I might live in a house whose mistress had bashed me like an animal to eat. I needed no deliberation, for I had received enlightenment. To save Eric, Elsie, and all the world's remaining witches, the Rathel would have to pass away to God's hands. Being a proven murderer, I deserved to send her. Praise God for designs only He could fashion, only He could fathom. When again able to walk properly, I planned my departure, on a selected day dressing to exit the house and have the prickless Rathel killed by demons.

Though continually uncomfortable, I was growing strong, having been walking about the garden, intentionally passing much time away from my chamber and Elsie until the separation became common. Mainly I was feeling normal except for a stiff mouth and facial swelling that remained. But I brushed my hair as Elsie had when I was unable, and did the stuff up to be covered by a hat, finding a detestable looking-glass to make certain I appeared the lady, that I was passable in English society.

I was not. In the mirror I found myself comical, for no longer was I pale. Much of my face was blue-grey with dark purples and red seams from gashes and bruises' discoloration. One eye was a slit, my forehead bulged above it, a scarred rent in the brow and beside my nose, which was both flat and crooked (therefore resembling Mother's), my lips cracked with bloody healing. Regardless, my only needed modification was a thick facial net draped from my hat—and where had I learned that deceit?—downstairs a day when Rathel was absent, hiring a coach with her remaining pence, into the city and gone for Penstone Place.

Because the driver was adamant about not entering Penstone, I allowed him to leave me on its periphery without the retribution this cowardly sinner deserved. I was not afraid to walk amongst criminals—how could I be when I sought them?

Near my objective, a portion of the city to house no ladies, a child screamed, screamed as though dying. And I thought: Yes, I have the correct locale, one of sinners' death. But after screaming further, the same child laughed as though insane. But madness seemed no less appropriate, for my plan itself was senseless.

Few people walked these streets, but only I passed without skulking against the walls. The farther I walked, the more I became the prime object of these persons' attention. None of the many comments heard did I acknowledge: staring men croaking for me to come with them, as though my companionship would be humorous, what with their laughter. Remarks from a woman as to my being a "tart of no doubt great expense." Surely this was true, for whereas the cheap whore speaking gave only pleasure and took metal, I provided ultimates, and my fee was death.

How boring was the criminal's surprise. On that barren street of burned and crumbled structures I had traversed before, out from a building's niche like a cockroach from a kitchen crack leapt Giraffe.

"Good morning to you, foul sinner," I told him before he could initiate his base speaking. "Next occasion come to me immediately so that we might begin our business without delay."

"And what do you say, mad girl, that you have business with

me? Mine is the business, and yes, I shall have it of you," and he stepped nearer.

"Very well, cretin," I continued quickly without one step's retreat, without a moment's shown fear. "Presumably you would care to have me."

That operatic line halted him, the male creature requiring a moment for his slow comprehension to grow. The basic content of my speaking, however, was well accepted.

"Then I am taking you, girl, despite what you say," and he stepped another pace nearer.

"Very well, Sir Criminal, you will have me as though a husband, but I expect payment," I declared, halting the male with my words. "For taking my sex at your pleasure, you must kill a person for me. Thereafter, my sexual portions shall be readily available to you."

"Why don't I just take you now and mark it on your tab?" Giraffe sneered, and stepped toward me with no further restraint.

I pulled forth the cold firearm stolen from the drawing room and pointed it low, toward his body.

"Because I will shoot your prick off, blackguard, if you touch me wrongly. Now, will you have my baby slot or not?"

Then I lifted my skirt to reveal a dearth of underthings below, only a realm of secret hair and flesh to draw men like flies to spoilt meat.

"Lap me here till dry, cretin," I said, my phrase gained from this beast's bulkier colleague during a previous sojourn.

The male agreed, nearly throwing himself onto his knees before me, thrusting out his face, mouth open as he grasped my hips and began burrowing between my legs. No mention was made of skin like winter. Of course, even a witch's vagina is as warm as the lust expended upon it, and this criminal had some heat. Against my bottom's thin lips he placed his own, emitting strange sounds from his throat and mouth as he sucked me as though nursing, eating my sex milk that was only lust, a ludicrous language of passion no witch knew.

I rapped his head with the pistol's barrel, and we separated.

"Enough of your consuming me, starving beast. If you would

290

rub your man stick in me and completely, you will do the deed I require. You will kill a woman as she exits a coach before her home the upcoming Friday. She returns from the opera, perhaps with an older gentleman, whom you must not harm at the peril of your passion. Only the woman is to be killed, and she must be thoroughly murdered."

"And after I cut her neck off, you will have me better when?"

"The day after she dies, I will be here for you to take. You see I have no pause in receiving you within me," I declared, and with the pistol yet aimed toward the kneeling male, I thrust my bottom against his face, the uncooked meat for his perusal now, and later for the promised consumption, a great insertion of his tongue well aimed into my baby passage. Then I rapped his head again and pulled away.

"Kill her this Friday, and the following day you might mate with me till you die," I concluded, gave good specifics as to address and identity of the victim, then walked away, looking over my shoulder to the criminal as though a skulking sinner myself. Giraffe did not follow.

Upon fully accepting that the man had not damaged me, I felt a grand relief approaching humor at my survival. But I understood that my resolve was a hiding device, for terror was in this locale, and behind my demand for justice I hid my fear. Surviving the criminal was revelatory, exposing my dread of Giraffe: from his visage and smell, his touch as he held me between his hands with strength enough to lift me from the ground. Only his sexual contact seemed undangerous, for there he was a pet controlled by his own desires via a master's taunting. Controlled by me. But the only pride I took in my power was the expected salvation of my friends from sending Rathel toward God's realm and away from ours.

With a light step, I quit the criminal, needing but a moment's walk to be in London's better segments. But too near a disheveled building I stepped while too much in Penstone Place, and there was a monkey with his hands on me, arms wrapped about my torso to drag me into his home.

He threw me to the floor with more force than required to control me, the pistol slipping in my bodice but remaining.

291

Monkey then looked down to speak, bending from a curious distance to view past my disarrayed veil.

"Cor, what an ugly one, your face. A dead dog's arse is better," he spat. "But weren't I about to fuck that arse of yours when you were lovely? I bet your undoggy arse yet be lovely enough for my blind cock."

I would have no business with this male—I would have survival. Before he could step nearer, I stopped him with a sight by spreading my knees, pulling the fabric from my bottom to display his spoken goal.

"Here is my sex grand enough to kill so lowly a cretin as you," I spake, and he looked at my pulchritude, the gnarly muscle he loved.

"I'll kill you with my fucking," he growled, and began to uncover his own sex. Therefore, I revealed my small but previously convincing weapon.

"Yes, please reveal your baby stick so that I may shoot it away."

With scarcely a pause, looking between my half-hidden face and the firearm, this monkey replied, "I believe not the thing can fire or you can aim it, wench lady."

"Your desire lies where, blackguard, with my vagina or this trifling metal? Will you have a ball in your brain or your prick in my arse?"

This last speaking of mine influenced him to full attention, those words and the firearm detaining him as I stood.

"You will have me, sir, for a price."

"You're no whore. I can smell a whore, and you be clean."

"Never will you fuck a lady like this," I averred, and lifted my skirt in an instant to let it fall as quickly, the monkey watching that flesh revealed, then hidden. "But my cunt and arse are for your taking if you're man enough to kill a killer."

"I'm man enough for more than you can imagine."

"Then imagine killing an enemy for me, then mating with me till your phallus falls off, if you are so complete a man."

This business arrangement was the same as for the previous creature. Monkey's response was similar to his brother beast's.

"How do I know you'll do the bargain once the wench

292

is cut dead?"

"I presume myself worth the wager," I replied. "In proof, why not taste my sex muscle and tell yourself you would not kill to exhaustively, ecstatically fuck me." Then up with the dress, down with the man, around and in with his mouth portions, the male seemingly tearful once my taste had penetrated his coarse sensations. And despite my ambient coolness, he found a local warmth.

I rapped him with the barrel, which he barely felt, but enough for me to move away, the criminal remaining on the floor, another sinner on his knees as though praying, having worshiped the altar of my baby bump.

"Ah, your cunt is sweet, bitch, but not to the death. I'll have a fuck from you first, and another after the killing. Murder is worth more than a suck of your sex juice."

"Fool I would be to let you take your payment in advance. I shall let you hold the coin in your pocket, however, by holding your stick in that desired receptacle a time."

"And what are you saying, taunter of good cock meat, bitch?"

"I say this," I replied, and reclined on my back, legs upward, nude buttocks exposed. "I say you might find my fundament most voluptuous, yet without excessive girth. I say to insert your limb to see whether the fit be acceptable, but no endless rubbing. And touch not my vagina, sir, for it's as damaged within as my face's surface, and full of ointment to burn you. The firearm I'll keep aimed at your brain, if you please."

He was pleased enough to fall before me, spreading his knees so that his buttocks were flat to the floor, and at my arse he went with his pink stick. From Marybelle's examination, I knew to make loose those tight muscles, but no practice had I, and no gentility this cretin. He rammed his limb into me like a knife, the pain such that I would have shot him had my pistol been primed. Too much pain for him, perhaps, for soon after the initial rubbing, Monkey found that he had made a fire, as though rubbing two sticks together instead of burying one. Therefore, the felon extinguished the heat by spitting on his removed phallus, his fingers coating saliva on the tip and along the length of that fat finger, then again inside me with much

293

smoother rubbing. Clearly here was a cretin who knew his perversion. But as his rubbing continued with force enough to bruise my back, I wondered if he would ever exit, no longer certain that this fecal path was different from my sex hole regarding killing. So I thrust both feet with utter strength against his shoulders, and the two of us were free of one another.

"Ah, you near broke my prick off!" he barked, though his damage was no greater than mine.

"Next instance your man stick will fall away from my arse's love," I declared. "If you'll have more of my fecal sex, then kill the woman as I've described. Then here I'll return with no less modesty, but a more enduring arse for you."

I ran away, and was not followed by this monkey. Running now was somewhat painful, for my rectal muscle was so sore that I limped. But my greater pain was from Rathel's bashing, a deep, oppressive ache returned from my exertion.

Though having successfully withdrawn from a criminal whose sex part had been within me, I felt no relief, only fear. I continued moving rapidly, for my immediate future was all foreboding and was shaped like an animal. Somewhere near was the unnamed elephant, and would not this last attacker be the one to succeed in taking me wholly, and thus either killing me or dying? But as I ran without being attacked, I saw potential for ensuring Rathel's demise; for whereas one of the two criminals might consummate the murder, were not my opportunities for success doubled with my doubling the Rathel's potential killers? This concept filled me for a moment, the notion literally coming to me that the likelihood of success would be superior when trebled—and did I have a choice? for here came Elephant.

He ran from a crumbling building—and I ran toward him. Seeing the male approach, I was astonished by another nightmare's coming true. And I was angered. I ran to him with my pistol drawn, not concerned with citizens who might see.

"Welcome, blackguard, to my sex," I hissed, words to halt his every move. "You'll recollect near fucking me before, and I am here again to collect your prick. Will you have it in me or have it shot away?"

"Ugly girl, you are without thinking," he responded, thereby

294

denoting the condition of my veil. "Being shot by one incompetent is no wish if instead I'm to be fucked by one even if hideous."

I gestured for him to return into his building of concealment. Then I revealed myself.

"This is your notion of ugly, Sir Satan?" I pronounced, and the hirsute view was all beauty to him.

We proceeded with business. A few crotch hairs in his teeth were not enough for this animal. As though reading the same script as Monkey, the current cretin stated that coupling after the death was not enough to inspire him toward murder. Therefore, I told him a great deal of truth.

"The baby port is impossible, being damaged inside as is my head, and the arse is too sore from my receiving another animal recently. Therefore, retain your dealings; and I, my pistol, and my vagina shall retire."

"But you've got another lodging for my prick, woman girl."

"Rotter, I'll not be accepting your limb in my ear."

"No, mad bitch, within your mouth I would stick it."

"Insane cur you are to suggest I take your urine limb between my lips."

"Pissing can't be done when the stick is set for sex, ignorant slut. And can living flesh be worse than the butchered beef and pork you stuff within your mouth all your wealthy day?"

Likely not.

"A fool I'd be to let you crash your phallus throughout my mouth as did the other bastard my buttocks. All my teeth I'd lose plus my tongue."

"No, ignorant bitch: The prick I hold still while you move your mouth along it and again."

"I nonetheless see no method of applying myself to your baby stick without being in jeopardy from your battering me with your other limbs."

"And why would I do so when I'm getting me prick sucked, witch?"

Witch?

"And if I accomplish this mouthing, do you then kill the

woman?"

"Dead as my father hanged years ago."

"The accommodations therefore be these: I shall tie your wrists and ankles as you lie along the length of your spine. Then I will, er, move my mouth along your baby stick enough to prove the function satisfying, to convince you that more is desirable. Further of my mouth's activity you shall receive when I receive knowledge of the Rathel's death."

"And it's jeopardy you fear with but my prick in your mouth when you'd have me bound hand and foot on me own arse?"

"As well, of course, I shall have the firearm trained against your testicles."

"A damned fool I am to such an agreement," Elephant snapped.

"At this moment I have the pistol, cretin. Had I intended to harm you, by now you would be bleeding and dead."

"And how do I know in certain that you'll untie me when done?"

"Are you not man enough to handle a girl's bonds? If not, then surely you're not man enough to handle her cunt."

I tied his ankles with his jacket and his wrists with his shirt after Elephant had loosed into the air his own and now firm baby limb. Secured on his back the man lay when I kneeled above his crotch and found his uniqueness. About his short and curly hair, beyond his normal testicles, was a ring of scars on his inner thighs and lower abdomen, as though a crown for his cock. I had no idea why this sinner had been marked so specifically, for I was occupied with my latest nightmare: I would have to smell his sex odor, and this seemed immediately worse than his piss in my mouth. But as I bent over the sinner, I found his smell less than intense. The cause of this mildness, however, was more likely my own perception rather than his lack of stench, for my nose was not fully healed to its former sensitivity. Regardless, I accepted his warm and salty meat into my mouth, as well as his complaints.

"Ah! hold the teeth, wench! You're not to be chewing the thing—it ain't your bleeding breakfast sausage!"

I thus attempted to apply the movement Elephant had mentioned. Successfully, it seemed, for his further description contained a satisfaction to weaken him.

"Yes, that's it: You're to suck it some and hold it with your lips and inner mouth and—Jesus bless, yes—your tongue and move along it and again, yes, like that, God bless, yes. . . ."

Reasonably the thing had no taste, in that I was not consuming it. The salty moistness about the stick was no more than sweat, and the small amount of sticky fluid at its end no more than snot. The sensation was strange, for the flesh of this limb remained stationary while the skin held with my mouth moved against it. And I had no curiosity of God's making such massage so pleasurable, for in the first moments of the toothless portion of my rubbing, the man went both stiff and weak in his body and had no emotion within him but sinning ecstasy. My only emotion was relief to find that the man's meat was no worse than the chicken bits Miss Elsie during my illness had attempted to slip within me, relief because my mouth did not lock upon this stick never to release it; and what a superior receptacle for manifesting the special sex of the white witch.

More of this meal was coming. I was aware that males eventually deposit a quantity of fluid for making offspring within the female. I imagined a bucket of sex snot rushing within me to bloat my cheeks like a pregnant woman's belly. I imagined the essence of male sinner sitting in my stomach until a criminal began growing there, and when next I vomited, it would be a baby cretin I puked out, and part mine.

"Enough demonstration, cur," I said after spitting his limb away. I then stood, leaving the criminal to his knotwork. "If you find the sex of my tongue satisfactory, more shall you receive along with vagina and buttocks or bloody ear, if you so desire, soon after the Rathel dies."

"Oh, yes, God bless, yes . . ." he promised; and with his moans, my chances were trebled.

The hour was not late upon my return, but into the basement I went to wait and later be found. Then came a thought. Though not expected to be present, perhaps the Rathel had returned and now prepared to entrap me, having posted her sinning servants about the household to view my ingress. Concealing my wares in the basement, I moved through the gate again, then around to my side window. Up the wall I clambered, not a sinner on the street to view me, my move surely no more foolish than fucking felons.

My next decision was to wear gloves when again handling a prick, for the smell was on my fingers, though no taste remained after that inner licking and swallowing I had commenced once away from Penstone, Penistone. Beneath the bed I moved, a place over cleaned by some servant other than Elsie in my illness as ordered by Rathel, Satan take her soul soon to be available. With the nasty smell of wood soap and oil about me, I sneered as though a criminal myself, sneered at the Penstone Place too social for Rathel but worthy of me with all my killing deals. Would not Amanda be proud of her daughter's business? Would not my business eliminate her pride? Would not the world be a safer, less sinful place with Rathel removed to God's hands? Yes, please dear Lord, yes. Pray God accept her generously.

Weary from my divine dealings, I felt the safety of my bed's bottom, though not of my greater home, for I had never been more damaged than when in the Rathel's abode. My ideas were so unpleasant that I left them only by leaving awareness, sleeping although afloat in oil as though greased in a pot for cooking, until Elsie entered and called for her lass.

"Alba, child, are you truly not in here yet?"

"Present I am, miss," I announced through the bed's fabric draped to the floor.

"So, how long are you in here, girl, and are you too ill to be elsewhere?" Elsie called without bothering to bend toward the bed cave.

"In and out of this room I have been the day, beneath the bed now to be alone for sleeping. Though more weary than usual, I am ill only due to the excess oil which I absorb like a wick. I suggest you bring no candle near, lest I illuminate all of London."

"Ah, and you're saying my presence is so bad that you're

needing to hide from me? And I thought it was months ago that you're abandoning this wild state."

"Kindly induce me less often into announcing that you alone of the persons in this household I would have about me. I thought that during those same months past you had learned that we are friends, and that I am a person with continual regard for both the wilds and for my occasional solitude."

"Aye, I'm allowing you this, girl, if only because from my place our speaking is ridiculous, one of us is talking as though to an empty room, and the other like a dust ball beneath the bed."

As she began sighing and turning away, I told her, "Incorrect, miss, for no dust exists beneath this bed, the floor polished as though a surface for eating, and therefore no longer quite a place of my own."

Then Elsie spoke again, and most sadly.

"And it's correct you are, girl, for all of this locale is the Rathel's."

Then she departed, unable to hear my final phrase.

"But you and I, miss, are not the Rathel's for long."

Two days later was the Friday of my arrangement. That afternoon was not useless for me, for therein I culminated my concern. Around and around my considerations chased me, here another waking dream, one of morality, for I yet regarded myself superior to the criminal creatures who had worshiped me from below. Objectively, however, because of the nature and purpose of my influence, I was inferior to them in God's sublime eye. This was the emotion that alternated with my throwing a hand against my mouth lest the household hear me cackle, for those sinners sucking me like a treat for kitty were clearly more ludicrous than any human ever seen by a witch, even more so than that whore sucking the elephant's prick; for she was the beastmaster—beastmistress—not he, the trainer in control of the sexual menagerie. But the felons' foolishness was not their aspect I encouraged. By promoting their continual evil, I positioned myself below them morally as I crammed my desires into

299

their persons to be spit out as murder against the Rathel's face.

These conflicting responses were nothing new. From the beginnings of my plan, I had retained my self-revulsion from plotting murder. How holy I was to save my friends from Rathel by emulating Rathel, Satan's purest sinner. But when the time came for Rathel to die, the time came for me to find God again instead of Satan, whom I had disguised as the Deity. Finally I came aware that I had been dealing with the devil, not sinning criminals. Sinning me. When Rathel with Lord Andrew departed to the opera, I nearly achieved panic, for I had missed my best opportunity to save the mistress. Therefore, I waited with dread outside the Rathel's home those following hours with no complex plan, my new business only to warn her of death and have the coachman drive her away upon hearing my screaming to flee for her literal life.

I positioned myself early in fear of being late, slipping into a neighbor's privet hedge, hidden from those social folk to pass me, some silent, some with pleasant chatting as though a witch and a doomed boy whispering at night. Houses away I waited to gain Rathel before the expected criminals met her at the door, my intention to gain her carriage as it slowed while turning the nearest corner. And there I was at the proper time when Rathel came home from the opposite direction.

Though other vehicles were out this night, not until I heard one halting behind did I fling myself about to see Rathel's taken coach before her house. Too far away and too late to be screaming, I leapt out and ran to the coach, Rathel alone within, the driver stepping down to the passenger's door as three exotic animals converged on the mistress.

From a hedge before me ran Giraffe, who saw Monkey running toward him, swinging a knife. Giraffe's weapon remained sheathed until he saw the armed man, and clearly each was attacking his alternate, so the operatic scene appeared even to me. They met before the coach to call out vicious oaths to one another, then swing uneventfully with their knives before flinging themselves about and away, desperate to avoid the corresponding assassin. This was the true arrangement I had made in the eyes of Elephant, who ran from across the street as I proceeded to Rathel's vehicle, this last animal hissing that I was a "vengeful witch" and stabbing at me with his own knife, but missing because his greatest effort was in fleeing a scene surely arranged by the lady wench to gain vengeance on three males who had attacked her months ago, these being the thoughts I read in some mind, perhaps my own, as four running bodies fled from the static coach, the criminals in three dissimilar directions, the witch slipping into the spot by her neighbor's kitchen recently vacated by Giraffe, in that she no more than the other criminals desired to be caught making business at night.

No hopeful prayer did I offer for my safety, in that greater relief had been delivered, the panting, frightened witch praising God for fulfilling her ultimate plan, that of saving evil Rathel.

"Madam, madam! Are you safe?" the coachman called out as he looked everywhere for further flying demons. No knives seen, however, and no animals, the Rathel climbing out on her own and running to her doorway.

"Off with you before the next attack!" she shouted to the driver, then beat on her door for entry, the house opening as the coachman whipped his horse, which flew past me as though a fleeing criminal; and I wondered what this harnessed creature thought of our theater.

Stepping backward like a cat, I returned to my best shelter—the Rathel's home—but found each door locked, including the basement entry. So up the wall I climbed like my former spider to discover my window latched. Then I recalled my own doing, for I had feared that one of the criminals might surmise the residents here and come looking. Unfortunately, the curious criminal was I.

To the Giraffe's kitchen niche I would retire, slipping to sleep until morning when I would stealthily move inside the house as though never gone. A single step I took toward the neighbor's before smiling and running like a horse to Rathel's front door.

"It is I, Alba!" I hollered while violently rapping the knocker.

"What? Who? Why . . . ?" came replies from numerous voices within before one of the anguished women understood my screaming to be genuine, opening the door a crack to first view, then fully receive the daughter.

I was the one to slam and bolt the door as Elsie, Rathel, and Delilah asked of the meaning. But I had no answers for them, only condemnation.

"Out I run to see the loud activity, espying two criminal men, when here is a third running directly toward me. Tremendously I flee from his knife, yet when I am returned and desperate to enter my home, *you have locked me out!* Am I a part of that band of thieves that I must live on the streets?!" I yelped, then stalked angrily to my chamber, firm in my demand not to cackle until upon my bed, slamming the door behind, my face in the pillow as I laughed enough to tire me; but before sleeping, thankful prayers to Lord God that He deserved, even though from a sinner.

Twenty

How simple my dreams became. No ship's chain to entangle me, no bridge, no salt water, no drowning, no attempted escape. No failure, only pain, and all from smelling a witch burn. In this era, I was smelling Lucinda die, my dreams of the agony I had felt upon sensing her odor. Perhaps the misery remaining from Rathel's securing me in her home was inspirational, at night drawing similarities from a remote, more permanent damage. Often I slept well through evenings, but when I slept poorly, I slept not at all, sensing a sister ablaze.

No further tutoring was I given, though my thoughts of geography continued. Rathel and I scarcely spoke to one another, and were never together alone. Elsie had no further justification for Rathel's evil acts' being caused by a heart hurt long before. Never in my healing did Elsie speak of the mistress in fine terms. Neutral she was but no better, and therein equal to me, for I had no more liberal reviling of Rathel. Student Elsie had been tutored by her own observation to understand the truth of Rathel's heart. But we shared no hatred, for neither was capable of altering her servitude to the sinning mistress.

Less intently I looked through my window, no studious stares for witches and boys unheard of since their departing an era of education ago. Such a thing as letters existed but had never been promised. And if sent, might not Rathel intercept them as part of her business of which I was an instrument, a dupe? Perhaps I missed Eric's company, and I would never neglect the godly revelation provided by this male who seemed less foreign a beast than other sinners: less than Rathel and that zoo lapping at me in Penstone. But being with me would mean Eric's death, I was certain, and I was saving my wares for other men.

Fleeing London became the center of my existence. Unlike my early days in the city, I now had great confidence, having learned all the vagaries of British business. Only for my strength I waited, in that I required more energy to fuck my way out of London.

In this manner my plan proceeded. One morning, feeling nearly strong enough to begin my seduction of the city, I gazed through my window at passing sinners. One woman was walking herself like a dog, for stiffly past she stepped in her decent dress, later returning. Then came a coach for Rathel, our mistress entering and gone. A moment later, as though predictive, I turned from the window to see Elsie enter my chamber. Surprised she was that a lady from church sought to visit me though aware that Rathel was absent. A woman unknown, but who was Elsie to argue with a fellow parishioner on God's business? After my accident, some religious guests had come in the way of normal, soulful visitation of one ill, but orders from the Rathel were to disallow such intrusion, using the pretext of the girl's yet being too delicate about English society to be swimming in it hideous. The lastest visitor, however, had been adamant: not in seeing me, but in having the servant deliver her name. So up comes Elsie prepared to go down as soon as I give the order, as surely I would have except for that proper word brought me, the name Marybelle having me run downstairs like an animal.

A woman dressed as though a merchant's wife, and veiled, but no witch I knew, not with my improving nose sensing no sister's odor. A woman so timid as to remain outside, though requested to enter the foyer. Not timid was I, however, for out I went to close the door behind and lift that veil myself. And, yes, below the cloth was an ugly thing, and at this distance, having the faint but true smell of a sister.

"A rare salve applied on the skin when beneath the bright sun for the day," she described. "I learned that some dogs have been trained to smell us, and I would rather not be caught by an animal who should be friendly."

This witch I did not embrace. Perhaps no living person I should have loved more, but Marybelle should not have been living. She should not have been dressed as I nor walking so well, no cane used when stepping along the street, her clumsy boot of Man's Isle replaced by a normal shoe. But this sister, no less wise than before, was aware of my thinking.

"More of a witch you are now with your changed head. But even this bent face shows me your thoughts. What you would hear told can come later. But now we go."

"Go?" I asked. "Our destiny being . . . ?"

"A decent land with no streets, one made by God for His simple folk. A long journey we have, and must begin now."

"Now?"

"The servant of Lady Rathel has heard my name. Rathel will recall it from Man's Isle."

"Elsie will tell no one if I ask her to refrain."

"So thick you are with this sinner to trust her with my life?"

"In fact, so godly a person is she that I can trust her with both our lives. Regardless, why the jeopardy of using your true name?"

"Thereby I gained you now. Having done so, we must now depart. God would have us leave to be natural. Where would you be, Alba, with London and this servant?"

"I would be in a decent land with no streets, one made by God for His simple folk who yet include me, despite the complexities of my current life."

"Then abandon your complex living and return to God."

"You speak as though your meaning is immediacy."

"And when should we go if not now? Are you not prepared in your heart to regain our original life? If so, when better than immediately?"

"But I have to . . . first," I said, unable to enunciate the center of my feelings. Though my only need was to quit London, this need was only for myself, and therefore selfish, akin to lust. In this city, I lived not alone, but with friends. And how could I depart with a nightmare? How could I leave with someone whose death yet pained me waking and asleep?

"You hesitate, Alba."

"Often have I departed this house in order to exit London, though never successfully. Never have I made such attempts, however, without preparation, and therefore the notion of a simple exit is strange."

"You would kiss the sinner good-bye, perhaps, or bring your best gown? If you've money or jewels, bring all you can, but elsewise bring yourself."

"A veil at least I need to draw no attention through London."

"Agreed, yet you hesitate to run for this and be gone."

With the immediacy Marybelle sought, I announced, "You are dead," and understood that all along I had been staring at her, staring at a person often seen in my dreams. "You are dead, Marybelle. You died as—"

"I survived," she stated curtly. "I continue to live as God intends, so do not argue with my life unless you would argue with Him. And to His land we now should journey."

So I ran away. I turned and hastened upstairs to my chamber, taking veil and hat and cloak, also a bag. Yes, from a massive chest I took a bag, one for holidays in the countryside, and placed within a fine gown, my most comfortable shoes, but no mementos. The Rathel had jewels, and since I would no longer be living in her London, I need not fear being discovered, arrested, enjailed. But I had no jewels, and was too much the sinner in having killed and stolen to become a greater felon. Downstairs I ran, below to the foyer and Elsie.

Hesitation is not the term for my response, for Elsie looked at the apparel in my hand, saw the bag, and knew my goal. So I ran to her, dropping my items, and embraced the woman as I had no one since Lucinda. I embraced Elsie with no explanation of my intents, only of our lives.

"Never mention that this person gave her name," I whispered while looking into the sinner's eyes, my friend's eyes. "And never forget I love you." And I kissed her face, kissed her well and loved her better, then ran away before she could reply, through the doorway and to Marybelle.

We began walking at once. Marybelle, stepping stiffly with long, certain strides, first moved to a brick post supporting the fence of Rathel's neighbor where criminals of failed killing had previously hidden. From this niche she gained her own luggage, more of a handled sack for potatoes than my embroidery and brocade finery. Then she wordlessly continued, and I followed. I followed, but expected that door behind to open, expected Elsie to look or call out, but she did not. Wise Miss Elsie knew again what was best for her Alba. So did Marybelle, for she had summoned a brown carriage, instructing the driver to take us to an unfamiliar address. Then she provided the coachman with coin. And away.

"You have funds?" I asked her.

"From stealing the sinners' belongings. Long have I prepared this leaving with you, but felt it best not to burden you with knowledge of me, lest you or I become like Lucinda."

"You know this person?" I immediately returned.

"Not enough. This one was too thickly in London to save. God grant her the rest she could not gain alive. Was it with her you made like preparations?"

"Yes, but the Rathel and my sex had me fail."

"You have been killing sinners with this sex?"

"Only one, and only thereafter did I understand it was I who had killed him. God forgive me, but I did not know."

"Concern yourself not with God's forgiving you for your ignorance. He is the greatest Lord, not a superior person, and understands us better than we. When you begin killing from desire, then beg for God to understand, though He shall not."

"I wonder, however, why I was not told of this sexual characteristic by my superiors on Man's Isle."

"Perhaps because those witches were disrupted before the time of your learning. Perhaps because we failed you by not teaching you sooner. So know ye the remainder of your sex, Alba, that if you will be having with men, use any way but your child passage. Your purpose with any sexing remains with you and God, but the sinner will survive your hand and anus."

Managing not to say, "And mouth," I instead returned to a significant subject.

"We travel where with your coin?"

"Wales is our goal as an end, though we begin by leaving

307

London."

"Not to Man's Isle?"

"That place is become too small for both witches and sinners. The sinners have little interest in Wales near the mountains, which is not near us, but not across a sea. I crossed the Irish Sea twice, once fully on a sinners' boat, and before that part way, but walking. But that is done and now we are away from the tale."

Despite the veil obscuring her visage, from this witch I could sense the memory of an illness whose influence remained; and healed enough was my nose to smell her pain.

"Wales was the locale of my arrangements with a Mr. Wroth, of which Rathel became aware," I informed Marybelle. "The town's name I cannot pronounce, likely not recognize, but the Rathel would. The village is that in Wales nearest London, due west. If we journey to the same place, are we not to fear being followed?"

"I spoke with this Wroth. I learned of the same village, but more, that it is built on the edge of a path through the mountains, and thus traveled by sinners. We go farther south."

"But where do we go that we are not gained? Being aware of Mortwaite as a rare provider of extended land conveyance, Rathel via the magistrate will have any recent departure followed by horses bearing only men. We would thus be gained despite an advanced exit of hours."

"We would, but shall not, in that I have not hired Mortwaite," Marybelle replied. "I knew better upon learning of a person with your face and an aunt, of wild land sought, of your promising Lucinda a way to the wilds. But our travel to Wales is only the end. We begin by going to Bournchester. That is another of the sinners' great villages. But people often travel to and from these cities. The Lady Rathel and all of England's magistrates cannot seek every route in England for us if she knows not our destination."

"What business is arranged for us in this second city?"

"None yet, for I've never been there. But our travel is simple: We continue toward Wales, but not where we might be expected. True, someone seeing us leave the sinner Rathel's home could follow us, but I sense none. So inform me if any should be expected. Has your favorite servant run to the constables and directed English law behind us?"

"She has not and shall not. None from Rathel's household would so actively attack except the Rathel, and she was not present in her home. As per your planning."

"Help correct me if I lead us wrongly, Alba, for we are together and will suffer together if found. Though our way to Wales is longer than Mortwaite's, it yet is safer, I believe. As long as we are in the cities, we are lost amongst the sinners."

"No better thinking have I, Marybelle, and would praise God for my wisdom if I could contemplate so completely. Since I remain average, I will praise Him for a superior idea, that glorious notion of your survival. No fact could fulfill me more than your remaining on this world instead of being lost as were too many sisters."

"Praise Him for all life, Alba, for even sinners deserve the breath He gave them. And none deserves a life more than you. Thank God for the idea that is Alba."

How appropriately unemotional was all this praising of life, for Marybelle's life remained unbelievable to me. But praise God I did for the opportunity to accept her living, and thereby reject her previous visitations in distressing dreams of guilt.

Odd this carriage was to leave us with another. After a lengthy ride through those dense, connected villages comprising London, we arrived at a vehicular agency dissimilar to Wroth's, these small stables neat as chalets, the one coach seen more akin to Rathel's furniture than Mortwaite's rolling sheds. Nearby this vehicle we halted to exit. Requiring four horses for pulling, the massive box was tall with a folding step for entry, its roof purposeful and flat, supportive of luggage.

Marybelle took her sack and bid me follow, moving to a tall man standing near the great coach. Though he looked to Marybelle, she was unrecognized due to her veil. Therefore, the witch introduced herself.

"Here, sir, I am, Madam Belle and her charge of whom I

told you. Prepared we are to depart for Bournchester."

Then the sinner scolded her.

"Schedule, schedule, schedule," he intoned as though singing, looking down to Marybelle from his giraffe-like height. "A business of moving folk runs not on wheels but on schedules, Madam Belle, and most relieved I am with your sight, in that our schedule you nearly made us lose."

"The graveyard is filled with folk who nearly lived another day," Marybelle replied. "Might we then board and thereby keep our schedule schedule schedule?"

No further words had this sinner for the witch. His following speech was for a man on the coach's outer seat to stand down and take these ladies' parcels, up with them onto the roof and secured, then covered with a coarse fabric. The tall man completed his schedule by proving himself worthy of the name Giraffe when applied to male sinners. Opening the door for his final passengers, he aided Marybelle with a hand on hers, assisting the companion with fingers beneath her left buttock, a firm grasp and a hearty push into the coach, close the door, step backward to call up to his driver to be off, wave good-bye.

I drew no handling from the passengers. Two were women and the third an old man concerned only with his shallow breathing, his mouth opening and closing as though biting pieces of air. The English ladies began conversing with one another and the unknown witches as to the destination and relatives temporarily left behind, a church project to have all of London pray for the eradication of ants, and so on. I was least social in this cab by achieving silence. In answer to a smiling sinner's inquiry as to my opinions of the hellish nature of insects, I described my current difficulty in thinking due to a recent illness of my head, which I displayed by lifting my veil. Thereafter, no conversation came to my family.

The following, familiar scenery was not longingly viewed, for I prayed to never view it again. This future was not easily believed, however, for London seemed permanent, my own attempts at departure having been so difficult that surely this current journey came with the ease of desire, not the stress of the real. But my real life would not become proper without an

310

ending dream, for soon we arrived at a bridge. I then discovered why our initial retreat had been filled with ease—because now it would be filled with death. I knew that we would cross the Thames only part way. We would be on the bridge when it collapsed. We would fall into the water and all survive, for all in this coach could swim except the witches. This would be my final nightmare by being my final event.

Without viewing the expected death in my eyes, Marybelle knew. Smelling my change, she turned to look, but said nothing. I only waited. Waited until we drove past the bridge. Drove past the bridge without crossing. Drove past that presumed death to continue with God's living.

My last dream in London was no nightmare. Before I could fully accept that we would not die from a bridge, we arrived at nature. Across the Thames I viewed a landscape that had bid me before and drew me again, a breadth of wild field that seemed nearly adequate for my living with its lack of structures. But, of course, even if Gravesbury Reach were to become my home, I would need cross that river to gain it, and thus it was Heaven, requiring one's death for salvation.

God's evolving house was expected. This aspect of London was no horror, though in returning the past to me it seemed a dream itself. The edifice had grown, but my greatest concern for this space of God was to leave it behind. As we passed, I looked to the laboring sinners with bare backs, saw a clerically dressed man, saw a type of artist beside him seen before and smelled. I saw my betrothed's Father laughing heartily in his profession, saw him in a happy state I would never see again.

BOOK THREE: WALES

Twenty-one

The witches gained Bournchester with enough daylight remaining to find an empty portico for the night's sleeping. Nothing fearful found us that evening, Bournchester seeming no more than an edge of London. My resting was reminiscent of Rathel's basement, for despite all the exterior air, the smell was of buildings. As I slept, I seemed in a dream because my dead sister had returned, my greatest desires were being manifested, and the extremes of my beliefs in the reality of the world were found limited; for when had last a dream come true that was not a nightmare?

Up with the sun and the earliest sinners, Marybelle and I walked until finding a coach out for its day of work, whereupon we sought passage to our next goal, the city of Oxford. Why, this man's very company would take us that far, though not in this local carriage. Conveyed to the driver's office, Marybelle made arrangements while I avoided males. Walking nowhere as we waited for our next conveyance, Marybelle and I discovered a woman selling produce from a cart, and feast we did on cucumbers. Fatted on natural food, the satisfied youth could not resist chatting on previous theater.

"Your being alive I find inconceivable," I told Marybelle. "If acceptable, I would know of your living since that last instance on the sinners' boat when I lost you."

"From that instance shall be a gap in my telling, Alba, for the task of losing the rock and gaining land is one I cannot describe. When thoughts of that journey come, I pray God

315

only that they leave. Yet because I did gain land again, at times I feel I have complete power over God's waters. At others I feel the first drop will kill me."

"No more shall I inquire of that wet journey, for I have a similar sense of water's terror, and can imagine your survival no more than you can describe it. But I will ask of that following era, wondering how again I became part of your living."

"This tale I will tell, in that you are either the center or the end. Once out of the sea and learning how to breathe again, I continued with my old living. Peace I then had, but not lasting, in that a blight on the sinners' potato growings came that they believed was caused by witches. Many sinners and most witches of the island were killed thereafter, and this was the devil's stroke to tell me to leave. Thus, I became a demon, the type you and I call sinner; for I became a thief, and thieving is an act of sinners. But steal I did in Jonsway until with money enough to buy passage across the sea. Stealing is safe for us, because sinners think it too 'human' for witches, and we are not blamed. In greater England, I deemed London the best place to go, for there lived the Lady Rathel, and you. No other witch was known to me. Poverty was ever my way, and I lived between buildings, seeking the smell of criminals. In London is Penstone Place and the thickest part of criminals. There I lived."

"I know of Penstone," I confessed, not mentioning my own thievery.

"The criminals have their own society in Penstone, though little to admire. But I lived safely, the criminals not seeking me. Well they know their wares, not bothering to steal from those who have naught. Near them if not with them I lived and learned to steal better, this being aided by my smelling, in that dogs for guarding and folk hiding in wait I knew where sinners could not. I clothed myself decently to pass better, and lived in a building even the criminals rejected, in that it was marked as carrying plague before the great burning, and did not burn enough to ruin the warning signs. But no witch need fear a sickness carried by rats."

316

"How did you find that house in which I lived in London?"

"The Lady Rathel's name is no mystery in her city. I needed only to dress so that people would listen when I asked of her. Then I stole enough to afford this passage, and came for you."

"The other witch, Lucinda, you also found."

"Near the Lady Rathel's household. As I moved there one day to study your locale, I smelled her remnants. This was not you, but a wild witch. That night I returned in hopes of gaining her. When Lucinda came, I had difficulty in convincing her I was the witch, with my salve of no smell. Only with sensing my bottom did she believe, and I was told she awaited you. I remained with her, but you did not come—the constables came at dawn, and then we had to flee. Lucinda ran away like a natural creature, whereas I hid like one social. But Lucinda ran toward the constables. The rest you must know. And for you I returned in the brightest light to be unseen by sinners looking for concealed demons. But I smelled you to be most sickly. This had me feel good, for witches recover, but inside a house you would not be found with witches or looking for them or out amongst sinners with your sex. When you were smelling better, I made complete my plans, then came for you, and we are here."

This tale was astounding to me in its ease, and though I was filled with curiosity, I retained my questions. Since Marybelle asked nothing of my own, longer and more complex life in London—no queries even about my scars—I remained silent. Then I felt dejection. Had I not failed in London from being less of a witch than Marybelle? How ironical that she had succeeded by being a complete witch and thus undesired by sinners; whereas I was so popular as to have entire families living their lives about my center, my end. But I was equally popular with Marybelle, and thereby had been saved, saved from my own killing. And though somehow I would thank Marybelle, first I praised God for a witch's love.

Far from the carriage station we walked, as though practicing the great distance we would ultimately travel without aid of horse. Nevertheless, we did not fail our schedule. Schedule, schedule. When the sinning passengers converged on their

317

conveyance, the witches were also present. As we boarded, Marybelle pressed herself against me to preclude my being sexually aided. Then we repeated our previous day, journeying in a large coach out of the city, through nearly wild land and to Oxford. This great village we gained with daylight enough for Marybelle and me to find a vacant commons for our sleeping. And a chill I had that night, though not from the cool dew; for I felt myself wild, felt myself disbelieving the complete ease of our passage away from Rathel and to God, away from fears and toward fond wishes. About us were trees and bushes, the sound of nesting birds and largish bugs, the smell of a snake. And to think the remainder of my life might be so fine . . . except for the passing drunk coughing and pissing near enough for us to smell and hear nothing else. Up in the night myself to defecate in the chamber pot of a grass thatch, the next morning feasting on squash in the streets, find a coach, then on to the business of true wilderness.

"But, Madam Belle, without arranging aforehand, I cannot carry you today where you would go. In two mornings, however, I can have my son tote you in his wagon. But you must be as hardy as you say, for you would ride behind with cockles and ported barrels. You are fortunate, though, for he goes to Whitford but fortnightly. But no farther. That place is what you seek in being as far west that we carry. Therein you are sure to find conveyance to take you over the Wye River and into Wales."

"To gain this Wales, sir, we must cross a river and a bridge?"

My speaking was unexpected, for I had been described as having too damaged a face for conversation. Not even Marybelle presumed my words, she and the man of vehicles turning to me as I stood apart from the pair doing business at the sinner's desk. But I was not so far away as to cross rivers peacefully.

"And no, miss," the male answered. "In fact, the difficulty with crossing the Wye is that no bridge is there. Thus, a place

318

narrow and shallow enough for a wagon's fording must be used, and they be rare. One is near to Whitford, for that's how towns grow near rivers. But my wagon so swells up in the axles when wet that it would be ruint with such a crossing, so I must thank you, but no. Surely in Whitford you will find a more sturdy or less valuable transport to get you across into this part of Wales, which is not well lived in by folk. To Whitford will be no road, only trail. Beyond that is the Cambrian Mountains. Only donkey or feet will allow you to approach them. But, madam, I can help you little with that living of your life."

"Two days is too long to sleep in the commons without being caught as vagrants, then found to be witches. Thus, within a house we should stay."

Rooms to let for weary travelers? was our query to random sinners. Soon we were directed to an old couple willing to take in decent persons especially if female with a bit of funds. Scarcely could I imagine any person so social as the Rathel, her friends, or the Dentons accepting strangers even for the morning. Of course, those wealthy folk were in need of no extra coin, and had tremendous difficulty applying generosity and concern to their own families.

"Oh, and apologetic we are to burden your door with our presence, missus. But Mother and I traveling to be with kin find that no conveyance shall we gain today, and therefore require any simple spot to situate ourselves throughout the night as God watches over our sleeping, and harsh would be the streets and likely unlawful for our resting. Therefore, we thank you greatly for the bedding that you graciously provide, and bless you through Jesus. To display my appreciation, I shall burden you no more with my speaking, in that I require respite from movements of my head from a terrible accident that yet brings pain after a few sentences—see?" the young lady said, and lifted her veil, up to the tidy room, no thank you for the food either because we've recently eaten or would puke to have that grease within us, only one of the two

319

comments made by the girl, take her non-mother upstairs and wait for Thursday.

Out the next morning after thanking the missus, but we'd be taking no meal and especially no mead in that our faces were too sore for the eating, including that of the mother—see? Then to the streets of a more significant version of London than little Bournchester, Oxford having cathedrals and gardens of its own, an open market providing us with vegetables to feed us for days; for though soon to be in the wilds, we might require some time to become adjusted again to morsel of dulse. To the sinners' house for the waiting, into our hole for another day and night in which we mainly slept for the accumulated resting, eventually to the man with the wagon, all as per schedule. Schedule, schedule.

He relished me at once. Though cordial, this son was fully adult, and proceeded to waft out that sub-belly smell of males upon sensing me, although he was accompanied by his dour wife. Anxious the man was to aid me into the wagon beside his inhuman cargo of cockles. Most forward I was to walk within a hand's width of this male to speak as he deserved.

"Sir, one of your hands on my buttock and I shall beat you to death with this face," I whispered, and raised my veil. Under my own motive force, I climbed into the wagon, the father wondering why only Marybelle's entry was aided, wave good-bye, the wife soon complaining to her husband about a cargo to starve them were it not for the persons' fare behind, this very pair drawing stares from sinners on the streets who wondered of us amongst the seafood, through Oxford and out.

Thus began a journey lasting days. Even the first hours removed from Oxford were a thrill for me, in that our travel was through a land bordered by no buildings. The soil road led through an expanse of fields with no sinners and none of their noise, which was stunning. Though only massive church caves are perfect in their silence, God's wilds have a gentle lack of noise that the sinners' greatest city greens cannot duplicate even at night, for therein even a frog's croak reverberates against buildings and strikes back harshly. But in the open, all the sounds were soft, the wagon's creaking the last aspect of sin heard. Here as well was a lack of stink. Though the city smell was yet in my nose, the stench was replaced by specifiable fragrances of sap, small animals, and blossoms. I then gained a foretelling of even superior experience, for once away from cockles and males, would we not be in Heaven?

We soon came to humor, for I smelled water. Ahead was a river to cross—but, no, it was but a creek, one shallow enough to walk. Sodden logs had been secured across the bed, affording the wagon a shallow path not swelling the axles. As we entered the water, I cackled, the driver turning in wonderment of my sound. Laugh I did at this water I could safely leap into, water that would offer no threat if the wagon collapsed. The additional runnels in our days of travel brought me such high spirits that I fondly anticipated them, for here was relief from dreams of wet subjugation.

As though boasting to myself of our escape, I attempted to smell the sinners behind; and, yes, there was a city, but not London. Oxford I could smell, but the same as a person, land areas are individualistic, and London was not within my senses. And London was my home. Then within me peaked an emotion that I had been bearing long: the loss from being removed from normalcy. So abruptly had I left my established life that I felt lost. As we continued moving away, ever away, the fact of my having abandoned all contact with London by having lost its every scent was a blow to me as though I had lost a friend. And, truth be known by God, friends I had lost there. Only God, however, knew how many.

We rested in the day's center, the driver and wife sharing their bread and water. Marybelle and I offered them beans, which the sinners preferred cooked, thank you. Graze the horses in a natural land not wild enough to satisfy me, not with a wagon and sinners present; and had I been in the near-wilderness so long as to have acquired indulgent sensibilities? After another day's journey, would nothing please me but Man's Isle? This demeanor soon ended, for after boarding the wagon and proceeding, dusk brought a new smell of society, for ahead was a town. Gaining this settlement, the sinners parked near a barn to bed the horses and themselves for the night. Even the conveyed ladies were provided with a louse-infested cot, a good night's sleep with no misery from the bugs' biting us and not the first male slipping in to examine me tactually.

Out of town the next morning into extending wilderness, though not wild enough for a witch as long as sinners could infiltrate the land with horses and a bit of easy riding. This day was repetitive of the previous, including resting in the middle and gaining a village at day's end, one smaller than those before: our goal of Whitford. Jonsway's edges were reminiscent of this village: sparse, unsophisticated buildings not arranged with the formality of London. Few people were seen, the best dressed of them no more social in their attire than Elsie. The moderate gown I wore—with its velvet surface and full petticoats to promote a lady's shape—made me a cipher, especially since I was a wagon's cargo.

So small was Whitford as to have but one church and no glassblower. Similar to great London, this settlement was situated on a river. The driving couple would not cross this water, however, for Whitford was their end. Off to their home outside the village after securing for their passengers a shed for sleeping, thank you everso, and up the next morning for business, walk to the market where farmers gathered to exchange goods. There the witches sought transport to Wystghllaenniomb. One staring male offered to convey us to the village for a fee if only he could comprehend.

"I see ladies too finely dressing to be in the hill land of Wales. If you've kin there, why are they not named nor here to meet you? If you lived there afore, why is it I, who's been here an ever, have not seen—"

"Excuse me, sir," I interrupted, "but we have difficulty replying, in that being from London, we are unaccustomed to such rude intrusions into the personal affairs of ladies."

The farmers surrounded us, though all were hesitant to approach our veils. All of them wondered of our apparel, these people so innocent of society as to find Marybelle's common weave equal to my handhewn piping.

"Might any gentle person be amongst you to convey us to this village named and receive from us a grateful payment in metal coin as well as our kindest wishes and blessings of God?" I asked of all.

Aye, there were at least one, but he could not be leaved until days next. One old and knotted man with permanent amusement and no foolish questions could depart now with his fresh horse and be returned with coin instead of spending it on sea eatings only the wife relished and it did terrible things with the gas in her besides. Leave at once, through Whitford and to a river to kill us.

We journeyed in a small, flexible wagon with remarkably large wheels for extremes of landscape. The farmer offered an endless chat despite our poor interest in discourse, but Marybelle had to reply alone, for I knew our goal. I recalled the Wye, the killing river first mentioned by Wroth in London. My companion also knew, for she could smell my fear.

"We approach a river, sir?" she asked the farmer.

"We are, and a most beautiful and wild thing nearer the mountains."

"We cross this water with effort?"

"No, and ma'am, in that our path leads to the shallows that are most this dry season."

"I swim not, sir, and have a fear of needing to do so," Marybelle continued.

"Well, don't be fearing for that Wye which lies before us. Walking across it you could without getting your vest wet, though some water might be seeping up from the wagon's floor, so hold your goods high if they should be keeping dry."

Soon visible through the trees, the river proved to be narrow ahead, though it had an odor of wet bulk. The sound as well was mild: no raging currents to drag me under. But with all my fear as we approached, I found further emotion, found surprise at the sinner's lack of preparation, for he simply drove into the river. Up I stretched to view, seeing the far side of the Wye—as well as its bottom, so shallow and clear was the water. And I thought of a pool in a huge garden in some

323

opaque city left behind, but Pangham's had been water enough for drowning, despite its clear aspect. Then I settled within the wagon as we crossed, the single horse wet to its belly, the witches receiving some seeping as the farmer had warned, but no drowning as per Satan's nocturnal vows.

As we gained dry land, the farmer stated: "And this is Wales, ladies, once over the river, in that it be the border between England."

We proceeded to wilderness, a land I was finally able to contemplate, to feel. Only after crossing the river did I become aware that I had been regarding nothing but this water. During the day's travel, I had thought little of our goal, because I understood that any thinking would lead to a river's fear. But as we continued into Wales with all drowning behind, I sensed the countryside, seeing a wealth of deep greens ending with no brick building. I saw tall trees with countless peers, saw the land about me in rising, falling curves, hills never flattened for a cathedral's foundation. And where were the sinners? No road had they here, and scarcely a trail. This dent in the land we followed throughout the day, twice resting the farmer and his horse, the witches sitting on soft ground to smell cats of no London household, perhaps a bear, birds seen throughout the air, and enough insects to support them all. I also smelled a witch, in that Marybelle's salve was worn away so that again she smelled like family. Soon, cresting a hill like a tide to carry me high, not drown me below, I viewed through the trees a unique sight, an idea known but never experienced. In the distance were ragged, conical cliffs of enormous scope called mountains. And when the sinning farmer turned to me, I had no explanation for that terrible sound of cackling, Marybelle's only response a pleasure I could smell.

Days on wagons' bucking bottoms had yet to pain my bones, but soon my nose hurt. Deep into the day we gained a final settlement, the younger witch disheartened to be amongst sinners again. Wystghllaenniomb was no more than a supply center for the local horse ranchers whose mobile crop we also smelled. Unreadable words carved on the rare sign proved the foreignness of this region. The entirety of the village could be seen in a brief walk, no buildings here requiring stairs, no high roofs from which to observe more of the sinners' constructions. No gardens to give a witch respite, for sinners were the aberration here, and around them was God.

"And where about this place is it you go?" the farmer asked as he halted his horse at the village's far edge.

"We would go beyond this place," Marybelle replied; and I wondered when last I had heard her speak, but could not recall.

"Nothing past but farms," the man stated. "Toward which one would you go?"

"That one nearest the mountains," Marybelle answered. "My father has a cabin in the forest beyond. There I take the daughter for healing."

"A few farms be about, madam, and two that I know of toward the mountains. One lies there," he said, and pointed north, "the other there," and stretched his arm south.

After a pause, Marybelle replied, "I believe it the one southerly."

"And how is it we will know right or wrong, madam?"

"If correct, my father will appear with donkeys shortly."

"But what, missus, if the farm be incorrect?"

"I will know when we approach it. If incorrect, we shall hie to the other. Surely an extra fee shall be paid you if more toting is needed."

"Very well, and off we are, missus. And kindly speak to me of the wrong way as soon as it be known you."

We proceeded beyond the village toward the west and south. Before us was the same land seen for hours, hills increasing in size as the mountains grew nearer, the green of the foliage deep, the breeze clean and smelling more of horses than sinners, the mountains seemingly as expansive as the sky itself, a grey atmosphere of stone.

We continued for another hour, continued toward animals. Soon, small, dark horses were seen at pasture. We then arrived at a farm, its buildings well removed from the path we traveled. Having sensed about carefully,

Marybelle of course recognized the site.

"Yes, and this without question is the proper locale, sir, one not mistaken by me. Then we ask for you to travel as far as you might to the dense forest ahead."

He did, and we journeyed effortlessly, halting at the forest near dusk, stopping at wilderness.

"No farther can I travel, madam," the man announced, "what with having no path beyond. Yet I see no father nor donkey."

"Surely he is immediately about, or coming. If not, then we walk to his cabin which is exactly in that direction," Marybelle asserted, and pointed into a forest she had never seen before.

"And, madam, I have some concern if you may be wrong."

The younger traveler then provided an answer.

"Kind sir, your thoughtful generosity of concern we dismiss with appreciation and clear explanation; for if by rare chance we have the wrong locale, then return we shall to the passed farmhouse by walking."

"But, miss, you will be walking in the dark."

"Sir, we would be walking beneath the moon. If ever you had traveled in London at night with criminals likely to attack from every doorway, you would glory in the solitude of being away from true beasts. The horses about are safe, are they not, so what is to endanger persons?"

"No more than being lost, miss," he replied. Even the smell of this sinner's concern had become odd, for I was no longer of his people.

"Sufficiently lost, sir," I continued, "and we sleep until daylight, thereupon to gain the farm, or even the village if need be. But no longer shall we gain your concern, for we deserve no worry from you to make you suffer, in that no suffering shall burden us, I assure you. Therefore, with the grace of Lord Jesus we bid you adieu, and pray for your safety even as we pray for God's kindness toward you to never end."

Finally the talkative lass convinced the farmer to abandon us, though he refused the additional coin Marybelle offered, for his thoughtfulness would not be moderated by money. A tip of his hat, a wish for good waiting, and he was gone.

Marybelle looked toward the forest. I watched the farmer

depart. No horses were about, no farmhouse nearby, only a receding sinner returning to his world, leaving me for a wild land that seemed not only immediate, but infinitely beyond. The wagon left trails, but none existed past the forest entrance. Only untouched Earth and its remaining warmth of day, vines and grasses never seen by men, animals never corrupted nor killed by sinners, a new world so complex in its sensings and promise as to form a whole engulfing my perceptions. And all this world was ours.

"Can we be so safe so easily?" I pondered, speaking to Marybelle while facing the disappearing wagon and its dissolving sound.

"Only the end was easy," she replied.

"This area is unknown to us."

"Smells like God's Earth to me."

"In what manner do we select a direction?"

"Until the hills become mountains we walk. Farther than that, eating and water may be sparse. We move away from the sinner smell."

"And thereafter what is done?"

"We live. We live away from sinners. We walk and follow our sensings to the homesite that best fits us. We walk away from any trapper's cabin, any other poison in the natural land."

This was no Elsie. Marybelle lacked the servant's sweetness, but also her navet. As Marybelle removed her veil to relieve herself from having to hide, I saw how ugly she was, for the first instance in my life not finding a witch's true face pleasing in appearance. Elsie's and Rathel's and Eric's—faces like my own—were familiar and accepted, if not preferred; but was not this witch's visage of God's nature?

"We walk, then, into God's land," Marybelle stated.

"Away from Satan's," I replied. And we entered.

Twenty-two

We entered the forest to a depth precluding the view of sinners potentially approaching on horseback. Then we slept in the grass near the raised roots of huge oaks, an experience wholly unlike our night in Oxford's commons, for in these wilds we were not bounded by sinners. We slept until dawn was announced by birds with their flapping and insects abandoning their night buzz. Then we sought a home.

The Cambrian Mountains were not visible through the forest, but the pervasive stone smell of our site had a massive source I was eager to see again. Around us were parts of that range from its ancient past, mossy boulders separating the trees. Past these hard forms of God I walked with Marybelle, through a haze of tiny moths, beneath flitting swallows, frightening a rabbit, which brought a smile to me. I had forgotten how rapid and erratic were the moves of these beasts. But, of course, not erratic: Drunks in London were erratic; hares were precise in their complicated turnings. The witches themselves remained steady, having stuffed hats and vests into bags, proceeding through a land of true life.

"Not enough undergrowth to feed even two witches," I offered some unspecifiable time later when the coarse terrain had yet to change.

"We'll not settle in a place to starve us," Marybelle replied, "and not one so near a village and farm."

Walk we did. After significant travel, I found myself losing energy. Marybelle, however, was as constant as the ocean waves. So steady was her progress that she seemed familiar with this land, though in fact she was only decisive. Worse, she seemed tireless, and I wondered if I could sustain this rate considering my lax life in the city. But Marybelle became weary enough to cease before I collapsed.

"I will pee here, and then we might rest," she said.

"Excellent, in that I am less than accustomed to such hiking."

We dropped our baggage, then squatted in different areas for different deposits. When we returned to our paired bags, as though a witches' settlement, they became the subject of our speaking.

"If your bag be weighty, you might throw out what is useless," Marybelle submitted.

"Within I have additional clothes and shoes if those I wear become depleted. No mementos have I brought, nothing truly useless. For now I shall bear the weight."

"Are not all the dressing things beneath your gown excess?" Marybelle wondered. "Do they not interfere with your movement in a witches' land?"

"To some degree, but removing them entails removing my dress, a process elaborate enough for me to delay until our next night's sleeping. As well, divesting myself of underthings would necessitate my burying them, think ye not? Although I will leave my urine behind, liquids are worn away by the rain; whereas cloth remains to draw sinning curiosity."

"Agreed. We need not attract sinners, even those unseen. If none are in any area, they soon may be."

We had walked for hours. If in London, I would have a home to accept me after my efforts. This concern of shelter, however, was not entirely due to the sinners' influence on me, for all my life I had slept indoors: with Mother in a cabin, and later in a London town house. I mentioned this environmental change to Marybelle.

"With no roof above, we shall collect dew each night as we

did this last. Never have I cared for dampness. The Rathel's basement I found comforting, but the moisture there was in the air, not upon my skin."

"I fancy the dampness," Marybelle replied. "Even in London, with all its buildings, I oft slept out. But here we'll need a shelter, for the smell of this clime promises a much harsher cold than Man's Isle. Perhaps we'll find a cave."

"Having familiarity with such cliff holes from my past on the same isle, remaining within enough for a telling experience of their nature, I have come to understand that against my recently-stated preference, the average cave is not only damp in its nonabsorbency, but also typically dripping and puddling."

"Not so wet as the Irish Sea," Marybelle observed.

We ate our last cucumber. Continuing our trek, we soon came to ridged land with fewer trees, these stony ledges precluding my viewing our mountain goal. Marybelle offered her sensing of more verdant land ahead, believing this region we entered no more than a rocky foot to the mountains, the solid stone head well beyond separated by a richer torso. Often as we proceeded we needed to skirt sheer drops of several paces. Standing upon one of these minor heights, I glimpsed the mountains, then leapt upward for a superior view. Being poor at leaping, Marybelle could only listen to my descriptions and smile. No difficulty had she in walking, however.

And walking. Further mountain views continued to thrill, renewing my sense of goal. Before darkness, we halted to select a site for sleeping, but what was our choice? A thorny bush. A mass of smelly flock plants with sticky oil worse than that used by Elsie on my (my?) wooden floor. A rotten log with every type of bug, none of them appealing. Sharp, protruding ridges of stone. Marybelle moved directly to a tree, placing her bag against the exposed roots. I wondered what mystery was contained within her luggage so useful that Marybelle would not dispose of its mass as she had suggested of mine. Perhaps its only value was a pillow, for thereupon she settled, not opening her eyes until morning.

No bed here for me to be upon or below. Seeing Marybelle settle so easily, and being fully wearied, I lay upon a flat section of soil, brushing away stones poking my spine like a man's hands against my bosom. Feeling dampness collect on me at once, I leapt up to remove the extra dress from my bag and cover myself completely. Though I nearly smothered throughout the night, I had none of that wet river feel surrounding me, drowning me. I slept, no dreaming.

"Is our walking endless?" I asked Marybelle during our morning rest.

"We walk till we find an end."

"The smell of sinners is scarcely noticeable. Are we not sufficiently removed from them?"

"Not if they ride horses. Besides, the eating is poor here."

"So I've noticed, since not even sweet grass roots have I found about, only some small mushrooms that need be spat away."

"Once living in these wilds, you will have less of a sinners' need to eat throughout the day on some schedule."

"Living in these wilds in our current manner and I will require less sustenance by having less of a person in need of nutrition, my feet and legs falling off after further months of travel. And though I'll become accustomed to this endless walking by accomplishing same, how might we find our goal? Have we a better guide than randomness?"

"I follow my nose, which was not injured by the sinners as was yours."

"Equally impaired are my eyes, since they see only rock ahead. For a time I would be a bird flying above these trees to sight what lies beyond."

"My prayer for you to become a bird," Marybelle returned, "but I doubt it occurs."

"Then I climb a tree."

"I've no nimbleness for that."

"Not being constructed like an average witch, I've adequate

331

flexibility for such clambering, as perfected perhaps by climbing up and down the Rathel's wall from my chamber to the street in formulation of plans unfortunately less successful than yours."

"Yes," Marybelle replied.

Considering my mass of words, I waited for at least one more from the sister, but none came. How much like the land this woman was becoming to issue no verbalisms. Perhaps I should have brought Eric along.

We sought a suitable tree. Ahead was a steep and rocky rise, one we would normally avoid to eliminate excess climbing, but the upper plateau was well treed. There I ventured, Marybelle remaining below.

"I study signs while waiting," she noted, and began examining roots.

"Upward I go in a most vertical mode along the stone flatness to a tree of high scope, its selection dependent upon reachable limbs to facilitate my extended climbing and the desired viewing therefrom," I mentioned while looking only toward Marybelle.

"I look at signs," she replied, bending toward vines.

Climbing this rock was easier than Rathel's steeper wall, though the current journey was more lengthy. And the climb was finer, for instead of boring brick, before me was a continuum of Godly subtleties, none of which smelled of sinners' soot, but of soil and insect trails and growing molds, living aspects too small to be noticed by a sinner, but of import to any respectable witch, even one corrupted by major cities. Carefully I climbed, my feet on hard lumps, my hands in shallow dents. Disappointed I was to find upon that high plateau no view of the desired mountains, for even higher ground lay beyond. I then applied myself to a massive tree, up its trunk limb by limb, looking down for footing only to see Marybelle looking up toward me. I continued, manipulating myself up and around until achieving the best view.

The best view of more high land. As though on Rathel's roof, I saw extended sameness. Similar to that view of London beyond which was only more of London, here as well as a scene of further rocky land, greys with not enough greens. The same as Rathel's roof, the view afforded me no sight of home. Slowly I climbed down to my sister.

"Since you return no bird, we both walk," Marybelle said as I moved to her side. "Found ye a clear aim?"

"More of this," I muttered, and we continued.

With an endless journey before us assured, we sought eating to support us. After lapping a bit at a tiny spring, we searched for food in the land of rock. Succulent mosses we found, but they would offer little sustenance. Reluctantly I followed Marybelle's mealing on insects, the elder witch heartily chewing beetles. Though softer grubs were my preference, I accepted several young beetles that required no extensive toothing; and, no, I would never eat a spider. Due to my recent bugless diet, I first had to kill the insects by nipping off their heads with my fingers. Then I pulled the legs and wings off as though . . .

"Plucking a chicken," commented Marybelle, who popped a pair of bugs into her gullet.

In this manner our days proceeded. After two or four or a hundred, I became filled with this life and longed for Man's Isle, the comfortable terrain with abundant food, little stony ground to batter one's feet, no needed climbs and plunges up and down hard crests. London itself seemed nearly preferable, but the current environ so impressed me with its genuineness and peace that my full willingness was to continue. But after additional days — six or a thousand — so wearied had I become that I felt some further understanding of our progress was required. As we rested at the bottom of a long, rough slope to require further clambering, I found myself inquiring of my companion.

"If you would be so gracious as to aid my understanding, miss, so long was I in unnatural London that I remain these days uncertain as to the specifics of the environ we would seek in permanency, in that seemingly we've been walking eternally with no likelihood of finding a foothold superior to these which currently puncture our backsides."

"A clear stream of lasting size," Marybelle pronounced, attempting to eat a worm squirming from her fingers. "More and better things for eating than this. A shelter made by God, or things to make our own."

"In London, miss, I came to understand that all of England is islandic. Therefore, we will unavoidably gain the sea if our walking continues, for surely those mountains are beneath us this very moment. Since sinners love the ocean, we will have stepped into their social maw."

"We would smell it first, but I smell only mountain," she replied, and downed a dry, useless leaf.

"Of course we will not achieve the sea, for we starve first. If not, in winter we freeze in slush at the bottom of a gorge."

"We feel winter coming and prepare."

"Well, praise God for a change in weather, in that the current lovely clime is so grand I can scarcely bear it for another million days."

We continued. One day ended and the next began. The nights were separated by rocks. The rocks were connected by our feet. Whenever I found sufficient energy at day's end, I climbed a tall tree for observation, always viewing sameness beyond. Though I found no joy in exhaustive hiking, this dynamic situation was superior to my static state in London. Mainly in the great city I had suffered emotional lethargy when not out seeking salvation, which usually turned detrimental. Since I had neither the chores of Elsie nor the business of Rathel, I was often bored. But in these wilds with Marybelle, I relearned a witch's occupation: living. Gathering food and caring for one's home had been our need even on Man's Isle. Common living had always been an experience: wading in a creek or trekking to the shore to watch the sea waves, examining the changing states of God's seasons. Then I understood how much the sinner I had been in London. Rathel and her ilk could undertake their chosen activities because the tasks of daily sustenance were accomplished by inferiors. Chores were the servants' living, but witches were all peers.

And by accepting the position of a lady in London, my living had been that of a social sinner; for as long as Rathel had servants, so had I. Dear God, please allow Elsie to forgive me.

As though in a delirium, I found myself contemplating London's better aspects: the fine foods available, the dewless environ of Rathel's house, the days devoid of extensive treading. Then I received holy enlightenment in the form of objective truth. London was criminals and other gents to attack me. Animal flesh fried and metal burned. Beggars and drunks and tarts. Rathel and her plans for me to be killing whomever. What a place of torment this London was compared to the wild and wondrous land wherein God had now graced me to live! With this improved deportment, I continued with Marybelle for several more thousand days before I tired of forced comparisons, and my travel again became plodding.

Awakening late one day as though a socialite, I found Satan's worst witch, for there was Marybelle gnawing a lizard.

I was sickened.

"You eat an animal of God as though a sinner?" I blurted.

"God would not have me starve," she replied, and swallowed. "You find no similarity between insects and lizards?"

"I find similarity between witches and sinners, but not enough for me to build a city. If in our travels we find a horse, might you not consume it? How similar they are to lizards, with their equal number of legs and but the single tail." And I snatched a handful of grass to stuff into my mouth as I leapt up and began walking for another epoch.

The world changed. I cannot say the change was soon, for nothing came soon in this era: not the next step when the first of each day was an effort, not any hungered bite since the materials being eaten were neither gratifying in their flavor nor satisfying to my starving bowels. I therefore note that eventually the terrain began changing: first smelled, then seen, *finally* felt with our battered legs. The land became flatter, and we achieved our best view yet of the mountains, though they seemed no nearer. Some green thickness was seen at their base, but viewed we hill or forest or imagination? One full day of traversing the lowering land revealed flat greenness immediately beyond, which from my initial, distant espying seemed a satisfying field. But this emotion left with a good smell and one word from Marybelle.

"Swamp."

"My sense is that we should best proceed in such direction," I noted, pointing away from the swamp, "for there lies drier land."

"But I have seen kites and a swallow flying," Marybelle returned. "Their patterns say richer land direct ahead."

"Ah, following the blooming birdies has to be better than remaining with the ruddy rocks," I submitted, and tromped toward the swamp.

Mud with patchy, low grass was our changed terrain in the following hours. Then we traveled through higher, sharper grass that irritated exposed hands and concealed its deeper water until we were wet. Up to the waist we fell the first immersion, only I managing to keep my bag dry. Our next stumbling found the thin witch face first in murky water nonetheless cleaner than the Thames, with plant remains on the bottom instead of glassware. Thereby my bag became sodden and heavy, this wet collapsing continuing and never pleasant in its surprise. The submersions ended when the swamp became consistently deeper, we witches walking for hours with our knees never out of the water; and when our thighs were clear, we yet had to drag our sodden skirts. For our buttocks to be in the air was a holiday, and to carry our soaked bags at our sides instead of on our heads was cause for praising Lord God, Whose mess we were immersed in.

Night was coming with only unclean water about us. A stand of trees we espied on higher, drier ground was too distant. Nearer was more of that initial low grass denoting a solid patch of earth. Perhaps. Without comment, we proceeded toward the expected dryness, hoping for a sleeping place whereupon we might drain. Because light was ended as we approached this hopeful parcel, we could not view well ahead, though the massive snake swimming at me was not missed, not with my response of near drowning from flinging myself away from the creature in fear, for had Mother not warned me of that shape of head? And when we reached the presumably drier ground and dragged ourselves up the steep bank, to no surprise but to my utter disappointment I found myself collapsing onto mud.

Walking farther on this segment to find only similar mud, Marybelle settled anywhere. Before accepting this locale and falling into a sleep to claim my thinking, I offered a sensible notion.

"Might you deem it best, Miss Marybelle, to sleep standing upright in order to discourage poisonous snakes from attacking us?"

"Poisonous snakes attack no witches," she returned, prostrate on the mud.

"I suggest you not eat them despite this safety," I muttered, and slept in the dank and the mud and longed for the wettest cave in God's universe, or a bridge to sleep upon, or the bottom of the bleeding ocean, which in itself must be better than this.

In this manner our journey proceeded, only changing by becoming worse.

Gaining that previously-seen stand of trees the following day, we seemed on a sinners' ship to separate us from the surrounding swamp sea. Though the mountains were clearly seen, intervening land was not discernible due to the increasing trees, all unclimbable. Luxuriously we settled on dry soil a spell to contemplate our future course.

"Our simplest path to the mountains is unquestionable," I averred.

"We do not seek the mountains themselves in that they will be no better than the hard land recently left," Marybelle offered.

"Oh," I replied.

"We seek the best land near the mountains," she continued, becoming as talkative as a sinner. "Farthest from sinners yet

337

the best for our own living. Remote enough we are now to venture in any direction."

"Oh," I replied. "I believe the recent breeze brought a scent of the sea. Therefore, we should select a different direction."

"But the sea smelled is from over the mountains," Marybelle returned. "Nearer, toward the low warmth, is more animal activity, thus better land for the animals that we are."

"As long as we don't follow the snakes that would eat us," I muttered, and off I sloshed in Marybelle's direction.

Exiting the swamp after another day's walking, we achieved drier though scarcely superior ground. Before us lay a fog-covered expanse of soft, greyish brown, a gently rolling land that was visually comforting but stank of a different mud.

"In your vast experience with the wild lands of God's particular world known as the British Empire, might you have gleaned knowledge, miss, of an area such as that before us, and can you now describe what we face?"

"Bog," Marybelle said. "Slick and muddy."

So it was. The greater part of that day we traversed this semi-firm land, our journey begun in a fog and proceeding through drizzle, which at least washed the scum away from our frequent falls down slick slopes into a thick, blackish material covered with lichenous slime. At least our bags sank slowly enough for retrieval upon such slippage, and what a horror the thought of swimming in the stuff to retrieve our submerged belongings.

Necessarily we slept in the bog one night, on the firmest ground we found. The sole dry area available to collapsing witches, however, was scarcely large enough for our bags, much less our bodies. Therefore, we both accepted immediate, total stillness, since any tossing about would have us rolling down a slope toward appalling circumstances. And fully static I easily remained after falling asleep, for my mud coating dried to stiffen me, the sporadic drizzles that night only enough to irk my face from the moistened mud drooling into my eyes, such an annoyance as to attack me unconsciously; for one drop of mud I thought a blinding torrent set me into a

338

common state of nightmarish foolishness wherein I believed that a water snake was eating my eyes as I proved myself the sinner by swimming hellishly away. Then I semi-awakened only long enough to comprehend that the true difficulty was no more than stinging rain even as I rolled over to shield my face with my fingers, finding better use for that hand as I lost balance and began tumbling down the slope with no ability to cease, a mere witch's limbs inadequate for overcoming God's own gravity, into the muck, through the layer of slime, gagging at once in anticipation of having the stuff on my tongue and therefore spitting it out in advance, which only opened my mouth and thereby allowed a true ingestion, a most effortful gagging thus ensuing as I threw myself upward in a harsh awakening; for at first I thought myself in a dream wherein I slid from a sinners' ship into the Irish Sea to drown along with Elsie, whom I had adjudicated the witch for failing as a servant to clean the Thames's sludge flowing under my bed and over me. But so common was this nightmare that I ignored it until finding myself asleep breathing mud, up and awake and gagging in a flash, clambering up the slope to collapse face down, arms spread across God's mediocre Earth for support, mouth in the dirt, but how to tell with all the muck on the tongue from immersion? Marybelle did not bother to awaken through this, my only consolation being that at least my bag had not accompanied me, for I was determined to retain it, not losing nor abandoning it until Marybelle lost hers. But being so superior a witch as to sense a sister's thoughts in her sleep, Marybelle next rolled over, retaining her balance though she nudged my bag with her sinners' shoes enough for it to roll away and down, lost in the mud, the entire remaining night finding me concerned with the horrors of retrieving it in the morning, of having to dig through the muck and not discovering the bag for hours, having to search the slime with my face below the surface in order to reach bottom, eating scum all day only to sleep above it at night and again swim within the sludge during dreams of eating slime and swimming in muck the evening long. Therefore, at first light, having suffered through the unending night with partially-conscious though exhausted anticipation of waking horrors, up like a frog I leapt to tear myself from thoughts worse than nightmares or even operas in being true, worse for their describing not the past left behind, but the future to suffer through twice, once in the foretelling and the second in the upcoming experience, the former always worse by seeming endless and being repeated throughout the era of worry. To end this nightmarish foreboding, up I leapt at dawn to throw myself into the scum and thereby begin my torment immediately so as to end it as soon as possible, God willing, which He was not, though in a manner I was most successful, easily reaching upward from my position mired to the guts in the mud to grasp my case where it had lodged on a stone, remaining dry and muckless. But a failure I was by attempting to crawl out of the sludge with the bag instead of tossing it upward or asking Marybelle to remove it from my grasp, for too great was the weight for me to overcome the slippery bank, sliding backward and down, both myself and the bag well mired again in the sludge, this another instance in my doomed life of finding a nightmare come true to torment me, Marybelle by then awake and on her way, surely having reveled in the finest night's sleep of her lifetime, I bloody well hoped.

By noon we had exited the bog to enter less slippery land where we discovered a gritty creek that to the muck-witch sisters was surely God's most graceful river. Lolling within completely unclothed, we became decently clean and laughingly pleased, washing all our apparel including the semi-lady's underthings she would not bury, not if she had to dig in the mud, dry the frillies then into the bag for later secreting. First wash the luggage. Marybelle opened hers beyond my good view, though I saw items wrapped with waxen paper. Only her bag she cleaned, not its contents, which had been made impervious to mud not from the owner's great experience as a witch, but due to her opportunity to prepare, though I would have thought of no such wrapping regardless, therefore being inferior to this person as a witch even in a situation wherein such superiority seemed circumstantial. When we had been wet in the creek so long as to shrivel, out we came to lie on the stone bank, drying in the luxurious sunlight. And all the world was perfect, except for the starvation of those two witches somewhere in God's wilds whom Satan had not allowed to eat in days.

"Might I suggest, miss, if only in the way of fond, optimistic impression, that the worst of our travels be ended," I mentioned.

"You might not," Marybelle replied, "in that Satan has ears."

Again we walked, no longer approaching the mountains. From ahead, a light breeze brought a greater smell of animal warmth. As the land became less moist, our spirits became less slimy, especially when we smelled wild food, our small company of traveling theater witches moving up a rise to find and uproot groundbean plants, not a grand meal for Man's Isle, but wonderful after eating Satan's slime. Handfuls of the pale tubers we consumed, thereby gaining sustenance to support our further endless walking. Perhaps this eating was most satisfying because all our senses told us that the food ahead would be superior. Though bloated, we raised our bent torsos and attained a hearty rate of travel.

The marsh edge we traversed led to hilly land, gentle slopes of God's greenery, not the devil's stone. Eventually the gritty, grey earth changed to richer loam supporting plant life: clumps of the no-hue brush and wild grasses whose roots precluded a loosening of the soil with each rain. Low rockwood trees and brown oaks for birds and squirrels began appearing in our noses. Into the day I became concerned again, as though a business person worried of invoices and income. So improved was the land that I wondered of proceeding so far as to find worse. Unfit for sinners in that no flat space was available for them to drag their horses and carts upon, the locale revealed to me no gross features detrimental to our living. Then I sought my missing thinking, wondering what inferior trait of this region I had overlooked that Marybelle would instantly fling before me after I revealed myself as foolish. None found, I proceeded with my mouth.

"I might ask, Miss Marybelle, whether we are so set in our traipsing that we can no longer understand settling."

"I would seek a stream instead of these wet ditches," she informed me.

"Yes, miss, thank you, miss," the fool replied.

The next day we found an excellent brook flanked by bright grasses and numerous trees. Into the rising ground the brook inversely disappeared, its source revealed by our walking: a bubbling spring producing a lovely pond with tiny fishes in clear water infinitely superior to Pangham Gardens or the Irish Sea.

So pleasing was this perfect water that my continued walking became lighthearted, for I hoped to discover further aspects of this land equally rewarding. Next encountered were bright blossoms and shading trees, and, yes, various berries and silkshoots for the nibbling. Most important was the greater fact of our being within rich forest land promising fine living for God's good animals—and what could be better? To find my own answer, I proceeded ever more rapidly, bag on my hip, happy strides carrying me onward, ever onward, only to become aware in the following moment that I was walking alone.

I turned. Behind me stood Marybelle by the pond, her bag on the ground. In the speckled shade of a yew, with the water's crisp music behind her, Marybelle stood looking toward me, toward bright Alba in a spot of sunlight on her endless way.

"Why go farther?" spake loquacious Marybelle.

Since her speaking was obviously a witches' test of some cruel nature, I paused to consider the ramifications hidden within Marybelle's apparently simple verbalities, convinced that cryptic notions lay therein to flog me with my own ignorance. From my brilliance, I thus gained full comprehension, replying with an idea to save me.

"We stand on the sight line of a sinners' roadway under construction and approaching this very moment."

"I smell nothing of them."

"Immediately beyond our sight, hidden by high ground and prevailing breezes to carry the smell away, lies a small village populated only by bishops, magistrates, and tormented lovers."

"Doubtful, but yonder tree will tell with its climbing," Marybelle returned, and pointed toward a grand hill some distance removed that held a towering plane tree with branches reachable by a flexible witch.

"No taller tree nor higher hill I find about," she added. "No better view would be afforded."

"True, miss, but a journey will be required for me to achieve the hill, its upperside, and then the treetop."

"Yes," verbose Marybelle replied. So I dropped my bag and moved away with firm strides and the semi-satisfied sense of having appeared less of a fool than possible, for my possibilities were boundless.

What an odd hill was this to become no larger in appearance as I approached, my impression due to the hill's being so removed and huge that I traveled an era and was blind from exhaustion by the time I reached its slopes. Around me I saw only forest. Taking no rest, I began the steep climbing, looking behind until espying Marybelle, for her sight was my first goal. Halting to look toward my sister, I was surprised to find her so tiny as to be viewable by only birds and witches. Again I was thrilled by God's great creation of distance, that substance of space, as tactile as water and wind, especially cherished by me then because nothing but distance separated us witches, no sinners' smoke nor haze nor city street, only God's singular color of multiple greens, only waving leaves and impassive tree trunks, only insects and birds and hiding marmots. With a brief wave to my sister, I turned to the hillside and continued climbing, cackling loudly, foolishly, so lustful to be so pleased.

Once on the hill's upper level, I became childish, intending to reserve my best sight for the end. Therefore, I only glimpsed the vista about me as I chose a tree and clambered, determining to be less giddy lest I miss a step and take a tumble down the hill to receive a greater beating than inconsequential Rathel had delivered. And this thoughtfulness was required, for the climbing was difficult with limbs too thick to readily grasp. So I proceeded in a businesslike manner, as though a widowed English lady plotting a bit of vengeful death for the day. But once up the tree and lodged in a crotch, I laughed at the thought of Rathel; for no sinner was in sight, nothing but a perfect view of home. The mountains were so near as to induce my gasp. Here was God's greatest exemplar of space, the mountains in fact being so distant that trees on their slopes seemed buds, though that impassive mass of grey and streaked green crowned with white seemed at the end of the limb that held me. And I laughed from the joy in my life and my pride in great God, then ceased cackling upon slipping to nearly fall and break my back on a limb below. Then behind I turned, seeing far away a bog, then a swamp, and I laughed at Satan's rejected land, turning again toward God's. The remaining views about me presented only forest like the land below, perfect land to require no more endless walking, only endless life.

No words had I for these sights, for this total experience— and none was needed, for I was composing no opera. I was alive as though only now living. The details of shadow and light, of dark green and wilted grass, of bugs and birds and furry creatures, were all delightful. Nothing seemed static. The trees had rustling leaves, the animals and clouds were moving uniquely, and the Earth itself seemed to vibrate with life, as though having heart and lungs, fluids flowing warmly within.

Though joyous and well satisfied, I understood my position to have been mandated by serious, saving concerns. Apart from a vantage of pleasure, I had the business of searching for sinners. Therefore, I carefully looked and smelled for any sign of sinning bodies and their products: cut trees, paths in the

344

land, smoke from cooking, smells of droppings, unsensed activity causing poor growth in plants and fearful activity in animals. Thorough I was in waiting a true extent, long enough for the breezes to shift as they might and bring fragrant news: of a dead squirrel and a fox eating it before the carcass rotted, of the wild potato flower blooming, of a salt lick and some unidentifiable animal there I knew to be anything but a sinner. Then, being satisfied that creatures of God were alone in these wilds, I turned to glimpse Marybelle, the woman yet to move. Then down the tree and the hill I moved and through our home to my sister.

Twenty-three

"Either an especially damp, especially unseen cloud had passed by, or the beginning of cool weather I sense; do I not, Miss Marybelle?"

"Fall coming," she replied.

"Now that we have tacitly accepted this locale for living, I must suggest that shelter of some nature be sought; for although I well appreciate the advantages of our wild environment, let us not suffer therefrom. Let us not become inundated by the rain and snow, the hail and sleet, the ice and slush of winter."

"A cave might be sought."

"Having familiarity with such cliff holes from my past on Man's Isle, remaining within enough for a telling experience, I have come to understand that against my preference, the average cave is not only damp from nonabsorbency, but also too often dripping and puddling."

"Not so wet as the Irish Sea," Marybelle replied.

"No abandoned hut is to be found?"

"Not where sinners have never been."

"We thus concede that the sinners are alone amongst humans in their ability to use God's given materials for their own sheltering benefit."

"Say you this after condemning me for a single lizard eaten?"

"My meaning is not to promote the destruction of God's complex creatures with our teeth nor the vanquishing of trees

346

with any extremity. However, not only multiple limbs but entire trees are known to fall without a witch's aid, and lesser branches can be broken away without crippling the bearing plant. As well, have not the sinners displayed the alternate possibility of laying stones together?"

"No mason am I nor carpenter," Marybelle mentioned.

"But fine cave-finders we shall prove to be," I declared, "even though our days here have not revealed the first crack expansive enough for a half-eaten lizard," and I stomped toward the nearest hillside.

Together we sought a stone cave for our dwelling. An era was required to search the local hillsides, Marybelle having to overcome her difficulties with climbing; and how fit for the Earth she was in her solidity and stiffness, like a stump. And though I desired no cave, neither would I accept defeat in another challenge, having previously lost those of exiting London, selecting the proper town in Wales, determining the best direction for walking, halting at the obvious locale for a home, surviving the bog, and so on. But after too many days of seeing countless fallen limbs and stones of a size to be handled, no more than several cracks in the hills had I found, some large enough to hold a single, folded witch, but no chamber to make even a cramped, uncomfortable dwelling.

Marybelle concluded our search by saying, "The land never did smell like one for caves this far from the mountains."

"Yet by your own suggestion we passed weeks or months in fruitless search when you never expected to achieve success?" I wondered.

"My expectation was to be on Man's Isle until my death."

"Mine was for you to reside in the Irish Sea forever, and praise God for that mistake. And since we've both been proven imperfect in our expecting, let us attempt to progress with intellection instead of dreams. Rational examination of the lost past you mentioned is that on the former island, you had a home of sorts as built either by yourself, some other witch, a herd of sinners, or other living creatures, did you not?"

"Built by God Himself, in that it was a cave," she said.

"Ah, and thus your predilection for wet holes. But since

347

we'll not be transporting your former home here for our usage, and lacking both a selection of caves and a desire to live on the bare mountainside, might we not activate some further attainment of shelter? Though of course you be no carpenter nor mason—as I surmise from the great randomness of my guesswork thinking—might your vast and deservedly gained though less than ebullient collected knowledge contain details of how we might construct a type of shelter without being considered sinning carpenter nor blinking mason, neither of which you likely are, as I might presume without further intimations on your part?"

"Yes," she replied.

"And thank you, miss, for such relief, in that no longer do I fear becoming either a craftsman or an ice floe."

"You're welcome," she replied.

During the following days or decades, we proceeded to construct an unnatural shelter. My first notion was to duplicate Mother's cabin on Man's Isle, having scant desire for such an oppressive manse as the Rathel's. First we selected a reasonable locale.

"Here, miss, where the ground is firm and flat to allow us space without interference of growing trees," I suggested.

"Too low, it'll flood."

"Thank you everso, Marybelle, for saving us from a bog of our own making," I replied.

After further search, I offered an additional proposal.

"Up yon, Miss Marybelle, might be an acceptable locale, in being high to obviate flooding and the onset of glaciers, though protected from blowing snows by the surrounding trees and additional thick foliage."

"They be the runningvine bush, which grows so fast as to overrun us during first spring."

"Aye, and it's not the dreaded runningvine bush we're desiring to grow up our noses, is it, miss?" I Elsied my everknowing sister.

"No," she replied.

Searching for a superior site, I found myself in another challenge, and finally understood their nature. Neither Mary-

348

belle nor the world around us was offering such tests, but the flexible witch herself, as though a type of emotional self-mutilation.

"I suggest, Miss Marybelle, that we plant our home on the bottom of that rocky hill; for with the first storm of rain or half-eaten lizards from Hell will come an avalanche to flood and kill us, and thus I will be unable to rant on further in response to your fine knowledge and moderate disposition, which pray God I will learn to better appreciate if ever I stop talking."

"You speak well, Alba."

"You speak perfectly, Marybelle."

Eventually Marybelle discovered our site.

"Against that hill, on the side where the sun shines to warm us. No bank above is there for rains to run down or snow to collect and melt. Yet the low and straight hillside and huge boulder there give us the most part of two walls for our beginning."

"Ah! Miss Marybelle, your learned and lucid erudition describing cleanly the criteria for our homesite is such a composition as to be theatrical, and thereby I determine your insistence upon refuting yourself as carpenter or mason, for in fact you are the composer of opera!"

"I go for limbs," she said, and I was certain she suppressed a cackle of glee at my ration of meager humor.

I aided, beginning a task requiring years, it seemed. So far from Marybelle I roamed that she could not be smelled. Initially, however, nearby limbs were gathered, my first loads judged by my colleague.

"These be too small, and scarcely useful," she reported.

"Yes, miss, and thank you."

"And this large one is—"

"Is easy to bear, though of a grand mass."

"Easy to bear because the worms have eaten it inside, and soon it will be naught but pulp."

"Thank you, miss, and I thought you were no carpenter."

After carrying those useless loads in my arms, I was shown by Marybelle how to bundle limbs together, tie them with vines, and drag them behind me, a greater quantity thus transported with each journey.

"And how, miss, am I to gain segments of these tough and green vines?"

"If the yellow ones are not to be found, search for these but in a brownish state and thus breakable in places," she replied, "or cut them with your knife." And from her bag Marybelle pulled forth a waxed bundle that she uncovered to reveal a blade.

"Where is yours?" she asked.

I refused to be astonished.

"Not being an eater of lizards, I have no need for weapons to butcher them," I asserted, and withdrew to find a town house exactly like Rathel's.

So massive was my next heap of limbs that I did not return until overnight. And pleased I was to have found a type of vine breakable with repetitive bends. Marybelle, however, submitted that these vines were not the best sort, for the yellowish she had found were more flexible yet equally sturdy and could be achieved even by someone with no knife.

"Yes, miss, and thank God you are no mason, lest I be dragging the wrong color brick halfway across Earth," I mentioned, and left her sight for the night to return with a tremendous load of sticks whose dragging seemed enough to kill me, but Marybelle had remained nearer our site, finding several sources so that her multiple loads conspired to lose mine in their shadow, away with me again for two full days, not caring to return with a single flipping limb, but by the grace of God hoping to find a way to avoid contests I had begun whose rules I could not determine.

"Presumably we next begin piling them, leaning some straight and vertical against our great boulder here, others against the hill's edge, then tying the lot together with vines of the proper pink and blue color."

"We begin," Marybelle replied.

Quite content was I to allow Marybelle to supply guidance

while I accomplished most of the physical chores—and was not the cause here my guilt for having taken advantage of Elsie, my (my!) servant? But caring for me was a task she cherished, even as I cherished mine, for the obvious motive of producing an abode, for the secondary cause of ethical shame and social retribution and flipping bog muck philosophy I suppose.

Our home would require two full and one partial wall plus a roof, the former made carefully straight so as not to fall and crush the inhabitants, the latter angled from the hill to guide water away. And what had I learned from observing a certain cathedral constructed by dissimilar sweating bodies? The basic outlines we established by holding limbs upright, setting others thereupon as supported by knotty protrusions and tied fast with flexible, yellow vines so strong as to retain their innumerable leaves interminably, cleared with difficulty by the pale witch pink with exertion who had no knife and by the devil would not use the one offered her, every leaf necessarily removed to promote better tying and placate the ancient architect; and surely a few cathedrals of her own Miss Marybelle had tossed together in her day.

After the frame was up like a skeleton, I asked Marybelle of the particular nature of our abode: town house, chalet, or. . . ?

"Hut," she replied.

"Might we arrange for a window?" I suggested. "How pleasant to look from our home onto the realm that God has provided us."

"We'll have a door, which is needed, but I fear making a window also in that the wall might no longer be sturdy."

"Therefore, am I to expect no upper story of my own? No basement nor interior balcony shall be provided? No cornices and columns, no drawing room and lady's chambers?"

"I be no carpenter."

"Nor mason I might surmise in a fantastical bout of waking dream."

"Nor mason," she agreed.

After uncounted days, our house was recognizable as a hut,

but a chalet for any witch accustomed to sleeping in bogs.

"Am I correct, Miss Marybelle, in surmising that an exceptional wind might take our house along with it like constables an unwilling prisoner?"

"The bottom we will bond to the earth with clay."

"Being myself but a common witch at heart, if not in the crotch, I know little of clay, since I am no mason."

"Yonder lies good, grey stuff."

"None yellow? Recently this has been my favorite color for building materials."

"Grey," she replied.

This specifically grey clay we transported with a small sled made of limbs too tiny for the hut brought early in the construction process by the white—not yellow—witch, its surface covered with a weave of leaves, though not the tiny sort stripped from our attaching vines whose hue I could scarcely be expected to recall.

Our hands were the implements for digging the sticky clay from the ground and applying the material along the hut's base and those edges attached to the great boulder and adjacent hillside. After the task was completed months or millennia later, I noted to Marybelle that the walls were porous, for I could see through both simultaneously.

"We seal them with clay," she said.

"How is it, miss, I understand your meaning, in that I am no mason?" I wondered.

Before completing this sealing coat, our crew ran short of clay, and had to search a day to find a new source hours removed from our home, thank you, Satan. The roof then followed in losing its porosity. Here I was greatly disappointed, for I had a certain expertise in repairing thatched roofs as learned on my Man's Isle abode. But no palm trees grew in the Cambrian Mountains, and our roof was not thatch, but pottery. Praise God Marybelle knew nothing of blown glass. Regardless, I heartily applied my efforts toward the particular roof she designed without thoughts of Edward Denton.

We made our door large enough to overlap its opening on

all sides including the bottom where we formed a high, clay sill. Secured on the inner side with vines and stick wedges, the door provided an acceptable though imperfect seal, a bit of light leaking through about the edges. The remainder of our shack was dark, this being descriptive of security from the weather, and perhaps suffocation if the door were made to seal more tightly.

The weather became cool, though no snow fell before our home was completed. Before we had fully engineered the mechanics of the door's latching, we slept within, being certain the sealing clay layers were well dried, since neither witch desired to awaken bonded to the floor for a very long life. Soft, strawlike grasses we collected and brought into the hut, along with our bags and their contents. We witches selected separate sites inside, wandering about until randomly dropping our bedding. So voluminous was our house that another pair of women could have joined us, though my four-poster in the Rathel's was too long. Apart from beds like nests, no additional furnishing was considered. Therein we lay, sunlight lolling through the open doorway to fill our house; and there was comfort, satisfaction enough to lull us to easy sleep.

Awakening near dusk, we found little activity to occupy us. The door panel required drying before we designed the hinging; and though no mason nor carpenter was present, did not the hut's populace include an expert in latchwork? Therefore, we lounged about on our grass piles like useless sinners, Marybelle nibbling a sweet shoot, offering me a bite for which I thanked her no, this witch's belly yet full of a new berry discovered only after eating to be indigestible. After a walk merely to verify the world outside as ours, we returned for the night's sleeping, the door opening providing a moonlit view of our domain throughout the evening.

Days later, our door now dried, we were able to secure it from within via Marybelle's design of vine ties and a stick latch I invented, harrumph. Surely our home would now provide security against the snows and freezing winds sensed coming, cold weather worse than any of Man's Isle. The witch without fat's padding especially desired to separate herself from upcoming icy conditions, being shy a coat and shawl like a sinning lady, yet having lived protected in society too long.

Studying the completed house, I determined the true nature of our construction. With its solid, windowless walls, "hut" was no proper term. Neither did we sit within a manse or hovel or witches' castle. Again I had found a challenge, one soon failed: not the building of this house, but its design, its idea.

Suddenly I turned to Marybelle and called out sharply, "Now I see, Miss Marybelle, that despite your lack of carpentry and masonry skills, you reveal yourself a virtual deity; for you have formed not a hut, but created a cave!"

"I fancy the damp," she confessed.

The seasonal differences seemed to make our stay in this land more genuine. The leaves' changing in color predicted their fall, plant life grew slowly or not at all, and extant animals other than witches prepared to settle in shelters against the approaching cold. During this ending season, an important task for Marybelle and me was collecting foodstuffs to last through a winter's deadness. Each sister had her preferences for eating, Marybelle mentioning that my chosen sky berries and soft nuts would spoil in weeks and be inedible. Thank you everso, miss witch. Soon I began another task, one Marybelle considered as evil as her eating a lizard had been to me.

I undertook a new construction. So long did I work on this item that Marybelle was forced to become both curious and loquacious.

"You make a large vessel of clay and with a lid. For storage it be?"

"For deposit, Marybelle, in that I make us a chamber pot."

"The thing sinners empty on the street?"

"Swank sinners bury their swill, and we have no streets to soil."

"Do you say we are to use it?"

"If the cold comes so intensely that we cannot quit the cave, our bowels might be emptied herein."

"You say we shit in our new house?"

"Only under drastic conditions."

"So long you've been in London as to be unable to hold your pee a freezing season in which you are nothing but asleep?"

"We white witches are different from you commoners, perhaps," I returned, and continued with my project. Marybelle left my sight aghast enough to eat fried cattle.

Exceptional was the winter that came to our domain. Yet no suffering befell me, for I had not been in London long enough to lose my natural immunities. No standing in a heated room looking out to snow made the last winter preferable to this, nor did my renewed exposure to nature after an interval of pampered society make the current winter more bitter than its objective temperature. Although our house was high, soon it was covered with snow, though the air itself seemed colder than the ice coating our land. So changed was our world in its colors and textures that it seemed another new domain. But our house seemed as old and sturdy as its supporting hill, the door leaking little until the edges were blown filled with snow, then not at all. Surely our homesite became so ensconced with snow as to be hidden, for the door opened a crack revealed a white wall blocking our view, not a glimpse of the grey sky to be seen, a wall so solid it did not collapse to fill our hut, our home.

On the rare day early in this season when the dry snow could be pressed away, Marybelle and I moved outside: to chew snow for its water, and for the required bodily drainage that could not transpire within our house, since my chamber pot was a container for food's storage until an emergency, so displeased was Marybelle's smell regarding this sinning device. Another cause for exiting was observation and existence, for this land was our home and we intended to live therein, not hide. Little wandering about we undertook, for I especially had no preference for bare limbs, birdless skies, and white ground revealing scarcely any life except the occasional rabbit's footprints. But the land remained natural even in its severity, and I continued to love it. Then the cold came so bitter that we dared not leave, placing our two beds and bodies together in order to retain the warmth that God's animal creatures produce with their blood and flesh.

How easily time is discerned in the wilds, for therein are readily distinguished seasons, clear distinctions of month according to the moon, day and night as delivered by the sun, minutes too inconsequential to be countable even by an educated witch. Moments were everywhere, and winter was our longest.

Our attitude of mutual holding became an occupation seldom left by the witches who slept through entire days scarcely moving to avoid exposing new areas of flesh not previously chilled, and no true desire for a fireplace in the adjacent room had I, merely random thoughts. None of our extra clothing we wore, for that would have proven our failure to secure adequate bedding. With all our sleeping, we required little eating, most of our collected food unnecessary, and the chamber pot was merely another unopened bag. Eventually the season became static, a permanent, blowing cold to render the witches in their home like the trees outside, equally active, equally warm. And I could only wonder of other animals: Along with bears and witches, did elephants hibernate? But soon we were no more aware than those trees and bears, for we fell asleep so deeply as to not awaken until another year.

Twenty-four

So stiff were we upon awakening that sitting was an effort, and standing did not come early that day. Freezing was not the cause, but weeks of stillness to lock our joints as though parts of a sinning latchwork rusted together. Surely the young witch was no more supple now than the stiff hag beside her, our poses so comical that Marybelle and I cackled together, but only briefly, for here was another act to pain us.

Next came eating. Well hungered we were, though not starving, since our meager activity had required scant nourishment. Unfortunately I found another failed contest before food, for the berries in my chamber pot had spoiled, tainting the remaining victuals. And though Marybelle recognized the odor immediately as I lifted the lid, no gloating came from her, only a silkshoot tossed my way. And thanks again, miss. May you and most superior God forgive me for my foolishness.

Though immediately outside was unpleasant slush, beyond were signs to enliven us: tracks of not only the winter's rabbit, but also lynx cats and turtles. Farther was the tiny dark spot of a ptarmigan in the receding whiteness, and there a squirrel with a thickened winter coat. Smelled beyond sight was a flock of swallows returned too early in the spring, though they were not so untimely as to meet their own freezing.

Once the cold vacated our realm, Marybelle and I lived unclothed in order to save our shoes and sinners' attire for the next winter. As well, the additional clothing in our bags was not worn due to sinners, because if we again had cause to approach them, no unnoticed passage would we achieve if nude. The lack of inhibition in my moving through our world with exposed skin I found satisfying as long as brambles and bogs were avoided.

As spring became summer, our greatest achievements had passed: first achieving our land, then constructing a house, passing through winter alive, and renewing our persons with the spring. Thereafter, we were able merely to live, having vanquished the struggle called survival. From this source of unstressed living, however, came a change to my natural life; for having been rewarded by God for strenuous work and prayerful living, I was delivered by Satan with his curse of boredom.

A day came when I was warm and well rested, without the need to seek food, or build, or flee. Walking with no aim in the lowlands, I passed some stagnant water whose wellhead had evaporated. A frog's leaping there activated the water's odor, and I smelled it fully. Then I was transported. That smell I knew, though its source was not this ditch, but the River Thames, for the odors seemed identical. And I was conveyed a world away by a simple sensation as complex as life, suddenly feeling London about me as though my spirit were present there. With Elsie I stood on the river's bank, an untrue experience so convincing that I remained utterly still to retain the sensation. The power of this unique impression was of the original experience, an old living so rich as to survive into my succeeding life. Exact details were not of import here—the wharf's timbers and Elsie's clothing—for I was moved by return, not reproduction. I received again that previous moment, reliving the instant, all my bodily and spiritual aspects located in London, by the River Thames, with Miss Elsie, my friend.

Captured by conviction, I remained until the vividness was reduced from reality to recollection. In this state, I was passively delivered with unsought memories of every aspect of my living with sinners, all their social and material and falsely familial constructs. Remembrance came so quickly that I was astonished in a changing array, astonished at Elsie and the genuine love we had shared—and, yes, continued to share, for

I yet loved this woman, enough to weep for her had I been a sinner. Being as human as any, my emotion was the same, even in the next moment when I recalled Elsie's smell, the terrible odor of sinners. Further thoughts of London immediately followed: Rathel's distressed romance and her ultimate goal: for me to kill the Eric boy. And I nearly laughed to recall Eric, for whereas Elsie was the most beloved person in that world, Eric was the most entertaining. I then recalled in renewed astonishment the change he had elicited within me that made my living lighter: his profound impression that after I died, had not God so made love a part of His human world that my love would continue, even as I loved Mother although her body was gone?

I was delivered from this reverie of remembrance by its initiating emotion: boredom. Thoughts of my current home's simple living returned me there. Never during the winter controlling us completely had we reasonably feared dying; whereas each day in London was a challenge to survive. Surely this strife was the source of my entering contests with Marybelle seemingly against her. In London, had I not been presented with the constant challenge of continued living against Rathel and her society? Unkind the devil was to have me even obliquely compare Marybelle and the enemy, Rathel. Thank God for His following revelation, that my witches-in-the-wilds self-contests were akin to the gamelike confrontations I had so often undertaken with Miss Elsie.

I was then astonished by my greatest games in London: my trials to achieve the survival of escape. Pawnbrokers and criminals and coachmen. Here were recollections of fear, and I was astounded by the reckless acts I had willfully entered. Less astounding was my having killed a man, for therein I had been unwilling and ignorant. From this death I was more sorrowful than repentant, for God or His chief devil seemed the cause more than this misused witch. Finally I could only pray God for His greater way of kindness to be done in my world and in Satan's.

The latter's realm remained in my thinking, for certain aspects of the sinners were yet desirable though their living was unnatural. How often had any witch astounded me with religious revelation as had Eric? Could the sinners be completely decrepit if Elsie were a member, a friend as loyal and loving as any sister? And though most sinning productions were wasteful, had not great cathedrals moved me? Was not our hut the same as any sinners' dwelling in sheltering its residents? Were not sinners also human?

Eventually these impressions left, my tangible state again becoming foremost. And reasonably so, for whereas London's torments were more influential than its satisfactions, my current world held no danger, the boredom of this land next impressing me as a mildness to satisfy in a Godly manner. How could I not well love a land that so kindly kept me? Like a mother.

No more powerful sense of return to London had I in the wilds than those impressions engendered by boredom and a smell. Occasionally thereafter I returned to that stagnant water, though never was the evocation so intense as the first. With no intent, however, I often recalled the sinners' great city, and often felt boredom in my latest realm. But I had learned to respond to that boredom with a sensible appreciation of my moderate life.

In this manner the months proceeded. To alleviate my tedium, I initiated a hobby: seeking each type of mobile creature in the domain by walking circularly around the hovel-manse, first cataloging the largest variety: rarely-seen small bears I notated via droppings and lairs in caves Marybelle and I had not previously found – and would not be living in now, considering those unsharing inhabitants. Besides, we had a cave. But friendly I would remain with these furry bear beasts, since we were so similar as to share sleeping habits, perhaps along with elephants.

The second-largest creature was a type of lynx cat, like our own from Man's Isle, and therefore happily reminiscent. This beast I appreciated less upon learning it ate lizards. Smaller yet were two varieties of fox that hid in dead trees, and a type of marmot residing in burrows. None of these animals had interest in me, avoiding the witch even after my smell and demeanor proved me harmless. No Randolph were they. Perhaps the same as London, I would be appreciated more after I was gone, and the beasts became bored with their dull life without me.

London.

Soon I lost the fine spirits I held in this enterprise, for upon discovering a third variety of squirrel, a black moth flitted by of a type not observed before. The remainder of the day I thus sought only moths. Despair set in shortly, for of the countless moths seen, the different types seemed as numerous as the individual members of any breed—what then of flies and half-eaten lizards?

But never did I find a monkey.

Marybelle had no similar activity, being so fine as to enjoy her safe life painlessly. Not painless was mine after endless moths turned my hobby into a chore, into another contest I would certainly lose; for how many decades would I need to discover the final animal when each day a new bird was observed, though weeks ago I had proceeded to toads? And, no, this self-inflicted hobby had nothing to do with my surviving in London by becoming aware of coachmen and clergy and constables. The possible truth I next considered hardly relieved my anxiety. I came to believe that neither boredom nor my retrieved past was the cause of these contests, but a curse from Satan for my not killing enough sinners when he had given me opportunity.

With this response, the understanding of my past most likely to come seemed madness—and thank you, Satan, for your latest enlightenment. To encourage my own survival of mind, I thus abandoned my animalistic hobby while I yet had the abilities to count and account for, and what a relief not to have reached ants.

This relief, unfortunately, came too early in the year, for I retained my hobby until early autumn. Therefore, the greater part of a season lay for me to pass before winter brought its suffering. And come winter did, with more intensity than the former. Again we became like bears, but before sleeping we suffered, for not even witches can comfortably accept a cold to paralyze furred creatures. All our clothing we donned, including shoes and pantaloons. Lying together in our mutual bed, my belly against Marybelle's back, painful shivering struck completely through us. And though I longed for spring and the warmth of new life, not in the least did I desire London, not even the Rathel's house with its superior warmth. The only removal from this cold I craved was a season of heat. But first came sleep and with it comfort.

Soon after Marybelle and I awoke the following spring, I determined to love the present season and avoid both old and new anxieties. I thus pursued no further hobbies. Sinners and their cities were not my concern. The same as Marybelle, I proceeded with full appreciation of our common living. Then came summer, and another stench to change my life.

Early in the season came a tremendous passing of birds, a type of kite with abbreviated tail, the flock so massive as to inhibit sunlight like a cloud. Though the fascinated witches denoted no untoward occurrence, the white one had further curiosity of this natural passage.

"The previous year we were present in this land, Marybelle, yet no such passage was seen."

"And before that we doubtless missed their return."

"I beg pardon, miss, but I fail to glean your meaning."

"For birds to go one way now means their later returning. But the cycle may not be a year, but two or three. Perhaps they returned at a time before our arrival below them."

"Know ye of other animal cycles so lengthy?"

"In nature's whole, more than creatures are of a cycle. Winds high and low can come each year or once a lifetime. The sun does things difficult to sense but every decade or more. Certain animals find the need to mate but once in their life, or once young and again before dying."

"If recollection supports my knowledge correctly, thrice in my life on Man's Isle were tides of equal intervals so low as to expand beaches."

362

"Yes," she replied.

"Furthermore, is not my recollection accurate of a crab with long legs seen only with these tides?"

"Oft the things come not alone, but engender other parts of nature toward their own cycles."

"Might we then expect a companion effect with this massed flying, perhaps tornadoes or hail—or an influx of giraffes into our land? Oh, please, miss. No more delightful sight could I imagine than scores of giraffes descending from the mountains."

" 'Giraffes'?" Marybelle retorted. "Be this something the sinners make? Expect ye metalwork or furniture to be coming our way?"

With a delight equal to my having seen the wonderful creatures, I explained giraffes—and elephants also. Marybelle at first considered my speaking mere humor, but the monkeys I also mentioned were beasts she had sensed before. I therefore proceeded in a wondrous but accurate manner to describe my every sight and smell of the animals, pleased Marybelle becoming most interested. Not mentioned, however, were auxiliary facts: about viewing the creatures with a sinner boy and being ravaged by their trainer, about naming my personal semi-killers after these animals, this an insult for which I would doubtless never redeem myself in the eyes of God.

Though assured by Marybelle that no such exotic beasts would be seen flocking to England, the imagining was nevertheless so fine that oft I literally looked beyond in a game of seeing giraffes and elephants come quietly approaching. On a hill one day to search for mushrooms that never grew low, I sensed a strong, hot breeze from along the mountains' lay. With this wind came an odor I thought at first to be of giraffes, so odd and old it was, though known. With more thought, however, I found it unpleasant, therefore not belonging to these favorite creatures, but more akin to . . . stagnant water. Comprehension of this identifying scent then returned, for even diluted by distance and mixed with intervening odors, the smell of sinners was recognized.

Long enough I remained high to return with an assured story

363

for Marybelle, who thereafter climbed the hill with me. Thereupon she worked her nose and lungs only to unfortunately agree.

"Do you find their distance significant, Marybelle?"

"Not great enough to make us fearless."

"But the smell I find static, and not of a moving herd."

"No better is this, for the smell is not of simple human animals, but sinners' products. We smell an establishment, not a pack. This scent I fear to be of a village," Marybelle determined.

"Not smelled before, I presume, because of this extra-seasonable wind come to frighten us. Nevertheless, the intervening distance should not currently distress us."

"Not now, but as any plague, a sinners' village spreads and devours nature before it."

"What then might be our active response to this unpleasant knowledge?"

"Worry little and remain alert."

"And if the plague of sinners infests our domain?"

"Move if we can away and deeper into this land."

"And live thereafter on the bog? Rather would I be taken by sinners," I retorted.

"Not into the bog, but to the far side, beyond our current sensing."

"The direction I mentioned when this one was chosen instead. Praise God we did not proceed that way, for surely we would now be standing in a major city."

"Doubtful," Marybelle replied.

Guided by good sense, Marybelle and I remained cognizant of the sinning smell without becoming so concerned as to modify our lives. Never did the older witch need to climb high ground to denote the sinners' state, for her curious sister kept vigil, finding herself perhaps too often on that hill. Marybelle did not bother to inquire of these observations, aware that I would describe any significant changes in the sinning situation. And silent I remained because the sinners retained their position, allowing us to retain our land.

364

During that summer, I developed the notion of insufficient concern. What sinners were we concerned with? I wondered. How were we to understand the potential problem beyond when our knowledge of same was diluted by distance? Would we witches not improve our defense by learning more of the specific sinners, their number and potential approach? To do so, some sister would have to near that smell, and what was dangerous about a walk in warm weather?

Naught of this idea I mentioned to Marybelle, preferring not to display my overconcern and thereby fail another unintended contest. Nevertheless, to prepare for dreadful circumstance, I examined my sinning apparel without my sister's notice. My brown woollen dress approached shabbiness with its shredded ends and translucent areas where the witch had rubbed her environ. Apparently new, however, was my medium-blue gown of a cut not so stylish as to stop the River Thames. But had I grown so massive that the item would no longer fit? What value the apparel in coming winters if I could not pull it over my form? But fit me it did, though tightly. No shawl had I, and no jacket for my torso, so how much of the lady was I? A cloak and hat, however, I had retained, adequate for societies shy of London's. Since at the time I lived in God's society, I undressed with the knowledge that if need be, I again could pass amongst sinners without their presuming me the witch.

After days of believing that increased knowledge of the sinners would benefit us witches, my moral sense revealed additional emotion, for desire was included, the need to understand what value I yet found in the sinners and their manufactured lives. For days, this self-comprehension satisfied me as a mark of my becoming more ethical in God's moral world. As though an expert in understanding, however, I gained even greater comprehension, though it seemed detrimental to my ethics. My desire to find a proper place with the sinners by understanding the past and predicting the future was not only moral education, but an attempt to justify my acceptance of certain sinning values. Therefore, I dealt not with mores, but lust. My attraction to sinners was like Londoners and their liquor, which made them fine yet made them mad, and eventually could kill. As though drunk myself, I had only to decide if I were insane enough to approach the sinners, or witch enough to remain apart. Before mentioning my passion to Marybelle, the sinning witch had decided.

"Despite my lack of objectivity, Marybelle, I confess that I fear the sinners, their potential and proximity."

"I also, but little."

"My belief is that our fears would be alleviated by our learning more of this nearby populace."

"True, so tell me news when you smell it, in that often you are high."

"Since I am also distant from these people, my suggestion is to approach them to learn more with better smelling, perhaps with sight."

"Being no fool, I'll not go to sinners who would kill me."

"I would offer myself for this venture, Marybelle. Since I resemble these folk, my appearance would not draw them."

"The white witch draws them with her smell."

"Only when near to the touch, and I would remain at distant sight."

"What if you are espied yourself and followed here?"

"I would run."

"Not from horses."

"Horses I would smell before their riders could observe me. I would remain beyond sight if horses be present."

"The value is not enough for the risk," Marybelle insisted, "not if you are followed here and our home and ourselves be destroyed."

"Approaching so near as to allow following would in fact be foolish. Being no fool, I would remain well removed."

"If sense you do have, you remain away until they present danger."

"We wait, then, for the sinners to attack us?"

"We wait for them to leave their settlement and near us."

"But we would be too late if mounted hunters discover us hated witches."

"If men come with horses and metal weapons, we will not be able to flee enough. Even sinners can move through a bog. We would have to hide away, perhaps bury ourselves a time."

"But if we were sufficiently removed, we would have no necessity to disrupt our lives."

"Much farther and we have no good food."

"Farther, Marybelle, and we have no need to retreat because we would be well separated from the sinners. And if we had knowledge of them beyond our current ignorance, we would not require such endless speech."

"I travel to no sinners for the sake of fear's fantasy. And neither do you unless you have a craving of their ways."

"I have no craving for sinners, in that most of their ways I find offensive."

"And the remaining ways which offend you not? Do these draw desire from you?"

"Your question is the very fantastical fear you mentioned, Marybelle. The craving I have regarding sinners is to know what they would do against me before they begin. The craving I have is to be neither killed nor vanquished from my home. Surely you have the same intent in living."

"Surely you intend to hie toward the sinners despite any of my speaking."

"Since you have convinced me of the value, Marybelle, I leave tomorrow."

"You go alone, girl, and go more of a liar than a fool," Marybelle declared. "Your words were given with care, but you smell of desire. The sinners have something you would have or would seek, and I will be no part of your finding it. Go if you must, but justify it not with our safety, but fault the devil for your lust. You go without true concern for my speaking, but you will never be so fine with words as to have me agree. Sinners dupe one another with speeches, but they do not hoax witches with words. I am the witch and remain the witch—what person are ye?"

With all our firm words, we parted without a spoken decision. And though I felt Marybelle was not too displeased, mainly I hoped that she was not disappointed in me, disappointed in her sister.

Twenty-five

The walking was easy, despite the burden of a new possession. The morning I departed—Marybelle out in the land and out of my sight—I found a defense against sinners left as I slept. In my bag was a Bible, a magic notion to protect me, since no witch would carry a Bible. Marybelle thereby revealed her concern, for I would have no need for the sinners' talisman unless they detected me, and thus she expected me to approach too near for a witch, near enough for a fool.

The travel would require days. No difficulty did the terrain present, except for a river. A river I followed for a half day before finding a crossing. This site was not shallow, only narrow, and would require my submersion. Through the water I would need walk with my bag held above the surface and my head below.

So much the witch had I become again that bridges were forgotten. Discomfort in crossing this river I predicted, but the horror of water I had misplaced. Since living in the wilderness, my dreams had been rare; and though occasionally unpleasant, never were they nightmares to ruin my thinking. This water held no fear for me, being clean and sparkling, unlike the fetid Thames. But as I entered, this different immersion became equal to my dreams.

As though a typical bathing it began, a gentle current surrounding my legs and bubbling about my breasts. Further steps, however, brought my chin near the surface, and I wondered why in dreams I continually thought of Mother on the ocean floor when she had never been there. I wondered why these dreams could not become a peaceful part of my life by being understood as false. But this contemplation led only to my sinking.

As the water covered my head and the inherent fear of immersions rushed through me, I gave every effort to undertake that strange combination of breathing water yet not breathing, that horrible state of having to survive. After one step with water like thick air pressing against my open eyes, I thought of returning, of searching further for a place to allow my crossing and breathing simultaneously, for I was suffering. My chest and all my innards felt sodden, and I shuddered from the unnatural impression. Then the past struck again, but one never experienced by me; for I recalled that Marybelle had saved herself by walking beneath the salt ocean as though along this river, not across, and so deep she could never have considered leaping up to gain a taste of air. Because my task in comparison was shamefully minor, I forced myself to be sensible and continue, accepting the proper technique of allowing water inside my mouth, allowing it to come and go and bring air to seep into my lungs, proceeding with a strength provided by Marybelle's saving feat.

Once my head was in the air again, I rushed through the river, for no longer could I bear the wetness about me. After achieving God's glorious, pellucid air, I thanked Him for survival, but not until I was on the bank and away from Satan's wet suffocation. Again I was moved by Marybelle's accomplishment, one beyond my imagining. And I knew that I was not the same witch as she, knew that upon my return I would walk for days if required until finding a section of the river no deeper than breathing.

Eventually the sinner smell was evident without my gaining high ground. And when the scent of a sinners' village became clear, I returned to London. Again I smelled glass and saw carriages and sinners and recalled their acts. I felt the fear of being in such an incredible, evil midst, felt the lifting of my awareness from having emulated the unnatural in order to survive. To understand that I was again moving toward this life, not away, engendered such foreboding in me that I determined to

370

have exceptional caution in approaching the settlement lest I find myself entrapped amongst God's poorly souled creatures.

Days later, I first sensed individual sinners by their odor. Studying the smell, I understood that they were not approaching me, but traveled in an oblique direction that would not lead to our witches' home. This was not the odor to have drawn my notice on the hill: Beyond was a village situated amongst farms. Feeling safe, I continued with a modified course that would lead me to the settlement beyond, but away from these nearest sinners.

After another day's walking, I made myself acceptable in the eyes of sinners who might espy me before I them. I donned not my fine attire, but my worn dress used for our journey through the wilds. I would be seen as a woman, not a lady. How bizarre to find even imperfect wool amongst the poison sumac. A camisole I had retained, and though normally meant to cover a corset, the latter was an enclosure rejected by this witch. So the camisole covered only pale skin much browner now that the sun had been influential on its hue. A petticoat I also wore, and what a strange sensation to have this cloth against me. With this feel came old thoughts of Miss Elsie's attempting to make me the lady with the same frilly linen. But she had failed, and I remained the witch at times and at others the sinner; therefore, neither woman had been successful.

The veil and hat in my bag next became decisive. Poor farm women do not wear veils. Besides, by touch I had discerned that my head had healed to some extent, so perhaps I was presently only homely instead of revolting. How perfect that would be: not so lovely as to draw appreciation, nor so ugly as to draw derision. I decided to wear only the hat into which I stuffed my hair, for only wanton women allow their locks loose in the social air, the witch leaving a bit of the black stuff out in a curvacious layer about the ears and nape, cramming the rest in for an additional cause; for not even baseborn folk allow their hair to go unbrushed an interval of years—and what would Miss Elsie think of that? Smile I did to imagine her horror if one day had passed in London without her lass's grooming properly. What a brushing she would have given as a lesson, setting me before her and attacking from above like a hawk snagging a rat with its talons, Elsie constantly complaining, and I would be in pain like that rodent. And with Lord God as witness, in some way I would enjoy it—but what way? For being with a friend, being amused by taunting someone, or being waited upon by a servant?

The next morning, I came upon a trail with wagon tracks that certainly led to the village whose odor was ever intensifying. My choice was to follow this path, a bold move since the land was so open that were an urgent horse rider to come along, I would have scant opportunity to hide. Therefore, I moved with caution, especially toward noon when I arrived at a farm for food things in the ground. And I smelled manna—I smelled onions, and considered digging through the soil for that necessity of life I had been deprived of for decades. But, no, I would consume only the succulents and berries that had been my recent eating instead of throwing myself into the sinners' peripheral society.

I hid near the farm until nightfall, then walked beside the trail, paces away to leave no footprints, continually smelling about me for sinners out late. The following day found me hiding from men on a wagon with straw and brick their cargo. Their loud approach precluded my surprise, and here was a factor to strike me. With all of my talking in the wilds to Marybelle's detriment, never had I produced such a noise as those two males with their raucous laughing and loud, useless hollering about the worthlessness of a third.

So decisive was this loud experience that after the wagon's withdrawal, I stopped to contemplate until coming aware that toward men like these I journeyed. The danger ahead was not in being captured by passing men, but attempting to pass amongst them; for if continuing in this manner, I would come to people so numerous that not all could be avoided. But would the sinners' discovering me amongst them not be superior to their finding me hiding in the brush? Better was the pretense that I had nothing to hide. Best perhaps was returning to Marybelle, but that would teach me nothing.

The question was no longer whether I would enter the village,

372

but the manner in which I would present myself. Then with a sigh I became weary of the minor guilts coming with every step. Nevertheless, this marked me as moral, and should not deliver me with shame. The shame came from my lust for the sinners' ways. Being aware of this, more remorse I received, more sighing, and along the trail I proceeded.

When the land became flatter and the trail straight, sight became more valuable a perception than smell, for no odor can measure buildings. Beyond I saw a mass of them, some of two or more stories. The buildings of this settlement, as with Jonsway, became larger and more numerous as one neared, the road widening as other trails joined to cross and increase it. The populace was also sparse on the edges, becoming denser along with the buildings. Surely I would not continue this walking to be confronted by all the folk I saw moving beyond, for a young woman alone and unknown would literally be questionable; and I had no desire to be explaining myself, a burden often and unintentionally generated in London.

Then I was struck with a pride to pain me, for with my thoughts of London came a comparison: that I was of a city so great that this village was unworthy of compare, London a land of mansions versus a tract of huts. But at once I became remorseful for considering myself part of London, for was not even that greatest city another sinning business?

The reasonable procedure came to me of approaching the town at night, then hiding until morning when the populace inhabited the street and I could slip amongst them. Thereafter, I would proceed with my business: I would look for hunters and explorers. I would become aware of the sinners' dispersal into the land God had given me and Marybelle. Then I would return home. Having decided my course, I settled behind expansive trees, reclining and attempting to rest, becoming so successful as to fall asleep, not waking until morning when sinners attacked me.

In a dream, London's populace demanded my identity, brandishing lances toward me while insisting that I respond. Then I awoke with a start to see a girl prodding me with a stick and saying, "Miss? Miss?"

Looking past her, I saw a waiting one-horse wagon loaded with an adult man and woman. Instead of danger, I felt foolishness: How could I pass safely through a town if I were so worthless as to fall asleep and not notice an entire pack of sinners approaching in a noisy wagon drawn by a smelly horse? Had I been dead the evening? To preclude my suffering that undesirable state, I decided at once to quit this world, to return to my home and Miss Marybelle, whom I loved in that moment more than ever before. And I would have returned had I not been captured.

No longer prodding me with her stick, the girl looked down to sitting me and spoke further.

"Miss, are you harmed here, miss? I had to wet and Father ceased the wagon and over here I find you. Are you not ill, then?"

My racing thought was that these sinners would pee less if they ate as God intended, but desperation replaced frivolity in my thinking. The possibilities of explaining myself to these people came and left upon my thinking that the exegesis should be reversed, for this nation was foreign Wales, yet the girl spoke English. Could that river crossed and breathed by me have been the Wye, and therefore again I was in England? Being a sophisticate from England's greatest city, at once I devised the perfect plan for outwitting these baseborn folk, and again I was in a contest whose rules I would have to invent as I failed them.

As the girl last spoke, the woman had stepped down from the wagon to approach, craning her neck ahead like a snake, reaching out with her face as though to protect her body by sacrificing her head. Halting shy of the girl, she remained well removed from the stranger; and I understood her true courage, true sacrifice. She would allow her own daughter to face the alien alone. I thus attacked the youthful sinner.

"I am sorry," I told her, "but I speak no English."

The girl's reply was to look behind, seeking parental support. Her safely removed mother was the sinner next to speak.

"What are you telling us, in that you talk it good?" she asked me from afar.

"I am sorry, but I speak no English," I repeated, then added a sound imitative of Continental folk heard garbling in London.

After a pause to contemplate my words and that odd, accompanying noise, the woman turned to run halfway to her husband as though for superior communication, explaining as she galloped.

"Good Lord, husband, we find a German miss!"

"French, you twit," I muttered, but only Satan and I heard that language.

Then the father, so brilliant a person as to be worthy of his kin, called out to the intermediary mother.

"Ask if she's dying or near it, lest we be late for the town meeting."

"How do I ask her if she is German, husband?" the woman returned in a testy tone. "She has said she don't speak our English language. Can you not understand that, sir?"

"Then ask if she is toward Lucansbludge, and would be taken in a wagon," the male intoned.

So reasonable this seemed, as though conveyance were a more Germanic idea than dying, that the woman turned to her daughter, relaying the family's most recent semi-notion.

"Child, ask her if she would go with us to Lucansbludge."

Becoming a universal translator was no burden for this girl who perhaps all her life had waited for so intellectual a challenge. Displaying neither timidity nor hesitation, she initiated a series of senseless gestures surely meant to signify transport.

"Do you," she said, pointing to me, "would go with us," and she pointed to herself, "to Lucansbludge," arms aimed along the trail, "in our wagon," ending with both hands directed to the wooden box.

Because sinners, as I learned from my tutor, have no measure for moments less than a second, no more time than this did I consider refusing the sinners' offer. Thereafter, I smiled to the girl and nodded affirmatively as I told her "yes" in French.

"Man sawyer," I pronounced, the girl smiling in return as she led me to the wagon.

I sat in the rear and conversed with the girl by answering,

"Tray bean" and "Bow coot" to everything said. Uncomprehending I attempted to appear as the daughter spoke mainly by repeating her mother's words, asking where I was going, where I was from, as though the girl had some special ability to communicate; for although she used the same words as her mother, did not the gestures make all the difference?

In this bout of communicating, the father revealed himself as brilliant by saying nothing. Then we entered the town, and I reached my latest predicament, for the wife was saying to the husband: "She is got to have somewhere to go. She must know where she is going."

Having failed to impress the husband with her concern, the wife finally turned to her daughter.

"Ask the young Gerwoman where she is going here, Jezebel."

Scarcely could I restrain myself from leaping out to thus avoid the next translation. Looking about, I saw this area of Lucansbludge to be businesslike with decently dressed men and women and no apparent hoodlums. Therefore, I pointed toward the nearest building and shouted, "Can of sewer! Can of sewer!" to the wagon family, aware that "Jaw Thames" would mean nothing to them in that it referred to a London river.

"You would have out at the barber shop?" the mother asked with some uncertainty.

"Maybe it be her father who works there," the husband replied, having become an instant genius. "Those Continentals are good with hair."

As soon as the man stopped the wagon, down to the street I stepped, moving off the roadway as I waved and blew kisses to the farming family, calling out, "Mare sea, mare sea!" while smiling, receiving good-byes and waves from the females, a tip of the hat from the father. Then I turned to move along the walkway as the horse was urged on by its master.

No farther had I cared to travel with these folk, for the deeper into Lucansbludge I moved, the farther through it I would have to journey upon exiting. As well, the wagon family's conversational habits were largely unfulfilling to a lady so social as myself.

This was no foreign country. A herd of people across the

street laughed and gossiped in English. The sign in the barber's window was readable by the nonalien girl. This was England, and none of the British sinners took great notice of the unforeign witch as I walked. The farming family had not been amazed at my appearance, only my roadside locale and alien tongue. The people on this street were occupied with sinning affairs: loading wagons, berating their children, selling revelatory pamphlets direct from London . . . The local loiterers seemed no dangerous type, mostly older folk with no better activity than viewing their peers. Walking was my activity, and quickly I moved, as though having some significant appointment to keep at the street's end. Despite radiating an aloof demeanor, I nodded to the rare couple whose male half tipped his hat while the wife smiled, providing only the first pair with a "Man sawyer" before understanding that this false identity was best left on the wagon.

An important question then occurred to me, for I wondered what I was doing. To reconnoiter the city properly, would I not have to traverse it end to end? How long could I continue before passing a male sinner sensitive to my crotch? Perhaps I would remain safe, but become bored here even as I had in the wilds, and finally be finished with the sinners. Was such an achievement not a goal of mine? But this village was no fair site for such an important self-contest, in that no great buildings like London's were present, and none of the society. About me were working people with only common scents, a minimum of snuff, none of the periwigs and glossy canes and cloaks of Londoners. On the street's far side was an open market, but not the first pomegranate was being sold, only lettuce. Only onions, but I was without coin. The nearby plant life consisted of weeds besides buildings, not the elaborate hedges and gardens of fine London estates, not the first refreshing green seen at any street's end. With all of its mediocrity, how could Lucansbludge offer a test of my feelings toward sinners equal to those available in London, my home as a lady?

Those feelings were then tested by an odor. Approaching a shop, a dead, cold smell to unsettle my stomach reached me. Inside the shop I saw a dog chained to a ribcage, a large and raw side of one of God's murdered creatures, the living animal seeming to pay no heed to all that dead flesh for its taking. No person would steal this meat as well guarded by an exceptionally trained canine, and pity I felt for the beast who was made to behave so unnaturally. Then I thought of Randolph and his unnatural life that at least was made pleasant by Eric.

This experience inspired me to emphasize my business, that of a witch's survival. My only intent was to search for aspects of this town that might lead to an attack against my home and my sister. I then surmised that a random route would likely lead to worse sections of Lucansbludge. Reasonably I would return to the town's edge and espy about the periphery at a distance, allowing no sinner to notice my cryptic positions. A few days of skulking would be time well spent in the knowledge gained. Then I would return to Marybelle and our home, hopefully with news only of boredom.

I continued in my quick rate, reliving the sensations of a sinners' community, from broken glass to burnt tobacco to buildings of brick and timber. But no part of this town impressed me toward fondness. Then, after one street in Lucansbludge, I came aware that the most important parts of any community are its people. Elsie and Eric and the two elder women conveying me to Rathel's after Satan through my bottom had murdered. The coachman who lost himself attempting to aid me. But this sort of sinner lived not only in London. Since the kindly family thinking me Germanic were of this community, certainly more of their type were about. But one did not find such folk as though opera performed at a set date: They were met in the process of living with their ilk, which included suffering from their inferiors. To keep my wild living fine, I turned from this populace, intent upon espying at the town's edge as per my planning. Behind me, however, was a force as familiar as flies to feces.

"I would ask you, miss, of your business in my town."

Some sinning male smelling of fried tobacco and rare meat was immediate as I turned to a voice too near to ignore. Though drawn to my aspects, not likely was he following my wool.

"And a fine town you have, sir," I replied to the average,

discomforting male. "How wealthy you must be to own an entire township. Be ye also so gracious as to identify yourself to an unmet lady?"

Tipping his hat as though dreading the move, the sinner stated, "I am an associate of the constable's office, miss, and would ask of your business, in that I see you have a bag."

"Sir, are you so determined to begin some professional venture that you verbally accost any prospective customer with luggage?"

"Miss, accosting business is right what I am after," he answered harshly, "for certain youths gone to stealing are those I seek."

Immediately I threw my bag down and opened it.

"Near all my life's possessions are here, and of these I have no hiding. My best velvet dress, my Sunday shoes, a pantaloon God Himself would not ask to see, and my mother's Bible from which I might read you a passage regarding humility." After pulling forth each item, I stuffed the lot into the bag again, leaving it open before the male.

What blushing overcame him with the revelation of my underthing. The crowd as well had a sharp, joint inhalation. Ah, yes, in town but a minute and an accumulation of sinners I had drawn, like flies to so on. At least in this less sophisticated community they remained paces removed so as not to jostle the semi-official male and me, most folks attempting to conceal their gaping, which shamed them. And though they desired to retain their comments, one too many and too loud was emitted, and heard by this constable's affiliate.

"Might she be, I'd ask, of the Lutheran persuasion?"

Like a dog my inquisitor then pricked his ears for better hearing.

"And your business in this town is what, you say, miss?" he asked, pricking his tongue for better speaking.

"I am seeking my aunt who concludes the affairs of my late uncle's estate, a business to bring such tears and torment to me that Auntie insisted I not attend. By the butcher shop I was to wait, though why she selected this site when I am terrified of dogs, I know not."

"Are you Lutherans then to come into Lucansbludge as though to disrupt our town by settling?" he of the constable's office asked.

"Sir, my grandparents have a home well removed, so herein we have no desire to live, and thank you. As for my religion, there is only one God for us all to worship, and He is of Jesus and England. Therefore, sir, in that you find me not so heinous as to be either Lutheran or criminal, may I be allowed to depart your perusal? May I continue in my Christian way and pursue the death of a loved one?"

"About your business then go, miss," he stated firmly, and walked away with no further salutation. Being a lady, however, and prideful in my etiquette, I was not so quick to release him, being also a bit of a fool.

"In final greetings, sir, I thank you for the gracious welcome given me by this town you allege to own, and wish you godspeed on your official concerns as paid for, I hope, not by decent taxpayers, who are civil."

Then I closed my baggage, lifted it, and left, the crowd thereafter dispersing. Behind me, the constable-oriented male watched, but did not follow as I passed the butcher shop, the barber, and vacated his town.

So displeased was I as to lose my design. From distaste would I depart Lucansbludge, thereby returning to Marybelle with insufficient knowledge? But what was our concern with these sinners unable to worship God without worrying of His foreign supporters?

I exited via the same route of my entry, remaining on the trail's surface as though I belonged there. Outside the town, I sensed two male riders who passed only to return and ask with smelly smiles if I required some assistance.

"No English I speak, sinners," I retorted, and waved at their horses with my bag, the animals bucking, though controlled by the men and their reins. These males then continued on their way with no further interest shown me, though they were certain to spur their mounts so that dust was kicked against my face, the devil take their Lutheran souls.

Once calming my ire so that sensibility was revealed on the

volatile patina of my personality, I left the trail proper and moved out of vision of travelers. Near dusk, I stopped in a stand of diseased trees whose rotten husks offered a fine hiding site against sinners surely disappreciative of this odor more natural and inoffensive than their own. Confused and displeased, I determined to give my position proper consideration after a renewing sleep, hoping to wake in the morn with a fresh view of my journey. But when I awoke, it was not morning, and I did not wake alone.

That evening I dreamed. Through the water I walked, but no salt was present, the fluid about me so diseased as to be nearly black. My journey was reduced to a few final steps before I would gain the bank and good air. But though opaque beyond seeing, the water transmitted smell; thereby was I aware that on the bank stood a dog, one trained to guard anchor chains by sinners who coated the links with grease. Though harmless to me, the creature was a terror because in London I had told the magistrate that I was fearful of the beasts whom in fact I appreciated, what with their long necks and stripes. But because I had lied to another human in the official society of his ownership and then berated him in God's name, my lie had come true in reality, the reality of this dream that was currently my life. So drown or face a fear to make dying preferable were my choices as I took my final step toward the bank.

Then I awoke. Before me was a huge dog wagging his tail as he sniffed loudly in my direction. But not even waking to suddenly see this creature did I fear it. The dog was tied with a strap, the strap held by a man, and here was terror and hatred. The man was of the constable's office in Lucansbludge. And the despised smell of this person was not of sinners, but of a male aroused in his body.

"The heathen is now found by a true man of God," he loudly called down to me. "The Lutheran who tells folk that English is not her language—and is this lie not true? German you are, or is it the devil's tongue you hold in your mouth? But yet in England is no law against Lutherans who worship dissent more than Jesus. So arrest you I cannot, but my duty is to deliver you with God's truth and the laws of morality through a lesson your kind deserves."

Then the man exposed the source of his hated stench, entering a hand into his pants to step toward me with his baby stick grasped, a Godly part held in Satan's fingers.

Up I leapt to run without confronting this sinner with anger or words. Up I ran, leaving my bag, having finally decided to end my journey by absolutely rejecting the sinners' realm. But only one step I took before the dog bit my ankle. His hold was nearly playful, though, for I was being tripped, not mutilated. Then the man was on me, but he displayed no gentility; his entire weight thrown against my back abolished my breathing. Though I knew by this sinner's grunting that he had harmed himself as well, the male was not so damaged as to discontinue his perversion. My only wish was to continue breathing, for the blow to my torso had ended my lungs' movement, and I felt myself suffocating on nothing. And I prayed God only for my breath to return, my terror so great that I could feel no concern for the foolish sinner who even then was killing himself on me.

Moments later when I breathed again, the dog was lapping my face. Though yet to fear this creature, I was terrified of Satan, for I felt in my loins a pain only the devil could envision. Agony averted my regarding the male's tragedy as he became trapped within me, for I longed to be merely breathless, merely drowning on nothing. So tightly did my baby muscles clench that a vision came of my innards exploding, as though an insect stepped upon and splattered. The sinner's grinding my breasts with both hands like pig meat for sausage passed me unfelt, for bodily pain is naught compared to the torment of an internal demon.

The agony continued along with the male's thrusting until I thrust in return. Such torture I felt that I prayed for both parties to die, but then I felt strength. Desperation was this idea, for God might end my torment if only I aided Him. Here my assistance was not selfish, but moral, for the strength I gained was that of righteous life, which is continued living; so I rejected the future that was not my further agony, but this male person's death. I insisted upon rejecting him, pushing him away while he yet was whole. But not with both hands on his shoul-

382

ders could I press strongly enough to move the sinner, and my legs were so separated by his torso that I could not arrange my feet to kick at him. But somehow I managed to roll over. The man had quit his thrusting, my vagina locked on him in an agony to kill my senses, kill his, kill him, managed to roll over to sit on the male and press with both hands against his chest, press with both feet against the Earth using all the effort of my legs, my life, to separate the conjoined, killing persons, press so utterly that I stood, lifting the man's hips with me, moving up and down as he groped with both arms, attempting more poorly than I to depart. I shook myself while standing as though fucking this man, as though a child riding a broomstick, moved up and down attempting to drop him. But the witch succeeded where the woman failed, for having intentionally exerted to the absolute, my body continued beyond desire. My crotch continued as I fell upon the male no longer attempting to extricate himself. Having failed to save him, I was left with torture, and prayed God for the sinner to die soon so that I might live, convinced that no sort of human could save him, God's will be done, prayed that if this pain were to continue, dear Lord take my life instead of the sinner's. But the only angel receiving prayers on this occasion was the black prince who had me suffer so long that when the sinner and I fell apart, my senses left also. Unconscious I was though deeply aware of a torture passed though permanent in its trauma, my innards feeling like spoilt meat, dead and rotting. When again I awoke to an awareness of agony, the dog was lapping my tormented bottom, the sinner relieved to find himself away from my cunt and with his master, Satan, in Hell.

Again a sinner had brought me revelation, this bloodless male displaying with his passive body the effortless intent of our greatest Lord. No sufficient thinking could I procure to comprehend a man's lax piety heinous enough to make him worthy of so devilish a demise, one provided by the Creator without effort. No lust and self-concern of my own so compiled an immoral mass to condemn me as a continual killer. Only the Deity kills with impunity and implies it exalted plan; and how casual was God's correctness to equate in castigation His sinner and

His witch, unequal people made similar by enhancing the devil's domain.

In the darkness near dawn, I arose with my bag to crawl away, then collapse, having to void my stomach of its most miserable contents, a rushing gush so painful that my very internals seemed rejected. Then away from this mess I rolled, moments later able to stand, but soon I was followed by a beast. First the dog ran to me and barked in no threatening manner, then returned to my stomach's contents to smell there a moment and then consume, eating some portion of my vomit as though my previous meal were not all digested. Away from him I moved as rapidly as my weakness allowed, but the dog followed in a most dedicated manner, his eating done and the play commencing. Since I ignored him, the dog made himself better known by leaping against me, disrupting my walking. I then made to gain his leash and tie him anywhere. But this he understood, running away with a wagging tail as I stepped toward him, the dog believing that I was playing. So I chased him as best I could with body bruised enough to be blackened, chased the dog that leapt and barked and would not allow me to near him nor allow me to leave, for it ran before me and blocked my path. When I turned away, it ran from behind to jump against my legs, knocking me down. When I stood to begin running, this proved to the dog that I was playing in return, the creature demonstrating himself better at this game by running faster than I to trip me or throw me to the ground again.

This contest continued until I could no longer run, could no longer walk, collapsing in the grass to make senseless noises as though mad, grunts of exasperation to a God Who had deserted me. Then He returned in the form of a dog who approached to lick my face. With the first kiss, I grasped his leg; and though the dog yelped and bit me bloody, I held him firmly, feeling anger enough to pull his leg off if need be; but there was the leash, and then in my hand. As I stood with a firm grip on the strap, I was prepared to drag the dog with all my force to the nearest site for tying. But as soon as I jerked his leash, the creature followed; and I walked away with him, leaving the open ground for the nearest tree. What a sight this would have been, the witch with a face seemingly grieved over a dog with wagging tail whom she followed to his dead master.

The man had moved. After ravaging me, the male had taken his reduced form and walked away; and I imagined him stumbling off in shock as his blood leaked out, collapsing only to die. Perhaps I had passed him unnoticed as I stumbled away myself, for he was between me and the stand of trees. Somehow he had managed to secure his pants about his hips again, so I had no view of his damage in moonlight adequate to reveal a horror. And I knew him dead from his stillness, not through smelling; for there is no smell of death in a living world, since death is a removal.

I tied the dog to the dead man's ankle. I tied him to his owner with no concern for the man's lost life nor the dog's potential starvation. After all, if no one found him, he could always eat the man, unless this dog had been trained by a butcher. I tied the dog and stumbled away, to my bag and then toward home, the secured dog yapping after me both happy and sad.

This walking was difficult, in that my body below the waist was a sack of raw parts rubbing together. But I removed myself far from the scene, lest the dog loose himself and follow. Then I forgot how to plan, to think, to feel. When next I was able to consider myself, I was awakening in a new day, and behind me was a broad creek I had crossed, not recalling my sense in so hiding my odor. Wet the witch was on one side where she lay against the ground, yet dry where exposed to God's sun or perhaps Satan's breath at her back, which surely followed her through life.

To the stream I returned and drank, smelling and viewing around me as I moved, sensing no other persons nearby, no barking dogs. With no thought in any sinning or witch's world except returning home, I grasped my bag and walked. Then I halted, for I was lost. One glimpse to the sky, and the sun told me my direction, that I would have to cross this stream again, and soon, for its path was divergent to mine; and any unneeded distance traversed might allow sinners to gain me if they were out with humorous, uningratiating canines.

After fording the shallow creek, much walking brought me to the same trail to Lucansbludge I had first followed. This trail I was best to cross, for my original course to it was too round-about. But now I sensed a farmhouse ahead, and though I saw no populace, drawing near would surely draw the sinners near me. Being eager for rapidity, I crossed a field with insufficient trees to conceal me, another contest lost, for a sound behind of feet revealed a sinner running toward me pell mell.

The girl of the wagon. My immediate thought was to crush her head with my bag and be away, but this was foolish fear, not intent, and gone only to be replaced with dejection. If I ran from her, I would thereby reveal the exact path I traveled. As she neared, however, I sensed no intent to capture in her manner; for she seemed frightened enough to be running away from a horror, not toward one.

"Miss! Miss!" she called out while yet moving. "Oh, if only you could hear English talking!" Then she halted nearby, panting, looking toward me as though I required salvation.

"A little I know your speaking," I told her, and the girl was encouraged to continue.

"Oh, praise God, I saw you here and had to tell you what we have learned of terrors nearby."

"Terrors? What terrors these?" I responded.

"Demons, miss!" she hissed, looking about as though one might hear. "Demons in women or pure witches are about, and one has killed a town man."

"Kill?" I replied, truly distressed by that idea. "Someone is killed?"

"Yes, a man killed dead nearby—and Satan in human form they say the cause. Townfolk are out now with dogs looking for the evil folk, but if the demon finds you first . . . I saw you, miss, and began fearing for ye!"

"No more kind a girl . . ." I said, thanking the sinner for her concern.

"Oh, miss, you must go home, or perhaps returning to my farm until the demons are driven off. Heretofore

386

one is captured, but if others be about . . ."

Some entity of superior strength struck me with a blow of certain knowledge enough to stop my heart a beat, yet I had to ask the girl explicitly.

"One captured? You tell me."

"Oh, miss," she began, leaning near and glimpsing about as though not to spill her demonology too far. "Oh, miss, I have not seen her, but talk is of a most ugly creature, one like a bent woman, and with a woman's clothes, but it is a demon inside her that makes her look so."

Then the girl stepped away from me, looking to my face in confusion because of my odd response.

"Miss," she asked, "why is it you smile so?"

"God is too wise for me, too wise," I replied, unable to explain the association between humor and madness that was being taught me; for anything can be humorous to those insane, and humor most extreme is madness.

"Thank you, kind girl, and I go now to be safe," I concluded, and began walking, stepping past her toward the trail. A moment later, the girl called out.

"But, miss, have you a place to go?"

"To safe now, no fear, you kind," I said, and I waved to her, continuing out of sight.

I stepped to the trail, then into the wilds and toward Lucansbludge. Correct that child had been, for I smelled sinners and dogs, but remained too distant to view them. I walked a great distance, my route circumvential, for I would approach Lucansbludge from a different direction, a different trail. The entire night I waited before entering, but I had no rest, no sleep, only previous dreams of awakening wherein I entered the town and again was with my Marybelle. Donning my best attire, I placed the hat with care, though I wore no veil in that my face was no part to be concealing. In the morning I entered Lucansbludge not as a witch, but a lady.

Twenty-six

"Sir, I would beg your aid, in that I have lost my aunt, and having searched for days, I was told by townfolk to seek Magistrate Waingrow."

A citizen had directed me to this authority's office. After hearing my description that matched Marybelle's bodily appearance and her best sinner's dress, Waingrow shared some official view with a constable standing in the doorway. He then stared at me vaguely with no smell of sex, only apprehension. His allegations, however, were not vague, not surprising.

"Miss Alba Landham, your aunt we have here, held in Queen Anne's custody," the magistrate reported; and I wondered of King William, thinking that truly this might be Wales, thus having a separate monarchy. "But the name given is Mary Belle, not Marybelle Landham."

"Landham, sir, is my name, and my aunt's name after marriage," I told him, detesting the need to invent stories instantaneously. "With my uncle's recent death, Auntie felt herself separated from her husband, even to his name. And God help me thank you, sir, for watching over my lost family. Might we then be on our way? Now that I am here, Auntie shall—"

"Miss Alba Landham," Waingrow interrupted, "in explanation I must say that your aunt is here because we fear she has been taken by demons."

I stared at the man as though he had slapped me, thereafter displaying confusion in my speaking.

"Taken? Sir, and I thought my aunt was here. . . ."

"The word, Miss Landham, is possessed," the magistrate returned. "We of this office have assertions by witnessing folk and also ministers that a demon from Satan has gone into your aunt and caused her to kill a man."

So long did I stare at Waingrow that a sinner's clock would be required to denote the duration, and even then my look was of a mild lady lost, utterly lost. Finally the magistrate spoke, for someone had to.

"Miss Alba Landham, I tell that your aunt must stand accused in trial before a court of Queen Anne for having associations with Satan."

After another extended pause, I responded, "Queen Anne accused my aunt?"

"Before Queen Anne in Lord God's name she stands accused. A just and reasonable trial she must be given, and accused of witchcraft she must be."

"I will see my aunt?" I asked, speaking as though not having heard Waingrow's speaking. "I would see my aunt and speak with my last loved one on God's Earth."

"You may, miss, but first we would query you to learn of your—"

And I screamed. The questions asked would be the same as those directed to Marybelle, and since our answers could not match, I sought her presence for discussion. Therefore, I screamed, and swooned, my hands to my face, my words more pitiable shrieks of a tortured lass than mere words.

"Jesus! Great God help me through Your son! Help me lest every person in the world I love should die of plague and consumption and now the devil! You have let the devil kill my aunt?" With that final phrase, I was no longer speaking to God, but accusing Waingrow.

"Calm, miss, your aunt is not—"

And I shouted again.

"Please, if you know Jesus, let me see my aunt before you kill her!"

So he did, perhaps to appease my panic. I was led to an area worse than those simple rooms in Jonsway where we witches had been detained, for these townfolk were more earnest about incarceration. Down a corridor with the smells of ill and revolting men we walked, air as dense as stagnant water, walked to a thick door with iron locks so massive I could nearly taste the metal odor, and I was let inside.

I ran to Aunt Marybelle before she could stand, and a loving reunion we commenced. Though Waingrow had his jailor close the door behind, we witches knew the sinners were listening. I began by asking whether my dear aunt were harmed, expressing all sorrow for not tending to her better. Aunt Marybelle attempted to soothe me, not allowing her niece to accept blame. After praying together for God to give guidance, we spoke of the magistrate's mistaken allegations, which Auntie could not explain, the dear innocent. Then the trial was mentioned and fear together we did, and pray again with weeping words until we smelled that the sinners had departed. Then we attempted to save our lives.

No passion was between us when we began whispering gravely. Marybelle first repeated the exact tale told to Waingrow: alone in the world, her husband dead in London, she and the niece quitting that disruptive city to seek peace in her father's cabin beyond Lucansbludge, here but days and separated, and further details not readily verified by authorities. Neither could these baseborn officials prove her a witch; but, of course, they did not need to.

"I die at a trial," Marybelle said. "I can smell a fear in these sinners enough to kill me. A knowing person as the Lady Rathel would condemn me accurately, but I die regardless. My only salvation, then, is to choose my death, as on Man's Isle."

"But no sea is hereabouts," I replied.

"The death I choose is then another. I will have them behead me."

"This you call salvation?" I groaned.

"Perhaps, if you and God can heal me."

I looked toward her as I had the magistrate, my disbelief utterly genuine now.

"God makes miracles, Marybelle, but I am not one," I told her.

"God makes witches, and makes them special. How special is not a thing completely known to me in experience, only in tale. I've heard as you that a witch might live if only beheaded, not also quartered or burned."

"How a witch might live if 'only' beheaded is a question beyond my thinking."

"Beyond my thinking, also, but not my belief. If God makes us so reparable, let us make use of His wisdom, not our own. I know not how to learn this, but you do."

"I? Marybelle, I know nothing," I whispered in return, "nothing but how greatly I desire to have you live."

"If this desire be strong enough, then perhaps your love may succeed. But remember our makings on Man's Isle and the pain it cost. Men you have killed with your body. As Satan has used you for death, pray that God may use you for life. Your person is the embodiment of all our forces, our love and worship and magic. Think ye, girl, of killing men and make your feeling reversed, for you are this witch, the invert witch; for are you not the same as I, but different? Have certainty, however, that you would dare the attempt; for though die you shan't, succeed or not, the great feeling required as an effort will change you ever."

"I could be much worse than I presently am and yet live well," I said. "What is to be done?"

"I have the sinners kill me in my manner," she described. "As well, I beg them to allow you to bury me in the wilds near my father's home. Thus, they will give you the burial box with me inside, and my bag which you must demand. If the coin within is left by the sinners, purchase transport for the coffin. In the wilds, take the casket and my bag. Therein might be things of godly power to you, though the sinners find them common. In the wilds do the magical thing."

"Do what magical thing?"

"Replace my head and have me begin healing."

"In the name of God, Marybelle, how—"

"In the name of God," Marybelle stated loudly, and continued with a prayer for the benefit of an odor come again, that of sinners remaining beyond our sight. As though coincidence, as soon as the prayer was complete, the jailor entered to remove me, leaving my aunt.

I was well questioned, my despondency easily projected. And though my answers were consistent and came easily, as important were my comments wherein I appropriated for Marybelle not innocence, but guilt.

"No, my great-uncle is not yet so found as to join me. Being a dumb person unable to speak, however, he will tell little. How

391

strange that my aunt has also been speaking poorly, though in a completely different manner. Think ye, sir, that her newly strange speech is due to exertion?"

Here was a topic for the magistrate's inquiries more interesting than unmet uncles. Mumbling, I told him. My aunt has been mumbling no words known to me. Then I extended his interest.

"My aunt's desire to eat raw meat: This was not an attempt to settle an undue stomach?"

More of this he inquired, whereupon I told him of pork without heat, of a squirrel eaten by the aunt yet with fur. And a horrible laugh coming from her on occasion: Would more sunlight perhaps cure this?

Then our conversation, which had come to fascinate Waingrow, was interrupted by the jailor who asked for his superior's presence in the corridor. None of their further speaking I heard, but I knew the message: The Landham woman is frantic.

The jailor bid me wait, in that the magistrate had been called away for a moment. But this moment was too long, for after Marybelle's frenzied speech of Jesus for the magistrate's ears, a resolution was required. A superior in English law was beckoned, also one in the rules of Heaven. To circumvent a trial, Marybelle would have to appear immediately dangerous, perhaps thrashing about the cell, even attacking the minister accompanying the magistrate and justice. How strange was this thinking of mine, as though dream or recollection, every detail before me and understood. So convincing were my thoughts that I was nearly able to speak for Waingrow a long hour later when he returned to state that our interview was concluded.

"Have you a place to remain this night within or about Lucansbludge?" he asked.

"I do, Lord Magistrate, and will return, perhaps with my aged great-uncle, to learn of the schedule for this trial. Upon my coming tomorrow, will you be able to tell of the agenda?"

"This following morning we will have scheduled all things, and then will inform you," Waingrow stated; but was it a smell or that facial cast like a crust that promised not the future, but finality?

I walked no farther than necessary from the town before hiding in the wilds and waiting for morn. Sleep was a part of this interval no more than cogitation. On my bag I sat, aimed at a community not seen, only smelled, one whose sinner-fresh portions were rancid to any witch. No hope had I, only confident expectation that the more profound smell of Marybelle's black body would not arrive. With the same predictiveness felt in Waingrow's office, I surmised the night, one to end with my sister's parts in a box. Strange were my perceivings, for though sounds of insects and animals were discerned, they seemed more story told than true experience, as though my predictions were the genuine facts of this evening.

This witch in the wilds was a dew keeper again, becoming more damp than any cave could render her. As though dead myself I sat that night, impenetrable to common signs of life, for I was expecting signs of death; and what does one butcher a witch with? An axe, perhaps, that utensil for removing limbs from a trunk. Here was an activity I would not be smelling: Blood has no odor to carry for miles, not even that of a sister. Waiting for a terminal hour, I used no sinners' device to track time, because I counted no minutes. The moment's measure was God's, called a life, variable in length; and if His will be done the same as Marybelle's, extendable as well, like a cold creature returned from hibernation. The degree of my waiting was an evening, so with the sun I returned to Lucansbludge. No sinner bothered me there, none asking of my dampness, for perhaps my wetness had come from all extensive tears. But what sorrow could I have while aware that English law would give my aunt her due?

Along with Waingrow, I was met by a cleric in the magistrate's office. Was Waingrow more respectful to me this morn, as though accepting the proper mien to face a young miss whose kin had passed on recently—but passed on where? To a box like a pot for dead meat, directly to Hell—or to a trial, as promised? As I sat before Waingrow at his desk, the thought enough to startle me came that these plans of Marybelle's would function less fully than those of the past, that I had overestimated her intellection, that her current idea was too foolish to be realized. How many sinners were so inane as to be convinced by a witch unfamiliar with their ways? I was the witch who had passed as a sinner, yet Marybelle felt herself able to dupe all those to pain her in this world. Utterly foolish was her ultimate survival, for the beginning was death, to be followed absurdly by the notion that death might be impermanent. Even the pseudo-mystic sinners had but one person in their history to return from the dead, this Jesus. Most inane was the method of Marybelle's planned resurrection—me, the witch more familiar with sinners' ways than those of her own kind. Yet with no idea of magic herself and with no instructions from her superior, the girl was to retrieve her sister from God's second greatest power, that of death, via his greatest ability of life as though Lord God Himself. Worst of all was my disappointment at Marybelle's undergoing a trial instead of dying at once, for my undertaking her mad plan would therefore be delayed. This seemed more distressing than the blatant fact of any trial's ending with Marybelle's burning. Of course, by then sinners more sensible than these two idiot witches would discover me evil and have me burned as well.

All these thoughts passed through me in the moment of my settling before Waingrow. Another moment passed before he spoke of the trial I had come to expect.

"Miss Alba Landham, with regret I do apprise that your aunt is dead, killed by the devil within her."

I paused for his words to be ingested, for his speaking was so odd that I could not comprehend. Therefore, I began the predicted, sensible conversation myself.

"You said when, sir, that my aunt's trial is scheduled?"

"Miss Alba Landham, please hear me when I speak that your aunt is dead, as seen fit by God to defeat the devil within her."

And I shouted, "Previously you said that the devil killed her from within, and now it is God from without?! I understand not what you say, sir. When is the promised trial?"

The clergyman present then offered his piety.

"She heard you not, Lord Waingrow, in that grief makes these things unbelievable. I will pray with the girl and have her understand."

Quickly the minister moved to bow and take my hand, holding it firmly with his hot palms.

"Miss Landham, look to me and see that your aunt was so filled with a demon that God told her to beg for her own execution, in that no other method could remove Satan. Such a fury

394

she began in bloodying herself and assaulting me and the magistrate with her very teeth that her conflict could only have been between God and Satan, and thank Jesus the former won."

Then deeper he bowed, commencing to pray for me to understand and for God to aid my soul, but no longer did he hold my hand. One of his sinning arms had moved around my shoulders to squeeze me in emphasis of his words, the other paw rising from mine to surround my breast, emphasizing only that faint stench rising from his bottom.

To help him pray in his selected manner, I slipped my hand to the source of the holy priest's evil fragrance, squeezing the one finger there as he had my hand. And, lo, as though an arm it became, with its size and firmness; and was I not practicing for my planned resurrection by giving life to his sex with but a touch?

I then pulled away from the minister to call out sharply, "Amen!"

The protrusion in the priest's apparel was as evident as his crucifix, viewed by the magistrate with clenched jaw. I considered feigning a collapse, but knew both sinners would be fucking me.

Holding out both hands as though needing to fend the men off, I displayed with my visage that my speaking must be heard, that no grieving girl was confronting them.

"You murdered my aunt without allowing me to tell her of my love?"

"Before your Aunt Marybelle Landham pleaded with us to release her soul, she—" was Waingrow's attempted explanation, a lie I interrupted loudly and with the force of love.

"Before you killed her said she what, Lord Magistrate? For murdering her did she praise you? And was my name mentioned, or only those of your affiliates, Queen Anne and the demon you discovered? Did this minister aid my aunt pray, and had he his hand on her bleeding cunt as he did mine?!" I screamed, and pointed to the pious penis. "Was the devil more completely in my aunt than in this false priest? So evident is Satan in his limb, will you not cut it off as you did my aunt's?!"

The priest then quit the room, holding his mouth instead of his groin. And I wondered if his guilt were so great that he wished to puke up his phallus and be rid of it. Holy revelation I gained with this operatic scene, aware that with woman or man, witch or sinner, Satan's cave is the crotch.

"Have you burned my aunt yet, Lord Murderer, or are you not finished butchering her body?" I shouted. "If you were truly a man of God and Jesus in this enterprise, at least you would allow me my aunt's . . . person," I averred.

How pleased the magistrate became to receive relief from me instead of passion. As though an oil lamp wicked up, his face grew bright; for the sinner was allowed to prove his decency, speaking quickly so I would have no opportunity to strike him down again with my voice.

"You aunt's last request we accorded her, Miss Landham, on behalf of her final godliness. That her body be buried near her father's home we promised, and this vow I pass to you with Jesus as my proof. Within a coffin she lies now, to be carried by citizens at your bidding and buried with a minister before her grave at the site of your choice."

"Your minister would be guiding her soul to Hell with his immoral pointing," I retorted. "My grand-uncle and myself with our hands and hearts will bury our beloved Marybelle, and for your death box and the conveyance I shall pay you coin. Being Christians loved by God as we love Him, we shall pray her poor soul to Heaven ourselves, as aided only by Jesus."

"No price need be paid," the magistrate responded with more kindness than before, "in that we accept responsibilities beyond mere law."

"Beyond mere life, so it seems, Lord Holiness," I harshly returned. "But I thank you true for requiring no payment, in that all our funds were in my aunt's bag, which is not in my possession."

"Yet it is, miss, yes," Waingrow quickly replied, stepping away to a tall cabinet, removing Marybelle's bag, which he provided me. "As well I say you shall find the contents undisturbed."

"God bless you, sir, for your aid, but neither you nor a decent minister will relieve me of the grief within me that I pray God I might survive. And since my heart will not begin to heal until my aunt is buried and her soul released to Jesus, I would accept her . . . person . . . soon, please; for truly the more I consider this dying, the more agony I feel."

"Within moments, Miss Alba Landham, your aunt's remains

shall be brought before this office in a wagon. Then you might go at your own speed, your own manner, and . . ."

Waingrow found himself alone at his sentence's end, for I had grasped Marybelle's bag and walked away. Stepping outside, I waited on the walkway, the magistrate sending a constable to accompany me, but he remained apart. When a wagon came with the box, I was surprised at the fine construction of this pauper's coffin. Smooth but not polished with wax, its craftsmanship approached the Rathel's furniture, but made to contain no linen, no life. Should its color therefore have been red, or black?

Waingrow's man instructed the driver and his assistant to convey me and the casket wherever I desired. And though the constable placed my bags within the wagon, when he offered his hand that I might sit with the two sinners ahead, I stepped around to climb into the rear unaided, settling myself beside the casket.

"I sit with my love, sir," I told the male quietly; and with a salute from him as though I were an officer, I was taken with my love away.

The village sinners stared at me as though I were royalty expected. Since no smoke nor smell of blood was rising from the box, why did I achieve their attention? Only due to my odd position behind with death? No grieving did I display, no spastic weaving of hands before my weeping eyes. No interest had I in feigning sufficient grief, for interval was my only challenge, this contest akin to that of the previous night in which I had survived duration. Fearful of the subject, I avoided thoughts of Marybelle's plan, fearful because my solitary actions would be required, and I remained ignorant. But would a vapid state provide adequate love for Marybelle, and what quantity could be proper for her condition? Was she alive or dead, retrievable or returning? And poor was my heart that my best hope was to find Marybelle in only two pieces.

Past the farm we moved and those sinners who had allowed my ruin by cooperating with my lustful journey to their town. Far from the trail, the family stood before their home as though official folk. Looking to me, the girl raised her hand in a gesture filled with a pity sad enough to smell. Then she bowed her head, covering her face with both hands. Not touched by either parent, the girl looked up to see me blow her a kiss. This was no aid, for her shoulders and all her body shook with weeping; but, yes, aid it was, for the mother then drew her daughter near.

As though a dream, I suffered a reliving, but this as inverted as I. Again I was in a wagon dragged by horses to the edge of the sinners' land with Marybelle and our baggage. As kind as our previous driver, these males asked of the casket after placing it on the grass, or was this mere curiosity? As far as possible we had traveled before coarse land stopped the wagon. My great-uncle comes, I lied, and they asked his source. A cabin yon, I replied, and waved my arm nowhere. How is the box carried? they asked. By a sled for dragging, I said, and if they had further queries, to ask Jesus for inspiration; and the sinners knew to depart.

I waited for them to leave my sight. This was my initial decision. Next I looked toward the coffin, for the first instance with deliberation. Then, with no forethought, I achieved unspoken words, and was this scream in my head not a prayer? When can I love her last? I thought. When can I grieve in my heart to myself, and not with a lying mouth to sinners? Then, as though granted revelation by God Himself, I knew that I would have to earn my grief by disposing of my guilt.

I was staring at this box, another wooden cave Marybelle slept in, like that home of her own conception. I was staring at her bag, then grasped it as though food required for my survival, understanding how easy examining this container would be compared to the other. So I opened it greedily, needing an action to begin, for the sooner started the sooner complete. Within were Marybelle's garments and shoes, her Bible missing because it had been given me, and one of those wax-wrapped items, narrow and dense. Of course, Marybelle's knife. Another wrapped parcel held coins, but the luggage held no magic. None besides the knife, for with its sight I understood the future, and that was the casket. I would have to open the box, but nailed tightly it was, like a crate, as though containing porcelain items shipped from the Continent. Whatever shattering had occurred therein I had to see, for repair thereof was my expected expertise. I imagined opening the thing even as sinners rode by to ask in Jesus's name of my actions. I imagined opening the coffin even if alone in the world, and found I was not prepared to think further.

I would have to move the coffin deeper into the wilds. Alternately I could remove Marybelle's . . . person . . . and carry her and our two bags, leaving the casket to be found empty by sinners. Or I could drag the crate far enough for it to be hidden from easy view, leave the bags temporarily, then move Marybelle to a remote locale and . . .

I discerned its asymmetrical shape. The coffin's narrow end was literally fit for legs placed together, the other broader for shoulders. I approached the former, presuming it lighter. Grasping the lumber's edges, I lifted the coffin, stepping firmly, but had to drop the weight after only two paces. With further attempts, I learned that long, reverse thrusts wherein I grimaced and nearly ran were most effective; so into the bushes I moved and through, deep, deep breaths not of effort but pain, around this tree in a final spurt before dropping the box, and me.

I sat on the casket where I had placed the bags, which had fallen off. Standing to retrieve the luggage, I found my legs as heavy as the coffin and as limp as water. Only to the far end of the casket did I move before collapsing to bend double, breaths moving through me as though the sea currents in a nightmare. But no longer was I on the narrow end. I imagined the box below, imagined sitting on Marybelle's face, on her head that was no longer . . .

My body was the next burden I dragged, to the paired bags that I could scarcely move. So I hid them in the brush, for not all of these containers could I be conveying at once. Then I returned to the coffin. Lifting the narrow end, I attempted to pull, but could not; so I dropped the box, nearly smashing my feet. Since holding up the coffin was no longer possible, I jerked it along with low, wrenching moves. In this manner I proceeded over rocks to trip me and vines to entangle my feet, jerking along until I collapsed onto my back, so exhausted as to be astounded by the thought that ever again I could lift my arms. Too uncomfortable to be still, I rolled my head every way as though to find an angle whereby air might more easily enter. Racked with pain I lay as though I had just killed another man; but, no, not so great was my distress. Why, then, did I receive the impression that pain of this nature would come?

I opened my eyes, rising on one elbow to look about for a new path. To the incline past the thickets down the slope. There I walked with a slowness unmatched in my recollection. Yes, at the bottom I would find easier passage. Then proceed north, deliberating my further course upon reaching that bend. Return to the box to continue dragging.

This lifting had become the same as a blow, as though I were hitting myself with timbers instead of moving them. For a moment, I nearly smiled, so ludicrous were the sounds I produced, as though animal croaks or muted curses spoken in no language known. I nearly laughed from the absurdity of so punishing myself; and again I found a connectivity between humor and madness I could not quite comprehend, not while experiencing it.

To the slope I struggled with the coffin, hoping to recall the location of the baggage. How far had I gone? What distance had I dragged my impossible burden, what interval or era? At the incline with the box, I decided to push the thing with a controlled sliding, God's natural force of downward attraction to aid me. But after the lift and pull was a required drop, and here the box I sat heavily upon my feet, immediately struggling to lift the casket before I was crushed. But not flat enough on the slope's edge was the coffin for such rough handling. Once lifted from my feet and dropped, the crate came down on a corner, then fell unbalanced to one side, angling to slip down the slope uncontrolled. Grab for it and hold I did until the box was lost, tumbling loudly twice; and with the second, had I not heard a thumping from within?

Gently the casket landed. Sliding down with care, I found the box inverted, and then I had to right it. Though a difficult task without the constraints of cautious handling, even greater was my stress from rolling the coffin so gently that nothing inside would be jostled; yet as the box rolled came another thud, and this I felt within me.

At once I began dragging the casket so as not to ponder that sound, so that the pain in my body would overwhelm the pain in my heart, my spirit. To the bend of the terrain I moved with the box, falling motionless only twice, gaining my latest goal late in the afternoon to find beyond a ledge, one much lower than my height, but as possible to climb with the coffin as a tree.

I wished to go farther. I wished to move the casket that entire day, and the next, and next; because when finally I ceased, I would have to open it. Then I would find Marybelle within. But I knew I could not continue forever, could not allow Marybelle to go long without repair; for eventually would she not truly be dead, permanently dead, and become spoiled the same as any old meat?

I had to open the box at that instant, no longer at some indefinite end. I had to open the box immediately, but could not, for so securely nailed was the lid that no human hands could pry it up. Only thick splinters split by nails could I remove with my fingers. In a grand feeling of mad relief, I came aware that I had left the knife with Marybelle's bag, and would have to return for this prying implement. But my return was a holiday, a mad emotion in which I delayed the true end of my journey. Satisfying was the excellent distance I had traveled, and no difficulty was encountered in my finding the hidden bags. But returning with them was a chore, though I valued the pain, the torment of my arms hiding the horror of my journey's conclusion; for there was the box, and since I had the knife, I could open the lid, and must.

Dusk had approached. With further delay, I would find myself in darkness. What thoughts were these to consider night beneficial for its blindness, rendering me unable to see dead, half-dead Marybelle, see her parts? But wherein the disadvantage when I had no idea how to proceed with her . . . person? But I required no idea, for eventually I found feeling.

With a lethargy of the mind fit my exhausted body, I began removing the coffin's lid. Holding the knife was unpleasant, for in this natural land, its metal smell seemed perverse—yet how fitting this trait was considering the usage. And why did I feel a distress like drowning when I began to pick at the casket's lid, feel as though I were stabbing myself?

My lethargy decreased in proportion to my failure, for the lid had been fitted so well that even finding a beginning was difficult. At the end split by nails, I managed to insert the knife, but my initial prying was fruitless because I split more wood away without forming any gap between lid and box. This useless poking then became intimidating, for would I be knifing the thing until Marybelle rotted and the sinners found me robbing graves? Replacing anxiety with activity, I began pounding on the hilt, first with my palm, then with a rock. I pried by leaning on the knife with all the force I could apply. And when I had formed space enough for my fingers to be inserted, I understood this end of the casket to be the wider; so I moved to the opposite and successfully pried until breaking the knife.

Exactly at the hilt it snapped, and I was astonished to find this sinning metal little stronger than wood. Attempting to use the implement with no handle, I cut my palm, bleeding on the sticks I next gathered, inserting them into my gap and prying, then using larger limbs that functioned better because of their length. And though my hand was a viscous, reddish mess sticking to the wood, the pain was not important, not with the greater pain to come from within that box when I opened it.

Limb after limb I broke, others I had to discard, being too brittle or too flexible, like a frail and weak witch. Up the slope, slipping and crawling into the forest time after time, during my later returns simply sliding down and scraping myself bloody. In another contest was I, a failing challenge with the sun, for I would not be repairing the dark. And I did not wish to fail. I did not wish to fight nightfall and magic and Satan and the sinners' work all together against me. So I sought limbs, but the best was too large for my narrow gap, and those thinner broke and broke. Therefore, I used my hands and nearly broke them, so that as well as cut and bloody, the one became so swollen and sore I could scarcely close it. Crawling to the trees again, I returned with as fine a limb as any, but too large. So I entered the crack with my bent arm, and with my shoulder at the lid's edge, I stressed every muscle in my back and side until some part of my flesh came loose enough to have me gasp and go rigid; but there was a space as though part of God's sky, enough for my best tree limb. Inserting the stick, I was pained by my side and my hand as I pried along the lid's perimeter in a strong continuity of movement, aware that this great effort was required merely to open the coffin; and there was the lid on the ground and Marybelle before me.

Not so dim was the remaining day that I could not see perfectly, see all of Marybelle's . . . person. Her parts. Everywhere within were lengths of broken tree limbs, on Marybelle's legs and torso, one on her neck, her empty neck. There on her crotch was

402

Marybelle's head, askew, the cut end a plane of red flesh and vessels as though from a beast half eaten by predators, but cut so cleanly, like a butchered animal in a sinners' shop. But the first astonishment was her face, the lips partly open, eyes closed, but the cheeks and nose were smashed and bruised, and must have been terribly painful—but what could she feel? And I knew the source. Marybelle's thrashing before the magistrate had not caused this damage, but my own mishandling, Marybelle's ruin due to my rush, my hurry to avoid her sight, herself.

Death has no smell, for death is nothing, but I was sickened by Marybelle's subtle odor, that personal fragrance of her body, my sister's body, and her blood, so meager a smell that she could only be dead, she would always be dead. I was sickened because here was all my love in the world, that love for my departed mother and minor love for Elsie incomparable to the desperate love I felt for Marybelle, my sister so great a portion of my life that she seemed yet living. And I fell away from the casket and to God's ground and vomited nothing, for I was empty of food but filled with agony, my body retching in spasms to force up none of the poison within me, for it was that very love to sicken me, and would remain. But was I most ill because I knew Marybelle to be gone, or because I believed her ideas of magic, believed her to be partially present; and the only force in God's universe to save her continued living was me, though I could not, not in my ignorance, weakness, my imperfection as a witch? But I wished to, desiring her life enough to kill myself instead of accept her death.

Ah, bless you, Lord God, this knife would do, and I reached for the broken metal, having begun the contest of ending Marybelle's death by somehow killing it. Once in my hand, did not the metal feel fine? Yes, but also cold—like my flesh—then hot—like the metal's forged source—too hot, so hot I perspired as I stared at the metal in my palm where it never belonged until now and thereafter would never have a better place. So hot I perspired and my mouth salivated as though trying to aid me sweat. So hot I became that I removed my clothing to remove some discomfort, all my clothes except my shoes, which were too difficult to dislodge, as though nailed on, coffin lids of leather. Then I wiped the sweat away, wiped it from my neck and shoulders and then my chest, and that hand on my bosom seemed the sinner's, a touch I recognized; for surely males had touched me there more thoroughly and often than I. That hand was a sinner's by being mine, for I was part sinner, in my blood and my desire for their life, that hand on me a sinner's because it remained and fondled and squeezed the flesh made to encapture sinners, kneading my breast as had those men who died from the touch—and was this not the death I sought? Yes, and from the nearest sinner—me—came the smell of sex at the body's bottom, but different here; for all the others had been male and this was a woman's, my smell different by being invert.

Hot was my breast in one sinning hand and my baby slot in the other, for that was the next goal of sinners conveying their lust along my torso, and my lust was life, was death. One hand on my breast and one on my cunt as I looked to Marybelle, her head on her crotch like that sinner's hand on mine. And here were the rules of my evil challenge, for could not some exchange be arranged in that I wished to displace deaths? Why not limb for limb, for were these not the parts transmitting death to men and Marybelle? Yes, so I continued that conveyance of lust, lust of love, along my body as I had conveyed the coffin's opening, proceeding from end to end, from teat to groin, taking Marybelle's head with no remorse nor fondness to stick the bloody end between my legs while that sinner continued to squeeze my breast. Since one hand held Marybelle's person, the other was required to hold the knife, and that was the sinning one against my bosom unable to resist my white flesh. So it continued to squeeze metal and flesh as I pressed Marybelle against me to have her love as near as possible, the emotion conveyed so profoundly that I hoped for her to grow there. The season above was not that of new growth, however, but autumn, the one of fall, in that my parts were dropping, not so neatly as the leaves via God nor Marybelle's head via Satan; but there was my breast hanging only by skin, no smell of fresh blood noticed, no sound of meat being cut away. No perceptions had I, for all were occupied by this incredible screaming, such a vibration that my spine shook and my jaws were locked open, and the cry was terrifying; but how was I to notice even so frightening a response when the devil was cutting me asunder? How could I feel mere demonic sex when I was dying by mutilation?

Though the witch in me could not scream enough to obscure that agonized idea, perhaps my audience could cry better; for either Satan had sent demons or God His angels to observe, and actively, for they as well were screaming. They as well seemed mad, for these aides from Hell or Heaven in the guise of sinning males rushed down the slope less neatly than I to approach me as though desperate to gain part of my dying before it became alive, thus dead. But too late they were, for I was finished as they arrived, my breast dropping onto Marybelle's face and remaining, stuck, as my vagina contracted against her neck like a fist to squeeze an animal dead. And there came the blood, squeezed from my sex by my sex into Marybelle's throat as the angels came to take me away.

Twenty-seven

No more peaceful sleep could I have achieved than in that era devoid of troubling dreams. But forgetfulness did not survive the night, for ignorance participates not in understanding, and the latter was my characteristic concern. Therefore, when I awoke, I remembered everything, details of the attempted repair recalled by my corporeal outcome.

So extensive was my misery that I discovered no single prevalent pain to consider. My attention was on a general agony impossible to sleep through, despite my need to implement healing by rest, healing of damage notated by pain, by suffering within me, that was me. And when recollection began, I was grateful for silence, thankful for the absence of the sound of that torture I had invoked not in the name of Satan, but of living and therefore God.

Less gratitude had I after dropping my dress to discover one breast and one wet scar, finding that a part of me was not damaged, but departed. With that madness came an accompanying humor surely from Satan that had me consider this bodily lack beneficial, for sinning men would now have less of me to molest. Thereafter, in all graveness and begging love, I prayed Lord God for that breast to have done my sister good.

"What manner of fiend are you to slaughter me in my sleep as you did my aunt?"

This was my greeting for the jailor who entered my cell as I examined my chest. Literally I had nothing to hide, and allowed him to enter with no change in my audit. Rapidly he departed, having seen my hand near flat gore that should have been feminine. Returning soon, he was accompanied by the magistrate and a priest not seen before, even as that erect member of the clergy was never seen again by me. As the males entered, my story came forth—came first—but it was accusation.

Despite my stern intents, I could not avoid a mien of pleading, for the small effort of looking up stretched my side enough to astonish me with pain, and I felt violated.

"How long I have slept I do not know, but God I bless forever for allowing me peaceful recovery," I began. "Each second asleep I knew the truth, that part of me was asunder, for the revelation was divine, praise Lord Jesus. And praise His Father to have His good men of English church and law explain why they have butchered me."

So astonished that they lost their questioning, the magistrate and priest respectively explained that my damage had been inflicted by myself, by Satan. Then the constable to lead my captors was summoned, his witnessing a settling tale; for though horrid, did it not combine the two official views in a type of descriptive peace?

"The poor Belle woman did seem a person in her death," he began, looking anywhere but at the fallen lass. "Even if not, no fiend if ever human could deserve the vile acts done by that young lady, whom I pray God was taken by Satan himself, for that screaming from within her—Jesus please us—was the sound of Hell itself. Such were the deeds that the miss did force herself with every breath—I swear of Jesus—to resist, so firm was her desire to be merely human. Lord Magistrate, if you were Lord God Himself I could be no more certain than to tell you the truth I saw, that this miss was taken by a sinister power beyond my understanding which did force her to have at these acts. And if you saw her face and heard her screaming, you would know as well as I that the miss was being tormented and reviled beyond her will to be what her common soul would never have her be."

"As you removed her from the activity," the magistrate asked with no emotion, "was the fiend within her seen to depart?"

"Everything seemed to depart inside her, Lord Waingrow, including her life, in that once we pulled her away, she collapsed like death, so much that we listened to hear her breathing. Then wrapped her naked form well we did, in her gown and our own jerkins, and bring her gently here. In truth, Lord Magistrate, to look at her screaming was to see Satan himself but see him attacking a lady. And when he left and left her calm, only the lady did we have, and pitiful she was to make every man weep what with her sweetness so ruined, and blood complete all over."

"No further sign of Satan was seen thereafter," the magistrate continued, "in the wagon as you brought the Alba Landham person here?"

"No sign saw we of anything but a pitiful miss, Lord. And in the belongings of the two was nothing devilish. The other woman, though, was naught but an executed folk that we could see. But so devilish was the previous activity with her that my distraught men could scarcely find the effort to bury her. But they did, these good men, with much prayer for everyone about, alive and dead, for peace and all good spirits to go to God. And I tell, sir, that I was gladdened to be taking the girl and not burying the other, for those men had to pick up the portions and place them all in the casket with their hands with some puking done, God bless them, before the hole was dug and filled with the poor woman."

Gracious God be thanked, I prayed, for not allowing them to have cut her further or burned her body. Blessed Lord be praised for giving my most extremely unrealistic hopes new life.

Though the magistrate spoke again, I heard only the end of his query about my having truck with ungodly spirits, for I was occupied with worship.

"I desire only for God to be within me, not Satan, whom certainly you are more familiar with than I," was my displeased response. "Perhaps more than familiarity you have influence over the devil, for all my godly recollection describes me as whole upon leaving the wagon with my aunt's casket, yet violated and in pieces when placed therein again by men of yours, not by Satan, men with their hands against my tortured, naked body."

So distraught the rescuing constable became from my moral deprecation that his spirit was damaged, pain seen in his moist, disbelieving eyes as he looked to me when before he had been unable. Thus, I blessed him as though the nearby priest.

"Good sir, cure thine own distress with the presence of God within you and find in me no condemnation. Whereas 'tis true that my flesh being taken I do not recall, more sensible it seems that I was mutilated by men rather than Satan; for the devil I know not, yet

408

you males cut my aunt worse than I lay butchered now, and before God must acknowledge. But you, sir, are an individual of such exuded Godliness that I disbelieve you responsible even if witnessed with my own eyes."

"God be with you miss," the constable pronounced; and though he might have gained some of the relief I wished for him, he yet retained a distress from his witnessing.

Perhaps his greater relief was in quitting this experience, for with his telling done, he was ordered away by Waingrow. Thereafter, the magistrate queried me as to potions, spells, chants, and charms for all demonic occasions, to which I shook my head not in rejection, but pity. And what aid to English law was the available priest who asked nothing and displayed no expertise in seeking the devil? A poor observer he would be if I moved against him via Satan, for the priest looked to God with closed eyes, his hands clasped before him no preventative for oncoming evil.

"I know nothing of these things," I retorted to Waingrow. "How bizarre you are to mutilate me then ascribe responsibility to your victim."

Undaunted, the magistrate continued to interview me as to my recollection, my interest in the forest, my great-uncle.

"A man never seen, a part of our family promised by my aunt."

"Yet you professed to me having seen him," the magistrate returned. "What other lies have you to tell?"

"None besides the fallacy that your sense of Jesus is deeper than that of Satan, for the latter alone you seek. And since by your own description my aunt was stolen by Satan, how could I of such youthful experience not believe her corrupted words? She instructed me to profess having met Grand-uncle so as not to appear the gypsy and thus become the receptacle of prejudice. But not so receptive of your bigotry am I as to allow you to place Satan in my mouth to thereby justify cutting him away. You might have begun your mutilations with a sexual part to please your manhood, but with God's strength and Jesus's love, I'll not seek your further slaughter."

Experienced in his official ways, the magistrate continued to confront me, no longer abated by my reversals whereby I observed the demon within him. Eventually, with no verbal aid from the prayerful priest, Waingrow presented me with a public trial, and before a justice of the Court of King's Bench I would tell my story and see how intimidated God, the English public, and Queen Anne's law would be by my speaking. Therein adjudicated would be my responsibility for the demonic things done to myself and my aunt as she lived and thereafter, and the initiating crime that was the murder of an associate of the constable's office, Daniel Cameron.

As though sickened by his allegations, I told Waingrow, "Jesus save your soul that now you accuse me not only of slaughtering myself and being demonic to my dead aunt, but doing so in advance and thus causing her execution. Her blood was drawn by your hand, Lord Killer, an achievement that in your secret thoughts perhaps you find prideful. As for the English public, more impressed might they be with the magistrate's handiwork on lady prisoners," I returned, then succumbed to presenting my best weapon, reaching for my dress above that missing breast, reaching with that cut hand as though to apply gore on gore in mutual attraction.

With my move, the priest held his hands out, fingers twitching, for me to not, not reveal this, a plea without words before his speaking.

"Blessed Jesus, she could be free!" he insisted, his words meant to divert my gore's exposure with their invocation. And no gore was forthcoming, since the priest seemed to be associating his Jesus with me.

"Lord Waingrow," he added quickly, "known well to us all is a demon's overcoming a person to perform a sinister crime and thereafter vacating, do you say?"

"True are your words, priest," Waingrow agreed, "but this Satan that you know in spirit I know better in flesh. Firm he is in retaining a body once acquired. Hide well he does, often imitating the piety and fine speech of God's ministers. He now could be speaking with this very girl's mouth. Despite her words, we know she cut herself, as certain as Jesus."

"But certainly Satan was the cause," my clerical benefactor submitted.

"Without question he was," Waingrow returned without agreeing. "Our only uncertainty, then, is this demon's location: yet within her or absconded? Retreat is difficult for the devil; this I know. English law and secular history tell that killing the body is oft required. The demon in Marybelle Landham convinced us to kill her as a ruse, for this girl was available to receive it. The question for the court is how receptive she was, whether a dark magic in her desired a Satanic conjoining. A further query is whether this devil yet remains with her, desired or not. These things shall the trial determine, for therein God and Jesus and English law will weigh against one devil."

Then I was stricken with enlightenment, but remained uncertain whether its source were God or Satan, for which entity would inspire me toward salvation by having me evoke the worst demon in my life?

"And holy you are, sir, for pitting God against me, as though you were His master instead of He thine," I declared to the magistrate. "But God knows I accept Him as my maker and glorify in His superiority. With me shall He and Jesus reside during the trial, with all of you opposing Him. But since most of England's populace you might very well possess, I would request one of them particularly to stand with me at the bar."

"And what person would this be, Alba Landham?"

"My reference is to an individual of London, the Lady Amanda Rathel. This woman had adopted me beyond my choosing, and knows of demons more than you might imagine. To the extent that one accused of having killed a loved relative and part of her feminine self can be vouched for by established expertise, the lady shall so do."

"Your life thus changes again," the magistrate contended. "Though you alleged all to be dead, here is another example of your family, and perhaps another lie."

Referring to me as a liar so filled me with hot fury that I reached harshly despite the pain to rip loose my gown and dressing to reveal my bosom, not the half considered shapely by sinners, but the reddish gash revolting to humans.

"This is the truth I tell, killer of women!" I cried, and quickly recovered myself, Waingrow snorting in disgust, the priest falling to his knees, looking to the floor, not me, praying with pressing hands clasped before his eyes.

As though a miracle, the priest immediately stood, but his strength was a war, for this man preferred his collapse. For this sinner, I felt true pity, for though his godliness was modest, when facing horrors he demanded courage.

"Ah," he began, sighing or moaning, looking away from me and

411

high. "Ah," he said, a word to give him breathing and an ability to speak further. "Magistrate, I believe this Lady Rathel is a person as spoken, one known to be an enemy of demons."

Waingrow then looked closely to the priest, not having expected so pious a source to support my lies. The magistrate, however, was not one to disagree with God.

"This Lady Rathel is then a person to learn of," Waingrow stated, "and well study and seek if she be aware of the Miss Alba Landham. And a blessing this search will be to begin now, and a blessing it is to be away from one so maddening." Waingrow then abandoned me as threatened, with no salutation due a lady, no curse due the devil. Only the priest had words, crossing himself then waving that same hand toward my head, praying for my peace and all our holiness, speaking quickly by necessity; for the other human by then had left, and the priest would not be alone with me; for devil or lady, I was yet a witch.

"Ah! beat me your bleeding beast, you fiend—I'll yet be killing you!"

Outside my cell, a criminal resistive to incarceration assaulted his captors who responded with kicks and clubs. Thereafter, I smelled new blood. After being locked in his cell, the criminal remained loud, calling out oaths and convincing screams. Around him—and me, for I was of this populace—came murderous cries that the respondents, too, would be killing the bastard jailors with any opportunity. Other males shouted to this pack to be quietening their farting mouths lest the current speakers get out and teach them about interrupting a true man's peace. Soon the sinners' speech became less intellectual and more virile, for ladies were the subject of their discourse.

"Quiet these blackguards, jailor! Drag the lout into the hall and kick his bloody mouth silent!"

"Aye, Lord Jailor arse faces! Then bring out the witch to fix her difficulty. Bring her out where we see what remains of the slim bitch!"

"Oh! Lord Waingrow, the queen's bastard! Yes to let the witch out, for I smell her problem and it be wet cunt for me to lap as though holy water!"

So great was the following, collective response of mad laughter as to mask the sound of clomping boots. The guards arrived to pull forth several occupants, replacing the sounds of their sex nonsense with that first criminal's noise: moans of pain to occupy even a sexual man more than silly fantasies about one young woman partially in the vicinity.

Those mad calls for me and the jailors' tactile response reduced my breathing, for I did not care to be sensed, hiding in my cave lest I attract the exterior beasts. Though I appreciated the relative silence to have come, the justice delivered remained undetermined; for whereas thoughts of my being ravished made me further ill, did I wish these sinners beaten only for their foolish speaking? Had the constable who captured me been one to beat his fellow males? And which scenes to him were more distressful: Marybelle's repair or the criminals' groans? Could this violent settling of prisoners be normal for guards, whereas a witch's way with her body was demonic? My screaming could not have aggrieved the emotive constable, for this product was common here. Must be, I thought, the loosened body parts, for even men can be mutilated and therefore commiserate with cut ladies.

Not unique was this day in having me the center of men's fantasies, though felons were not alone in subjecting me to their imaginings. Outside my door day by day were prayers whispered by a known voice, for the priest oft returned to speak of me with God. Though this minister smelled only of regard for the prisoner within, I would change his subject. My great desire was to convince him of the superior need of a superior person, hoping that the priest might pray for Marybelle.

In this manner my days proceeded. Twice each week a jailor came for my chamber pot's contents, though I knew by the shouting how unfairly I was treated, the other criminals crying out at the dog bitch jailor for taking their pissy shit but once a season. Daily the guard would leave a plate of usually rancid gruel, but we criminals were all equal in received cuisine. Occasionally water was added to my bucket, the green slime therein appealing in its natural aspects, though drawing commentary from without as to the arse face jailor's allowing the other prisoners to die of drying. Later the priest might come to pray in my vicinity, though never near enough to bleed upon. Oft his presence was first made known by precursors of prayer not so well spoken, coming from the secular state of criminality. All the prisoners had good words for the priest, for the same as I, they desired his special qualities. And though I heard him pray over only the witch, I knew his blessings went to all the felons, knew by their hoarse thanks that made them seem nearly semi-human. But what sort of humor had me wondering of the priest's ultimate reward for these blessings? Since prayer was his employment, when found to be blessing a creature born soulless, would he not be construed as having failed his job, and thus be dunned for his time with God instead of rewarded?

Though I retained my silence, I was potentially as noisome as any criminal. Each day I would find the flesh of my chest not damaged but destroyed, any movement of my side or arm delivering new agony. My moans were unavoidable, though I reduced them to prevent the prisoners' joyous response from hearing me. Since I could reduce my sounds but not eliminate my pain, I ejected the excess agony with my face, producing grimaces so intense they hurt me additionally. But even these responses I avoided that day a woman came, a nurse who placed fresh salve upon my chewed chest, new fabric on my raw ribs and slit hand. After wondering of my rapid healing, the woman was quickly gone; for perhaps she did in fact apply her nursing to a demon, Satan himself the true healer, a smile for the girl regardless for her being so pitiful a lass, out the door and seen by only one sinning prisoner commenting on his desire to roll his balls up her baby gouge, no physician returning thereafter.

I imagined my future. In a massive room before barristers and the populace of Lucansbludge, I would speak as I had in my cell, with equal anger due to my foolishness, my inability to be sensibly temperate. Accused I would be of housing a demon, and yea, he would yet be found within me, since he had never been seen to depart. Most vivid in this imagining was the sound of the best crowd ever drawn by me, a mass of godly sinners crying out at my story exactly as these criminals had cried out at my slimness, my cunt. The final noise would be of air seeping into my veins as my blood rushed out, following my rolling head. And with no witch sister left to repair me, I would not achieve the current condition of dear Marybelle so remarkably healed as though reborn in her box. Except for that separation, the one between body and head, between Marybelle and life.

Dreams I had, of course, for what better opportunity than sleep for Satan to taunt me? On the sea bottom I sat, criminals collecting at the top of the anchor chain before me. To make my hiding from the felons complete, I inhaled not a breath, or was this lack of respiring due to my drowning? And there was the shore mere paces away and with it salvation, but not a step could I take, because the priest was finally praying for Marybelle's soul, and I would not disrupt his spiritual repair with my own difficulties, own death.

In this manner my dreams proceeded. Came the day in which my side no longer anchored me static with pain. I thus could stand with but a wince. Pleased with my healing, I examined the wound not viewed since the first day of my awakening. Removing the dressing, I saw that the reddish patch was now a drying, rough crust. I also viewed destruction. As though only now comprehending, I saw that all my dishonest words to the magistrate had been accurate. Then I was struck with a new grimace as fierce as any from agony, for I found mutilation, and I was sickened. Near ill enough to vomit, I fell to the bed and covered the wound with its dressing and above that my own clothing, being utterly certain not to touch my injury, my mutilation. Then my gown I plucked up to falsely produce my former shape as though I could replace it, plucked up the fabric to fill that void of flesh with air. My discovery was that the mutilation, though by my own hand, was the sinners' responsibility. The sinners had assaulted me again, nearly killing me, though they were killing me regardless in pieces. And I knew that the sinners had also violated Marybelle. But I had killed her. Even as the sinners had been the implement, I had been the cause. Yet so unjust was this sinning world that Marybelle was dead while I had escaped with but a wound. So at my bodice I plucked and plucked till my arm was so sore that I could no longer move it, but when my hand dropped, it fell not against my chest, for all of me would have to die before I allowed that contact.

Only in dreams did the trial beleaguer me. The king's justice was Cameron, his periwig my breast dropped onto his head when last he had been between my legs. Cameron accused me of inspiring Godly thoughts from priests though as a witch I was due devilish considerations. No refute had I, finally controlling my glib tongue better than the priest his praying, the man unseen outside my courtroom. And this was best because his nature was my mother's, and I did not wish to see her in him, so long had she been dead that all of Mother would resemble my chest. Representing London was Magistrate Naylor, who had never been allowed a fair turn at my soot, practicing his verdict by blowing glass, his adjudication being that clearly this witch deserved a burning. As Elsie pulled tight my corset ties so that I would be burned as a lady without my torso pressing out everywhere, though less was recently available for protruding, the Rathel entered my cell to tell me there must be no trial, for surely not even she could have me survive.

"Alba? Alba, do you hear?"

"Of course I hear my own flipping dream," I mumbled to the demon in my head interrupting my nightmare. Then I awoke to feel a great hatred for those dreams whose ends turned real, for they could not be escaped by waking. Especially evil was the ending here as personified, for there was the Rathel awakening me.

What a crowd I had collected now, for in my cell stood the magistrate and priest and mistress, leaving scant space for even a slim witch with half a bosom, scant space for God, Who of course had invented distance. And since God could not be present, there was His substitute, the second most powerful entity in the world, Amanda Rathel, speaking to me as Waingrow observed. Then my hatred for the nightmare vanished, for as I awoke came a new dream in which I would be able to participate by my own selection, for I smelled this Lady Rathel entering a . . . composition.

"Alba, dear Alba, I am here to help you, child. The evil demon who took you now is gone, and therefore her spell over you is vanquished. Do you recall me, dear, and our lovely life in London? Do you recall the witch who stole you from our home?"

Damned straight, wench.

With all the speed my stiff pain could procure, I threw myself to the woman and well wrapped the one arm leading to a true breast around her, embracing a sinner I usually considered equal to puke, but better with her in London killing Eric than burned to charcoal in Lucansbludge. And whine I did as a replacement for weeping, feigning a tender return, though Rathel's odor beneath her false scents was scarcely better than a sinner's prick smell. But not enough hatred had I for the Rathel that I would not well love her in

416

this contest rather than accept a denouement as hot as blown glass, though blacker.

"Remember?" I replied with my sweetest voice. "Of course I remember the finest home in England and the love there, Mistress Amanda."

"And well have I missed you, precious child," my, er, mother averred, "and have come to return you to our home and love you well again."

Oh, how moving was her voice. And how loving was my disposition as I pulled away from the stench wench to look longingly into her eyes, holding her shoulder only with my bloody hand as I spoke again.

"But, Mother, I cannot go with you because these men wish to kill me more than you wish to love me."

"No, child, these decent men wish to rid their community of demons, not of a fine English miss."

"But they killed my aunt."

"Alba, dear, you have no aunt."

"Of course, mistress, my Aunt Marybelle from Man's Isle. She had come to London to take me into the wilds and live away from society."

"But, Alba, your aunt was a demon."

"Please, mistress, as much as I love you, Aunt Marybelle was true family of mine."

"No, Alba, no bodily resemblance had you to this creature and no blood shared. As I was not fully able to make you understand, this witch took you from your true mother when you were but a babe. And when through me you escaped her heathen control, she stole you again in London, murdered a man here who was Queen Anne's representative, then attempted to kill you when she herself was ended. Again she stole your mind, Alba, and I have come to return it with the aid of these excelling men. And this I may do, for through God's grace the witch and her master were unable to gain your soul, which is yet within you and holy. Do you understand, dear Alba? Do you now comprehend what occurred with Satan and the witch?"

"Certain of these entities I do not understand, my lady. God and Jesus ever within me I accept better than breathing, but witches and demons . . . no. No, I comprehend none of that. My true belief differs, and this I must state despite the magistrate before me, the

417

truth of all I know and saw: that his men alone have damaged me, for I viewed no one but constables. I believe these men have killed me, mistress."

The Rathel then stood to confront the male audience with all of her expertise.

"She cannot understand," she told the magistrate, then turned to the priest. "Father, could you understand the act? To find the devil in your own hand cutting away your own body? Could even you, a most Godly priest, find reason and acceptance in the devil mutilating yourself by your own hand but not your doing?"

"To myself?" the priest replied as though he had been accused. "To my own self, ask you, Lady Amanda? No, no, this not even a minister of God could readily believe. Only by the greatest grace of Jesus and equal effort in praying could I accept such a horror. With this same force of my spirit have I prayed continually to God and Jesus for understanding and for this girl to regain her soul, yet I remain astonished."

What sense this lady had to judge Waingrow a nonbeliever in the religion of his prisoner. As before, the priest's smell was all concern for things to be proper and set Holy again; and, yes, his concern was for me. Though he spoke no word, Waingrow had a mien I could read, the magistrate a more dangerous male than before. He was the official of my dreams, a glassblower hot for my soot, the forger of witches. Rathel had sensed this as well, and spoke to Waingrow only in rejection.

"The situation you surmise of the devil's being within this girl is sensible only in the past, Lord Magistrate. Her very survival proves Satan to have been expelled. In my studious years confronting witches, I have gained knowledge where you possess only presumption. Yet this story needs no interpretation, for the truth is known as soon as the telling. This I explained to you before the girl was ever seen, and have no fear of repeating in her presence, for Alba has God enough to give her strength. And this is the force that allowed her survival although attacked by Satan: God, His love and her fear of Him. God and Savior Jesus have allowed the girl to live despite a demonic entry. After you executed Satan's witch, this frail one of innocence with her tender soul was blamed most wrongly; for never has the devil achieved his way with her, not on Man's Isle nor in Lucansbludge. When Satan failed to win her via his representative witch, he leapt from that dead body to attempt his best to finish Alba. And through God alone giving her strength did she survive the perversion with only a wound, but her spirit intact."

Only a wound? I thought. Where had I heard that before? But I refrained from ripping off my dress to display the demon meal that had been my nipple.

Having dismissed the magistrate's opinion, Rathel returned to the priest's preferable nature.

"As expected from so pious a minister, you've a spiritual ability to feel the truth when God and Satan have conflict. Therefore, I am certain that through your Godly understanding and my documented expertise the truth of this girl's spirit will be revealed."

"Pray Jesus it be so, Lady Amanda," the priest replied. With no further look to me by any person, all the crowd departed, Rathel and the minister chatting like sisters, the magistrate remaining quiet and cold.

I waited. Not for the future was I expectant, but for the continuation of that same day. Upright on my bed, I awaited some part of that trio to return, for finally I had gained anxiety while awake. Rathel had been a name mentioned countless days before, but upon becoming real again, she brought me the interest in living that was salvation, and with it potential failure. Surely an authority would return to inform me of schedule: the magistrate to prepare me for trial and death, the Rathel for additional utter lies, the priest for my soul to be cleansed. Perhaps scrolls would be delivered with horn blares and oral pronouncements from England's new queen, but all that came were rancid slop and more crotch craving from criminals. When finally night arrived but no official acts, I became well peeved at having to wait further before beginning that lengthy, public affair that could well be my end.

The next morning came the jailor, not for my pot, but for me. Follow along, was all he said; and I wondered bizarrely whether the magistrate had deigned to circumvent official English law and have his own way with the witch. Would I be taken behind the prison for a head chopping neater than my breast's? And yes, there was Waingrow before me, but no axe, and he was not alone. I was led to his office wherein a crowd had gathered around the dung of my dropped head before it hit ground. The minister and magistrate and Rathel and two unknown sinning males. Then all of this talking commenced. Here was officialdom, and there the scroll, one of the extra males reading from it (without fanfare). My name was pronounced, and I was asked to agree to this, which I did, being certain that no lying as to my own name need be done. Then came opera. The composition of the reading clerk portrayed my living on Man's Isle, being stolen by witches—body and mind but never spirit—the Rathel's taking me to London, my living there as well regarded by parish priest and Sir Jacob Naylor, prime magistrate of London herself. Then stolen by the witch Marybelle of Man's Isle (body and mind, but not soul), forced to live in the wilds in hopes that an animal state would make her (me) susceptible to Satan. Escaped to Lucansbludge, though yet controlled by the witch in the mind, but not quite the body, and never the soul. Witch Marybelle then came to retrieve her, but was captured by Magistrate Waingrow after the female demon had murdered his man for discovering her malice. Then death to the witch, whereafter Miss Alba Landham—yet taken in the mind, mostly in the body, but never the soul—was attacked by Satan and mutilated whereby she might die. But the devil failed since Alba's spirit was not available, for it yet belonged to Jesus, though not her mind in this activity, only the body, and but a portion of the latter did Satan gain, exiting thereafter when confronted by Waingrow's constables, the girl imprisoned for trial, her unravaged soul awaiting while the mind and body returned through the vigilant prayer of the priest and the watchful incarceration (no cuisine being mentioned) of the magistrate, the Alba Landham thereby made whole again with God and England: yea or nay?

Everyone in the room then looked toward me. Static as tree trunks they were and staring. The reading clerk lowered his scroll so that he might see the prisoner over it, see the witch who refrained from saying, "Damned straight," only, "Yea," and then was silent.

The other stranger who had yet to speak then said by God's graces and the laws of England and Queen Anne the prisoner would be released under the auspices of Lady Amanda Rathel, and good morning all.

No one looked at me thereafter. This last man turned to Waingrow and began chatting amicably about a dart tournament his son had won. Though I made no comment as to having avoided another impossible contest, the magistrate bemoaned having missed the final tourney. During this discourse, the reading male approached

420

Rathel with papers to sign, and comply she did. The clerk then stepped to the unknown talker, who was too involved with his own challenge of chatting to allow such interruption, the reader having to await the conversation's end in which Waingrow smelled of darts, his interest in a new and common subject allowed by his odorous relief in being rid of exceptional me. The priest's mark, once gained, was doubtless so wobbly as to be illegible; for when the yea came out of me, so had the devil this holy man truly believed present, and nearly faint he did from having Satan lifted from both our lives.

After receiving a paper, the Rathel as though late for church ushered me away. Only then did I understand that the trial had come and gone. But I was dissatisfied with the outcome. Therefore, I halted, the Rathel nearly tumbling over me, so sudden was I in turning to the magistrate to ask, "Might I have my bags?" And the mistress jerked me through the doorway, all the way to London.

BOOK FOUR:
MARRIAGE

Twenty-eight

More deluxe than my fleeing was my return to London, the expensive Rathel obtaining rich accommodations: a succession of enclosed coaches with no companions, fine hostelry rooms without barred doors. No extensive speaking had we, the Rathel too occupied with her smirking, so pleased was she to have regained her vengeful instrument. As though yet in the wilds and bored, I undertook the self-contest of comparing modes of transport: What interval in this coach drawn by horses equaled what distance through the wilderness with a casket dragged by a single witch? This thought challenge occupied me enough to avoid the subject of Marybelle. Because I was so cowardly as to consider her possibly healing, I had no need to contemplate my sister's demise, that she was gone, though I knew it true, Marybelle as departed as half my bosom. Neither did thoughts of Eric's profundity ease me in my selfishness, for even if Marybelle's love for God and her family lay on the land like a haze, this state was no person as before, with breath and body like mine, exactly like mine.

The first evening, residing in a rented room, Rathel described how I might insert a rag into my bodice to preclude drawing attention to my . . . unevenness. Sensible was this idea to me, for my tendency to attract sinners had been too great before. But callous I was to take a towel and drop my dress so that Rathel could see my scar, my mutilation not from Satan, but from love. Look she did a glimpse before quitting the room, and though her composure was contained, every deep part of her went weak, for Rathel was a woman also.

London I smelled from a distance. This was no simplistic Lucansbludge. First came the Thames. In previous days I had seen this body, but now we approached familiar sections. Along the river we traveled toward Hershford Bridge, and I knew the route, knew we need not cross that terror. Thankful I was, for the river and that bridge were all my lives and deaths together, too much for one witch to experience collectively. There was the water of my dreams, of Marybelle's ocean survival, of Elsie's proof, the river that had led me to Lucansbludge and my sister's death. This bridge was the sinners' control over all these disparate aspects, connecting and conniving the world's parts. And in the depths of this impression I drowned, my feelings so intense that I wished to be a sinner only so that I could weep.

I nearly killed the woman when I saw her. No ambivalence had I toward Elsie, for witch or sinner, she was well loved. I recalled my last seeing her, the lost nature of her visage. But now I found only joy in her, and this we shared. As we ran together outside the Rathel's home to embrace, we both laughed and one of us wept, and well I understood Elsie's place in my world, my diminished world; for therein Elsie was not a fine friend, but my greatest. Never would she replace Marybelle, but before that sister's return, Elsie had been of tremendous value in my life, and hereafter would be appreciated properly.

As Elsie pulled away, she held my face to examine me from chin to brow and state, "Ah! girl, and I'm looking at you now to see you more beautiful than ever, what with God's healing you perfect."

No knowledge had I of such complete repair, but I answered the woman by saying, "Well, not perfect, miss," and smiling nastily. The slight wag of her head and mellowing of her smile revealed that Elsie did not glean my greater meaning. My bandaged hand meant little in that I held her with it firmly, but what of other pieces? Of course: Rathel's initial summoning had not included every scene of my theater. And pained I was to presume Elsie's state once learning of her lass, her imperfect lass.

Lady Rathel had us enter, and how pleasant she was, though yet smirking in her brain. The remaining countless servants were present to greet me warmly, and I they, all those two sinners I had scant regard for, and vice versa. But Delilah had been sweet in the kitchen a time, and were they not all capable of being Elsie? Not quite, but even the priest who would have killed me had been in some ways a fine person, so why not they? Was being a sinner so great an impediment to also being human?

Determining that the travelers would partake of some refreshment, the servants departed for the kitchen. Rathel, however, took Elsie aside for private speaking whose content I could sense as though a sleeping composition. Rathel would have her servant remain calm to avoid upsetting Miss Alba, poor, bloody Miss Alba. But not so quiet could such a friend be that her muffled weeping was not heard a half house removed, for the Rathel had been so cruel as to convey the truth. And though Rathel took no pleasure in the telling, was she providing kindness, or being efficient in another business enterprise?

Often the remainder of that day I saw Elsie, who with difficulty retained her tears and her knowledge, not allowing her eyes to fall below my face. About my bedchamber I moved, learning again of fine furniture's precision, the smooth surfaces and joinery approaching nature in excellence and far beyond the abilities of village coffinmakers. Again I found the chamber's smells striking: the wood's glossy varnishes, the pillows and bed of fowl down—and me, for an odor remained of my former presence. Not a bit of grime nor a single spider was seen, but the room remained mine; for even as Rathel and Elsie, it had been waiting for my return, its loyalty due to momentum as though God's gravity pulling things ever together. Beneath the bed was no dust, but a clear lack of oil and wax, and this was Elsie's doing. But not even this extreme tidiness that had been foreign to my previous lives in the wilds and in Lucansbludge could inspire me toward discomfort with the pretension of social sinners' ways. God forgive me, I was home.

With difficulty, I retained my cackles upon receiving onions and foreign fruit from Elsie. Tea was a surprise, however, for I had not recalled the product's being so natural. Less natural was the ending of day, for then I made ready for sleep, and that would include my disrobing.

Elsie was stressed in offering me aid, in remaining nearby with nudity implied. I considered telling her that she need not see. But, of course, one day she would; for whether my servant or my friend, her position would not allow her to avoid this sight forever.

427

And how long to stretch this dead occasion as though a loving era to linger over when in fact all my dead parts had fallen away? The remainder was yet alive.

"Your suffering more than I is not remotely just," I told Elsie, "and for me the injury remains but a . . . bruise."

No extravagant unveiling was required. My only extra apparel was that round rag I mentioned as it fell onto my hand: Oh, the Rathel demonstrated how I might shape myself to appear normal in public, and here is the cloth.

And there was the flesh, the former flesh, now scarred as though a diseased tree, the bark having fallen away. There was the flat scab as though my chest were a pale floor upon whose surface appeared a great cockroach that was stepped upon, its sticky residue never quite drying.

"You see, miss?" I offered as I continued to disrobe, not dwelling on my battlefield. "The appearance is of no consequence, though the area and much of my side remain tender." And I did not conceal the pain of moving my arm to undress. Having looked upon my lost bosom with a conflict of fear and revulsion, Elsie quickly moved to aid me.

"Don't be stressing yourself now, lass, in that you've yet a bit of healing to be done." And she lowered my arm, taking great care with that cut hand as though in fact it were my cut chest. Off with the dress, on with the sleeping gown, the great horror nearly complete. Complete in revelation, but not in deed nor words.

"But no matter how you're feeling, lass, tomorrow we begin on that hair, which is such a riot I'm hearing it."

"Yes, miss," I smiled, and made to turn away, toward that plush bed and a sleep I was anticipating. But Elsie grasped me as I turned, holding my face with both hands to kiss my jaw so firmly that I could feel her teeth. Then quickly she left my presence for the evening.

I fit again into English society with minor effort, my ease in oozing through London like the everpresent fog stemming from my need to recuperate from former lives. But soon came a new life, one never experienced but promised long, for it was vengeance.

After satisfying herself with my hair's progress, Elsie proceeded to the next extremity. With those calluses, the hands on the end of my arms belonged to no lady, but a blacksmith. And praise Jesus Elsie did that shoes were ever worn in London, for how else to hide feet more like hooves than a part of any person, lady or not? And your carriage is lost, girl, though at least you've good color, despite your . . .

Any activity in my bedchamber brought reminiscing of times passed in that space. I could not open my window without recollections entering, thoughts of Lucinda's smell, Eric's visits, the first sight of the garden, my departures and the disasters begun by breaking that plane. But I was not so fearful of the past as to hide from mere remembrance, not when night fog and buzzing, nocturnal bugs were out for the sensing. And since the smell of my chamber and me was scarcely other than sinners, what had the witch of value to the greater world to retain in her box?

Sleep I did, and dream. In my prison cave in Lucansbludge, I sat still so as not to draw the criminals outside heard screaming prayers to Jesus's crotch. But imperfect was my hiding, for although I was slim as a scroll from sexual starvation—not having eaten a man with my baby gouge in days—my huge bosom pressed outward as though to trip sinners. And though the opaque cave door blocked any view, being no thicker than I, it passed odor like paper, like me, my sex odor transmitted from a damp breast to silence the criminals who approached with no more prayers screamed lest they warn their victim. Their approach was foretold by their increasing smell, the sex smell of a woman though these were men, the sinners clambering nearer, nearer, unable to smell me because too much of me had been cut away. Thus, they would find me by sight, that dark paper door an untrue impediment, the prisoners so longing to see that their eyes became as large as my chest's gesture.

I awoke only to exhale a snarl, needing to express my displeasure with that rancid dream. But when I harshly rolled over to fling myself again into sleep, the turning caused a pain that snatched me like a bite from within my bones, so that most gently thereafter I reclined on that side, catching a glimpse of eyes above my windowsill as I settled.

All static and breathless I stared, wondering how frightened to be or how mad I had become before blinking and awakening further to determine the true nature of those eyes; for they were neither huge nor savage, being part of a head belonging to Eric.

Dark it might have been, but no lady should have risen without first concealing her nightclothes with a robe, without further concealing her ribs formerly hidden by a mammary.

As I neared, those eyes turned lingual.

"I have come for the witch," they uttered.

"Sir Eyes, as I have been adjudicated innocent of such an identity through godly interpretation of English law, I suggest you seek demons elsewhere. Perhaps grave robbers rather than ladies would be of value."

With the bridge of a nose now visible above the windowsill, the eyes' owner then replied, "Perhaps, in that fascinating lives they surely lead, but none so enticing nor feminine as the pale person within."

"Who is not so enticing as before, if you've heard enough stories to deem me a witch," I said. The strangest look then threatened those sill eyes, but my speaking continued. "In this chamber lies neither fascination nor demonology, but a boring lass with too many words and not enough breasts. So if you've the temerity, enter as you would an open grave, to join a corpse." And I stepped away from the window.

More than before, Eric's face suggested Edward's, the entire lot of Denton males with pale hair and mild, sinning features. This Eric who entered was larger than the last, but did his growth also measure maturity? But man or boy, that countenance was a combination: the same timidity seen in our early meetings, but now accompanied by too much of an adult concern. Enter he did, but with that demeanor, what next could he accomplish? And did my body not gain his glimpse as he passed? I attacked not his vision, however, but his gloom.

"Sir, what best I recall about you is that no other person in this city could I speak with fully and gain equitable response. The Rathel's speech is curt business phraseology, for despite her intellect, the mistress's speaking is limited by her heart, which in itself is curtailed business. If you've some opposite problem and your heart is overly filled with feeling as though a chamber pot to require emptying, I would have you bury it in your own garden. If

430

here you've come for friendly discourse, then welcome. But if you would purge yourself of passion, do it on the breast of mine that's gone."

Eric then smiled, but from surprise more than humor. Perhaps that comic correlation with madness he as well had learned.

"Tender is your mind, Miss Alba. If I am welcome from friendliness in this manner, may England's army assist your enemies."

"If you have concluded dismissing my etiquette, then turn up the lamp so I might have something to view in my sleepwalking. Fear not the neighbors, sir, I've nothing to hide. At least, less than before."

Eric did not near me as he stepped to the bureau's lamp to touch a metal handle I would not, producing a light bright enough to prove my impressions of him. A man, yes, there the timidity, there the concern. Handsome or not I could not discern, for this was a sinners' fashion too subtle for me. But this older Eric seemed uninterested in vision despite his formerly gigantic eyes, for after increasing the lamp's output, he remained turned away from his hostess. Even less interested did he seem in speaking, for the next words he began were a jumble.

"Oh, Miss Alba, I had heard, and thought I could . . ." Then the boy was weeping, the man so needing to control this response that nothing followed but choking. And from me, displeasure.

"Sir! you will end this sorrow or leave my presence with a leap through that window," I stated with the harshest sound a whisper to keep the household asleep could be.

"But miss," he cried, literally cried, his back to my breast, "so pitiful you are that—"

And my anger interrupted.

"If ever again in your life you weep before me like a sickened elder, I shall spit on you. Miss Elsie with her weak emotions was never such a cad, not even upon viewing my gory, titless chest."

"I am sorry, miss, but I, it is that . . ." but no end could he find to his speaking. Therefore, I aided him.

"I will not have such weakness in a friend. The blackguards in Lucansbludge's jail were stronger than you in having brass enough to acknowledge their desire, despite the demonology presumed of me and the wound they knew to be true."

This person of indeterminate maturity then turned to me as im-

431

passioned as before, though perhaps less saddened. And exactly at my chest he looked without staring, as though having seen it forever, his demeanor not changing as he spoke, Eric seeing nothing but his own sorrow.

"I will bear all your unkindness, Alba, if it will aid you. I only mean aid. With my words, my heart . . ." and near to weeping again he came. But before he could sicken me, I stopped him.

"Never have *I* wept over me, sir; so I'll take no tears from you. If you are so bold as to stare at my chest, then learn to accept the view."

"I leave, then," he whispered sadly, and did so, hands on his face either to preclude his seeing my bosom or revealing his tears. To the window, out, and gone. Then close the thing I did, and no dreaming.

The bleeding lamp I had to leave bright, not being enough of a sinner to handle fire, merely enough of a woman to reject a man's tears.

"Coo, girl, you were known before for your life in the wilds, but everyone in London knows you now. People have been coming to hear your story and one from them newsing papers, but away we've chased them. But, forgive me if you must, I've told the tale meself to only friends, for our mistress did explain to all her servants so we would not be surprised by gossip. And since all she told us be the truth, would we not be telling these truths so as not to agree with outside lies?"

"Philosophy could be your profession, Delilah, instead of dumping chamber pots. But, no, I've no need to forgive you for your tales. All of London loves opera."

The later morning found my bedchamber infringed upon by another servant, Miss Elsie tearing through my doorway as though to proclaim the house's burning and my necessary exit.

"Alba, Alba, the young man is coming now to be official!"

"I beg your pardon, miss, you mean some official youth approaches? The amateur children therefore remain away?"

"No, no, Alba, and you'd best be serious now, for young Eric is here to be speaking with the mistress."

"Eric? Eric? Is that not the neighbor's dog?"

432

"Alba, I'm saying the boy is here to ask for your hand—I'm knowing it, girl."

"Praise God he won't be asking for a breast, since I no longer have a spare."

Having battled me poorly with my selected weapon of syntax and syllable, Elsie won the war by applying superior strategy: She took my ear and began pulling it downstairs. To retain the attachment of this body part, follow it I did.

At the stair's base, Elsie moved her hold to my elbow—but the wrong one, that near the tender scab, the wince I emitted most genuine. With a flash of remorse, Elsie released me to step around to the opposite side and grasp that elbow even more firmly, dragging me along with all the tenderness of an African slave driver in search of exotic animals to encage.

"And thank you, miss, for your thoughtful gentility to a wounded lass," I told her.

Approaching the drawing room, Elsie took me aside, fussing with my collar enough to collapse the lace, shaking her head as she spat on her fingers and attempted to batten down my hair.

"You look the dog," she declared, and pushed me inside.

Within sat two persons so pleased in their faces as to sicken me. As I entered, Eric popped up from his chair as though a spring had come loose and thrust him forth like a catapult.

"Ah, and by the happy faces seen I must presume an exceptional enemy has died—eh wot?" spake I.

Ha-ha the two did laugh, Eric with true humor, Rathel attempting to remain the superior by not encouraging my comedy nor discouraging me, her instrument. Away from them both I sat, speaking thereafter to Eric.

"Sir, you then come to notify me of the funeral schedule—schedule, schedule—or be there another trial first?"

Ha-ha from the pair, and Eric began, officially.

"Lady Amanda must forgive me, and you as well, Miss Alba, for I remain uncertain as to the proper procedures in these social affairs."

"Well, sir, the process is simple," I replied. "You mention who has expired, explain the cause, and we pray for his soul, then have a spot of tea, and off with you for more dog walking."

Only smiles now, no more of the flipping ha-ha, in that Eric was

433

ripe for his speaking, and Rathel was anxious to hear.

"No, miss, I am pleased to say that none known me has died, except for Eric as a boy."

"Oh, dear, but better he than me," I returned, then looked about the room for a servant. "Do I call for tea, then?"

Eric rapidly continued, no longer speaking or looking to the witch.

"Lady Amanda, as I before promised with all myself and in document, your daughter Alba I have come to seek in marriage, and no other lady could I or shall I ever desire."

Rathel then clapped her hands, radiating additional joy (though no ha-ha); and was not some impassioned inhaling heard from beyond the room?

"Oh, Eric, my lad, my future son," the mistress crooned, and stood in a flurry to grasp the boy's shoulders and kiss his forehead. "No greater joy could I have than for you and my Alba to wed."

"All that remains, I believe," Eric added, attempting to look or not look toward me, "is for the daughter to respond."

"Well, if you'll cease kissing my mother, perhaps I'd consider your suggestion," I huffed.

Rathel then sat again, but now in a winged chair near Eric so that her face was unseen to me.

"Alba?" the invisible woman sweetly pronounced, "can you reply to the lad and his great question?"

"Presently, perhaps, in that I now am cogitating," I answered, and in fact I was. How odd, as though I had a choice, yet this was my true impression. The Rathel's having me revealed and executed was no fear of mine. My thoughts were of choosing between my established life and beginning again in a new household. What social situation could English marriage involve besides that man smell ever about the premises? Would not a home with Eric be preferable to one controlled by Rathel? Besides momentum, what in Satan's world could keep me here?

Then from within me swelled a tremendous idea, revealed to all as a brilliant smile. At once, I stepped near Rathel, looking closely to her eyes as I gave my reply.

"Why, yes, yes I shall marry this person—if only my dear mother provides me a desired wedding gift."

Knowing herself formidably attacked, the Rathel returned my

gaze, searching from chin to brow for my weapon as she replied.

"Why, dear Alba, whatever in the world could I refuse you if your happiness be at stake?"

"Mistress, I smell fear from you as though I might request your liver. But something more valuable to me that you own now strikes me as a gift so fine as to inspire my acceptance of this gent's most generous, semi-permanent offer."

Surviving well despite my torture, the stiff lady replied, "What then is so dear that you would marry to possess?"

"Why, dear mother, I will marry this superlative gent if you allow me to take Miss Elsie as my personal servant."

And here was proof of eavesdropping, for throughout the house was heard a poorly stifled gasp.

"Why . . . why, of course, dear Alba," Rathel replied uncertainly. "Miss Elsie shall go live with you, if only your new husband agrees."

Both wenches then turned to Eric, who could scarcely wait to spit out his reply.

"Since no finer woman friend and servant could there be for Alba than Miss Elsie, I myself could wish for no more satisfying offer."

"It is done, then!" Rathel cried, and stood too spryly for one so reserved. "Alba and Eric Denton will wed!"

Eric then stood to applaud, as though at a blooming opera. And outside this room, what other sinner was part of our audience?

When Rathel and Eric settled thereafter to mere relieved smiling and wringing hands, I whispered to the unoccupied doorway.

"Tea now, please."

"Yes, miss," came the quiet reply, and refreshments were brought by my (my) servant.

Twenty-nine

The Rathel achieved such an attitude of success that I thought she would choke on her gloating. Though equally impressed, Elsie was less assured of her specific satisfaction. Basically she was overjoyed at my having acquired an English lady's ultimate achievement: an English gent. But as well she was distressed at having to leave her home of years to begin anew—for therein she might be given more responsibility than her meager bones could handle. On and on Elsie would fret until I threatened to beat her, for certainly Eric would establish this practice in our new home if this be the only servant's attitude.

Our new home. Of course, this witch had concern as well, but aligned with Rathel's revenge, not Elsie's household management. The social aspects of marriage were problems I would easily overcome. My concern was in revealing myself to Eric without inspiring Rathel to kill me. Such were the difficulties of the wedded witch: to avoid murdering her husband and to arrange for that revelation to be other than suicidal.

British custom provided an interval for my revelation: the courting of the damsel. Good Miss Elsie explained the purpose thereof: for the conjugal couple to become acquainted with one another, and for London society to view them as a proper pair.

Elsie endured distinct parameters in accepting her duty as chaperone. First she became as delighted as a child attending an animal faire whose exotic creatures were man and beast, er, wife. Nothing but pleasure had she to be traveling with these dear youths and their heartfelt emotions, and so on. Upon Eric's arrival that first day of courting, however, Miss Elsie changed, becoming firm and proper. Once in the carriage, she insisted that Eric and I not sit so near each other—even inserting her parasol between us. And when the conversation lit upon Randolph, the miss across our way condemned us for not speaking of serious things, such as the wedding party and dowry and flipping so on. I was thus inspired toward discussing grave family affairs.

"Eric, I must ask whether your parents both continue to hate me."

"Yes, both," he answered.

Elsie with this speaking reddened and began chastising me as to the proper discourse in such a social clime. But who was she to chastise a, er, superior?

"Master Eric, should we not implement the preventative idea of thrashing the more rowdy servants on the Sabbath to inspire them toward quiescence through the week?"

"No, Miss Alba, in that we can set the dog to biting their legs."

Eric and I changed this first day's courting into a contest wherein we lanced hapless Elsie with our tongues. Soon becoming vanquished, Elsie ignored our tiny, syllabic feet dancing about her sensibilities, defeating Eric and me by removing our target. Thereafter, the future husband and I entertained one another as we had in the past, with oblique references to dogs and monkeys, but no talk of households.

Returning to our temporary lodging of the Rathel's town house, Elsie and I had only to bid the Eric person a pleasant good afternoon before supping like normal sinners. As Eric grasped my hand for a buss with no terror of my icy fingers, he emitted a low odor instead of an ending salutation, a stench never again to be ignored by the rape witch.

"And it's a good day we wish you," I told him curtly, snatching my hand from Eric, stepping past with too quick a gait to be less than rude; and the servant came chasing after.

Eric made to save face by calling out for us both to be well. And though Elsie was distressed by my peevish attitude, no mention was made of my change in demeanor, change in smelling.

That night my sleeping was delayed, for the future wife was waiting. The lamp I had Elsie leave burning, for company was expected. Thus, I was not surprised to see undreamed-of eyes propped with their brows upon my windowsill.

"Come have I for cruel and vain Alba," they said.

"The wrong window has then lured you, sir, for this plane contains only the cruel one, a vain Alba being beyond my acquaintance."

Eric then entered to stand in my chamber brushing at his waistcoat with his palms, perhaps removing building crumbs.

"And a great humorist I am to so brand you, miss, for I have seen paintings near as beautiful as you with more vanity, and they be dead. But not inert is this Alba, not with her considered thoughtlessness."

"Is considering this thoughtlessness your purpose here?"

"The humorist quits me, miss, for you state my very intent. I have come with the idea of speaking, but at this hour and alone in order to arrive at some content beyond comedy."

"Might we walk in this English night without fear of attack by a social brew, the criminal dregs to settle against our persons and form a crusty stain on our lives?"

"Away to the streets, then," he replied, "to wager our entities against the London fog and the vertical creatures it cannot conceal."

"I am first, then, to preclude your cruel searching up my dress to gain a vision most criminal, since not yet are we wed. And no hand in aid, sir, if this be your prime intent in luring me to climbing, for well have you learned the wildness that creeps across me along with your fingers."

Over the sill I moved, climbing a path unnatural for London. Once on the ground, I looked up to see confidence in Eric's climbing, thinking that he might fit in the wilderness. As he stepped beside me, he brushed away further building crumbs that were imaginary, for I had none though my climbing was equal. But, then, I was not so apprehensive as he.

With a nod, I led Eric to the street's center, bright smears about from rare lamps behind windows, our feet making a meager crush as though compressing crisp snow. And where was the air? Only tiny drops of water were in this atmosphere, one to chill a sinner and enthrall a witch.

"Too cool you might be, miss, with your neck so exposed," Eric mentioned as he turned up his collar.

"Scant sensitivity have I to cold," I replied, "and herein I am comfortable. So let us proceed with this speaking and be grave—if you can bear the trait fully loosed in me, for you know how earnest a person I can be."

"I know how unkind you can allow yourself to become. So if you temper this and expose only truth, we both might learn each others' ideas."

"We begin with the wedding," I stated. "What of your father?"

"Previously he is wed."

"And bore a hilarious boy the marriage did," I groaned. "I mean to ask the degree to which your parents agree with your nuptial notions."

"They agree in the negative. In truth, they disbelieve my intents, and attempt to convince me of my falseness. But they shall not. And if I am tossed from the household because of my conjugal plans, I go elsewhere, for London is large."

"Aye, we've room in the basement. But enough damp comedy. We now return to your first-mentioned topic: my peeved and thoughtless manner achieved as you touched me this noon."

"An excellent progression, and one whose explication I fear from a future wife," Eric admitted. "And the future bodes poorly for me if you shirk so simple a touch. Was I too coarse with your fingers?"

"Too coarse with your emotions, for along with your touch, I sensed your lust. And with ambient God as your judge, sir, lie to neither of us."

"No lying need be done to save my soul, miss, for I have no shame in feeling passion toward the woman I will marry. As well, I would desire that touching be part of your married pleasure with me."

439

"Exceptional I am with the menfolk for drawing this passion, sir, as you recollect from Mr. Gosdale and the trainer of exotic ladies. This latter man had his finger far enough within me to touch my breakfast, and you were present to observe. Can you question, then, my distaste for the pleasure of men?"

"The pleasure of your husband is our topic, for the basis here is not lust, but love."

"Elsie loves me, but has no desire to lie with me."

"Do you believe I care for you less than your servant?"

"Your concern is dissimilar in its selfishness. Because Elsie loves me, she desires to be with me; whereas you desire to be within me."

"But the question ultimately is love, not procreation, Alba. Praise your heart and Elsie's that you have each other to love, for you both deserve the best emotion. But can your love for your parents and for Elsie not allow room for another? Can you not love me as I do you? Never so explicit have I been in saying this, but only because I thought you might not accept the potential, and now I fear it. Think not that gender is the basis of my passion, for no more than Elsie's is my love sourced in lust. In the frank truth you so admire, I must say that most English men would reject you for your disfigurement, your false history of demons, and for the trainer who so pressed toward you that some fools would call you ruined as a wife and not worthy of bearing their children."

Abruptly I halted, turning to Eric as though maddened or amused.

"Then laugh I do, sir, at your own social position, for the woman you're vowed to is no more virginal than a cow, for no untouched land lies between my thighs. The trainer's offense was slight compared to the violent rape I suffered by a man outside Lucansbludge. As for offspring, gain ye a greater set of dogs if I am to be your wife and you require further family, for my innards are such that children will no more come from me than milk from that missing nipple."

As though transformed by God into a boulder, Eric became still and lost his breathing. He then fell to his knees and grasped my dress as though about to pull it off, grasped it like

440

a rapist. Then the weeping began, an unloud wailing to sicken me.

Because this man was defiling me in his own, emotional manner, one no more acceptable than if his prick were stabbing me, I pushed him away with some violence while calling down forcefully.

"Bleeding well, you'll not be slobbering on my hem! I'll curse your soul as black if you weep at my every problem I have willfully accepted!"

Eric looked up to me as though a child chastised for a wrongdoing not fully understood, then moaned, "From Elsie you allow weeping, but not a tear can come from me? Is the truth that she is allowed to love you more than I? Surely it cannot be that I am a man and should be different from womenfolk in emotion, for heretofore you have implied that men and their manners you hate."

"By the God of Heaven, sir, never would my *mother* weep on me, and I can praise you no more than by that comparison. Heartfully embrace me she would, then share with me the satisfaction in my strength. After counting my breasts, Mother would have laughed with joy at all of her Alba remaining. But never, never would she or I collapse in misery, for such emotion is a sodden selfishness to steal the value of my fortitude. And though Miss Elsie's heart is so sweet as to make mine seem decrepit, she yet is no equal to me in the mind. Therefore, sir, I honor you by expecting you to secure the same living strength as mine. By God, no servant of love will this person be — and none to a husband, despite the low level in which English society might place me. And by your own Jesus's name, confront me not with accusations of cruelty, for again you have heard but truth from me."

As suddenly as he had thrown himself down, Eric leapt upward to stand with the passion perhaps of idea, but no further tears.

"The greatest truth is that you have no love for me, yet you consent to wed. The utter truth of your heart you spoke when I sought your hand, that you would only agree if given the servant. Therefore, into an unloved marriage you enter

441

by bringing your own love, none from me required."

"Might you infer with your brilliant sensitivity that my agreement to wed stems from my preferring to live with you rather than Rathel?"

"Ah, the fact is simple, then: Live with Eric instead of the miserable Rathel woman. And all be well as long as you have the bleeding Elsie."

"I've done enough bleeding for us all, sir, so resort not to a criminal's obscenities. Selfish you are, Eric, if you will have me as a wife and also demand my worship. I say that we have insufficient investment in each other to have formed a mutual love of spirit. Long has Elsie been my aid and guide, and though oft attempting things not fit me, never has she sought any benefit but mine. She lacks the passion of the crotch to provoke a love as yours was surely engendered. Despite your appreciating my additional traits, initially you sought me as a female, not a friend. Deny this truth to God if Hell be your chosen eternity."

"I deny not the natural desire between genders, and reasonably so herein, for your most evident trait is comeliness. But your unique wit and telling speech I also well love, Satan receive my mediocre soul if this not be true. But since reason compels even you to admit that my love for you exists beyond passion, the query for us is your love toward me, for this greatest emotion must be mutual between man and wife."

"In London I have learned that certain people must exist with others in order to be sheltered by a stronger will. Such a person is Elsie, but I am of a different sort. Though I appreciate companionship, I require no sustenance from an alternate person's strength. And though Elsie's friendship I treasure, I would have you as a companion of peerage rather than any other person I know to be alive."

"Though I as well cherish your company, do not consider me selfish to also desire a love of touching between us, for this is only normal."

"Oh," I replied sharply, "I now have a true view of this passion, for I was thinking only of the mating sort. Your meaning is additionally the preliminary things that young lovers sweetly display when not seen by society, with their squeezing and rubbing and slobbering about each others' mouths. Ah! here's a third type of loving to challenge me, but one too many, sir. Beyond the love of character that I mutually grant you, as wife I might also provide that part of marriage required by society called mating. But, sir, whereas I might well fuck you, do not expect me to kiss you also."

Before aghast Eric could return with some astonished speaking, we were accosted. A man with a familiar type of staff and doublet ran toward us, calling loudly to gain all of our attention and fear.

"Eh! and what is your standing in the street's center? This is no hour for legal passage, and I will have your explaining."

So explain to him I did.

"Our identity, Sir Constable, is that of a recently wed pair having misgivings to sort away from the remaining family. Pray God that English law will ever allow us harmless citizens access to Queen Anne's streets."

Approaching, the constable replied to the talking woman.

"Harmless folk are no difficulty, missus, but those lower persons who would thieve from you. In such dark and with no populace about, you cannot be expecting us constables to protect you from so large a city."

"If we are attacked, fellow citizen," I continued, "we shall personally subdue the felons and send their remains for your disposal."

"No other aid need ye be, sir," Eric stated, a citizenly demeanor replacing that former disposition of the lover derided.

We then walked away, leaving the constable to stare after us and mutter from our unfoundedness. After a separation from the officer and our previous distress, the, er, lovers began speaking again.

"Returning, sir, to love and its lack, more people emote in this wedding than we. Of your parents lacking love for me, what precisely do they portray as causal?"

"They say that your history of living with witches renders your soul suspect. Though Lady Amanda has briefly described your past living, I seek your own version. And I expect you to

443

find no offense in my asking, since you are so cold and severe with things as minor as a suffering life."

"I would first ask what tale the Rathel has given you, for thus I know what to lie of."

"Depicted was a girl whose parents were lost and whose person was stolen by females later deduced demonic, said girl thus removed from them by English law. Later, Lady Amanda accepted same girl into London for a superior life. How agreeable are you with this story, Alba?"

"The Rathel lies enough to make me puke," I answered with that cold severity mentioned.

"Jesus calm your soul, Alba. I've not heard such crudities from baseborn beggars."

"Less crude in their mouths they might be, though I doubt they compare in the areas of wit, charm, and remaining chest. Certainly in seeking money alone, they have more integrity than the devious, dishonest Rathel."

"How then, miss, would you modify her tale?"

"I would begin with the parents. And bear down upon your tender spirit and watery eyes, Eric, for comes my next fact to damage your heart. The utter truth is that I know not my father—nor did my mother, for I sprang from a rape, of which God and Satan are equally cognizant. Are the nuptials therefore dismissed?"

Eric's response was to accept a fact to brutalize the average English fiancé, looking down to shake his head in a motion virtually unseen, though understood. When he replied, his speaking seemed objective, lacking both severity and coldness.

"Despite its personal import, you provide an addition to Lady Rathel's story, not a refuting as I see it."

"Then see this next addition as emotion, for it deals with my mother. And, sir, if ever I come to love you half as much as I yet love my mother, you will have more emotion from me than you can imagine. In fact, my mother I well knew into my young adulthood until we were separated by mad English officials who condemned her as a witch and had her burned. Sir, yes, beheaded and burned as though the most wicked murderer instead of a thoughtful mother, killed dead along with our

444

friends on Man's Isle. And the person to convince the authorities of this demonology was Amanda Rathel. The person who allowed my mother to be butchered and burned was the woman from whom you seek my hand. Only after destroying my family did the heinous Rathel conduct me to London. And if you do not believe in demons, sir, then you are a fool, for no demon ever existed more evil of spirit than Rathel. Now, sir, go ye home for your best weeping ever. Look first at your mother, however, and imagine her beneath the executioner's axe, imagine her in ashes. Think of your mother and her love, and as you love your mother living, therefore weep for mine."

No courting or communication occurred the following day. My only thoughts of the previous evening's damp discussion were of humor. What would come of the Rathel's plans if Eric rejected me for promising him my crotch but not my heart? This jest remained until night delivered a pair of eyes and one nose to my sill.

"I come for the wife."

"Wrong sill, intrusive face. Lovers alone reside here."

"Then the daughter boasting of mother's love. In the street do we meet?"

"If you rhyme no other time."

After the eyes disappeared, down the wall I crawled, again cursed with verse.

Quietly we walked in the street's center, avoiding all words as though in a quiet contest, a challenge I abandoned by calling out with voice enough to startle Eric.

"Any constables please note that our event is but marital difficulties discussed by decent folk."

Then from a side street came that voice of the previous night.

"And well, but speak lightly, in that untroubled persons be asleep."

After Eric and I laughed lightly as instructed, I confronted the male with a history I desired to conclude in order to proceed with the future.

445

"Sir, I proffered not the total truth of my emotion when implying I had scant love for you. What I did say remains true in that your companionship is more desirable than that of any other man alive, but as well I have a genuine fondness for you."

"This I wish to hear, Alba," Eric returned with a serious sort of enthusiasm. "I would hear this and desire to believe it more than life itself, it sometimes seems, certain times at night when I can—"

"No more interruptions for loose emoting," I chastised, "for my idea is not yet expressed. Because I have appreciation for your character and some fondness thereof, I wish no harm to reach you, not before we are wed nor thereafter. Thus, you must know of the Rathel's design with our lives so that we may avoid it and formulate our own."

"Describe this design, then, Alba, but provide it as observation; for despite all your graveness, you remain a person of extreme emotion."

I then stepped before Eric and turned so that he could see nothing but my face.

"The truth of Rathel is that your parents are correct, and you are a fool."

"A fool I am now because I know not your meaning."

"You remain unaware, sir, for you've not the preparation to believe, but this I will establish. To know the cruel truths I have for you that will pain you soon and save you later, you must come to me with a new ability to accept. This you shall gain elsewhere, from a trustworthy person you will not disbelieve."

"How am I to learn, and from whom?"

"From my pet."

"The spider?"

"Miss Elsie. The spider was ravaged by Rathel, as she has ravaged all my loved ones. As she would ravage you. But before being sent along for a lesson of preparedness, you must promise me a thing."

"The promise is then made," Eric returned. "Now may you say in advance the suffering to be caused by that vow?"

446

"None worse than you've received on this street, but perhaps no better."

"Perhaps I should then rescind my vow, for I've not been well treated by these nights."

"No, you shall not rescind the vow, which is to speak with Miss Elsie and insist that she tell you dispassionately of the Rathel's response toward me upon learning of your departing for distant schooling. Question her thusly tomorrow when the mistress is not about. Come to my window that night, and in further vow, bring no tears. I have your total promise, then?"

"You do, miss, and in truth you have my fear. If more tears are expected of me, then Miss Elsie's speaking I would avoid."

"You would, sir, but shall not, for you have vowed to hear. The purpose in this lesson is to foment your belief in the Rathel's greater truth that Miss Elsie cannot describe. But this present lady can, and shall tomorrow evening. Bring with you then some strength, and all the objectivity you can gather; for no story told by Elsie will be more true or more damaging than that you shall receive from me."

The day of learning I remained in my chamber to avoid interfering with Eric's visit. Trust him I did to fulfill his vow, though I caught no sight nor scent of him. And though Elsie was too quiet through the remaining day, not until evening did she reveal her distress.

"Dear Alba—dear God—and why were you having the boy demand such a story? There was no relenting in him, and each of us told all. And I'm never seeing a young man with more torment, no matter how much he was holding it in. Alba, girl, I'm not knowing your purpose in bringing forth such pain and giving it to your future husband."

"I will not conceal so significant a story from Eric exactly because he is my future husband," I truthfully explained. "Regarding the event you depicted to him, either the Rathel or I was evil, and I will have none believing it me. Trust me, miss, that in having this man know me fully, the two of us will be safer."

"And you think he's to be knowing you so completely, girl? Even husbands and wives can be decently keeping secrets of themselves. We're talking of marriage, Alba, not God's own judgment. And, dear God, I'm fearing you'll next be telling him that story of being a witch—and how that would be ruining poor Eric and the wedding."

"Why worry of that tale, miss, for did it not improve our friendship? But save yourself harm in your heart by trusting the true friend that I am, and believe that in this instance I am cautious to do what is proper. You are well convinced of my morality's depth, are you not, miss?"

"Aye, and I'm ever praying you hold it, Alba."

"Then understand I jeopardize my Godly heart in no manner, but seek that Eric might understand my true decency. Go then, miss, and worry as little as possible, no more than you must. And when last you pray this evening, ask God not that I achieve the best tonight, but only what I deserve."

"I come with no speaking," the eyes stated hours later. "I come to hear."

Neither had I words, only a gesture, a throwing motion as though Eric should fling himself to the street. There I flew to join him, down the vertical hill of this social wilderness. No fog this evening, but a drizzling rain as though a gift from God for my refreshment. And the air seemed cleansed, the city's building crumbs washed elsewhere, perhaps to the wilds where no witches lived. Of course, all these folk were in London or in Hell.

"I could not call you by an identity," Eric began, "for I know not whether you be demon or fiancée or loved one. The last is true, and I pray the second remains. The first, however, seems characteristic of your surrounds, not yourself, as you have maintained."

Eric could bear some refreshing himself, for about him was a haze of brooding, as though a light burned within him that coated his chimney with soot.

"Miss Elsie, I presume, attempted kindness toward her mistress."

"In her generosity, she did, but found difficulty in surmounting a continuing disappointment in the lady's actions," Eric pronounced, sounding weary. "Her ending of the tale portrayed a damaged woman stricken in the soul. Perhaps I've some understanding of this."

"Perhaps implies perhaps not," I offered. "But I must add how controlled you are, sir, a condition I expect you to retain as we conclude our composition."

"Very well," Eric remarked, "let us be on with the show, with your exotic creatures of revelation."

"Should not young lovers be holding hands when walking and speaking most intimately?" I replied.

"They should, but mature folk so established in their marriages that they've difficulty with them have less of this tactile romance."

"Praise Jesus, for did I not mention how I detest such contact?"

"You did, miss, noting the acceptability of intercourse, another activity of young marrieds; whereas ancient folk battered by life's turns find themselves to be people of discourse. Surely this is the source of your repartee, in that you have lived forever. You must have for so many sinister events to have befallen you."

"Either you attempt to develop a method for purging your emotional regret at my life's small disasters without slobbering from your eyes, or else you are cursed with verse again."

"I am cursed with the exquisite Alba, but even in my innocence I can imagine far worse burdens."

"And one might be?"

"To have Lady Amanda as the superior in my household."

"But it seems she is superior in your household, for is it not the Rathel who has turned your parents against the fiancée?"

"I am certain, yes, but her greater intent escapes me."

"The intent is to torment your father. Certainly you know of his former partner in business, the former Franklin Rathel, but know ye the business between Amanda and your father?"

"I know of no business between them as persons, no."

"Then I tell you, sir, the business is that most fugitive kind of entailing a vow, regarding the friendship between Franklin and Edward, though the vow was from the latter to the former's wife."

"If you have tales of these people as a triptych, I would hear of your source in advance, for the method of your having prepared me causes disquiet. Pray God, Alba, I now fear of my own father's . . . misdeeds."

"A misdeed be his, I believe, though the evil was all Amanda's. My source, I say, was Miss Elsie, from her years with the Rathel family, lord and lady. A second source was a woman of my blood, as was she with whom I lived those previous years in the wilds."

"The tale I have of that time is of your being stolen."

"In fact, I freely lived with a person of family, returning only upon her death. But you were a young man then, now having lost that trait, for you are but a man, and so your innocence dies as did my family."

"I am, of course, to fully trust your sources for my dying innocence?"

"Especially the last, for he is your father."

"How might this be, Miss Alba?"

"On a carriage ride to view Christ's Cathedral, I was confronted by your Mr. Denton. His purpose—or his duty—was to reveal his past with the Rathel, and to dissuade me from cooperating with her desire for me to wed the Eric boy."

"What has our marriage to do with my father's vow to Amanda?"

"He vowed in his generosity to care for her well-being if the worst should occur to ill Franklin. Now we arrive at discrepancy. The meaning of 'worst' to your father was Lord Rathel's inability to continue with their mutual business. Death was the idea dreamed of only by Amanda. During Franklin's ill era, she learned that a fever of youth had caused him to be incapable of procreation; whereas Franklin had ever allowed his wife to believe that the fault was her womb. Since a child of her own was all Amanda desired from marriage, she found in your

450

father's vow an opportunity to achieve a more fertile person, one promised to care for her."

"In your composition, Lord Franklin next arbitrarily dies?"

"His death was composed, exactly. Believe you, sir, that from an unlying source I have learned that Lady Rathel sought a material, as though a poison, to kill her husband. But the material given was to Amanda in order to make her forget her deadly intents. It failed, however, though causing her alleged barrenness to become factual."

"Alba, no tale of the real world could be this fantastical."

"I laugh, sir, at your reality, for not a thing bizarre have you heard, but the sort of personal business transpiring between sinners each day in London—do you doubt it?"

"The generality, no, but I would more easily believe Amanda's malice if you would better identify your unlying source."

"She was the person of my blood come to London as you departed for school. I swear to you, sir, of her honesty; yet she had most to lose in conveying this tale, for she had provided Lady Rathel with the killing material under threat of her own death."

"Alba, how can an average person be threatened with death so easily? In England are laws to protect people from threats of murder."

"But the Rathel made no such threat. Her promise was to reveal. You know of Lady Rathel's particular expertise?"

"That of demonology, which I find akin to the carnival and the fat man."

"No, sir, her expertise is in witchcraft, and surely you understand how powerful a belief this is in England. Even if no witch be real, consider the many poor women who have died by the accusation. You think such executions do not occur?"

"I know they have, but they stem from the failings of lawmakers who allow impious mobs to form, and therein lies the evil: ignorant, unjust hatred direct from Satan."

"And as real as that black angel regardless. Thus, you understand the power of Lady Rathel's threats to allege my friend the witch, a believable charge because of this person's unbeauteous form and the Rathel's established expertise."

451

"Yes, this now seems more believable."

"Now that you better comprehend, envision this past business: Not at first did Rathel discover her barrenness. Therefore, she returned to my friend to continue her plan, promising this person a certain death via English law and its hatred of things demonic. Amanda thus received for her threats a true poison with which she killed her husband."

"Alba, Alba, these words are incredible, unbelievable."

"She murdered her husband, I say, via means supplied by my friend, Lucinda, whose choice was to allow death or die herself. And since the way selected was immoral and illegal, why would Lucinda admit the act to be her own if not?"

"I know not, Alba. I know only what you say."

"Sir, know ye not that Rathel near beat me dead? Are you such a fool as to disbelieve this?"

"I believe, I do believe this," he whispered. "But I've not heard your version of the cause."

"Elsie's, I assume, was one of liquor's temporary affliction."

"It was, exactly."

"And not untrue, though morally incomplete, and innocent in not asserting the Rathel to be ever mad."

"You allege that she is?"

"What term be yours to describe her killing her husband to gain a father for her womb? What word besides madness for her further insanities?"

"And my father's part in this madness?"

"After Franklin died evidently from his illness, Amanda confronted your father with an extreme denouement of his vow: With the husband gone, does not your promise mean that you shall care for me in the form of marriage? Edward agreed from his own desire, since he considered the time for marriage come if the bond would provide him with an heir; for even as Lady Rathel, Edward had no desire to wed unless its product be a child. But Edward soon learned that Amanda's belly was barren. Then his vow was not rescinded, but reduced; for although Lady Rathel was given the benefits of Franklin's business, Edward would no longer consent to wed her. Being then exiled from her only true desire—a child—perhaps the Lady Rathel did indeed go mad, and came to feel ill toward your father. But not until his marriage did she hate him. Not until he married a lass who near instantly bore this Eric did mad Amanda produce a vow herself, one against Edward, not from his rejecting her marriage, but because he achieved the offspring she could not."

"These things are preposterous," Eric scoffed.

"Far removed from maturity you are to disbelieve the possibility of such things, for these are the lives of sinners. And to receive a further verity, you might well discuss my charges with your father."

"My God, Alba, why not ask me to assault him with my hands?"

"You are the preposterous one now—what has he to hide? Ask of the vow, of his knowledge of Amanda's barrenness, and whether he therefore refrained from marrying her. If some shame he finds therein, then shame he deserves; and as a moral man you will understand and forgive him. But ask not of things he could not know. Especially make no mention of Lord Rathel's murder, for even if your father suspects, no proof exists."

"But there should be proof and is, Alba, for despite this Lucinda's honesty, she was yet accomplice to a murder, and must be held accountable along with Lady Amanda."

"Held accountable she was, sir, and not along with Rathel, but by the Rathel. Know ye, sir, that Lucinda was trapped in London and wished to exit in peace. But Rathel swore this woman a witch, and thereby was she executed."

"The, the woman then executed for killing a man was, was this Lucinda?" Eric returned with difficult speaking. "I heard of this woman—I heard of the hideous method whereby she murdered a person."

"Lucinda had no part in that murder, by God's own knowledge. Being poor and ugly, however, she was arrested in suspicion of being a witch. Lady Rathel was the one to thus identify Lucinda. And exactly as she allowed my mother to die, Rathel condemned Lucinda to execution."

"By the God of Heaven, Alba, you will kill me with these

incredulities. What part had your mother in Lord Rathel's demise?"

"None, none—the Rathel knew naught of my mother until Franklin was years dead. That part of my mother the Rathel desired was me."

"And for what unbelievable purpose?"

"Why, to marry you."

"What sin be this?"

"Your father is one for demonology, Eric, as you are aware. Surely he suspects Amanda's causing his partner's death, and well he knows her hatred for his rejection. Rathel has ever allowed your father to believe that I came from a clan of demons. Recall our first meeting and my speaking thus? I did so because I had heard this talk from the Rathel. Recall as well your father's distress to find you drawn to me. What a fine punishment for Edward would be his son's marrying the daughter of a woman who hates him and has long implied revenge. But your father believes more: He believes that I, the demon, shall kill you in marriage. But the Rathel will have no further murder. Not if I am to be the cause."

"B-but what now?" anxious Eric asked. "Without my death, Father will come to accept our marriage, in that no other lady could make me so ecstatic as you, despite your, your . . ."

"Demonic coldness, perhaps?" I said as I halted my walking to confront Eric's face. "My promising you my groin but not my lips?"

Eric then turned away, unable to suffer my demonic truth.

"I will marry you," he said as though accepting a prison sentence.

"Was your father's voice so damaged when he promised to wed Amanda? You might ask him this as well."

"And let us seek comparison here," Eric replied with some pain as he looked to me again. "My father sought nothing but an heir, but with you I have long sworn my desire: for you, not your womb. And without love, there is no humanity; witness Lady Amanda and her lack. You might correct me in our future, Alba, but now I feel that your killing me would be necessary to end my emotion for you."

454

"Your speaking is passionless, Eric. Are you condemned to this love?"

"I can count, and as objective as quantity is the measure of my emotion. One day I may enjoy it more, but even now I have insufficient suffering from it."

"Grown old you have this evening, Eric."

"Surely in my lifetime less than you in the previous few years. I have a fantasy, though, that the very decrepitude of your experience causes you to be abnormally distant in your person, though not your words. Pray God we become married soon so that I might sooner become accustomed to your uniqueness."

"Well and good. But since you and Rathel are the ones for arrangements, may the expediting be your responsibility. And along with your comfort in our marriage will come your parents' understanding that you always shall be safe with me. Then the Rathel will be alone with her torment, and God remove it from her if He can."

Thirty

"Miss Elsie, I would request of you that I be allowed to speak with Alba a moment only to ourselves. No contact will we make nor fiendish plans plot against you."

"Aye, and it's a moment I'm giving you, lad, but your every move I'm watching from behind the window."

As per Eric's request, I spoke with him outside the Rathel's home, Elsie behind glass seeking misplaced digits. Though nothing untoward was to be seen, Elsie surely preferred the silence, aware that no comfortable topics were being discussed.

"The speaking with my father went poorly," Eric began.

"How so?"

"He freely conceded all I asked of him, but painfully. I mentioned only what he could directly know; and though none of these things I held before him with distaste, his own confessions carried sufficient consequence for shame. More important, there was no dissuading him of believing in your evil. Though too painful for him to say outright, the fear that you shall kill me is the greatest emotion in his life."

"You had quarreling?"

"No, we had weeping—on his part, the type you would condemn me for. And with him, Alba, your position became fully mine; for I would rather have accepted his screams than his tears. But strength you have taught me, miss, and I would admire your education if only you could instruct me with some method other than misery."

Since Elsie remained distraught from exposing Rathel's thrash-

456

ing me to Eric, I was pleased to see this demeanor leave when Eric described our day, for therein he would lead his future women to their upcoming home.

Such a squeal the servant emitted that I thought a seat spring had popped up to stab her derriere. But, no, this was mere uncontrollable excitement, one to set Eric into pleasurable laughing and me toward wondering of these sinners' façade of maturity concealing a childish state.

"Are you not pleased, Miss Alba, in that you've not even a smile?" Eric wondered as Elsie continued with her sprightly giggling.

"Extreme joy I do predict," I stated glumly, "in that any cave would be better than this box we're ever passing time in." And away in the wheeled armoire we rolled.

To my surprise, it was a cave. To an area of booteries and cutlery stores we traveled (by the dint of God's grace not crossing the Thames), a locale too businesslike to have the green frontages of Rathel's neighborhood. Eric had the carriage driver halt before a jewelry store behind whose glass front lay shinies for ladies.

"Eric, my semi-love, you've achieved a display window for our living!" I pronounced.

"Thanks for your appreciation, miss, and therein may you happily abide. Elsie and I, however, will reside in the tenement above." And upward he gestured toward the true windows behind which we would live.

Craning to see this proper glass, Elsie gained renewed delight at even so base a view, oohing and cooing enough to embarrass any decent witch.

"No need for such rapture, dear," I told her as Eric aided me from the carriage with no fondling. "No angels are flitting around up there, only flies, and well I recall your dislike for crawlies," and I made a gesture as though grabbing a bug from the air to pop it between my teeth.

What a callous person she was to ignore me, her own mistress.

Eric had entered the sparkly store, exiting after some boisterous laughing by a sinner within, sauntering toward us with a key.

"Be so bold as to follow me, kind ladies, up the stairs about

457

yon corner," he advised. And away with a stride of prideful confidence he led his, er, family.

"Not since he showed me his dog," I told Elsie, "have I seen him so arrogant."

"Your own home, miss," Elsie whispered, having ignored me again, pressing against me to squeeze both my hands. "I could just weep now, I could."

"And you could gain a flogging for it," I scolded, "for in my household will be no opera and no tears. Since beating I well learned from my current mother, I know it to be proper."

That comment she heard perfectly, Elsie giving me a look to break a display window, releasing me with a huff. So I pinched her ribs sharply enough for her to yelp, as though another spring had been loosed against her fleshy carriage.

Up the stairs on the building's outer wall we went, onto a landing and soon through a doorway. Since Elsie was struck with a bout of swooning once in the foyer (which was no more than a corner of the semi-great room beyond), I pushed her firmly within so that I as well could enter. The servant then began a slow dance (more of a waddle), Eric with the same happy pride leading us from the main chamber to the kitchen and the two small sites for sleeping, the troupe finally arriving at a cavelike locale with no windows that Eric referred to as his "study." Elsie immediately noted the two wood stoves, one each in the kitchen and non-great room. Praise God for no fireplace, I murmured. But tidy the household was, with a clean, unworn carpet in each chamber (except the cave), though scarcely enough furnishings for even a small family. One of us women looked about inside with rapture, the other with even less objectivity; for whereas Elsie found herself in a manse, I found myself in a construction worthy of Marybelle.

"Eric, dear, is this what is known as a 'hovel'?" I inquired.

With semi-uncomfortable laughter, Eric termed the place a "flat," but Elsie was not so amused.

"Miss Alba! a most ingrateful person you are to be speaking so of your lovely new home."

"But where is the basement for me to hide when you have been traipsing about my chamber too long?" I asked.

"Here it is called a display window," Eric submitted.

"Then no escape shall I have from this person," I scowled. "And with only two bedchambers, where does the dog sleep?"

"Wherever he so chooses, miss," Eric informed me.

"Then I will find his unending tongue lapping at my face the sleeping night," I grumbled. "Well, better him than the other pet panting and pawing as I dream. At least Elsie has her own room."

The servant waddled away, having enough of my unconscionable comedy, gone to pant and paw within that aforementioned chamber. Then I was alone with the future husband who would have my genuine opinion of his manse.

"I remain uncertain as to interpreting your true attitude toward such an abode," he told me, "considering your disdain for things richly physical, and your having lived and loved the wilderness. Nevertheless, Lady Amanda's town house is most elegant. But on my salary as a draftsman with my father, naught else can I afford. I know your humor, miss, but how foolish am I to fear your disappointment?"

"Sir, you fail to understand. I expect this family shortly to move into the deepest wilds and live in a . . . a tent. I would have said 'cave,' but I abhor caves; therefore, have your dank study with my blessing. But until we abandon London to live as natural animals, well will I be satisfied here. After all, you've made no provision for the Rathel, so why should I complain?"

"Oh, and well I would embrace you, miss," he beamed, "if I thought you would not flog me."

"If only Randolph were present, you could have at your embracing till your hugging mechanism ached, and be kissing him also to your lips' withering, in that he's the tongue for it."

"Bless you, wife," Eric muttered as Elsie with renewed pleasure regained the tiny great-room.

We womenfolk proceeded with further examination, the witch especially fascinated by the palest green spider housed on a pantry shelf. Guiding Elsie to this sub-dwelling, I warned the servant severely.

"Here is a friend to the mistress of this household, and if eradicated by any pet with any quantity of legs, I shall display such distress as to embarrass you before the master."

"Ah, with your jesting, you're tormenting me constant, so how could a bit of embarrassment make me suffer worse? Your very self is the greatest embarrassment in my poor life, even when

459

you're thinking yourself kind." And with a cackle, Elsie sidled away.

"Bloody witch," I mumbled to the spider, and it could not disagree.

Then the cackling and humor ceased, for Eric glimpsed through the window a sight to send him at once to the door where he made to lock the entry with grave movements and a most concerned smell. But too late, for the door opened as he reached it, and face to face were two men, my upcoming husband and this child's present father.

How short the latter had become, but this first thought of mine was only a fantasy. Eric was the one to have grown, and the sinners were now similar in size. And similar in distress as the senior spoke.

"I would speak with you alone," Edward stated with no comfort.

"I am here with my future wife and our chaperone, sir, and will allow you to greet them before our speaking."

Edward could have viewed me by turning slightly, but as though he could smell my position, he moved his head not a degree. I remained invisible to him, a specter who could haunt without being seen.

"My best to your chaperone, but to the other person I cannot speak, and this you know," he told his son, whose reply came the next instant.

"Sir, if you have not the capacity for such a simple courtesy, then you have no place in a gentleman's abode."

"Young sir, this place is not let by you if you've no payment for it. Since from this moment you have no employment with my firm, you'd best return home where you are well loved and cared for. But despair not in your finances, sir, for if you marry this woman, you will have no need of economics, because dear God knows that *Satan will have her kill you!*"

His last words were a shout, but Eric's next were nearly a yelp.

"And well loved I am by you to condemn my marriage and a lady no less profoundly excellent than any you can imagine!"

Edward then continued harshly, "I have learned, sir, with no aid from my imagination, only the magistrate's office, that in the town Lucansbludge where this person lived and was imprisoned, a man was murdered in the same, demonic manner as the poor Bitford fellow slaughtered heinously at a time when your fiancée was in this city."

"How repulsive you are, sir, to speak of murder and Miss Alba in the same raving speech."

I then began to move, revealing the specter whom Edward yet ignored, for all his senses were directed toward his son. And between these males was a passion that seemed evil—then between them was their subject. As though an emotional force, I literally intervened in this family, pressing the men away as I looked up to their faces. Before they could continue with their passion, the witch had her say.

"Here's a pair that should be flogged like cruel children attacking pets. One so in love with fear that he'll draw his son's suffering from imaginary demons, the other so in love with an unknown woman as to lose his father. Well, by the grace of God, I curse the devil you form between you, sirs, for above all other responses I gain from this scene is the recollection of my departed mother and the love we shared. That is the creation between parent and child, and if you pair destroy your own, more heinous fiends you are than any devil could be."

With my speaking, I viewed them each, looking side to side. When Edward finally noticed me and looked toward my face, his response was to flee, as though I were a fiend. Sensed in him that instant, however, was no fear, but pain, an emotional creature bequeathed to his son, Eric accepting it for his new family.

Eric moved into the flat as I closed the door with no force. The master now had nothing to say, rubbing his face as though exhausted beyond sleep, unable to awaken. Appearing genuinely flogged, Elsie looked between future husband and promised wife, and in her searching was the first to find words.

"Time will help him," she pleaded, "God in His time will be helping the man to understand."

"I believe I've heard that notion before," Eric stated with a deep, fatigued voice, now appearing more distracted than destroyed.

Intervening again, I stepped between Eric and Elsie, who were separated by the room's length, but bonded by emotion.

"Enough with these harsh feelings," I stated as though a child with her fill of chores. "Let us *carouse*," I suggested. "How does one accomplish this? Let us become drunk and beat upon one another, perhaps." But Eric had not concluded his exhaustion.

"I am afraid we've more harshness to confront," he told Elsie and me, and I sensed a new remorse in his voice or smell or the squeezing of his hands. "My father has made this threat before, but now I believe it a promise. With this trouble, Alba, there may be some delay in our marriage. Other employment I will gain, and have prepared for this release from my current work. But delay there shall be in my accumulating funds. And, and—I'll not be able to afford Miss Elsie's services."

"But, Master Eric, I would need no—"

Eric then cried, "I could not afford to *feed* you, miss!"

Such a blow were his words that Elsie suffered a near tactile shock, but recovered her poise as though God's greatest lady.

"But, but, there's no concern, now, for Mistress Amanda is yet good to me, and might be turning lonely without more folks about her home. Especially she's being fine to me now, for I'm never seeing her so joyed as she is at this marriage."

Having again felt too many emotions flung past me, I accepted a lighter air, flitting about Eric and Elsie as though an angel.

"How painful I am to interrupt this mass of tender feelings, but such is the way of wise people when confronting the ignorant. For this false dilemma I have an evident solution, one named Amanda. So complete a business person is Rathel that a loan might be proffered the new couple until their finances finally be firmly . . . finished."

"Alba, I would be shamed to ask your mistress for a loan of money."

"You asked for me permanent, did you not, sir? Am I not of greater value than glossy coins and bank notes? Besides, I expect more of a dowry from the Rathel estate than this single spare servant."

As Eric settled into thoughts of a shamed life of begging for pennies enough to feed his pets day to day, while Elsie was feeling bolstered in her presumptive spirits in that perhaps, yea, perhaps this tiny home might yet have space for her, I shooed them both out the door.

"Away we are!" I told the pair. "Lock the door behind us, sir, so

462

that no thieves will steal my spider. Then to the street for passage to the Rathel's." Disallowing their queries, I insisted they follow my guidance.

Gain a carriage and gone, Eric not yet so bankrupt as to find only walking affordable. A pleasant journey to the Rathel's— pleasant if one considers a box full of troubled sinners an especial joy—and to home again. With my family lagging behind, I leapt from the carriage—one brown, not black—to march post-haste to the front door, which of course was bleeding well locked, thereupon to pound loudly and blare out a demand for entry. Relieved was Delilah to find three semi-friendly faces on her stoop instead of the invading army from Africa she reasonably expected.

"My dearest mother is in?" I asked while handing Delilah my cloak. "I must see her in desperation," and into the house I swept as though I owned the place.

"Well, uh, and yes, Miss Alba," Delilah replied, "but, er, no, she is resting now, and of course you understand."

"Of course, I understand that I should not bother you to wake the mistress, for the act shall be a pleasure of my own."

Flying up the stairs went I with the most ludicrous of haughty miens, nose and bent wrist poised precisely so as I strode to the Rathel's bedchamber, observing with removed glimpses that my army followed, one not of Africa though led by an exotic beast. Against the proper door I rapped to enter without acknowledgment, having the invading forces wait in the corridor for their leader.

Reclining on the bed, Rathel lifted one shoulder, attempting to awaken, attempting to ask, "What? What is . . . ?"

"Beg pardon, mistress, for this veritable intrusion, but a true emergency has thrown itself upon us."

"Alba, what do you speak of?" the Rathel demanded, finally awake and adequately aware.

"Currently outside your door are Miss Elsie and Master Eric, who shall prove themselves extant with only hallooing, having too much courtesy to be intruding as does your daughter." Then over my shoulder I called.

"Outside, there, are persons waiting?"

" 'Tis I, mistress," Elsie squeaked.

"The best wishes for you, ma'am," Eric followed with scarcely more certainty.

Rathel then looked toward me with fierce interest as I continued.

"We three have come from our lovely abode wherein we shall live once wed. The reason for our flight was Edward Denton's having come there in distress, unfortunately finding it necessary to dismiss son Eric from the family business. Therefore, no wedding shall occur because no funds exist for us to affix the flat as legally let. My presumption being that nothing in this world—nor any other you own—would please your kindness more than to see the daughter wed this incomparable, incontrovertible lad, might you make arrangements for a bit of a loan before we starve?"

Through all the flurrying words, Rathel most clearly comprehended that the father was so distraught as to have chucked his very son. Expert in emotion was the mistress to conceal her inner gloating.

"Why, dear Alba, all along I've intended to set you well financially. Do you believe the only dowry I would provide you is Miss Elsie?" And, yes, the Rathel then laughed—how polite, how ladylike!—and along with her I tittered until her further speaking. "No difficulties so inconsequential as funds shall be allowed when grand love is available."

Then I rejected my silly smile, stepping beside the bed so that only Rathel would hear my following words. Seeing my face change, so did hers; and in that moment in which I neared, she searched me and waited, for much waiting can transpire in a moment that threatens loss.

"Another thing, mistress, with no humor. I think it best this male and I be wed without extravagant ceremony, for this is a process, and the more we proceed, the more interference shall we find. I suggest that your arrangements be for a simple, immediate ritual. Can you comply?"

"I can and will, if the boy agrees to such haste and simplicity."

"Do your part with the ceremony as I go now for mine."

I retained that grave visage upon quitting the chamber. Closing the door behind, I spoke to Elsie.

"Be relieved, miss, and be comfortable because your life of the future shall be as the near past so pleasantly offered. And since

464

no more traveling will you accomplish today, go about your internal affairs while I speak with this male outside in some privacy."

"Oh, and praising Jesus I am, miss, in that I did so much wish to be part of your home."

"You know my feelings to be identical, Elsie, and praise God for your sweet nature. Now, off we are for a time, and if I vanish from the grounds, the fault will not be yours."

Before Elsie could transform herself from friend to chaperone, I grasped Eric's cuff and led him outdoors.

"We are conversing again, miss, and alone?" he wondered.

"We shall be alone, true," I intoned, and Eric sensed my changed manner. "Call us a carriage, sir, and we're off."

"Destination, miss?"

"To a place you have never been, not even in your dreams."

An utter stranger would have sensed my distress. What a mistake, I thought, to allow Eric to gain an open carriage, for now nothing existed to hold me in, to keep the water out, keep the bridge away from me. As we crossed Hershford Bridge, I thought of Marybelle in her own open box, and felt my end would be no better; for my impressions were of never breathing again and feeling each extended moment of being without air as I suffered and suffocated and lived the dead nightmare of a wet agony to end me.

This sinner was staring at me as I remained abjectly still, hand on my brow as though to shield myself. I could not accept his ease. No fool was he for not fearing the water—in this relationship, I had the excess emotion. Then I had to look toward him, for was he not my only sanctity?

"Sir, I fear bridges as any person living fears an upcoming death," I said, then moved to him, remaining low and compact to minimize the risk of being thrown out, into the water, off the bridge, toward death. I moved against him as though a spider in a corner, and spoke again.

"Sir, you will hold me with your arm and no passion, the object to reduce these passions of mine."

And he did, Eric placed both arms about me to draw me near. Throughout him rushed emotions I could sense with only our

465

mutual touch, a vibration of his body that told me, yes, I will secure you and love any strength I may impart, and aid us both in this shared embrace. And though crossing that bridge remained a sort of terror, for one of us it became a type of joy.

No persons were at Gravesbury Reach, none within smell or sight. Upon our arrival, I instructed the coachman to be off yet return in an hour, and Jesus bear witness that he keep his observations to himself.

Christ's Cathedral I viewed, the edifice so removed as to seem average in size; but was this a building constructed or demolished? It seemed such a piecemeal thing, a collection of parts. So I looked away, for in London was more life than this stone pile, and life remained a mystery. I looked away, and listened. Far, far down the river came a massive sound. Nearer to me was Eric, Eric speaking, questioning. But I held out my hand for him to cease, for I had turned toward that sound, and here was my effort, my interest. Huge barges were against the bank, along the opposing side, but too far for clear sight. And though here my best sense was hearing, I could not determine that rhythmic sound, the source of a thudding to cover the Thames.

"What product do they unload, sir, so massive as to sound greatly upon the docks, yet not be ruined by coarse dropping?"

"I cannot guess, miss, and cannot care, for surely you've not brought me here to experience the silence that these boatmen disturb."

"I have not, sir, no; this is but distraction. My purpose here is swimming." And quickly I turned to Eric. "Can you, Master Eric?"

"Can I swim, miss? You ask whether I can swim?"

"I do, and a simple query."

"Why, yes, I am able, enough to save myself if found in the water, though I could not be placed in competition."

"I cannot," I said, and looked away, again toward that sound.

"You cannot, miss? You cannot . . . ?"

"I cannot swim. No witch can swim, this being a trait to separate us from sinners."

"Dear God, Alba, do not go mad on me now, not when again I

466

am so near to wedding you."

"Oh, and wed me you shall, sir, but not easily. First you must prove your love—not to me, but to yourself. Then the madness shall be yours."

Then I stepped near him, looking to his eyes so that he could see nothing but me; but, truly, from the first his only vision was mine.

"And how do you love me, sir?"

"How? I love you absolutely, Alba. I love you—"

"Enough to pledge your soul?"

"My soul? Alba, I cannot understand you. Your manner in this moment is—"

"This moment is your life," I stated loudly. "Nothing in all your prior existence is more important than this moment. You must ignore your confusion at my strange words and listen to each, for they have meaning. Understand the importance of this instant and tell me: Do you love me enough to pledge your immortal soul on the emotion?"

"God help me, miss, I do."

"You will require God's aid in the next era I present you, sir, for by your endless soul you must pledge me a thing."

"Miss Alba, I yet recall previous vows you forced upon me."

"From them you should have learned to trust me to improve our mutual understanding, and again I demand that trust. Now, think carefully, and be concerned with your future, not mine. I depart for a time, but will return. I—"

"You go where?"

And I leapt to grasp his arm and shout directly at his head.

"I go to scream in your ear, sir, if you cannot listen to my simple words!"

The force of my shouting was such that Eric had to jerk away from me. When we both had settled, I continued.

"I depart, sir, and promise no one will be harmed, though it may seem otherwise. Therefore, I will have you pledge on your immortal soul not to come for me, not to interfere in any manner, though one will soon become evident. You must understand that though I leave, I return briefly and unharmed. As you wait, however, the thought shall come that I die, that I must be dying, but I do not. And with God as my love and my witness, I swear that only your emotions will be pained, not my bodily health. Do you understand this, sir?"

"I do not, of course I do not understand, no matter how carefully I consider your words. But as I love you as much as my soul, I do pledge to fulfill your wishes, and wait for you without attempting to follow."

"Very well," I concluded, and stepped away, kneeling to unfasten my shoes. "Your heart must retain the vow, and your mind the recollection of my promise that no harm will come to me, only distress to your senses."

"Why, miss, do you remove your shoes?"

"Elsie would be most upset to see me soaked with water, for she would understand the deed presented, in that years ago I offered her this very demonstration."

Off with the cloak, then to the gown, my hands behind to the closures.

"What demonstration, miss? What precisely are you showing?"

But he knew, knew I was revealing body; and his breaths were strange, his stance doubtful, though none of that man smell could come, not through his apprehension, not through his knowledge that a certain part of my body would never be seen, for it was missing.

"Incidentally I reveal what eventually you must see as a husband, for Satan knows we shall be wed," and from my gown I stepped. "But moreover I reveal yourself as a fool, fool enough to allow your own death were it not for my salvation." With those words, I lowered my vapid underthing, lowered the fabric that had covered my skin no longer so white in places, lowered the garment to reveal my half bosom, half disaster.

Eric was not breathing. No tears nor screaming came, and neither did that bottom odor. Not even when the remainder of my apparel fell, and all of his wife was revealed. Never would he likely see me so clearly again, in the open day with all of God's light and space surrounding me, white light for my ambience, white apparel as my base, white skin the center of Eric's world. Now to show the devil's black reveal.

"I go to swim, sir, and since I cannot, you will panic. But recall your vow, recall your immortal soul." And I moved into the river.

"Alba?" he called out behind me, his sound an expression, not a name, a conveyance of consequence.

I lodged myself in that water before entering. Warm it was, but I felt nothing of this river nor those past, and this was my intent: not to allow the waters of my dreams to drown me when real water never had; for with each crossing the water became more murderous, and I more fearful. And I knew that dream and reality would one day meet, the conjoined water finding me on its bottom to crush me softly with fluid.

All my thoughts were on the process: open my mouth and allow the water in. And I began, this wet acceptance not yet a terror, eyes closed, slow movements. But I refrained from allowing the water's air to mingle with the remaining air of my lungs. Fearful comprehension had struck me, the knowledge that breathing air is life continued, but breathing water is death postponed; and how long can a person save herself? Through how many rivers, how many dreams?

The striking act needed to drive away my panic was the acceptance of wet air within me. At once I felt drowning, but also air, for so long had I retained the old breath that the new, wet one was sustaining. I found myself alive, though barely, surviving more than living. So I determined not to move about as I had with Elsie, remaining stationary to thereby require less air. Standing still on that unexamined river bottom, I began emulating an era by imagining walking up the Rathel's stairs and down, through the kitchen and corridor, into the garden and about the house, through the gate and around, into the foyer and great room to the library, always breathing, always needing to concentrate on that unnatural fluid as I stepped along the street with Eric, understanding that I breathed water and was able to do so, though barely, though I could lose this survival with a lack of effort, the slightest allowance of panic, the briefest thought of seeking true air, true breathing, true life, as I entered my bedchamber to find Eric at the window.

Eric underwater was thrashing and bubbling, and finally grasping me. I pushed away from him to step quickly toward the bank and out before I lost my calm. As I stood upright, Eric quit the river to thrash on land as though he were yet submerged.

So sharp and rich is the air of the sky that upon leaving the water, a witch must breathe slowly and with calmness, lest she pass out as though drowning on air. I thus appeared the opposite of Eric, who was gasping for breath. Then I had to yawn, for Eric had been drowning and needed recovery; whereas I had been breathing as though asleep.

"Is your soul as worthless as your life to so abandon both?" I confronted him. "Is your love equally impoverished?"

Wiping the water from his face as he supported himself on one elbow, no longer refraining from staring at his woman, Eric replied.

"My love is enough to provide me with reason for failing a vow. You are not God to have control of my soul; so no failure on my part will have me lose it on your account—you've not the power. But, God tell me, Alba, what power is yours to go without breathing?"

"But, sir, being only human, I was breathing through necessity."

"Are you a *fish?*"

"Continue your verse, poor poet, and find in time the rhyme, for I am no fish, but a witch."

"Jesus help me, woman—what are you *saying?*"

"I am speaking the whole truth, whereas before you heard but a portion. The Rathel has known of me from the first, and brought me to London in order for you to die, for few men can resist the white witch if she applies herself toward them. The Rathel's intended vengeance on your father was not your marriage into her family, but your death on our wedding bed, for I am the white witch who kills men with sex."

Though breath was no problem, Eric appeared drowned and unable to recover as he spoke.

"My God, Alba, you have gone mad! You speak of dreams."

"No dream allowed me to breathe those many minutes you observed. None of my life's terrors have been dreams, not even the last told by your father, for well he learned. His speaking of the men killed in Lucansbludge and London was most accurate, for both males died by me, though I murdered neither."

"You assert that these men you *killed?* You could not murder—how could a miss my wife ever—"

"With me they had the marital intercourse, though I was so devastated that only afterward did I learn the truth of Satan within me. The second man raped me through a lust worse than yours and thereby died. The first act you correctly heard described at the time: This Percival's manhood was cut away from him and thus he bled to death. With both men, this was true."

"You cut two men to death?" incredulous Eric groaned. "I am to believe that you knifed two men and—"

"I knifed no one, sir, for I am the sex witch, not a butcher of swine. I did not cut the men—I *fucked* them to death, and my vagina is such as to have pinched their pricks off as a child pulls away the wings of flies. But the difference is moral, sir, and immortal. The child has the power to cease his act, yet accepts the initiative of intention; whereas I have neither. Never would I choose to kill a male in any manner, yet when the marital act begins, I have no control, only torture of my own. Therefore, sir, do you not care to fuck me? Previously I have promised the husband my cunt."

I sat upon my backside, settling on my gown with legs spread, leaning backward with my weight on my hands, knees upward.

"I've another wound for you to view, sir, one you've dreamed of long, I know."

I could smell his man fumes now, though Eric seemed not excited but devastated, leaning on his elbow as he stared at me—my face and lower, much lower—with that same appearance of having drowned.

"There's been enough waiting by you and the Lady Rathel, Eric. And I think her correct. I think you can resist me never, not even aware of my murders. You call this love, but perhaps it's only lust, no more than sin. Now come to the wife and foretell the marriage. Come to the witch and see if you can live with her."

I told him to approach me and lower his pants. And he did, moving as though walking in his sleep, walking underwater. Step to me he did and unclothe himself, revealing his lust, his demon; and was that man stick held before him more of a sword or a cross?

"On your knees and well spread your legs," I instructed, for I had become expert in taking men. Eric complied. As he knelt before me, flat upon my back I lay, knees well up and above my hips. But when Eric placed his reddish glans against my vagina, I reached down to grasp the shaft in my hand and guide him toward

471

perversion, Eric removed from death by a bit of flesh, separated from a demon by a segment of God's profound space.

I had him spit on me. I had him spit on my anus and his phallus as per the lessons of one illegal animal. Then that central buttock muscle I endeavored to relax as Eric arrived at the safe entrance. No more instructions need be given, for Eric was then moving on his own, entering me completely with a strong thrust, and his entry was painful. His entry hurt because that orifice despite relaxation was too constricted to comfortably accept such a function. This pain, however, is not my best recollection. Most I remember his testicles against me, soft, a type of caress. As he began a thrusting known to men deeper than dreams, I looked away. Eric was desperate, it seemed, for I saw no joy, and was able to ignore his lust because no one was dying. I gained a sore muscle below, that soft kiss of his testicles antithetical to his grinding at my buttocks and his spearing within and the shuddering of his entire body. This force I recognized. His hard breathing had a different timbre and the rate had increased, but was not the nature of this thumping akin to the barge's unloading we had heard? A sound gone while I was submerged, as though drowned.

Eric soon achieved a lesser shudder, one I felt within, but mild compared to his great thrusting. Why, then, had the new movement such influence over the lad as to make his face go mad, to take his body whole and grasp it as though choking him, as though the stabbing were in his heart instead of my arse? Then he slowed, that greater shudder having lost its strength, nearing completion; and I felt the lesser tremor squeezing outward from within me, then relax; reach, then return, again; Eric moving his man stick in close rhythm to this stretching as though practiced, slower, then ceasing, that last caress of his testicles held tightly in their softness against me, then stillness.

Only then did I notice that Eric had been supported by me, for he held my thighs in his hands, now moving his fingers slowly upward, away from the welt formed with his grasp, moving his hands along my legs, and he seemed elsewhere. Eric's view was of no area seen before, his hands unconscious as they rubbed toward my welt, passing the pained area to aggravate the bruise, then continued only to return, gone, return, and I would not find this touch offensive.

His legs were the damaged pair when Eric made to stand, for though flesh, they now seemed boneless, giant mansticks more limp than his small limb. After an unbalanced step backward, Eric gained enough solidity for him to bend and aid my rising. Not toward each other did we look, but with all the feeling, with all the *understanding*, what was left to see? Then he embraced me more fully than when upon the bridge, embraced me with both arms and all of his body, as firm yet as tender as his testicles' kissing me, Eric with his head against mine, holding his lady with all of his heart; and again he was weeping, barely heard though unmistaken, but this occasion accepted by the wife.

Thirty-one

Hiding in the shadows like any decent demon was I when Eric arrived the next morning. As a gentleman he appeared, not a pained lover; and, yes, he was present for business, not passion, in that no mention was made of me. Eric sought audience with Lady Rathel, waiting for her in the foyer instead of entering deeper to find greater comfort, greater love.

As Elsie proceeded to the Rathel's chamber, I revealed my position behind the short wall near the library. After a gleefully evil look to her, I vanished from her sight. Though not revealing myself to Eric, when Rathel oozed from the upper floor to the lower, I casually encircled her with graceless steps before returning to my hiding.

The mistress continued without acknowledgment, exchanging brief cordialities with her guest before Eric began his business.

"No longer am I allowed to live within my father's house," he told the mistress. "Therefore shall I move to the home of my true family, and that is myself and my wife. Of course, nothing with my parents has changed to improve my position as a future head of household."

"Previously I have vouched that your finances will not be problematic," Rathel conveyed. "Not so long as I am your mother-in-law."

"Your generosity is beyond words, Lady Amanda. But con-

474

cern yourself not that I might be a drain on your life, as though a leech to let your blood. Currently I am negotiating for good employ with an enterprise requiring a man educated in sums, which is not beyond my ability. But I fear the legal force of my father, that he may find a way to make a marriage bond between myself and Miss Alba most difficult."

"We are yet to suffer from his thoughts of averting the marriage. Perhaps we never shall, for as determined the previous day, the wedding will come quickly. As soon as our speaking is complete, I depart for the city clerk to conclude the legalities of marriage. Thereafter will we have a schedule."

Schedule, schedule.

"My speaking will end by allowing you to continue with Alba's benefit and mine; and with my great thanks, I depart." Eric then bowed, the gent, though not taking the lady's hand; for how could he kiss the knuckles that had thrashed his love?

As Eric departed, the lady quit the foyer from one direction, and I entered from the opposite. There a door closed toward my face, but not a hair of me did Eric see. Therefore, I silently followed him out; but as I gained his side, why did I have this feeling of mad humor, and why did I need to suppress a cackle?

"I confront you, sir," I told him, smiling as Eric halted to look toward me. "Do you seek to run from the woman you must love?"

Shaking his head like a rag to be freed of crumbs—perhaps building crumbs—Eric smiled as though mad himself, and spoke.

"What a great man I am," he said, "not to hate you till your death," and laughed uncomfortably.

"Your passion was then dispelled yesterday, sir, so that your heart may think more clearly?"

"As well you know, and through your own intent, that prior day was no end, but a beginning."

"With all my murder you can yet bear my sight?"

"All your unintended killing seems enough to kill me, but you have proven yourself as innocent as any lady, and as honest."

Then all my humor expired as I spoke with the exact honesty Eric mentioned.

"Your suffering from me is displeasing, sir, but since it cannot be ended, I pray you might comprehend and control through God's aid and mine."

"I pray equally that I never lose the comprehension you've provided, that mine is no life of agony. I've naught been raped nor beaten near death nor had my body torn most cruelly. Never have I killed a man nor had one killed through me, thereafter having to live with my murderous guilt; so who am I to do other than love you? Yesterday was the schooling you knew it should be, and perhaps I might thank you. But despite that culminated pain and passion, I have more lust for you now than ever before, and God help me, more love as well."

Eric then turned away, toward the street and his waiting carriage; but the witch was not through with her victim.

"Sir, I'll have another word with you," I said, and grasped his arm to turn him again toward me. "With all the passion of that prior day, did one event you not forget?"

"Pray no, miss, for no more could I bear."

"A little thing of thine own desire I know little of, but will offer for you to learn yourself. Here, sir, you may kiss the bleeding bride." And I offered him my mouth.

He also seized my body, Eric at once pressing his torso against mine, surrounding my shoulders with his arms, and I was entirely against him, especially the mouth. I had been ignorant before of the exact activity sinners pursue with their kissing, but from Eric I felt only his lips against me like his testicles against that other end, a soft yet firm pressure. Some movement he produced with his face, but the greater sensing for me was his emotion. That man smell I did not notice, but Eric breathed as though praying for someone's salvation. And all his holding was not crushing, but containment, perhaps not the finest home in God's world, but as safe as the Rathel's compared to the jails of Lucansbludge. After all, this home was my husband; and though I found no joy in knowing that the future would bring more of this kissing, I was amazed to feel no revulsion for having this sinner in my mouth.

I rarely saw Eric those following days. The Rathel had him once for some legal signing, and again for arrangements of finance, areas beneath me as a current lady and upcoming bride. Wagons of hire came to the Rathel's and went to the Dentons', Elsie a fount of accomplishment here with all her ordering and arrangements. Into the tenement thus entered Elsie's few things (including hair not her own), but all my clothes along with their armoire set in the non-great room, for none other had enough of God's space to contain it. This thing I determined to burn with all its contents rather than have it in my (my?) new home, as though a monument of past death or a recently grown mountain surely containing a dank cave on one unexamined slope. And what of my personal chamber pot, my bloody bed?

They came as well. No bloody bed, since one adequate for a close couple and their close coupling resided in the spouses' chamber. But since scarcely more than straight chairs were our new home's furnishings, the pseudo-mother of mine insisted that my very secretary accompany me, as well as a fine divan from the basement, two stuffed chairs, some low though not lowly tables, and so on, including the girl's pot, which was a comfort in that it had her smell, similar here to certain parts of Eric.

A pair of hired sinning males transported our belongings, Eric coming and going about the flat with no kissing, only anxiety. I attended only those journeys in which Elsie complained least about the upcoming ceremony's being too curt for a London lady. One junket revealed a superior ceremony at the homestead, Elsie and I observing a second pair of bulky sinning men heave a great oaken bed up the stairs to find the door locked.

"Ah! and it's a most beautiful wedding bed—how much the lad does love you, miss!"

This was joyous Elsie's effervescent blubbering as she simultaneously gossiped about Eric's devotion and expense (thank the Rathel's funds), while leaping up the steps in no ladylike gallop to insert herself between the bed and God's plain air twenty feet above the alley, thereafter opening the door so that the sinners might enter with the bed before either dying from holding it interminably or dropping it upon me and the carriage below. The next ceremony was the males' eventual success in passing through the doorway with this furniture, the stairs nearly smashed flat, but all survived except the meager great-room, which disappeared once the bed was situated therein, so monumental was its girth, especially considering the previously-residing armoire mountain.

Next in the progression of ceremonious buffooneries was these bulky sinners' removal of the current bed from its place and past the latest monument without destroying the household, my burly armoire, or especially unburly Elsie, who near lost her heart as a functioning device as the men threatened the kitchen walls, the bedposts, our best front window, all the divans and wing chairs that were no longer the Rathel's, but mine, and therefore Elsie's. Nonetheless, through manipulation that seemed more happenstance than expertise, the men succeeded; and there sat two beds in one room, scarcely any of God's space remaining for mere persons.

The males would continue after breathing tremendously for minutes. Finding that they either had to sit or drop as though dead, the ravaged pair began to lower themselves upon the new bed until Elsie emitted such a screech that up they leapt before contacting wood as she came at them in a fury enough to frighten them heartless, though each had sufficient bulk to squash the miss with their fingers. But Elsie would have neither these commoners nor even Jesus sit upon this bed that would hold the newlyweds and no other pair of breathing souls, the men shooed to the floor, and there with relief they settled.

After a sinners' instant, Miss Slave Driver shooed the two up to their deadened legs and into the bedchamber with the bed hulk, the same scene repeated but in reverse, both Elsie and the men surviving, though no mention did the latter make as to aiding the young couple in any further way, and a good day one and all.

Within the bedchamber, Elsie began fondling and cooing over the grand oaken creation, the soft surface for sleeping and nightmaring. I noted to the miss that although large, the bed was not expansive enough for husband, wife, and pet. Therefore, the dog would sleep with her. Elsie, however, would not allow my paltry humor to mar her next ceremony, which was lavishly coating the mattress with our finest bed coverings from Rathel's.

So gracious was I as to wait until Elsie completed her pleasing task before dragging her into the kitchen to demand the whereabouts of my spider.

"And I'm setting the beast outside, I did, by having it crawl on a stick with no harm. And I'm not seeking it, Miss Alba, nor replacing the thing, no matter how many dogs I'm forced to sleep with."

In this manner our home was prepared. For days the process continued, Elsie in charge, Rathel plotting, Alba disinterested. I became more aware one morning upon finding all the sinning women of the Rathel household attacking me with fabric as though a new bed, no particular day except that it would see me wed. And there I was in a coach with the mistress, exiting at a small chapel with a roof not high and pointy enough to impress the God of mountains. Into the chapel where sinners normally begged the greatest Lord forgive their iniquities on their way to promulgate their further sins. The holy business that noon, however, was a witch.

I was made to enter a nave full of Elsies. Eric's family was not present, but all of Rathel's countless servants. Had I been more the lady, surely their presence would have impressed me as unseemly, since their station was in some rear room with grease. At least they had been conveyed in their own carriage—brown, if any justice existed on Earth. But being a mere person and no lady, I was pleased at their attendance, for they reeked of satisfaction. No astonishing joy attacked me, but I was only the bride. Nearby stood my mother weeping to lose her daughter; but, no, this was Elsie; and I could not determine whether she wept because the event was most joyous for her dear lass, or because the occasion was not worthy of the lady same.

Eric was then hied along to stand beside me, the Rathel also proximate; and being so near the pulpit, would we be allowed to preach? Evidently not, for here was the minister who commenced to provide Eric and me with a personal sermon directly at our faces. Since the man had been eating onions lately, I allowed him to breathe in my vicinity without questioning any secret allegiance of his toward Lutherans. The service provided was most odd in my experience, for Eric and I were quizzed, queried, and made to answer. As though this chapel were the wilds beyond London, I found myself in another contest not of my choosing nor comprehension. Certainly our (our?) Rathel was the ringleader of this animal faire with its exotic creatures. As well she seemed the seller of tickets (as made obvious by the audience), and purveyor of rules. But no more challenges would I accept, so this one I abandoned by answering the minister's questions exactly as I thought he desired, regardless of the consequences to follow. Yet to my most ironical bemusement, I found myself victorious, for I won Eric. All he got was to kiss the bloody bride.

Elsie I removed from the chapel via the medium of her pinched and pulled ear, such a fussing of tears she effected as though a contest not to end until she drowned from the weeping, as though proving herself the witch in the river of her face. Scarcely less pleased was the Rathel, who was gloating enough to choke, nothing hidden. But whereas Rathel I could leave, Elsie I was required to take along, for she was the additional prize I had been connived into accepting. The contest, I discovered too late, was for the ownership of a pack of sinners, and foolishly I had won. Then home to a domestic situation.

"God help me against the devil who attacks!" Elsie shrieked as she retreated from Randolph, who graciously wagged his tail, presenting his snout for Elsie's petting as she stepped against the window, thereafter to either cease her retreat or learn to fly.

"Whyever would this dog's presence be such a terror, Miss Elsie?" the master of both dog and household inquired.

"Because dogs are hating me, sir, long have and ever shall—

as proven by this beast's latest attack!"

The "attack" was Randolph's rearing upon his hind legs to paw the air scant feet from Elsie's heart. As Eric produced a talented snapping sound with his fingers, Randolph proceeded to his master's side, receiving a fine scratching for his obedience. The identical gesture on my part and firm pointing toward my feet eventually brought Elsie to my vicinity. Pet her I did not, though I urged the woman to become friends with this creature, who was surely no more wild than I. Grumbling that she might best have remained with Mistress Amanda rather than suffer a toothy death at the mouth of a demon, off she shuffled, but away from the dog.

After dog was poorly met by servant, husband and wife received a guest, for Lady Rathel presented herself to conduct the glorious couple to a wedding party at a dining hall resembling St. Nicholas Cathedral. Within were all the persons Rathel had ever met in her universal career as a London lady, though scarcely an acquaintance of Eric. Thoughtfully had Rathel designed the meal, for the witch and her brood were served a casserole with no fat, a salad with no hidden meat; whereas the remaining sinners inhaled puissance of partridge and so on. Then came a toast by Rathel, whose convincing sentiments connived the audience into standing and cheering for the newlyweds, though no males made their way toward me for breast grasping, a rare lack for a British crowd, though one made more difficult by my recently reduced bosom. A fine toast wherein I found myself sipping this liquor champagne that made me sneeze and made me consider spitting. *Eventually* Rathel delivered husband and witch to their flat with little speaking, a certain volume of gloating. Therein, the pets were supping, Elsie for the first instance in her arduous existence with me explicitly obeying my request; for the dog and she had become fast friends, the former because of the tremendous bone he had received, the latter due to the furry affection lavished toward her in return.

The marrieds then practiced nuptial boredom. Miss Elsie herein became anxious, fidgeting around the household, needing to straighten each drape and attack dust in every crevice with a wad of feathers on a stick. Chatter away she did, but who was to hear with our lugubrious ears? Not misplaced Eric or the dog so bored he fell asleep, not the wife who secretly laughed at the sinners' discomfort. Heaven this was compared to the boredom and anxiety their witch had suffered in previous lives.

What a brief eternity till nightfall when the sinners' apprehension intensified, Elsie's tiny, quick breaths supplying her insufficient air for endless chattering, Eric's slow, shallow respiration fit for a river's bottom. Eventually Elsie's twitching and fidgeting peaked, for after rubbing her apron till her fingers were surely worn, she reached around the apparel for the strings to remove the item and fold it scrupulously before describing her plans.

"And it's home I'm go—. It's to Mistress Amanda's I'm leaving, now, to return the morning—please." Then she stepped to the door.

Having been seated on one of the countless divans with sleeping Randolph as Eric and Elsie respectively dragged and flitted about the tenement, I responded to the servant's proffered departure.

"No coach will you find at this late hour, miss, and no need for an exit regardless."

"Aye, but the walking is brief, miss—mistress—for a hearty sort such as myself."

"Yes, I have noticed that the heart is quite significant in your system, but less of a purpose I discern in your fleeing. Have you some explicable cause?"

"I—I can't be staying your wedding night, I can't be staying," she reported, and hurriedly made to exit.

"What a tremendous coward I find you, miss, to abandon me alone with such a swarthy male."

"I—I cannot remain, lass—mistress—not on this night," Elsie repeated, and through the doorway she stepped, only to be followed by Eric.

"Wait, Miss Elsie. If you so insist, at least I shall walk with you and ensure your safety."

And so he did. The traitorous dog followed. Not

even a spider had I left for companionship.

Late was the hour of Eric's return. I had not moved, Randolph regaining his place as though never having abandoned me, and no mention was made by either party of treachery toward the new mistress. Eric's reply to my asking of his tardiness was of a walk longer than predicted.

"How strange that a daytime distance increases at night," I responded. "Perhaps your having wandered across half the city is a factor. So fearful are you, sir, of one thin witch? I am the same woman you fully possessed but days before while receiving no damage to your person. I bite, sir, no more than the dog."

"Through good fortune, I am at my new employ tomorrow," Eric replied with unconvincingly tempered emotions. "Truly I feel uncomfortable at being in debt to Lady Amanda."

"Because she is a woman and your wife's relative, or because she is the person who beat me bloody and to this moment longs for your death?"

"Please, Alba, not tonight with this talk," he sighed, and stepped across the room. "All your truths I shall bear, but grant me some interval before I acquire your bold manner of acceptance."

"What a pity to be so burdened by the potentials of an improved life. But the present that remains is that of your wedding day, sir; and to extend those most felicitous nuptials into this connubial evening, shall we hereupon not fuck the master dry to remove his bloody pouting?"

I stood to remove my nonbloody clothing. Though Eric understood, he remained confused, looking at me as I had Marybelle upon finding her eating a lizard. Did Eric so fear I would consume him?

"Your visage is scarcely one of passion," I remarked as my velvet vest dropped beside the dog. "But even now I smell lust rising from between your legs, and sense your man stick firming in preparation." Then the unique bosom was exposed, and soon, all the pale body.

"Witches have an exceptional capacity to sense via smelling," I informed him, "so your sex interest I note by odor. But, in a marital inversion whereby we might better comprehend one another, how does the witch smell to sinners? Appropriately here, how does her sex smell, have you noticed?" Then I placed my hand against my vulva, my temperate vulva, coming away with a sex scent on my fingers that I held before Eric's face.

He took my hand with both of his and inhaled as though to overcome all those shallow breaths of the evening. Kiss my palm he did as though needing to eat it, my hand a sex scrap for this carnivorous beast.

"Here, sir, smell better below and learn of the witch," I intoned, and pressed his shoulders until the man was on his knees. Then I moved my belly forward, Eric's face going lower, fingers on my buttocks and squeezing as he began kissing the folds of my sexual area. And his head rolled and his mouth was more alive than ever with mere eating, the wife finding this passion remarkable as Eric manipulated the cleft of my buttocks as though dirt to be dug through for treasure. I was moved at the power of my baby slash to so incite a sinner, but only he of those males to have slobbered and sucked on me was a friend. Only this man was my husband; but since the relationship was one of the sinners' society, I did not cherish the bond, did not love my husband's lust. All that mouth against me and his tongue so far inside my crevice seemed useless, especially with all of his intensity, as though he dealt with massive masonry needing to be cut and firmly moved in order to construct a cathedral. But though I took no pleasure from all these coupling lips, I was more bemused than upset, and truly pleased because distraught Eric was being relieved of his anxiety; for in this day and the world of our marriage, Eric had finally found his place.

Away from him I stepped and to the bedchamber. Upon our new monument of sleeping and sex I reclined, for the first instance in my life imagining myself in the same position taken by Mother at my birth. But no baby vacated my body, for here was only entry, that naked person no child, but Eric nude with his tongue lapping in and around me as though Randolph digging toward the middle of a bone for marrow. I considered Eric's tasteful organ entering too far, for too great a period, thereafter eaten by me, my sex lips making a meal of his mouth.

As though from uncertainty and needing to observe my response, the man soon looked upward. My face, however, was not first seen, but my bosom; and some part of Eric had him continue viewing that scar. But sensible enough was this sex sinner to understand that superior sights were available, Eric looking toward that adjacent, adequate breast—and of course there was the groin, Eric viewing high then low in a reciprocation to be eventually paralleled sexually, the husband on a holiday in a foreign land with too many exotic sights to see.

Again Eric had his hands on me, my belly and vulva, holding his plate so that no person would remove his meal. How base this unsocial male was to be eating with no utensils. And I could only wonder how long he would be supping on me, the vaginal victuals required for his sexual sustenance. Sex, the nourishment of sinners' marriage, so long neglected in his diet that years of chaste starvation Eric now made to undo. Yet I was the wife here and felt no need—was this due to my bottom's previous eatings, male meals of a cunt cave no heroic man could enter and quit whole? No, the cause was that I was not wed. Only Eric here was married.

Since such concealed flesh is tender even on a witch, I eventually encouraged Eric to apply himself toward my alternate entry with his second, stiffer tongue, that poor beggar below equally red but now drooling. Not enough, however, to provide smooth access to my interior; and how proud I was of this ever-thoughtful lad who had well accepted his tutoring; for there he was attempting to spit upon his vibrating shaft and missing, spitting on the wife instead, on my belly and finally his fingers, transferring the lubricant to his headed tongue and about my tunnel entry, Eric like a boy all concerned with his adult craft, a sensitive aesthetic attempted with a cumbersome paw. And, oh, the fond effort on his face; but finally his instrument was against me and moving within, and I placed my legs comfortably about the husband as Eric began renewed

485

grasping of one thigh and the single breast, his nervous phallus pacing to and fro inside me, falling out of my dung cave on occasion only to search for the door and reenter, more worry and pacing about my bowels until the dog came.

Effortlessly Randolph leapt upon the bed, instantly moving to my face to sniff once and thereafter begin his own lapping, as though I were to be shared – and was this a cryptic part of the marriage agreement only now revealed to torment the wife? The well-covered tail waved about to strike Eric's face, a gentle but annoying hair whip. The master, however, could not postpone his activity to prevent that whipping, could only continue with the demon within him by pumping the thing until it expired from the thrashing, Eric holding me with one hand while attempting to press away that flying tail with the other. This target was not stationary, however, but moving around and around to thrash the master again and again, as though a hairy and roundabout imitation of intercourse. Less occupied than Eric, I was the one to move the dog, pulling the beast near till Eric's face was in clear air. Randolph then reclined, looking at me with a canine smile and an occasional lap, contemplating my situation. Thoughts then came of another dog, one equally friendly though not exactly a friend. Not of the dying I thought, only the dog, praise God I thought only of the dog and not my chasing him, only the lapping; but here it was good, so I laughed and loved it.

After a look to wonder of the comedy, wonder of being the fool or the victim, deeply occupied Eric occupied with my depths seemed to approach imminent collapse in that he was leaning forward, slack of posture. Therefore, I pressed my legs together, and upon my knees Eric leaned with his shoulders until slumping away and lying beside me.

With Eric's full nude body now against mine, I received further perceptual details of the species of male sinner. No horror here, for the man's odor of exerted perspiration was virtually relieving in its naturalness, as though the smell of the wilds, of stagnant water, perhaps; and his breath was of cooked vegetables, not fats turned rancid betwixt the teeth. Randolph, however, was now less interested in me and more in his master, who again was available in his passivity, what with all the thrashing ended. And though I ignored the man beast, the dog was concerned, clambering upon me to reach his master's sinning body, specifically that part of the rising odor not quite so firm as before. There the pet began his sniffing and licking only to receive a non-fond push from Eric as the master rolled onto his side, displaying his spine to the family. Randolph then quit the chamber, bored or offended.

With no business to conclude nor carriage required to carry us away, I was uncertain of the procedure to properly follow this act, now that it was legal and non-murderous. Perhaps the husband knew, for although less familiar with sex than I, nevertheless, more of a social creature was he. And correct I was, for the master turned to begin a most social progression even I was familiar with.

"You've yet to kill me, miss," he noted with a most brilliantly astute observation, and rolled onto his side again.

"Missus," I said.

"Though I appreciate these temporary jaunts near Heaven," he added. "You are allowed, miss—"

"Missus."

"You are allowed to enjoy this process as does the husband," he submitted, having turned enough to observe the ceiling, settling again after his words.

I wondered whether Eric were aware of taking his turns in a conversation in which he was the only participant. But when next he lifted his head to proceed with his speech, I produced a better say.

"I pray I've not been too harsh with my, my . . ."

"Do you yet love me, sir, or are you merely satisfied with your lust?" I asked.

With my beginning words, Eric stiffened in parts other than the phallus, his head held suspended to hear me, doubtless with no comfort.

"I love you no less, Alba, because I am not imaginative enough to love you more. But greater comfort I have with this love the more you relieve my fear."

"Greater comfort you would have to lower your head and

487

avoid a strained neck. As for relief, do you not in fact mean relief of the great pressure of passion within you released as thrashing and fluids as though a popped pimple?"

"What I mean, miss, is—"

"What you mean, missus. What I mean, sir, is to ask you to tell me most truly, as you would yourself or your God, whether you would wish not to love me. Would you choose this emotion to be unnecessary toward me, but better saved for another woman?"

"You mean one with more numerous breasts?"

"No, one with fewer murders."

Then Eric sternly sighed, rising from the bed, moving to his attire so that he could clothe himself and be gone. With no intent of dressing or allowing his, I erupted from the bed like puke or a gushing sinner's prick to rush around before him and educate the boy again.

"Sir, this pitiful sensitivity I suggest you outgrow. My mad humor you shall allow me, and not go pouting off as though a disciplined child when the comedy comes to irritate your tender heart. The distress you feel for having need of such a wife and all her horrors is but a joke compared to my having experienced those horrors. So when you find yourself beside a person with neither blood nor life and find that Satan through your own body has cut and killed that man, then you, sir, be the one to run from the terror."

After a brief pause for staring toward me, the husband reacted.

"Very well, missus, my running away shall be to the bed." And move there he did, pausing after the first step to turn and point toward my superior breast.

"By the way, Mrs. Denton, despite my consequential love for you and my glory in living with this," he spake, then moved his gesture to the scab, "the alternate I find absolutely grotesque." And the bed's surface he regained, lying in the same position as before, settling on the identical side.

I also returned, same locale, similar position, though not one scrap of skin did I allow against the sinner.

"Another response, missus, before you fume away your consciousness," Eric said with lifted head and breaking neck for all I cared. "When again the great pressure of my fluid lust accumulates, oh, within the hour, might you be so connubial as to drain the boil of my passion?" And laugh this foolish sinner did, giggling over his new toy before the mistreated pet could answer. But not one single instance again that night would I be his receptacle, as though a chamber pot. Not once, but twice.

Thirty-two

The one day lived in our new home would evidently be our last, for the next dawn we were accosted by criminals so fearless as to beat upon our door and demand entry. Despite the dog's ferocious audible protection, the beating and murderous shouting outside did not cease. Rape and pillaging were no concern, in that I had become accustomed to the former during the night, and nothing in the home existed to be stolen except clothes that would not likely fit the average cretin. This last was certain, for the entire horde of crazed criminals had come to awaken her master lest the fool be late his first day of new employ.

"Kill!" was my instruction to Randolph upon opening the door, and a good licking he gave the servant, who then set to giggling worse than Eric had after each instance of ravishing me throughout the evening.

Into the bedchamber went I with the dog, who evidently had slept the night upon me, in that I was covered with his fur. Into the bedchamber to have Randolph leap upon his master's spine and bark enough to arouse the dead. But Eric was not dead, only, er, drained; and only after I struck his flank with his own boot did the cur consent to awaken, aware then of his dilemma, up and on with his clothes, his wife pleased to see that for once in their married life his man stick was a twig and not a trunk.

An astonishing change this sinner had undergone during the night, for hair had appeared on his face. I thought the dog had slept upon him as well, all that beast fur against his skin causing a hirsute growth to ensue; and should I therefore expect a

490

coat to arise from my entire person any moment? But, no, these males had hair on their faces as though an average animal, though Godly beasts do not scrape the stuff off each morning. And so did Eric proceed, Elsie down to the common well to retrieve water thereafter heated for the master on one of our two personal wood stoves whose fire was enclosed, praise God, though the entire thing was metal, curse the devil. After lathering his face with a fattish smelling soap, Eric nearly killed me. A horrifying knife he began rubbing against a piece of dead animal hide, and then—and then he cut away at his face as though skinning himself or murdering himself or cutting his own breast away, own cheeks and neck away. I could not look, though he did, staring into a looking glass to make certain that he slaughtered himself properly. Immediately I searched for a bag wherein I could pack my things and abscond, but since nothing was present I cared for, I would exit alone; but Miss Elsie would not allow this because I was yet in my nightclothes: no running away from the beard until properly dressed. And wait till he's nicking himself, missus; then you're truly to be upset.

So mad was all this humor that I determined to remain, for Eric was departing regardless.

At least he wore no wig.

Out the door with him and away from my body. Then to convince the servant that my wedding night was as fabulously joyous as she wished it. Now straighten the bed, miss, for this be the servant's chore, and I care not what horrors you find there.

Eventually I settled in this day by awakening fully, the poor disposition brought by the criminal horde at my door and the one in my bed dissipating. Unfortunately it was replaced by a more intrusive emotion, one to have nearly vanquished me before, in an even wilder environ. I envisioned boredom. Was the previous night the measure of my married life to come? Would my existence be one of buttocks so constantly sore that I could only walk obliquely, Elsie thinking that I was ever lost, when in fact my bottom was simply impossible to guide? This sexual exposure had so entrenched Eric's gender stench in my own skin's crevices that the first morning after our marriage's consummation, I well took to sprinkling myself with a lady's powdered scent, but only after first applying ground tea, a preferable material that unfortunately would not adhere. Observing this activity, Elsie gained great satisfaction along with enlightenment, understanding that no more was required to make me a lady than a million consecutive butt couplings, and so might society be defined.

In this manner my days proceeded. My greatest concern was Rathel's response to learn that after all her years of devious effort, after planting the killer witch upon her victim's very baby stick, Eric yet remained alive. This fear of Rathel's further vengeance was more discomforting than any tribulation of my average married day. Eric awoke each morning with difficulty only to be at his face with a Satanic blade and then vanish for the day. After his exit, the dog and I would walk endlessly while Elsie ruined the home by making it spotless, stoking the fire, emptying the chamber pots, washing the laundry and thereby removing my own smell from my own apparel. Toward the day's end, Eric would return from his accounting. Then we would eat, speak of nothing, and soon the odor in the man would rise, his wife thereafter walking the dog until she could no longer stand, returning home to receive her husband's smells within her warehouse (rear entry) until she could no longer recline.

As part of ruining the household, Elsie prepared meals, and I nearly wept to find that my own personal home would not be free of burnt animal flesh. Elsie and Eric insisted that the race of sinners could not live without meat longer than a few days, so a few days after the wedding, fat they did seek. In my foolishness, I believed the traitors until Elsie came home with chops, which immediately I wrested from her and hurled through the open window onto the street, thereafter wiping my hands madly across my hem until the death smell was off me; and damned be my spirit if I would allow Randolph out the door to gain the flesh himself. Then I shouted in a sane fury that I would take all of Eric's flesh infinitely within me and accept Elsie's having her way throughout the house, but with

492

God as my moral support, no living creature would eat another in my home unless I was killed and eaten first. Thereby did I become mistress of the household.

From that tirade on, I became known by my own husband as the little Rathel. The Dentons remained vegetarians, however, though the heinous dog was oft found sneaking home with lizards on his breath, but he had an excuse in being only human. Everyone else but me was a sinner. And I was gaining vast power over these people. So much they loved me, I believed, that through my own implacable will and crafty wisdom I would connive them into abandoning London and venturing with me to live in the wilds. Yes, with certainty I believed that I could so convince them, but knew in my heart that the three would kill and eat me first.

In this manner my weeks proceeded. Since Eric was too poor to afford the opera (praise God) despite his desire to attend this function with me, the husband and servant presumed that a substitute would be church attendance in the very chapel in which all three of us were wed. They did not understand, however, that my God lived in forests, not the caves of these sinners' buildings. But not being so foolish as to argue about God to thus be expelled from the household as a Lutheran, I did well attend services with my family. There came boredom again, though no desire had I to exchange the church choir for musical theater. More and more, however, I mentioned mountains.

Eventually I became better at this married life, if only because a quantity of Elsie's oil for cooking plant life I kept near the bed to dip the husband in too often each evening with no explanation to the servant and none dared sought. Occasionally Miss Elsie slipped over to the Rathel's to visit the local servant populace. Always did Rathel herself well meet the miss for news of the young marrieds, though no direct query was made as to the quantity of Eric's phalli. All was bliss according to Elsie, and never did she report to me of her former superior's achieving either frenzy or joy to learn of our household's fine condition, of Eric's continued wholeness. Then the other raft of relatives became subject in our tenement, for a side of this family existed apart from my (my?) own.

"Mrs. Denton," Eric offered one evening before molesting me throughout the night, "I am considering presenting ourselves to my parents' house to demonstrate how excellent a life we have achieved. Upon comprehending my safety and happiness, Father will not refer to you in the wicked manner as before, but well apologize in his goodness."

"Bless us all, sir, for your father's goodness, a mendacity so vast as to cure the world of its unkind emotions. But if you recall, Mr. Edward's previous characterizations of me were accurate. He might therefore apologize for what? After all, you were the one to steal his dog."

"He might have described the events about you with some accuracy, but no understanding existed in his descriptions of you. His talk was of murder and evil, whereas you are all sweetness and virtuous living—excluding your starving your only husband and raving on about hill land and the like."

"Sir, I am distressed not by your father's misconstruing me. But if ever again he applies to his son the hatred he displayed in this flat, I shall slap a sense of Jesus into his sinning mouth."

"Please, Alba, you speak of my father."

"Condemn not my mild words, sir. I would have said that I shall fuck him with my witch's cunt and snip him off at the balls, but did not in that he is my husband's father."

"And praise God you did not, woman, for such talk would have sickened me," Eric replied, and began a shaking of his head as though to jar my words loose from his ears.

"Make your own plans, sir, for our being received at the Dentons' household. During this visitation, if one befalls us, I shall remain most ladylike, for here I am glib and capable. But presume suffering, for what if we have not waited time enough for your parents to have accepted our connubiality? What gain in achieving nothing but your weeping, for which I, in my vast unkindness, shall berate you? Is your life so lacking in excitement that you seek parental agony? Am I not the one bored in

494

this household, whereas you and the pets are ever amused?"

"And how is it you are bored, miss?"

"Missus."

"How is it you are bored, missus, in that the suffering of your prior life should have provided you with excitement to last for at least one full marriage?"

"I am bored, sir, because women do not ejaculate," I retorted. But before he could implement his gender's endless capacity therein, the wife walked her dog for the evening.

After church one Sunday came a person to our door, most unusual in that the few visitors to our home were salesmen of useless household implements, except for the one so practical as to provide me with an instrument for his castration, in that his wares were razors for shaving. These vital business folk never appeared on the Sabbath for fear of being stricken to death by Jesus, no doubt, though other days were scarcely less provocative considering Elsie's commendable threats of sending Randolph's teeth directly into their goods or their guts. But the person coming that Sunday had most durable goods, so it seemed, in that Eric after opening the door grasped the man with an embrace I rarely allowed him, this entwining followed by glad speaking and happy laughter. And after the husband greeted his guest, the wife had a cackle to see Lord Andrew.

The gent was well set within our home, Elsie fulfilled to be serving tea to so fine a relative. To begin his conversing, Andrew stated his difficulty in finding us.

"For a month I've been asking Edward to describe your location clearly, but for some reason he has been unable. Finally I contacted Amanda Rathel, who has a better memory than my son. But at my age, this memory of mine is the least reputable of all. Forgive me, Eric, but I can scarcely recall attending the wedding myself, as though I were never present."

Though Lord Andrew's disposition was cordial, Eric knew to reply without humor.

"But, sir, could the world's greatest grandfather miss my life's only wedding? And how do you find your tea, Grand?"

Since Eric had demonstrated sufficient tact for an entire family, the conversation proceeded with ease. After a certain expected chatting regarding Eric's business, including Lord Andrew's pondering why Eric no longer was employed by his father, the guest quit this area of potential discomfort by asking the recently-wed couple how their life together proceeded.

"As perfectly as possible, Grand," Eric replied, "what with the unenvious and utterly gracious lady of the household—we are so fortunate to have Miss Elsie." And Lord Andrew laughed heartily as I made to throw my tepid tea against the heathen husband's face.

"In fact," Eric continued, "Alba herself is exactly descriptive of my life, and that is perfect, sir; though the wife makes implications of boredom, which I can scarcely comprehend."

Andrew then became nearly agitated as he looked up sharply from his saucer to declare, "But of course, the lass is correct! A lady's life is one of boredom when her husband works at his employment constantly. And knowing young Eric, he doubtless neglects his wife's affections."

After choking on my tea or those words, I introduced Lord Andrew to this man who was certainly not the young Eric he knew, offering next to display all the welts secured directly by Eric's affection.

"Then surely what you need, Alba," Lord Andrew replied after the men's laughter had subsided, "is to rest from this affection, and vacation on the sea. Yes, child, you and Eric must come sailing with me."

Eric then clapped his hands together as though at an opera's climax or one of his own, replying to his grandfather, "The idea you present is superlative, Grand, and most thankfully received."

"I hope you will find it so, Eric, in that a great interval has passed since last you sailed with me. I would also hope that the young wife will appreciate the notion."

"But of course she does," delighted Eric promised as he looked to me. "Constant are her expressions of love for the out of doors and wild land. What could be more wild and out than the English Channel?"

"Penstone Place," I muttered.

"But, Alba, you seem less than enthralled," Eric noticed. "I have seen you in the water, missus. Have you a specific aversion to the salt variety?"

"Sir, the ocean I well love—when standing at its edge. But I am incapable of being upon its expanse, for I have a great aversion toward drowning."

"You jest, ma'am," Eric returned. "I have seen you . . . swim . . . most spectacularly."

"Sir, that swimming you witnessed was each moment a struggle for my life not to be taken by water. With Lord God reading the deepest truths of my heart, I swear that no greater terror inhabits my dreams than the fear of being beneath water forever, and forever there being dead."

Eric was staring at me, reading my deepest truths, perhaps, staring at me with a neutral visage as he silently, profoundly accepted the latest lesson of his missus.

"Ah, and what a pity I find here, dear Alba," Andrew responded. "And this is no fear to be overcome?"

"No, sir, not within my allotted lifetime. Nonetheless, I truly thank you for the offer, and hope my incompatibility with water will not erode our felicitous bond."

"Never, Alba, for no decent man would fail to appreciate so comely and authentic a lass, no more than a poorly-remembering elder could forget her."

Into the sea of his tea Eric was now looking, and did he find me in this ocean? Was I the lemon slice perilous on the cup's edge, in some future to slide down the porcelain beach and be lost in the pekoe?

"Please, Lord Andrew, continue your warm and welcome conversing by speaking of those boats with which you are familiar."

"Familiar, missus," Eric responded, forging a new trail in our talking. "Why, this gentleman owns them."

"But a few," came Lord Andrew's modest reply.

His interest in this conversation improving, Eric mentioned a veritable fleet, boats small and large, including the grand Queen's Flight.

"This Queen's Flight might be especially what, sir?" I inquired of Lord Andrew.

"The Queen's Flight is a vessel of *proportion,* Alba. A ship of twelve masts and great grace in the water, of thousands of tons and many more thousands of knots of experience on the seas."

"The boat is very large, Alba, one rigged for sailing the deepest oceans," Eric added; and I could sense his desire to be speaking with Grand and me, though only now was he regaining the ability, so moved had he been by my . . . swimming.

"To what end, might I ask?" was my inquiry to either gentleman.

"Most recently to supply the American colonies with further populace and items for their living," Andrew replied.

"I have heard mention of this region, Lord Andrew," I continued, "but know not its nature."

"The politics might interest you," Andrew ventured.

"Preferably I would learn of the area's exotic animals and wild lands rather than be inundated with social implications, if you please. Have you lived there, sir?" I asked of Grand.

"I have not, Alba, in that the Americas are lands for younger folk—especially you. Since the societies there lack the sophistication and elegance of England, so virtuous and thinking a lady could only benefit their culture. There are cities and towns in the colonies, but none as great as London. As for wilds, why, there are more wild lands and more wondrously varied than all of England and the European continent. America is a land of deserts and forests, of mountains and tremendous lakes, of endless fields and infinite canyons."

Then I turned to Eric and ordered, "We depart tomorrow."

"Very well, missus," he replied, "but you will have to walk, in that you'll not allow yourself on shipboard."

"You'd best wait, my child, until you gain your sea legs," Andrew offered, "for walking those thousands of miles through the ocean might be most wearisome."

"I can well imagine," I said, then had to set my tea down because the liquid there bade me drown, a sea in my own home containing Marybelle and Mother. Too much of Eric's concern with . . . swimming . . . had emigrated to the colony of his wife.

The visit concluded with less weighty emotions, Lord Andrew's departure a privation to our family. I later asked Eric of the expense of this Queen's Flight type of vessel, and whether the impoverished might own one. Utterly not, in their great costliness, he replied. Then I inquired why we had not sought funds from Grand instead of Rathel, and whether potential existed for our procuring additional moneys if required from him. No, Eric answered, for then my father would hate both me and Grand.

Not until that evening and our own bed came mention of the remnants of that conversation, an early segment to have set the husband toward lasting distress.

Tightly had I wrapped my dressing gown about me as we lay in the dark, an abnormal state of attire in that usually Eric sat at my corpus with his own while I was yet in waking clothes. The source of Eric's restraint soon became evident.

"Of all the blatant torments you have calmly described from your past, I had no sufficient notion that your being in water was near their equal."

"Rather would I move through water than lose another body part; so though uncomfortable and haunting, the activity is not the ultimate distress."

"But when your dreams are nightmares, is the water not torture within that realm? Yes, it is, I know without your answering. Well have I come to understand this, Alba, by your change of voice and the difference in your eyes. And if you had not so abolished tears from me, I would now be weeping against you; for you are my wife and my love, and no pain is worthy of the one I hold most dear. So if in my sleep you notice me weep, understand I shall attempt to control this weakness, but moreover understand that my thoughts and love then are all for you."

Eric then rolled onto his side to face away from me. But within this marriage, Eric was not alone in connubial comprehension, for I as well had knowledge of my spouse. Eric, in his intended generosity, would not be having sex with me that night.

499

Not easily did I achieve sleep, in that my routine was disrupted because my buttocks were not. But eventually I arrived at slumber, well pleased to have sensed no tears from Eric.

And dream I did. Having tea with Edward, I often fell into my cup, and how delighted was Eric's father to see me nearly drown. But seldom was enough liquid in the cup to submerge me, and when the tea tide was high, I always landed upon the lemon rind, which floated and conveyed me near the colonies, as near as Eric, who did his best not to weep because the sour fruit burned my skin, he knew, and never before had he understood the torment of my life of eating no meat. Disembarking from the rind, I found myself upon a bed with twelve posts that rocked to and fro, for not enough sails had I to protect me from a hot wind that cut through me from head to groin, stabbed me like a corn cob, an arm with bark, a . . .

God alone could know the dream Eric was snatched from by my heart beating upon his shoulder, having pulled my baby slot away from his ready man stick, which had entered me normally but most unacceptably. And when Eric awakened enough to see and gasp and cower, I told the fool that I had not become his mother and thus could have no man named Eric inside my cunt without killing him, and finding oneself dead was no way to wake in the morning. Shake him I did most harshly until he acknowledged my words, that the loss from his taking me so would not be his pleasure, but his blood, literally his bleeding life; and did the beggar understand? Yes, missus, yes he did; anything to end the shouting and bruising, good evening to you, over he rolled and to sleep.

The next day I invented a new type of clothing, an inelegant rag to be wrapped about me before each night's sleeping, tied so as not to be removed without my knowledge. And as for inconvenience: Well, the husband would simply have to eject all of the lust from his system before the wife settled to slumber, lest he get all the blood out instead. But before I awoke to become a seamstress to Elsie's great curiosity, I dreamed. Of course, I dreamed again.

Insufficient clothes had I in my floating armoire to prevent sailors from populating my colony with their mizzenmasts, though I repelled most with the loudest tea in the wilds, that region settled by the one successful sailor being a new land less social than England, for he jibed me from the stern, not the sternum.

In this manner my life proceeded. Few thoughts had I of any past existence, preferring to wish for some superior life beyond the drudgery of London. But I could think of none, no specific world of nature, for what wild land would fit me now that I had a family? Would Elsie revert to eating lizards? Could Eric build so fine a timber cave as Marybelle? And how long would Randolph last before drowning in a bog? Neither could I abandon these friends, for so authentic was my love for them that truly they comprised a family; and this witch would accept no life, not even in Paradise, in which she was alone.

So bored I became that I nearly espoused the contest of needlework. Grandly satisfying herself by being too much of a servant for this family, Elsie walked through her chores as though a witch through a forest. Unlike the latter type of human, however, Elsie in any empty interval would settle with metal shard and thread to manufacture doilies and other flat constructions that the mistress was sure to insist she well loved draped all over her home. Soon I observed, however, that part of this activity was stabbing oneself occasionally in the finger — and was this not as bad as shaving? What tortuous metallic challenge of the sinning world would I next discover enamored them: eating coins? Fornicating with wood stoves?

So bored I became as to look forward to Eric's daily return so that we could torment each other with jest. But all my felicity was ruined the day I looked through the front window to see Eric on the street with his arms about another woman. Eric was embracing her absolutely, in a manner not allowed with me, and with equal intensity they were weeping, weeping and fruitlessly attempting to converse. Perhaps their failed speaking was not due to tears, but sourced from their foreignness; for were they not different types of persons, as though sinner and witch? Finally Eric with gentility pressed the woman away, and

501

with tears she departed, Eric turning to the steps and waiting, waiting until his face was dry before moving up to his tenement; for tears were not allowed with his wife as they were with his mother.

Poorly he concealed his distress, but I made no notice, attempting to respond to him normally. No explanation was given by the husband nor questions asked by the missus. And we retired that evening with none of that man smell from Eric and no penetration, for the first day in our wedded life Eric not making love with me, not even in his dreams.

"Surely, madam, you are neither so wealthy nor unkind as to refrain from granting this minor request."

"But I cannot contemplate why a lady such as yours would be seeing herself upon a rough and common wagon as mine."

"As heretofore provided in explanation, I have need of conveyance; yet despite my apparent social position, mine is a state of financial stress. Therefore, I offer you this coin to allow me to ride with you on your return journey from London."

"But, ma'am, I am taking to my farm these bad fish behind to help in growing things, and they are smelling now and will be doing it worse. And to ride beside me on this coarse seat of wood you might rip your fine dress, or worse, be seen by your social friends or minister."

"Enough discussion," I told this woman near ugly enough to be a witch, though none of their smell had she, and witches are never fat, as was she, extremely, in that they do not eat to excess, nor smoke, as did she, extremely. "Are we a pair of politicians going at each others' ears with inconsequential and repetitious words of scant content?" And up I clambered beside her. "Or are we but womenfolk about our affairs, you returning to your home, and I to Gravesbury Reach? The latter we are, and here is my coin and my words of thanks for your conveyance." Then, after pressing the money into her palm, I settled beside her, staring firmly ahead as though we were under way. With a tremendous sigh as though releasing all the pressure from the fat within her, this woman with word and gentle strap encouraged her elder horse to proceed.

As though animals, we went without speaking, the driver soon proving herself accurate in assessing my position. After a length of Hollet Street and a turn at Missingmile Avenue, we passed a person who well stared at me, for there was Theodosia rendered static by my sight. Though with that wide opening of her mouth she seemed fit for extensive speaking, the servant had no verbal response, as though weakened by the sight of an angel, barely managing to lift her hand toward me as I waved and heartily smiled.

And a fine ride it was, up in the air and open to all sensations, the rich smell of decaying fish following along as though a friendly pet traipsing after master. As though never before in London, I gained an unusual awareness of the society about me, understanding that these lovers and those businessmen all had families of their own, and when not on the streets, they were in their homes as though alternate worlds. Even the drunkards living in shrubs had families, though surely lost. Although proceeding out of the city, I had no feeling of quitting, for how could I forsake these families when one was mine? My intent was no more than respite, for I was on a morning's vacation. But abandoning London remained my true desire: not the physical means, but the emotional logistics.

"I am now to desert you here, miss?" the large woman confronted me. "All that is here is nothing. No persons pass near here except to pass by. And how is it you will be returning?"

"Being rationally adult, I shall accept the responsibility for myself, though you can scarcely imagine the honor I gain by your positing yourself as my mother. Be off, then, woman, and pray you may find good use for my pence. . . . And I pray that despite my unkind and needless remark about my own beloved mother, you will accept the truth of my appreciation for your transport and your kindly concern."

Then I was alone. An increasingly fine state I was gaining, though the woman's ending apprehension had nearly destroyed my prayerful pride in having survived another bridge. How strong I had felt to be so high and exposed on naught but a plank above the river yet pass over with no panic, no death. True, for those minutes I had scarcely breathed, feeling that too great an intake of air would disrupt our travel and spill me into the water, which I did not view, though I smelled it, did not feel though it touched me everywhere. What a religious accomplishment the crossing was, and for minutes thereafter I could only praise the greatest Lord and God for allowing me to live through another river.

Not so intense was the smell of sinners here, though across the Thames some massed construction was barely seen, between us a distance I cherished; for although not the same substance as that beyond Lucansbludge, it was more enrichening than the materialistic air above the Rathel's roof. Cleaner was the river here, lightly rippled by a breeze. Every swell I viewed, those beyond smaller as their distance from the observer increased, though each ripple seemed immediate, the separation of their quiet lives not removal, but a connection via God's glorious substance of space. Some activity I could sense far beyond, plumes of smoke from sinners, boat on the Thames, but none was strong in my experience. Behind, too ensconced on a sinners' roadway to be as wild as I, wagons passed as the woman said, gone without coming near. These as well I ignored until one approached to bring the Lady Rathel.

She formed her own space, instructing the coachman to move away, this distance to segregate the greater society of London from Rathel's particular life. The mistress then approached her daughter, a murderous witch not evil enough for the demon lady.

"You have come for a swim, then, madam," I spoke, "or might I hope you've dreams of drowning yourself?"

No reply had the Rathel for my smiled greeting, remaining calm as her norm. Then I saw her as never before, measuring the woman as though only now fully able to discern sinners. How remarkably young she appeared for all her living, but was her life not mainly of arrangements for other people to live and die? How handsome was this lady, even in her middle life, the short lives of sinners come and gone like a cut witch's tit. Well

504

could I understand how she had drawn men to herself—wealthy Franklin, vivid Edward—for despite all their feigned, Godly spiritualism, were sinners not a people to send body after body, passion after lust? How mundane for so well souled a race.

"Why is he not dead?" the social lady asked. "Why have you not proven yourself the witch I know you? Why does the bastard live?"

"Oh, and Mistress Amanda, never have I heard you curse. Lie, yes, and here again is your favorite trait; for the tremendous hatred you have is from Eric's legality, the very fact that from your baby slot he did not and could not issue."

"Much have you learned of my life, meddling witch."

"Bless your compliment, dear mother. As for lives, importantly I have learned of mine. Never would I have done so except for your machinations that forced my education. Therein I learned of witches, and through experience, the white one. Learn I did how Satan kills through them, and also how any man might survive."

"Not forever will this bastard avoid your sex. Kill him, witch, and depart from London. Sleep with him and be done with us all."

"Oh, but lady, sleeping kills no one. Not even your wretched soul could supply nightmares intense enough to kill. What you mean is another obscenity: You mean 'fuck.' But, mistress, this man is my husband and well we mate and often. Extraordinarily often, so I understand, compared to common women. But this woman is not common. She is the witch and the white witch to draw men to her cunt and consume them. But this joy you've expected for years I now deny you. Eric is drawn to my sex better than any man, for I allow and encourage his coupling in that the fine person is thereby pleased. But I have learned how the husband can avoid the deadly baby slot. Instead, the target allowed is the anus. Yes, Amanda, a man is perfectly safe fucking any witch within her arse's hole, and therein does Eric gain great ecstasy from me. Every night, often, and often in a dead sleep. So accomplished am I at saving my husband that even when he sticks his prick you would love on your mantel against the wrong entry, he finds a closed hole

505

he may not enter. Then to the rear does he march, and well up into my arse I take him, allowing his stick to wallow until his baby seed is accelerated far within me. So much of his seed I accept that it becomes my own fluid. To absorb his sperm makes me smile, mistress, if only because I can now spit his semen at you." And, yes, I spat at the Rathel's feet, though languidly, as though she were scarcely worth the effort.

At once she leapt toward me with a fury never seen, worse than during that clock beating, because then her abilities were tempered by drink, but here she was all hatred. But my front she faced now, so upon reaching out to strike me dead, the lady met my fingers. Both my palms I thrust to her cheeks and jaws, knocking Rathel to her backside. From this position, the startled sinner looked up to me as I commented on her situation.

"I suggest, lady, that you not assault a British citizen, lest Queen Anne herself spit in your direction."

"You Satanic bitch!" Rathel shouted, appearing less than the lady for sitting on her virgin arse in the dirt. "I will have you be what you are. You will kill the Eric bastard or your perverted arse shall be the soot beneath my mantel. Kill the bastard or I'll prove you the witch. I shall prove that you murdered Bitford to gain transport out of London, and murdered Cameron because he discovered your identity. I will have you burned without beheading, bitch, so that long you will suffer, more than you ever dreamed, more than your mother."

Being a lady, I replied mildly while straightening my cuffs, "Of course you shall, dear mistress, as soon as you teach Lord Naylor to become so complete a fool that he will overlook your pimping deaths. Wherever a man died by my body, you were the cause. Aware of your expertise in witches, all of London will believe that you ever understood me the killer. So tell your tale, Amanda, and you will die in more pieces than I. Until you choose your own suicide, become accustomed to Eric's happy life." And I stepped away with a smile, gesturing for the distant driver to return his charge to her home, to her dedicated hell.

Thirty-three

Days later, the Rathel attacked. Through the window I viewed two men with grave visages clomping up the stairs, one with fingers on his jerkin and a thumb lodged in his belt, the other leaning on a scabbard with his elbow as though the knife were a walking stick supporting his upper body. More descriptive of these males than their extremities was their attire, those jerkins and peaked hats signifying the magistrate's constables.

Elsie at her needlework well heard the sound of feet, but preferred in her uncertainty to wait for the additional noise of rapping. Like the dog, I could not wait passively. As Randolph set to his barking, I set to the door, opening the poor barrier to our home before it was violated.

"Might you have an exalted morning, gentlemen," I greeted the pair upon opening the door with their rapping hands hanging startled in the air. After the males tipped their hats and nodded, the scabbard leaner spoke.

"And well we might, mistress, with God's grace and your co-operation."

"Gracious you are to align me with Lord God as though we functioned together instead of I in His servitude as is the truth of my life."

"Very well, ma'am, and thank you for church this morning, but our business is the magistrate Sir Jacob Naylor, as we are his men, and come we did to inquire of the Eric Denton."

"A person currently at his employ, as you are, a person also my spouse, as you are not. Therefore, might your business with the Eric Denton be told his humble wife?"

"The concern placed before Magistrate Naylor is by one

507

Lady Amanda Rathel, that the Eric Denton has made himself indebted to this person and does now refuse to pay her in return what is due. Therefore, might we ask you his place of employ in that there we speak with him of things?"

"And if in distress from indebtedness my memory is so poorly returned as to negate my awareness of his profession, do I thereby incur your doubt?"

"No, missus, not doubt we achieve from you, but suspicion. And for incurring your humor shall we provide you with the true consideration your husband's debt deserves." And with a hat tip and head nod, the men quit my stairs.

The first consideration, however, was distress from Miss Elsie.

"Oh, and Miss — Mistress — Alba, am I not believing what I hear, for how is it the lady herself is invoking such a turn? Is her business going so bad that she's rendered poor and in need of every pence for survival?"

"As I have ever told you, miss, the problem is Eric's survival, for Rathel now comprehends that the man shall continue living. Therefore, she seeks to expel her wrath from failure as last she did upon my head. Perhaps that damage you have forgotten, Elsie. I have not."

"Oh, and Alba, what next is occurring with this funding? Are prison cells not made for paupers?"

"No, miss, made for paupers are special prisons with great spaces folk can mill about within. Cells like stone boxes are for witches and murderous women, but not for dogs and servants. These pets simply wander to the next house in the neighborhood."

"And are we waiting, now, for the master to return before great worry?"

"In fact, miss, have you not begun this response without him?"

But we had little waiting for any emotion, for soon to our abode came a pair of men last seen toting our belongings, now climbing our steps with new strength and a pair of constables met only hours before.

508

"And we come with paper, Mrs. Denton, as writ by Queen Anne's man the magistrate Sir Jacob Naylor and signed by he, upon which certain items are described and an order of us to be taking them as unpaid for."

At once I moved aside, waving for the sinners to enter, for I'd not be taken away instead of furniture due to my interference. Randolph bounced about the males' feet as though to aid them, so only Elsie was left to wail.

"Oh, Lord Jesus! To be taking a miss's dowry is most grievous and ungodly!" And damned if she did not step between the carrying men to block their path, clinging to the armoire as though varnish. But since no prisons existed for servants, but yea for folk denying constables their duty, I pulled her away from the traffic of men and furniture through the flat, then spoke with the woman.

Guiding the weeping miss to her chamber, I offered, "Ah, Elsie, what a fine opportunity we now have to move into the wilds as I have ever desired. How easy shall your life become when your only caretaking is for the one small cave and its single room."

Such a commotion transpired from Elsie that no ending could I achieve. Therefore, I left her with Randolph, and observed the pillaging of my (my?) home.

Outside the master's chamber, the two men of transport fiercely whispered while glimpsing within, attempting not to look toward the constables some distance removed. The carrying pair examined a paper, and here the witch could read their thoughts. They well recalled those weeks past and the recuperation required from manipulating that oaken tree in the guise of a sleeping instrument. Therefore, when the constables approached them to ask whether that bed were a piece written as to be taken, the transporters as though stuck with a pin or a pious revelation perked up to commence a denial while lowering the paper and stepping away from the room, down the stairs with them all.

The bed's salvation scarcely helped Miss Elsie settle into our lately threadbare flat. Painfully she wondered of Eric's knowledge of this predicament, wondered how he would react to see this barrenness. With outstretched arms, she longingly looked about at the space between our walls. Soon, however, we learned of Eric's exact response; for another pair of men we heard talking and walking up our affronted stairs, and one of them was the master.

Only this family person entered. The second male completed pleading his position, then returned to his jewelry store; for of this shop was he proprietor, and of the entire building owner. During his ending speech, he begged for Eric's understanding, for his bankers were insistent upon having his own debts called immediately due if the debtor above were not made to vacate the premises paid for with funds not his own.

A dreary master entered his former household to describe the family's new position.

"So generous is our manager that he shall allow our scant possessions to remain in the flat until tomorrow noon. So insistent were the bankers, however, that our bodies must be vacated by dark, for the constables at evening will come to clear the place of any persons remaining."

"We live on the street, then," I affirmed, "for a person of my wilderness knowledge can well teach her family to survive the pavements."

"No, missus, we do not," Eric sighed. "For at least one day, we shall present ourselves at my grandfather's house and allow him to aid us as well he would love."

"Then away we are," I affirmed again, "taking only what our figures wear, in that little can we pack for walking."

"No, missus," Eric sighed. "The distance is too great for us to walk."

"Not likely, sir, can I make arrangements as per my previous journey where a person's wagon was found in my path and gained for mere pence."

"What pence we have, we save," Eric added. "In advance I shall hire a carriage, and pay the fare upon our arrival, as borrowed from Grand."

"And I'm praying the man be home when you arrive," Elsie

prayed, "so as no further difficulty become you. As well I'm praying the Mistress Amanda will not be taking me in harshly when I retreat there, for in the past she has been decent to me."

Turning sharply to the husband, I demanded, "Sir, do we burden Lord Andrew with our pets?"

"We do not abandon our family, missus, neither to the Rathel nor to the streets. Instead, we allow my grandfather the generosity that is prideful to him as a gentleman, and present ourselves, all four."

"Oh, and please, Master Eric, do not be letting this dull woman so drag you —"

"This woman shall continue as our servant by determining with the missus what items we might take along, in that this task is one too many for me," Eric stated. Then he quit our major, former room, moving to one away from all family members except the dog, for Randolph would best accept his sorrow.

So pleased was Lord Andrew by our coming to him in our need that he nearly dragged the entire family into his fine home, paying the driver with his own hand perhaps too generous a gratuity, as though the transporter were responsible for our visit, as though he sought us out. What, then, would Grand pay in tribute to Lady Rathel, who had sent us here by happenstance, in that her true goal was jail — or Hell? Our only explication to Lord Andrew was that we were less than fortunate in moving from the former homesite, having been caught without a roof — and might we stay the day?

"I defy you to leave," he smiled happily, and welcomed us aboard.

Our family was provided with two chambers, Elsie situated in so grand a suite that she felt herself a queen, and felt herself weep. Such guilt she expressed to Lord Andrew's servants that they had no poor feelings toward her, despite their base lodgings. Being unfamiliar with his surrounds, the dog could

511

not decide which chamber to select. After much panting and prancing to and fro between those of his family, he bounded away, taking as his run the entire house.

Fed sublimely was this family, except Elsie, who insisted upon eating with the servants in the kitchen, in her cowardice running there instead of remaining to argue with me. The witch who had banished burned creatures from her own home nearly fainted onto the plate while picking for potatoes and peas, though so strong and brave she was that no puking ensued. Delirious were the males of the family for the same fleshy reasons, so grateful that not the first hurt glimpse was proffered the mistress.

What fine relaxation we had with our bellies filled with beast meat as we sat before the fireplace and gazed at the flames. None of these satisfactions for the witch, however, for she had eaten only vegetable slivers, avoiding their accompanying grease called gravy. And not near the flames retained only by an upward draft and God's grace would she sit, so far removed that none of its heat could be directly felt, so turned away as to see nothing burning in that square cave. What a terrible entity was fire when not contained by a solid metal stove—and what a sinner I had become to be lustful of iron. But neither did the husband gain relaxation, for with all of Lord Andrew's insistence upon the boy's remaining till babies were born and grew to adulthood, Eric was not a man with new lodgings, but a husband who had lost his home.

A demon was amongst us. Though from my corner I saw no flames, Randolph luxuriating before the fireplace provided me with the sight of sparks alighting on his coat, unfelt, and the smell of hide made unnaturally warm, thus emphasizing my belief that the beast, too long in society, had become a sinner.

In this manner our life proceeded. Since Eric retained employment, there he hied the morning after our first night of sleeping in a strange bed not so unusual as to preclude the husband from lustily coupling with my buttocks. Not so supportive of sex was this handsome bed as our own, however; for although sturdy as a whole, one piece was a threat, a particular

512

post so loose that all of Eric's repeated journeys within my tunnel had it totter side to side as though a sinner's testicles, implying that it might topple upon us. And please, Lord God, let it fall upon the male and put him to sleep and me to rest.

In the morning with Eric gone, Elsie became another worker out in the city, she and certain of Lord Andrew's male servants traveling in a hired wagon to return with our personal belongings from the former flat, bringing all but the gigantic bed, for no men animal enough had Grand to carry it. Therefore, Elsie returned in failure, she believed, having brought the family's artifacts, but leaving their greatest treasure. Pooh, I told her. You should have seen the handbuilt chamber pot I had to abandon in the wilds, and you worry about a stack of planks? Consider all the master's heinous, lustful fluids to have floated this bed as though a boat, then rethink your desire for that incarnate, oaken passion. Thereupon, Miss Elsie found such shame in my speaking that doubtless she wished the mistress to have been left behind instead of the furniture, and how wise was the witch to ease her friend's sorrow.

When the husband returned that evening, he displayed a pleasant countenance instead of brooding on his dread, a natural response considering his homeless state, the failure to provide for his new family, and social so on. Taking me aside, Eric told of the latest developments re our illegalities.

"I have arranged with the magistrate's financiers to end my indebtedness to Lady Rathel via my current employment. She would have us all in prison, but England's laws are more reasonable."

"Should we then subtly mention to Lord Andrew, rich in his money and generous love, that coins spilled upon our persons would be regarded?"

"Do you desire, ma'am, to experience a repeat of that event held between my father and myself on our doorstep?"

No word was spoken of Eric and his mother on the stair's bottom, but the event mentioned was enough to have me answer, "No, and sir, I do not. Nevertheless, the fault here is trebly yours. First, for marrying from lust instead of love; second, for wedding a witch though warned in advance by unique and suffocating proof of her identity; and third, for not accepting the wife's idea of withdrawing to the wilds and being away from Rathel's madness and your parents' incorrect emotions."

"Recently I have applied some thought to your wilderness, missus, and no longer find the notion fit for ridicule."

My only reply was, "Sir . . . ?"

"Mark this day well, Alba, for therein you have failed to reply elaborately to an idea of interest," Eric observed. "But to proceed beyond your graceless, open-mouthed staring: I continue to consider the utter wilderness unappealing; that is, residing beneath bushes. But a type of simple cabin in the vicinity of acceptable foodstuffs . . . perhaps. After all, you and your mother lived for years in this manner and endured. I am not unlike you in certain respects."

"Not in respect to being a witch."

"These persons eat differently than I have since our marriage?"

"Have you spoken with Elsie about me and insects?"

"Missus, you would sicken me when I speak gravely? Do you say I must consume crawling bugs once stepping beyond London's bounds?"

"No, sir, and forgive me for my comedy. In fact, abundant are the foods to eat in the wilds, and well I know the nourishing plant life most sinners would pass by even if starving."

"And if these sinners did not pass by, but stopped to dine, would they expire whereas the witch would not?"

"Perhaps regarding certain forms; but, then, we would have Miss Elsie for experimentation."

"One severe failure and she would be dead, leaving us without further studies."

"One severe failure of our genders and you would be dead, and this family without employ. But another method of wild living is applicable to us, since we are not known as witches. Without need to conceal ourselves, we might reside near enough farms to have available those common eatings that sinners desire."

514

"Being near farms, could I not slip away for a rib on occasion?"

"You could return with fatty flesh on your breath to find yourself in bed with Miss Elsie."

"At least with her I could procure that normal sort of sex I've known only by accident with you and for a moment."

"But you would have no benefit of her buttocks except for deriding you upon mentioning them in the same sentence as your maleness."

Due to my arse's being unavailable, Eric set upon my mouth with his, willfully pressing his tongue against mine; and in his breath was passion, as well as some fat from breakfast. Rarely did I allow the male within me so, but return his moves I did, holding his head as he held mine, my tongue dancing within his mouth, and so on. The satisfaction I achieved, however, was not of sex, but of my emotions; for as the husband well loved this kissing, I was pleased to satisfy him, though such generosity could not last forever. Not with a witch.

Pulling away from the slobbering sinner, I remarked as would any unenvious lady.

"I think you would find this well worth a lack of dead beast in your diet, for no meat will you find more alive than mine. But let us end this facial sucking, lest master or servant discover us and you suffer a sinner's embarrassment."

"Embarrassment from kissing? Since we are wed, kissing is no great shame if pursued within the bounds of one's home and not in broad and public places."

"True, but I doubt you would have any part of London gain a view of your pants with that current peak, for without looking, I notice lustful fumes rising from a certain lump."

Then Eric looked down, arranging his little limb and clothing so that the former was barely noticeable by sight.

"What a nose you have, missus. Some use might be found for this talent."

"Please, sir, be satisfied with the sex you achieve with the rest of my portions, and leave one part of my body in peace."

Thereafter, we proceeded with our business of appearing

515

pleased with our lives, although impoverished and without home, although pursued by the Satanic Rathel. For the witch, at least, the ongoing task came with less effort because of the future, a superior life suggested by the husband, a life removed and wild. Then I wondered of a more immediate future, when Eric was without debt and again we might settle in a home our own. How likely would that home be in London rather than in God's natural world?

Contemplating a wild life implied but not likely supplied by the husband was my main activity in the following days. Soon my pondering turned to moping, my concerns continuing one evening as I sat with the husband well away from the fire. So established was this dejection that it remained until driven away by visitors, family members so social as to bring hatred to their kin.

Thirty-four

To the door came paired guests well entered by a servant of Lord Andrew, and pleasant was their discourse to this chamberlain until as pleasantly he mentioned that their son was present.

Ah, the silence of unsettled hearts, the stillness of the racing brain. And the oblivion of innocence. As though the walking dead unable to lift their feet, Mr. and Mrs. Denton dragged themselves to the drawing room, led by the servant who pleasantly called out the visitors' introduction. Dull, dull were these people, as was their son, who forgot how to breathe those moments. Happy Grand, however, was all spritely as he moved to his guests and fully embraced them. How pleasant to be holding zombies, I thought, for the wife was stiff, Edward more of a torso than a son. Here Lord Andrew seemed another dog, for Randolph also knew these folk, running to them while yapping his love. Down to him both visitors stared, thereby avoiding a deeper look into the room, toward the son and his wife. Toward the witch and her man. Was natural Andrew so innocent of society's policies that he could only yap happily to his family when he should be separating its members? No segregation here, for Grand with a hand on either back pressed Hanna and Edward into the drawing room toward those other social folk.

Eric rose as though drawn from the grave, for dead he was to this meeting. Being tutored in etiquette, his wife remained seated, though she was certainly no lady with that smile, a

517

common expression as brazen as a cackle considering that fiends should display only shame.

"Come, come—all of you now!" Andrew called out brightly as he pressed the moving zombies toward their static son. "I am aware that some differences lie amongst you young folk, but for this evening, let us well rejoice in our common love, and allow any discord to settle." He then had the mother embrace her boy—and how loving these two sacks of meat were, rubbing as though mutually allergic. Then father and son were made to clasp hands, but could they even feel each other with that limp connection? All of this was colder than my holding Marybelle's head to my crotch, for at least one of us had been alive.

Unsocial was Lord Andrew to have the lady greeted last, but she was so far removed, though truly central. No more than the slightest nod and bow I received from Hanna and Edward. I, at least, had the courtesy to call to them each a good evening; and here the salutations ended. As soon as the latest Dentons faced me, Randolph ran to his new mistress as though to ask whether he were yet part of her family, in that the previous seemed to have abandoned him. Though his coat remained hot from the fire, his spirit was warm from his love, and this I acknowledged, rubbing Randolph's neck and looking to him with a smile and with thanks for his genuineness, as Lord Andrew had the zombies seated.

Performing all the speech in this cemetery, Lord Andrew called for tea, then asked his son of business, how well the great cathedral was progressing, and how unfortunate that the grandson was no longer with him, continuing in his father's profession no more than the last had with his, but again setting out on his own. But, come, come, here was too much difference, since Eric was but an assistant to an accountant, and when would he return to his father's firm where he belonged?

"Please, Father," Edward urged in reply. "You must know better than to ask of such subjects. Ask for the tea again instead."

"Ah, but I need not request the tea twice, in that so well I

518

called the first instance that its delivery be assured. Perhaps I should ask better of family business, in that my initial mention did not receive comprehensive response."

"And exactly appropriate, Father," Edward returned, "in that the previous family business of rearing a son turned out to be a task poorly accepted by the youth."

"Drink your tea, Father," Eric remarked as the servant entered, "and rest your weary brain."

The chamberlain and his refreshments should have been a pause in the conversation, but such was the stress of the Dentons that their nerves never faltered, Hanna responding as a cup came toward her.

"Very well, Eric, then aid your father in his exhausted intellection by returning home where you belong—with your family."

"And poor my rearing would be if I were to forsake my current and truest family now that I've achieved a servant plus the pet to care for—oh, yes, and the single wife."

"End your jesting, son, and we can end your true difficulty," Edward added. "In this England are acceptable means for allowing you to return home gracefully. If you would leave this woman through a legal and understandable annulment, your difficulties would be ended."

"And therefore abandon the person I have selected above all others to live with forever?" Eric returned, his humor ended as requested. "You forget that I was born to you and your wife without being given the choice. But I would leave you and have done so rather than desert the greatest receptor of my love."

"Eric! Would you destroy your mother's soul by alleging to love this person more than she who gave you birth?" Hanna cried. "Would you lie to me and Jesus by saying that this woman could love you more than I?"

"Would you measure these respective loves as though accounts at a bank?" tense Eric returned. "The measure I make is not numerical, but emotional; for if Alba has never loved me more than you, she has never been so thoughtless as to engender my torment and call it love."

519

Quickly I rose from my chair to glimpse down to the tea at my side, then toward the congregation, the audience this witch had drawn.

"No lemon?" I inquired.

"In the weeks of this new life of yours," Edward said as though I had spoken no more than a painting on the wall, "she has worsened your ridiculous mind, for you believe that living with her is not dangerous."

"To be ridiculous, I must have been encamped in your surrounds," Eric answered, "since you have become the total fool." And Hanna gasped enough to choke. "How long must I live with this woman to prove that she brings no danger? The only damage in this marriage is from your foolish thinking and incorrect fears that each day my wife proves false."

"Evil does not always attack in a strike," Hanna averred, "but can increase in force as though a slow poison. Witness how that person more and more ruins our family."

"The poison consumed in this family is fear and by yourselves," Eric admonished. "So fully are you addicted to this sinister liquor that you foment its increase, for the poison is a hatred that fills you and which you find nourishing. And yet you continue your unhealthy beliefs, as though a religion wherein Lord God is not worshiped, but some devil."

"You sleep with a devil and call me a fool!" his father shouted.

"I sleep with an angel, previous sir, and since you've no experience beside my wife, I demand that you never again refer to her maliciously, for thereafter you will no longer be called Father by me."

"And you've not been my son since marrying your own death!" Edward shouted, his face a bluster.

So great was Edward's intensity in this conversation that his body shuddered with every word, his limbs forming inspecific gestures that signified distress. Sitting beside her husband, Hanna found herself but one gesticulation removed; for with Edward's quaking, she received blows on her shoulders sufficient to upset her carriage. But she moved no farther from him, for beyond she would be alone. Before the noisy pair could further devastate each other, the men were approached by three persons: Lord Andrew, who so much desired to smile; the young witch, who was taking her husband and cheerfully quitting this house; and the chamberlain, who gave notice that Lady Amanda Rathel had arrived.

An impoverished conglomerate was this to consider the provider of all their demons a relief. Only Lord Andrew's greetings, however, were as cordial as due a guest, though perhaps done too grandly, as though to relieve him of the previous operatic tension.

The lady had brought gifts, Andrew's servant guiding Rathel into the drawing room while bearing an intricate tray whose engraved and raised edges retained a pair of clear decanters, their contents of different hues. Rathel explained their intended dispensing in advance, her speech welcome, for none of the previous guests cared to hear more of their own anger.

"Allow me to apologize for my intrusion, while conceding how a portion was in fact intended. That is, I knew beforehand that the young wedded pair had come here as though in refuge. My purpose in following is not to justify their current difficulties, but my part therein. I would attempt to explain that my business was not intended to damage their happy marriage. Constables and financiers, however, apply themselves too strictly on occasion. But seeing that I now add to a present tension, I shall retain my justification. Instead, allow me to provide a thing to soothe us all and perhaps bond us together in relaxation. Being only drink, however, we cannot expect it to make all our lives as one, though it might make them a bit milder for this evening."

"Here, here," Lord Andrew responded agreeably, then lightly clapped his hands together, he the most appreciative member of the audience at this opera, at Rathel's overture.

"Very well, then," the mistress continued brightly, her speech surely a bout of acting, for the woman was vivacious only when gloating—but what cause had she for satisfaction? Was her plan to so drunken us all that we might set to one another

521

with clocks? "Here are my rare selections, seldom seen in this country." And she raised a decanter to pour a clear fluid; and what sort of mouth could a sinner have to blow a square bottle with facets? "From Siberia comes this vodka with its uncommon warmth of anise to restrain the spirits' strength. This for the Dentons: Hanna, Edward, and Eric." After filling three moderate metal chalices included on her tray, she proceeded to the next bottle. "From Persia, a liqueur made from figs, dark and sweet, but mild in its alcohol. This for the folks who should have a minimum of spirits: our senior, Lord Andrew, and Lady Amanda, who understands that her drinking itself must be rare, and our natural Alba, who imbibes only from etiquette."

Rathel then flitted about to deliver her spirits, which had begun to fume the room. "God bless you," she said to each person receiving a container, all but the last, who received instead a quiet warning.

"Drink not the entirety, Alba, in that liquor makes the true witch ill," and she gave me a small but thick glass. No metal.

Then to our general center did Rathel journey, lifting her hand with goblet and her voice with toast, one of family love in God's eyes, of marital satisfaction in peaceful homes beneath the watchful stare of England, and so on, up with their little buckets one and all, and well set to drinking did some. Not I, who would not render myself sodden despite distrusting Rathel's advice. Nevertheless, my drink smelled only subtly of spirits, being sweetly rich with the taste of liquid figs. I thus partook of a second swallow although the pledge had ended, thinking that this sipping would occupy me. But could I not have mimicked the drinking and retained a dry mouth? What guilt had I for being a witch who enjoyed her imbibing? Not alone was I in this fluid satisfaction, though supposedly alone in being a witch.

"This is most delicious," Edward submitted quietly, looking down to his rounded trough to sniff the fumes.

One sip later and the group began to separate as though a herd of creatures scattered about a pasture, as though a stew spread by the consuming child: fat to one side, vegetables another, meat directly into the mouth. The parental Dentons, so continually together as to be of one body, floated away from their son, Rathel espying a painting adjacent to the fireplace, having Lord Andrew join her for a view. Amanda then proudly mentioned a special piece, the portrait of Spanish royalty painted by a Portuguese master whose brushwork was most ferocious, as though attacking with his tools. Ah, but the Portuguese school characteristically employs this technique, Lord Andrew replied. Note, however, how this exceptional Iberian craftsman tempers his ferocity with fine layers of glazes that soothe the colors, and so on.

The best flotsam drifted my way. Looking to both sides to see that he was no longer surrounded, Eric slowly approached the wife, much to her satisfaction; for were not these folks of two but relatively similar minds? The traitorous dog followed the Rathel about, sniffing at her heels as though she had recently stepped on his girlfriend.

Eric and I stood as though imitating his parents, shoulders nuzzling as we leaned toward each other and whispered, vessels inches from our lips as though to conceal our words.

"Thoughts had I of escaping this dungeon," Eric said quietly with his liquor breath, "until coming aware that it now is our home."

"Escape is no matter," I replied with wet figs on my lips, glimpsing the other parties, "for the Rathel has poisoned us all, and we die before the fire in one family heap."

Then Eric submitted, "Incorrect, missus, in that she and you be saved, for your drink is different. My word, woman, and I see it vanished as well," he noticed upon looking into my empty goblet. "Your kind, then, are lushful drinkers?"

"Worry of your own kind, sir, for you are the one poisoned. Not likely is Rathel sending herself to Hell merely to deliver me to a similar vicinity. Yours, after all, is the death she desires, though only as punition to your father. So here she has arranged for both males and the extra woman to succumb. Be wise and drink no further."

"No wisdom needed, missus, you will observe," he said, and gave a nod toward Rathel, who was chatting anew with Lord Andrew after filling her goblet with anise vodka; and what had become of her moderation?

"The poisoned one must be me," the wife surmised, "and the Rathel has achieved madness to the degree called suicide."

"Then consume no more, wise missus."

"Ah, fear anew, for the enemy attacks our position," I noticed, for the Rathel—accompanied by Andrew—approached to fill Eric's chalice. Graciously I demurred. Surely as sublimely crafted a compilation of lucid glazes and ferocious though oily spirits as ever imbibed, I replied, Grand and the Rathel chuckling off to the next couple.

"Their thinking be yours," I remarked to Eric, referring to his parents. "Note how they view the room's personal contents from the tops of their eyes which float above their goblets. As you before, they plot their exit, and well regret their blunder in being so kindly as to have visited family."

As though complete with her own plotting, Rathel aroused the crowd by announcing her exit, in that her welcome should not be elongated, enjoy all ye the remaining liquor, and away she moved, through the foyer and gone. Before the sound of the door's closing had faded in the air, the older couple announced a similar plot, remaining to one side of the room to wish those walls, perhaps, a good evening, so impersonal was their salutation. Then off they slank as though spiders chased from the kitchen by Miss Elsie. The dog remained.

Having made a move to see his youngster to the door, but failing when the man *cum* wife hastened away with a partial wave, Lord Andrew was left with no visitors in his home, only boarders. Remaining quiet, the older gent sipped at his drink; and I knew he was not mimicking, having greater integrity than the local witch. Eric, espying about with crass turns of his neck, well reeked of relief as he called out loudly.

"Now that the troublemakers are gone, let us carouse at a boisterous rate!" And he followed his speech by snaring my goblet to throw the thing into the fireplace, knowing his own metal cup would not histrionically shatter, my glass bounding amongst the logs without a crack forming in the thick crystal; and surely this was some augury of Eric's ability to succeed in life. Lord Andrew became so amused as to laugh and bend double, his face all in joy and tears, though his sound was so quiet that I was made to laugh myself, the dog noticing none of these makings, not being a creature fit for gallivanting, as boring as the purest witch.

"With the misfits fled, we may well enjoy ourselves," Eric added with a full voice, a most pleasant sound after that hidden whispering, "an especial possibility considering that they left the grog." Decisively he then stepped to the tray, lifting the darker decanter to open it and smell.

"Ooh, what a nasty stuff we have here," he muttered, and returned the bottle. Gaining the second, he found himself with no receptacle, having banished mine and lost his own. The Rathel had abandoned hers nearby, but Eric was aware of its user, looking past it toward that pair left by his parents. Lift one he did, only to recall the words to have come from the mouths against those vessels. He thus turned to Grand with empty hands.

"Have you a cup, sir?" he asked pompously, and Lord Andrew at once pointed toward Eric's chalice.

"Now let us all sit before the fire and speak with humor of nothing," Andrew offered with a smile as warm as the dog's coat.

"Well, not all of us, sir," Eric replied, "in that the wife dreads fire as much as drowning. Unfortunate too, in that her skin is the crust of winter, and well would I wish to warm it."

"But the lass has a heart that radiates a warmth beyond the coarse heat of this blaze," Lord Andrew intoned, smiling broadly toward me.

"Encore, Sir Opera," I replied, and bowed deeply toward Andrew as he raised his chalice to me, Eric thereafter speaking between swallows.

"True enough, Grand, but on a chilly evening in bed, she's but another icicle with hair." Then he raised and sloshed his vessel in my direction, looking wherever his face was pointing.

"We shall compromise," I suggested, stepping beside the husband, "for this is the source of a marriage's happy, albeit bored, continuity."

I then commenced to arrange Grand's furniture, pulling a settee farther from the fire so that a witch upon it would not suffer from being social. Thereupon I situated the husband, gesturing for Lord Andrew to be seated in an adjacent chair. The men then sat, Eric placing one arm about the wife to pull her near as I turned hip to hip in order not to face the fire while retaining Eric's desired contact. Eventually I settled in a pose not fit a lady, though acceptable for a wife with family.

Chatting was our activity, though no great measure came from myself, mostly a proffering of ignorance regarding art and other forms of painting—or vice versa—for this was the subject examined to no true depth by the menfolk as the woman avoided sights of that fire even as the previous audience had attempted not to view certain other members thereof. Not even the dog could I give a deprecating glare, for Randolph again was parked before the flames, static as a log.

A pose we soon imitated. Andrew was the first to find a deep sleep welling within himself, and no one had to inquire of its source. His age, the Rathel's drink, his family's unkind emotions so foreign to this kindly man were causal here. Eric soon followed his kin in declaring a need to retire, and his cause as well was clear: The flexing of his wrist had well sloshed him toward a liquor smell to permeate him as though a stain on his skin. And though my own condition agreed with these males', too weary was I for self-philosophy.

As we three traversed the stairway to our chambers, I wondered of Elsie, but surely her vanishing had coincided with the Dentons' visit. Randolph also had interest in our second pet, for to her door he moved, looking longingly there for us to allow his entry.

"Let us not bother the blissful," I told him, so the dog with easy obedience accompanied Eric and me, and from our weari-

526

ness, was allowed to occupy more of the bed than one canine body required.

Eric seemed near asleep while undressing, tottering to every side, though never stumbling. Carefully I watched, waiting for the man to fall onto his head, for a great laugh I intended to loose on him. But as though accustomed to being unsober, the male did not relinquish his balance until leaning toward the mattress, clothed in only stockings and undershirt. Whisking aside the counterpane, I threw the fabric over fallen Eric, who slowly dug his way out as I undressed, donning a thick and soft sleeping gown, hoping this night to be a good one for retaining the sanctity of my sphincter, tie my body rag about my butt lest the husband awaken not drunk enough to resist my tunnels, and to bed.

Stealthily I slipped beneath the cover, but Eric was facing me. Though he seemed asleep, immediately he slid against my person. I could thus select from a pair of poses: lying flat to smell this drunken sinner breathing upon me the entire night, or turning away to present my rear, which contained an orifice or two generally sought. The latter position I chose, Eric immediately moving to conform to my shape, pressing himself tightly against me. And though the contact toward my bottom was most intimate in a marital manner, Eric made no attempt to enter my garment or myself. Securely in his arms I became enswathed, Eric so familiar with my form that his hand went directly to that remaining breast. There we lay, the witch only partially successful in her placement; for although I was not penetrated by the man, no comfortable pose had I with this sinner draped upon me like long hair down my back made wet and dank by immersion in booze. And though above all other men in the world I appreciated Eric, I did not care to wear him the evening.

"Bite this person smothering me, will you, Randolph? At least pull him away a few inches and insert your own form within the gap." This mumbling of mine, however, went unnoticed by the natural creature who should have been my ally, though was he not too social to be in league with a witch?

527

After all, was he not also male? Eric then spoke, not replying to me, but expressing thoughts of a previous subject, his words rather clear for a sot.

"In the wild places you speak of, Alba, does liquor exist?"

"Perhaps, sir, but no crystalline decanters, and certainly no persons to drive folks from their home, then follow to the next in order to dispense a poison of torment."

"Then a wild place in the forest seems most natural and ever more desirable. Are large and comfortable beds of this sort also available?"

"Comfortable enough for you, I say, in that you mainly sleep upon me, and I'll be there. How viable, then, are your thoughts of living a simpler life, one not so burdened by society?"

"Stronger now than before, but so is the fog in my head. Regardless, the idea was initiated in sobriety, and will not vanish along with this lax state of thinking."

No more could I draw from Eric on this topic, for he sighed deeply and seemed unable to hear me further, as though having exhausted his best effort in that wild conversation. Minutes later, however, he had a final thought, his speaking again not the mindless speech produced by liquor, but a comment from his spirit.

"Pray God I might forget the pain of this evening," Eric whispered, Eric prayed. Then he squeezed me well, and no longer had I concerns for my own discomfort, being so virtuous as to suffer his smell.

Soon I seemed unnaturally taken by sleep. Awake or not, however, I had no natural method to understand that Lord Andrew slept more immediately and deeply than I, to be later awakened by people who wondered how a bit of drink could render even an elder person so unavailable to the waking world. Neither had I means to see the Rathel arrive at her home to immediately swallow a potion to make her vomit, for she did not wish to be sleeping unnaturally, in that sought news should arrive the next morning. No witch could know these things aware, so were they not revealed in a dream?

528

The Rathel was present, though not puking. In her carriage, she had come to retrieve her belongings; so there went Miss Elsie and the dog. I knew the anguish they would suffer in that home: Randolph would be placed with cats to claw his face like a dropped clock, and Elsie would never be startled by a wilderness mistress again, thus turning old from boredom and dying, for without her family she had no life. To save lifeless Elsie and cut Randolph, I journeyed to the Rathel's at night, having crawled through the window of my cave-manse like a spider demoted from its home, and correctly so, for I was no creature of society. I was a creature for collecting and killing bugs. There went I, the spider, to gather Elsie and Randolph in the web bed of the wagon's straw that was identical to my bed on Man's Isle, wherein I had collected a social man of God so entranced by religion as to have joined it for infinity with my body the conveyance. I would have been considered holy for the act of sending a bishop to Heaven had my deity not been Satan, who had me kill via nightmare, which thus could only be understood when mentioned by a dream; and for what further life had this death been practice? I was unable to save Elsie in this bishop manner because she had no man stick to pinch off, and I could not save Randolph because he slept too near the fire, and being half sinner and half witch, I could only approach halfway. With the dog and servant lost, what family member remained for me to save?

Marybelle. Marybelle with her head regrown on her crotch, for after my successful magic, the Lucansbludge constables had tossed her head into the casket instead of placing it properly, lovingly, upon her neck. Marybelle walked London's streets, setting up a smell outside my window not noticed because the window was never opened again, for I had lost too many family members through that plane, first the witch, then the lady, only the wife remaining. But so true was Marybelle to my family that she deigned to return, outside my window spinning a web to entrap my attention. Since I was half sinner, half witch, Marybelle could only approach me halfway, unable to climb the social flank of London because that head between her crotch made it impossible to move through society without being entrapped, for easy prey was a smelling witch with her nose at cunt level. I thus would save her by taking her within me and away from a city she could not survive. But I could not accept her because my vagina was too tight from not having killed a sinner in seasons. To save my family, I would have to become practiced again in my most natural act, the contest of life and therefore death. I would save my family's greatest member by practicing on a lesser. Only two remained: the colorless witch who had failed in her previous salvation of Marybelle by allowing her to live, for death would have transformed her to the superior state of evocative love forever on Earth as prescribed by a bastard preacher whose mother was right in being wronged. He was the last family member; so I would send Marybelle to nature by killing her naturally, practicing by having nature with Eric.

Eric's ministry was proven again by his offering himself to aid in saving Marybelle. But having married me, Eric seemed only half sinner, because the wrong half of my pair of webs he made to enter. Into my baby web he headed, and I—desiring to not fail him as I had Elsie and Randolph and Marybelle— would not accept him so maritally, which would ruin his marriage by killing him like the dead food shat out the hole within which I placed him again and again until finally I convinced him that he was a turd; so he properly dropped into the chamber pot of my buttocks, and I saved him by inversely shitting his prick. But minor this salvation was compared to all my failures, for where were Chloe and Miranda and my mother except dead in Hell and burning in the fireplace? Yet so poor a sister was I as to park before the flames only to placate a sinner, a false family member I had been unable to murder these months, though through Eric's own ministry I was finally saving him by working to release his love across the Earth. Now I was succeeding—and suffering—for in order to kill him, I again had to near the fireplace of Hell, and I was hot, catching sparks on my coat, each a limb or eye of my burning mother, each one burning me: not my hide, but my soul. My mother's embers so collected against me that they burned through my skin directly to my heart, which was in my crotch, for there was my love, in that love was killing Eric. My failing to save by succeeding at murder was Hell itself, for I was in torment, a torture I had felt before, felt in the death of my mother, felt in my cunt as Satan had killed through me. Yes, the fires of Hell were present, but not for me, though the smell of a person burning was unmistakable. Then my nightmare deteriorated, for after smelling death, I had to hear it, for there was Miss Elsie screaming murderously. My torment became so great that it wrenched me from the dream; yet when I awoke to gasp and blink, the nightmare worsened, for I found that I was killing Eric.

How could Eric draw a person to save him when he made not a sound? The dog had heard, however, had heard that flow from his master's crotch: not the normal, nightly one of semen, but blood. Perhaps the dog was upset by the smell or the color, for he was barking at Eric's crotch; but now there was less to bark at, for part of the master was within me.

How rich are a person's sensibilities to so notice yet suffer at once. On my back I lay in a cold sweat and heat to kill me, the pain from my body so great I prayed God to let me die. But I also noticed the barking, then heard Elsie at the doorway screaming—but I could not even desire to understand, so intense was the agony grasping me in orgasmic contractions. I could not understand that Elsie with her lamp ran first to me, after one scream of hesitation, ran to search through my clothing until finding blood, finding me heinously ill, but not dying. Eric was dying. Eric was the source of my blood, and there did Elsie look next. And who could comprehend her horror to dig at a man's crotch to find no limb, but a wound? Who could duplicate her courage upon discovering a damage that destroyed her senses but not her spirit? With metaphysical courage, she wept and wailed, barely able to move, but moving enough. With every limb shaking, she wiped at Eric's wound until seeing that the bleeding would not stop, then covered the red welling with a sheet to contain the flow, not hide it, Elsie next

531

releasing some of the horror flowing from Eric into herself by screaming, screaming at the servants in the doorway, persons unable to duplicate her horror. But such was her noise that it made them flee. She made them flee according to her orders, for they returned with a knife held in the flames of the fireplace long enough to cook meat, and Eric here was Elsie's meal; for she held the bright blade against him to stop his blood, retain his life, and she could not hear his flesh sizzle. None other in the chamber could hear with Elsie's wailing as she stared at her work and prayed to her God while burning the devil from her master, this man a demonic meal that Satan would never gain.

BOOK FIVE: MONTCLAIRE

Thirty-five

So complete was the accused's laughter that the magistrate and attending constable believed she might choke herself to unconsciousness. Or had she found in their allegations the ultimate level of insane humor, achieving absolute humor by going utterly mad?

"You say that I chewed my husband's phallus off and spit it away?"

"You find humor in this horror?" Sir Jacob responded.

"I find foolishness in your descriptions."

In the spacious cell, the magistrate then turned to the constable, transmitting a comprehensible question by pronouncing but a generic name.

"Constable."

"With my own unhindered eyes, I saw that this person as she was being led to this facility did eject from her own mouth a man's member of procreation onto the street, and this I say in certainty."

The magistrate then turned to inquire more complexly of the prisoner.

"Either you bit away your husband's male portion or cut it off with an implement, thereafter concealing the flesh within your mouth in order to hide your murderous act. Or have you a superior explanation of this professional man's witnessing?"

"He witnessed no murder. He observed but a sickness caused by the true butchering; for after she cut the phallus away, Amanda Rathel forced me to swallow the thing as allowed by the opiate she had placed within my drink. This was the cause for my being near asleep when you arrived, for Lord Andrew Denton's being oblivious even longer. Did you not examine the liqueur brought by Lady Rathel?"

"We did, and our man who sampled the material slept most lengthily, but this is proof only that Lady Amanda had you sleep. The purpose thereof, as she sensibly poses, was to end the family difficulties all your people were suffering."

"And what does the victim recall of this assault?"

"Eric Denton has no recollection of the event before awakening to find himself smoldering. Have you no interest in him besides a potential alibi? Is this man not your husband whom you love?"

"Of all the people alive in this world, I love but two, and Eric is one. With God as my truth, Eric is one."

"Who might that second person be?"

"She who saved my husband from death. And with her life Lord God reveals Himself so great as to be beyond my comprehension, for how could He not accept her immediately into Heaven?"

"Easier is your loving her now, for Elsie Rowell is but two cells removed."

"What fool idea has taken you to bring the woman here, Naylor? Elsie is more than innocent; she is a saint."

"She is a suspect, being that individual nearest the victim, along with yourself. Despite your allegations, Amanda Rathel at that time was witnessed asleep in her own household. Therefore, why should we not believe that you and Rowell were aligned in this assault?"

"Very well you should if you are a paradigm of asinine thinking. As for greater inanities, what might the Rathel's opinion of this slaughter be? Where in her testimony are Miss Elsie and I situated?"

"She says nothing of Elsie Rowell that the servant does not. As for yourself, Lady Amanda can only surmise that you are mad. Your bizarre laughter in response to the slaughter in itself describes you as abnormal."

"And no hint of demonology has Rathel found in assessing the crime?"

"None beyond the demon of human evil that Satan places in many. And since Lady Amanda is long the expert here, I have no quarrel with her wisdom. She was not found with a prick in her mouth."

"Ah, but one is found in yours, obscene magistrate. But since my husband is full in his gentlemanship, likely he will forgive your foul reference."

"But this Eric Denton is no 'him,' for no longer has he gender. Can you imagine? Can you understand how important it is to be a man in this world, made by God beneath His vision, in His image, then suddenly to no longer be a man, but a . . . a neuter person?"

These were not questions, for imagination was present and was Naylor's, the magistrate—the man—looking toward me but seeing himself with a scab on his crotch like Eric's.

"Do you understand how important it is to leave for your nation an heir, yet be incapable? Do you understand that a surgeon was required to bore a hole into this person so that he might pass his body's water? Can you imagine being so . . . hopeless that the remainder of his life he will spew urine from a scar?"

"Yes, this I can imagine, for half of God's persons pass water in this manner. They are called women. Perhaps you have some obscenities for your mother as you did my husband since she as well has no limb between her legs. But no human with Eric's spiritual courage would accept for his life the curse from ignorant men of being hopeless. No man could have sufficient flesh between his legs to make himself superior to my husband."

"And there is a bond as changeable as his sex. England and its Church hold laws for a marriage's dissolution. Certainly no justification could be greater than that defined by Eric Denton's injury. In your love for your husband, you might wonder of his further desire to be wed to you."

537

"Is your equating love with legal bonding a perversion of your soul or a corruption from your profession? My concern for Eric is not his concern for me. Through God's grace and Eric's own considerable strength, I pray that his permanent damage soon becomes no more than an inconvenience; for that flesh gone shall not return, and I would have Eric replace it with acceptance."

"How blithely you assert this hope, as though classical philosophy. But no woman can imagine the horror of being so torn asunder. Yet you, in your objective, acting mode, would have the former man simply accept."

At once I began tearing at my clothing as though seeking a treasure in a rag sack. But I sought a terror, for I reached within to find hard flesh for Naylor, displaying that boyish bosom which seemed an eaten carcass.

"I am certain that Eric's horror is worse than *this*," I barked, providing Naylor and his silent man Satanic visions, for according to their faces they saw this ultimate fiend. "More intrinsic to Eric was his manly portion now gone, but I've some idea of his loss in that my breast was not unwomanly. Am I therefore half a woman for being without *this?*" I shouted, and thrust my chest toward the sinners. And retreat they did a step from a fear no actor in an opera could duplicate.

With anger, I reclothed myself, covering Satan and thereby saving these whole men, these complete sinners, from religious terror. Since they had no capacity for speech, I continued for them.

"Against no human of either gender would I wish my own distress, but even as God has allowed me to accept my damage, I pray He provides Eric with the awareness that no removable portion of his person equals his life. I pray Eric might continue living with the wit and love he held before, even if my part therein is only to aid with absolute hope and constant prayer for his success."

And they left. With no further word, the magistrate turned

538

from my covered carcass and stepped to the cell door, followed by the constable. Then I was alone with my scars, and with Eric's.

They left me in a manse. Expansive was this cell compared to that of Lucansbludge, with a larger window so distant from the door as to imply God's substance of space. Through the thick door's iron accoutrements came quietude, not crying, no mention made of the killer witch and her one acceptable nipple. The greatest difference between these hard environs was the latest bed, which I rejected because its odor of sinning men was other than my husband's. I would sleep on the floor.

How fine this site would be for my remaining life. What a cave for hiding, a wilderness compared to grander London. But within these wilds could I hide not from the sinners but from my sin? Here in my selfishness might I hide from Eric, from that man I knew to be uniquely virtuous, no more ambitious than a witch. Here might I remain in my confusion, not knowing whether to pray God in thanks for Eric's survival, or scream to Satan's maker why, why this most decent friend had been stricken, why I had been the vehicle for his needless harm, why the perverted Rathel had finally succeeded in evil, why overtly excellent Eric lay in torment and despair to make my state seem heavenly. How could I thank God for Eric's survival without implying that his state was acceptable?

All these feelings came to me again and again, as though different diseases to strike separate parts of the body—here the head incredibly aching, there the stomach vomiting into knots. With a basis of bereavement, I prayed with effort that my idea to the magistrate come true, that Eric would survive and accept his torment as I had mine. Of course, Eric's loss was unquestionably worse; for I had no use for that breast, whereas Eric well loved his sex with me. From his mutilation, Eric had received nothing but senseless torture; whereas I yet felt the righteousness of having attempted to heal a friend. But might not his superior personality overcome his greater torment? Then I prayed again for him to become no worse, please, dear

539

Lord God, let Eric's anguish come to me as an evil I deserved, since Satan lay within me, was part of me. And I thought of my husband needing to weep but being unable, for I had tutored him in my ways. I had ruined even this sinners' relief for Eric, and pray God I did with utter thanks that I had no such ability, for I knew that if my weeping began it would never cease, no more than my regret.

Then came the next demon in my cycle—false imagination, impossible notions of making the present unreal by changing the past, thoughts of Eric before, of how fine he would currently be if only I had recognized Rathel's evil intents and slapped her brew away or simply quit the room, and never accepted Rathel's control, accepted her demon. Or if I had not slept with Eric but moved away from him before the Rathel's potion took me, hiding in a closet or beneath the stairs or in the alley or the wilds or bloody goddamned Hell rather than remain beside Eric. Had I been less stupid and cowardly, I could have avoided Eric's damage, his permanent torture—but, no, dear Lord, not permanent, not torment without end. No man stick forever, so must it be, but not endless misery—let him have ease, for he had felt evil enough. Then in my ludicrous state I attempted to outwit God by thinking for Him, deciding that, yes, Eric had suffered enough and required no more. Therefore, the husband would accept in his heart and be healed in the spirit, though the combined recuperation would not have been needed had I only averted the Rathel's plan, her success stemming from my foolishness, a weakness allowing her influence first and then Eric's torment, torture, impossible loss.

On and on I deservedly suffered, but not enough, never enough to equal Eric. Pray God send me Eric's torment, enough to kill me, thank You, if it would remove from Eric the terror he did not deserve. On and on, sick and sore in the body, then night, pray for sleep, pray for Eric, pray I might regain time and kill Rathel or myself or Satan rather than drink Rathel's murder or sleep with the husband thereafter, pray God to recreate the era of my evil, return the opportunity to be bored and become so righteous as to suffer only boredom. On and on until the restless night ended, until sinners came I could not ignore, the one speaking immediately hated for interfering with my misery, for it was pious.

"You are ill, missus?"

Sir Jacob had returned with significant company. Along with a guard, Naylor had brought a bishop, a man new to the diocese; for a demon had murdered his predecessor, murdered him in the same Satanic manner as that used against my husband. Since this bishop knew me as present in both killing vicinities, had he some strong feeling for my guilt, for the devil accompanying me in the form of witches? This man of God might have had me in mind, but in his mouth was his master, for Bishop Dysart stood praying by the door as Naylor spoke with the prisoner.

"Missus, I ask whether you are ill. Can you not hear?"

"Ill with evil," I muttered, then noticed the magistrate looking down toward me with wonder; and I would not accept his curiosity. Painfully I sat upright with the proper carriage learned by all ladies for sitting on a prison floor. Situating myself as though on a brocade divan, I feigned normalcy, though I was not normal, and felt I never would be.

"I have no illness, only poor sleeping."

I knew he looked toward my chest, though I viewed him not, Naylor an oblique peripheral in my sight. The cloth to shape me I had not replaced, and Sir Jacob looked, attempting not to see. After that raw sight of my breast, however, he would not step near, not after my threat of applying my scar like a contagious fever.

"With no illness, you then will speak. I seek more words from you, and would have your cooperation."

"I shall cooperate, but first you must tell me of Eric."

"The former man you love? Your concern is such—"

"I will learn of Eric's condition through the previous night, or naught will you receive from me but scabs," I demanded. "I

541

will hear of him regardless of my love, your authority, or the evil you seem to promote more than alleviate. You will tell me of Eric's health or receive no further words from me unless you cut them out." Then I firmly stood, nearly touching Naylor as I stepped past him.

As though I had brandished a blade with my breast, the magistrate leaned backward with an abnormal breath. But quickly he settled, calm and official again as he continued his interrogation.

"The Denton person is of acceptable health, not yet with infection and offering no fear of demise to his physician. Of his spirits I cannot speak, except that he seems uncertain of himself. This I well understand. Nothing further do I learn from him, for he asserts to have no recollection of his attack in that it came in sleep. And the victim cannot state who was present during the assault but you. Therefore, I will have more speaking from you, but no more of health's interest."

The most reverend then spoke, "We shall pray first," and stepped near the prisoner, though not near enough to touch her. Lowering himself to both knees, he clasped his hands, again closing his eyes. But with his head all bowed, was he looking toward his God or away from my bodice?

Without thought, I moved to sit before him. I then bent my neck and well desired to pray, for though the sinning reverend and I were different people, our God was yet the same.

Naylor lowered himself to one knee as the bishop began his praying; and though the reverend's phrases were mostly rote, the man seemed to hold God as his love, not merely his profession. In my silent praying with this sinner, I emphasized the notions we shared, those of guidance and salvation, an increase of righteousness to replace the ambient evil, amen, the bishop surely feeling better, the jailor and his witch unchanged in their corruption.

As though having completed the nasty chore of groveling on his knees, Sir Jacob rose to begin his speaking anew.

"I say again, missus—"

"I say first, Lord Magistrate, that you might begin by ending, by revealing to me likely conclusions to this tale. That is to say, if I am adjudicated guilty of this crime, what be my legal punition?"

"Since no life was taken, neither would yours be," Naylor stated, suavely accepting my interruption. "But doubtless you would never leave this prison."

"Intense thought have I given this matter. Therefore, I think it best that you speak with me alone."

"A great truth is best given with witness to eliminate misunderstandings."

"How subtle you are, Lord Magistrate, to have said 'great truth' instead of 'confession.' Is the great truth, however, that you fear having parts removed by this thin woman your prisoner?"

"I fear no person, only God."

"How fearless are you with Satan?"

"Satan is not to be feared, but, with God's aid, despised."

"Then dismiss these men and remain with me and God to discuss the devil. If you've the spirit for it."

Long did the magistrate view my face, but not for a blink did I avert my eyes. But in my visage did the sinner find a challenge to his courage or his soul?

Turning to his holy associate as though ordering tea served, Naylor said, "Reverend Dysart, this constable will lead you away for a time. Pray God I do in thanks for your continued counsel with Jesus."

"But Lord Magistrate," the constable replied from across the cell, looking to me as though I were a weapon, "this person has—"

"Leave, and have less concern with persons who would have your concern."

As we were made alone, Naylor faced the door, not me. He faced the door as though beyond lay an area to his preference, but no further evidence of fear did I sense in him. Nevertheless, it was not his courage but my words to turn him from

543

that temporary wall.

"I ask, Sir Jacob, of your interest in witches. I ask of the value you would find in gaining a personal expertise in that race you find exceptionally wicked, these witches you believe responsible for a death in your family."

Stinking of interest, the magistrate faced me better, becoming so weak as to seat himself on a low stool, though the lady yet stood. In several manners he was then situated beneath my level.

"This is no subject on which I shall accept your lies, and I'll not further respond prior to comprehending your intent."

"I explain, then, in question. If you were the captor of a witch whose identity was proven, would you allow her to live if she provided knowledge of witches beyond what the lying Rathel could ever imagine?"

"I would, undoubtedly, and consider the price worth and well paid."

"But you might lie. What sin exists in deceiving one sinister? Surely Lord God would forgive such a paltry iniquity with barely a prayer. What would preclude your lying to a witch; and, after gaining her knowledge, taking her head as well?"

"That type of dishonesty is one of criminals, and equal in malice to their deeds. My entire life supports integrity, and thereby have I attained a respected position in great England's greatest city as appointed by King William and verified by Queen Anne. Only one long seduced by dishonesty would consider evil acceptable, even when dealing with Satan. In fact, immoralities are not overcome with the treachery they promote, but with the very integrity they would damage."

"In fact, your integrity I must infer; whereas I reside in your control. No lie of yours will have us exchange positions, and my best truth will not free me from your cave."

"And what best truth do you have, woman, with all your talk of honesty? Where is that previous speaking of witches, a subject you well know to impassion me?"

"The subject was potential agreement between London's magistrate and a new expert in witches yet revealed as verifiably extant. Now that your honesty is accepted, shall we proceed to detail a contractual vow toward which you might dispense your powers, those to punish and to free?"

"The former more than the latter considering that we deal with witches and near murders. But continue with your potentials if they include topics to interest me concretely. Your fine speaking reveals a learnedness best applied toward the bishop, who is a man of ideas. I am more of God's world wherein His ideas of grace and happy living are seldom applied except in wishful prayer. What thus of Satan and his applicators, these witches?"

"You then vow before God—not me, not the bishop, but before God and Jesus—that if I confront you with a witch who killed by act of Satan that you would spare her life to learn completely of her race?"

"Before you, Dysart, or Jesus are all the same in receiving my integrity, and such a moral pact I would make, as witnessed by all and pleasing to God. But no witch a Satanic killer would I set loose upon England. Such a creature's life I might spare upon learning all of her people, but she would live within these walls till death, and before Satan and God that be another vow."

"One understandable. But understand also, Lord Magistrate, that the people of my husband's life are not all felicitously disposed toward one another. By dint of your business with Lady Rathel, you are one of these persons. Therein lies potential for such prejudice in receiving tales that you might doubt even great truths proffered that, if fully accepted, would send another person to this prison cave."

"Which person do you sentence, as though a magistrate yourself?"

"I am wondering now of the verity required to have the Lady Rathel become your prisoner."

"Any genuineness proving a second person worthy of incarceration would suffice. But no lie could be subtle or strong enough for me to imprison a great lady."

"And a great truth it must be to convince you that my base objective is not vengeance. Well would you contemplate the condemnation of a 'great lady' by one despising her."

"Your philosophy is sensible, but I am ever convinced by fact. Seldom, however, am I made a fool by vengeance. Have you a person for me, then, a witch to tell of witches? Or have you more philosophy? Perhaps you might convince me further; specifically, by describing the cause for a witch confessing murder when none has been committed nor alleged."

I then looked away from this sinner. What contest was I entering with my life when naught had the playing magistrate to lose, and nothing had I to gain but vengeance toward the Rathel, whether termed "justice" or not? One basis of this dangerous game was foreboding, the belief that my legal future would include witnesses to swear my proximity to Percival and Cameron before and after their deaths, testimony Naylor would well receive in light of Eric's harm. Surely I was best to protect myself from these associations in advance. But beyond self-protection, an additional influence existed to make me casual with my flesh.

Too long was I speechless for Naylor to peaceably remain without due attention. Therefore, he viewed the woman who looked away.

"What illness has taken you now without your mention? I see no philosophy in your demeanor, perhaps weariness instead. Are you exhausted, woman, from diatribes or the devil?"

What courtesy does God deserve before one contemplates wagering the life only He supplies? Was I so set toward justice that Rathel need be revealed? Could I not be satisfied with my life in this cave with only my guilt and away from my damage, suffering from my latest mutilation without seeing the scar, without being shown by the husband who insisted that I no longer weep for his damage—but I had never wept, and never would. What element was left to cogitate before the prisoner would present the witch? Then I knew without thought, unavoidably bending to grasp my head, crying out with honesty for the benefit of no one in that cave.

"God, I wish Eric to be well!"

Convinced or not with no concern from me, the magistrate replied after a sinners' instant.

"With all your intense sorrow, you shed no tear. Not from the torment you were found in this morning nor the similar anguish you now vent toward God. But not even you are so beauteous as to dupe me with forced emotion, no more than with revenge. If the former be true, how can your eyes remain clear when your heart is darkened?"

"Because though well they feel all of God's emotions, no more than visit Heaven do witches weep."

"Fool you are, woman, to mention witch and yourself. A proof you must have as sure as numbers for me to believe you so, for this is unbelievable. Well I expected your accusing the Rowell servant, and set was I for firm convincing even with that person. All my life I've known evil, but never a woman with your mien who was not inherently a lady, despite a crime caused by temporary moral weakness. You do in my belief possess sufficient evil to have cut your husband horribly, but the lie you now fabricate comes from your hatred of Lady Amanda. Denton's assault was from envy or anger as aided by Satan, but not from your being his witch."

"Proof I have as sure as numbers, and they be three, for that is the quantity of pricks I have cut away with my own body."

"Woman, you'll not be striking me with coarse speech, for I have heard worse, even from—"

"The best proof you could have is to fuck me, Lord Magistrate, Lord Bleeding Magistrate whose queen is an arse with her head stuffed with shit and his bishop a knave, no more holy than the pricks I've spat out."

Naylor was now struck enough to leap to his feet, his face ruddy, his personage stuffed with enough integrity to come rushing out like blood from a cut limb. But I was stricken equally, vaulting forward a long step to speak first.

547

"By the grace of true God, you will hear the truth I posit in terms of my choosing, for it was my body taken by Satan and forced to kill, and my mouth through which male members left with enough horror to strike me mad. Nothing have you suffered for me to placate your upset sensibilities; and by God's power to control even fools, the Lord will take your soul as dung if you fail your vow after I have proven myself."

Removing myself a distance more comfortable to the magistrate, I continued with my speaking, my voice official as though I were the authority, the man a fire before me consuming itself.

"I am the witch and the white witch. I am the sex witch who kills with intercourse. Proof I will give of my being a witch, but none of this sex killing, for the act tortures me as though tearing my innards, an agony I will demonstrate not even to save my life. But with facts for you to verify, I will convince you of this sex, and when done, you will believe me as though I've counted you like a simple number."

The magistrate then sat, no longer so startled. Exhausted from my words, he was also filled with energy, that of knowledge and fear, a contradiction appropriate for a lady witch who slaughtered.

"Never have I heard of such an . . . entity," Naylor stated plainly, "not even from Amanda Rathel, though she has mentioned some of the connection between sexuality and witches."

"Lady Rathel has told you little of witches. This you can understand, in that the greater your knowledge, the lesser her influence over you, and the less her ultimate gain."

"But what kind of creature could one be to so ravage a man?"

"Call me not 'creature,' unknowing sinner, for in this prison are persons of your own kind who have murdered through pure intent; whereas I have been most pitifully the vehicle of Satan through no desire of my own."

"How is it, then, you summon Lucifer when the killing is to be done?"

548

"Magistrate fool!" I screamed. "I will not have you blaspheme God by impugning one of His worshipers who in her heart and mind completely loves peace."

"Yet you also assert to be the sex witch who kills? A human who well loves God yet consumes men?"

"In His fantastical wisdom, God allows Satan to enter my sexual parts to injure male persons. Were this a desire of mine, every hour I would pass coupled with men to come away with their man sticks in my sex lips. But this or any act of damage is a horror to me, and my life I have constantly made to avoid men. After being wed, I lived for months with my husband before Rathel supplied a potion so that Eric might be harmed."

"Missus, for all your charges of my ignorance, I remain well thinking and experienced, my beliefs and observations reasonable. Rational thought guides me to believe you no 'sex witch,' but a madwoman who plucked away her husband's manly member, and in her madness would convince both herself and me of a false story tremendous in its telling. But I will have my proof before hearing further."

"Then this proving you shall have, Sir Jacob, my truth to take two forms. To begin, I shall prove myself the medium through which Satan destroyed the men Percival Bitford and a constable's affiliate in Lucansbludge."

Herein was Naylor's interest provoked as though a desire for my sex; for although deaths were common to him, these two were special, one for being within his own city, the latter a killing of a person his kind.

"Tell me of the former," he instructed, looking to me as though I truly were a murderess.

"That person procured from me the sexual intercourse, which killed him through no advance knowledge nor intent of mine. Though executed for this death, the woman Lucinda was innocent of any connection. Proof of my responsibility will be found in the testimony of one Mr. Wroth, who spoke with me in the same room as Percival minutes before the latter's death. Further witnessing might come from two fine ladies who con-

549

veyed my person ill from that death to the Rathel's household shortly after the incident."

"And this 'constable's affiliate' from Lucansbludge?"

"His was a later death, and sorrowful despite the man's own immorality; for this Cameron followed me into wild land after I had quit his village, and therein harshly raped me, dying from the act through no will of mine. The individuals to interview are those of my detention within the Lucansbludge prison. The magistrate of that locale is named Waingrow, and was with minister. For their litigation I was released by a certain Lady Rathel's swearing my integrity, proof again that she has fomented plots even against England for me to fulfill her vengeance."

Sir Jacob then gave his best interpretation of my truth.

"Your prejudice toward witches is well understood, but stems from your delusions, not your blood. Your time gone from London was truthfully explained by Lady Amanda, for the same as in your youthful days you were taken by true witches. In this later instance, the thieving witches murdered the poor folk you described, then were executed for their crimes, having been proven guilty and proven to fit the accurate, established description of witches as adjudicated by English law."

"And by the expert Lady Rathel, who, by insisting upon my innocence, also asserts her own."

"For myriad reasons, Lady Amanda's tale sings truer than yours. First is the fact of your stories' being unoriginal, in that each I have heard before. After Bitford's death, I interviewed his employer, Mr. Wroth, who mentioned a belle even then recalling your appearance. Though now I learn of your presence there, I learn nothing to dissuade me from the truth of the witch Lucinda's having done the killing, thereafter being discovered and punished appropriately. Thus proven are both Lady Amanda's expertise in describing your delusion, as well as the efficacy of my own constables and English law. As for the man of Lucansbludge, through my very office did Magistrate Waingrow seek Lady Amanda, and thereby I heard of your situation before she. Sensibly explained by all was that witches from your past had found you again, and again one had murdered in your vicinity. Furthermore, an obvious witch was discovered nearby and adjudged guilty of a killing. That ending part of your molesting yourself only proves that you were taken by a witch's influence, for never have I known a witch to harm itself—they only harm others, even if using human folk to harm themselves via their auspices. As for tales with less corroboration than those mentioned, Lady Amanda's views are to be accepted above yours, for her basis of belief is a life of integrity; whereas your life's great influence is witches and their heinous ways."

"In your bland professionalism you then believe it coincidental that these deaths were equal to Eric's injury, and though most immediately present, I was uninvolved?"

"I believe that these witches were so decrepit as to kill average men and influence you evilly, perhaps even teaching the lovely sinner to imitate them in malice. In fact, that single assault for which you stand accused proves by its limited nature that you are less than a true witch, for these friends of yours, being truly evil, well managed to kill their men; whereas the common, deluded woman—being merely human—could only wound hers."

"How brilliant of compositional effort you are to have created an operatic defense for me as extemporaneous as it is false, and surely as fluent in its own glib conviction as any story told you by the Rathel, that demon to have influenced you toward self-deception, deposing you from your place in English law and God's justice. Therefore, I hope my further proof, being purely deed, shall convince you better toward the accuracy of my life, not your view."

"The deed of which you speak, and endlessly, is other than that act of sexual mutilation itself? But, of course, for previously you swore not to display this act even to save your life. How brilliantly convenient in that your future life is now saved, by my vow but your arranging. How additionally convenient

551

since you could offer no such proof regardless, for this delimbing cannot be done with the sex of any woman. Perhaps by a witch, but you are no witch, only a deluded and vengeful child."

"In your incompetent adjudication, you have no interest in my additional verity as yet undescribed?"

"Describe it first, then be on with your deed if not adjudged by me specious before displayed."

"I shall swim for you, Sir Jacob."

"How entertaining that might be, but wherein lies proof of your occultism?"

"Occultism is an invention of sinners' imagination. My surviving is proof of the witch, for no sinner can breathe within water."

"That no person can breathe water is true, but entertainers can well be convincing in their false depiction of truly impossible acts. Shall I therefore bring a bucket for your head's immersion?"

"Perhaps you will entertain other sinners with your bland attempts at comedy; but witches, being disposed toward humor, not farce, shall remain unimpressed. I will impress the comical magistrate, however, with a deed inexplicable as entertainment; for I shall be completely and visibly immersed in water for so great an occasion as to confirm myself no member of your species."

"Proving yourself the frog will not make Amanda Rathel a prisoner for your own entertainment."

"Will you have this proof, or will you have more comedy, frivolous sinner?"

"I will have the former, and warn you first that no more of your own frivolity shall I accept before depending upon God's perfection to forgive me for breaking a vow. Now, on with the particulars of your proof."

I then described that to some body of clean water I should be conveyed, preferably one so clear that I might be seen by those observers without. So shallow that I might leap up into

552

God's air as required by panic. This last was not mentioned, however, only that any place would do but Gravesbury Reach; and no explanation was provided for this parameter. Then away was Naylor to formulate logistics, my accompaniment by official men, enough to succumb even a witch, even a deluded, mad and maddening woman. And with a bow and verbal salutation surely provided no other prisoner, the magistrate left me alone with my cyclical despair.

My prison home seemed so unclean compared to rural London, compared to Pangham Gardens where I was delivered in a wooden cave, a dark coach with a miniscule window, a blank interior, and an outer lock on the single door. Though the coachman was a constable, he offered the lady a hand for her entry—or was his hand for the sex witch and the inferred sublimity of her crotch? Being neither lady nor witch, but a criminal, I entered with no aid. But even locked in that box I felt the beauty of spacial volume, of distance, having stepped from the prison into an alley to find space about me and beyond. Then into the box that reeked of men's sweat and sorrow, and on with the unpleasant ride.

The pool was strange to be so contained, its walls whiter than sand, straighter than any cliff leading to an ocean. This reduction of messy details sinners deem elegance, but how elegant is the finest clock compared to the average vegetable? Compare the smells: acidic metal ever hot versus the cool confinement of sweet moistness.

"You will be on with your proving, missus."

Around me were sinners, all men. Vapid an art is philosophy to remove one mentally from the real. As I stood prepared to immerse myself, my thoughts of the pool replaced my concern for drowning, no shuddering heart, no stuttering lungs. But with the magistrate's words, I was returned to my most recent life of evil disbelieved.

"Missus, does this water body then fit your occult requirements?"

The constables were mixed with prison guards, dull doublets versus thick, loose shirting of a reddish brown. With Naylor and this army, I stood before a geometric pool with floating, living plants pressed toward one end, and golden fishes—more magical and beautiful than the whitest witch—swimming at my behest, it seemed, dazzling me to my preference.

"The selection is good."

Though a slight accumulation of fungi grew at the pool's edges, this water was more clear and clean than any to *drown* me before.

"You might proceed, missus, instead of staring down so intently. The fishes will offer no harm."

"Where the fishes breathe, therein might I . . . not," were my words, too quiet for anyone but the immediate witch. To my side stood the magistrate, but unseen, for into that contained river I stared.

"Missus," Sir Jacob continued more loudly, "you will—"

"Have you dry apparel for me? The cold I do not mind, but I cannot bear to be damp, as though a lichen in a cave."

"Missus, shall you wet yourself and prove your truth, or—"

"Yes, Naylor, I shall drown for you now."

Toward the pool I stepped, kneeling to remove my lady's footwear. This dweller of Montclaire wore excellent clothing because her mother was wealthy and influential; and what a hag the Rathel would seem if failing to provide her daughter with fine attire and bedding despite the youth's incarceration. To save my shoes, I removed them, for they were insulation against Montclaire's hard, damp floor; and being a sinner, I preferred my amenities.

"Shoes so retain moisture," I mentioned, but whose voice was this with such lethargy? Was the witch poisoned again by Rathel's potions, or merely by future water, an upcoming moisture to drape her lungs and drown her thinking, her philosophy? And what of the constables so enthused to see my feet

554

that they swayed as though toxic themselves? Did I not smell a low odor from them that only my husband was due to project? But, no, of course not, for my husband from that region had only the smell of gore.

"Woman, you delay as though—"

"I delay as though I were about to drown myself, magistrate," I retorted. "Believe ye my immersion for long minutes is less of a chore than an illness that might kill if not soon cured. Remove a fish there from its atmosphere and place the beast upon this pavement. As you study the creature's throes, understand that it does not flop about carelessly, but is drowning in air, is dying."

"Missus, I say it is *your* assertion of an ability to survive within water," the magistrate declared, "yet now you say you are stepping toward a drowning death? Be ye a witch or not?"

Then I sharply turned, stepping firmly away from Naylor and his water.

"No, I am no sort of witch. I am a fool to value justice toward Rathel above my own torment. Rather than feel myself drowning for a moment, I will feel myself dry in your prison for a life."

"Drown no more shall I in your words, missus, in your madness and maddening contradictions," loud Naylor retorted, and signaled with a harsh gesture for the military men to approach me.

"Immerse this woman until she proves herself either especial witch or common mortal," he demanded. And his men, his sinners, stepped with haste to take me.

How legal were these males to receive me by my groin and bosom? What of that hand grasping the flattened scar on my chest to release the hold after a moment's tactile study, as though the fingers had found heat too great for a mortal hand? Those other hands continued, lifting me with such combined force and speed that my resistance was to no avail. Then I was in the pool, wettened and submerged.

As soon as I was within the pool from violence and held

555

immersed with force, all my breathing's aspects ceased, locking like some solid box containing a sinner's jewels. The box of my body held only fear, however, exuded as violence; for I struck at these men holding me, struck and kicked as I twisted from one to move better into the grasp of two others, all my moves made slower by that thick atmosphere; while somewhere beyond, true fishes of gold moved effortlessly away with surprise. Thrusting with my entire person, I dove below the sinners, managing to free myself. And I was able to continue, for the guards' efforts to retain me were as full of effort as my own, and all of us were immersed, were drowning.

Once at the pool's far side, I reentered air, gasping as I pulled myself upward with hands on the stone ledge, looking up to see another constable prepared to grasp me, three guards in the pool now gaining my position. Then, with no visage of a lady, I sought the magistrate, inhaling a final gasp of air to allow my speaking.

"Please!" I begged him, looking to his eyes with my word. "Please, lord, you will wait." Then all the infinite constables had me again, those three immersed making their own gasping sounds, wet breaths of water's choking and anger from being deposed by a woman, a prisoner, a witch.

"Constables, hold away!" Naylor instructed loudly. "Move from her, then, and allow her breathing."

The magistrate seemed angered at his associates, looking down harshly to shake his head. Then a pacing he began as though a forceful version of the guards' movements as they stepped from the prisoner, displeased themselves by the magistrate's command or by my power of fear, my fearful power that controlled them all.

Eventually Naylor looked toward me only to pronounce, "Woman, you are a witch." Then he continued pacing.

Was the sharp gesture Sir Jacob next made — his hand moving upward as he looked to his constables — one of consternation or defeat?

"Out with her, then, and again to Montclaire's building for

556

her to live dry every day further she might breathe." But disagreement came after this order.

"No," I told him, glimpsing the magistrate. "Allow me calm breathing for a time, then you shall have your proof."

Sir Jacob then ceased his stalking, looking toward me rigidly to call with force, "Woman, not again will I have your—"

"Words," I concluded for him, looking up to this sinner, then again between my hands, which held the pool's edge as though I would fall without this support, though upon the bottom I stood. "Endless words. Current words are only for distress, and none to follow my proof will be required. But I tell you, sir, my older words must be recalled. Recall and then be ashamed for being made the fool by Rathel. Then, sir, quantify your pride that finds Rathel a peer, for what sort of man will you be?"

After staring at me a sinners' moment, Sir Jacob with a sneer gesticulated for his constables to exit the water. And despite the sex therein to be held in their hands, they were not displeased to leave.

Soon my breathing was mild, and this was intended, for deep inhalations would disrupt that insulating layer of water immediately against me made warm from my body, my own cool body having more heat than this freezing corpus that held me like the hands of sinners meant to chill me with their law. Having set myself in preparation, I turned so Naylor would look toward his prisoner to see her become a witch. This single glimpse was all the lure required for me to gain Sir Jacob's attention as I moved away from the air and prayed God for my survival. And madly it seemed that my prayer was to survive not my drowning, but my hatred of things damp.

I had intended a straightforward process with this proving, my desire to be on with the distress so that it might sooner end. But as I sank to the pool's bottom and accepted water into my throat, I found myself drowning. All hope left with my last breath's ending, for the water rushing within me was a damp fiber to clog and kill, containing life for fishes, but none for

557

me.

Astonished to find myself committing suicide, my only thought was to be within the air again. Yet I feared moving lest that held water be replaced by worse, by an airless mass sucked dead by fishes. So I waited in fear for some air to seep within me, waited but a moment, a dying human's moment, and enough, for no breathing I found. Potential was no longer sufficient, for I required true substance to support my life, but not enough tangible air was forthcoming for me to remain for what purpose? Then I knew. Having no thoughts of the magistrate astonished, of Rathel enjailed, of Elsie released, I flexed to press upward with my legs and thought of Eric, Eric staring down to his body and receiving greater torment than when first confronted by my scab. Therefore, I remained below because in this wet world I could not cause Eric further harm, and would never see him in the flesh, the scar. And if my confirmation were to fail, I would then be in a world even more perfectly devoid of his presence, for pious, precious Eric would never be found in Hell.

No thinking had I for the longest era likely extending from one moment to another, but no counting by me, only the task of seeping in air, the duty of avoiding Eric. My demeanor soon approached a different panic, one of failure through neglect; for how long would I need to remain submerged to prove myself sinister? If apart from air too long, would I not drown despite an established authenticity?

With fish breathing again set well within me, I replaced my upset thinking with contemplation of time as though distance, this tactic of duration successfully applied before in drowning eras. History then arrived in my thinking, for there was our cabin on Man's Isle, and I turned toward the dense growth of difficult walking that nonetheless provided the most concise route to those several shallow hills upon whose northern slopes grew a mossy grass too soft for any plant, it seemed, and impossibly green. Completely through the thicket, below those vines to snarl the pesty hair Mother insisted remain kempt, east around the great dry gulch to trip a witch, up the ridge across the narrow field to the hills of mossy grass, gather a huge armful and return, track and retrace every pace, what a chore with this burden, one worsening with each step, the burden of my breathing, not this grass, continue with the work, the aggravation, until home was in sight, through the thicket with some loss of my load, between those spindly trees toward the cabin; and there was Mother, drop the load before her to finish a convincing distance of drowning, one final step directly upward and into the natural air.

Surely a saint or demon left that pool according to the sinners' manner of viewing. The leader was yet Naylor, for his view, being most studious, was also the most revelatory; but of what type of creature, type of human? One to be touched by none of these sinners, not a word given nor received, only dry apparel not donned till the lady again was in her prison. Yet in the coach and during that long journey, no dampness was felt.

Thirty-six

Fish heads I snipped away with the toothed baby in my belly as I sat on my soot-cell bed, the mattress made mine because I was forced to lie with it, the previous-prisoner stink my responsibility as I ate peers with my bowels, Sir Jacob Satan entering with a new prisoner each day: a bishop prisoner presuming Heaven, a driver prisoner conveyed to Hell, a constable prisoner seeking legality along the trail but finding a golden dog eating prick heads while moving well in its medium of play, fins wagging as its smiling gills barked, and a husband prisoner presuming to provide sufficient love to fertilize the wife's wildness and promote a love returned, but no.

The castigation all these crimes deserved was proof, and the only proof was demonstration. Refusing again to eat meat, I was therefore made to repeat. So there I sat looking up through Satan's space at the inquisitor through an atmosphere made hazy by its disrupted upper surface, all that swimming smoke making sight difficult in that I was burning and would continue until I proved myself guilty. And yes for the bishop fish as I snipped his pink metal head off and screamed enough to break my lungs. Yes for my guilt in again baby-biting away the driver's mane with my crotch mouth that was sweet meat to some as I bit my own soul simultaneously, therefore screaming enough to break my spirit. And yes with regret for dropping the semi-constable from between my legs without a baby maker as a pain bounced upward and inside me that was misery to make me wish my mother had never lived so that I had never. And yes for the husband with his selfish aggravation removed, not again to bother the wife with his distant education of the Continental cunt. Now his boredom and mine would be equal, his scar and mine would be equal, as I made the husband not a witch nor the wife a sinner but both of them a different race, and wept enough to break my heart.

Waking from that life was no disappointment, not even to find myself social fungus in Montclaire cave. Upon leaving that dream, I moved to the window only to stand in the volume of entering light, to be part of God's geometry; for I was more alive than before in that cell, since now my life was revealed, my true life of a witch. Despite the current cooling weather, I was warm within, for I was completely dry. So alive was I—and so social—that I used the brush provided by my mother Rathel, for I was her only daughter and a most successful sort of vengeance; for when had all the Dentons ever felt such horror? Abuse my scalp I did to relieve my coif of tangles from sleeping on a wet head. Praise God my lungs were dry, unlike in my dreams—and what of Naylor's dreams? Did he see wet witches pinching limbs off English victims like a child denuding a bug of inconsequential parts? Or was he more concerned with my waking hair? Here was Naylor's attention, Sir Jacob entering to stare at that black mass which in his eyes could have been gold, such was its value, not the gold of decorative fishes, but of precious emotions, bejeweled ideas.

Before the door's loud opening and Naylor's footfalls, I knew his approach, knew from his particular sinning smell. And with my back toward him as the sunlight surrounded me, I sensed his gaze, not at the witch but the woman, her white skin and black gold. Not willing to be a feminine demonstration to this sinner, I ceased my brushing as though ending an annoying chore, moving away from that cubical light toward the dark where sinners belong.

"I would speak with you of yesterday," the magistrate began, his voice unaffected by his eyes and mind, by the sight of that woman, thoughts of that witch.

"We shall, if first you tell me of Eric."

"Missus, we shall continue with our established business, not the pretense of—"

"Missus is correct, magistrate. As before, you will tell me of my

561

husband's condition without questions of my fidelity or curious demeanor. God will concern Himself with my true emotion toward Eric without the aid of English law. Supply me, please, with the factual status of my husband, for which I thank you in advance."

"At your pleasure, Mrs. Denton. I say your husband is as before, alert though unmoving in bed, injured but healing."

"Why, magistrate, have you such reluctance to tell me of Eric without difficult queries? Have you some bizarre notion from your British law or deceased Jesus that precludes a simple depicting? Or are you especially fond of my pleading with words?"

"Missus, never have you pleaded with words, only with an emotion yesterday when you begged for me to leave you undrowned, and then no sound was needed. And there you were correct in your desire to live, for being alive, now you have further opportunity to prove yourself a witch."

Not likely had Naylor ever been more struck by my revelations than I by his comment. Perhaps I seemed the social sinner in my response, staring at Naylor with ignorance of his customs, his mentality or madness. So taken was I by his words that I had none myself, allowing the magistrate to converse for us both.

"Before your . . . swimming of the previous day, I presented skepticism as to being shown not occult proof but mere entertainment. Having passed from that time wherein I was affected by the immediacy of your demonstration through a night and day wherein I could contemplate, I must say I find myself most impressed, but less than satisfied."

"You say, then, that some entertaining trickster of your knowledge could duplicate my accomplishment?"

"I say that the possibility of such a duplication is more believable than your being a witch."

"Then provide me with a numerical understanding, magistrate, as to the quantity of women you have executed as witches with less confirmation given of their race than I have displayed."

"The proof I have ever had with witches is an evil event and a wicked person nearby; whereas Denton could have been harmed by human means. And you I adjudge human, for neither yourself nor any expert has verified your being a witch."

562

"You know of no expert but the Rathel?"

"None is required but Lady Amanda, who describes you not as demonic, but brilliant."

"And where within my malice lies genius?"

"Amanda avers you well hate her, and knowing yourself settled within Montclaire for life, you convinced me toward a vow to disallow your execution, your purpose to have your enemy incarcerated also. And clear sense has the lady's explanation, for you have nothing to lose by being the witch, only she. Were her daughter adjudged Satanic, Amanda would lose her freedom by being an accomplice to a demon's life in London."

"You must agree that God and England would suffer if the lady be as guilty as I allege yet goes unpunished."

"I agree with your fantasy, but it remains a lie. As for now, you remain within this cell a mutilator, not a witch."

"But if Rathel assesses me as human, and my proving was inadequate to you, do we not all concede that I am no witch, merely a fool to have mentioned myself and witches? What could be your goal in pursuing the subject? In fact, do you not reek less of integrity and more of lust? Confess your desire not to prove the witch but to have the wench. Why else your insistence upon my no longer being a mere woman?"

"Because I know that neither in your flesh nor mind are you 'merely' a woman. Despite Lady Amanda's expertise, I believe you do possess some occult powers that you concealed by sublimely presenting a proof you knew I would disbelieve. By your failure, you would convince me of your innocence so that further allegations by any party of your being sinister I would reject."

"How contemplative you are, sir, to make such a net of simple notions. If truly a witch, why should I fail the proof, since you have vowed on your soul not to slaughter me for being occult? Either you have gained a new career in which you are decrepit, or I have no punition to fear for being the witch. What purpose would I have in concealing myself?"

"Your purpose is a form of salvation, for you would avoid suffering. Witch or not, that water breathing of yours was torment. When you stepped near the pool and recalled the immersion's pain, you dismissed your personal interests in proving yourself occult. And though your swimming was in fact a near drowning, that further proof available would be even worse. During a pained moment when your speaking was all honest, you allowed me a revelation I yet believe. Reasonable you are to avoid suffering, but how much reason or easy living should a witch be allowed? As for my career, its purpose has not changed: I well serve England and God by learning all of witches a mortal can. To further disprove your envious gibes at my integrity, I shall again allow you to convince me occultly. Therefore, kindly demonstrate your abilities that are magical."

"I know less of magic than you do of witches. I can swim better than perform magic, yet the former did not impress you. Therefore, you might select failure as a further topic, accepting me as the same human as you, God forgive me."

"In fact, I accept as your next topic that remaining area of expertise. Therefore, I offer to provide you with a criminal due certain execution whom you shall demonically reduce with sex as you did your husband."

Not a sinners' moment did I hesitate, speaking next with true hatefulness to the magistrate, but with less hatred than he deserved.

"Only a worshiper of Satan could be heinous enough to seek torture for a person doomed. The only evil more thorough would be subjecting a woman prisoner to tortuous rape by a criminal so fiendish as to be worthy of death. Therefore, whether I am the woman or witch, *you* are the evil creature to mutilate either the man or me, and likely not even God in His infinite understanding will be able to fathom a method for forgiving you. But, of course, you would not ask dear God, for with such ideas only Satan could be your deity."

"How pious you are for one admittedly a killer of men via sex. This latter I believe, and know you avoid the demonic coupling because it brings you pain. This was your admission, woman, and a true one from your black heart. But being a person pious in truth, not merely in words, I shall allow you to avoid the tortuous deed. By your own behest you may select another method for confirming yourself the witch. If you do not, I shall, and the subject will be legal death, a man with no future living."

"What I select, then, is your contradiction, that you allege piety, yet promise evil. Therefore, the choice be yours. If a godly man, you reject rape and killing. If ye be evil, let Satan choose your topic. If God is your creator, you select me as a lady."

Naylor then laughed with his mouth closed, his smile so meager he seemed to be conferring politeness toward poor humor. And that smile and all his words Sir Jacob retained as he turned from me and quit the cell.

The next man to enter brought mainly his prick. A male so accustomed to lying that his visage did not reveal his age entered in prison garb so contrasting with my fine woolen dress that further conflict was demanded. Immediately he sought me, and found disbelief, the man startled that so comely a lass would be offered for his leisure activity. Meat for the animal's eating was I, the starving sinner staring at me with no embarrassment as he neared, as he made to join me on the stage of my bed. Despite the histrionics, the audience retained its response; for behind that temporary hole stood the magistrate, his face hidden by the corridor's darkness, his smell penetrating that meshed opening the same as shadow and sound.

As though a site selected for this lovers' tryst, the bed saw us meet at its edge. Performing my practiced role, I sat on the cot and lifted my legs toward the second actor; and with no lady's undergarments worn in this society, what was to interfere with his gaining my meat? Well rehearsed was this actor who knelt to consummate the scene or consume the scenery. He found, however, not the fulfillment implied first by my beauty, then by my spreading, but a composer's climax wherein taunting was merely a segue to a sexless denouement equitable with the surrounds; for I kicked him like a crime, striking him full in the face with both feet as he knelt. As the actor stumbled backwards from the energy of my orgasm, I proved myself so aesthetic as to leap up and perform a variation on my theme, stepping to the man with no overture to kick him well again, now to his sensitive, smelly crotch. In this role, I had no concern for the male, my only intent to avoid killing

565

sex; and here was society's evil: to foster disregard in folk by encouraging mutual attacks among members, then punishing the troupe with each other. How pleased, then, was the audience at the composition's turn, expecting a romance yet finding tragedy? No booing ensued when the act progressed from bodies to bodily function; for noting the criminal about to rise, I met his shoulder with my chamber pot, both items damaged by the contact, but only the latter past repair. Then the sinner forgot my femininity despite gaining a great smell of my lower regions in that he was coated with my piss, a minor revision compared to that of his arm so wrenched the man could not lift it, could not modify his expression from one of unrehearsed pain.

The scene ended as though a curtain closed, two stagehands entering to change scenery, a pair of sinners who looked at me, then the man, removing this latter prop by dragging him by his side without shit, without breakage, act one, scene one, more tragedy to follow.

I had no regret for saving myself from the torture of that evil sex. Praise God, I implied, for saving that man from Eric's mutilation, from Percival's death. Naylor's promise of the criminal's forthcoming, official death had no effect on my emotion. Most significant was a new aspect of my life, for I had never before attacked a person with brutal intent. The men I had killed were Satan's work. The boy flogged in the park was mere punition. Slapping Rathel was direct defense, but the prisoner I had devastated. What sort of person had I become to attack without so much as contemplating avoidance? True evil is evil's self-justification, and though I felt shame from the assault, I also felt relief from averting my own injury—but was that small salvation worth the man's damage? As though Eric in my hands, here was another man partially destroyed, this crime more morally heinous by being intended. Eric had been injured from foolishness, a criminal lack of thought avoidable if the evil witch had only rejected the Rathel's drink, rejected Rathel. But, no, in her socialness the witch allowed her husband's destruction, which led to her causing further injury, that to her identity given by God; for never had I been more of a sinner than when damaging one in their own manner.

566

***

I waited for Naylor. Surely he would provide a new process for the witch now that lust had failed. But only a guard came that day, cleaning my split dung bucket, leaving me grease food, exchanging my water crock for one whose content was too fresh to support the greenish cast of a previous wet body, that pool where I had not failed to prove myself the witch, but failed to prove myself witch enough.

I would not eat that sinners' grease until near starvation. And though unhungered, I prepared for my future sustenance by hieing toward the nearest insect, gaining the flying beetle to bite its belly, bite the creature to find myself eating a bug as though I were an animal — but I was worse, for in being revolted by this natural consumption, I again was a sinner, folk who would likely eat each others' heads rather than bug guts and call the feeding Continental. As punishment for being a sinner, I decided to starve, and tossed the dead insect through the window, having swallowed only the single bite, which in fact was less than tasty. As though refuting or refusing my own witchness, I proceeded to the water bucket and well cleansed my palate, further proving myself the sinner by being unable to accept the taste of God's true food.

The magistrate returned that night, for I found him in my dreams, that most heinous sort of being real. Therein he first visited another cell, one identical to the Rathel's kitchen, to obtain a lethargic drink, but not for himself. As though more concerned with my dreams than his own reality, he had come to feed a certain ignorant prisoner, one so deluded as to believe herself a sinner, when in fact the magistrate knew her to be a common criminal. To prove her identity, he would connive her toward sleep, for therein she would dream of escape and thereby prove the justification for her incarceration in bed.

Having achieved my sleeping, the magistrate observed by sending an actor to participate in my dreams of eating raw meat, though in the future he would grieve over that role, for the eaten meat was his. From my crystalline crotch, I decunted dreams of witchcraft that this sinner sipped, though my groin fumes were so biting he

567

should have refrained from imbibing, his failure one of etiquette, a failure in thinking he could control the flow of sex liquor, later to wonder why he had not simply refrained, simply quit my bed, simply refused my crotch or spilled it. But too politely did he pour himself into my cuntainer that held but a small part of him, but held it completely. Then he danced on the stage of my sex a non-musical opera that turned to tragedy; and I, the unappreciative audience, suffered. Lodged in my balcony bed, I felt the same torment that this player portrayed; and what God did he seek to redeem himself? What prayer do men have when their manliness dies, their offspring deceased without being born? The sinner was a bug on me feeling its leg bitten away. This creature meat was made into a meal by devil Rathel, a family member who according to history was a chef so rank as to revolt the diner from the bottom up, the invert person from her stomach out disposing of the criminal consumed, the man a meal puked away as warm mush, no longer imprisoned within the witch, though not precisely free, his limb exchanged for tactile regret, limbo mush nightmare remorse for accepting the sleeper and suffering her dream.

So tormenting was this nightmare as to be in two acts. After the meal came a loss of employment. Since the spy had been too social for the law of Naylor, no pardon was forthcoming despite the spy's tremendous outcry of bloody tears from his crotch face that lacked a nose, his response one from remorse, for he hated a dampness composed of his blood. Sentencing the actor to silence, Naylor ended his crotch-face conflict by separating the pieces, and successfully, for no longer did the man cry Great God, Lord Jesus, and Blessed Mother for having his manhood cut away. Surely this lack was no longer a problem, for now he had both noses removed, the one to be smelling my decunter and the one sniffling all those tears, Great God, Lord Jesus, Blessed Mother, because both sneezed only blood, the latter from its newly cut bottom, inverted, and the man did not care to be a white witch, in that one had pulled his nose off, Great God, scabbed Jesus, and the witch's bloody mother with her pieces in a grave, in pieces like this man, but all sooty was she, dirty and not to be touched lest fingerprints be left on everything touched thereafter, throughout one's life, her daughter's life, fingerprints of soot left wherever Mother touched her after death, in all her daughter's lives, darkened smears like bruises from within the flesh, welts on her spirit's sensibilities, bruises on her love, sooty blood as dark as the devil left as clear as tears on that white skin, black body.

How saddening a composition the magistrate created, one to move me toward tears, but not near enough, for my tears were golden fish unable to pass through my eyes, remaining in my head as though a nightmare to swim round and round, rooted by the black gold of hair as though a familial source. Most vivid was this dream for the pain it brought me, as though I had been mutilated instead of the nightmare spy, as though I had lost a limb when in fact I had gained one. Though having difficulty in distinguishing this dream of pain from my tormented sleeping, I finally awoke to see my keeper cleaning a meal thrown onto the floor whose consumption I could not recall; for why would I eat such a mush made of water and bile whose only distinguishable portion appeared to be a nailless thumb? Perhaps this was the guard's own vomit, for his entire body retched and trembled, though no part of him expressed enough revulsion to fit one beauteous of view who in her heart was a cannibal.

Thirty-seven

Miss Elsie looked up from the street, but could not see her lass. This was no dream. Since the window's bezel was set deeply within the wall, I could not press forward into light; so in shadow I stood to look down upon Elsie. Her clothing was typical for a servant, not the dull greyness fit a jail; but then, Elsie was no longer a prisoner. Miss Elsie had been released from this home of mine, though too long after being captured by Naylor's morality. But what force had rejected her? There she stood in the narrow street's center, a wagon passing by, a carriage, not enough traffic to oust her as she stared upward to Montclaire's building. But was the woman looking up to see the cave that had held her for days, an era, a life, or was she looking for me? And what should my appropriate response entail? Should I scream out: Here I am, the one who loves you yet near killed my husband your master! Or should I hide from shame and regret, do nothing, no response, mentioning naught of the history to bring us there not to be changed. But, no, some past aspect was different, some conviction or belief modified, and the potentially guilty Miss Elsie had been released. One belief, however, would never change, one of mine: that this woman I did love, should love, and no remorse had I for my conviction.

Standing in my cave to see Elsie in the world to fit her, I loved her better for the justice she had received, loved the relief I felt for her release, and was satisfied. Yet Elsie was looking, not for an object unless that object be as alive as her own emotion. So in my selfishness I called her name, no more, no pledge of love nor desire for forgiveness. I spoke her name again, more loudly, then louder yet, until the sound was no longer a name but a cry, a plea. And the sinner heard me, this woman, this friend; for no longer did she cast her view along the wall, but gave all of her attention to a sound, a spot, a dark shadow that was my cave's passage for remorse. There she looked in silence, toward silence; for having gained her attention, I gave nothing further, considering reaching out for her to see my hand, but nothing, did nothing; so we shared God's space, a medium that was loneliness, a distance of despair.

She looked away. Sharply Elsie moved her gaze to the street's level, for as though male sex fumes came loud orders from Montclaire's bottom for the woman to be on her way lest she return for a greater stay, what with all her fondness. Then Miss Elsie turned to leave, lifting her hand to produce some gesture; but with nothing left to hear and no one to be seen, the woman had no goal but a black hole that was me, Elsie departing with only her freedom, her half-raised hand returned to her side as she left my world, left me.

"As sure as God lives, He will have your soul, murderous cur, and send it to Satan where the spirit of such an immoral hypocrite belongs."

No surprise did Naylor display at my condemning him, a vow from me on the Lord's behalf that I desired as though lust. The magistrate, however, was either accustomed to such condemnations or familiar with my rash assertions, my liberal philosophy. Or in truth was he less surprised at my words than my special speaking, that murmuring of my lower lips he had witnessed having effected within him true belief, a proof to last his entire life of occult concern, his long career of questionable integrity? And did I not discern a new attitude on his part signified by a whiff of fear? Those two males within my cell near the door: Did their presence not prove the magistrate's caution, his cowardice? What form did his fear take that he was not accompanied by a man of God, only those of crime?

"Your response may be too strong, missus. No cleric would

condemn me, and surely they know Jesus better than you—
better than I, for we all have limited areas of expertise. The
previous night you were finally able to prove your own, for
which I thank you as well as praise God. And He will accept
my praise with none of the rejection you seek, for I have
fulfilled my duty as one of His men by executing the barbarous
criminal who this morning was passed to greater hands."

"And during the night was tortured. My God vilifies all
torturers. Does yours, being Satan, perhaps praise them instead?"

"If true, he would be praising you, missus, for you are the
person to have done the bloody deed."

"My person was the *implement*, vile Naylor, dishonest in
your sinister philosophy by which you and the devil destroyed
one of God's people. No willingness had I as proven by your
requiring a potion to steal my body. No less than the blade
wielded to kill the man was my person a tool unwillingly used
for slaughter."

"But even as the metal blade slices naturally, proven equally
natural is your ability—your need—to slaughter men."

"The *need* be yours, heinous Naylor, and the ability is mine
the same as any person with a blade has the capacity to
slaughter, but only those vile have the need."

"Enough of this pious expertise, missus, from one residing in
an English prison for having mutilated her husband. I did not
make your torso such a weapon. But I have verified its capacity as you previously maintained. Thus, we proceed with the
area of your person, not your philosophy; the area of witches,
not of humans. Therefore, avail yourself in good detail to
correct my misjudgments of your true nature, for this be the
vow made us one another. Despite your initial doubt, my
integrity in keeping my word is now proven. All that remains
is your testimony."

"With all of your integrity, you take pride in never having
pledged to refrain from using me heinously?"

"Be a good blade, missus, and feign not that your edge has
no dried blood from previously occult displays. Hereafter you
will deny that your own husband's male member was separated

572

by his wife's body. If a Satanic force overcame your pious will and caused you to slaughter, then be it part of your description, part of your vow."

"And your vow is to allow me life. How generous when without Eric's death you cannot kill me—cannot *legally* kill me. But, then, a magistrate of your bloody career can interpret the law according to his own integrity—and who's to restrain him: the God he praises or the devil he manipulates?"

"Your own lax philosophy will not change the honesty of our mutual pledge, nor my accurate recollection thereof. Your life I have promised to spare not as due to be taken for your husband's assault, but for those other sheer murders last night proven true. For those deaths you receive no punition from England. At your life's end, Lord God will have His own interpretation, but His justice is not for magistrates to question. My place with you now is to receive your own expert and most thorough knowledge pledged in description of your race and all their occult secrets."

"My own, accurate recollection provides for further accomplishment on your part. Or has your memory vanished with your integrity?"

"All my requirements regarding our vow I have realized. Your 'saint,' this Elsie Rowell, was released today with no harm done. Proof might be offered you from a trusted exterior person as to this Rowell's living freely in London."

"No verification is required in that I saw her depart, and pray God that she more than you receives from life what her pious heart deserves."

"From further observation did you note this prison's latest guest arrive? Did you observe my remaining vow's fulfillment?"

"I did not."

"As Elsie Rowell vacated her cell, the woman was replaced by one now considered less expert than before. A formal English trial awaits Amanda Rathel, who is charged with conspiracy to murder, and additionally, with harboring a murderess and dealing with occult forces at the cost of human life."

"How might this trial damage me since often there I'll be discussed?"

"Well accepted legally will be that your dealings with Lady Rathel are separate and fulfilled with justice in the eyes of Queen Anne and her law."

"This Rathel, then, will not manipulate you as often she has during your career of integrity?"

"Lady Rathel shall receive a justice due her that you will not, for only your testament saves you. But Amanda . . . No words shall I accept from her, no expertise. As you wished for Rowell, the Lady Rathel will receive her deserved results in life. To prove my expertise in arraignment, shall I display the prisoner and have you understand my contractual completion?"

"You may."

The magistrate then stepped away, moving to his guards with whom he had quiet speaking. I discerned no words, but Naylor's voice sought me, his deep tone projecting an unsegmented sound. Then the door was opened, one guard leaving, the second remaining with Sir Jacob.

"You will accompany us, missus," he offered, and held forth his arm as though for a lady. For this prisoner, however, his arm would not contact, but denote; and I followed not by his side, but in his direction.

Guards infiltrated the prison's halls like rats, internal constables observing at every cell; and I wondered how often they had stared into mine. Now they gained good viewing, looking closely not to their superior, but to his most beauteous charge. And what had they heard of this prisoner to set them to wonder? Though that unpadded, half-flat bosom was readily seen, did they also stare at my pelvis as I passed to wonder of pricks contained herein, like sweetmeat in a crockery jar, cockery jar? Did they look behind me for sexual members dribbled from my bottom, jostled loose by the movement of my legs, the swaying of my hips they well desired to imprison with their senses? And what was the source of Naylor's pride I smelled: from accompanying a blatant beauty, or controlling a proven witch?

As though on a street we came to an intersection, our party turning left, north, that side of landforms where mosses grow best. What formation of Earth was this mountain for its caves

574

to house social ladies of the Rathel's stature? One promoting natural senses, it seemed, for through the fog of man fume I discerned a whiff of a woman known in all my lives wherein death had settled, an order of violence promoted by a lady now correctly situated, for her new stone home was meant to contain only those sinister. Therein we would live together, separated by a maze of mountain walls, connected by crime.

"You would speak with this woman? She is yet your legal mother, is she not?"

This was Naylor's query as we stopped before a door much like my own, for were not the respective tenants peers?

"Of no living creature could she be mother, for the Rathel is barren of life regardless of her womb," I replied as though she and I were not peers here as well, for my crotch supplied only killing. "I'll not speak with this sinner, for our business is ended by God."

"Then you would look past this iron to see that justice through your own auspices has gained the specific person."

"I take no pride in so placing her. My imaginative preference is for Rathel to be as pious as Elsie or Eric, but that desire is so fantastical as to be opera. And I need not view her, for I can smell her moving." And, yes, I could readily sense every turn the woman made, for Rathel was hot, stalking as though searching for some creature on the floor to eat, something new to kill.

"You will not speak, then?" Naylor asked.

"I have no words for her," I said. And though this statement was honest, I yet had a sound; for despite a true pity I felt not for Rathel's position but for her acts, I nonetheless found a new bout of mad humor most recently seen in my dreams. As I paused before the Rathel's household, a sick smile and demonic laugh came that drew the attention of the legal men surrounding me; for no expert in occultism was required to recognize the sound as a cackle, its source therefore a witch.

"Witches can write with an ability equal to their smelling?"

"This one can," I replied to Naylor's query.

575

"What further surprises have you for me?"

"An abundance, no doubt, to be divulged herein," I responded, and nodded toward that stack of paper the magistrate had supplied, fine writing surfaces worthy of so unique a lady. My additional tools of composition fit me in a different manner. The desk brought by Naylor's men was simple, common, yet as artificial as London, the chair comfortable though composed of slain trees. The quills, perhaps, were most appropriate, for though ostensibly natural, were they not plucked away in either death or mutilation, and for all their beauty, was each not tipped with metal? Small blades for cutting like my cunt, removing the artificial postures that had adorned and obscured my life. But what had I to currently, continually hide, when no truth would have me removed from my home? This cave was mine forever, this living a type to last, one in which I had no better effort than to apply black prints to clean paper, like the marks of those I had burned left upon my own skin, stains on my sensibilities. Dead these words were compared to my past acts. Like the Rathel, I was barren of life, having destroyed my family not through vengeance nor failure, but a misapplication of love.

Thirty-eight

As though being punished for her desperation, Elsie arrived at the Rathel's town house to find her original mistress removed, and in a mad way the servant was relieved. Nevertheless, was she not also mutilated to discover that her home was no more? The remaining servants rambled on in a fluster as to how Mistress Amanda's estate would be taken by English law and dispersed. Though not yet mandated to leave, the servants expected this legal instruction, for whom would they serve in that their mistress and her moneys would not return? Surely Miss Elsie could remain as long as any, for all were friends and more of a family than ever before. Not past the next morning, however, did the former prisoner remain before seeking not new employ, but another family. This house was yet a home to her, though comfortable only compared to prison, its value diminished because the occupants, though admired, were not to her preference. Home, mistress, and life: All of Elsie's were wrong. That first woman had not been Elsie's mistress for a life, but how could Alba be? And she recalled the sound of her name called and called again from the prison, as though the entire wall were Alba, her Miss Alba, but removed by such a distance that even a building's loud voice was soft to hear. Soft to the ears, but damaging. And the sound came to Elsie again, a noise enough to stop her heart, for how in any life, any world, could she be part of a family not including Alba?

With no more family of blood in London than Rathel herself, Elsie would not find her affairs looked after by any sanction except the state, and that meant a home for the poor. That meant another prison. So Elsie found the truth of desperation in her life, departing the next morning for a walk never taken before, one to tire her little but frighten her immensely, Elsie seeking the last member of her family, journeying to the house of Mr. and Mrs. Edward Denton.

The chamberlain answering the door was not alone, but had a companion to make Elsie weep, for there was Randolph to well greet his friend. What could the Dentons' servant think of this common woman who fell to her knees and wept over the family dog? Thereafter, what did this visitor think of the answer to her seeking company with Master Eric? A person not receiving guests, what with his . . . illness, in that he was yet confined to bed. Kindly, then, asked the woman, inquire of Master Eric as to whether he might have a message for Miss Elsie.

He did. The door closed calmly in her face, Elsie found this wooden panel not a temporary hole, but a barrier between herself and Randolph, perhaps one permanent. Soon, however, the chamberlain returned with two notes. In the first, Eric ordered Elsie to leave. She would not enter to be confronted by his parents who hated everything about Lady Rathel and Alba including their shared servant. Therefore, Elsie should proceed to Lord Andrew's house, giving the grandfather the second note wherein Eric requested Grand to temporarily house this servant who was indeed part of Eric's married family. And what did the chamberlain think of this woman's weeping anew? Terrible news she must have received, for after her reading, the woman departed with a thank-you barely audible through her sobbing. Then Elsie turned to walk away only to whirl and dive for the doorway, embracing the dog with a farewell not meant to be final.

Lord Andrew would have received Elsie better if only he recalled her. Speaking with her at the door, Andrew had to read his grandson's note before recollection was sparked within him, and sorrowful he felt for his lapse of recognition. But with old thought released, Grand received this woman into his home, there to live as part of his own family until further requests from her master, and that was only Eric.

No guest would Elsie be, though Andrew had no orders for his own servants as to her hierarchical position. An elder lot the same as their master, these folk would allow the woman to fit as she pleased, but Elsie was only pleased to be sweeping and scrubbing and peeling vegetables, the latter especially reminiscent of her previous home, that one most true and most false. But this home required little maintenance in that neither witches nor vengeance were housed therein. Thus, the newcomer was told to refrain from performing all the household's work herself, lest the current servants feel so useless as to leave for Miss Elsie's previous residence. But, no, they would not likely seek that abode, she told them, and within days found a position at Lord Andrew's to please all those present; and wait she did for further instructions from her superior, not that lost lady, but the reduced man.

These instructions came soon enough even for a woman unable to wait as well as a witch. Active in the household though no longer a storm, Elsie one day answered the door to find a young gent able to walk only poorly; for as soon as he found command of his legs, Eric quit his parents' home, for he could not live with people who hated his wife.

The reunion between servant and master was warm, yet diminished by that person missing, tempered by the man's insistence on not being wept over. Randolph here was like a child who in his innocence had no accompanying sadness, no regret for that family member presently untouchable. Having joy for those about him, Randolph was no barrier between Eric and Elsie, but a medium to aid their pleasure's transfer without the burden that was Alba's memory. My memory.

With his grandfather's welcome acceptance, Eric had no thoughts of his parents, their pain at his rejection. Businesslike in his leaving, Eric had alleged that he would find more comfort at Grand's, for in his original home was too much consideration given the cause of his injury as though others had been more damaged than he. Perhaps they had, but none were parents. Gone was that felicitous relationship between parent and child, a common yet profound state whose deterioration had begun with the future wife's entering London and Eric's life. Here the parents were to blame; for they, unlike Elsie, had believed in Rathel's potential, her hatred a religion whose iconology had convinced them. Yet for all their courage in defying ignorant Eric, Hanna and Edward had lost their place with him now held by passive Elsie. Separated by conviction, the parents hated Alba too fully

579

to be accepted by their prejudicial son. But with all the love and defiance from friend and family, no one had saved Eric from his own lust and love, from his wife's inadequacies, the limbo lady neither sinner nor witch, Eric no longer the son he had been nor the man God had made him.

Not until Eric began healing his life, not his body, was a missing person mentioned: the unladylike Rathel. Queried by Eric as to Rathel's position, Elsie described that for his very injury the woman was now incarcerated, her responsibility the oldest and most basic in this opera, exactly as maintained by Alba from her first days in London. Exactly as described by most honest Alba to a faithless servant who had not been friend enough to believe the lass her superior in both intellect and courage. No opinion had Eric of the wife's alleged superiority, only mentioning Elsie's aspects, that this friend and servant was wholly without blame. Only the witch herself was not morally situated within this conversation, for it ended with Rathel. Therefore, my place was lost, my name not soon mentioned again, and then not by the husband.

The progress of Eric's healing was noted not only by a hired physician, but also London's prime magistrate, who occasionally visited Eric at Lord Andrew's residence. When presuming the victim healed enough to accept strong subjects, Naylor brazenly, frightfully mentioned the wife: not her damage, but her identity.

"Mr. Denton, those rumored accounts as to your wife's being associated with witch persons I know to be true," Naylor stated.

At once he knew. In a strike of enlightenment, Eric came aware that his wife was known to be the witch, and would therefore receive the typical, permanent punishment due her kind. Retaining a calm strength with difficulty, Eric responded to Naylor.

"Is this foolish belief the cause for her remaining imprisoned?"

"Sir, feign not a coy attitude we know to be false. By her own verity, your wife is proven the witch and accepted as such by English law. Regardless, she shall not be executed for her identity, and her punition of life's imprisonment for having damaged you shall not change."

Stunned was Eric as he instantly accepted the fact of my latest demonstration, yet relieved he was to learn of my survival, these confused emotions so strong as to weaken him. Nevertheless, his speaking was firm.

"Wherein your purpose, Sir Jacob, in tormenting me with this subject? In fact, the identity of my wife is verified as a person pious with God, who remains morally incorrupt despite your commentary of witches."

With new intensity, Naylor then declared, "By the grace of God, Denton, your wife was not the witch without your knowledge; yet through all my inquiries, you never condemned her first aspect, and now virtually forgive her assault."

"I do not forgive the damage, sir, I do not. But I will not have my wife blamed when she is not at fault, not in her heart nor her intent."

"Thus, my intention: to learn why you apply mildness toward a woman who nearly killed you. I would in some way know the man who has lived as husband with this witch, and who, having been cut away until no longer a bodily man, yet has no condemnation for her. What sort of person are you, sir, to have such remarkable qualities?"

"The true question sought is misstated, Lord Naylor, but nonetheless I comprehend. In fact, you would not inquire of my special qualities, but of the unapproachable personality who is my wife. That unique character I cannot be expected to describe, not so soon after suffering from the evil to inhabit her. And suffer I do, sir, to a degree I believe unimaginable to those without equal experience. But when I come to suffer less, perhaps I might gain some understanding of Alba for us all. Perhaps not. But I suggest you prepare for a consequential waiting, for as long as I know of this woman, in some ways I shall suffer from her. After this has ended, sir, let us be pleased to speak again."

Eric learned from Naylor that only Rathel, not the wife, would receive a public trial. Though no request was made for his testimony, Eric had thoughts of another person who might bear witness against the evil expert. Eric had thoughts of the wife's attendance, and therefore imagined being amongst the audience. Observing the witch was an irresistible idea to him, yet how in God's world could he ever bear to see her again?

With the conflictual anxiety of needing to see an impossible sight, Eric attended the affair to find disappointment. This was no trial, but a sentencing. No testimony would be given by any person, only documents presented by Naylor's aide. No personal testimony meant no person the witch to appear where she could be seen by all of London. Here exactly was Naylor's intent, for a significant audience awaited the demon. The Lady Rathel was present, and was made to stand before the well-wigged justices like a row of social gods seated in a wooden heaven. With no word asked from her, Rathel was sentenced to a stay of two hundred months for her sought cooperation with demonic forces promoting the death of one Percival Bitford and the grievous injury of Eric Denton.

What a murmur went through the audience of commonfolk and gentry packed together within a room too small for unequal classes. Such is the power of witches, the exact force sought by this congregation, the greatest crowd ever drawn by the particular sister, and this without her presence, though not without her name. As the crowd began its complex sound induplicable by natural entities, the available wench replied. Led away by flanking guards, the Rathel heard murmurs of ". . . witch . . ." never spoken by English official, and turn she did to confiscate the crowd as she had my life, calling toward them in outrage.

"Yes, the witch! Where is the witch and her deserved death when I am imprisoned enough to kill me?!"

Then the screaming began, followed by enough of a rush to imply a riot. Early to exit was unrecognized Eric, the audience not seeking the husband before he was gone. Also promoting their safety via fleeing were the barristers. Behind doors they hid themselves before the crowd arrived at the lockwork to shout past the constables for justice, for the witch, these two notions combined meaning the latter's head in their hands.

Though well heated in their pious emotions, the audience was not so volatile as to crush through legal doorways and have at the hiding men. Therefore, the constables allowed them to mull about and cry epithets until becoming bored enough to vacate the legal chambers; and what poor beggars would clear the disarrayed benches and broken chairs? Who would clear from these citizens' hearts an idea never to bore them, that of hated witches and an evil individual yet to be given her proper, deadly due?

Since all of London was the source of this crowd, great was the rabble becoming distressed at a fine lady's being punished; whereas the witch was bloody well lounging on a throne for all they knew. Through the streets they paraded their concern, some with songs of justice portraying the Rathel's release and the witch's permanent mutilation. Outside the prison they caroused, but the wrong side, for the witch was in a rear cell, yet her detractors marched on the wider boulevard before Montclaire. Scarcely did I notice them, being occupied with writing, my composition's heroine yet on Man's Isle, perhaps, affixed in a theater piece lusted over by Naylor daily.

How remarkable to be unaffected by a crowd to kill me when these same persons brought Eric a regard that harmed. Poor Miss Elsie was answering the door that day a throng appeared to burst past her and infiltrate the household, searching every room until Eric was found. With God in their mouths, they pressed Eric to his knees enough to wrench his back as all went down for Jesus's sake, commencing a prayer. Several at once, for this church lacked the refined formality of a true congregation's clerical process. Then up with him as though a sack of beans, and the inquisition began, harsh, hot breaths so near Eric that their smell was left on him. Questioning Eric's salvation, the voices sought his continual prayer to purge the witch's evil. Then a separate sect formed to shout an unorthodox view: Since the man had taken sex with the woman witch, had not she left something within him instead of taking a piece? Mad humor this was as though a witch had been tutoring the sinners; but were they not squabbling over the same victim, under the auspices of the single, presumed Jesus?

Then began a mutual persecution, for these sects of anti-witch, pro-victim began a pushing to accompany their shouts, followed by smacks of fist on face. A third type of fanatic, Eric gained a salvation that situated him in his future world. As though enlightened by God Himself, Eric found the power to proceed in life, all his remorse and confusion replaced by anger. As the secular confrontations continued, Eric implemented their ending.

Elsie had long before gone running for the constables. The other servants, being elder and intelligent, well hid themselves lest they suffer from a witch scarcely seen. Proving himself father to Edward, Lord Andrew pressed forcefully through the crowd as best he could, demanding folk leave as he pulled them away; but Grand was too elderly for great success, his efforts absorbed by the mass. So were Eric's, but poorly; for with the beginning violence, he moved from the corridor into a bedchamber that had once been ours though never again slept in by the husband, removing that loose bedpost and presenting it to the crowd with concise, controlled swings to the nearest backs and shoulders, poking the wood toward faces and bellies; and what mad humor for him to be praying with a stick not crossed in its middle. The congregation, large for a hallway, became small for all of Eric's anger, which passed like a sea wave over the audience members, its medium of transference pain. Then all who could stand ran from the house, not a crowd now but individuals with no religious affiliation beyond sole survival, each running for salvation, though not through Jesus.

When constables came in carriages with Naylor and Elsie, recuperating Eric was found with his grandfather cleaning the mess, these two weakened men sufficiently strong to drag the wounded intruders from their home with scant regard for injuries; for Eric had begun to rearrange his life, and would not end until only family members remained.

The trial in which Eric had failed to see the wife had been his last failure, the congregation she had indirectly sent delivering this message. Though exhausted and sickened by his exertion, Eric had fully recuperated, if not in the body, then in his heart. Eric had come to understand that his health and profession were insignificant, for he would spend the remainder of his days not working nor healing, but loving Alba. In an instantaneous, completing view of his future, Eric accepted that he would not pass his life pining over this ultimate love vanished as though a crowd of evil haters praying via trespass too late to change the court's adjudications. This decision was not only for Alba, but from her, Eric recalling the instances wherein she had refused in anger his lax, useless feelings, yet with a most subtle and special love accepted his best emotions, whether she agreed with them or not. And, yes, he knew it to be love, a type of love, an enhancing and fulfilling and desirable love that the wife had felt for him, this the very force allowing her to remain with an alien in an alien land. For this man and woman were together not merely in England's registers, but also in their hearts, a bond now obvious to the husband aware of his wife's emotion through her own peculiar manner that was no longer unique, for Eric had learned. The husband understood only when the wife was gone that they were truly wed, Eric ascertaining my desired position in his life not through a detailed cognition, but a subtle revelation of love.

The correct position of his personal witch was not in Eric's heart, but in his house. She should not be lodged in his emotions, but should live along with him, at his side. Together they should be on God's Earth, not within some sinning philosophy. Separating them now, however, was no bridgeable distance, but the space of English law, Eric coming to feel for the situation an emotion the wife might not approve of, though it was one she often displayed. Within him seethed anger, a demeanor that issued an intent of equal strength, one not to be quenched by love, but only fulfilled by achievement. Only with an act as intense and absolute as those initiated by the wife for her own survival would Eric save himself from the sinners' morality that had split his family. As though suffering from mad humor, Eric came to understand that since English law would not release his wife, he would have to take her.

Thirty-nine

"I shall now determine the size of your heart."

"And I'm begging your pardon, sir?"

"The size of your soul, miss, and the substance thereof."

"Ah, sir, but you're saying what I cannot understand."

"Miss, I will soon describe how the life of my family shall proceed in its following years, and will know your part therein. My family consists of myself, Randolph, yourself, and your mistress, Alba."

"Oh, and Master Eric, and Alba is enjailed now, like a tomb, and not to be released, and my fear has always been that you would be keeping her there if given the choice."

"No choice am I allowed by English law; therefore, I shall force upon society the selection of my family's ways. My choice, then, is to have the wife returned to her family with whom she belongs. And I ask you now if you can live and cooperate with the fact that I shall have my wife's release, even if criminality is required on my part."

"Oh, great Jesus, Master Eric, why should I be living free if Mistress Alba is not? No more injustice I can't be thinking than Alba not living as best a person can. God knows I've oft prayed to put me in her place and be releasing the girl if only you would accept her again."

"I think we both understand that a person in my reduced condition cannot be expected to desire such a woman beside him ever again. Nevertheless, despite how she has pained me, Alba is my life's continuing love. Herein I have no choice, though perhaps I would select no other, for Alba's life has surely been more distraught than mine. Therefore, I will have her returned despite the legalities that retain her wrongly. But from you I ask no criminality, Elsie, only your cooperation in spirit."

"But if I'm only praying for you, sir, then I'm doing not enough, for I can be praying in me sleep. If you're having Mistress Alba removed from the prison, then you're dealing with something beyond me, sir. But I would learn. I would learn in order to remain in this family."

"Thus are we conjoined in ignorance," Eric told her, and took Elsie's hand as though clasping a man to consummate a business venture. But Eric's exuded confidence made the servant no less fearful, for here the master had the force of anger, not cunning, a reversed demeanor fit the inverted wife, the lost companion.

He was certain no legal venue would release the wife. Too satisfied was the magistrate with his new expert to relinquish her, an impossible dismissal considering her confessions of Satanic murder. And dangerous her freedom would be, for though the parading of pious folk seeking her neck had subsided, alive in London during the following months were stories of the witch living in Montclaire Prison as though a hosteled queen. And Eric knew better than to draw further attention to the witch's husband, his secretive plans thus to be surmised by curious, clever sinners.

Though innocent of prison ways, sufficiently familiar was Eric with the greater realm of British society for him to deduce his task's beginning: finance. Not seeking employment in that payment for his talents would not support his fiscal needs, Eric approached the blessed Grand with lies, portraying himself as a man requiring funds to provide his wife with legal defense. Moved by Eric's forgiveness and fidelity, Lord Andrew allowed his grandson access to a sinners' bank, generous accounts therein to afford Eric that unparalleled power of ready currency, if only he could determine how to apply his new wealth.

Solicitors reinforced Eric's idea that the wife would not be legally released. The expertise Eric thereafter considered was not in English law, but appropriately its invert, the realm of crime. But what professionals could be sought on this subject? Constables were expert in felony, even moreso than barristers, who were insulated from criminal locales by the architecture of the courthouse. But obtaining the services of a constable willing to reject his profession for superior funding seemed unlikely to Eric as well as dangerous. Doubtless he would find honest lawmen before those corrupted, and therefore never gain the latter due to his being incarcerated by the former.

Cognitive Eric adjudged he was best to proceed by seeking established, not potential, criminals. No great enthusiasm enveloped him with this decision, but his life beyond the upcoming corruption would not be endured without his spouse. And who could be more fitting for him than the sex witch who hated sex? With no gender limb on the husband to require satisfaction, the married pair would likely live more comfortably than during that initial, raw-arsed time of marriage. Comfort, however, was not Eric's prime concern. That anger within him was both guide and torment, an emotion he would follow to its end.

Even a sinner could smell the difference. The bodily wastes and food remains tossed at the street's edges formed a sensual ambience, and that burned background was natural for no city. Surely the buildings themselves housed worse elements than their peripheral artifacts. Therefore, Eric traversed this street by remaining paces away from the buildings, away from the dogs whose bared teeth and low growlings threatened the interloper walking with no goal, his oldest clothes too good for this society.

Long he walked without seeing any person, though from the buildings' depths came anonymous threats to have his goddamned kidney cut out and et cetera. His first response was relief for having brought no money along, for at least he would not be robbed. One epithet was shouted so near Eric that he seemed to smell its source. Leaping sideways with a start, Eric saw but a hint of a man in the shadows, a man with no intent of retreating though his position be revealed. Here was a person to meet, perhaps, in that he neither attacked nor fled. But since he had also shouted obscenities worse than any of the wife's when most upset, Eric felt that some superior example of semi-humanity surely lay ahead.

Moving a few alleys north—as though seeking certain mosses—Eric came to a broader street with equal squalor and more human noise. Espying children playing with ungrowling dogs no more fetid than themselves, Eric presumed greater safety here, and a greater opportunity for success, in that the base of people for his communicating was increased. Thus, he walked several minutes before two men assaulted him with saps, in a flurry of activity clubbing the manless man to the ground, searching every portion of his attire for purses and watches; then, finding nothing, off with his boots to run away like playing children.

Foolish he felt to be sprawled on the street with no gentlemanly pose. No elite Londoners, however, were about for embarrassment. Even the former populace had now departed, as though refusing to be seen with a man so uncouth as to lie in the dirt and spit blood. But Eric was not concerned with etiquette, for he was seeking pain. His balance poor, Eric stood with difficulty; but with his left eye swollen shut and his jaws stiff and inoperable, why had he only numbness?

So pervasive was his dullness that Eric had no shame in shoeless walking. In fact, he was virtually pleased at the people staring in better London, for they would not harm him. And once in a coach and before Lord Andrew's house, he well felt at home. If this be so, however, why the delay in leaving the cab, as though he had adhered to the seat? But no surprise had Eric here, for danger had been his expectation, though he was displeased to lose those boots; and what a fool to wear an ancient westcoat but excellent footwear. Having never gained mad humor despite long exposure to Alba, Miss Elsie had no understanding of Eric's stumbling into the house chuckling, mumbling about returning to Penstone with no shoes, but then they would steal his pants. And no explanation had he for that blood sputtering down his chin with the chortling, though Elsie guessed the source to be other than criminals, perhaps a witch.

"And, sir, it is I notice you in our area before, and wonder if you come for the selling. It may be some cooking wares you mean to peddle."

After recuperating from his latest damage, Eric returned to a similar section of Penstone Place. Two days of questing found him approached by a surprisingly young man with excellent teeth and perhaps the clothes he was given at birth, such was their age, youthful for criminals but not for their artificial hides.

"I've a proposition for a genuine man, but not a coward nor a fool."

"Well, sir, and if you're giving me payment to be aiding you, genuinely I can do all you may wish, after a decent meal to get me thinking straight, which I've not had in some time."

"Your lack of straight thinking is readily seen. Therefore your difficulty in recalling my previous speaking wherein I rejected those foolish, a category likely to include you amongst its members."

"Well, and, sir, you did seem less than the gent that day without your boots, and now with lumps yet showing on your nut."

Eric then stepped nearer the man to immediately state, "Sir, this day again I wear fine boots. Would you alone care to examine their fit?"

Not so foolish as to measure the emotion guiding Eric, the young man answered, "Perhaps not, sir, but perhaps I am not alone here."

"Then bring your mother out to aid you, child," Eric replied with mild, perhaps mad, laughter.

"She was in an English prison at my birth, sir, and scarcely has been out since. More in than out. But she reared me to the business of this place, and so might I aid you here, for Jesus can see you're not doing well on your own."

"Aid me then, youth, by finding for me a man expert enough to enter Montclaire Prison and not leave alone."

Laughing himself, the young man returned, "And, sir, if you think to rob London's best prison, have in waiting a fee so generous you can't carry it, for you would set men toward death or an endless stay there."

"A business I do know is paying a man well for his arduous tasks. If you've familiarity with the sort of man I seek, send him to me, tomorrow, on the corner of Harborough Street near the museum. Attend and you shall have your fee. If you've no capacity for this chore or know less of this region than you maintain, visit your mother instead."

Eric then turned to leave, the youth watching his initial steps, staring with a small laughter barely escaping his lips.

The typical London bustle at this corner was heartening to Eric in its security. What a change of mien the people about him displayed, moving and speaking as though having nothing to conceal, nothing to hide from. Common here were courteous gents bending toward Eric to wish him a fine good day, Eric replying by tipping his hat, always with a deeper bow and broader smile, his lengthier greetings stemming only from his pleasure at saluting decent peers.

A peer of that young Penstone man soon approached Eric, alone. Not only his simplified clothing—no waistcoat or jacket, only a jerkin and poor hat—but also the containment of his personality as he looked about without moving his head described him as not fitting this locale. No felicitous greetings had he for passing folks, only a cold query to a waiting man.

"You're of the prisons?"

He had stopped by Eric's side to remain unseeable by the gent unless the latter turned. Eric viewed a heavy, not youthful man whose head's hair was as short as his beard was long. What of his countenance made this man seem a criminal and not merely baseborn? Was the difference his viewing folk as though he would rather spit at them? Standing beside a gentleman, a commoner would present his front at an acceptable distance; whereas this man was askew and too near, as though to conceal himself behind the gent.

"I am the man of the prison," Eric stated, viewing the stranger's thick ear. "And what man are you?"

"I am one who knows you."

"How are you familiar with me?"

"I know the business you seek. I know you would have your wife away from Montclaire. I know she is called a witch by all of London."

Remaining calm though this man seemed to read his mind, Eric thought that somehow his plan had been made known to general London, so that any moment would find him confronted by constables, not criminals. But this rapid thinking was more guilt's concern than good idea, and was ignored by Eric, who continued with his business.

"I would know the source of your notions," he urged.

"No matter. What I know is the truth, and you need know no more."

"As long as I am the subject of your familiarity and the source of cash to support my plans, I will either learn of your knowledge or retain my finances for one more cooperative."

After a pause for irritation, not cogitation, the hirsute man replied.

"I was at this Lady Rathel's trial and did see you. That you would have your wife away from Montclaire is easy thinking. I doubt you'd want this Rathel instead when I have seen both."

"My wife was not at any trial. How, then, do you maintain to have seen her?"

"I was in the same prison and saw her walking past."

This clear description was no ending to his speech, the man yet to overcome his irritation. Therefore he added: "Will you hear this, or hear the truth?"

"Regardless of your difficulty in producing true speech, I would have us continue in an honest vein. Tell, then, of your seeing my wife."

"In that she came to Penstone and find me for business, as did you."

"What business was hers and when?"

"Years before, when with the Lady Rathel she did live. Her business was for me to kill that woman."

Eric could not retain his surprise, though it was only revealed by a stark stillness and too long a pause before his response.

"Your only appropriate idea is the mention of Montclaire. If in fact I had payment for a person's release from this building, how might you manifest this notion, and how in advance could you convince me of a success not to place us all within the bounds of prison?"

"This jail I've been in, long and recent. A good plan I could make and have it succeed with the work of others known me. The plan's good job I could convince you of, but you would have to pay for it, and for these other persons to do their parts."

"Now we arrive at your most expert aspect, which is accepting money."

"What money do you offer?"

"What sum would you accept?"

592

The criminal then stated a price. Eric laughed and cut two-thirds away. This sum the criminal doubled, which Eric somewhat reduced. After this mutual tutoring for a doctorate in pawning, the men had the beginnings of a figure. Apart from an understanding of funds, a broader agreement was yet to come.

"The fee I would charge is low," the criminal asserted, "too low for the price of failure."

"One sentence ago we had a virtual contract, and now the sum becomes unworthy. Is part of your illegality to seduce your employer?"

"The sum is too low for your task, and any man in my place would agree. I tell you, then, I would work for less if given other payment."

"My word, man, would you require classical paintings from my wall, or perhaps the dining room's candelabra?"

"No, I would have your wife. Again."

Eric was so startled that his mouth without bidding opened; but was his greater surprise from the first idea or that ending word?

Only then did the felon turn to look at Eric, one gaze at his face before turning away to speak again.

"You say to know none of your wife's sex doings? With them she did nearly kill you, yet you have surprise."

"We'll not bother with her dealings, but with yours. You've mentioned the sought killing of Lady Rathel—what now of my wife and sex?"

"No coin did she offer me to kill that woman, but sex instead. And in advance did she give me, allowing me manself into her mouth as I would have it again, and therefore challenge Montclaire Prison. And do not tell me of not knowing these things or things like them, for you are no virgin with that woman, and she's no common wife like others. Why are you without limb beneath your belly and her in jail forever if she's the average lady? Insult me not with your ignorance."

In another rush of absolute decision, Eric had rapid orders for his future employee.

"Find me at Penstone's edge tomorrow, near the warehouse without roof. There will I have your initial payment, not to be transferred in the midst of London's populace. Small it shall be, but a good beginning."

With no further word, Eric returned to his grandfather's home. Entering the kitchen, his thoughts were of the wife's expertise in unnatural intercourse, not the kind to kill a man, but to please him, more than one, gents and criminals. An implement for cooking Eric attained, then to the bank for currency, returning to practice the entire day handing the criminal his payment. Until sore in his arms, he reached into his coat, then out to that felon.

Even upon retiring, Eric gave effort toward his wife's release. In bed he found no sleeping, only a part-waking dream that constantly displayed the criminal with the short and long hair. All Eric heard was the felon boasting of sex with the wife, describing the acts with such disdain that he could not face Eric, all the while astonished at the husband's virginity. A greater distress was not from imagining sex between Alba and the Elephant as though I were practicing for pleasure, but my having intercourse simply to live out a life meant to torment me first, Eric later, and please a criminal enough for him to risk his own arse to come and rescue mine, to come within mine, that prick in my mouth not Eric's, that man meat and semen eaten like the animal flesh and gravy I refused, refused fine beef though I would consume a fiend's fetid cock, taking his rotten sperm on my tongue though rarely allowing Eric even a cursory kiss.

Not even these scenes caused Eric's greatest torment. Though seeing me couple with baseborn blackguard curs often enough that night for an army of tongues and turds to be procreated, Eric's worst pain came from the man's *conveying* this tale as though Eric were so poor a husband that he would not mind the wife's extraneous fucking. After all, since he had married a witch who pinched his prick off, was he not less than human himself? Worse was the cad's implication that Eric had never been quite human, and therefore was less of a person than this bristly low-life cretin who had raped his wife in her ear for all that Eric knew. Through the night, he suffered from criminal dreams until he was rolling from side to side in torment, the pains from his wound coming next a moderation of agony in comparison. But never in the night did Eric imagine the upcoming contract's denouement, for some things are best left unexamined, especially the precious wife's having fucked a fiend.

The next morning in Penstone, wearied from his embattled

594

sleep, Eric accepted exhaustion, thereby avoiding the reasonable thinking of a freshened mind. When the criminal appeared as though a grubby vision presumed in sleep too often, Eric achieved the striking thought that he had no name for this person, one surely less of a man than himself, despite any quantity of penises. A person too lowly to have a name caused such repugnance in Eric that all the upcoming business seemed tainted, even the exalted project of releasing the wife. Therefore, Eric would be on with the transaction and off with himself, having no torment now beyond distaste (though not from thoughts of manly fluid in anyone's mouth). When the felon in disdain moved not to Eric's face but his side while asking for the promised payment, the husband gruffly waved him on with no word. Looking about an alley later to find no superfluous persons, Eric revealed the blatant bundle of currency in his greatcoat exactly as he stopped, turning toward the felon. Accepting his payment, the man held the printed pile with every finger as though a precious living thing, perhaps an exceptional vulva, certainly a rare surprise, for never had the criminal seen such a sum nor expected one from Eric. Though immensely satisfying, the booty was not long retained; for as the criminal's interest peaked, Eric reached for his kitchenware, which he applied to the felon with a certainty to convince potential observers that Eric typically stabbed men in the chest with a parer.

He did not wait for the man to die. Immediately after stabbing, Eric released the knife lodged between ribs and began thrusting with both fists against the criminal's head. As the semi-human pulled away, collapsing, the semi-man allowed him no opportunity to attack, for the cad was reaching out with one hand, reaching for the hilt with the second. But Eric by then was kicking the felon with force enough to strain his joints, strain his injured crotch, his face revealing the exertion of kicking the man's stomach inches from the utensil poking out like a readied baby meat.

This was their business, one erect stick exchanged for another, Eric's lost prick replaced by this blade. Culminating their contract, Eric ceased his bludgeoning only when the man was static, his breaths like a dead frog's twitches of remaining nerve. Half closed were the felon's eyes when Eric pulled the knife out, but Eric had no thoughts of man and beef being parallel in the butchering, only parallel ideas of his wedded mutilation, an instant dream wherein he ripped the cad's pants off, reaching in to cut away that soft stick with the knife as though grinding, sawing, as though chewing it off, inserting the prick into the felon's mouth until he choked dead on it. But only in a dream and an instant was this scene, for Eric's true conclusion was to drop the knife by the grunting man's side and retrieve his currency yet bundled by the bank with paper at its middle even as this cretin was girded with blood. Then away he fled with no fear, no regret, only a businesslike gait through Penstone Place, then a sore walk into real London, moves made stiff by the force required for his surpassing success, an achievement never gained by the wife, for Eric had vanquished from his life a dream.

Forty

"So could we not be sending things to Mistress Alba to make her stay easier? Some attire, I'm thinking, or the fresh fruits she well loves but is surely not getting. Now that we're admitting how much she should be with us, are we not helping her discomfort?"

"No, miss, for several reasons. First, we would have English law believe that we've rejected Alba, for thereby ours is the advantage of surprise when we come for the prisoner. Furthermore, consider Alba those years in the wilds when she likely had not even a roof to shield her person. Additionally, might not our thoughts of her current discomfort inspire us toward greater activity as we fulfill our designs?"

"Ah, but what design is this we're having, sir? Well I'm seeing you out and doing things, but no task am I receiving; so I'm beginning to feel the nerves in me, because of my uselessness."

"Your spirit ever supports me, Elsie, so accept less anxiety. As well, be certain that your time for true activity comes. If in your heart you then remain prepared to aid the missus, be assured that your hands will have no difficulty in following your spirit."

Despite his enthusiastic talk to Elsie, Eric could no longer envision a time for true activity that would lead to anything but further violence in Penstone Place. And though having failed in his initial stage of releasing the wife, he could conceive of no better means than his original, criminal plan. Having undiminished desire to free the wife, Eric felt devoid not of idea, but of spirit. For days after the stabbing, static Eric remained in Lord Andrew's study, responding pleasantly toward his grandfather and the servants while wishing to be with none of them. Often Elsie saw him at the window looking at the closed curtains as though desiring not the view outside, but whatever light the imperfect opacity of the fabrics transmitted. Too often was Eric seen moving his head side to side as though rejecting some new scheme or pitying his lack of thinking. Not until days later was Eric set again on his path toward reestablishing his marriage, a renewed direction provided not by the brilliance of his intellection, but the persistence of that broader genre called family.

A pair of old visitors come anew were met poorly by Miss Elsie, the servant able to greet them only after substantial pause, for at Lord Andrew's door stood Mr. Edward Denton and Mrs. Hanna.

How removed the offspring remained considering the familial proximity, Eric unable to approach, standing in the great room as though a timid boy, his legs dead. He thought of the wife, and what a loss she was, but what of this parallel loss, that of his original love, the parents? Families should not be exchanged, Eric knew, but increased, the spouse adding to the parents, not overthrowing them. Then all of his losses became active at once, Eric so disheartened that he could only feel, not speak, only look to his parents and see me, see nothing.

"We would hope, son," his father began softly, "that we all might speak again."

"We would hope to all be together again," his mother added, the concern in her eyes so intense that she seemed to be pained by the sight of her only child.

"Now that . . . she . . . is away and gone. . . ."

"Can we not be together as a family is due?"

Eric then spoke strangely, for his smile seemed facetious. This mad humor was from his parents' stating that the wife was gone, as though done and gone, Eric therefore considering them fools. But, no, only innocent, Eric in a rush of certainty feeling that the wife was not gone, merely apart, to be returned as he willed, if only he could will enough.

"I do love you well and always, both," Eric told them with that smile changed to fondness, "but you must learn to love me equally."

"But, Eric, we love you more than—"

"Not enough, Mother, to respect my own love, that which I have always felt for my wife."

"Son, you cannot be so distressed as to love one who would kill you," astonished Edward returned.

"A devil in the form of Amanda Rathel made to kill me," Eric declared. "You are certainly aware, Father, that this woman resides in prison for that crime against me, and more than anyone you know her cause—yourself, you and that family never gained by Lady Rathel for which she could never forgive you."

"I cannot deny Amanda's part as adjudicated by law, Eric, but she was not the one to, to . . ."

"Alba was the vehicle, but no more to blame than any knife wielded by a criminal. Your accepting this fact might be difficult, but understand that you must come to believe for us to be as we were before. For in fact, dear Father, all your long assertions of Alba's danger even considering my wound were not proven true. Only verified is my love for her, a love that remains though my lust is impossible. Praise God for moderated flesh and a strong heart of love. And now, my parents, I accurately offer you my love, and suggest that you might not visit me again until willing to visit my wife in her home."

The morrow found Eric preparing for Penstone, for his parents' visit had set him toward activity. After seeing the pair and suffering that shared, imperfect love, Eric found he could no longer remain indoors and merely cogitate. Instead, he had to initiate his next beginning, and therefore would proceed to that land of loose illegality to achieve its freer aspects for the wife.

No hat nor cane would he require for this inelegant journey, Eric approaching the front door as a knocking came. Startled and stopping with his hand at the latch, Eric in a flash believed that the skewered criminal had come for revenge. The man of criminality to come, however, was inverted, for there on Grand's stoop was a most legal magistrate.

"I would speak with you, Mr. Denton, of a certain interest your wife of late attracts."

Eric had Sir Jacob enter, responding to his guest with courtesy but no conviction, since his main response was fearful confusion. Guiding Lord Naylor to the drawing room, Eric wondered of the wife's "attracting," imagining guards drawn to their loveliest lodger, imagining her sex attacked, the men's genitals accommodated as his own.

"Mr. Denton, could you kindly explain the intents of your parents for them to seek audience with your wife?"

Convincing even to magistrates was Eric's confounded visage, his lack of speech. Naylor thus continued without Eric's reply.

"You have no knowledge of your parents' requesting of me with some firmness that they be allowed to visit your wife?"

"Utterly, absolutely I have no idea that any such request transpired."

"Might you explain, then, why the woman remains your wife? No record exists of your seeking dissolution of that marriage."

"The rearing within my home and England's great church is that marriages once made beneath God's eyes are permanent. And no need have I for shameful annulment when the marriage's continuation is impossible. Legally or not, Alba and I are not husband and wife."

"But your parents' pronouncement was precisely that the prisoner remains their son's wife. Whyfor, then, would they seek the person who in marriage you reject?"

"I conclude that their feelings stem from a comment of mine. My damage was caused by the devil in Alba, not the woman herself. The parents, however, place all responsibility on Alba as though she were evil incarnate. Between parents and son is a stress sourced by the former's failing to accept that Satan not only can reside in average folk, but seeks their companionship."

"Mr. Denton, I interrupt for a reminding, in that you and I know equally that your wife is not average, for she is the witch."

"Before Satan's attacking me via Alba—witch or not—the woman was a peaceful, Godly sort. As for the parents, they disloved her always, even when believing her essentially a woman."

"This comment, then, that so inspired your parents to seek Alba via my office?"

"I remarked that until they understood the evil to damage me enough for them to visit my wife, the parents should not visit the son yet affected by that woman."

"Affected in what manner?"

"By her aspects evident to any man: her decisive intellect and uncommon beauty. These traits yet move me, but not so deeply that I misconstrue them as being less weighty than my scars. Therefore, Lord Magistrate, though my parents would visit Alba to reduce my oppression, I cannot imagine associating with your prisoner regardless of her beauty or wit or that recorded paper we share. That, sir, is ink," Eric added, then pointed to his crotch. "And this is blood."

Naylor was convinced of Eric's partial notion that he desired no company with the prisoner. The husband's greater idea, however, was that he would live with her forever once she became the wife again. Adequately satisfied, the magistrate departed before tea, a fluid of less concern than Eric's blood and Naylor's ink, two materials I handled profoundly.

The following morn found Eric in Penstone Place. Anxious for action, his taut emotion a type of energy itself, Eric proceeded for deeper sites, not concerned with further bouts of cutlery's display. Fortunate he considered himself to soon arrive at a voice that fit his desires.

"Eh—and if you're of prisons, enter to speak with me."

Not so foolish as to enter unaware, Eric cautiously stepped into a sagging building to find a man prepared to kill him.

Due to his youth or the attacker's own wound, Eric avoided a thrusting knife by dropping to the floor's rubble. By then he had recognized the man as a seeker of his wife's gender, having known it from previous commerce. Poorly stabbed had he been according to his minor stiffness, his imperfect movements all anger and force. Up and around the two males proceeded, Eric intending only to run away, but the felon was between him and the door. All of this in seconds, Eric stumbling deeper into the building, his assailant following with unpleasant grunts as

601

though a mad animal defending itself with desperation, but only sinners become desperate for vengeance, not God's natural creatures. Another exit Eric sought as he avoided the knife's loud swings, its screams through the air for his entrails. After a quick beginning, the two men danced within, never but nearly together, Eric crawling over a timber even as the felon lunged with an ugly grunt of satisfaction, a failed sound since Eric again avoided the blade.

Eventually Eric understood that the man seldom moved directly toward him, always remaining between the gent and the door, that single path of escape excluding the roof; and Eric had thoughts of flying, of clambering up fallen rafter and thatch pile to the outside world. But no opportunity had he for this attempt, the felon sliding left and right, his mass expertly balanced over his feet, amateur Eric not considering attack, only survival, not contemplating grasping that beam as a weapon nor throwing those bricks, only seeking the door, only seeing that sliding knife.

Stepping backward, Eric stumbled to his knees—and the man was on him, Eric throwing himself at the felon's shins, barely tripping him as the knife ripped near enough his head for Eric to smell metal. With each following lunge and stumble, Eric seemed slower, now attacked by that anxiety of his parents' visit wherein he had lost his legs, but this poor moving would lose his heart as slit by the criminal. And again he was in his bloody bed, part awakening to find himself part missing; and how would such damage feel to one fully aware? Each rough breath by the attacker was as frightening as a scream, Eric sensing efficiency in the felon's sliding moves, in his careful view of his victim's feet, Eric sensing disaster, a cut to come that he would feel, feel absolutely, as he ran to the man's side and leapt over a chair only to be met upon landing. And there was Eric hurling himself over that same chair backward, an unlovely move that saved his life. Eric again had avoided the one blatant mistake to be his last; and how would their audience observe his mutilation?

Came a woman so blatant as to enter through heaven, which was the door, a Jesus door to save him. This audience carefully approached the felon's back. Immediately Eric thought her

Elsie; but, no, this person he had never seen and could not study now, not with his needing to match the killer's every lunge, needing to hear this every grunt, the soundless woman with a shadowlike appearance grasping the timber Eric had failed to gain, striking the criminal against his shoulder.

The felon gasped but retained his knife. Turning to face the woman, he made to strike her as she stepped away to swing the timber again, but these two were not alone in their lunging. Immediately upon seeing the killer's back, Eric thrust a fist against his ear. This blow so stunned the man that he failed to elude the timber, which struck him near the neck, nearly cutting Eric's face with a protruding nail, Eric instead striking the man to the nose, a slap to splatter the felon with blood and preclude his avoiding a timber blow that felled him.

At once the man began to rise, but slowly, Eric immediately on with his exit, grasping the unknown woman's wrist and pulling her along. Not light nor agile was she, though neither was she plodding, Eric viewing the damaged felon, then glimpsing the woman, a face never seen—a creature never seen. This was Eric's startled thought as he clambered about debris toward the door, watching the felon, his spur, then the woman, his horror. A horror because when this woman looked about, she did so literally, her head swiveling past Eric but not stopping, rotating too far, too impossibly far, until her face was parallel with her back. And when looking about again, her head came comfortably to rest toward Eric at her side, her face pointing at him bizarrely, chin rubbing her neck—like an owl, not like any human. Then they were through that Jesus door and into the heaven of continued life.

Quickly they stepped from the building, Eric certain to remain ahead so he would not see the woman look devilishly behind. He looked ahead to guide them, then briefly to her face seen as most ugly in day's light, but at least pointing toward him, not Satan.

"I have sought this man with the witch," she spoke to Eric as they slowed, her voice revealing the stress of combat and flight. "Tell me your house so there we speak again, for Alba is mine to save with you or despite you."

After a pause for slow understanding, Eric stated his grandfather's address. Then, after a glimpse behind by the woman that sickened Eric, the literal stranger concluded.

"Common sinners can't aid in your desire. We go to our own places now, but prepare for your future. If you will save the witch, prepare to lose some in exchange, for this is the way of nature." Then she ran past, turning only her head to look over her back and warn Eric finally.

"To gain your wife, expect to lose as much as me." And to her place she ran, one Eric prayed God he would never need achieve.

Forty-one

With difficulty, Master Eric explained to his only servant how to prepare herself for a future guest.

"And I'm to be upset, now, because this woman is unhandsome?" Elsie replied. "You're noticing, sir, that I'm no beauty meself, though I'm frightening no people with my appearance."

"But a beauty you are, miss, compared to this woman who in her great courage saved my person as surely as Jesus has saved my soul."

"Oh, and Master Eric, I'm worrying to near stop my heart whenever you're gone to that place, and I'm fearing you've not told me half the times you've been attacked and I'd be fearful to hear them regardless. So what's the terror in a woman coming here of no beauty? If she's aiding in our planning, then I'm finding her handsome enough."

"In truth, Miss Elsie, this person's lack of facial beauty is not her most distressing aspect. Instead, 'tis her neck most strangely bent; and—more unfortunate for her than any observer—also . . . twisted."

"And it's twisted, you're saying, sir?"

"I do say, and say further that from kindliness you must absorb your distress upon seeing this woman to avoid a mutual embarrassment she especially does not deserve, in that I believe her likely the most important resource in our freeing Mrs. Denton."

What a life of doors had Eric for these swinging walls to present him alternately with anxiety and stressed love. Next to arrive at Grand's stoop was the macabre, for Elsie one day approached Eric to state with a whisper and pale visage that a lady had come, no name given.

Solemn Eric approached the foyer to find Lord Andrew chatting with the saving woman as though the two were friends seen each week in church. How *decent* was the weather, they decided, with the clouds only occasionally drizzling. What exceptional strength had Grand, determined Eric, to pleasantly converse with a woman completely repellent, from her hideous face to her soiled apparel, to her neck so canted that her head seemed about to fall. She did, however, face Grand at an angle so that her head turned obliquely across her body seemed natural, surely a decently comfortable positioning for one whose face was usually directed to the side. Andrew then stated to Eric that this fine and friendly woman was known to him, and her purpose was business. Summoning some courtesy, Eric agreed with a smile inferior to Grand's, the latter bowing to Eric's guest, stating he would leave them and the drawing room for their discussion, exiting their presence with no hand kissing. As the two colleagues in crime began to step away, Eric was elated that the woman's first words for him had not been given Grand as well.

"I know Alba in that she and I are as family. On Man's Isle we lived, not persons of the same blood, but the same type of humans we be."

Not delicately settling as a lady, the woman placed her weight on a chair as did the wife; and were not the two of one nature? Thoughtful this woman was, Eric knew, to look over her shoulder instead of her back.

"Saying you are the same type of person as Alba is to say you are equally the witch."

"No more pride could I have than to be friend to Alba's mother," the woman replied. "And God forgive my boasting to say that I am the same person as the daughter, the same witch as she."

"To what extent are you the same as she, madam? Do you have equivalently within you a physical surge that mutilates fools?"

Though stern before, the woman achieved an unpleasant tone when next replying.

"Alba can annoy with all her words, but I will take them from a sister. No more of sinners' words will I suffer from a man. When I suffer next again, it shall be blood for blood."

The woman was becoming filled with emotions, a type of anger seen in her eyes, and in her voice perhaps some hatred — or was it love?

"I would have no further suffering," Eric told her, "for we all have suffered beyond normal living. So tell me, friend and family of Alba, how might we release this person to a freer world without more torment befalling us?"

"Before have I told you that suffering has only begun. To free Alba, you must not only accept torment, but seek it."

"Here I travel with difficulty, since I've less of the estimable courage that you witches so pridelessly display."

"Boast before you lie, man. Those in Penstone know your courage, thinking you foolhardy enough to live there. When that knifer succumbed, a coward would have left alone. What were you, then, to pull me along and thereby slow yourself?"

"What I was I remain, a foolhardy man who thanks you to his heart for allowing me to live via the force of your own courageous actions. If all witches be the same people as you and Alba, then praise God for witches."

"Courageous words are those in a land of sinners, but we've told of your courage. Next to be measured is your love, and with it your desperation, for not love and courage together will free the sister. Your taste of death given by Satan through Alba must come again. No weaker force will break the bonds that hold her, for they take the hateful form of society. Sinners' justice is not changed by mere permanent love."

"Emotion for Alba is no lack within me, but it has no tactile state. How, then, shall we manifest our emotion? Pure feeling is pure nothing compared to the passionless building that holds her in its heart."

"We free the witch from sinners not with their means, but those traits of their best prisoner: with that unpleasant state of magic."

"Magic is known to me only as superstition, a groundless rumor on the lips of the ignorant. Alba herself asserted to me that she knows no more of magic than I, and I believe her honest."

"Honest she is, but oft incomplete, for with her long wording, she can have one hear things not said. Enough you've heard her to know this."

"As well, madam, you might understand that my own affected

607

speech is due directly to Alba's lingual influence."

"I am no madam," she returned, "but named Marybelle."

"A name I have heard," Eric mused, then paused to study either that face or deeper for identity. "God of Heaven, you are the one to take her and live in the wilderness. But unless Alba is the absolute liar, you should be dead, for this was her most saddening belief."

"Sinner, I am dead," Marybelle declared, her sound like a sentence of further execution. "Dead she yet believes me, but I walk because of her. Death I neared because of you, sinner, for your kind had all the hatred to remove my head, even as we must have the love to give Alba further life."

Eric's reply was to move his head side to side as he stared at Marybelle, her neck, able to say no more than, "No such thing is possible . . ." in a strangely firm whisper. Firm in her living, Marybelle replied more certainly.

"The sinning men of Lucansbludge placed my head in the casket against me, but with no more care than needed for the dead, and so it grew, though decently it functions. And all from Alba, for though unaware of magic she remains, the force of God's greater nature came to her through a love and panic to cure me."

"Marybelle, please tell me anything but that Alba via magic reattached your head," Eric returned, those last words nearly choked out.

Then the woman stood to approach Eric, turning her back toward him, but also her face.

"Sinner, I come from the grave to free my sister, and no less a passion would have brought me from that repose. For days with bloody fingers I dug through the wood and soil above to gain clean air, and only because I knew that Alba one day would need equal to what she gave me. Now, male, I come for my sister and will use you if only in slaughter to free one who to her shit is your better."

Sitting strictly upright, Eric stared at that face too near, that back too improper, stared at the witch to declare:

"Marybelle, you could have no more desire than mine for Alba's release, for with the woman I lived in love, and with God's grace shall do so again."

"Boast not on your lust, sinner, for your love is mere fucking, and ye shall have no more of that. Your prick is gone to never return, but Alba is retrievable. But not forever. Too much passion has this magistrate to retain the witch long. So much he wants the sex with her that only killing Alba will end it, unless you think he'll cut his own prick off. Pray your Jesus she rambles well with the writing he's having from her, for thereafter he has her burned like the animals you sinners eat, and God has given not even Satan the power to retrieve a person from ashes."

"I will have her out, I tell you," Eric croaked, wishing to shout yet wishing to retain this conversation within the room. "But you speak of impossibilities and ask me to agree when I have no ability."

"Alba knew no ability to save me, yet save me she did with a strength of spirit a sinner would die to experience. So if you aid me, male, be prepared to approach some loss that seems death."

Marybelle then stepped even nearer, her ugliness and perversely canted neck not hiding the humanity of her emotion, perfectly normal except for an intensity that seemed enough to kill.

"If you save the wife as I save the witch, prepare to lose as she did to save me. And that was no small body part taken in sleep by Satan. What she lost was the sanity and sanctity of loving her own life, for she exchanged it for a blade, exchanged it for my head, exchanged it with a sinners' knife to kill her. But, no, instead she lived for me."

Eric made to speak again, but Marybelle stopped him insanely.

"With her own hand and own volition she did cut away herself to save me, sinner, so in your love to release her life, what gift have ye for Satan?"

Eric then leapt to his feet, brushing past Marybelle as he stepped away, having to halt because of the pain that bent his body, the pain in his head that turned visual; for he saw the wife hacking her breast with a blade, Eric's greatest pain that he could not imagine mine, not with all his fine intelligence. Great was his torment because it was not his own. And so genuine was his love that Eric rejected the tears coming enough to drown him; for in surviving that wetting, he proved himself the witch, finding again the anger that drove him, drove him to me.

He turned in a rush, facing oblique Marybelle to wipe his face as though slapping himself, speaking with a power equal to the witch's previous harshness.

"By any God or Jesus, I'll not weep my brain away. And if

609

metaphysics be needed, beware of my magic, woman, for the power of sinners is death, and nothing else can be nearer Satan."

Marybelle then smiled, a normally hideous sight now adding to Eric's strength. And when she turned to leave without a word, her move was accompanied by a type of mad laughter heard before by Eric, but only from his wife.

Marybelle returned one evening. As instructed by Eric, Elsie would be the sole servant to answer the door, but finding Marybelle outside at night was a terror to the miss; for despite her faith in Eric that this woman would be their greatest resource, Elsie found Marybelle intrinsically a source of fear. From that night visit on, Elsie found a dread of evening as though a too-imaginative child.

Eric and Marybelle spoke outside away from light.

"Are you set, sinner, for evil? Have you readied the husband?"

"We meet the devil now if it be best for Alba. We leave with but our scars and spirits, and I am prepared."

"I smell your anger, man, and it be dangerous. But this type is needed, for you must place yourself with danger. But never will we meet the devil, for he is holding Alba. To free the witch, we meet with God, as near to Him as to each other now, and no force of terror is greater in the world, for He made all the world, made Satan himself."

"Though I believe your speaking true, I can bring only ignorance. What I have to free Alba with is not knowledge. Bring guidance for us all, woman. Depend on my passion as I upon your expertise."

"Be expert in your living, man. Dying in pieces is easy when you have a killing love. So begin your part of this release beyond the end, and expect to live after Alba is out. If as a pair you be together again, find a place not knowing her, and that excludes most of England. What you do with her then is your planning, for it won't be magic, but social. Find a place in this world for Alba, then together we'll deliver her."

Marybelle then departed, Eric expecting her to return typically at night. And well the darkness hid her darkness, concealing her freakish cant, her pocked and pitted visage. The night that obscured her visage supported the person, emphasizing the witch's rich voice, which made her seem as magical as expected. But with the magic gone, Eric was left with society, needing to become mundane again after expecting the metaphysics of evil. Now he would need to be so social as to find a niche for a woman retrievable only with panic.

The day was brilliant in light and life as Eric journeyed to a friend, the supervisor of Grand's shipping enterprise; for although Andrew yet owned the company, in activity he was retired. Only for scattered moments during his journey was Eric happily impressed by London, the sounds of people leading their own imperfect lives that were heavenly in not being based upon mutilation, in not seeking torture but avoiding such heinous aspects. How magical of these common folk to emphasize felicity.

Strange that a seafaring concern should have its offices in London's center, removed not only from the ocean, but away from the Thames, a lake, a pond. Perhaps the office for transportation Eric entered was like that of Mr. Wroth where I had dealt so poorly; but did this concern have wharves behind where lustful pilots might partake of their final and wettest sex?

"Mr. Eastman, I seek passage for my family to America, and must request that my father's family does not learn of this business."

At his desk, Mr. Eastmon settled in a gloom, as though a ship harboring in a fog bank. Eastmon's distress was from good thinking and gossip, for most of London had heard of Montclaire's evilest inhabitant.

"Some part of this arrangement I can fulfill, Eric, but certain aspects I must question. I knew your father before you could walk, and his, of course. These people I will not harm, not even to aid you."

"I ask you neither to lie nor falsify recordings, but only retain these truths until the ship leaves."

"If only this suspect morality you seek, I might comply, for confidentiality does not equal dishonesty. Not quite. Nevertheless, great consideration shall I apply before aiding the separation of Lord Andrew and Edward and yourself. Therefore, I must query

611

your further motives. Above all, Eric, I will not jeopardize my place in God's Heaven by supporting Satan's evil."

"Supplying passage for myself, my servant, and her sister in no way approaches the illegal."

"And what of immorality, Eric? What if one of these women upon approaching my dock is seen to be your wife, a prisoner for life in Montclaire? Why else, sir, would a man take his servant and her kin to America but no family member of his own?"

"Because he has no other family, sir, and because that servant prevented his dying from blood's loss. As for my spouse, since she resides in Montclaire for life, expect her not to be traipsing upon your dock. Having never met this woman, you know her not; so if you find my servant or her sister suspect, I suggest you pray God for Him to rid you of suspicion, for this is a notion as evil as any."

"Eric, your business I would only satisfy if your requesting contains a vow to Jesus that I do not support Satan's evil, which would infect all our lives."

Eric then knelt, clasping his hands on Eastmon's desk, speaking to the man and his Deity.

"My prayers are equal to your thoughts, for with God's help, I seek to *retrieve* my life from the evil infesting me through my wife. Understand my joy to be far away from she who has made me a lesser man. Understand the embarrassment I would flee, that from harming my father and his. Then pray with me, sir, that I succeed in rejecting evil from my life, and that with my retreat, Satan's remnants in me be left in England."

Eastmon moved to his knees with reluctance, since his religion was too sophisticated for such passionate displays. Joining Eric, he heard pleas for evil's release and thanks to Jesus for the strength to reject Satan's temptation and torment. Then the men rose to deal with finance, not metaphysics, Eric reserving future passage for his family, needing only to purchase one member's freedom, and the price would be pain.

"Strong forces of God's nature are set by God, not humans. Magic is most natural and has its own schedule."

"You say we cannot have Alba's release coincide with the ship's departure? That date I cannot modify, since the voyages are rare and set well in advance. To leave one's country requires much preparation, and must occur at the best season for sailing so vast a distance."

"You would hear what I say if you'd keep your interruptions. My feeling is that we deal not only with nature, but with your sinning society. As well, such a journey is itself a season, and to return would be disastrous for she who escaped. I sense of this voyage the strength of a new life begun, an old one ended, of release from the devil and a fleeing toward God. Yes," she concluded, "I sense that this boat's disappearing from our homeland will fit well with our made disaster."

"Now that we have schedule, Marybelle, what is to be done for procedure? Is this magic to be some extended process, or a brief striking of forces? What materials deemed magical will we use?"

"You say magic yet speak of building, sinner," she retorted. "We need draw no plans and cut no timber, for our magic be a type of prayer. You sinners build things even to worship your Maker, but the truest church is the Earth, and there we apply ourselves. The goal is the same: to have Alba from the prison's evil, from the magistrate's upcoming death for her. The doing we shall know as it is being done if our preparing be correct, and this we do not with tools, but our hearts. This magic we must worry on, and never bother to seek itself, only its success. And failure we must fear, for that means Alba lost to dead Satan. The love we must feel for her these weeks shall be painful, and we must think of saving her with ideas as crooked as my neck, for nothing comes unless we love and pray utterly and hate Satan enough to drive him from our lives with our lives. This be our planning, then, and never wait. Never wait with calm for the time when Alba shall leave, for she will only leave if we take her, steal her, force her away from Satan by using the devil's very force against him, tempered by God's greater strength and guided by our panicked love."

Seriously construing Marybelle's speaking, Eric waited for magic with anxiety. His first difficulty was in relaxing before sleep, for thereby he sensed future relief, in that soon the waiting and worry would be over. Since optimism was detrimental to anxious magic, Eric with practice made himself so miserable at night that he suffered ugly dreams, visions of human limbs dropping like tears, fiery incantations led by Marybelle, whose head swiveled around and round, her chin nicking her shoulder with each rotation. His dreams worsening with every day, Eric suffered screeching chants by Marybelle, whose face was a scab like my chest and Eric's groin, Eric reduced to a limbless torso clambering like a stout snake beneath the guards' feet and into their prison only to find the wife fucked to death by Naylor months before, rotted now to nothing but a scar on a naked cot, retrievable from death only by her own magic, but she was dead, so could save no one.

Marybelle did not return, having scheduled no visitation. No great loss was her absence, Marybelle frightening to Elsie and distressful to Eric, the dog ever hiding in the pantry when the witch was smelled, having none of the furious, toothy response first given the wife. And here was Eric angered, since Randolph in compare should have attempted sheer murder against hideous Marybelle. But, no, the asinine beast had reserved his boastful anger for the lovely witch, the one so witty and passionate that sexless Eric recalled her sex, recalled his face between the wife's legs lapping her gloriously, these thoughts bringing to Eric the feel of a sexual erection. But, no, that was impossible, for scars do not drool semen, only pus. Upon understanding that he could have no more unnatural intercourse with the wife's voluptuous fundament, Eric would fall to fitful sleep as he was due in this era of strain, his dreams ending at his crotch where my utterly desirable mouth open and moist would spit upon him since nothing he had there but a scab to sicken. And after Marybelle's magic, what of Eric would remain to revolt me?

"Yes, miss, the woman is the same to have taken Alba to the wilds, and pray God she takes her again for us all. Correct again, fearful Elsie, the woman is a witch as is Alba, but here only to help us. No, not through plague nor brimstone will she foment this release. No, I cannot say of chants and charms, only evil, that Miss Marybelle hates Satan and worships God as well as Alba, as well as we."

He informed the servant that she accompanied them at her choosing, being part of the family and important; but if she desired to remain, he and Alba would both understand and yet love her. But Elsie had nothing to remain for, had no one to keep her but her current family, which was Alba's. And pray God she did to give her strength to follow the young couple to a new land. Bless you then and good, quoth Eric, in that your passage has been booked. Then a sentimental weeping Elsie commenced, which ended with Eric's comment that Marybelle as well attended.

Elsie's era of distress increased with the awareness that she would abandon her country, never to return, for she would be accomplice to a crime. She would leave not that shack of her childhood, but her fine home of London, of England, that truest part of God's world, leave for the wilderness exactly as Alba had ever desired, as she had sought and gained with this very witch now come again, the hideous creature come to steal them all — and was Eric correct? Was this woman truly as God fearing as Elsie? How fearful of God could a witch be? But Alba was a witch — yes, dear Jesus — Alba was a witch as always maintained, yet had never promoted evil beyond pinching her own husband's prick off with her cunt.

Of course, Elsie knew that Satan had been creator of that most heinous deed, not Alba, Elsie convinced by the sight of the missus on her husband's mutilation night, that lost look of ignorance and illness, Elsie convinced by that last word spoken from the prison: her name, only her name, but a sound so pitiful as to cramp Elsie with tears from her spirit. Then completely did she pray God in thanks for sending the witch Marybelle to release her dear Alba, pray God make her the best witch ever; and to any end of Earth would Elsie follow that woman if it meant the dearest girl's release.

Elsie queried Eric of their packing. His curt reply was typical of his ongoing melancholy. Take whatever you can carry and yet run, he answered, which seemed to Elsie a clear explanation of their upcoming lives.

Her despondency was displaced the day Eric came to her nearly weeping, frightened like a boy in the night with creatures about. Most sincerely he convinced the miss of their wrongness in being normal, for they had returned to eating meat. According to Marybelle, they must set themselves solely toward Alba — yet here they were consuming animal flesh — and was this carnage fit the mistress? Of course not, Elsie agreed, from that day hence neither person eating meat, Eric explaining to Grand that this abstinence was in memory of the former wife, a vegetarian. Lord Andrew seemed to understand, though not the servants, Elsie's similar explanation to them receiving near derision, a response she found appropriate for such a strange religion.

Their weeks of nervous gloom continued. Even Randolph seemed dejected, if only because his family's main activity was fomenting their own distress. As for Eric's family, at one midday meal, Grand mentioned how pale the boy appeared, that his health would improve if he ate but a bit of meat, for would any wife have him starve in memorial? Yes, Eric thought, one would. Additionally, Lord Andrew continued, his strength might improve if he left the house more often. And his spirits as well if he gained some activity for his thinking, perhaps employment in an area to interest him. For example, his own business concern might hire . . .

How influential was Lord Andrew to so activate his grandson, for Eric at once bolted from the table, the town house, toward a carriage and to London's center, an office of the ocean dryly misplaced, Eric present not to seek employ, but to verify his previous spending. And what did Mr. Eastmon think of this thin man pale as an invert witch who entered his office in a panic and left praising God like an evangelist for Eastmon's having kept his schedule, kept his secrecy?

How terrible for Eric to wake from nights to well please Lord Andrew with their activity, in that Eric crawled and rolled across his bed as though employed in nocturnal marching, only to wake to a day worse in its anxiety, for Eric could experience torment better when not weighted down by nightmares. In this manner his days proceeded, Eric's apprehension increasing in proportion to the calendar, as the time for the voyage approached. As the time for magic neared, Eric had more and more attacks of acutely unpleasant ideas: those of the ship's schedule, of Eastmon's describing his passengers to all of London, of Eric's not having prepared himself adequately, spiritually, of Marybelle's being mistaken or false or incompetent, of her being absolutely genuine, yet failing due to Eric's inadequacy, his lack of will, lack of love.

Elsie fared little better. As though an exchange had occurred between servant and master, Elsie began plying the anger that had been Eric's center; whereas he became so timid as to fear each small aspect of living, feeling dread to eat another meal, sleep through further, fretful dreams, or face his grandfather who would certainly rebuke him for his laggardness, his sloth, his blatant support for the very devil in the form of his wedded witch. Though usually a smoldering coal in this latest epoch, Elsie would spark sharply into bright anger whenever some servant would inquire of her laundering the master's wardrobe again when he wore but one suit. Then the miss would reply as to the questioner's lazy, godless life with no activity but demeaning a man with more love in his dirty pants than this fool's entire existence. One too many humorless comments of her eating no meat received a response of onion shoots tossed against the face, which Elsie herself swept from the floor, since the young mistress well loved her onions, did she not? All of this in tears, of course, for Elsie was poor at anger, a failure at retribution.

This reversal ended with Eric's awareness that the weeks before their voyage had turned to days, his heart a crash in his chest when he thought that his foreboding nightmares would soon turn real, for Marybelle would return and bring evil, bring forth evil from him.

Eric would be leaving, he knew it, felt it, felt he was leaving not only his land, but his life, for he was also leaving his parents. How could he finally tell them of his love? And Eric was struck with the fantasy to have driven him from his home. With so brief a time together, had that name ever truly been a wife? Even if she had been his spouse in the past, why bother with the future—what purpose was a wife to one with no gender? But this thought was quashed by the accuracy of Eric's turmoil, for beyond false impressions stemming from separation, ever near him was the knowledge that his wife was his life's most genuine part; and though his desire for her was yet sexual, his need seemed religious, as genuine as God.

Then the days were two. The second day would see the Queen's Flight depart. With this awareness came a dread to stop Eric's heart as though struck by the devil, for he felt that his entire existence was one day ahead, and if his life were not proper then, never would his torment end, for never again would he be with Alba. But this final panic was neither fear of Naylor's killing Alba nor of Marybelle's failure to return, but the absolute conviction that no opportunity, person, nor planning would come other than Marybelle, that return she would to end his anguish climactically, bringing devices not of person nor planning, but evil, a magic for the wife's release that would not be equivocal, but absolute.

Eric determined to make certain there was yet a ship, a schedule, a place for him and his. Even his quitting the house was despairing, for outside he could not suffer his preparation as painfully as within Grand's madhouse. To a dry office for wetness he hied, gaining data from a subordinate of absent Eastmon, then via carriage to the dock on the Thames where the ship would depart. And there, the particular vessel, a wooden crate rocking in the breeze. Here was the very captain to invite the passenger aboard to view his lodgings. Though Mr. Denton did not care to visit this cave, this prison, he acquiesced for sake of further business, Eric applying his knowledge of ocean conveyance, hearing that—yes, indeed—on occasion a person is found stowed away, an additional passenger rarely accepted for a fee and an additional fee, since a ship's stores and space are limited for any voyage. Then the captain offered how discreet a person he was, especially when dealing with an appreciative colleague, such as this gent Denton, who provided him with a golden gratuity.

Eric then left to conclude his designs. He hired a covered wagon and purchased a mariner's chest that Eric prayed would not become a coffin. Having expunged all of his activity, Eric then returned to Miss Elsie for more apprehensive despondency, a contradictory evil of mistreated hearts.

No nightmares struck Eric that night, for no sleep would come. Neither did Marybelle the following day. For some unspeakable, spiritual reason, he was not surprised. Throughout that day, Elsie remained near her master, often looking toward Eric, waiting for some speaking or sign, but silent Eric scarcely left his room, sitting in a narrow chair, staring through the window, certainly looking nowhere. The door he left open for Elsie to pass by and look within, for Elsie to come and see nothing.

That day disappeared. The next came for Eric after a sleep calm in that it seemed suffocation. The morning of the ship's schedule had arrived. Arising late for a day devoid of expectation, the husband was left only with the exquisite end to his despair, a denouement worthy of a man to have wed a witch.

His final inversion came with Elsie. Eric was dressed and staring at his chamber door when she appeared at that plane; and what geometry so conjoined them that their functions became reciprocal with their mutual view? Having been driven to him by another door, Elsie received his anxiety as she looked toward Eric, who truly seemed her master then, or was he a tormentor? For as soon as she approached him, he smiled, then laughed, not at her distress, but their mutual success, for he knew her message before it was spoken: The madam named Marybelle had arrived. But, no, he told her, this was no madam, but like Alba, called the miss. No miss neither of them, he laughed. Not miss, but witch. And was his laughter not a cackle?

Elsie lagged behind as Eric quit the room, the master moving downstairs with an unreadable mien, seeming to Elsie not spritely nor well humored, but having some mad implications of both. And when in the foyer Eric continued out with no glimpse to Marybelle a pace away, what did Elsie think of his thinking? What mad emotion had the servant when her sick though smiling master left her behind? What small, insane disappointment had she from not being taken to save the mistress? So there she waited, approaching the door moments later, prepared to move with the pair who frightened her while offering a salvation she could not understand, could not refuse. Later she moved into the house with no dejection, thinking then of baggage and mementos, formulating her own preparation for her family's exit from Hell.

Forty-two

On the floorboard lay a fabric bag of no great craftsmanship, its contents unrevealed to Eric as were his companion's thoughts; for not a word had she spoken, their destination also a mystery as they journeyed by carriage. But were they moving toward Alba, or away from her detention?

Marybelle's magic was first proven by their goal: Gravesbury Reach, where the wife had first revealed her own sorcery. How perfect was this Marybelle to select the sole locale of Eric's life that seemed mystical in itself, though in fact the source of that magic had not been the land, but its populace and her proving.

Eric stared at the receding driver, for with no word spoken, Marybelle had exited the wooden box with her bag and walked toward the Thames. Eric stepped from the carriage, and away the driver went as though having occult instructions instead of common recollection of previous orders.

She continued to an area free of tall growth, that very locale upon which Eric had first known his wife completely. There did Marybelle stop to place her bag as Eric remained by the path until the driver and carriage were near out of sight, no sound heard of that creaking cave, of the wife calling him toward magic.

He next found himself before bent Marybelle. The passage to her was not magical, though. Since he had stared at the woman with every step, there seemed no change in his position, their relative states, her apparent size increasing too gradually for notice, that medium of space and separation present even when he was near enough to vomit on her; for regardless of proximity, the two were not together.

Before her knees, she had collected bits of dry foliage as

though a nest. Then from her bag she removed a handsome, whitish bowl of blown glass, of a size to be supported by a single palm. This vessel accepted her foliage after she had placed the glass upon the ground. From her bag she then procured bits of hard rock, dark and sharp, which she struck together, sparks emitted as though from her fingers, tiny bright igniters falling to the bowl to light the dry tinder. But could the viewing man comprehend the true fire, which was terror in Marybelle? For she was a witch too alive despite past deaths to accept that worst dying for her kind. And was this male's ignorance the cause of this fire? For when the blaze became brilliantly established, Marybelle lifted the bowl to fling its hot contents against Eric's face.

Quickly she dropped the bowl, not only to prevent her hands from burning, but to aid Eric in an indirect, perhaps magical manner. At once he was slapping at his head because his hair was sizzling, the heat barely noticed but genuine in that his jacket as well was ablaze. Here Marybelle concentrated her aid, not by smothering the flames, but by attempting to jerk the garment off. Her accomplishment, though, was to entangle Eric's arms so that his own smothering became a failed tangle of elbows. Thus, the fabric began burning fully, Eric pushing away from Marybelle and rushing toward the water. A strange aid this woman was in continuing to hold the jacket so securely that Eric had to pull himself from beneath the garment to escape. With his hair and collar ablaze, he ran and stumbled to gain the river, becoming fully immersed for seconds, surfacing with little hair, curled and burned eyebrows, red patches most sore on the neck to scar him. Up into the air to see that Marybelle had kicked his jacket to her bare patch of ground, setting the bowl upon it as though to heat a pot for cooking.

No rush had Eric to gain the bank, for in the water he would not be burning. But from the Thames he rose, stepping bent to settle apart from Marybelle, who watched her glass pot boil air. Too steady was the jacket's burning, since the fire should have either died or increased to consume the fabric, yet it burned as though a candle, Marybelle stretching with her shoe to tuck a fold beneath the glass, certain to lean away with her person. But was she certain of Eric's beginning considering her words?

621

"No magic I find in you, in that you do not burn, but can swim. Therefore must you take the magic inside. So, witch's husband, get your deserts from your marriage. Come to the bag."

Eric complied, moving slowly due to the painful neck that hurt even from walking. But not mundane enough was he to touch that crinkled scalp.

"Reach in and take that item you touch."

He did, with his first contact becoming wary, for the object seemed a foodstuff, Eric thinking pork. Lift the item he did only to drop it and retch, for the thing was aged, depleted in mass, yet recognized; for that was the wife's particular nipple on the end of her vanquished breast.

"Now you have to contend with sand when you eat the thing," Marybelle pronounced.

Looking toward it, Eric found he could not look away, could not help but laugh. Of course, he was to eat the mutilation, and what could make more sense? Eric's mild laugh was mad enough to be a sinner's cackle, Marybelle continuing, though her words seemed known before spoken.

"This is a man's job. Oft you've sucked the wife's breast, so now conclude your nibbling. Only men find lust in a baby's meal, and only men are retaining our witch. Only males are there to cut her again and kill her, so you are our weapon against them, husband. Take this magic within you until you are sick of sinners torturing your wife."

With a laugh like a choke, Eric bent to lift the breast, lift it without looking because his eyes had lost their focus. And with a brush of his fingers as though removing building crumbs, breast crumbs, off went the sand and grass. Then bite this magic he did, and it was tough and stank, and chewing would be an era; so a huge bite he took, pulling between teeth and hand until much thickened tissue came away in his mouth.

Here was the cause of his terrified weeks, Eric now aware how deserving he had been of anguish. The wife's dead flesh he ate so that she would not become dead. Then he was weeping, for the breast was rancid, revolting, and—yes, dear Jesus, Father and Son—it smelled like Alba. Here he was eating her breast as though killing her, eating her meat when she would not allow him even fowl. But what was a bit of revolting perversion compared to Naylor's eating Alba with flames?

Gagging and shaking his head, Eric breathed like a rabid animal, mucus dripping from his nose, saliva from his lips. But the final bite he took with care, for here was the nipple, and gentle Eric would not be biting through my areola; so in completion, he swallowed it whole.

Marybelle ran to the sinner, grasping stumbling Eric with both arms to guide him into explosively vomiting my body part into the hot glass. Then drop him she did as though losing interest, Eric falling to his backside like a child sitting awkwardly at the shore's edge, staring at the glass container now unhandsome with that fluid slopped on its outer side hissing and turning dark from the flames, flames that continued to burn too long, one common jacket so full of sin as to provide Satan with energy enough to cook a meal, a repast of perversion.

Marybelle soon found new interest in Eric, though her concern seemed more disgust than appreciation of his aid.

"A poor husband you be to so reject the wife," she retorted, "and no true man to decline great sex. Not true enough for your own desires. Therefore, we shall make you a man, one enough for your wife and the magistrate's demon. So rise, sinner, and approach the baggage again. Therein find your true self or a false description. Look carefully, male, for no witch nor wife will benefit from your falseness."

He did not rise. Neither vanquished nor defiant, Eric accepted that least stressful posture of crawling, collapsing into an awkward sitting pose near Marybelle's bag. Though intending to continue as he must, Eric desired no further torment. Where, however, was his sensible hesitation? What witchcraft had he found to so cooperate with demon Marybelle that he reached succinctly into the bag for his authenticity, his identity? An imperfect magic, perhaps; for after pulling forth his own severed phallus, Eric had to drop it.

Insignificant of mass was this gore stump compared to the previous breast, but how would they compare as cuisine? For without a word from Marybelle, Eric knew he was to eat it.

"You will take yourself back inside and become the man needed to resurrect Alba."

A huge erection it became, as though sexually engorged and

about to be crammed into a baby's anus, tighter and tinier than the wife's cooperative tunnel; for without any change in size, it became impossible to fit his mouth. Impossible because this great aspect of his life had been irrevocably displaced, yet Eric here was inversely duplicating his greatest torture. No transferring of his senses to some dreamlike, dedicated state would come wherein Eric might process this act and this prick with scant notice in order to be on with the salvation. But not Marybelle's order nor his own cooperation made Eric lift the member. Only most unpleasant magic could connive Eric to subvert his decency, to surpass that perversion of eating me. As he lifted his own prick with its dried surface like a leather vegetable, why through his weeping were his clearest thoughts of his parents? Why was his only thought of me in death's prison not of the wife, but of the parents attempting in all sincerity to visit her? What force had this thought to allow Eric to lift that impossible burden those endless inches from the ground to his lips?

He saw the soil, expecting grit against his teeth, saw his phallus better than ever when attached, Eric feeling that the greater perversion was not the prick in his mouth, but the scar on his body, that former, forever loss, not this ludicrous regaining. Refusing to taste that sickness, Eric opened his mouth until his jaws cracked, for all his losses had begun with the body, remaining there despite endless mental reliving. Eric would not have his mutilated manhood against his tongue, and, no, never would he bite it. With the interior of his mouth extended like an empty bag, Eric accepted his phallus, weeping as he swallowed it whole, the pain from too great a gulp felt acutely, but not enough to conceal his torment. Eric then thought of the wife again, thought of her severing her own breast away, maiming herself to save Marybelle. And despite his best objectivity, for that second of his swallowing, Eric could not consider his own perverted burden a lesser sacrifice than mine; for he had found the limits of thoughtful generosity, found the limits of his love.

Did the witch intend compensation by kissing him? Surely this buss was no worse because of Marybelle's back facing Eric, her old inversion mild compared to his perverse, reverse eating. And what pride felt she to place her mouth against a sinner's? This was no social witch as the wife, but a pure sister surely sickened

624

by the contact, surely intending Eric further illness, not reward, the sinner's prick in his stomach so near its proper place before being thrown out again, expelled from his mouth into Marybelle's, who swallowed it. But no comparisons had Eric of kissing the wife, a click of the teeth when too much pressure was applied by Eric, the eager eater. The similarity was in retching, Marybelle throwing herself around to bend in the heat above the flames akin to those that had burned her friends, bend above the hot gasses to expel magic into the glass pot for melding, the Dentons' vomitous body parts now together again, as though married folk rejoined.

Both sinner and witch squatted on their shins with noxious mouths. Not so ill and weak were the pair as to be senseless, for Eric could smell himself and recall Marybelle's taste, noticing that the elder witch was so unsocial as to allow her head a comfortable cant toward her shoulder, her half-clasped hands resting on her skirt in a reminiscent twist. Though staring away from the fire, Marybelle was near enough the hated element to sense its incorrectness.

"Too much heat," she said. "You must temper the heat with your scar."

As though in a dream, dazed Eric envisioned himself straddling the fire nude, bending his legs to smother the flames with his groin, for there his only scar was situated. Would he thereby re-cauterize the urethra again, the hole closed so completely as to cure Eric of urinating? What physician was this Marybelle to heal so base a need?

"Stand at the fire and pee there, male. I know you've a sinner's piss in you in that I smell it. A wicked fluid it can be if left too long inside; so let's get it out and be on with our magic."

No hesitation had Eric, but no strength either, so his rising was slow as he stepped to the flames. No concern had he at having to lower his breeches instead of merely opening the front flap, for his scar would not fit through the gap. Considering his previous consumption, Eric found no shame in standing nude near the flames to squeeze his scab this way and that to better control the spewing as he wetted the fire and dripped within the bowl proper. Though the man desired that meal in his hand again, attached instead of that scar to his body, he nevertheless fulfilled

Miss Marybelle's directive, and Hell have all his shame.

As though displeased with his success, Marybelle ran low toward Eric to grasp his buttocks, pulling him toward her to bite his body, bite his scar, coming away with blood and urine, which she spat into the bowl as Eric screeched and stumbled backward, tripped by his own clothing. What now was left for him to feel? After perversion had come pain, after eating himself for Alba came Marybelle eating him, Eric on his backside reaching for his breeches, looking upward but not seeing God though his goal in this magic was righteousness, Eric with new misery recalling worse pain, greater torture between his legs. But even with this blatant evil, Satan was not found.

Next for him to feel was either God's glory of shared sexual love or Satan's wickedness of sex gone cruel and selfish; but was not Marybelle seeking to aid a sister when she sat on Eric's face? When pressing her vulva against Eric's mouth, certainly she sought no pleasure for herself, for this decent witch was naturally revolted by gratuitous sex.

His naked legs and blank bottom twitching on the dirt, his useless testicles caressing the soil as though kissing the wife's cleft, Eric found no sensation in Marybelle's skirt to equal Alba's, only a rancid smell and hair like bristle, loose flaps of tissue unseen in the darkness, her folds and clitoral bulge filling his mouth, clogging his nose, gentle Eric waiting until devoid of breath before biting. Drowning in her vagina, he bit the woman, eliciting from Marybelle a trebled ejaculation: a gasping shudder from above, and from below, drips of blood and a second fluid. And, yes, the bite made her move from him, the witch dragging weak Eric like a log to the fire to have him spit their shared fluids into the bowl that cooked for me, only me.

No more presumption would come to Eric. As Marybelle dropped him, his arm near enough the fire for more hair to be singed, Eric was fully resigned toward further torment even as the trial ended. Even as he surrendered to the magic, he found his aspect ending, the magic released on its own perusal of the world.

Persons in a wagon approached these people magicking, but could not near, could not travel the usual road leading to their home. Even as their horse, the people sensed a smell to be avoided, all the animals turning to a new route naturally, in the manner of sensible folk near a flame retaining their distance without deep cogitation. Only persons sinister with passion enter the evil parts of fire existing within us all, while those of God and normal sense remain removed.

Marybelle had moved. Shortly after settling, Eric came aware that the witch had looked to him, then walked away as though intentionally leaving his sight. Soundless she was, Eric assuming her still, not expecting further attack from the magician though not likely to be surprised by the next bite or blow, by any upcoming perversion.

None came. Soon he found himself waiting. Though unable to sense Marybelle behind him, Eric yet had her taste in his mouth, had her smell on his face as though a lady's grease for social occasions. Then came innocence returned, Eric thinking that never in his youth when a future family of his own seemed desirable had he presumed perversion. Never when considering the potential joy of marital sex had he imagined sucking an ancient witch's fetid crotch. How normal that inverted intercourse with the wife now seemed. But, then, none of that would again transpire, history itself, as useless as his boyhood thoughts. No intercourse, common or queer, would he accomplish with his scar, with that ubiquitous prick now boiling. To accommodate his future passion, Eric knew he would have to resort to kissing the wife's unscarred bottom. But after that more recent witch, sex seemed no more desirable than any other illness.

No dream held Eric when he sensed himself in London. He breathed as though sleeping, and noticed this respiring, but awake he remained and newly aware of himself, of his locale. Before him was the River Thames, wide here with weedy, boring banks. To the far side and beyond were low buildings with no people seen. Deeper into London was the prison that held him, held his life in a legal spell by having captured his wife existentially. Then along the river's flow he viewed, a swift and accurate move compared to the water's bobbling transport, Eric looking seaward where, beyond his sight, docks of a major port expected his departure. And he was stunned again, for within him were the thoughts of a lifetime, Eric recalling that this very day he and his family were scheduled to board a ship and leave their homeland

627

to never return. But with all of this disruption before him, Eric nevertheless had no need to panic, for no family had he as long as the wife remained in Montclaire. Yet no move the husband and racial sister made for her release, only perverse fucking and puking as though in self-castigation, as though for entertainment.

Without turning toward her, Eric nonetheless became attentive only to Marybelle. He wondered of his leader's next production, for in his family whose center was Alba, this sister witch had become the prime member. Out of his senses, however, she seemed out of his life, yet he denied her no control, for her means were also beyond him. And then she was beyond his contemplation, for Eric was asleep, exactly as in his most recent life having no influence over his dreams.

He walked within the prison. How surprised he was to find this building identical to his grandfather's home. The servants here wore drab jerkins, however, and each was a criminal seen before in Penstone Place, though in this building they were employed by English law. Each of these dishonest, powerful men stood before a door behind which lay Alba, the guards securing each others' legal privacy as in turn they had violent sex with the wife, conventional sex with common penises and not the first death, though Eric could hear their reciprocation as they moved toward their pleasure, away from her peace, toward their lust, away from her health, and so on. Scarcely could the husband wait to be stabbing these commoners, but they were so tall that Eric would need to reach up for their bellies. And though eager to be leaping with his large fork made for skewering meat above a flame, Eric would be disallowed this magic by his parents' parent, since Grandmother Marybelle refused the eating of meat within her home—and what a resurrection, for Grand's wife had been dead since Eric's infancy, even as his parents were dead within his current life, yet here she was returned as a witch to stop his stabbing, because his implement was made for fire, and fire was made for killing witches, not saving them.

Then came a guest to the door. Sir Jacob had come to deny Eric his wife's release in that Eric had come for a witch, and their pale woman could not be proven so because the tide had gone out, taking with it so much water to the sea that the River Thames was too low for any wet proof by God's permanent creatures. Then Eric turned to his grandmum to ask what further, following magic she had to save her sister, considering this latest event. In fact, Eric turned to describe their magic's condition, for he awoke to give Marybelle a charm.

She was looking toward him. The fire had gone out, and the Queen's Flight would soon follow the departing tide. Time enough had passed for Marybelle's fumes to infiltrate the air, and Eric was her clock. With no word, he looked to her and provided this knowledge. The two then rose together like that bodily, emotional mist they had injected into the atmosphere, and follow it they did, toward magic and toward me.

Forty-three

Not even the Sabbath gave Naylor respite from his occult duties. Each day from his first of providing me with the utilities of writing, he visited me as though a publisher of pamphlets come to make certain his creative charge's literary products were palatable. This imprisoned scribe, however, established the protocols of writing, for her experience was the only expertise in the desired subject of her life. So Naylor arrived each day to take my product and read with all concentration, never long remaining with the proven witch, and never without guards.

Once the magistrate had confirmed me officially occult, his disposition changed subtly in the immediacy while portending poorly for my future, for Naylor achieved a curiosity of my living aligned toward fear. Reasonable was this view from one to have observed me the killer of men. His fear, unfortunately, might actively protect the magistrate, for this was no man to wait for expected damage. To preserve himself, Sir Jacob would attack when some dangerous force found him its subject. And did he not wonder of the witch after ending her testimony directing her evil efforts toward that nearest man, her captor?

Sir Jacob's disposition I knew from his smell. That excited interest of finding papers stained with knowledge was ever tempered by distrust, fear for his ultimate well-being with the witch. This fear was best smelled when Naylor was least protective of himself, upon gaining satisfaction from my writings. Then his bright interest would become tainted by sex, the fear of illicit sex with a desirable woman, the fear of death from her sex as though holy in its immediate punition directed from God via his decrepit counterpart, Lord Satan. Not the plain sex smell roiling from males was uppermost here, but a subtle odor unusual because of its apparent source, for did not the magistrate have a rigid prick in his brain?

Believing that Naylor once done with me would have me well done, I should have procrastinated my tome's end. This I could not do. Montclaire's cave with its stench of criminals, with its leader Naylor and his vengeance-in-advance, was a misery chamber, more sepulcher than cave. My testimony in comparison was my life itself, which I experienced as God intended: with vigor and genuine morality, not some secular code idealized by sinners, but a desire to comprehend God through worship, a passion inherent to any true human.

At times I could not move the quill quickly enough to remove all my words, to settle them upon paper. Like ink's opacity, these words obscured my present, for when busied with the past I could scarcely notice upcoming terror. With each of Naylor's visits, I could better sense his odor, smell a lust unique since he would not quench it with my body and his sex, but eliminate his desire by eliminating me. Imperceptive he was not to sense the prisoner's entrapping him, for never could he reject the witch. I could not be avoided, for my home was the manse of the magistrate's career. We two could only be separated by killing the passion to bind us, but I had no lust for Naylor. Though he knew enough of my special sex to be coupling with me without dying, the married magistrate was too moral to accept intercourse out of wedlock. But what love had he to find me resistible only with death?

I knew myself special. According to my smell, no other prisoner of Montclaire was female except Rathel, but she was no concern of mine once settled in prison, though she had not settled so well as I. Had the magistrate personally asked her preferred eating in that he knew Montclaire's meals to be unfit a lady? Did the Rathel thereafter receive instead of felon slop fresh vegetables from the English countryside? Had Amanda been provided a desk of yew and all the ink her distressed spirit desired? Did the very magistrate visit her each day with a personal interest and a smell increasingly reminiscent of death?

631

What a torment that window was to pass implications of true living while allowing no experience. Between me and that life outside was not metal, but the devil; for the separating entity was tortuous, the space beyond not God's, but Satan's. Common sounds of wagons passing, lovely horses snorting and clomping, were alternately enlivening and distressing from describing a life to be loved while offering only separation. Sinners' voices I well treasured in that era, though most often they were heard due to increased volume, the cause thereof either traffic confrontations or excess gallivanting, though even mutual curses at failed horsemanship seemed more energetic than disputatious to me, the sober and drunk carousing more humorous than foolish; for who was I in my constrained existence to denigrate parenthetical results of genuine living?

Too often I dreamed. No new subjects came to my sleeping, a variety of old events tormenting me sequentially. Mother, Eric, ocean, ever. But no greater distress had I than to wake and find my nightmares real, to find myself always ill with a remorse as changeable as Mother's breathing, as Eric's manhood. Though I deserved to drown in these sins, I was not saint enough to accept my torment. In God's additive punition, I suffered from my suffering, and well prayed Him my apologies, not for myself but for those I had loved incorrectly.

An abject importance I learned was that the more I wrote, the less I dreamed.

What a smothering this writing became, and all selfishness I purveyed to endanger my truest race to avoid not my execution but my waking thoughts. For although I wrote factually, it all seemed story, an operatic composition to occupy my emotions, to conceal me from the real.

In this manner my days receded. Each hour disappeared into a future that would culminate my past. Recurring remorse I retained from my mentor, the magistrate's best suffering to come. Poor Naylor and his smelled guilt from having to snuff me. Sick Jacob reeking from pride at saving England from this bitch. Lovely God to enjoy all the thick living below Him. Thank you Satan for eating my tedium.

I could not write enough to dream nothing. Having reached that segment of my tome's chronology which equaled my time of life—writing then of my writing then—I received a dream appropriate in being an end, for therein I was released from prison—but was this foreboding of escape or execution?

A terrible smell came as I stood in my cell, for it was the odor of a person I had killed, a smell fit certain living folk, for in varying ways I had killed not every person ever known to me, but every person loved. Elsie I smelled, or Eric, or Marybelle—perhaps all three or some combination of their souls, their soot. The smell's increasing intensity indicated an approach. In my cell cave casket, I waited for the smoke and blood person to near. Soon came eyes at my door hole, a nose brow on my bars belonging to Eric.

I have come for my wife, the lashes said.

None exists, sir, I replied. Here is but a witch.

Then I shall take the witch and teach her the past, for in that realm she was my wife, and in the future shall be again.

Then, Sir Nostril, I go with you; for who is a prisoner to argue with the master of time?

Therefore, I opened the door to find Elsie in Lord Andrew's pantry attacking Randolph. Demanding that the dog accompany her, Elsie found him hiding, having smelled the missus; and knowing full well she had killed all the others she loved, he preferred to be the last alive, not the final murder. Ah, but he'd be coming with his family or remain with the bread sticks, and Elsie would be choosing for the blooming coward. Thus, the miss became forceful, first nudging the dog with one hand, then attempting to lift him, and Randolph growled. Then loudly she spoke with inadequate results. Therefore, the servant lifted the only member of the family her inferior, and the hair rose along his spine, and those were teeth displayed. But knowing the best for her dog lass, Elsie proceeded either to pinch his penis away or lift the heavy brute completely in her arms. And with the first full grasp of either his torso or phallus, the dog with surprising speed turned to bite Miss Elsie's arm, bite her fruitlessly; for although she yelped herself and began weeping, she continued either to pinch his prick off or lift him completely from the ground, and he ceased. Either Randolph quit his breathing in that he was bleeding instead, or the frightened dog came to understand that no choice had he in hiding from mere witches whose evil owned the world, at least every family he had known. Pull the maleness from his torso she did or his torso from the floor, Elsie with a heavy, stiff, and fearful item that she carried with tears and the one bleeding bite that hurt her to the bone, carried the foolish family member and here were two saved, neither allowed to submit to their fearful instincts, Elsie not abandoning her friend, Randolph not being so cowardly as to shun his family when an entire new world awaited them. If only he had sense enough not to slap Elsie's hand away when she came at him with salvation, sense enough not to refuse her after he had imbibed her act. Therefore, when Elsie conveyed the dog in her arms to Montclaire and me, I opened the door to find Naylor.

"You sleep in the day, missus," the magistrate stated in my unfortunate real. "Is your health therefore impaired?"

Not a word came as I arose, only a negating nod as I stepped from the bed, a new mattress from Naylor. Long enough had I slept there for the bed to smell of me: not man sweat and piss, but my sweat and piss, my blood and smoke.

"Understandable it is that you should be weary, for your effort expended toward writing is significant. But your latest, which I have read during your strong sleeping, contains nothing new. This also is understandable, since heretofore you have described your entire life. I find, missus, that nothing remains, in that you seem to have ended."

He smelled of future ashes. I wondered if common for this prison was a witch burned at dusk, or was it at the will of the magistrate, the master of time? And when he dragged me away like Elsie dragging Randolph, would I bite him? Would I find opportunity to pinch away some part of him before he removed my living?

Then came a new odor, another dream turned true, for through the air I sensed a fragrance to chill me from lost history; for never on Man's Isle did I notice that odor to change Lady Vidgeon. In this waking dream I smelled it, and was transported to that era of innocence wherein the people I knew in all the world were only witches. Now, however, the only persons known to me were sinners. Better they than Satan, however; so before the latter was delivered by this final sinner in my cell, I would write of that odor, I would convey my ending dream.

I stepped to my desk, beginning to write with no word from the magistrate. Perhaps I heard him sigh, but mainly I perceived that fragrant dream. Carefully I sat so as not to disturb the atmosphere of lost living, yet hurriedly I moved before the dream vanished, before I failed to secure that fragrance in the real.

The magistrate remained, but he did not read my rapid writing, for Naylor would never near me when I was active, lest I cut him with my quill cunt. The magistrate remained, and I queried him not of those activities I kept him from, not when they likely included me.

My lasting people were in this final dream, all of them dead in some manner; and how odd for vacated persons to be describing my life. Sensing Marybelle, I wrote of her. With Eric she was, an unusual pairing since these loved ones had never met in life. Marybelle and Eric were clambering up a great wagon they had convinced its driver to park against Montclaire's outer walls. Remarkably, Marybelle and Eric were not seen climbing the wall, in that the guards' backs were toward them. Up they climbed and down to the prison grounds, not seen by guards, whose backs were turned to the infiltrating pair. Exterior guards then ordered the wagon away. Unfortunately, it contained a mariner's box meant for comely cargo. Aware that his destination was ultimately the Thames's wharves, the driver hied there to wait for his employers, who then were occupied manifesting a dream.

To the prison entry they ran, but here was a massive door only to be unlocked from within as requested by an outer guard. Therefore, Eric shouted that the door be opened, and so it was, he and Marybelle entering with no guards noticing, since their backs were turned, and they smelled intruders poorly. The witch's location within was known from Elsie's stay and Marybelle's smelling, and there they ran. And though the pair moved through corridors populated with guards, moved through locked doors whose keys were smelled and found, no man sensed them, for all males in Montclaire had been connived by manless magic to turn away from my dreaming.

Nearest that dream, the magistrate became so courageous as to approach my drying pages, reaching the paper while viewing me closely so that I would not attack him with my imagining. Attack him I did with my words, for at his back came Marybelle and Eric, though not quite in his hearing did that screaming exist.

"Witch! Witch! A witch is in the prison and the other escapes!"

The screamer's back was not turned to the invisible infiltrators, for no man was she, Lady Rathel so dark as to be nocturnal and infer my dream. Therein seeing Marybelle and Eric pass her door unnoticed, she announced their presence with a cry.

The decider Marybelle said the husband should not face the magistrate beside his wife, said to silence the Rathel instead. The witch would busy herself with the witch. Retreating through passageways, my dream achieved a key known without examination guarded by a man emulating Marybelle by facing folk with his back. Dreamy Eric then ran to Rathel's cell as Marybelle opened mine, seeing me write her name a final time before I faced her. Naylor could not see my move, not with his back to my family's passion. The sinner could not see me depart with my crooked sister, past jailors blinded by a dream.

Though the Rathel's cave was on our path, Marybelle had us continue without halting, allowing Eric to conclude his task while my sister completed hers. The one to live here must leave first, before becoming seeable. Therefore, we rushed through Montclaire and to its outer wall, whereupon Marybelle hollered for the guards outside to open. They did, seeing not enough. Less charmed than Marybelle and Eric for being no magical producer in this dream, I was the one to be set in a box in a wagon and sent to a certain wharf, a specific ship. My sea cave, however, was missing. Dreaming that it was on the docks, my crooked sister sent me straight to the wharves and bid me wait for her as she returned for my husband, her invert lover.

Less than deeply moved was the magistrate to read another of the witch's dreams. But *eventually* he sensed a discrepancy, for Naylor was reading of Lady Rathel's screaming though nowhere on the paper was it writ. Only when understanding that he stood beside a prisoner no longer present did Naylor reach my final word, and then he escaped as well.

Wiry was the Rathel when attacked, and stunningly loud, but Eric silenced her despite his approval of ladies. This one, after all, had been known to lie. Scarcely a bruise did he render the

636

woman, Eric simply leaping upon her, collapsing Amanda with his weight. Out went her breath, which ended her screaming. Then Eric tied her with bedding until she resembled upholstery, the lady not moving until Eric had turned to the door to see Naylor run past.

The magistrate attempted to awaken the guards from my dream, but since the topic was magic, the sinners failed to notice. Though listening to the magistrate, they knew not where to run, since nowhere in Montclaire were misplaced persons. Not being with Marybelle, Eric was misplaced, becoming frightened and cautious of Naylor, who now could turn, who now could see him.

Aware that loose persons would leave, Sir Jacob hied to the prison exit. Ignorant guards heard his orders and followed, but only Naylor of the pack was not blind to Eric. Therefore, the husband ran between guards with their confused activity of looking for whom where, ran past loud boots, but not so near the magistrate as to be seen. Run they all did, an increasing lot soon at the prison exit, Eric wondering how he would ever pass the seeing leader. But Naylor was not seeing once at that barricade, for he was drowning in my dream, smothering in apparel; for a witch had fallen from the sky onto his face, Marybelle having dropped from the stone wall. Eric then guided several guards into stumbling over their magistrate until the lot was a heap, Marybelle calling for the gate to be opened. The magic pair in their implied innocence then walked calmly, briskly away, to a carriage and to me.

So wide was the Thames near its ocean outlet that the river could not be seen across, and smell it did of brine. Busy was the water, its traffic boats large and small for transporting hay and for fishing. The largest, for conveying people to distant lands, was mine, and I hated it. Gently, precariously, it moved side to side. With all its huge timbers for sails situated so high above the hull proper, clearly the boat was unstable. A mobile bridge it was, meant to travel far from land before collapsing to toss its passengers into the water with no hope of returning, for no solid bridge existed to grasp and pull oneself upon and then walk back to land.

Aboard this huge armoire, this closet cave for drowning, stood people appearing like frogs on a log about to leap away from their unsteady perch. The only familiar persons in this dream were dead, my nightmare coming true most falsely in having begun with dead Marybelle returned in a silly shape accompanied by the ridiculous smell of Eric's assistance as though he were yet a whole person with some interest in the wife. Especially foolish was this dream's intent, since clearly my former loves meant to drown me. But there would be no drowning in most solid Montclaire. Therefore, I requested that the sinning coachman return to being fatefully real by returning me to my home.

How typical of a dream to be more convincing than established life, that tilting bridge behind me more of a threat than Naylor's smell. But, after all, I was witch or sinner according to the disadvantage of the identity. In this regard, who was I to so determine a sinner as to judge Naylor prepared to roast me? In fact, was he not merely contemplating a change in my living? Perhaps a new cell, one smaller and with a worse view. One my length made of wood with no windows and a sky of soil. Not so disastrous would this be, I deemed, since Marybelle had survived her lodging in such a cave. And what if a few of my body parts were removed by Naylor first? After all, Marybelle had survived into my dream with no head. Eric had continued to seek my window though lacking a unique limb. Then I imagined these semi-living seeming-witches dragging my box from the dirt, performing magic to reinstate my pieces. But in fact had they not previously attempted that painful worship and thereby entered the cave of Montclaire? What items of their lives had they lost for me that now I vomited at their faces? How saintly was I to refuse their pieces and their tilting ship? How demonic was I to reject that final drowning I had ever dreamed and thereby reject their love?

"You say, miss, that I'm to be returning to the wharves again?"

I did. I had the sinner return this witch to her massive casket so social with all its white apparel.

"You say, miss—. Beg pardon. You say, missus, that I am to wait while you gain your fare from your husband on the Queen's Flight? The very ship under way now?"

The grandest vessel on the Thames seemed much less massive once removed to the river's center. To the nearest boatman I called in question whether that ship be the one my dream believed, and yes. How typical of my dreaming for a sinning male to know more of my own casket than I. How typical of my living to have such difficulty dying.

I found myself without further dream, further instructions. I had been told only to wait, but my family had not, could not. Of course, while I had been wavering in my dream, the partially alive pair of Eric and Marybelle had gained the Queen's Flight. Having procured magic for only the prison, they could not delay a sailing. And since they had departed on their bridge without me, I found that again I could return to that static home which fit. But, no, my dreaming changed once more, for the Queen's Flight was now static itself. Her sails were being lowered, and witch eyes could see a great iron hook tossed over like Marybelle and her stone. This metal was attached with a chain dreamed before, all that mass arresting the boat; and clear was this event. Though Eric had failed to detain the boat, at least he had managed to halt it, waiting for the wife; and who was she to reject time's master?

From box to box I moved, stepping from the coach to floating caskets with staring, sinning men. With my influential visage, no difficulty had I in achieving a craft and its crew for the purposes of conveying me to the Queen's Flight, a spry boat with fine sails sure to catch the cumbersome Queen in brief minutes, miss. Er, missus.

Since my dream presumed no drowning from this smaller coffin, scant terror had I upon dropping over the gunnel without allowing any sailor's hand in aid. And well I settled on a hard plank with minor regard for the boat's rolling side to side, for it seemed well attached to the river, even as these sinners were attached to me.

Typical they were to discuss transporting me gratis if only they could fuck me lifeless. Typical they were to be unconcerned with that flat chest when the other was well lumped, and always the fundament remained for kneading and the thighs for fingers to crawl upon and gain the graveyard of my vulva. Typical was I to kick their testicles and jab their faces with my fingernails, and Jesus cure them as he had cured me. Unacceptable business was this, however, for the males shoved me harshly to the boat's bot-

639

tom where that desired end of mine became wet. Thereafter, with unpleasant speaking, they denied me further courtesy, for they returned to the dock despite all the world's gold available to pay them for taking the wench to the Queen's Flight—let her swim. Of course, she could not.

No hand these sinners offered as the lady quit their crate; and who could say of other sailors staring even more sexually at that wet fabric clinging to and thereby revealing the buttocks below? The witch could, presuming her further dream, one of endless males at her gender while in their boat caves. Nevertheless, the husband and sister awaited on that static casket; and who was I to deny them my dying after having killed them so often? But with no boat available, I would have to swim.

Of course, I could not.

The populace of the Queen's deck stared. Not so acute were my eyes in this realized dream to distinguish their faces, but certainly they saw me, and were shouting and gesturing at the wife, the sister, to join, if only I were witch enough, family enough. If only I would not fail again. If only I could find enough love to accomplish an act instead of merely emoting, merely suffering, merely performing philosophy. If only on this last occasion I could love someone more than I loved myself.

Active were the docks with men unloading boats, all of them moving and sweating, most staring at me, some with loud voices mentioning their desire, mentioning my organs. Therefore, sinners' minutes I walked before finding a tall stack of crates to hide my entry into the Thames. What a terrible dream this was to be so falsely real, for with all my nightmares of drowning in the ocean exactly as had no one in my life—not Mother nor Marybelle nor any witch nor sinner I knew—I would be the first, drowning not in the ocean, but the broad Thames so appropriate in being a sinners' thoroughfare more than God's body. Therefore, I entered the river with no alternative, for this was not my life, but a nightmare; not my living, but my death. Into the water I stepped to walk farther than I could see. Into the water to find the nature of nightmares, for when they end, the real begins, a realm superior in strength to dreams by being their source, nightmares being minor imaginings compared to the waking torments to have caused them. Into the water I moved to find myself awake, find that final instance of a nightmare turned real, and appropriately turned inverted; for I found my reality nightmarish. Enter the Thames to end my dreams, along with my living.

"Yes, sir, and that be a generous sum to end my worry, for you know the funds go to my employing company and not to me. For meself—"

"Are you sure the woman is as described?"

"A most comely and youthful person she be, sir, with the pale skin and most black hair you tell of. And, with my apologies, she did have to correct me for saying her a miss by telling me she be a missus."

"And she said she would achieve funds from her husband on the Queen's Flight and then return to you? Did in fact you see this journey of hers?"

"No, and, sir, I did not. A waiting I continued, but with all of these boats and people here walking about, I lost her sight amongst them."

This was the second of two land vehicles waiting for Eric at the docks. As the husband sought a sailor, Marybelle proceeded to the first vehicle, the covered wagon of bad happenstance.

She would enter the cave in my place. Before the imperfect dreaming, the plan had been for Marybelle to pass as "the servant's sister" as per Eric's booking, while the thin witch played the stowaway in a mariner's cave, and the true servant boarded normally. But Alba was now chasing after the belief that all of her family had departed. Marybelle would thus box herself in a coffin more comfortable than the last.

"Aye, gent, and I saw your very missus headed out with two sailors of my acquaintance. I am presuming that the Queen they have reached by now and perhaps returned, though I see them not on the water nor along the wharves. A great lot of water we have here, mate, and likely they're out on it again. But if you've a need to be at the Queen's Flight, sir, well, my own craft is available for an easy voyage. It seems the Queen is anchored now, and probably waiting for your very self, sir."

"I welcome your offer, sailor, but I've a further problem. Not only did I fail to board the Queen's Flight, but so did a most important chest. A fine fee I have for he who conveys me and this weighty item to the Queen."

"Well, sir, and my brother is with me here. I see it not on the dock—can two good men handle the chest, then?"

They could with Eric's help and Grand's money. And a thing of heft it was, the sailors moving the chest from the wagon and into the boat with no damage, Eric and the other males out to the Queen's Flight to find the wife there.

But she was not. Eric learned this before boarding by looking up to Elsie with a questioning expression, receiving a negative gesture. Then came difficulty with the chest: The captain would not have it until Eric had a good fee for him, the sailors of Eric's conveyance and those of the Queen's Flight requiring true exertion to load the thing, but on board it was with no damage, then dragged below decks into storage.

As this activity commenced, Eric heard Elsie's story. She told of all the anguished pleading required to convince the captain into lowering the anchor. But praise God you're reaching us, sir, and you say the missus is released? Pray Jesus, have they taken her back? You're saying she was seen on a boat coming here and never arrived? Oh, and sir, are you thinking with her poor swimming that . . . ?

The captain was saying they could tarry no longer. Eric replied that another person was due to fill his booking. The captain was saying they could tarry no longer—until Eric silenced him with currency. Nevertheless, they could not miss the tide despite any passenger's generosity. As Eric considered returning with the boat whose sailors had remained at his request, the other passengers began wondering of the delay. For whom were they waiting now? they demanded. The answer, however, was readily evident. Of course, they awaited Lord Magistrate Naylor, for there he came now.

Every idea in Eric's life seemed to rush through him at once, and all were useless. His stepping toward Lord Naylor was no surrender, however, but attack. At the boarding ladder, Eric accused the magistrate of tormenting him—on my way to a new land and away from these troubles, yet you follow me? No, Naylor had no allegations for Mr. Denton. As for his official business, since Denton had no part in it, he would best be away from the magistrate, who would accept no further difficulties for his own life.

Sir Jacob spoke with the Queen's captain. How many in the Denton party? Three, but only two present. The third being? The servant's sister whom Mr. Denton says may yet arrive; therefore we wait—but cannot for long. The magistrate then inquired as to the Dentons' baggage: One large chest stored away but minutes ago.

The captain would know of English law's interest in his ship, but Naylor would not say. Sir Jacob would not admit that his most important prisoner had escaped, that he had allowed her heinous evil to again be set loose in London.

As these men spoke, Naylor's party moved throughout the ship, their orders given on land: to search for a particular face, one known by all, for these males were guards from Montclaire Prison well familiar with the comely escapee. Though a few handsome women were discovered, none resembled the witch, the wife. The chest was readily found, found to contain two smaller crates much like the remaining cargo in the hold. Nothing there contained any prisoner, any untoward person—and neither did any other niche of the Queen's Flight, for all were searched.

More than ever before in his career of integrity, the magistrate knew his witches. Standing at the deck rail, he waited with the passengers for that missing person, the one due. Naylor recalled the witch's first, inferior proof of her race, and looked to the Thames, recalling her distress at simply waiting on a clear pool's bottom. If she attempted to walk this far, he thought, she would surely die. Therefore, Naylor was certain that he need only wait; and without his activity, the witch would be ended, out of his life, his land.

Not long was his waiting. Minutes later, Naylor stepped to the anchor chain, for how else would she board? Looking down, he saw a dark shape against that chain, too high to be the anchor. Unclear, but clear enough. The shape was covered with apparel—it wore a dress. The shape had dark hair, hands holding the thick metal. Distorted from the water's movement, the shape was thick one ripple and thin the next—but what shape could it be except the one Sir Jacob had lost?

He looked away, and waited. He looked away, and was uncertain of his view. The witch was seen, yes, but more than her face, more than her appearance. The magistrate as well saw her danger. He saw his parent dead. He saw her killing a man. He saw all the men who would kill her, the latter perhaps including himself. Walk that far and die, he had thought, but the magistrate had been wrong again. Perhaps, perhaps, he thought, if she can remain breathing water long enough for me to decide her, then she deserves to live; and this was a new idea within him.

He looked down to the shape another instance, then moved away so that he could not see. He instructed his men to continue searching even though they had searched everywhere often. He told the captain to have his passengers quit their complaining, for he was in no position to accept such criticisms, not with space in Montclaire, more space than that morning, too much of God's separation.

He sent Eric's boat away. No further use had any passengers for these sailors, correct? the magistrate asked; and no one disagreed, not Mr. Denton, who was within hearing, though not nearby.

Nothing changed for Naylor, for no thoughts came, no decision. Nevertheless, after a sinners' moment—a moral moment—he found relief, certain that no longer would the witch be his concern. Then he ordered all the guards into the boat again, and joined them in returning to London.

"I suggest, captain," Naylor called up to the Queen's Flight, "that you weigh anchor and be on with your journey, for it is long and will never begin if you continue waiting for nothing."

The captain could not disagree. As Sir Jacob and his people retreated, the captain ordered the Queen's anchor raised. Naylor looked. Naylor viewed the chain on the ship's opposite side reach deck with no shape attached but that bare anchor on the end. Then Sir Jacob looked away, not turning again to the great vessel.

The captain could not disagree, but Eric could. As he turned to his first mate to have the sails raised, the captain was interrupted by Eric. Further waiting would net the captain further currency. The situation now, the ship's master insisted, is one wherein all these paying passengers must be convinced—have you enough funds for that, sir? But Eric had not. Therefore, he ran to the rail near the anchor chain, looking down to harshly call back to the captain that a person was swimming below. A loud response ensued amongst the sailors of the Queen's Flight, but none could see a person on the Thames. Below, the person is below the surface, Eric insisted. You must lower the anchor again to allow the person a path upward. Foolish this seemed to the sailors, but Mr. Denton proved himself most serious by removing his shoes and gently dropping overboard, for near enough was the magistrate's starboard boat for its passengers to hear a port commotion. Once in the water, Eric called out that, yes! indeed a person was here and the anchor must be lowered since the person was sinking. And who was the captain to argue with a wealthy man attempting to save an invisible person from drowning?

Down, down he dove, but the Thames was too deep here for him to gain bottom. But he could see, see a witch pull herself up the anchor, her head *eventually* gaining good air. Astounded were all those on board the Queen's Flight to see this rescue, though none heard her speak, heard her describe her sighting to Eric. And when the ugly woman was brought aboard, none of Mr. Denton's further odd observations were doubted.

Forty-four

I could hear the harbor voices through the salt. This was my first thought upon entering the Thames; my second was a poor reinforcement: that this submerging was exactly as terrible as I had dreamed, had recalled, had experienced and now lived again, for this was no dream. At once I recognized the day's entire truth: that Marybelle lived, somehow lived, praise God yet lived, and that she and Eric had released me from prison, that we all would leave for America as carefully planned by my family. We all would continue living if only I could save myself, if I were witch enough to breathe the ocean that had killed my nights.

Immediately after this recognition came dying, the experience of breathing nothing, of being a fish, a fish dragged onto dry land and drowning on air. Instant flashes of panic assaulted me: of walking farther than I had ever imagined, nearly as far as Marybelle in the Irish Sea, an experience so deathly she could not describe it to her sister. A second panic was the impossibility of my leaping up for God's pure air, for the smothering brine was too deep, an atmosphere above me. Then I forced myself to consider as well as fear, forced myself to accept the needed water, easing my breath out and the water in, air from the water seeping into my lungs. But this was intent, not emotion; for I was so frightened I felt an infant with sinners before me, a race never seen before stinking to scare me breathless; and so I was.

My only goal was to retrieve a known process, that of breathing not water, but the air in water, an activity never to have failed me, never to come easily. I became thoughtless, having no idea of other people living or dead, for the only person I knew was me, and she was dying. No thoughts of Marybelle impossibly alive had I. No notion of Eric so foolish as to desire me continually came. No idea passed of Naylor seeking my ashes. Only I existed, and I was drowning; but with all my intense feeling, the process of breathing water was not forgotten, was not rejected, eventually becoming manifested in the real, for I found myself surviving. Then came the next panic, for I recognized my mediocrity, the witch achieving air but typically little, not enough for walking forever, all the way to God or Satan.

I was walking: away from pilings, over mortar and brick shards, across depressions and mounds in the river's bottom as though it were land, dry land with air; but no. Wet it was with only hints of air, scarcely enough to support me even if all my effort went to avoiding those panicked thoughts one failed breath away, one bad emotion removed. All of my effort was required to continue systematically with the process of moving my cheeks, holding my throat in a particular manner, allowing water to move in and out and that air to seep farther, but not water, allow air into my lungs alone lest I gag as though puking up a sinner's prick. Then I would choke, and then I would die.

I was walking, and no more of the sinners' words could be heard. Darker my atmosphere became, for above was deeper water, no cleaner here, and my eyes and nose were smarting. Carefully I reached to pinch my nostrils together, not accomplishing this closure before since all of my effort had been required for the mechanics of water breathing, effort required to avert that panic behind my mind, the panic of failing with some small aspect of my mouth or throat or lungs, thereafter to choke and gag and goddamned die. But so superior did my nose feel that I was able to continue with better control of that imminent panic. Sensing my body beyond fear, I thought of closing my eyes, which were stinging, and would have done so had I not needed vision to guide me to the Queen's Flight. But close my eyes I might have regardless, for no boat did I see ahead, and I knew not where the ship was situated. Being lost, I became too frightened, so frightened that I stifled on water and nearly choked. Nearly choked, and then I turned immortal, impossible; for I became totally filled with prayer for great God to aid me, yet was totally filled with awareness of the upcoming drowning, and was totally filled with such terror that I could have nothing else within me, terror I could not consider, only feel, feel the panic as all in a witch's moment I gasped and then was completely filled with the need to save myself, for there was not enough air.

Becoming a genius, I stopped while I drowned so as not to lose my way. I stopped and pinched my nostrils hard, painfully hard, though I could only feel my drowning, stopped to close my eyes so forcefully that I saw flashes against my lids' inner sides. Gasp and stop to pray God to control it, allow none other, no further choking, as I halted all my breathing a moment, a sinner's or a witch's or a Holy moment to wait, wait an instant or an era for my panic to subside. I waited without breathing, and found improvement. Praise God, no breathing was an improvement; and I felt myself nearly dead, for such was the utter lack of everything I required. An absence of every movement was needed to quash the choke with calmness; and the gagging ended. All of it, the single gasp to nearly kill me with fear and with drowning, come and gone in the space of a breath.

Slowly water with its meager air again came in and out, though the act remained difficult. Not readily reestablishing water breathing was disappointing, a poor foreboding for my further journey if I could barely survive one small gasp; and what difference regardless? For I partially opened my eyes to see I knew not where I walked, and thereby became so panicked that I nearly choked again, which would drown me the next instance, the last.

No, I had not turned, but walked straight. Yes, I was a witch, and knew directions above a river or below. After all, the ship was stationary: They had not raised the anchor and drifted away. And neither would I. No with the turning and yes with the witch and please God retain that panic. Yes with the walking. Yes with breathing water. Yes with smothering in salt. Yes with needing to be perfect in my mechanics or fail my life. Yes in hating this difficulty, hating this smothering.

Yes with arduously following the proper direction. Yes in breathing damp, choking suffocation and needing to continue the stifling breaths. Yes with having no choice, with having placed myself in a situation, a life, wherein I could only smother on misery or die, suffocate even with my finest effort, and worse would be failing to smother. This was the horror I hated: If I lost that smothering, no air at all would I gain, only a choke, a cough, a gag and gasp, and then would come panic to have me breathe water, which I could not, thus my living would be so much worse, for I would be breathing nothing, and would not be living, but dead.

On and on in this manner my horrid and false breathing continued until becoming worse. *Eventually*, after hours or days or an entire life, I became exhausted. Walking through water is difficult unless one's head is submerged, and then it is torture. Torture from the smothering, for there is no breathing. Torment from the suffocation, for there is no air. Weary I became from the walking, and therefore an even greater effort of thought and will was required for me to proceed with the simple act of moving water in and digging for its tiny air, greater effort needed to reject that panic, though the discomfort remained, remained so long it worsened, becoming pain: pain in my legs and even my shoulders from moving them, pain in my neck and throat from that confined attitude I demanded of them, pain throughout my chest, my torso, my lungs pained from being checked, being denied their full and proper movement. Pain from that most important lack of movement, the refusal to allow panic's moving near, a panic to weaken me enough to lose effort, for with effort lost would go breathing and come choking. And with no surface nor riverbank to gain, I would breathe only water, no air, gag and choke and constrict to die on the river bottom.

Then I was burdened further, for I found myself filled, not with water, but words. All the words of my testament that had saved me from death now threatened to drown me, for every syllable written I felt, and they were too many to breathe, though by describing my life they now seemed my life, which was dying, a life only to end properly if writ to completion, but I could not write dead, and smothering me was too much briny ink to pass through in one mere lifetime.

The oppression improved, for it was killing me. The massive torment improved toward its victim by killing my senses until I felt nothing of my body. I felt emotion, however, and it was the horror of knowing that my senses' dying meant that my brain was dying, and with it my heart, my spirit, me. But, of course, my brain was dead, for I knew not the ship's location. In limbo I was, not a river, and beyond was Hell.

So slowly was I moving that my steps had ceased, and next I would collapse. So meager was my breathing that I might as well halt, for with no bodily effort, no air did I need, being dead. And no fear had I of that threatening panic, for torment had smothered all of my intensity; therefore, I would never choke, for gagging is an acute response of life.

My last thought was of Mother. The final understanding came that I had not allowed her to die, for nothing in her death could I have changed. And here was peace, for no person I had killed was as important as my mother. Surely not her daughter. With her death, too, would come peace, and an acceptance granted by God. And peace I would have gained by collapsing onto the river bottom to breathe eternity if Mother had not been weeping. Mother was weeping because no, no, I had never failed her, not in my heart, not in my spirit. Not until now. Mother was weeping across Earth and its waters in the form of God's greatest emotion of love. Mother was weeping because now she would be alone. She would be alone, for not enough love had I to verify my spirit by surviving. No spirit of family emotion had I to selfishly accept an eternal peace without this wet misery instead of surviving for Mother thereby to love her as she deserved. Therefore, though all of my failures toward Mother were proven false, here at my end I rejected her finally by rejecting her love. But no misery had I in this recognition. No remorse came to me for my ultimate failure. No guilt did I achieve, for I was too angered.

This dying fool I wished to kill. So scurrilous was this sick bitch that she could not love the best mother on Earth with her dying breath, for to love Mother properly I would have to reject that dying breath and accept new torment. Accept more pain of breathing water, enough water to sustain me to the ship and the sinners there. But after that initial anger, I had no thoughts of Mother, for she was dead. Alive were Eric and Marybelle and they had saved me, and by the God Who had made me and in His glorious generosity would accept my life, I would *not* fail Marybelle again. I would *not* allow her to die again. And Eric, Eric, I would *not* snatch away his heart as I had his phallus. I would *not* kill his love for the wife, for every part of me was inferior to that emotion. I would *not* fail my remaining family, would *not* reject their love, would *not* die easily, but suffer continued living. I would *not* panic and choke, would not fall to the river's bottom and would not lose my way. But I had.

I halted. Intentionally I ceased in order to regain my direction. There, that direction, yes, at an angle to my path; for so immoral had I been as to walk away from my family instead of toward them. So I began walking accurately, and I breathed, breathed water. Then came a new torment, one of impossibility; for although my insistence upon living was now reestablished, it did not make me God. My great desire for life provided me with no powers over living, and I felt that despite my best intents and an anger to drive me onward, I would not be able to overcome the world, the natural world wherein people strive as best they can yet die, always die, and so would I. But even as God gave me life, in my selfishness I would not abandon it, but make Him take it from me.

I would not fail God after having discovered that never in life had I failed Mother until accepting my own death. I would not fail my family and our Maker, and would have no more negation, for I would. I would walk in that proper direction. I would continue breathing as I must, as I could. I would achieve the sinners' ship and with it my love. I would not broach feelings of impossibility – if God had impossibility prepared for my success, then He could implement it without my aid. I would live as best I could, and if I died therefrom, praise God for being superior to us all in His ability to decide. But I was inferior and would live my life without further presuming God. So I walked and breathed and Satan knows I suffered. Walked and breathed and felt dead, was surprised I was not dead considering how slowly I moved, no longer able

651

to keep my eyes constantly open, blinking now and again, again and now, all limp in every portion of myself, not having pinched my nose shut in my memory. Walked and breathed until I heard a noise of another person's drowning.

The sound's source was the ship. Walk there and breathe and suffer, too dull and dead for panic. Too full of dying for further acute anger. Breathe and drag myself along the river bottom until espying a rope to hang me. A dark rope all in knots and above it a noise. A splashing noise as I dragged and nearly breathed. A noise denoting an item falling into the water and thrashing only to rise. Activity ahead as I dragged and nearly breathed, nearly failed to breathe. A milder sound of movement within the water body, for ahead was a fish swimming. Ahead was a sinner swimming. Near the metal rope of dark knots with a huge hook swam a sinner looking toward me, unable to see because of my distance, my depth, this the sound of another fool moving impossibly in the water. And a sight. The sight of human gesticulation, for an arm was waving me toward the rope. Then up the sinner went for God's air and I had no jealousy. Then down came the person more alive than the walker to look for me, look at me, waving me toward the hard hook at the rope's bottom, the river's bottom. What a fine sound this splashing, for it was air and water mingling. What a fine sound for being above me, for the rope was at my feet. And I knew. I understood. This was a fisher. Some sinning fisher had lured me to his line, lured me to his metal, and so insistent was he with his attractive immersion that I could not resist. Lure me to his line he did, for I stepped upon that hook and held the rope, and then the fisher snatched me up onto dry land where I drowned in air.

Upward I was pulled into an unknown medium, for it was so thin and dry as to pain me with its sharp substance. Up into Satan's trait of separation, for around me was air, yet I could not breathe it. So long had I respired water that I had forgotten normal living, and I recalled Marybelle's having to relearn breath, recalled her inability to speak further on the subject, and neither could I, the invert witch inversely suffocating on too much air as the sinners lifted their chain, a specific person I should have known holding the rope and a wife who could not breathe. Up onto the flat surface of a floating box as pulled by many sinners' hands, all of them on my genitals or digging through my heart for all I cared, since I was dying again in another new manner. Flat on my back on the wooden deck and there was a witch beside me having everyone else retreat. No care had I for her as I stared at the darkening sky with absolutely open eyes to search for God's knowledge of living. All those muscles in my mouth and throat and atrophied lungs that so long, too long, had been stressed to a near static state were now cramped beyond proper function, for I had forgotten how to breathe. But, of course, I remembered how to die.

"Breathe water, believe that you are yet breathing water," the witch beside me known by odor hissed. "Breathe even as you did below, then slowly regain the breathing of air."

And I did. As though in the water again, I applied that smothering process, but odd, oddly painful it was, as though the material I allowed into my lungs were fire—yes, burn my lungs it did, this fire air, cold flames burning my internal meat. So intense was this pain that I stared upward and saw nothing, breathing with all my concerted effort yet gaining scarcely a morsel of air. And here was a new form of panic, for upon choking would I need to save myself by leaping into the water to gag on brine? Would I have to save myself in this atmosphere by drowning in one inferior?

My eyes were closed. Eventually I understood that I was breathing air, yet useless it seemed, since my entire person— from mind to heart to spirit to emotion—was devoid of energy. Scarcely could I discern my state, my position. I could neither open my eyes nor feel any sensation. I was nothing but utter loss: of effort, energy, interest, intent. No feeling had I for survival. No feeling had I. Where or who or how I was meant nothing. On and on this state continued instantly or endlessly until I nearly felt peace. Then I opened my eyes to turn toward a smell.

Sinners stood everywhere, but beside me was a sitting witch. One with a neck as crooked as my underwater walking. Behind her were strangers made to remain away by kin. Above the sister stood a woman who had grown with me until we formed a family. Beside her was a married man. All intent and serious were these folk as they stared, but not a tear, for I had taught them better. All so utterly intense were these people as they stared at whatever that I had to laugh. And when a true witch laughs, it comes a cackle. I continued laughing although some sinner leapt upon me, grasping my throat with his teeth, commencing to lick my face as though he were in need of salt, and wag his long and lovely tail.

"Stop, Eric," I told Randolph as I touched his fur. "Not again tonight," and came another cackle.

"I do so hate that sound, miss," the husband whispered.

"Missus," I replied, and laughed again, all my family members now smiling, and some of them to later weep. Not the white one, however, floating unafraid on a sea that had saved her despite all its space, the witch in transition from world to world via the passion of living, a verified life, all my love lodged heavenly, ensconced in a clear spirit, black body.

THE BEST IN CONTEMPORARY SUSPENSE

WHERE'S MOMMY NOW?   (366, $4.50)
by Rochelle Majer Krich

Kate Bauers couldn't be a Superwoman any more. Her job, her demanding husband, and her two children were too much to manage on her own. Kate did what she swore she'd never do: let a stranger into her home to care for her children. *Enter Janine.*

Suddenly Kate's world began to fall apart. Her energy and health were slipping away, and the pills her husband gave her and the cocoa Janine gave her made her feel worse. Kate was so sleepy she couldn't concentrate on the little things — like a missing photo, a pair of broken glasses, a nightgown that smelled of a perfume she never wore. Nobody could blame Janine. Everyone loved her. Who could suspect a loving, generous, jewel of a mother's helper?

COME NIGHTFALL   (340, $3.95)
by Gary Amo

Kathryn liked her life as a successful prosecuting attorney. She was a perfect professional and never got personally involved with her cases. Until now. As she viewed the bloody devastation at a rape victim's home, Kathryn swore to the victim to put the rapist behind bars. But she faced an agonizing decision: insist her client testify or to allow her to forget the shattering nightmare.

Soon it was too late for decisions: one of the killers was out on bail, and he knew where Kathryn lived. . . .

FAMILY REUNION   (375, $3.95)
by Nicholas Sarazen

Investigative reporter Stephanie Kenyon loved her job, her apartment, her career. Then she met a homeless drifter with a story to tell. Suddenly, Stephanie knew more than she should, but she was determined to get this story on the front page. She ignored her editor's misgivings, her lover's concerns, even her own sense of danger, and began to piece together a hideous crime that had been committed twenty years ago.

Then the chilling phone calls began. And the threatening letters were delivered. And the box of red roses . . . dyed black. Stephanie began to fear that she would not live to see her story in print.

Available wherever paperbacks are sold, or order direct from the Publisher. Send cover price plus 50¢ per copy for mailing and handling to Pinnacle Books, Dept. 17-505, 475 Park Avenue South, New York, N.Y. 10016. Residents of New York, New Jersey and Pennsylvania must include sales tax. DO NOT SEND CASH.